Treachery's Tools

Tor Books by L. E. Modesitt, Jr.

Treachery's Tools

The Tenth Book of the
Imager Portfolio

L. E. MODESITT, JR.

TOR

A TOM DOHERTY ASSOCIATES BOOK

NEW YORK

TREACHERY'S TOOLS

Copyright © 2016 by L. E. Modesitt, Jr.

All rights reserved.

Map by Jon Lansberg

A Tor Book
Published by Tom Doherty Associates
175 Fifth Avenue
New York, NY 10010

www.tor-forge.com

Tor® is a registered trademark of Macmillan Publishing Group, LLC.

The Library of Congress Cataloging-in-Publication Data
is available upon request.

ISBN 978-0-7653-8540-6 (hardcover)
ISBN 978-0-7653-8542-0 (e-book)

Our books may be purchased in bulk for promotional, educational, or business use. Please contact your local bookseller or the Macmillan Corporate and Premium Sales Department at 1-800-221-7945, extension 5442, or by e-mail at MacmillanSpecialMarkets@macmillan.com.

First Edition: October 2016

Printed in the United States of America

0 9 8 7 6 5 4 3 2 1

For Dashiell

CHARACTERS

REX

LORIEN D'REX   Rex of Solidar
CHELIA'D'LORIEN   Lorien's wife, sister of High Holder Ryel
CHARYN D'LORIEN   Eldest son of Lorien
BHAYRN D'LORIEN   Second son of Lorien
ALORYANA D'LORIEN   Daughter of Lorien

HIGH HOLDERS

AISHFORD D'ALTE   Nordeau
BRUESSYRD D'ALTE   Liantiago
CAEMRYN D'ALTE   Yapres
CAERVYN D'ALTE   Fleuryn
CALKORAN D'ALTE   Vaestora
CRANSYR D'ALTE   Head, High Holder's Council, Ilyum
DELCOEUR D'ALTE   L'Excelsis
GUERDYN D'ALTE   Nacliano
HAEBYN D'ALTE   Piedryn
LAEVORYN D'ALTE   L'Excelsis
MOERYN D'ALTE   Khelgror
MEINYT D'ALTE   High Councilor, Alkyra
NACRYON D'ALTE   Mantes
NUALT D'ALTE   Barna
OLEFSYRT D'ALTE   High Councilor, Noira
PAELLYT D'ALTE   Sommeil
REGIAL D'ALTE   Montagne
RUELYR D'ALTE   Ruile

RYEL D'ALTE   Rivages
SOUVEN D'ALTE   High Councilor, Dueraan
STAENDEN D'ALTE   High Councilor, Tacqueville
THYSOR D'ALTE   Extela
THURL D'ALTE   Extela
VAUN D'ALTE   Tilbora
ZAERLYN D'ALTE   Rivages, brother of Alyna

IMAGERS

AKORYT   Maitre D'Structure
ALASTAR   Maitre D'Image
ALYNA   Maitre D'Esprit, wife of Alastar
ARION   Maitre D'Structure
CYRAN   Maitre D'Esprit, Senior Imager
GAELLEN   Maitre D'Structure, healer
KHAELIS   Maitre D'Structure
OBSOLYM   Maitre D'Structure
SHAELYT   Maitre D'Structure
TARYN   Maitre D'Structure
TIRANYA   Maitre D'Structure

ARTHOS   Maitre D'Aspect
BELSIOR   Maitre D'Aspect
BETTAUR   Maitre D'Aspect
CELIENA   Maitre D'Aspect
CHERVYT   Maitre D'Aspect
CLAEYND   Maitre D'Aspect
DYLERT   Maitre D'Aspect
JULYAN   Maitre D'Aspect
LHENDYR   Maitre D'Aspect
NARRYN   Maitre D'Aspect
PETROS   Maitre D'Aspect, stablemaster
SELIORA   Maitre D'Aspect
TAUREK   Maitre D'Aspect
THELIA   Maitre D'Aspect, Collegium bookkeeper
WARRYK   Maitre D'Aspect

CHARLINA   Tertia
DAREYN   Secondus, Aide to Maitre

ISKHAR   Chorister of the Collegium
KAYLET   Tertius, assistant stablemaster
LYNZIA   Tertius
LYSTARA   Seconda, daughter of Alastar and Alyna
ZHELAN   Maitre of Westisle Collegium

FACTORS

CUIPRYN D'FACTORIUS   Brass/copper
DUURMYN D'FACTORIUS   Livestock, stockyards
ELTHYRD D'FACTORIUS   Timber, lumber, Factors' Council
ESTAFEN D'FACTORIUS   Banque D'Excelsis
GOERYND D'FACTORIUS   Pumps, plows, implements, Factors' Council
HULET D'FACTORIUS   Grain and maize, Chief, Factors' Council
KARL D'FACTORIUS   Iron, smelting
KATHILA D'FACTORIA   Spices, scents, and oils, Factors' Council
MAARTYN D'FACTORIUS   Brick and stone
NAATHYN D'FACTORIUS   Coaches, carriages, wagons
VASCHET D'FACTORIUS   Machinery and armaments
WEEZYR D'FACTORIUS   Banque D'Aluse
WYLUM D'FACTORIUS   Woolens and cloth, Factors' Council

OTHERS

HEHNSYN D'CORPS   Subcommander, procurement, son of High
   Holder Cransyr
HEISYT D'PATROL   Captain, Civic Patrol
LYTARRL D'ANOMEN   Chorister, Anomen D'Excelsis, brother of
   Elthyrd
MARRYT D'CORPS   Commander, Chief of Staff, son of High Holder
   Caervyn
MAUREK D'CORPS   Commander
MURRANYT D'PATROL   Commander, Civic Patrol, L'Excelsis
SAERLET D'ANOMEN   Chorister, Anomen D'Rex
TYNAN D'NAVIA   Sea Marshal
VAELLN D'CORPS   Vice Marshal
WILKORN D'CORPS   Marshal of the Armies

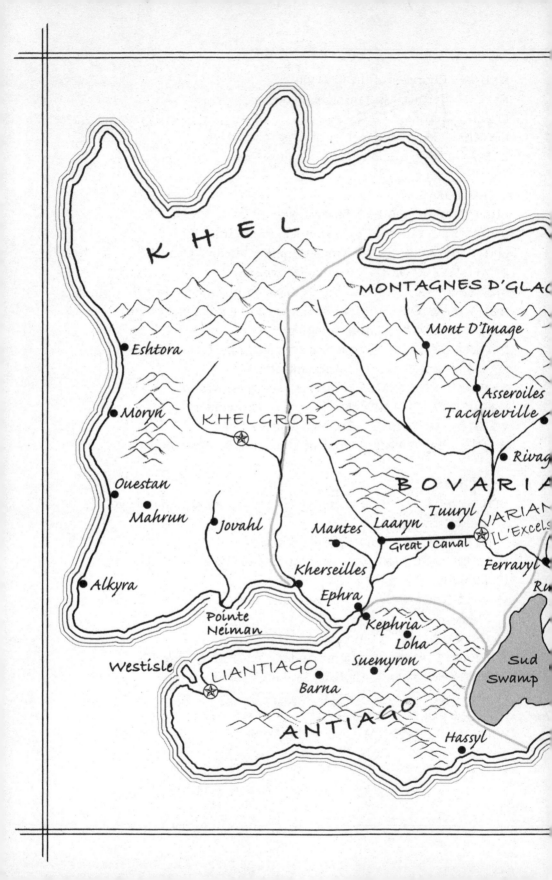

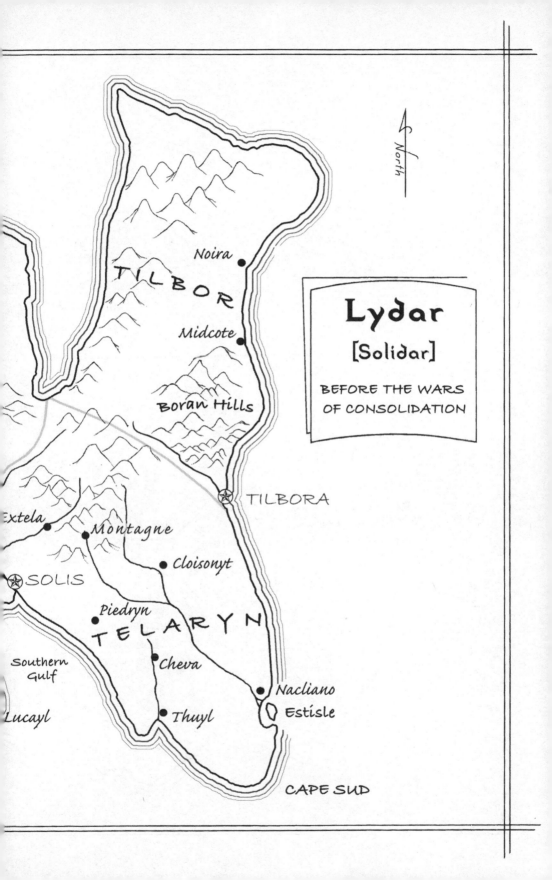

Treachery's Tools

1

In the deep gray before dawn on Mardi morning, Alastar stood at the
bedchamber window. Beyond the glass, water poured out of the sky in
a rush that suggested a waterfall more than mere rain. So heavy was the
downpour that Alastar could barely make out the stone-paved walkway
that led from the covered porch below the window south toward the
center of the Collegium, but he didn't have to see in order to know that
the twin lanes flanking the green that led past the cottages of the master
imagers were at least boot-deep in rushing water being channeled to
the River Aluse, a river that, after the continual rains of the past week, was
less than two yards from the top of the high granite riverwalls that surrounded Imagisle. So much rain in late Agostos was bound to destroy
much of the grain harvest in the areas around L'Excelsis—and everywhere
the near-continual downpour had struck.

As if matters weren't unsettled enough.

He turned from the window to find that Alyna was sitting on the side
of the bed looking at him.

"You're not going running in that, I hope?"

Alastar shook his head. "Running in drizzle or light rain is one thing.
Running through a torrent is another."

"Sometimes . . ." Alyna paused. "You're worried . . . again."

He nodded. "The rains . . . and Chief Factor Hulet . . . and High
Holder Cransyr. I'm afraid matters are going to get worse."

"You'll figure a way through it." Her words were warm.

Alastar just looked at her for a long moment, a slender, almost petite
woman, with short brown hair and black eyes . . . and with physical
strength, determination, and imaging ability so at odds with her appearance, as many had discovered, at times fatally. He chuckled. "No . . . *we'll*
find a way through it."

Less than a glass later, after a hot breakfast, Alastar and Alyna stood
in the front foyer as their daughter, Lystara, hurried down the stairs
toward the front door.

"Don't forget to wear your waterproof," said Alyna evenly. "And don't make that face again. I know the oilskin coat smells of fish oil. That's what keeps the rain from soaking through."

"And don't forget your oiled boots, either," added Alastar, "the way you did so conveniently yesterday."

"You don't—" Lystara broke off her words abruptly, her black eyes going from her father to her mother and back again.

"Don't understand?" Alastar's voice was dry. He wasn't about to mention that he and Alyna already wore the less than stylish and rather odoriferous oiled boots

"The other seconds . . ." Lystara began, then stopped.

"The other seconds don't have to walk half a mille in ankle-deep water. They might get damp running from the dining hall to the administration building. You'll be soaked all the way through, and if you keep imaging the water out of your grays the way you did yesterday, you'll destroy the cloth, and all your coppers won't be enough to pay for new grays." Alastar managed to keep his voice level, a far harder chore with his own daughter than with the imagers over whom he served as the Collegium Maitre.

"Getting soaked and chilled won't help your health or your studies," added Alyna.

Lystara tried not to frown. "It's just water."

"As your father has pointed out more than once, Lystara dear, there is water in everything. You're not skilled enough as an imager to take out just enough water."

"Mother . . ." Lystara's voice turned pleading. "Everyone will think I'm a baby. I'm already the youngest by two years anyway."

"You didn't want to be held back with the primes," Alyna pointed out.

"I'm as good an imager as some of the thirds." At the look on Alastar's face, Lystara quickly added, "I know I shouldn't be a third yet, but I just couldn't stay with the primes. I wasn't learning anything . . . or not much. It was too painful."

Alastar understood all too well what she meant. "We gave you the choice of whether you wanted to stay a prime." The fact that their daughter was barely ten had concerned both Alyna and him, although she was already as tall as many of the seconds, and taller than a few, but Lystara had pushed.

"If you can't do what's right and what's right for your health now when it's just a matter of what you wear . . ." began Alastar.

"Lystara dear, would you like your father to walk you to the administration building?"

The dark-haired ten-year-old stiffened. "No, thank you. I can stand up for myself." She turned and walked to the front foyer, seated herself on the bench, and pulled on the oiled calf-high boots. Then she stood and took the hooded oilskin cloak off the peg and slipped it on. Finally, she turned to her parents. "There are two other oilskin cloaks in the back closet." She grinned, then turned and hurried out the front door.

"Shall we go?" asked Alastar, turning to Alyna.

"Of course. After you fetch the oilskins."

They both laughed.

In moments, Alastar returned with the oilskins, fishy as they smelled, and the two stepped out onto the covered porch. Although Alastar and Alyna had to be at the administration building at seventh glass, as did Lystara, for the past year their daughter had insisted on walking alone. In turn, Alastar had insisted that, if Lystara wished to go by herself, she needed to leave before her parents.

As Alastar stepped out into the sheeting rain, he said, "She takes after both of us." Before Alyna could reply, he went on, "Your looks and quick wit, my stubbornness, and both of our imaging abilities."

"She does have a certain firmness of will, but her similarity to me, dearest, is limited largely to her hair and eyes."

"She has your mouth and lips, too."

"And your chin and bones. She's already tall, even taller than some of the other seconds. That makes fitting in harder for her."

"Besides being our daughter," Alastar added, "and knowing too much too soon and being too much in a hurry to grow up."

"We've pushed her a bit."

"As I recall, my dearest, we agreed on that."

Alyna did not quite sigh. "I don't think we had that much choice."

Left unspoken were the other problems Lystara would face.

"What are you going to bring up at the senior imagers' meeting?" asked Alyna after several moments.

"Lorien will likely request that we repair some of the damage caused by the rains, especially in L'Excelsis."

"He'll ask for us to repair all of it, and you'll have to decline doing everything, if only on principle."

Alastar inclined his head. "Thank you for spelling out my position." He smiled broadly before reaching out and taking her hand for a moment.

"Who else would dare?" She returned his smile with one of her own that held a hint of impish mischief.

"Arion would, if politely. Tiranya or Shaelyt might."

"*Might* is a very accurate way of putting it."

Alastar laughed. So did Alyna.

When the two reached the administration building, Alastar watched for a moment as Alyna headed toward the stairs to the upper level and her study. He still never tired of watching her. Then he made his way from the entry hall down the corridor and into the antechamber to the Maitre's study.

Dareyn, the white-haired secondus who had served as Alastar's only clerk and assistant from the time he had become Maitre, smiled warmly. "I'm glad to see you wore oilskins, sir. It's like walking through a cataract out there."

"My daughter and my wife didn't leave me much choice with the oilskins."

"Neither did Elmya," replied Dareyn.

"Any messages from anyone?"

"Nothing so far, sir."

"The rain may have slowed them."

Dareyn frowned.

"I can't imagine any good coming from a week of solid heavy rain, but I could be mistaken." Alastar took off the oilskin cloak and walked to the heavy wooden rack at one side of the anteroom where he hung it next to Dareyn's. "I'm sorry for the smell."

"Two's no worse than one."

Alastar smiled at his assistant's words. "I'm going to check one thing in the study. Then I'll be in the conference room. Just have the seniors come in as they arrive."

Dareyn nodded.

Alastar stepped into the study, gloomy because of the weather and the fact that none of the lamps was lit. He didn't bother imaging one into light. That would just have wasted lamp oil. He opened the second desk drawer and slipped out the folder with his notes for the meeting, then walked to the side door of the study that led into the conference room, opened it, and then closed it behind him. He walked to the head of the long table. Rather than sit, he stood beside his chair, thinking.

Less than a fraction of a quint later, the door from the hall opened, and the first of the senior imagers entered—the ancient Obsolym, white-haired, his face gaunt, but with watery blue eyes that missed nothing. "Good morning, Maitre."

"Good morning, you ancient troublemaker."

"The same to you, most venerable font of destruction."

Alastar couldn't help grinning at Obsolym's gruff words, although both of them knew that neither would have exchanged quite the same set of pleasantries had anyone else been present.

"I'll be seeing your daughter at eighth glass."

"Don't let her argue or charm you out of learning her history."

"So far that hasn't been a problem. She seems to want to know more about everything."

Alastar frowned. "She's not being a know-it-all, is she?"

Obsolym shook his head. "She's quiet, but not too quiet. She's been reading history on the side . . . or one of you has been tutoring her."

"No. Whenever she asks a question, I tell her where she might look to find the answer." Alastar would have said more, but Cyran, the senior imager of the Collegium, stepped into the conference room, followed by Akoryt and Alyna. In moments, the other senior imagers, those ranked as Maitre D'Structure or higher, had entered and seated themselves at the long table, with Cyran on Alastar's right and Alyna on his left, not because she was his wife, but because she and Cyran were the only Maitres D'Esprit at the Collegium—and that was more than had been at the Collegium in more than a generation . . . or perhaps since the time of the first Maitre.

Alastar looked down the table, taking in the ten other imagers. Even thirteen years after he'd taken over as Maitre, there were too few senior imagers. *But there are many new junior maitres and a goodly number of solid thirds.* Those thoughts reminded him of just how hard—and time-consuming—it was to rebuild something. *And how quickly things can deteriorate under poor leadership and adverse conditions.* He cleared his throat. "The good news is that no new difficulties have been brought to the attention of the Collegium. The bad news is that there will be." He offered a wry smile. "The rains have brought the River Aluse to the highest flood stage in hundreds of years. Recent dispatches from the west indicate that both the Phraan River and the River Laar are flooding as well. For the most part, the land on both sides of the Laar south from Laaryn is flat. Much of it is fertile bottom-land, but when the river rises . . ."

"The bottomland floods," finished Obsolym. "Happens every ten years or so. Just long enough that no one remembers how bad it was."

"This time looks worse than ever," added Alastar. "What's more of a problem is that last year was so dry there isn't much grain laid up."

"They had a bumper crop in Piedryn last year, and the harvest there is good this year," said Shaelyt.

"That's part of the problem," replied Alastar. "Some of the large grain factors here in L'Excelsis and in Ferravyl bought everything they could last year and have again this year, even taking contracts on grain that hasn't been harvested. And that was before the rains came, when it looked like the price would stay low."

"Sir . . ." began Khaelis, one of the more junior Maitres D'Structure. "I can see that this will make life very hard on the poor, and on some members of the Guilds . . ."

"You're wondering what it has to do with the Collegium, I take it?"

"Yes, sir."

Alastar would have been happy to explain at length, but a shorter answer was better for the moment. "The droughts of the past few years have left little grain here in the west of Solidar. The High Holders here in old Bovaria sold most of their surplus stocks earlier this year, and made a handsome profit on that grain. The larger grain factors held their stocks, Chief Factor Hulet, especially. They wagered on another bad harvest, and they bought up much of the harvest from Piedryn and the lands around Ferravyl. Now, a number of those High Holders will have to buy grain, and possibly other produce, on the terms set by the factors. Some will have difficulty in raising the golds. They may have to borrow. . . ." Alastar nodded to Alyna for her to continue.

"Many of the High Holders have remained landowners and little more. The High Council decided almost ten years ago not to allow factors to become High Holders unless they also held significant lands. Many factors decided against becoming landholders and put their golds into trade and manufacturing enterprises. Trade, especially the spice trade with various countries in Otelyrn, has allowed several factors to become wealthier than the majority of High Holders, and many to have more golds for immediate use than many High Holders. Those golds have been used at times to the distinct disadvantage of the High Holders."

This time, Alastar observed, more than a few present seemed puzzled, although Arion, the most recent imager to become a Maitre D'Structure, nodded knowingly, not surprising given that he, like Alyna, had come from a High Holder's family.

Before Alastar could say anything, Alyna went on. "Trade and commerce require both banques and exchanges. The banques and exchanges are controlled largely by factors. Traders can spread and lessen their risk on a given voyage, say to Otelyrn, by selling shares of the entire cargo. They can also speculate, by agreeing to sell or buy goods at predetermined prices at a given future date."

"But can't High Holders do the same?" asked Taryn.

"Some do," agreed Alyna cheerfully, "but using the exchanges means buying a seat on the exchange or buying or selling through someone who does have a seat. In both cases, that requires golds, knowledge, or trust in someone who does have knowledge. It also requires a presence in L'Excelsis, Solis, Nacliano, Liantiago, Eshtora, or Tilbora. That is where the larger exchanges in Solidar are located."

One of those who did trade through the exchanges, most successfully, Alastar knew, was his wife's brother.

"You're implying that most High Holders are at a disadvantage because their lands are distant from those cities," suggested Shaelyt.

"Prices on the exchanges can shift quickly," Alastar said. "Most High Holders have handled their lands as if they were barely part of Solidar. The original Codex established by the first Rex Regis let them retain the right of low justice. The terms of remaining a High Holder effectively require a certain amount of land, and the High Council has refused to lower that. Very few High Holders trust others with their resources. If a High Holder comes to L'Excelsis to deal in trade and the exchanges, he loses touch with his heritage and he must trust others to manage the lands. If he stays on his lands, then he must trust his agent in L'Excelsis or elsewhere . . . and any trade or exchange business that would be significant in improving his assets would be large enough to cost him dearly."

"So the High Holders are trapped, in a way, by their very holdings?" asked Tiranya, the only other woman who was a senior maitre.

"That's a very good way of putting it," agreed Alyna.

"And by the long-standing tradition that the High Holder is the only decider of anything of worth on the holding," added Alastar dryly.

"What do you think will happen?" asked Cyran.

Alastar had several ideas about what could happen, but because any or none might come to pass, he wasn't about to speculate, except in private and to Alyna. "All that is certain is that a great number of High Holders are likely to be in very difficult financial positions before long, owing large sums to banques and factors, without any way to repay what they owe." *Except by selling large parcels of land at very low prices or surrendering them outright to clear the debts.*

"Some may survive by starving their tenants." Those words came from Khaelis, broad-shouldered and burly. "They have before."

Alastar had the feeling Khaelis spoke from experience as a child, although Khaelis had consistently avoided speaking of his childhood, and the Collegium records only indicated that he came from a small town near Ruile. "Some may try that again. In any event, I wanted you all to be aware that it could be a difficult autumn and winter, and the Collegium as well will likely have to cut back on what we spend."

"Even stipends?" asked Gaellen.

"I hope not, but it is possible." Alastar paused. "Is there anything any of you feel the rest of us should know?"

Tiranya glanced at Alyna for just an instant, then said, "I have some concerns about Maitre Bettaur."

"What concerns, exactly?" asked Alastar.

"He teaches the primes grammar and writing. He's very good at it. They all enjoy the work, but . . ." Tiranya shook her head. "I can't explain it."

Alastar understood exactly why she couldn't, because he'd asked her, years ago, not to reveal her past experiences and misgivings about Bettaur to anyone, and only to consider acts or words after Bettaur had become a Maitre D'Aspect. "You feel that you're missing something? Or that he's hiding something?"

"It could just be me. That's why . . . I don't want to be unfair, but I don't want anything to happen, the way it did with Desyrk."

Alastar nodded. "I don't want gossip about Bettaur. He works hard. At the same time, it would be better—*much better*—if we didn't have another incident like the one Desyrk caused. If anyone sees anything that seems strange, I'd appreciate it—very much—if you did not talk about it, but let me, Maitre Cyran, or Maitre Alyna know." He paused. "Is there anything else?"

"It's not about imaging, Maitre," began Gaellen, "but there has been an infestation of lice, and even some fleas, among the primes, especially among those who have not been as . . . well, they haven't been as scrupulous in cleaning themselves as they should be. I'm thinking that the only way to stop this might be to cut their hair very short. I'd prefer to announce that any I have to treat a second time will be required to have their hair cut to a digit in length."

"That might be a good idea for all student imagers," said Tiranya. "Some of them try to avoid bathing or showering."

"Does anyone have a concern about what Gaellen proposes?" asked Alastar.

"Cold showers never hurt anyone," said Obsolym. "Some of the ones from factoring families seem to want hot baths . . . even before they can image warm water."

Alastar managed not to smile at Obsolym's curmudgeonly tone as he looked to Gaellen. "Go ahead. But that has to include the young women as well." After a moment of silence, he asked once more, "Is there anything else?"

When no one spoke up, Alastar cleared his throat. "Thank you all." With that, he stood, glad that the weekly meeting was over, a day earlier than usual.

Alyna followed him into his study after all the others had left the conference room.

"Was my reply to Tiranya acceptable?"

"You didn't have much of an alternative, dear Maitre. It won't stop the gossip, but it will likely mute it."

"Which is what you had in mind when you arranged for Tiranya to ask that question."

"Of course."

"You don't think Bettaur's really changed at all, do you?"

She smiled sadly. "Do you? Did his father ever change?"

"No, but I could hope." After a moment, he said, "How are the thirds coming on their advanced mathematics?"

"All are doing well at the calculations, but quite a few are having trouble with the geometric idea of having to prove something they already know."

Alastar nodded. "That's true in other fields as well. They need to learn that you don't really understand something until you can prove it—or explain it clearly—to others."

As soon as Alyna had left the study, Dareyn knocked on the frame of the half-open door and, holding an envelope, said, almost apologetically, "Maitre, during the meeting, a chateau guard brought this message from the rex."

"How long ago?"

"Less than a quint."

"Anything this early from Lorien is a problem of some sort." The rex was anything but a dawn-riser, unlike his ill-fated sire, and a message from him arriving before midmorning was definitely unusual, and most likely a harbinger of trouble. Alastar walked from where he stood beside the desk to the doorway and took the envelope, looked at the seal, then broke it and extracted the single sheet. His lips twisted slightly. "Rex Lorien would appreciate my presence at my earliest convenience. If you'd arrange for two escorts and my mount."

"Yes, sir." Dareyn did not move, a quizzical expression on his face.

"He didn't say why, Dareyn." *And he doesn't regard rain as an inconvenience to others, all too like his father in that regard.*

"Yes, sir."

"Let me know when the escorts are ready for me." Alastar wasn't exactly thrilled about a ride to the Chateau D'Rex in the rain that continued to rush down.

By the time the two imager thirds arrived outside the main entrance to the administration building with Alastar's mount, the rain had subsided slightly—from sheets of water to a mere steady downpour. Alastar donned his hooded oilskin and hurried toward the gray gelding—the second one he'd had since becoming Maitre, and another symbol of sorts.

"Good morning, Maitre!" called out Konan, the slightly younger of the two thirds, his voice strong but respectful. The other escort, who nodded politely but did not speak, was Beltran, sober, dedicated, and actually a year or so older than Konan.

"Good morning to you both," returned Alastar, who had always appreciated Konan's quiet solidity. He mounted quickly, and the three rode directly to the Bridge of Desires.

As they crossed the River Aluse, Alastar not only checked to make sure that he was carrying full imaging shields, but also looked down at the water level, slightly higher than the day before, but still almost two yards below the top of the stone riverwall, a yard above the highest level recorded since the founding of the Collegium. The height of the riverwall and its solid structure were just additional reminders of the power and foresight of the first Maitre, whose name and exploits were already forgotten outside of Imagisle and remembered only hazily even by too many imagers.

Once across the river, the three rode along the Boulevard D'Rex Ryen, although Alastar was more than happy that most people—with the strong exception of Rex Lorien—just called it the Boulevard D'Rex. The boulevard ended at the ring road that encircled the Chateau D'Rex, and less than half a quint later, Alastar reined up at the foot of the long white stone steps leading up to the main entrance of the chateau.

"Wait in the chateau stables," Alastar said as he dismounted. "I'll meet you there."

"Yes, sir." Konan actually grinned.

Alastar made his way up the steps swiftly but carefully, mindful that he was no longer quite so young as he thought he was, a fact about which Alyna gently, but frequently, reminded him. While the hooded oilskin had kept his upper body and clothes largely dry, his trousers below the knees were soaked. He didn't image them totally clear of water when he stepped into the entry hall of the chateau, but left them slightly damp.

The two chateau guards looked surprised at his oilskin clad–figure, then nodded as they recognized Alastar.

"Rex Lorien is in his study, Maitre. Ah . . . we could take your oil-skin. . . ." offered the shorter guard.

"Thank you. I would appreciate that."

Moments later, Alastar was climbing the grand staircase and then making his way eastward along the north corridor toward the rex's private study, outside of which was stationed another guard.

At Alastar's appearance, the guard immediately rapped on the door. "The Maitre is here, sire." Then he opened the door for Alastar, who entered the study.

Lorien sat behind the modest goldenwood table desk, the same desk he had used almost every day since he had become rex. Set near the west end of the chamber was a circular conference table with four chairs, all also of goldenwood. The study was gloomy, illuminated by only a single brass lamp set in a wall sconce to the left of the rex. The matching lamp to the right was unlit. The rex motioned for Alastar to join him.

As Alastar seated himself across from Lorien in one of the two straight-backed goldenwood chairs before the table desk, he noted, for the first time, scattered silver-gray hairs interspersed with the lank black hair that the rex had always had, at least for the thirteen years that Alastar had known him. "You requested my presence."

"You're always most deferential and punctual, Maitre. I suppose it's better that way, for both of us."

"I've always felt that the Collegium should remain as much in the background as possible," replied Alastar, with words similar to those used on more than a few occasions over the past thirteen years. "How are Charyn, Bhayrn, and Aloryana?"

"Charyn reminds me of an old man, and he's barely sixteen. Bhayrn's Bhayrn, always looking for something to put together or take apart." Lorien smiled. "You know how I feel about Aloryana, young as she is."

That youth might just be why you feel that way. But Alastar had to admit that the six-year-old was both mannered and charming, or had been on the very few occasions he had seen her . . . and Lorien's reactions. "She lights up every chamber she enters." *Apparently just the way her grandfather did.*

"I can often use a little light, especially with all the trials that come with being rex." Lorien coughed several times, then cleared his throat before continuing. "Marshal Wilkorn is making noises about it being time for him to receive his stipend . . . if not more."

"He's served you loyally and well, at times when neither was easy."

"That's true enough. It's not that. . . ."

"You don't have a spare chateau or the like?"

"More than enough chateaux. Not enough lands to support them, and what's the point of giving him something that will beggar him?"

"There is that. But he wouldn't expect the kind of revenues most High Holders get. You might give him a holding that would support itself and a bit more."

"I'll think about it. I worry about Vice Marshal Vaelln. He's from a factoring background. . . ."

"You'd worry just as much about Commander Marryt. Isn't he the second son of a High Holder?"

"Caervyn. Lots of lands southeast of Montagne." Lorien shook his head. "Besides that worry, and more pressing, I've received petitions from more than a score of High Holders, asking for a temporary reduction in their annual tariffs. You'd think I was bleeding them dry, when it's more the other way around."

"Do they give a reason?"

"The High Council sent a missive requesting that I not grant individual relief, but suggesting strongly that, if any relief from tariffs is merited, it must be applied to all High Holders."

"The High Council didn't mention factors, I take it?"

"Ha! Cransyr's behind this." Lorien grimaced, then massaged his forehead with his left hand. "He'd use any excuse to get me to reduce tariffs . . . and then . . ." He shook his head.

Alastar knew exactly what Lorien meant and dared not say—the same situation that had led to the death of Lorien's father. "No matter what they say, those who have managed their lands and their golds well can afford to pay their tariffs. Reducing tariffs for all to help those who managed poorly will hurt Solidar and only postpone the results of poor management."

"What about the factors?" asked Lorien.

"The same is true of them."

The rex looked slightly surprised.

"Many of the High Holders made substantial profits when they sold their surplus earlier this year. Now, facing a poor or ruined harvest, they want you to make up their losses," offered Alastar. "Some factors likely face the same difficulty."

"That's not the problem. The problem is that the more wealthy factors have bought up all the grain they can. The poor will go hungry. Even guilders may suffer."

"You didn't sell your stocks, did you?"

"You advised me not to. I didn't."

"Then, you can sell some of it to the guilds. At a profit, but not enough that they can't afford it. If matters get dangerous by midwinter, have the regial kitchens bake a lot of bread and distribute it to the poor a few times."

"What good will that do?"

"It will buy you goodwill. You can also then suggest that the wealthier factors might follow your lead. Most High Holders can't or won't do so."

"I still don't see . . ." Lorien shook his head.

"The factors are growing stronger. They're not strong enough, and you don't want to use the army to stop the High Holders from uniting against the factors." *Especially since it's not large enough to deal with all the High Holders at once . . . and not with senior officers who are the sons of High Holders scattered through the army, possibly even as regimental commanders.*

"You're the one who insisted the army was too large."

"I did. So did a number of others. As a result, you have a surplus of golds, far more than you're letting on. Using some of them is far cheaper than using the army. . . ." Alastar went on to explain.

Even so, he felt exhausted when he left the study more than a glass later and headed down the grand staircase and then to the center north door that opened into the rear courtyard. The good thing was that the rain had diminished to more of a drizzle.

When Alastar and Alyna set out from the Maitre's dwelling on Meredi morning, the drizzle had faded into a foggy mist, thick enough that he could only see the faint outlines of the nearest cottages of the married imagers. Lystara had departed less than a tenth of a quint earlier, wearing only her imager grays, with a spring in her step that had definitely been missing during the more than a week of heavy rain.

"She was more cheerful this morning," observed Alastar. "I don't think it was just because she didn't have to run with us this morning or wear her oilskin."

"I haven't minded the break, either," replied Alyna, with the half-mischievous smile that Alastar so enjoyed. "She imaged a set of jet buttons. Each had an embedded brass shank."

"You were there, I hope?"

"I was. She was worried that she might not be able to do them. The other junior seconds have been doing buttons at the factorage for over a month. Hers were perfect." Alyna paused, then added, "The second time around. She shouldn't have any trouble keeping up with the others when they do their afternoon duties."

"You had better fortune than I did. Her essay for rhetoric was grammatically good, but her penmanship . . ." Alastar shook his head. "She's even more in a hurry than I was at her age."

"Dearest, I doubt you were ever in a hurry. I fear that trait comes from me. I hated penmanship. Father had to switch me once."

"You?" That did surprise Alastar, given how deliberate his wife had always been, since he'd known her, anyway.

"Me." Alyna offered a rueful grin. "Deliberation has never come naturally. I've told you that before. It was so hard to be deliberate with you. Some nights I came back to the cottage and almost sobbed. I knew it was for the best, but . . ."

"Almost sobbed, except you didn't want to let Tiranya know?" Alastar had heard it before, but still liked to hear it again.

"I just couldn't." In a voice that was more subdued, she added, "Call it pride."

"You weren't the only one who didn't want to be deliberate . . . but you've known that all along."

"I did get that idea, but you were so polite about it."

"I'd never been really in love before. I do believe I did mention that."

"Once or twice . . . perhaps more than that."

They were both smiling as they walked the few remaining yards to the administration building.

Once there, Alastar said, "I hope today goes better with your mathematics session." He opened the door for her, then followed her into the entry hall.

"It will."

Alastar smiled and watched as she headed to the hallway on the right toward the chamber where, shortly, primes and seconds would appear and realize, again, that they had no choice but to learn.

Alastar's first task, once he reached his study, was to review the Collegium's finances, but the white-haired Dareyn was standing and waiting.

"Is there a problem?"

"No, sir." The old second paused, then added, "Factorius Hulet has requested a meeting with you at your earliest convenience. He'll come to Imagisle."

The fact that the chief of the Factors' Council not only wanted to see Alastar, but was willing to come to Imagisle, was a definite concern. Since becoming chief of the council, Hulet had not followed the practices of Elthyrd, his predecessor, and had avoided meeting with the Maitre whenever possible. "Did he say when he'd like to meet?"

"Today, if possible. His messenger is waiting in the reception hall to take back word."

"First glass of the afternoon, then."

"I'll tell the messenger."

"Thank you." Alastar turned and entered the study, leaving the door ajar. Sitting on the corner of his desk was his copy of the master ledger. Beside it was a single-sheet, badly printed broadsheet, with the one word in bold script across the top—*Veritum*. Alastar picked up the newsheet carefully, by the edges of the flimsy paper. He'd learned that the ink came off on his fingers all too easily. The newssheet—or scandal-sheet, as Dareyn called it—had begun appearing in late Juyn or early Agostos twice a week, usually on Mardi and Vendrei, and cost half a copper. Alastar had no idea who published it, but had found it was occasionally useful in providing information that might not have come to his attention until later.

The first story was about the flood damage caused to the livestock pens behind the old piers on the south side of the River Aluse downstream of the Sud Bridge . . . and how Factorius Duurmyn claimed he'd end up paying for all the repairs because, while High Holders had the rights to use the pens, they weren't obligated to pay for repairs, and had already informed him that they would not pay higher usage rates. There was also a story about "The Impersonator"—a risqué comic drama at The Yellow Rose about the daughter of a High Holder who posed as a wealthy factor's son in order to make her fortune before being married off to a dissolute widowed High Holder.

Given the subject matter, it must be very comic and even more risqué.

And there was something new—a black-lined box around some text that was definitely not gossip or news, headed by larger type—"The Finest in Men's Tailoring." The remainder of the text extolled the fine fabrics and fit provided by one Raabyrt, located at the corner of the Boulevard D'Este and Tailors' Lane.

Alastar nodded. Presumably Raabyrt was paying the publisher, and before long, at least if Raabyrt's business improved, there would be others.

After setting aside the newssheet, Alastar picked up the ledger and began to go through the receipts column, a column that thirteen years earlier had shown nothing but a monthly allowance from the rex. He was again reminded of the differences as he noted the receipts from the sales of fine papers, and especially of buttons. The buttons had come as an indirect result of the reason for Thelia's discovery as an imager. Thelia had mentioned that she had tried to image buttons for her mother, the Factoria Kathila, because Kathila had been complaining about how difficult it was to find suitable and durable buttons to supply to the fashionable women of L'Excelsis. The result had been the small factorage near the stables, where seconds and thirds imaged small items of value for a glass a day as part of their training. Factoria Kathila had been skeptical at first when approached by Alastar and her daughter, but after being presented with a matched set of jade-like buttons set in pewter, she had agreed to purchase and resell the buttons.

Before long, the golds brought in by the button-making, as well as other items suggested by Kathila, had quickly outstripped the amount brought in by the sale of high-quality paper, better than anything the papermakers, at least in Solidar, could provide, and far cheaper than parchment. In addition, the careful application of imaging to meeting the needs of the Collegium, in such matters as candles, lamp oil, furnishings, and repairs, had reduced the amount of outside purchases.

Even so, the Collegium still depended on the monthly payment from the rex for more than half of its expenses. *A far sight better than when you arrived.* The problem remained that, despite having been forced to show the power of the Collegium after the death of Rex Ryen, who was still referred to in many quarters as Rex Dafou, and as much as because of that power, Alastar was cautious about what he had the imagers do or make to raise funds, because all too many goods or services would have infringed on the Guilds, the factors, or the High Holders, and the Collegium's survival had already hung once on little more than a thread and the ability of a few imagers.

You still need to make the Collegium less dependent on the rex. He smiled ironically at the thought, since it was one he had often.

"Maitre Alastar . . ." Dareyn stood at the door, an apologetic expression on his face.

"Yes, Dareyn?"

"Maitre Bettaur hopes he might have a few moments of your time."

Why now? Especially so soon after the senior maitres expressed concern about him? "Have him come in."

Dareyn moved aside.

In moments, Bettaur slipped into the study, quietly closing the door behind himself. As Bettaur had grown older, Alastar reflected, not for the first time, the Maitre D'Aspect had grown even more handsome than he had been when Alastar had first encountered him as a third. Bettaur was broad-shouldered, yet trimly muscular. His strong and square chin had a slight dimple. A straight and modest nose was set off by striking brilliant blue eyes, a fair complexion with the slightest shade of honey, and fine blond hair. He was always impeccably groomed as well.

"Have a seat, Bettaur."

"Thank you, sir." The younger maitre's speaking voice was a pleasant baritone, and he looked directly and openly at Alastar as he settled into the chair directly across the desk. He also waited for an invitation to speak.

"What do you have in mind?" asked Alastar.

"Ever since that trouble when you first came here, sir, I've done my very best to live up to the requirements and precepts you set forth. I'm not looking for praise, but I'd like to ask if what I've done meets with your standards and approval."

"I'd have to say that your conduct and devotion to the Collegium have been exemplary." *Even if you don't trust the motivations behind his actions.* "Might I ask why you have brought this up?"

"Yes, sir, you might. I know I made a terrible mistake, and you and Maitre Alyna were more than fair in giving me a chance to redeem myself. I've worked hard to justify your faith in me." Bettaur paused. "But, sir, I have this feeling that everyone keeps looking at me, that no one will ever forget what happened."

"We often can't escape fully the effects of our early mistakes in life." *As you well know, Alastar.* "But you've done well."

"Sir . . . I was thinking, if you would consider allowing us—Linzya and me—to leave L'Excelsis and become a part of the Collegium in Westisle. We'd still be imagers there, with all the obligations and requirements, but people wouldn't always be looking at me and wondering about the past. It would be good for Linzya, too. You'd never know. . . ." Bettaur did not finish that sentence.

Alastar knew at what Bettaur was hinting. Linzya had come a long way from the illiterate girl barely better than the street urchin that she had been. Still . . . He nodded and paused for several moments before replying. "I wouldn't have thought of it like that, but I can certainly see how that would make sense on several levels. And you have been most diligent. At the same time, useful and attractive as the idea is, I'd like to think it over. I won't tell anyone else, except Maitre Alyna, and she won't tell anyone else, either. That way, whatever I decide, there won't be any other reasons for anyone to look at you and wonder about something else."

Bettaur nodded and smiled warmly. "Thank you, Maitre. I do appreciate the consideration."

"You're more than welcome." Alastar slowly rose and watched as the Maitre D'Aspect left the study, again carefully closing the door behind himself.

Now what was all that about? Alastar could understand the feeling of others always watching. Certainly, he often felt that way, with the High Holders and factors scrutinizing everything he did, not to mention Lorien. He still felt that there was more here. *But is that because of what happened . . .*

or because you distrust his bloodlines? And is that fair? But then, that was one reason why he'd wanted to think over Bettaur's request.

After a time, he sat down and returned to the master ledger.

Slightly less than a glass later, he set it aside again. While he had not
had any difficulty with Rex Lorien, that was because of Alastar himself,
as well as Alyna, even if few beyond Imagisle knew that, not because of
the strength of the Collegium, and Alastar wanted to leave the Collegium
far stronger than he had found it. That would require more income than
the Collegium currently created.

You have some time. He pushed that thought away. Maitre Fhaen had likely
thought the same thing, and he'd died at about the age Alastar was now.

Before he knew it, the anomen bells were sounding the ten chimes
that signified noon, and he realized, belatedly, that he'd meant to find
Akoryt and have lunch with him. The last bell was ringing when he
hurried up the stairs to the upper level of the administration building,
hoping to find Akoryt.

The red-haired Maitre D'Structure was just leaving his study when
Alastar appeared.

"I'd hoped we could talk over the midday meal," offered Alastar.

"That's the best offer I've had," quipped Akoryt. "It's also the only
one."

The two headed for the main staircase.

Alastar and Akoryt were later than Alastar would have liked in getting
to the dining hall. He saw that Alyna was already seated at the maitres'
table, with Tiranya at her left, and Seliora at her right. To Seliora's right
was Celiena, who had just become a Maitre D'Aspect, and who looked
a little awed, it seemed to Alastar, to be seated so close to the Maitre
D'Esprit who was also the Maitre's wife.

Alyna looked up to see Alastar and smiled, the expression that had
intrigued and warmed him almost from the moment he had seen her
smile . . . and still did. He couldn't help but smile back before he sat down
next to Akoryt near the end of the table. Immediately a second hurried
over and placed a pitcher and a mug before him.

Alastar glanced at the mug, definitely one of the better efforts of the
imager seconds, then filled it with dark lager, offering the pitcher to
Akoryt in a gesture of politeness, although he knew that the Maitre
D'Structure preferred the amber lager.

"You always offer, Maitre . . ." Akoryt laughed softly.

"I know. But I feel discourteous just ignoring you." Alastar waited until Tiranya handed the pitcher holding the lighter lager to Akoryt and he filled his mug. "How's that new prima doing . . ." For a moment, Alastar struggled to remember the girl's name. "Janya."

"She's doing better. Charlina has taken her in. She's even had her to dinner at her mother's cottage. On end-days, of course. Matriana Carmina's more than happy to feed Charlina's friends."

Alastar nodded. "That's good. How is Charlina doing with her own studies and imaging?"

"She's doing better since she took an interest in Janya. Janya adores her." Akoryt brushed back a wisp of fine red hair, hair that was beginning to show signs of gray, just as his face was showing lines from his eyes.

And it doesn't seem that long ago when he was the youngest of the senior maitres, reflected Alastar. "So long as it's good for both of them."

"I'll keep a close watch. Seliora and Tiranya are also keeping an eye on Charlina."

That wasn't totally surprising, given that Charlina's father had been well liked and respected and had died years before defending the Collegium. "Do you think that will help . . . ?" Alastar took a healthy swallow of the dark lager.

"Charlina has the talent to be a maitre, but . . . she's never really pushed herself. That has to come from inside."

Alastar nodded. That, he knew all too well. He waited as the server set platters in front of him and then Akoryt, containing what looked to be a sauced ragout over noodles. As usual, Dhelia was doing her best to use everything. He took a mouthful, discovering that the rather messy-looking dish was comparatively tasty. *At least it isn't refried squash and parsnips.*

The two ate for a time before Alastar spoke again. "On another subject, have you thought over the matter of training thirds to live inconspicuously off Imagisle?"

"You're talking about training those with solid normal skills but limited imaging abilities to act as spies, aren't you?"

"No. Not as spies. Much more as observers who can report from other large cities. I worry that all we really know is what is happening in L'Excelsis. I don't trust what I hear from the rex, or from the marshal, or from the factors. Nacliano and Ouestan might as well be in Jariola, Ferrum, or Otelyrn, for all we know."

"How soon would you want this to happen?"

"Not that soon. I think it will take years to do it right." Alastar could see the tenseness leave Akoryt.

"Why . . . ?"

"Why now? Because I'd like to get the Collegium used to anticipating problems, rather than reacting at the last moment."

"So I have some time to think this over?"

"Take as much time as you need." Alastar wouldn't have used those words with everyone, but Akoryt was not the type to stall or procrastinate.

"I'd like that. What you have in mind will require . . . consideration."

"That's why I asked you."

"I appreciate the confidence." Akoryt took a swallow from his mug. "Is there anything else?"

"No . . . not unless you want me to come up with additional duties for you."

"I'll pass on that, thank you."

At that moment, Alyna rose and slipped up behind Alastar, putting a hand on his shoulder and squeezing gently before leaning down and saying quietly, "Tiranya's asked me to spend some time observing the tertias during their work period at the factorage. Will you be in your study until fifth glass?"

"I will."

"Then I'll see you there when I finish."

By slightly more than a quint later, Alastar was back in his study, this time wondering exactly what he might expect from the outspoken and rough-hewn grain factor, a far less well-spoken man than Elthyrd was.

At a tenth before the first glass of the afternoon, Dareyn knocked gently on Alastar's study door. "Factorius Hulet is here, Maitre."

"Have him come in." Out of courtesy, Alastar stood, but did not move from behind his desk as Hulet stepped into the study.

The grain factor was lean, a good head taller than Alastar, who was anything but small or short, and his hair was the color of ripened wheat corn. Hulet's eyes were granite gray, and he immediately fixed them on the Maitre as he strode to the seats before the desk.

"Good day, Chief Factor." Alastar motioned to the chairs, then seated himself.

Hulet took the chair directly facing Alastar. "I understand you prefer directness, Maitre. So do I. I'll come right to the point. I understand that a number of High Holders have petitioned the rex to have their tariffs reduced because of the poor harvests in many parts of Solidar. Have I been misinformed?"

"You have not." Rather than explain his discussion with Lorien, Alastar merely said, "Apparently, many High Holders in this part of Solidar have lost most of their harvests, as have many smaller holders, I understand."

"They have thousands of golds laid up, all of them, and at the first sign that they might have to use them, they come to the rex asking for favors." Hulet's tone was scornful.

"What are your concerns?"

"We've all suffered as well. We've suffered more than the High Holders have, and we've been rebuffed on our tariffs being lowered."

While Lorien hadn't mentioned that, Alastar couldn't say that he was surprised. Although less secretive than his late sire, at times Lorien didn't inform Alastar of matters he considered not of import to the Collegium. "That's not all, is it?"

"What do you know that you're not saying, Maitre?"

"Nothing. I only know you wouldn't be here if you didn't think I should know something else about the tariff situation. Or am I mistaken?"

"The whole way tariffs are determined has been . . . shaky. It's gotten shakier, rotten even . . . and now the High Holders are sticking us even worse."

"How so?" asked Alastar evenly.

"I won't be telling you what you don't know . . . or should know. There's two parts to tariffs. First part is the annual levy on the worth of the land, buildings, and property. That's fixed for each High Holder. Doesn't change. For factors, it's two coppers on a gold's worth of land or buildings. Second part is the levy on how much you make. That's a silver and a copper on a gold, for us and for them."

Alastar waited.

"There's a passel of problems there, Maitre. First thing is that the High Holders have built factorages of their own on their lands."

"All of them?"

"Enough. We build something new or add something, and the Finance Minister's collectors make sure we get tariffed on it. Never happens, or almost never happens, when the High Holders do it. They can keep anyone they want off their lands. That's part of that so-called low justice privilege they got. If that isn't bad enough, they've come up with a way of not reporting all of what they make."

"How is that?" asked Alastar, intrigued by Hulet's revelations, and having the feeling he wasn't going to like what was coming.

"When they sell stuff to other High Holders, lots of times, they don't pay hard metal. They use bills of exchange, and they trade them among themselves, like the paper was golds. The Codex says tariffs get collected on the amount of golds, silvers, and coppers you make."

"And there's no mention of bills of exchange?"

"Not a word."

"What does Minister Sanafryt say?"

"He says he has to go by the Codex Legis." Hulet snorted loudly. "That's not all, either."

"Oh?"

"He claims that, even if the rex changes the Codex, the changes don't take effect until next year's tariffs are due."

"He's right about that," said Alastar. "Otherwise the rex could change tariffs the day before they're due, and then charge penalties for under-payment." *Among other things.*

"Suppose that makes sense. Don't have to like it, though."

"What do you propose?" Alastar didn't feel like fencing.

"Either reduce our tariffs or change the base tariff for High Holders. The way things are, they pay a lot less in tariffs than we do for the same buildings, lands, and profits."

"I can only advise the rex."

"He listens to you. May not like it, but he does."

"I doubt that he'll reduce tariffs for anyone," Alastar said evenly.

"Then he'd best increase them for those blood-sucking High Holders, otherwise . . ."

"Otherwise?"

"There's a lot more factors than High Holders. A lot more."

"I can only convey your thoughts and concerns, and I will."

"All I can ask. Right now."

Alastar was all too certain that the chief factor would be back . . . especially when it became clear how matters would likely develop. But then, Hulet doubtless already knew that and was laying the groundwork for later. "Is there anything else?"

"Not for now. I've said my piece." Hulet looked over his shoulder, in the direction of the door.

"You've made the situation very clear, and I do appreciate that." Alastar stood. "I wish you a good day, Chief Factor."

"Same to you, Maitre."

Alastar had hardly seated himself after Hulet had departed when Dareyn reentered the study with another envelope in hand.

"This came by private messenger, sir. The messenger presented this and left. He said he wasn't at liberty to disclose the sender."

Not at liberty to disclose the sender? Why would he say that when reading the missive would reveal that . . . unless it was anonymous. Alastar took the sealed envelope. Written in an elegant hand on the outside were the words

ALASTAR D'IMAGISLE
MAITRE D'IMAGE

Alastar didn't recognize the seal boldly stamped into the red wax. Finally, he opened it, careful to preserve the seal, and began to read.

> Maitre—
> The High Council has already informed His Grace Lorien, Rex Regis, of certain matters that may well affect the Collegium as well.
> If you are interested in these and other developments that may relate, I would be pleased to receive you tomorrow at first glass at the Chateau D'Council for an informal discussion, or, if that time is inconvenient, at any other time that is mutually agreeable.
> I look forward to your response.

The signature was that of High Holder Cransyr, and the seal was that of the High Council. Alastar couldn't help but wonder at the timing of the missive, arriving almost immediately after Chief Factor Hulet had departed. *Suggesting that Cransyr knows exactly what the factors are doing.*

But then, it might not be that at all, although Alastar wasn't about to wager anything on that thought. *Not at all.*

By just after noon on Jeudi, all signs of the clouds that had cloaked
L'Excelsis for more than a week had vanished, and Alastar rode northward on the West River Road, accompanied by two imager thirds, Oestyl
and Harl. Several blocks north of the Bridge of Desires, they rode past a
lane flanked by a bistro and a bakery, both of which Alastar remembered
all too well. The day was warm, as was usual during mid-harvest, and
he was more than glad he had worn his lightest set of imager grays, especially since, on hot days especially, the effort of maintaining his shields
tended to make him feel hotter. Perhaps because of the rains of the past
week, the shops on the west side of the road, particularly the bakery
and bistro, seemed more crowded than was often the case.

Two quints later, the three imagers crossed the Boulevard D'Ouest.
Alastar glanced at the Nord Bridge, repaired several years earlier by imagers, and nodded. Then his eyes focused on the Chateau D'Council, set
on a low rise more than a half mille ahead on the left. Since the events
immediately after the death of Rex Ryen, Alastar had been to the chateau only a handful of times in the succeeding thirteen years.

As always had been the case, however, two guards in maroon livery
opened the large, wrought-iron double gates hung on gray stone pillars
more than three yards high. Both nodded politely to the Maitre, then
closed them once the imagers had ridden past on the stone-paved lane
that separated two separate formal gardens. Alastar reined up under
the covered portico that could easily hold two carriages side by side.
Above the portico the dwelling itself rose another two stories. Imposing
as it was, with a frontage twice that of the Maitre's dwelling at the
Collegium, it was still too small to be considered a true chateau.

A footman walked in deliberate fashion from before the bronzed
double doors at the entry to the chateau and down three of the four wide
stone steps before inclining his head. "Maitre Alastar, welcome."

"Thank you." After handing the gray gelding's reins to Harl, Alastar
followed the footman up the steps and into the circular entry hall beyond the double doors. Out of habit, he tucked his visor cap under his

arm as he crossed the spacious hall, with its domed ceiling as high as the hall was across. The footman stopped outside the open third door on the right and gestured.

Alastar stepped into the receiving study. Almost nothing had changed there over the years. Two sets of armchairs were spaced in a circle around a low table on which refreshments might be placed. There were also higher tables set between the two chairs on each side. Those were newer, as evidenced by the lighter shade of the goldenwood.

High Holder Cransyr smiled politely, but not warmly from where he stood beside one of the side tables. His hair was as much silver as blond, and a straight nose accentuated the narrow set of his overlarge blue eyes. "Welcome, Maitre Alastar." He gestured toward the low table. "I understand you have a fondness for dark lager."

"Thank you for the invitation. And, yes, I do prefer dark lager."

"Excellent." Cransyr motioned toward the door of the study. Unlike some High Holders, who continued to wear doublets and hose, Cransyr wore an ivory shirt, with a bright green cravat, and a dark green jacket and trousers. His boots were black. He waited for Alastar to begin to seat himself, then did so at the same time.

In moments, an older woman appeared with a tray on which were two beakers of dark lager. She presented the tray to Alastar, who took the beaker fractionally nearer.

"We share the same preference in lager," said Cransyr mildly.

"So it appears," replied Alastar, suspecting that, while the High Holder might prefer dark lager to light, Cransyr most likely preferred wine to lager. Once Cransyr had a beaker in hand, Alastar raised his own beaker. "With my appreciation."

The two sipped.

Alastar found the lager excellent. He wouldn't have expected it to be otherwise. "Outstanding."

"I'd hope so."

"You suggested there are matters we might discuss."

"Ah, yes." Cransyr took another sip of lager before setting the beaker on the low table before him. "Matters that might affect the Collegium. Not that most matters, it appears, do not affect the Collegium in some fashion. I'm certain you have been following the questions of tariffs . . . and harvests."

"This year's harvests in the middle of Solidar have been largely ruined from what I can tell, although those in the east, especially around

Piedryn, have been excellent. It's still early for the harvests in the north-east."

"Some High Holders have petitioned the rex, individually, of course, and not with the blessing of the High Council, for relief of their tariffs. You are, I understand, aware of such petitions?"

"I am aware such petitions have been made. I have not seen any of them, nor is it likely that I ever will."

"I am also aware that, if he has not already done so, Chief Factor Hulet will approach you and Finance Minister Alucar in an effort to oppose any reduction in tariffs for High Holders." Cransyr smiled faintly. "He might even suggest reducing tariffs for factors, while raising them for High Holders."

"I don't know of a factor or High Holder who wouldn't be happier with lower tariffs." Alastar let a trace of irony creep into his voice. "The last time there was a problem with tariffs and no agreement could be reached, matters did not end well for anyone."

"We're not opposed to being tariffed fairly, Maitre. We are opposed to being tariffed unfairly. As High Holders, we have certain responsibilities that the factors do not have. We must provide more than wages. For those who live on the holding proper, we provide everything. Even those who have factorages on their lands provide housing and clean water and provisions for disposing of waste. Here in L'Excelsis, those who work for the factors must find their own housing, and the rex pays for roads, sewers, and even the water that flows from the public fountains. To pay for such, he uses the tariffs of both High Holders and factors. So the factors pay for such but once, while the High Holders pay twice."

"I wasn't aware that High Holders paid as much in wages as the factors do."

"When one considers housing, roads, and the ordered life on a holding, what workers get is about the same. That doesn't take into consideration the fact that our workers always have access to food and provisions, even when they have no coppers."

Alastar decided not to mention the fact that the "allowances" for food on most High Holdings valued basic goods at far higher levels than were the actual prices in L'Excelsis and other towns and cities. "What about the fact that the base levy for High Holders is fixed, regardless of what improvements have been made on the holding in terms of buildings, factorages, and the like?"

"That's what's in the Codex. It's been there for over four hundred years. Changing it because of a bad year isn't the best of ideas. If Rex Lorien does want to make changes in the Codex, then perhaps he should also change some of the provisions pertaining to factors. The High Council would be pleased to make suggestions there . . . in the interests of fairness, of course."

"I don't believe I suggested anything such as changes." The last thing Alastar wanted to do was to be caught in a position between the High Holders and factors, or either and Lorien. "I did note that the way tariffs are assessed on High Holders differs greatly from the method of assessment on factors . . . and it would seem that there is less difference, in terms of how each creates income, than there once was."

"There is one very basic difference, Maitre. A High Holder cannot sell off large portions of his lands and remain a High Holder. Nor can most holdings be divided between offspring. A factor can sell and buy as he wishes. That was and remains the rationale for fixing the base level of annual tariffs."

At that moment, Alastar realized something that he should have known years earlier, not that it would have made the slightest difference in what had transpired—that the tariff increases mandated by Lorien, and supported by the Collegium, had in fact struck the factors harder, because the increase was on the variable part of the tariff for High Holders, and not on the total, while it applied fully to both sections of the factors' tariffs.

"Don't look so surprised, Maitre. I assumed you knew that."

"I knew that," replied Alastar pleasantly. "I just had a twinge in my jaw. I was surprised. I was also thinking that, in a fashion, the rex is essentially a High Holder, since he is limited in what he can pass on to any children besides the one who succeeds him."

"Neither he nor his sire have seemed to have the same concerns as the council does," said Cransyr sardonically.

"Oh, but they have. Like you, they have wished to keep what they have and give up as little as possible. And that is true of the factors as well. The problem is, as you well know, that if no one gives up anything, roads cannot be built, navies maintained, smugglers halted . . . and many other matters would languish."

"That is true enough, but tariffing High Holders out of existence serves little purpose. I would suggest more revenue would be obtained, with less adverse consequences for all Solidar, by tariffing more highly those factors who have amassed hoards of gold because they underpay their workers and claim that they pay every idle relative, when in fact they pocket those golds, in order to reduce the profits they report to the Minister of Finance."

"You don't think terribly highly of some factors."

"Should I? Some of the most profitable factorages are stinking cesspits. You won't find anything like that on any High Holding."

Alastar was afraid, on that matter, Cransyr was largely correct.

"Even those factors who offer decent working conditions," Cransyr went on in a tone that suggested there were few such factors, "think nothing of the fact that most of their workers live in the worst of taudis, where cutpurses and villains of every stripe abound."

From what Alastar had learned from more than a few young student imagers, living conditions on many High Holdings were not much different from those in the worst of the taudis in L'Excelsis, except that there were fewer cutpurses, and also fewer young men who'd been suspected of such and who had "vanished" or "fled."

"You make good points," Alastar said mildly.

"You don't sound exactly convinced, Maitre." Cransyr's voice was dryly sardonic.

"I will admit that I recall too vividly the last time tariffs became an issue on which no one would yield."

"Both the factors and the High Holders agree now that tariffs should not be raised. We disagree on whose tariffs should be lowered."

"I can certainly convey your feelings on that to Rex Lorien, assuming you have not already done so."

"The council has conveyed its feelings to the rex. He has acknowledged our concerns and promised to give them the fullest consideration in light of all matters that must weigh in any decision."

Alastar could well imagine almost exactly those words coming from Lorien.

"In brief," continued Cransyr dryly, "he is likely to do nothing to alleviate the concerns of the more distressed High Holders. That being the case, the High Council would be even more concerned should he grant any form of relief to any factors or if he should, the Nameless forbid, add additional burdens to the excessive tariffs already paid by all High Holders."

"You've made your position quite clear," Alastar said with a cheerful tone he didn't feel.

"I fail to see that you have a position, Maitre, or that if you do, you have even intimated what it might be."

"The position of the Collegium remains, as it always has been, in favor of laws and actions that benefit all Solidar."

"I do not see, if you will pardon me, that you have articulated any such policies or actions." Cransyr's tone remained dryly sardonic.

"That well might be because I have not heard any such policies being put forth," replied Alastar, keeping his tone genial. "I have heard much about how either factors or High Holders wish to improve their position and how whatever the other has suggested is not in their own interest. I have yet to hear anything which goes beyond the interests of either, and I can only see that, at present, anything advocated by the Collegium would be attacked by anyone who perceived their interests as being affected adversely."

"Then perhaps you should offer an action which is indeed impartial."

As if anything impartial would be received as such. Alastar smiled, as warmly as he could. "Perhaps, in time, we shall. It might be best that the High Council and the Factors' Council consider additional possibilities first."

"Some might consider that a threat, Maitre."

"The Collegium endeavors not to make threats. We would prefer not to impose upon others unless they make it necessary."

"You are not offering much in the way of guidance, Maitre. Some might call that arrogance."

Alastar wanted to sigh. He did not. "I will observe that it takes a certain amount of golds to govern and administer Solidar. Rex Lorien has been far more prudent than his recent predecessors. He has reduced the amount of golds required for the maintenance of the Chateau D'Rex. He has cut the size of the armies in half, and moved the bulk of their forces where they are more effective in carrying out their duties. He has strengthened the navy and eliminated almost all piracy in the waters around Solidar. This has increased tariffs on trade, much of which was paid by merchants not from Solidar. He has made the justicers and the civic patrols in towns and cities far more impartial—"

"All of that benefits the factors and merchanters and costs the High Holders," interjected Cransyr tartly.

"He has greatly improved all of the main roads throughout Solidar," continued Alastar, not mentioning that the Collegium had also been helpful in that respect, particularly in improving the roads linking L'Excelsis

to other towns and cities, especially those nearby. "And he has eliminated the use of tariff farmers, and the surcharges they imposed on both
High Holders and factors. Tariffs are only a copper on a gold higher than
they were ten years ago."

"You're choosing your facts carefully, Maitre. Tariffs are six coppers
on a gold higher than they were fifteen years ago."

"And there had been no increase in tariffs for fifteen years before that.
An increase of six parts on a hundred over thirty years is scarcely excessive."

"To you and the Collegium, perhaps, since you pay none."

*No, we've all paid in blood and exile from the rest of Solidar, and in trying to keep you
and too many High Holders from destroying Solidar with your greed.* "There are different means of paying. Golds are by far the least onerous. I suggest you
also keep that in mind."

"Tariffs are only paid in hard metal, Maitre."

"I think you're missing something, Cransyr. I leave it to you to discover what that might be." Alastar rose, leaving the remainder of the
lager he'd barely sipped.

"Another of your famous cryptic utterances." Cransyr did not rise and
actually leaned back in his chair, almost languidly. "I will relay it to the
council." He paused. "Removing another High Councilor because he
did not bow to your whims, Maitre, might not be advisable."

"Removing *another* High Councilor?" Alastar laughed. "I wasn't aware
that I'd removed any. I did put a pair of daggers through a councilor's
boots, but that was after he tried to kill me."

"I was referring to High Holder Guerdyn."

"Guerdyn died of his own accord, as I recall. There was neither a
mark on his body nor a trace of poison. All that is well known."

"Every High Holder knows you were responsible."

Alastar shook his head. "A comparative handful of High Holders
believes that, but no one else does and, more to the point, no one else
cares."

"The High Council cares."

Alastar smiled politely again. "The High Council should also care
about what is best for Solidar, because that is far more in their interest
than what did or did not happen thirteen years ago."

"We shall see."

"That is true. I do appreciate your taking the time to make me aware of how the council feels, as well as your forthrightness in expressing it. I can only hope that you will consider all the matters involved before making any final decision." Alastar nodded politely.

"I would hope the same of you, Maitre. Good day."

Alastar nodded once again, then turned and left the receiving study. He smiled politely to the footman as he left the chateau, then mounted the gray. He had more than a few forebodings, given Cransyr's attitude and views. He hadn't expected much different, but Cransyr's polite implacability suggested that a clash between the High Holders and the great factors was inevitable . . . and that, for whatever reason, Cransyr was trying to goad the Collegium into reacting. On the surface, that didn't make sense, suggesting that there was much Alastar didn't know. Cransyr's attitude might be as simple as the fact that he only had one year left as head of the High Council, unless three of the other four councilors agreed on his continuing, and that might happen given that two of the other High Councilors, Olefsyrt and Staendyn, were largely dependent on the revenues from sales of grain, and other land-related produce. With High Holder Souven leaving the High Council at the end of the year, the only High Holder remaining with a more practical view was Meinyt.

On his return to the Collegium, Alastar rode directly to the stables, where he turned the gray over to one of the student imagers serving as an apprentice ostler. From there, he made his way along the stone walk from the stables past the brick walls of the refuse yard to the recently expanded "factorage."

Rather than disrupt the activities, after looking around and seeing no one nearby, Alastar raised a concealment before he neared the door to the building that had already been expanded twice since its creation more than ten years earlier. He waited several moments to see if anyone opened the door and left . . . and was about to open the door himself when a young imager third hurried out, headed toward the stables.

Moving quickly, Alastar slipped inside.

"Davour! Close the door, if you would."

Alastar recognized the speaker, Tertia Linzya, the recently wed wife of Maitre D'Aspect Bettaur. She stood at one end of the long table at which some eight older imager seconds sat. Before each was a small object, some circular, others square, and still others, Alastar knew, most likely hexagonal or octagonal. All the objects were buttons. At the end of the table were small bins, among them one filled with bone, another with various metal scraps, a third with shells, and a fourth with chunks of rock crystals of various shades.

Alastar eased around the table, watching and listening, until he stood slightly more than a yard from Linzya.

"Jaims . . . those aren't circles," said Linza politely. "If you cannot image a circle, try a hexagonal pattern. Keep the edges crisp."

Alastar smiled. The black-haired young woman who stood at the end of the table had come a long way from the illiterate boatman's daughter who'd had to scrimp and save every copper to send to her mother. He couldn't resist imaging a set of eight hexagonal buttons, each of black onyx, tightly rimmed in brass, laid out in two rows of four on the table just toward the middle from the two lines of small bins. As Linzya leaned forward, her mouth opening in surprise, he released the concealment.

While most of the seconds had been concentrating hard on imaging buttons, two of the eight looked up, eyes darting from Linzya to the Maitre. One—Howal—stifled a smile. The other was Yulla, who had been watching Howal.

Linzya turned, the surprise fading from her face. "Maitre . . . I . . . we didn't expect . . ."

"Of course not," Alastar replied with a warm smile. "Every once in a while, I need to surprise people." He looked directly at each second, pausing when he came to the fourth one. "Eskar . . . you really should have been concentrating on your imaging."

The long-faced blond youth swallowed.

Belatedly, Alastar saw two figures standing beside a high work table slightly behind and several yards to the east of Linzya. One was Charlina, and the eyes of the not-quite-stocky redhead were on him. From the way she studied him, he had the feeling she'd known he was there before he had dropped the concealment. The other figure was Janya, and her eyes were on Charlina.

Alastar forced his attention back to the seconds. "As Tertia Linzya doubtless told you, your best efforts at imaging buttons serve three purposes. They improve your precision in developing your own imaging abilities. They help support the Collegium. And they provide part of the coppers and silvers that you receive from the Collegium." He smiled. "They also provide a physical proof of your progress."

Linzya pointed at the eight perfect onyx buttons on the table. "You should notice that Maitre Alastar was able to image those while holding a concealment without any of you even knowing he was here."

Except for Charlina. And that brought up the question, again, of why the redhead was not progressing more, given what Alastar suspected were her true abilities. "It does take practice," he added in what he hoped was a humorous tone. "Since it does, I won't keep you all from continuing that practice." He turned to Linzya and murmured. "You're doing well with them." He frowned momentarily. "Aren't you doing something else . . . with some of the other thirds?"

"We're making fibulas. It was Maitre Thelia's idea."

"Fibulas?"

"They're like curved wire pins with a catch that holds the ends together. The small ones are used to pin clothing together, but you don't get stuck. Women like them decorative. The larger ones, that is." Linza blushed. "I didn't know that. Thelia had to tell me. Even Bettaur didn't know . . . or he pretended not to know so he wouldn't embarrass me. He's kind that way."

"I'm glad. Have you sold any of the fibulas?"

"Oh, yes. Factoria Kathila will take all we can supply, and each one brings in more than three matched sets of buttons."

"That's excellent." Alastar didn't have to feign the warmth in his words. That kind of initiative and result was what he'd been working to instill for years.

"Oh, thank you, Maitre."

"No . . . the thanks are mine." With a smile, Alastar eased past Linzya and walked toward the table where Charlina stood. "Good afternoon, Charlina . . . Janya."

"Good afternoon, Maitre," replied the imager third.

Janya nodded and said timidly, barely above a whisper, "Maitre, sir."

"How did you know I was there?" Alastar asked Charlina. "Under a concealment."

For a moment, Charlina did not reply.

Alastar waited, a pleasant expression on his face.

Finally, Charlina said, "I didn't know it was you, sir. I could just feel that someone was there, and I watched to see who it might be. It happens here in the factorage now and again. I began to notice when it happens in the last few months, especially the last week or two, but before, you never dropped the concealment."

Alastar managed not to show any surprise. He'd observed study sessions under concealment before, but hadn't visited the factorage using a concealment in months, not since spring, as he recalled. "Sometimes, it's necessary. Can you always sense a concealment?"

"No, sir. I don't think so. Just when someone's close, I mean."

"That might be a useful skill, Charlina. Most imagers can't sense that. Please keep working at it."

An expression of surprise crossed the third's face. "Yes, sir. Thank you, sir."

"But don't neglect developing your other imaging skills," Alastar added. "You have the potential to do much better than you've shown."

Charlina's eyes dropped. "Yes, Maitre."

"Having great potential is a terrible burden, young woman," Alastar went on dryly, "but you'll survive it. All the maitres have." With a parting smile, Alastar turned and slipped from the factorage. He had already decided not to make his way to the other end of the factorage where a handful of student thirds were working on imaging fine papers and stationery. At least one or more would have seen him, and he would have learned little that he did not know.

The fact that someone else was using a concealment to visit the factorage concerned him, unless it happened to be Akoryt, since overseeing student discipline and learning was his concern, but Akoryt hadn't mentioned doing so, and doing so without mentioning it would have been out of character. Still . . .

Once he was back in his study, Alastar wrote out a note to High Holder Meinyt, requesting a few moments of his time in the next few days, and then had Dareyn dispatch it with one of the older junior imagers used as couriers and messengers. The next task was considering with which other members of the Factors' Council he should meet. He was pondering whether to approach Factor Kathila or Factor Elthyrd first, when the study door opened slightly.

"Maitre . . ." Dareyn stood in the study doorway, holding an envelope. "This just arrived."

Even from his desk, Alastar could see the black and gray seal that signified that it had to have come from either the branch of the Collegium in Westisle or from Mont D'Glace, the remote imager facility set in the foothills of the Montaignes D'Glace far to the north where failed imagers, either blind or partly so, were exiled. "Mont D'Glace or Westisle?"

"Westisle, sir."

That could mean anything, but Alastar had a good idea what it might mean. *Either another appeal by Voltyrn to name a successor to Zhelan or a letter announcing Zhelan's death.* Alastar stood and took the envelope from Dareyn, then slit it open and began to read.

> *Maitre Alastar—*
> *With great regret, I must inform you that Maitre Zhelan died in his sleep last*
> *night. His steps had slowed some in the past year, but his mind remained sharp,*
> *and while we knew his days were numbered, the suddenness of his death came as*
> *a shock, beloved as he has been.*

Alastar wasn't that surprised. Maitre D'Esprit Zhelan had been in his early sixties when Alastar had left Westisle thirteen years ago. And, of course, Voltyrn's letter of a month earlier asking Alastar to appoint a successor foreshadowed the inevitable, but Alastar hadn't been about to do that while Zhelan was alive. Although Alastar and Zhelan had not been friends in any sense of the word, for just that reason, naming a successor while Zhelan was alive would have been cruel . . . and seen as such by those who did like him.

Then, too, while Zhelan had never overindulged in anything, he had been dubious about the value of exercise, especially for senior imagers, claiming that "imaging is more than enough exercise." That difference of opinion between Alastar and Zhelan had been one of a number that had led to Zhelan's suggestion that Alastar be considered to replace the dying Maitre Fhaen in L'Excelsis.

> *As you know, the most senior of the imagers here are Maitre Choran and*
> *myself . . .*

Alastar glanced to the bottom of the sheet and took in the signature just to make sure—that of Voltyrn, with the titles of Senior Imager, and acting co-Maitre of Westisle. He continued reading.

> *. . . and we are currently splitting the duties of the Westisle Maitre until the*
> *succession is determined.*

In short, which one of us are you going to pick? Because none of the other imagers presently at the Collegium in L'Excelsis had any knowledge of those at Westisle, the decision was up to Alastar, without the benefit of others' experiences, and the bulk of his knowledge rested on his growing up and spending his early years as an imager there . . . and on a visit made five years previously.

The sharing of duties by Choran and Voltyrn made it clear that Voltyrn, at least, believed that they were the only two viable candidates. Zhelan's infrequent reports had mentioned both Maitres D'Structure as capable, and since there was no one with the ability of a Maitre D'Esprit at West-isle, and the other Maitres D'Structure were much younger, Alastar had no doubts that he would have to pick between the two . . . unless he decided to send a Maitre D'Structure from Imagisle—and that would pose other problems. Then again, selecting a maitre from those in Westisle could well make matters worse.

So far as he knew, the Westisle Collegium was not overtly suffering, except perhaps from a lack of rigorous training that could produce a Maitre D'Esprit or even a Maitre D'Image, since it had become clear that Zhelan had slowly let lapse the training Alastar had initiated before he had left. Before Alastar's improvements, Zhelan had been having the imagers image what were effectively crossbow quarrels as a means of training and strengthening . . . and Antiagon Fire, which Alastar thought was self-defeating in the larger sense, because it spread and burned anything around it. While the quarrels were good for strengthening, they were totally useless for imagers who weren't essentially at least junior maitres. Of course, Alastar's change to iron darts hadn't set well with Zhelan, even if it had improved the training.

Alastar frowned. Voltyrn had been one of those close to Zhelan, and if he picked Voltyrn that also might make improving the training at West-isle a problem, since it appeared that the apparently less taxing training at Westisle might prove yet another problem, as it had been in L'Excelsis before Alastar had become Maitre. And then, there was the odd coincidence, if it were indeed coincidence, of Bettaur asking to go to Westisle. *He couldn't have been angling to be maitre there. He knows he's far too junior.* Coincidences did occur, but Alastar was dubious, even if he didn't know why.

Deciding to wait before making any decision, especially until after he discussed the matter with Alyna, he set the letter on the desk . . . realizing that Dareyn remained standing in the study. "Oh . . . the letter was to inform us that Maitre Zhelan had died."

"He was Maitre there for a long time."

"For over twenty years." Alastar decided against saying Zhelan would be missed. He certainly wouldn't miss a maitre who had resisted making changes at Westisle. "Thank you." He paused. "Don't send for him, but if Maitre Akoryt comes by, I'd like to see him for a moment."

"Yes, sir."

After Dareyn left, Alastar reread the brief letter again, then set it aside.

More than a glass later, the study door opened and Akoryt entered. "Dareyn said . . ."

"Thank you." Alastar gestured for him to close the door and then to sit down in one of the chairs across the desk from him. "This will only take a few moments." He waited until Akoryt settled himself. "I know that in the course of observing instructionals you have upon occasion used a concealment . . . as have I. What I need to know is whether you have done so recently in visiting the imager factorage."

Akoryt frowned, concentrating, before finally replying. "I've visited the factorage often, but only once under a concealment in the last month. It was on Meredi, the fourth, and I wanted to see how Belsior was presenting the materials instructional to the primes. He'd only been working with them a few weeks."

"How did he do?"

"Very well, I thought. He'll do better, but that comes with practice."

"No other times?"

"No . . . might I ask why?"

"Charlina apparently can sense concealments. She certainly sensed mine. When I asked her about it, she told me that someone had been visiting the factorage under a concealment often in the last few weeks. She said that I'd never dropped the concealment before. That was true, because I hadn't been there under a concealment."

Akoryt's frown deepened.

"As you can, I'd like you to approach Charlina at the factorage under concealment to see . . ."

"If she really can sense a concealment?"

"Exactly. If she can, it would be a valuable talent."

"You're thinking of Desyrk?"

Alastar nodded.

"If she can?"

"Then we may have another problem. I don't like the idea of an advanced third or even a maitre using concealments that way without letting anyone know, and especially not letting me or you or Cyran know."

"Neither do I, sir. I'll do what I can."

"Thank you. That's all I had."

Although his mind was still partly on Cransyr and the factors, not to mention the puzzle of the concealment, Alastar turned his attention, or most of it, to his copy of the Collegium's master ledger, now kept in Maitre Thelia's precise hand and script. While Thelia was doubtless far better at the accounts than Alastar would ever be, thanks to the training received from her mother, he still wanted to follow the expenditures and the modest income of the Collegium because they gave him a feel for what was happening in areas that he could not follow otherwise on a daily basis.

At a quint before fifth glass, Alyna eased into Alastar's study through the side door from the senior maitres' conference room.

Alastar stood immediately and moved toward her. He couldn't help but smile as she appeared. "It's good to see you."

"That means you've had a long day." Her smile was sympathetic. "What happened?"

"It began with a very hard meeting with High Holder Cransyr . . ." Alastar went over the details, ending with, "I got the definite impression that he was deliberately goading me."

"That's possible. He's not stupid, but he's also known to be intransigent about things he believes in."

"Intransigent enough to make someone who could remove him in an instant really angry?"

"You've made a point of being slow to anger, Maitre dear. At least in public."

"At least I've succeeded in publicly overcoming that fault."

"You also do well with Lystara."

"Even she is more reasonable than Cransyr or Hulet." He grinned. "But then, she is your daughter."

"My father would have disagreed with you about my reasonableness. What else happened?"

"I just received word of Zhelan's death."

"You did? He wasn't that old, as I recall."

"I never knew his exact age, but he wasn't eighty yet. That poses another problem. Perhaps two. There aren't any Maitres D'Esprit remaining at Westisle."

"There never have been many. You aren't thinking of sending me?" The mischievous smile played across her lips.

"Voltyrn and Choran deserve something like that . . . Voltyrn especially, but no, I'm not. You know I'd never let go of you . . . and that's what you wanted to hear." He put his arms around her.

"A woman likes to be appreciated." After holding him for several moments, she eased out of his arms. "Go on. You still have that look on your face."

"Voltyrn's been angling to be maitre there. I've mentioned it before."

"That bothers you."

"It does. He was close to Zhelan, and you know how I felt about Zhelan's views on training. Ancient quarrels, all because of tradition." Alastar snorted.

"There's also the fact that anyone who needs to push himself forward might not be the best person for the position if everything were to be considered."

"Very possibly. I'm going to have to think about it."

"There's more, I think. Bettaur?"

"You thought about that, too?"

"How could I not? It's a rather odd coincidence that he asked to be sent there the day before you receive word of Zhelan's death."

"It definitely is, but it just might be coincidence. Bettaur's far too smart to set up something that would look that obvious. Even if somehow he knew of Zhelan's death, and there's a real question of how he could even find that out before I did, he would know that making such a request so soon would raise far too many questions. He'd know that it would be far better to ask after whatever decision I make on the Westisle Maitre. If I pick someone from here, he could then volunteer to accompany them."

Alyna nodded. "You're right about that. But it is odd. What else?"

"I was at the factorage this afternoon, observing the younger seconds imaging buttons. Linzya was supervising them. Then I saw Charlina, and she informed me that someone's been using a concealment to observe students in the factorage. It wasn't me or Akoryt or you . . ."

Alyna said, "That's worrisome. Do you have any idea who it might be?" She paused. "If you don't know who it is, how do you know it was happening?"

Alastar told her.

When he finished, Alyna said, "Do you think Charlina can actually do that?"

"I think so, but I've asked Akoryt to look into it and see if she can sense him."

Alyna nodded. "Good."

"You have news of your own, don't you?"

"I just received a letter from Zaeryl." Alyna's lips turned up slightly at the corners, although her voice was normal enough.

"You occasionally do. This one must be different. What is on your brother's mind? Or is something wrong?"

"He's going to pay us a visit." Her noncommittal expression turned into an amused and wry smile. "You should read the letter yourself." She slipped the folded sheet from her light gray summer jacket and handed it to him.

Alastar took it and began to read.

Dear Alyna,

I've been remiss in writing. For that, I do apologize. The reason for that lack of sibling correspondence has been my preoccupation with several matters. I do trust you will understand, once I explain. I do not expect forgiveness, only understanding.

First is the matter of the porcelain manufacturing facility. Maarak has encountered some unusual difficulties. The nature of these difficulties is unprecedented, and I would like the opportunity to discuss them with you and with the Maitre.

Second is the matter of Malyna. She appears to take most strongly after her aunt, and a distant, if unrecognized, great-great-aunt . . .

Alastar managed not to laugh.

"You almost laughed," said Alyna.

"I see why you wanted me to read it."

"Go on. Finish it."

For these reasons, Malyna and I are traveling to L'Excelsis, and, while I could avail myself of the hospitality of others, I would prefer to be your guest, if this will not create any discomfort for you and your family. This journey will probably be the only one I will take to L'Excelsis at any time in the near or likely even the distant future. I would not be doing so if it were not necessary for the reasons I have mentioned, and several I have not.

"There's a family trait I see here," Alastar said dryly. "Several, in fact. He doesn't like to ask for assistance, either. Unless you see a reason to the contrary, your brother could certainly have the guest suite upstairs and Malyna the spare bedroom." He paused. "How old is your niece?"

"Twelve. Almost thirteen. She is his youngest, and was not expected." Alyna smiled. "You didn't finish."

Alastar resumed reading.

By the time you receive this, we will be close to halfway to L'Excelsis . . . I would not intrude unnecessarily, but some of the matters also bear upon the Collegium, beyond the obvious personal ones, of course. . . .

When he finished, he looked up. "I can't say that I'm not worried by this. Your brother, from all that I've heard over the years, seldom is ruffled by events. For him to undertake the journey here . . ." He paused. "We could foster Malyna."

"I'd very much like to . . ."

Alastar understood that. He also worried about how Alyna might feel if Malyna didn't wish to be fostered.

". . . but it might not be for the best."

"You want to meet her and talk to Zaeryl?"

Alyna nodded. "Also . . . Lystara might be a problem."

"Because she's so precocious in her imaging? Your brother suggested that Malyna was like you. That would mean she's talented." Alastar could tell that his wife did not want to hope too much.

"We need to see."

"We should tell Lystara."

"Tell me what, Father?" Lystara appeared in the main doorway to the study.

Appeared rather than stepped into the doorway, Alastar realized. "How long have you been able to handle concealments?" He realized his tone was harsh and added far more gently, "I'm not angry, only surprised."

"Just today, Father."

"Why today?" asked Alyna.

"Some of the thirds were talking about it this afternoon. Someone's been using a concealment to visit the factorage. They said it was Father." Lystara looked at Alastar. "I don't think it was."

"Today it was," Alastar admitted. "The other times it wasn't." He paused, then said, "Your mother and I would appreciate it if you would keep that to yourself for now . . . say for a month."

A slight frown creased Lystara's forehead. "Is it important?"

"It is," replied Alyna. "How did you learn about concealments? Just from listening?"

"It wasn't hard. The other day Maitre Shaelyt was telling the junior maitres about light, and how what we see is just the light that reflects from things. I got to thinking that if the light didn't reflect from me . . . if it avoided me . . . or sort of slid around me . . . then no one could see me." Lystara smiled shyly. "That was right, wasn't it?"

"It was indeed," declared Alastar. "Did Dareyn see you come in?"

"Oh, no. I waited in the outside corridor until no one was around, and then I slid the light around me, except it wasn't like that. I made a shield just for light, one that slid it around me. That's much easier."

Alastar managed to keep his jaw in place. Few thirds could manage that kind of concealment, and not even all Maitres D'Aspect. "I think you've inherited your mother's skills in imaging techniques."

"More likely your father's," said Alyna. "He was six when he first imaged things."

"Your technique, my age," replied Alastar.

"Father . . ." Lystara did not say more.

"We should go home," said Alyna. "You're both looking pinkish in the eyes." She glanced at her husband. "You haven't eaten since breakfast, have you?"

"I was a bit tied up with High Holder Cransyr." Alastar offered an embarrassed smile. Alyna always focused on his eyes to determine his state of health . . . and nourishment. "You're right. We should go."

Dareyn looked up as the three left the Maitre's study. "My eyes must be getting old. I didn't see Maitre Alyna and young Seconda Lystara enter the study."

"We came the other way," said Lystara. "We didn't want to bother you."

"It's all right if we're the ones intruding on the Maitre," added Alyna with a smile. "Good evening, Dareyn."

"The same to you."

Once they were in the corridor, Alastar leaned toward his daughter, "Nicely phrased."

"Thank you, Father."

Alastar straightened. *You only thought the problems with Lystara were subsiding.* Still . . . he smiled.

4

Later on Jeudi evening, well after Lystara had gone to sleep, Alastar and
Alyna sat in the matching armchairs in the sitting room adjoining their
bedchamber. A single oil lamp, set on the side table between their chairs,
provided the only light.

"She does take after you, dearest," said Alyna gently. "She's going
to be far taller than I am, physically stronger, and she began imaging
younger than I did."

"I could image coppers, but nothing like concealments," offered
Alastar.

"You might have been able to, if you'd known what she knows when
you were that young."

"She's far more precise than I was," protested Alastar. "That description of her concealment . . ."

Alyna laughed softly. "So she takes after both of us. That's likely to
mean trouble."

"She couldn't have been the one using concealments around the
factorage. She's never been free of supervision long enough . . ."

"Also . . . it was her overhearing others talking that inspired her to
try. I believe what she said. She's not that devious."

"Yet," added Alastar dryly.

"You still are rather skeptical of women, dear."

"Not of you. Not of Tiranya, and not of a few others, like Seliora or
Thelia . . . or Linzya."

"You've just named most of the maitres who are women."

Alastar found himself flushing. "You do have a way of bringing me
up short."

"Only in private, and only when necessary."

"For which I'm thankful."

"Sometimes that comes later," she added playfully.

Wanting to change the subject, if slightly, Alastar mused, thoughtfully he hoped, "I wonder how Quaeryt and Vaelora managed with two
daughters . . ."

"You only mentioned one."

"There are references to two daughters, but there's almost nothing about Vaerelya, except that she had 'some imaging talent,' according to Gauswn. Chaerilla was powerful enough to be senior imager for three maitres. They didn't rank imagers by ability the way we do now, but with what she did, she had to be the equivalent of a Maitre D'Esprit or even a Maitre D'Image. There might have been more about her, but . . ."

"Anything more would have been in the records that burned when Desyrk's cannon put the old administration building to flames," Alyna said. "Since our daughter can't be the imager who's prowling around under a concealment, who else do you think it might be?"

"In theory, any senior maitre and most of the junior ones. We can leave out Llendyr and Petros. Petros can't, and Llendyr can't hold anything but a blurring concealment for any length of time. Narryn isn't much better. As our daughter has shown, we also can't limit the possibilities to maitres. There are likely some thirds who might have figured it out on their own. They'd have to be strong or with good technique." Alastar frowned. "I can think of a number with the strength, but Linzya and Charlina, possibly Kaylet, are the only thirds with that kind of finesse."

"Kaylet's the main assistant to Petros, and the stable's close to the factorage."

"That's possible, but he doesn't seem the type."

"I'd agree, but . . . we just might be looking for someone who doesn't seem the type. The type who would seem the most obvious is—"

"Bettaur. But he knows we'd immediately think of him if he did something like that."

"I agree on that as well."

Alastar chuckled. "For now, we'll have to leave it at that. What are your thoughts on the succession at Westisle?"

"You know much more about that than I ever could. What do you think?"

"I'm afraid that either Voltyrn or Choran will continue Zhelan's practice of not challenging the younger imagers, and Westisle will end up the way Imagisle was before . . ." Alastar really didn't want to finish the sentence.

"Before you arrived and proceeded to upend everything for the better?"

"That's what I worry about."

"What about asking Smarthyl?"

Alastar shook his head. "He's got to be close to eighty. Even if he would take it, he likely wouldn't live long enough before I'd have to find a successor for him."

"Cyran won't do. He's a dear man and a good senior imager for you, and Meiryl has done so much so quietly, but . . ."

"He likes to be liked too much. He knows it, too. He'd do it if I asked, but he'd ask if it was a good idea."

"What about Taryn? He's solid and doesn't have that many ties here."

"He's a possibility. I worry that he's a bit like Cyran."

"I can see that, although he'd be better than Cyran. Who else is there? Anyone else with the ability to possibly become a Maitre D'Esprit is awfully young."

"You mean Arion or Shaelyt?"

"Arion would be a good choice. I'm not sure I'd want to lose Tiranya and Shaelyt."

"Then there's the problem of Bettaur," Alyna said blandly.

"He works hard, but only hard enough to get the job done." Alastar didn't have to mention that always pressing, if carefully, the limits of imaging ability was the only way for imagers to improve and strengthen their abilities. "Taurek's more likely to become a Maitre D'Esprit than Bettaur. If he were ten years older, I'd consider him. He's stubborn enough not to be worn down by imagers like Voltyrn and Choran."

"Oh . . . I forgot to tell you. Tiranya thinks that Linzya should be considered for Maitre D'Aspect in the next year."

"After she has her child, you mean?"

"You are the one who pointed out the dangers of excessive imaging on women with child."

"What do you think?" Alastar immediately asked. "About Linzya?"

"She's close to being ready, but she doesn't think she is."

"Like someone else?"

"I wasn't in a position to insist. Not until you came along, and then I didn't have to . . . and you know that, great and powerful Maitre."

Alastar winced. "Can you and Tiranya help there?"

"We're working on it." With barely a pause, Alyna asked, "Have you talked to Thelia about the factors . . . and why they're upset."

Meaning that you haven't and should . . . and that you don't want to talk more about Linzya right at the moment. "Not yet. I'll make a point of it tomorrow. I've also asked for a meeting with High Holder Meinyt. He's likely to be the only councilor even close to being reasonable—not that they all don't profess how reasonable they are and how unreasonable the factors are."

"Are the factors that much better?"

"Their range is greater," replied Alastar, "from totally unreasonable to absolutely logical . . . if based on incorrect assumptions."

"That sounds more like Lorien."

"He's been able to learn . . . at least a little. Too many of the High Holders have forgotten nothing and learned nothing. The factors, on the other hand, conveniently learn only what suits them."

"Is this going to be like it was with Rex Ryen?"

"What do you think?" countered Alastar.

"If it's about golds, and the factors and High Holders disagree, it could be worse, but in a different way."

"More indirectly?"

"More personally, with fewer obvious ties."

"Poisonings? Accidents?"

"And banque irregularities, perhaps failures, charges of manipulation of the exchanges, scandals, gossip . . . and in the end, High Holders trusting only High Holders, building up private armies, and withholding tariffs."

"With the factors pressing Lorien to use the army against recalcitrant High Holders?"

"It seems far-fetched, but . . ."

"You think it's possible," concluded Alastar.

"Possible, but not inevitable. You should talk to as many factors as you can before Zaeryl arrives. That way you will be able to present how the factors feel."

"And not just how we think they feel . . . or how Hulet claims they feel."

Alyna nodded. "You're tired. So am I." She rose from the armchair.

Alastar did not argue, but immediately stood as well, glad that she had extended her hand to him . . . and then imaged out the lamp.

5

Vendrei dawned clear and still, with a silvery haze to the sky that suggested that the mid-harvest day would be hot. When Alastar and Alyna left the Maitre's dwelling shortly after Lystara, Alastar found himself squinting against the early-morning glare.

As they neared the line of cottages inhabited by married imager maitres, Alyna spoke. "I need to talk to Tiranya."

"About Bettaur and Linzya?"

"What else?" She smiled. "That and a few other things."

"And I suppose Linzya insists everything is fine."

"Didn't she already tell you that? How could it not be?" replied Alyna sardonically. "She's married to the most handsome of maitres, the one that all the tertias swoon over and half the boys want to emulate. I'm certain he's as accomplished in the bedchamber as anywhere else."

"You still don't care much for him."

"Do you?"

"No," admitted Alastar, "but he's been absolutely faultless in his public conduct. He works hard, and he's willing to take on any task assigned to him. He's even suggested and accomplished some good projects that took a fair amount of work." *Not an exceptional amount, but solid effort.*

"So why did he marry Linzya?"

"You, dearest, would know that better than I. My masculine suspicion is that he had to. You told me that she's expecting. He likely felt that, if he didn't, we'd think much less of him."

"Shades of his father," Alyna said softly. "Even if he has no idea who his father was."

"That's definitely for the best." *For all concerned.* Alastar doubted that anyone living since Lady Asarya's "accidental" riding death, except himself and Alyna, knew that Bettaur and Lady Chelia were actually half-siblings. He didn't say more as he saw Alyna to the doorstep of Tiranya and Shaelyt's cottage, then continued on to the administration building—one designed and largely imaged into being by Alyna after the army's attack on Imagisle years before.

Dareyn was waiting with an envelope in hand. "It's from High Holder Meinyt, sir."

Alastar studied the seal and frowned. He'd never seen one like it, not that the design was complex. It wasn't. The wax was a grayish-green. The design didn't show a crest or some form of heraldry, just a single-span stone bridge under the two moons of Terahnar. *Trying to bridge between two shores . . . two views . . . two . . . somethings?*

He took his belt knife and slit the envelope. He definitely wanted to preserve that seal, at least for a while. After reading through the short note, he then turned to Dareyn. "High Holder Meinyt will see me at two quints past second glass. We don't have to send a messenger. He'll be expecting me unless I inform him otherwise. He's very practical." Alastar paused. "Is there anything else?"

"Maitre Cyran wanted a moment."

"That's fine. I'll see him immediately."

"Yes, sir."

In little more than moments, even before Alastar had a chance to look at the studies and discipline report left by Akoryt, Cyran was stepping into the study and closing the door behind himself.

"You're slowing down, Maitre. Some of the student thirds almost managed to keep up with you on your run this morning."

"They should be doing better than that. Compared to them, I'm ancient."

"I did mention that they should be able to keep up with a man twice their age."

More like three times the age of some. "What's on your mind?"

"You know I meet weekly with the commander of the Civic Patrol . . ."

Alastar nodded and waited.

"There have been a few . . . episodes . . . between young men in the last few weeks."

"Young men often have episodes, over either claims of physical prowess or women. Or over cheating at plaques. You're suggesting these are different."

Cyran offered a twisted smile. "These have been between the sons of wealthy factors and the sons of High Holders."

It took Alastar a moment before he said, "It has to be about plaques or bones and at the gaming houses. That's the only place . . . well, except at the Yellow Rose, but . . ."

"There was one episode at The Yellow Rose, but the others were at Alamara's and at Tydaael's."

"Alamara's? I thought they claimed to be factors of artworks."

"Smugglers of art and other items of dubious provenance, you mean?" asked Cyran. "That's the father. The son is Alamara the younger, and he has a tavern of some elegance, with several gaming rooms."

"I'm missing something, Cyran. Usually those establishments forbid weapons at the tables and enforce that with guards."

"They do. The incidents occurred later . . . outside."

"Has anyone been seriously hurt?"

"Commander Murranyt doesn't know. He thinks no one has been killed."

"Thinks? Commander Strosyl would have known."

"That's because Strosyl was once a street patroller."

"And Murranyt . . . I'd heard he only spent a few years on patrol before he went to headquarters. I can see him becoming commander, since he was the subcommander, but how did he get to be subcommander?"

"Favors and fortune, I'd guess. I asked after Strosyl's death. Things seemed to happen to people who crossed him."

"And he got promoted?"

"He never took a copper from anyone, anytime. Everyone knows that. He also was the one who cleaned up those patrollers who were shaking down the grain teamsters."

"A ruthless, honest patroller?" That combination of traits wasn't exactly to Alastar's liking, but honest and ruthless was better than dishonest and ruthless, and too many Civic Patrol commanders before Strosyl had been both. "It was too bad about Strosyl."

"The red flux isn't particular. Murranyt's worried someone's going to get killed if matters get more heated between the youngblood High Holders and the sons of wealthy factors. He didn't quite say it, but that's how I'd image it." The tall Maitre D'Esprit paused, then said, "There are over a hundred High Holders who maintain houses or chateaux in or close to L'Excelsis. There might be even more."

"That many?" While Alastar knew some High Holders who were not councilors had residences near the capital, that over a hundred did definitely surprised him. "And the incidents are increasing?"

"That's what Patrol Captain Heisyt told me."

"Do you think Alamara the younger would talk to me?"

Cyran chuckled. "There's no one in L'Excelsis in his right mind who wouldn't talk to you. Whether he'd tell you anything is something else."

"I might visit him."

"If anyone sees you . . ."

"I know. He'll likely say even less. I'll have to approach him in a fashion that few know who I am."

"That might be difficult."

Alastar shook his head. "There are more than a few gray-haired men in L'Excelsis. If no one sees the imager grays, who among those in the city would even look again?"

"I suppose that's true."

"If I carry full shields, the worse that can happen is that I'll be discovered."

Cyran frowned. "You think it's necessary?"

"I'm not certain, but it's better to look into matters that might not need looking into than to dismiss matters as unnecessary that prove otherwise. Is there anything else?"

"Not that I know of."

"Good. Let's hope it remains that way." Alastar doubted that it would.

After Cyran departed, Alastar walked out of the study. "Dareyn . . . I'm going to see Maitre Thelia. I shouldn't be that long."

Thelia had a small study off the main corridor, just south of and beside the senior imagers' conference room. She was seated behind a narrow table desk and looked up from what appeared to be a stack of invoices. "Maitre . . . what do you need?"

"Information . . . and after that, a cloak." Alastar settled into the single chair across the table from Thelia, a willowy Maitre D'Aspect with natural silver-blond hair and gray eyes, whose appearance and name had always left him slightly unsettled, no matter how much he reminded himself that she was absolutely no relation to Thealia. "The information first. I understand that you talk fairly often with your mother."

"Often. Less than many daughters do."

"Partly because your mother is a most successful factoria, I would gather."

"Partly." An amused smile crossed her thin lips.

"She has clients among both the wealthy factors and among a number of High Holders, I've heard. She is likely one of the few factors privy to overhearing observations and comments in a less rigid situation. I've received information that matters between a number of the more wealthy factors and High Holders are becoming increasingly strained. I wondered if she had mentioned anything along those lines to you."

"Maitre . . . such observations are possibly the last thing she would share with me. By mutual consent, we talk little beyond pleasantries, what is in fashion, and how the Collegium's factorage might provide goods to our mutual benefit."

"She should be proud of you," observed Alastar bluntly. "You're an imager maitre and have a position of responsibility."

"She is . . . now. But beyond abilities with numbers and the understanding of what lies behind trade, and the obvious tie of blood, we have little in common."

"Do you have siblings?"

"Ruel will inherit everything, obviously, since he is her only other child."

From Thelia's tone, Alastar suspected Thelia had doubts about her brother. "Then perhaps I should meet with her."

"I have no doubts that she'd be absolutely charming, Maitre. It would be best, I think, if you or Dareyn contacted her directly."

"I see." And Alastar did, even as he felt sorry for Thelia. "Would you rather have others . . . ?"

"Linzya is taking over more of that. She does it well."

"I did not mean . . ."

Thelia smiled, an unstrained expression. "I understand, Maitre. Mother and I are best with figures and ledgers between us and at being friends with a slight distance. I respect her great ability. She has come to respect my ability as an imager. Should I ever wed and have children, she will be a doting grandparent."

Alastar had wondered more than once why Thelia had not found someone. She was attractive and intelligent. But quietly strong-willed. "I'll take your advice. Now . . . about the cloak. I need one that would signify tasteful wealth and cover my imager grays."

"Meaning that you wish to be seen, noticed slightly, but not attract much attention."

"And not be completely out of place in an establishment less than perfectly suitable, perhaps as a father investigating the whereabouts of a son whose behavior he has doubts about."

"When do you need it?"

"Preferably before this evening."

Thelia nodded. "We can find or create something like that. Would fourth glass be sufficient?"

"More than sufficient. Thank you." Alastar rose.

Next, after stopping by his study and picking up the envelope with High Holder Meinyt's seal, he walked to the north end of the building where Obsolym had a study—and a private staircase and entry to the Collegium archives, some of whose records had been reconstructed, as possible, from Obsolym's recollections and research based on them.

The oldest Maitre looked up from the wide table desk and the stack of papers beside him. "Maitre . . . to what obscure question do you require an answer? Assuming I even know about it?"

Alastar extended the seal. "This is High Holder Meinyt's seal. Can you tell me anything about it?"

Obsolym studied the seal for a time before setting it on the table desk. "Meinyt . . . Meinyt." After a long pause, he said, "I can't be certain, but, as I recall, that High Holding was granted to the first regional governor of the lands that were Khel. "Other than that . . ." He shook his head. "Why do you ask?"

"I'm meeting with him later today, and I've never seen a seal like that. I wondered if there was a story behind it."

Obsolym laughed. "There must be, but it's not one that I've heard. If you find out, I'd like to know."

"You'll be the second one to know . . . if I find out."

"So long as it's your lady, that's fine with me."

Alastar was smiling as he made his way back to his study, but the smile vanished before he stopped at Dareyn's desk. "I'll need a rough map of the areas of L'Excelsis around Alamara's—that's the gaming house, not the 'artisans' factorage—and Tydaael's."

"Sir . . . ?"

"Maitre Cyran brought some problems the civic patrol is having there. The maps will be helpful. And . . . unhappily, I need them by around fourth glass. "I'll also need an escort, one of the thirds with strong shields, like Beltran or Noergyn, for an errand starting around two quints past fifth glass."

"Yes, sir." Dareyn's tone was not quite glum. "I'll take care of it."

"Thank you."

With that, Alastar returned to his study where he wrote out a note requesting a few quints with Factoria Kathila and then had Dareyn dispatch that. Seemingly before he knew it, he was riding north on the West River Road, accompanied by Beltran and Coermyd, both thirds who often served as his escorts.

High Holder Meinyt's dwelling in L'Excelsis was positively modest for a High Holder, roughly the size of the Maitre's house on Imagisle, a two-story gray stone structure overlooking the unnamed stream that fed into the River Aluse and located half a mille north and west of the Nord Bridge. The low iron gates were open, and the stone-paved lane led directly to a small covered portico on the east side of the main level.

A footman in green livery trimmed in gray appeared at the top of the portico steps just before Alastar reined up. "Welcome, Maitre."

The cheer in the footman's greeting was a rarity. In fact, offhand, Alastar couldn't remember the last time a High Holder's functionary had welcomed him so warmly. "Thank you." He dismounted and handed the gelding's reins to Coermyd.

"There'd be water for your men and mounts in back, sir."

"They'll appreciate it. So do I." Alastar gestured.

"Thank you," offered Beltran before the two eased the mounts forward and onto the lane that curved around the dwelling.

Alastar followed the footman through the door and into a comparatively narrow hallway floored in polished gray and white marble.

The footman stopped at the second doorway, where the door was open, and gestured. "High Holder Meinyt."

Alastar stepped into the very modest study, an oak-paneled room no more than six yards by four. Meinyt stood at one edge of a round table, a trim figure wearing gray trousers that were so dark they were almost black and a deep green jacket. He had graying brown hair and offered a pleasant smile. "Welcome, Maitre Alastar."

"I do appreciate your seeing me so quickly." Alastar had officially met the High Holder less than a handful of times, always at the annual year-turn ball held by the rex, and their conversations had been pleasant enough but short.

"I've heard that it's wise to meet with you, and always beneficial in one fashion or another." Meinyt motioned to the table. "Dark lager, I recall."

"You have a good memory."

"I have to work at it." Meinyt smiled wryly, then glanced toward the door, through which a serving woman walked with a tray on which were two lagers. "Talking can be a thirsty business." Once the server had left and closed the door, he lifted his beaker. "To useful conversation."

Alastar lifted his beaker as well.

They both drank.

"Good solid lager," said Alastar.

"It's an honest brew. You requested the meeting. What did you have in mind?"

"Finding out what I can from you about why Cransyr is trying to anger me and pick a fight with the wealthier factors."

"Fairly put, directly said." Meinyt nodded, took another swallow of lager, then set the beaker on the plain wooden square coaster that sat on the polished oak of the table. "The short answer is that I don't know. Cransyr claims that the factors are out to destroy the High Holders and that Rex Lorien is behind it all. That doesn't make sense. Lorien isn't the brightest flame in the fire, but he's not a clinker, either. Making you angry sounds stupid, and Cransyr's anything but that."

Alastar nodded and waited.

"I do know that Cransyr's not fond of imagers. I don't know why. Nualt claimed Cransyr's family has hated them for generations, but he didn't know why, either. Cransyr also doesn't much care for factors. Claims that they can do anything to make golds, and no one cares, and that there are lots of small factors who pay no tariffs at all."

"He's probably right that there are some," ventured Alastar. "Do you think there are that many?"

"More than the rex is tariffing. I could name a score in Alkyra. Even know a few here. I haven't gone out of my way to discover them."

"Why aren't the Factors' Councils collecting tariffs from them? What do they gain by letting them avoid tariffs?"

"Who elects the members of the Factors' Councils?" asked Meinyt.

Frig! That made a sad kind of sense, reflected Alastar.

"Obvious when you think of it that way, isn't it?"

"So Hulet here and other council members in the Factors' Councils in other cities feel the same way. If they add more members, the newer members have different concerns . . ."

". . . and the older and more established factors get replaced. The newer factors think that tariffs ought to be paid just on what they sell, and not partly on property and partly on sales."

Alastar had to think about that for a moment. "That's the same formula for both factors and High Holders, except the valuation on property is fixed for High Holders."

"It's fixed for factors, too," said Meinyt. "It's fixed at the value it cost when purchased, and that value includes large machines."

And the factors probably buy or make more of those . . . meaning the factors pay comparatively more on their property. "Even so, there's not that much difference in the way tariffs are calculated between those for some of the large and established old factors and High Holders." *Except over time, the High Holders do pay less, just as Hulet said, just not quite in the way he suggested.* "But for the more recently established and rapidly growing factorages . . ."

"There's more to it than that," Meinyt said, "but you get the idea."

"What happens when a wealthy factor becomes a High Holder?"

"That doesn't happen often. There's a definition in the Codex Legis . . . and if someone meets the definition, they still have to be approved by the High Council."

Alastar frowned. "Under the Codex Legis, the rex is the one who creates High Holders."

"He can create them and tariff them, but the High Council determines who can do more than that."

"You mean, be invited to balls and parties and help select members of the High Council? And trade directly with, bartering and the like?"

Meinyt nodded.

"I see. And since much of the value of being a High Holder is that association . . ." *It's not worth it for a factor to become a High Holder without it.* "When was the last time that happened?"

"Sometime before High Holder Guerdyn was head of the High Council."

That also explained another aspect of the resentment expressed by the larger established factors, not that any would actually admit to it, Alastar suspected. "What would you advise Rex Lorien to do?"

"I'm not about to advise anyone, Maitre, even you. Giving advice saddles one with all the blame and none of the credit."

"Then what aspects of the problem have not come to light that might make any decisions by the rex either less resented or at least more accepted."

"The word 'decision' suggests action."

Alastar shook his head. "To do nothing is also a decision, and sometimes that is the most difficult decision to defend, almost as difficult to justify as raising tariffs, or changing the tariff structure."

Meinyt laughed. "You've just covered all possibilities, without suggesting which course you might recommend."

"I may not be in a position to refrain from advising Rex Lorien. So if there is anything I have overlooked . . ."

"There's an implication behind your words."

"Since you're known to prefer plain-speaking, I'll say it directly, then. Because I will have to offer a recommendation based on what I've learned, I'll remember, and not fondly, anything that makes it more difficult for me to ascertain the facts about tariffs, and the assets and revenues on which they are based."

"That could be taken as a threat, Maitre."

"I don't make threats. I do my best to state matters factually. I said exactly how I would feel."

"I'm curious. Have you ever not removed someone who displeased you?"

"Quite a few times. High Holder Regial displeased me enormously. High Holder Haebyn shot and tried to kill me. Both are still alive, although I understand Haebyn occasionally limps. I found High Holder Nacryon to be callow, extraordinarily self-obsessed, and without almost a single redeeming quality. I've done nothing adverse to him. There are several others of position about whom I have similar feelings."

"And you have done nothing?" A smile played across Meinyt's lips.

"They did not threaten Solidar or the Collegium."

The High Holder picked up the beaker and took a small swallow. "You would judge what is best for Solidar?"

"That is one of the duties of the Maitre of the Collegium. The Collegium will not survive unless Solidar remains strong and united, with power spread between the rex, the High Holders, and the factors."

"The Codex Legis says little about the factors."

"Four hundred years ago, they did not have the power they do now or will have in the future. Neither the rex nor the High Council can afford to ignore that."

"What is the basis for that claim, if I might ask?"

"Tariff payments. Some years back, I persuaded the rex to let me look at the older tariff records. The amount of tariffs paid by factors has been growing for years, as have the number of factors paying tariffs. If the claims that some factors are not paying tariffs are true, then the growth and wealth of factors is increasing even more. At the same time, those tariffs paid by High Holders are remaining about the same."

"That would suggest that High Holder tariffs be reduced."

"A High Holder pays less in tariffs than a factor of comparable worth."

"A High Holder's assets are not so easily converted into golds."

Alastar smiled pleasantly. "I believe High Holder Cransyr has made that point most forcefully."

"You don't agree?"

"The point has some validity, but it's similar to claiming that a merchanter should pay lower import tariffs because he has a larger ship and thus fewer golds to spare. Carried to the extremes. . . ."

"You don't have to carry the point to extremes, Maitre. For all that you make interesting points, I fear that most High Holders will have difficulty accepting that factors must be considered as equals."

"I didn't say that. I suggested that the power of all factors will grow relative to that of all High Holders. Of course . . . if more of the wealthier factors became High Holders . . ."

Meinyt laughed, half sardonically, although also with a hint of amusement. "I've made that point myself before the High Council. I appear to be the only one who sees value in such a course of action."

"The rex could also lower the lands requirement for a High Holder, perhaps by also allowing larger tracts of land in cities to count additionally, perhaps two parts in five more."

"Some might accept that, if the rex didn't restrict the right of the High Council to approve possible new High Holders. Even so, Cransyr would be opposed to anything along those lines."

"Is he in favor of anything?"

"Besides double-tariffing factors? I doubt it. It's been rumored that's why Souven is leaving the council. That won't help settle matters, either. Souven must have half a score of factorages across the south."

"All of them in old Antiago?"

"Largely, I believe." Meinyt shifted his lean figure in the chair and glanced toward the door. "I don't know that I've been much help, Maitre." He took a last swallow from the beaker before replacing it on the table.

Alastar understood. "You've made a few things clearer. That's all I asked for." *Even if you did hope for more.* "You've been kind to see me. I did have one last question, out of curiosity."

"Oh?"

"You have a most interesting seal. Is there a story behind it?"

"There probably is," replied Meinyt with a laugh, "but what it might be I have no idea."

"I won't take more of your time." Alastar rose, then asked offhandedly, "Is the High Council scheduled to meet any time soon?"

Meinyt grinned as he stood. "Funny thing you asked. We're meeting next Meredi. Cransyr hasn't said why. Not yet, anyway. Wouldn't be surprised if we talked about tariffs along with whatever else the others want to bring up."

"I'd be surprised if it didn't come up," replied Alastar genially.

"There are always surprises in life, Maitre. You'd know that better than most."

Meinyt's parting words were still in Alastar's thoughts when he returned to the Collegium and made his way toward his study door.

"Maitre Thelia left the cloak you requested in your study, sir." Dareyn looked askance at Alastar. "The map is on your desk."

"Thank you. I have to meet someone who would rather not have it known that I'm meeting him." That was a partial truth, but Alastar didn't want to say more.

He was studying the map when Alyna arrived, this time through the main door, which she closed behind her gently. She glanced around the study, a frown appearing momentarily. "I see a cloak and a map. Are you wearing a long dagger?"

"Just a belt knife," replied Alastar with a smile.

"Does this have to do with what Cyran told you? You're going to Alamara's tonight?"

"I didn't tell him that."

"You didn't have to. You still have a tendency not to say everything until after it's over."

"I was about to tell you. I thought it might be more effective to play the role of the worried factor father to get to see Alamara the younger. Rather to get to the point of seeing him without the entire city knowing of it."

"Too many will still know within days. I'd say that I should go with you," said Alyna. "Except women don't accompany their husbands to such places, and, if they do go with a man, he's never their husband." She paused. "You will be careful, and carry full shields?"

"I always do, especially when I leave the Collegium."

"And don't drink anything . . . unless it's something you image yourself."

"You're worried."

"You're going someplace where no one knows who you are, and you'll look like you have golds. That can be very tempting."

"I understand, but I don't think I'll find out what I need to know unless I go, and the longer I wait, the worse things will get."

"You don't know that they're that bad."

"Tell me that again, dearest." Alastar looked directly into Alyna's deep black eyes.

Abruptly, she shook her head. "You're right. But I don't have to like it."

"Neither do I."

"I'll have Jienna keep some supper for you, just in case." She paused. "You are not to eat anywhere besides here tonight."

"I won't."

"Good." She softened the firmness of the single word by following it with a warm smile.

After she left, Alastar walked over to the dining hall and into the kitchen where he begged some bread and cheese and half a mug of dark lager. He hoped he wouldn't have to do much imaging, but if he did, he didn't want to do it on an empty stomach.

Noergyn, also wearing a cloak, if of brown, rode up outside the main entrance of the administration building just before two quints past fifth glass. "Where to, sir?"

"Alamara's Tavern. Do you know where it is?"

"It's in the theatre district. That's all I know."

After making one wrong turn, Alastar did find Alamara's, located on Players' Lane, a street unnamed anywhere except on the map that Dareyn had found for Alastar and located two blocks southeast of and running parallel to the Avenue D'Theatre. He reined up several yards from the brass-bound and dark oak double doors.

"Noergyn . . . just wait around here. I doubt that I'll be longer than a glass, possibly much less. Use a blurring shield on and off so that no one realizes you're here all the time."

"Yes, sir."

Alastar dismounted, then made his way to the doors. A pleasant-faced young man opened one for him without speaking. Beyond was a large public room, with solid but polished dark oak tables and chairs. About two-thirds of the tables were taken, but it was early, especially for a Vendrei, but a woman with a lutelin stood on a low platform, not even a dais, in the corner, singing.

. . . high upon headland, and clear out to sea,
my true love did sing out his song to me . . .
He sang and he wept and his words sounded true,
that never the night did I think I would rue . . .

Alastar recognized the song as an old folk tune, although he had no idea from where it had come, only that his mother had sung it at times. For a moment, he could say nothing, but he forced himself back to the task at hand as he scanned the room. From the layout, the gaming area was likely in the rear. He turned and made his way toward the archway on the left in the back, since he saw servers coming from the left archway with pitchers and trays.

"Sir . . . that's for gamers."

"I know. I'm looking for a gamester named Eleon . . . they say he's a friend of Estafen D'Elthyrd."

"Never heard of him," said the sweet-faced server, whose eyes were as cold as stone. "You need a pass to game."

"I'm not a gamer. I'm looking for someone."

The server eased aside, and from a recess just inside the archway stepped a large beefy man. "Sir, this is for invited gamers."

"I'm looking for a frequent gamer." Alastar stepped forward, using his shields to lever his way past the guard—or bouncer.

"Hold it. Right there."

Even in the dimness, Alastar could see the short, iron-headed cudgel.

"Don't care who you're looking for. You're leaving."

"I don't think so," Alastar said quietly, easing farther along the corridor, before stopping and anchoring his shields to the walls and floor.

The bouncer grabbed for Alastar's shoulder, but his hand slid off the shields. The cudgel came up, level with Alastar's eyes. The man tried to shove Alastar, who didn't move.

"Old man, you're going to move . . . or you're going to have a busted skull." The bouncer's spittle splattered off the shields, but the man seemed not to notice.

"I'll move," said Alastar, letting the cloak open to reveal grays beneath, but only to the bouncer, "but just to see Alamara the younger. If you use that cudgel, you'll break your wrist and look like a fool."

The bouncer attempted to knee Alastar, but staggered, his face turning white.

"I am an imager maitre, and if you don't take me to see him, you likely won't live the night."

The man was anything if not persistent and tried to jab Alastar in the gut.

Alastar imaged away the short cudgel. "Try anything else, and I'll image away a few fingers. Just yell out that the boss will take care of me and lead me there."

The bouncer swallowed, then finally swore, "You old goat! Let's see what the top has to say."

With those words, everyone looked away, except for the hard-eyed serving girl, who gave the smallest of headshakes.

Alastar unlocked the shields but kept them close to himself as he walked beside the clearly shaken guard along the corridor, past two more brass-bound doors, one on the left and the other on the right.

The guard paused at the last door, this one a shimmering black, but also brass-bound, then opened it and half-gestured, half-pushed Alastar into the chamber beyond, before following and closing the door. A gray-haired woman looked up from where she sat at a table desk placed just to the right of and forward of another door, this one of white oak. Against the wall to Alastar's right were three armless oak chairs.

"The top has to see him," the hapless guard announced.

The gray-haired woman looked coldly at Alastar.

He looked back evenly. "I'm here to see Alamara the younger. It's a matter of golds, of life, and, in a way, death. You don't want to know. You really don't."

Abruptly, the woman nodded. "Joast . . . get out of here. You forget you came here, and who you came with, and I'll forget about having you disappear."

"Yes, ma'am."

In instants, Alastar stood alone with the woman.

"Should I know you?"

"That's up to Alamara."

"Sometimes. This might be one of those times." She stood and rapped on the closed white oak door. "Someone to see you. Best you see him." She opened the door and gestured for Alastar to enter. He could see a chamber carpeted with a plush Jariolan tapestry rug, and a table desk shaped like a half-circle. As the door closed, he also saw that the man standing by the desk had a pistol pointed at his mid-section. Alamara the younger appeared scarcely older than some of the junior maitres, clean-shaven, with shortish brown hair and muddy brown eyes. He wore tight-fitting black trousers, a pale blue shirt with a black cravat, and a black vest.

Alamara wasn't quite what Alastar expected, although the pistol pointed at Alastar's mid-section was hardly unanticipated. Alastar imaged it out of the other's hand onto the table desk out of Alamara's easy reach, let the cloak slide open, then smiled. "I have no intention of causing a scene, other than the one I staged. Once we're through, you can tell everyone the obnoxious old man won't be causing anyone any trouble, that you took care of it."

"You could have asked for an appointment. I could scarcely have refused."

"It's better this way. You'd prefer that the Maitre of Collegium Imago not visit you openly—or you should—and I'd prefer that, for the moment, our discussion remain between the two of us. The reasons will, I trust, be clear before we finish."

"We could sit, like civilized men, Maitre." Alamara gestured toward the two chairs in front of the desk, taking one and turning it slightly sideways.

Alastar did the same with the second chair.

"Might I ask what you want?"

"Information . . . not anything that should provide a difficulty for you."

Alamara smiled openly. "What if I think differently?"

"I don't think you will, but feel free to suggest otherwise . . . after I explain. My first question is very straightforward. Have you noticed greater tensions or hostilities in the gaming rooms between those from a factoring background and those from a High Holder background?"

Alamara frowned. "I must say I didn't expect that question. Should I . . ." He paused. "You realize that we do not ask where our patrons were born or where they live, just that they establish that they have the funds to back what they wager."

"I understand that. I also have cause to believe that, with few exceptions, you and your people are likely excellent judges of backgrounds."

"Why do you say that?" An amused smile played across the younger Alamara's face.

"You are very successful." Alastar waited. "That means you understand both mathematics and people."

"Why did you come to me?"

"We've already talked to the Civic Patrol. There have been reports of . . . incidents . . . outside both Alamara's and Tydaael's. The patrol may not be as unbiased as you are."

Alamara laughed. "That may be one of the greatest compliments I'll ever receive."

"I suspect it's accurate. You judge people on their funds and behavior, not, as you said, on their background. That doesn't mean you don't know their background."

"Why are you asking me?"

"Because you'd be the first to see signs of hostility and anger between High Holders and factors. Your establishment is one of the few where the young men of means from both meet and interact."

Alamara paused. "I'd prefer not to be named."

Alastar was the one to laugh. "Accurate as I believe your judgments to be, there are others who would dispute my judgment. I have no interest whatsoever in naming you or Alamara's publicly. I do have great interest in knowing how the young men of wealth get on with each other."

"Some do. Most do." Again, the gaming factor paused. "We've had to separate more hotbloods in the past season or so than anyone can recall. It's usually always when a young factor or factor's son has more to wager than the son of a High Holder. There are table limits, but they're high at the most popular table."

"That's the most profitable one, of course."

"Of course. The girls do their best to keep things calm, and the guards are there just in case." After a moment, Alamara went on. "Several times last week, it could have gotten nasty. One of the factors told a young High Holder's son that he just couldn't buy a pot anymore. That wouldn't have been so bad, if he hadn't said something to the effect that young fops like him would have to get used to it."

Alastar let a wince show.

Alamara nodded.

"But part of the attraction is that those with factoring wealth want to use gaming to make points—and golds—from those they regard as the coddled offspring of High Holders?" Alastar raised his eyebrows.

"It might be. We don't ask. We're also very careful." Alamara smiled. "We've never seen an imager here. I assume that's your doing."

"A skilled imager would be unbeatable over time. He'd also be cheating in ways that aren't easily detectable. Gaming for gain is prohibited. Getting caught at it would mean that an imager would lose the ability to image."

"You'd kill them for that?"

Alastar shook his head. "Blur their vision or blind them. Then exile them to Mont D'Glace. The Collegium can't afford things like using imaging to cheat or deceive people."

"When was the last time you did that?" Alamara's tone was skeptical.

"Last month." Alastar didn't like mentioning Lannyt's blinding, even in general, but not admitting it would have be worse. "If we're fortunate, it isn't necessary very often, but there are always a few who don't listen or don't think the rules apply to them." *And then, there are those like Bettaur or Ashkyr, who are trouble waiting to happen.* But then, he worried that he was being unfair to Bettaur.

"It happens here, too, without imaging." Alamara lowered his voice. "We have our sources. One of them passed on a name. I won't say who. He's a factor's son who's a very skilled gamer. He makes a point of fleecing naïve High Holders. One of the highborn sheep tried to use a belt knife on him at Tydaael's. When either plays here, we've been putting an extra guard near their plaques table."

"What about outside, when they leave?"

"After ninth glass, there are two guards outside on the street. We can't patrol the city, but we don't want any incidents near the tavern."

"You used to only need one, didn't you?" Alastar had no idea if that happened to be the case.

"Only one . . . and only on end-day nights."

"When did you start adding the guards? Early summer?" That was another guess on Alastar's part.

"Toward the middle of Mayas."

Alastar nodded. "One last question. Are you seeing more factors' or factors' sons with more golds?"

"The numbers have been growing over the several years, especially in the last year. Quite a bit."

"Thank you. That's all I really needed to know."

"You're welcome, Maitre. In turn, might I ask why you're interested?"

"Because it appears that the factors and the High Holders are disagreeing on just about everything about how Solidar should be governed, and I wanted to see just how deep the disagreements run."

"And . . . ?"

"When people fight over the gaming tables more than they ever did, the level of disagreement is not likely to be trivial."

"It would seem that gaming might not be—"

"The best indicator? By itself, no. But it is an indicator, and there are others as well."

"I see." Alamara nodded.

Alastar could almost see the gaming factor calculating how to turn matters to his benefit. "I should go." He stood.

"How do you propose to leave here?" Alamara rose as well.

"You will escort me to the outer door of the chamber ruled by the gray-haired lady, bid me good-bye, and no one will even know I've been here, except for you and her, and she only knows I'm likely an imager."

"That simple?"

"Not simple. It just will appear that way." Alastar added a blurring shield around himself as Alamara opened the door to his personal study, and held it until he stood alone in the corridor leading back to the public room, when he converted it into a total concealment and edged his way along the side of the hallway.

Once outside, he eased from a full concealment to a blurring shield until he was within a yard of Noergyn, when he dropped it entirely.

"Sir . . . you surprised me."

"Good. Have you seen anything out of the ordinary?" Alastar mounted the gray.

"No, sir. Just well-dressed fellows who must have golds. And the two civic patrollers. One of them asked why I was here. He had trouble looking at me. I guess it was the blurring shield. I told them I was waiting for my master and wouldn't be long. He didn't come back."

"Just as well. Let's head back to the Collegium."

Samedi morning, Alastar and Alyna overslept and ended up being awakened enthusiastically by Lystara.

"Lystara," protested Alyna sleepily.

"Don't be so gleeful," mumbled Alastar.

"You always wake me up when I oversleep."

"Your father had a late night," explained Alyna, drawing a robe around her.

Alastar managed not to smile, since Alyna had also had a late night.

"You'll be late for breakfast," prophesied the ten-year-old.

"We won't. We won't run this morning," declared Alastar.

"You said it was best if we ran every morning."

Alastar sighed, and Alyna smiled.

Somehow, Alastar wasn't quite certain how, they all managed to get washed up, dressed, and eat breakfast in time to set out almost within a fraction of a quint of their usual time, with Alastar and Alyna only fifty yards behind Lystara, closer than their daughter would have preferred.

"She really enjoyed waking us up this morning," said Alastar.

"I'm glad you let her enjoy it."

"How could I not . . . at least after the first few moments?"

Alyna smiled. "The student imagers wouldn't believe you said something like that."

"That's probably a good thing. Right now, all Akoryt has to do is ask any who misbehave whether they'd like to explain things to me." Alastar's lips curled slightly. "Some actually shudder, he says."

"Everyone remembers that you're the one who turned an entire regiment and the whole River Aluse to solid ice."

"It wasn't the entire river—"

"Let them think it was."

"I might as well. Once I'm gone, or old and tottering, no one will even remember." *And that's likely to be sooner than you think.*

"You still think about Quaeryt and Vaelora, don't you?"

"How could I not? He killed over a hundred thousand men and imaged structures that will likely last aeons, not to mention single-handedly establishing Solidar . . . and almost no one knows his name. I killed a rebellious imager and army commander and one regiment, nothing compared to him." Alastar didn't want to dwell on that and immediately asked, "I take it that there's nothing new as far as Bettaur is concerned?"

"You wouldn't expect there to be, would you?"

He shook his head. "Even as a tertius, he left few traces. Now . . . I doubt if there will be any at all. That's what worries me. He could be every bit as devious as both of his parents put together; he's learned patience; and he's an imager."

"You know that there's no proof that he's Asarya's son?"

"Proof is confirmation of facts. That some facts cannot be confirmed doesn't mean they're not true. Asarya had a third child who supposedly died at birth, but no one ever actually witnessed the child's death, and Bettaur is the right age."

"It is suspicious that both Bettaur's guardians died suspiciously almost immediately after he came to Imagisle, but that could be coincidence."

"Do you think so?" asked Alastar.

"No, but what if we're wrong? Both about him and his birth?"

"Do you think we are?"

"No. That doesn't mean we're right, dear Maitre."

"I'd wager on your feelings."

"We can't discipline Bettaur on feelings," she pointed out.

"But we can look into things and prepare in case they turn out to be accurate."

"As you always have," she replied with a smile. "Are there any discipline hearings scheduled for next Jeudi?"

"Not at present. We've been fortunate this month. But after the mess with Lannyt . . ." Alastar shook his head. He still hated having had to mention it to Alamara.

"He should have known better . . . and then to . . ."

"There wasn't much else we could do, besides blur his vision and send him to Mont D'Image."

"Have you considered who could replace Smarthyl?"

"That's another problem. We don't have to face that yet, thankfully."

"Have you decided what to do about Westisle?"

"Nothing for the moment. Taryn would do well . . . but . . ."

Alyna nodded, understandingly.

"Besides, I have the feeling that this is one of those times to dither."

"Deliberate waiting is not dithering."

"That's what Voltyrn will call it. Choran will likely call it deliberative, since he'll take it as a sign that I have my doubts about Voltyrn, which I do."

"A day or two, even a week, won't matter. The same is true about Bettaur's request. Besides, you don't want to decide on that before deciding on the Maitre."

"And after that?" Alastar shook his head, then asked cheerfully, even though he well knew the answer to his query, "Geometry instructionals this morning?"

"And more on the basics of surveying, all of which you know, because I've muttered about the willful obstinacy of several. Most of them will silently groan and will try to ignore the fact—and the explanation—that knowing geometry can actually make you a better imager."

"If you learn it well enough and just don't go through the motions. And speaking of geometry and where you learned it, when do you think we can expect your brother?"

"He travels fast and light. Possibly even by Lundi night, no later than Meredi. That's if the weather holds."

"Is there anything about Malyna you haven't told me?"

"I don't think so. Remember, all I have to go on is Zaeryl's infrequent letters. She was born after we wed, and since Zaeryl hasn't been in L'Excelsis since he brought me here as a ten-year-old . . ."

"I don't think you ever mentioned that."

She laughed softly. "You didn't ask."

Alastar shook his head, mock-dramatically.

When they reached the administration building, Alyna headed for her study and Alastar for his.

"There's a message on your desk, sir," offered Maercyl, the older second seated behind Dareyn's table desk. "Dareyn was feeling unwell and asked if I would fill in."

"I hope it's not serious."

"He didn't say, sir."

"Let me know if you hear more . . . and thank you." Alastar nodded, worried about Dareyn. He didn't worry about Maercyl, since he had certainly taken over Dareyn's duties before without difficulty or incident.

The envelope on his desk was sealed with a lavender wax, a wax scented to match the seal. Alastar had no doubts who had written, and he opened the missive immediately and began to read.

Dear Maitre Alastar—
I would be more than pleased to receive you at the upper factorage at any glass on either Lundi or Mardi morning.

The signature was simply "Kathila, Factoria."

Alastar nodded and sat down to write a reply, one which, when he had finished, stated that, unless he heard otherwise, he would call upon Factoria Kathila at ninth glass on Lundi morning.

He was about to take the sealed reply out to Maercyl when the second appeared in the study doorway. "Maitre Akoryt would like a moment."

"Have him come in."

Akoryt closed the door as he entered, not the best of indications, then seated himself in front of the table desk.

"What else has gone wrong . . . or might?" asked Alastar dryly.

"Something unusual happened last night. Oestyl and Glaesyn wanted to get away. It was around fifth glass. They crossed the Bridge of Desires and walked up to that bistro on West River Road. The one where—"

"I remember." How could he have forgotten? "That's not a short walk."

"It's the best bistro on the west side of the Aluse, according to Oestyl. Anyway, he noticed a rider on a chestnut that seemed to be following them. Glaesyn thought that the man was just riding north and taking his time, but when they left the bistro, they could hear, at times, hoofs on the pavement behind them. Glaesyn can handle basic protective shields. He's hopeless with concealments. Oestyl can use a blurring shield, but not a full concealment. That was enough for them to slip into a side lane and then move to where the lamp from one of shops let them see that the same man was following them again.

"Oestyl kept up the blurring shield, and they took a back walkway for a time, but when they neared the Bridge of Desires, they spotted him again. He was waiting for them, but didn't see them. Oestyl used the blurring shield while they walked to the Bridge of Stones and crossed there."

"Does either of them owe anyone anything? Or been involved with someone's wife or lady friend?"

Akoryt shook his head. "They both say that they can't think of anything, even things that could be misunderstood. That's why they wanted to tell me."

"Can you think who might be following imagers, especially junior imagers who aren't students?"

"No, sir. Neither of them could, either."

"I can't, either. That makes it unusual, even worrisome. I don't want to make it a command"—*not yet*—"but I'd like you to suggest to the students and the other seconds and thirds that anyone who intends to be out off Imagisle after sunset either be with another imager or good friends. See if you can get to as many as possible this morning, since many will likely go out this afternoon and evening. You can tell them that there's been more violence in L'Excelsis lately, and we'd like them to be more careful for a while. That's definitely true, about the violence, from what Cyran reported yesterday."

"I can probably reach most of them."

"Good . . . and thank you."

After Akoryt left, Alastar sat back in his chair. Who had an interest in watching junior imagers? Was someone going to try assassinating less talented imagers? Or to discover if they used imaging in ways that could be used as a lever against the Collegium? Or merely to see if they could discover more about imaging?

The last seemed far-fetched, but he couldn't dismiss it out of hand. *Not yet.*

7

The remainder of Samedi went uneventfully, or at least with as little drama as was possible when a ten-year-old girl was involved, as did Solayi, even to the evening services at the anomen. Since, as Maitre of the Collegium, Alastar felt obligated to attend those services, he was grateful that Chorister Iskhar's homilies were largely focused on values, rather than upon the Nameless. That was as it should have been, given that the tenets of the Nameless opposed the glorification of the individual and centered on positive accomplishments, not that there hadn't been choristers in the history of Solidar who had focused on the ritual and not the meaning.

On Lundi morning, Alastar was still thinking about a variation on that theme when he entered the administration building and headed toward his study—perhaps because Iskhar had made the point in his Solayi homily that all too often ritual became a comfort that precluded action, as did day-to-day habits. *Have you become too settled in your ways to be as effective a Maitre as you could be . . . as you should be?*

That thought vanished as he saw Maercyl standing beside the desk outside his study. "Dareyn? How is he doing?"

"He's better, sir. Maitre Gaellen says it was the green flux, but he should be back to work in another few days. It might be longer, though."

The green flux? Alastar didn't like that at all. It wasn't nearly as deadly as the red variety, but it wasn't pleasant, in addition to being especially hard on infants and older people. And Dareyn was well beyond middle years . . . and then some. "Does anyone else have it?"

"Some of the primes have it. They're in the infirmary."

"Is there anything else?"

"No, sir."

"I'll be back in a few moments." Alastar turned and headed down the north corridor.

When he entered the archivist's study, Alastar didn't see anyone around. Nor did he hear anyone. He walked to the open door at the top of the steps down to the lower level and called, "Obsolym?"

"Coming! Coming . . ."

Before long, Obsolym trudged up the steps. He glared at Alastar. "If it's more history you want to know, you could have come down and saved an old maitre another climb up and down." For all the gruffness in his voice, the white-haired Maitre D'Structure smiled.

"It isn't that. I wanted you to know that several primes are down with the green flux—"

"I know. Gaellen came and told me. You two . . . you'd think I was ancient."

"You're the closest to an ancient we have, and I don't want you catching something like the green flux. I'd appreciate it if you kept some distance when you're doing your history instructionals for the primes."

"That's all you came to say, most masterful Maitre?"

"That's absolutely all, you intransigent intellectual," replied Alastar with a laugh.

"I'll think about it."

"Good . . . and keep thinking about it."

"You're not so young anymore, either," Obsolym said.

"But I've had the green flux, and most people who've had it don't get it again."

"Good thing for you."

"With a young daughter, yes, it is. Oh . . . that seal of High Holder Meinyt . . . he has no idea what it means or how it came to be."

"That doesn't surprise me."

"Now that I've disrupted the beginning of your day, I'll leave you in peace."

Obsolym shook his head mournfully. "That's what they all say."

Alastar couldn't help grinning as he turned and left.

Once back in his study, after instructing Maercyl to inform all the senior imagers that the next senior imagers' meeting would be on Jeudi morning, he went over the morning attendance report, although he was certain that Akoryt would have let him know immediately if any imagers were missing. Then he took out his copy of the Codex Legis and began to read. . . .

He'd been studying the Codex and had not found what he sought for less than a quint when a messenger from the Chateau D'Rex arrived with a request that Alastar meet with Lorien at the third glass of the afternoon. That would mean a long afternoon, since most meetings with Lorien were anything but short, and it took between two and three quints to ride back to Imagisle, even using the Boulevard D'Rex Ryen. Whatever Lorien wanted meant more work for Alastar, one way or the other, but since the rex seldom indicated what the difficulty might be, Alastar would just have to wait until after third glass.

He went back to searching the Codex.

At less than half a quint before ninth glass, Alastar dismounted before the "upper factorage" mentioned by the factoria—a low brick-walled structure just off the West River Road west and south of where the Sud Bridge spanned the River Aluse. He handed the gelding's reins to Aelbryt and walked toward the entry.

A young girl dressed in gray trousers and shirt stood on the single low front step of the factorage. Drab as her clothes were, they were clean and without holes or patches, and she wore sandals that had seen better days. Without a word, she opened the door for Alastar, but did not follow him inside.

"She's in her study, Maitre," said a white-haired woman who rose from the table desk in the small anteroom. "It's the first open door there."

"Thank you." Alastar tucked his visor cap under his arm as he made his way to the door and entered the study, closing the door after himself.

With a narrower face than her daughter, but with striking silver-gray hair, light gray eyes, and a slender but feminine figure, Factoria Kathila was an attractive woman. She rose gracefully from behind a jet-black table desk with wide rounded corners. The only objects on the desk were ten buttons, a broach, and what Alastar thought was a hair clasp, laid out on a dark green velvet cloth. All were silver.

"You closed the door, Maitre Alastar. Am I to assume either secrets or my daughter to be the subject?" She frowned momentarily, then smiled. "Secrets, most likely, since your actions suggest you're pleased with Thelia." She gestured to the single chair before the desk and reseated herself.

Alastar sat down and replied, "I'm more than pleased with her. You should be as well."

"You have a daughter. Are you pleased with her?"

"So far," replied Alastar with a smile. "There are times that I'm less pleased, but I suspect that's true of all parents."

"What if she were not an imager?"

"If she worked hard and did well at something else, I'd like to think I'd also be pleased." Before Kathila could say more, he went on. "Is it because she is so well suited to carry on what you have done and is precluded from doing so because she is an imager . . . and you're letting me know that?" *While not mentioning that your son is not half the person your daughter is.*

"You can build something that will outlast you."

"No, Factoria, I can build something that has the potential to outlast me . . . and it can be destroyed by poor decisions in years. It's almost happened several times." That might have been an exaggeration since Alastar only personally knew of one time. "I will grant that I have some greater say in grooming those who may succeed me, somewhat more than in the case for great factors and factorias, or High Holders."

Kathila gestured to the objects on the green velvet cloth. "They're solid silver, all of them, except for the broach. The stone is peridot. What do you think they're worth?"

"Whatever someone will pay for them. That much silver, unworked, is likely worth half a gold. I don't know gemstones."

"You're as cautious as my daughter claims. Strange for a man who risked his life to save a nearly worthless rex and a failing Collegium."

"Compare all that to unworked silver, Factoria."

Kathila's laugh was soft, but somehow slightly off-key. After a silence of several moments, she said, "I didn't have to say what I did, Maitre, and it's not that I'm not proud of Thelia."

"But she will never be Maitre of the Collegium, and she might have become a truly powerful and wealthy factoria."

Kathila nodded. "Now that I've explained that, what do you want from me?"

"Information and insight that will likely benefit us both."

"Such as?"

"Besides feeling that tariffs are too high . . . what do you feel should be done about them and why?"

"You won't support a reduction in them. Why should I say anything?"

"It's not possible to reduce them. It would make everyone's life easier if Rex Lorien could."

"You can always spend less. I know."

"One can always spend less by doing less. Do you wish fewer patrols in the Southern Gulf . . . and more piracy? Fewer warships, and Jariolan and Ferran privateers boarding more merchant ships? Less spent on roads and longer times in transporting goods? Less spent on the Civic Patrol and more brigandage? I've studied the matter for years. Rex Lorien has reduced spending wherever he can. The finances of Solidar are not perfect, but there are no great savings to be made without requiring far higher tariffs within a year or two."

"Then why ask?"

"As a starting point. I met with Chief Factor Hulet last week, ánd then with Chief High Councilor Cransyr."

"Were you not the fortunate one?" murmured Kathila.

"Each felt that his people were overtariffed and that the other's people were undertariffed. Both feel most strongly, more strongly than I've seen at any time since the last time tariffs were an issue."

"That surprises you?"

"No. But the degree of vitriol does concern me. That is why I wish your thoughts and observations."

The factoria nodded, but said nothing for several long moments. "Hulet is plainspoken. He is rough, but he has tried to keep tempers down in council. The last meeting . . . he was furious." She paused. "That was before he met with you. We have not met since."

"Did he say why he was so angry?"

"No. Elthyrd asked him. Hulet only said that it was past time that the High Holders could threaten and demand and expect factors to back down."

"I wonder who threatened him," mused Alastar.

"I thought the same, but I could not say."

"Did anyone ask him if he'd been faced with a demand or a threat?"

"Goeryn did. Hulet said that anytime anyone thought they could coerce him with threats was when the Nameless took up naming."

"Do you know of anyone else who's faced threats . . . or veiled hints?"

Kathila smiled sweetly. "I know less than anyone, except that which comes before the council and that which I've discovered from wives and daughters, and that is comparatively little."

"If that is so . . . ?"

"Why am I even on the council?" Her smile turned cold. "It might have something to do with my creation of various products in high demand, both for factorages . . . and other purposes, and I know who has used them and for what."

"It also might have to do with the facts that you are one of the wealthiest of factors and that you maintain ties with your daughter, who is an imager maitre."

"You already knew much of that."

"What else do you know about . . . shall we say stresses between various factors and High Holders?"

"Hulet holds significant notes from several High Holders. So do Estafen and Weezyr—even if his Banque D'Aluse is only five years old."

Weezyr? Estafen? After an instant, Alastar recalled the second name. "That's Elthyrd's son, the one who has the Banque D'Excelsis? Is it true that he's already far wealthier than many High Holders?" Again, that was a guess on Alastar's part.

"Many? Who would know. Certainly, he's better off than Paellyt, Laevoryn, Delcoeur, or Aishford."

The quick listing of High Holders revealed just how many Alastar still didn't know, since the only names he recognized were those of Delcoeur and Aishford. "Delcoeur? I haven't heard that name in years."

"The late Lady Asarya's brother keeps a very low profile. Wouldn't you, in his position?"

"Do his financial straits come from the dowry her father . . . ?"

"That is doubtless part of the problem. The major difficulty is that most bulls have more intelligence. Lady Delcoeur—Elacia—manages the lands well, but not well enough to support all Delcoeur's habits."

"He games excessively?"

"Two nights out of seven he'll be at Tydaal's or Alamara's. The other nights . . . few are spent with Elacia."

"Are Tydaal and Alamara considered factors?"

"So long as they pay their dues to the council."

Almost a glass later, Alastar stood. "I must thank you. You've been most helpful."

"How could I not, Maitre, if I want both my children's futures to be bright?" Kathila rose gracefully in a manner vaguely familiar, yet not exactly. It took Alastar a moment to recognize from where he'd recalled that almost sinuous grace—*Thealia*. Somehow the past was never always past.

"Maitre . . . did I offend you?"

Alastar laughed. "No . . . not in the slightest. Sometimes . . . let us just say that some matters that should remain ashes don't always."

"Too many, at times." She smiled. "I may have kept you too long."

"Not at all."

"You will think about what else I suggested?"

"At some point, before year-turn, you will receive what I promised." Alastar wasn't quite certain why he'd agreed to image a pair of formal boot or shoe buckles, except that he was obligated for the wealth of information, and rather than play favorites among factors, providing a good was a better alternative—although he had no doubts that Kathila would sell the buckles discreetly . . . and for far more than they were worth.

There was also the fact that he'd always been slightly susceptible to manipulation by women, which was one reason he found Alyna so attractive. Not that she couldn't manipulate, Alastar suspected, but she found it distasteful in dealing with those she respected or loved and lowering herself in dealing with those whom she found unworthy of respect.

As he departed, Alastar did note the faint but amused smile on Kathila's face. He had no doubts that she felt she had the better end of the bargain . . . and, if he had been a factor, she certainly would have, but so much of what was mere gossip about what was commonly known among factors did not often reach Alastar, or anyone on Imagisle. *Something else that needs remedying.* He'd known that for years, but he'd felt that until the Collegium had more mature imagers and depended less on Lorien's financial support, developing what amounted to an intelligence network would have been unwise, especially if discovered, and not worth the risk. In addition, selecting and training such imagers would also take years.

He was still thinking about the lack of information when he reached his study and found Cyran waiting for him in the anteroom. "You can come into the study and tell me what else went wrong while I was gone."

"You know me too well," said the senior imager as he closed the door behind himself. He did not sit down but stood beside the desk and said, "A merchanter's son is missing."

"Don't tell me. He won at the tables from some High Holder's spoiled offspring, left either Alamara's or Tydaal's, and vanished."

"Alamara's. Early on Solayi morning, just after midnight. A beggar claimed to have seen a coach stop by a man and that two others jumped out and grabbed him and threw him inside. The coach drove off. The patrollers don't doubt the beggar, but it was dim and at a distance, and it could have been men grabbing a friend . . . or grabbing the young man. There was nothing special about the coach."

"What about the horses or the driver?"

"The beggar couldn't tell, and no one else saw it . . . or wants to say anything about it. The street couldn't have been empty, but so far no one else seems to have seen what happened."

That didn't surprise Alastar. "A merchanter's son . . . not a factor's son?"

"The young man's grandfather was a factor. The son fell on hard times, but he has a shop that sells and tailors garments. Not all that far from the theatre district."

"That suggests that the young man was either very good at plaques or very skilled at cheating at plaques."

"Both, according to Patrol Captain Heisyt. But it wasn't plaques. It was bones. Tydaal's men have been watching him, but they can't figure out how he does it."

A low-level imager who hid his talent? "I doubt it matters anymore. His body might turn up downstream if they didn't weight it enough."

"You know that?"

"It's just a guess, but that's how most people disappear in L'Excelsis, just like most of those who disappear in Westisle end up as fish food."

"Why a merchanter's son?" asked Cyran.

"As a warning, I'd guess. Both to others who are too good for their luck and talent, and to factors' offspring who win too much. It's bad enough for a High Holder's offspring to lose to a factor's son, but to a mere merchanter's brat. . . ." Alastar shook his head. "The gaming houses will let anyone in who is moderately well dressed and has golds or silvers and is willing to hazard them. Very few who are not well-off have either the talent or the golds to last long in gaming."

"The problem is that more and more factors' sons have both golds and skill?"

"That's what Alamara as much as said. I'd be very surprised if Captain Heisyt doesn't have more problems in the months ahead." *If not sooner.* "And so will we."

"Sir . . . ?"

"I hope I'm mistaken, but I think there's more going on than we have any real idea about. It may even involve Lorien. He's asked for a meeting this afternoon. He never asks for meetings anymore unless there's a problem that he can't handle . . . or doesn't want to."

"You'll let us know?"

"Whatever it is that the rex wants . . . hopefully not something like more road repairs or an expansion of the paving in the chateau courtyard."

Alastar's last words were acidically dry. The stone repaving and expansion of the chateau stables the previous year had not been one of his favorite imager projects, possibly because the rex had kept changing his mind.

Cyran's face registered dismay. "I hope not. Anything but something like that."

"That's not even the worst. The stable business was irritating, annoying, and frustrating, but limited. We could face something like the tariff disaster when Guerdyn defied the rex."

"Cransyr can't be that stupid, can he?"

"He's more arrogant than Guerdyn and colder. At times, there's not much difference between arrogance and stupidity. Arrogance, though, is the brother to treachery. I'll let you know, either this afternoon or tomorrow, depending on how long it all takes."

After Cyran left, Alastar just sat behind the desk thinking, before going back to search the Codex Legis.

What with one thing and another, he had to hurry to get out of his study by a quint past second glass to meet with Konan and Borlan, who had his gray waiting outside the administration building.

He reined up at the foot of the unblemished and apparently indestructible stone steps leading up to the main entry of the chateau less than half a quint before the glass, and reached the top of the grand staircase, only to find Lady Chelia standing there with her three children. At sixteen, Charyn was already taller than either of his parents, but thankfully, so far as Alastar was concerned, his eyes were green, and his hair thick and sandy blond, unlike that of his mother—and her other male relations. Bhayrn was slightly built, more like his father, with dark hair, but blue eyes, while Aloryana was blond and blue-eyed. She smiled at Alastar, but the expression was both tentative and mischievous.

He smiled back, then asked Chelia, "To what do I owe the honor of encountering the whole family?"

"Mere chance, Maitre Alastar . . . and Aloryana's desire to meet a 'real imager.' We won't keep you."

"It is good to see you all in good health." Alastar inclined his head, then turned toward the north hall. He could hear Aloryana's words to her mother behind him.

". . . he's old . . ."

Alastar winced. He wasn't that ancient.

He barely made it to Lorien's study before the bells chimed out third glass.

"No one anywhere is satisfied, except perhaps for you, Maitre Alastar," said Lorien as Alastar sat down in front of the goldenwood table desk. The rex brushed back a lock of limp black and silver hair from his forehead. "The factors are unhappy with tariffs. The High Holders are unhappy as well and are demanding that, if tariffs are to be increased, the increases fall on the factors . . ."

But Meinyt said that the High Council wasn't to meet until Meredi. Was Cransyr acting alone and claiming the council was behind him?

". . . and the High Council's latest petition is demanding that, as rex, I override the Chief Justicer's decision that any case of murder on High Holder lands must be tried in a justicing court and is not within the purview of traditional low justice." Lorien glared at Alastar.

"From the first, under the Codex Legis, murder cases have never been the under the low justice authority of the High Holders. That's all you have to write in upholding the Chief Justicer."

"Easy enough for you to say. High Holder Lenglan was charged with murdering his lady after he found her in bed with the younger son of High Holder Farlan. Lenglan claims it wasn't murder, but self-defense, because they were conspiring to murder him, and that it falls under low justice because it was on his lands and his holding was therefore threatened."

"So why did it even come to the High Justicer?"

"Because the late High Holder Farlan insisted. He also likely bribed more than a few people, including Justicer Kastelyn. I've heard rumors, but . . ." Lorien shrugged. "Anyway, Farlan's son was crippled. Lenglan beat them both with a blunt blade while they were asleep. At least they were asleep when he started. Lenglan closed his gates and retreated behind his considerable walls. Farlan had no other options but to insist on a trial. He also persuaded all the exchanges and the local banque to refuse any transactions by Lenglan."

"What happened to Farlan?"

"He had a seizure in the hearing before the regional justicer in Daaren, who also vanished mysteriously after rendering the verdict of deliberate murder against Lenglan. Farlan died later, but his eldest son filed his own petition requesting that Lenglan's appeal be denied."

"It does sound messy." Alastar kept his voice level, although the ramifications of what had started as a simple but deadly love triangle were looking to be staggering.

"I asked Chief Justicer Veblynt about it. No High Holder has ever been charged with murder before the High Court . . . or any regial court."

"In over four hundred years with more than fifteen hundred High Holders?" Alastar didn't find it so surprising that some deaths had never come to official light—or to court—but that none had was certainly indicative that the High Holders of Solidar regarded themselves as sovereigns over their own lands. "Why now?" His voice turned ironic.

"Partly because the Factors' Council in Daaren petitioned the High Justicer not to allow the claim of self-defense to be a matter of low justice. They also pointed out that Lenglan has a long history of refusing to obey the regional justicer's findings that Lenglan owes more than a thousand golds to members of the local Factors' Council."

"Murder and a power struggle over golds."

"I see that. I can't let a High Holder get away with something like that, but I'll probably have to send a battalion of troops—and some cannon—to drag the bastard out of his holding." Lorien snorted. "Every High Holder will claim that I'm using what was a killing out of self-defense and infidelity to allow factors unlimited use of the high court to exact damages from High Holders."

"He owes the golds and won't pay them?"

Lorien rummaged through the papers on his desk, finally finding what he sought and thrust it at Alastar. "Read it."

Alastar took the single sheet and began to read.

Lorien, Rex Regis D'Solidar
Your Grace—
It has come to the attention of the High Council that the Factors' Council of the river village of Daaren has lodged petitions with you and with the High Justicer in the pending appeal of High Holder Lenglan . . .
Upholding even the trial of a High Holder for murder in a case where that High Holder was threatened and dealing with spousal infidelity is a clear and obvious violation of the provisions of the Codex Legis that reaffirm the long-standing practice of low justice administered by each and every High Holder.
In addition, the attempt by small and local factors to link their claim of fiduciary jurisdiction over High Holders by regional justicers is a clear attempt to invalidate the right of locus dominatus by High Holders . . .

"*Locus dominatus?*"

"It's an old Tellan legal term meaning the total legal right to all justicing. I had to have Sanafryt look it up."

"That was invalidated by the Codex Legis. So they're trying to . . ." Alastar broke off.

"What? I hate it when you get an idea and leave me hanging."

"It's all a legal ploy to get back what they think are the rights of low justice, and the right to answer effectively to no one on their own lands."

"The High Council claims that trying a High Holder infringes the rights of all High Holders."

"As you have told me," Alastar said evenly, "Lenglan found his wife and her lover asleep and beat them so badly with a blunt sword that the wife died and the young man is crippled. I have difficulty with seeing how that equates to self-defense."

"I agree," replied Lorien wearily. "The problem is that the High Council is staking out a position to establish that practically nothing they do can be tried before any court, even the High Court."

"This is only the first step," Alastar pointed out. "They're trying to put you in a position where each action you take will anger more and more High Holders."

"I won't have it. You can't have it, either."

He's right. "Have you received any other petitions or communications from the High Council or any High Holder?"

"What does that have to do . . . ?" Lorien frowned. "High Holder Ruelyr has requested the right to reinstate tolls on the section of the roads built on his causeways. That's the only one."

"I'd wager that levying tolls on the rex's highways that pass through their lands was another privilege revoked by the Codex Legis."

"Then you believe they will besiege me with all manner of requests and petitions? That each will seem reasonable to other High Holders?"

"It would not surprise me," replied Alastar cautiously.

"Nothing all those greedy bastards would do could surprise me."

Certainly nothing that some High Holders might do would surprise Alastar, especially Cransyr or Haebyn, or their allies, but he wasn't yet willing to image all of them ice black.

"They might even raise an army against me," declared Lorien. "I have little more than a regiment of troopers remaining in L'Excelsis. Six battalions at most. *That* is what comes of following your 'advice,' Maitre."

"Over two thousand men. That should be more than sufficient, considering that none of the High Holders can raise more than a few hundred." *And if they raised a force large enough to be a threat, they'd spend more time arguing over who would lead it than planning what to do.*

"If they turn the Civic Patrol against me?"

"They won't. The Patrol has less than two hundred men." *And enough of them know what imagers can do.*

"You have an answer for everything, don't you? Except all your answers haven't solved the problem. Why not?"

"Because the times are changing again. The High Holders haven't lost power, but they can see that they will. That's making them angry. The factors and merchanters can see that they aren't being treated fairly, and if matters continue as they are going, they'll get even angrier. If matters are made more fair, then the High Holders will get even angrier. If you or the Collegium acts in a way that greatly favors either side, that side will attack you. If you try to suppress both . . . or do nothing, they'll eventually unite, if only temporarily, and attempt to remove you."

"You're saying anything I do will make matters worse! So what am I supposed to do?"

"Nothing for the moment. We need to let them play a plaque or two." Alastar just hoped he could find a way to turn those plays into ways to channel or deflect the anger into something less destructive.

"I don't like it, Maitre. I'm getting petitions from factors in Estisle and Nacliano. They're complaining that High Holders are refusing to pay for goods in a timely fashion, waiting seasons, even. All of this is just another set of trials . . . one after another." Lorien sighed, then looked toward the open north window.

By the time Alastar finished listening to Lorien and then rode back to Imagisle, it was well past fifth glass, and he rode directly home, where he dismounted, and let Konan and Borlan take the gelding back to the stables.

Alyna was waiting for him in the front hall. "There's a pitcher of dark lager waiting for us in the study, with biscuits. Dinner won't be ready for another glass, and you look like you need both."

"That good?"

"I knew you met with Factoria Kathila and with Lorien."

Alastar followed her into the study, where a platter of biscuits, two beakers, and a pitcher were set out on a tray. They took the two chairs in front of the desk.

Alyna poured the lager. She said nothing until Alastar had taken a long swallow. "I imagine it's been a very long day."

Alastar nodded and took another swallow of the lager before replying. "I have the feeling that matters will get worse."

"Because of what Kathila said . . . or Lorien? Or both?"

"Both."

"What did you discover from Kathila, and what did it cost you?"

Alastar told her, beginning with Kathila's observations about Hulet, and the threats apparently made to the grain factor, and the debts owed by various High Holders as well as all the other details . . . "and in the end, I did promise to image a set of ornate silver boot buckles, sometime before year-turn." He paused. "I'd appreciate it if you'd make a design. Something uniquely geometrical."

"I can do that, but I'm not so certain I shouldn't accompany you on your next visit."

"That might be for the best," Alastar agreed. "I'm also worried about Dareyn and some of the young imagers. The green flux has showed up, and Dareyn has it. He's not a young man."

"Neither are you. You should stay away from him until he's well."

"I'm a good fifteen years younger than Dareyn." Alastar decided against mentioning that he'd already had the green flux.

"And you've been working harder for all of those fifteen years."

Alastar wasn't about to argue when her voice turned that firm. "There's also something else you should know. It's something I think we should discuss with your brother when he arrives. The High Holders are in effect petitioning for the return of their standing above the law of the rex . . ." He went on to explain what he and Lorien had discussed.

Alyna waited until he finished before saying, "They want to turn Solidar into fifteen hundred little rexdoms. That would destroy Solidar."

"And in time, the Collegium," added Alastar. "What do you think?"

"It's likely."

"What do you think we should do?"

"Nothing . . . for the moment." She paused. "Nothing obvious. Isn't that what you've already decided?" The mischievous smile he enjoyed seeing appeared, but immediately vanished.

"Unless you had thought otherwise."

"I haven't."

"You can see why I'd like to hear what your brother might say. Do you have any idea of what he might have in mind . . . besides Malyna?"

"Only that it won't be something trivial. He might have accompanied Malyna even if there were no other reason, but then he wouldn't have mentioned that he wanted to discuss other matters." She paused. "In a bit we should join Lystara. She's dying to tell you about her day."

Left unsaid, and emphasized by Alyna's setting matters up so that they could talk before dinner, was the fact they would maintain the practice of not discussing Collegium matters at dinner.

That was definitely for the best.

8

Alastar had no more than entered his Collegium study on Mardi morning and seated himself behind his desk than Maercyl appeared in the half-open doorway.

"Estafen D'Factorius is waiting outside, sir. He says that he knows he does not have an appointment, but that the matter is urgent."

Estafen . . . and not his father? Still . . . given that Estafen headed the Banque D'Excelsis, whatever he had to say would likely be informative. "Have him come in by all means."

Maercyl stepped aside and gestured.

A moment later, Estafen entered the study, then carefully closed the door. He looked to be a good ten years younger than Alastar, despite the well-trimmed black beard that well might have been cultivated to make him appear older. He nodded respectfully as he approached the desk. "I must thank you for seeing me without my making arrangements."

As he gestured for Estafen to take a seat, Alastar couldn't help but contrast the politeness exhibited by Estafen to the abruptness with which his sire had plunged into the study years earlier. But there had been an honesty about Elthyrd, and Alastar had to wonder if that honesty existed in the son. "You're welcome. I'm glad I was able to see you. Maercyl indicated that the matter is urgent."

"In more ways than one, I believe. On first glance, it might seem almost trivial, petty, in fact. I do not believe it to be so. The Banque D'Excelsis safeguards the funds of those who deposit them with us. We also lend some of those funds to others, but we require collateral in some fashion or another. Often that collateral takes the form of contracts to deliver grains, livestock, wool, timber, by a certain date, or at times, liens on such."

"Still exchange contracts, in effect," said Alastar, "since you're not a produce or livestock factor."

"Exactly. I have a number of such contracts on grain, with liens on livestock . . . and other goods as collateral for loans. After last year's poor harvest, I made more loans to High Holders, and even more early in the spring. Now, quite a number will not pay. They even refuse to pay default interest. The interest is not usurious. The regional justicer won't make a judgment until Rex Lorien rules on a series of petitions that claim such disputes can only be judged if they apply to debts between High Holders . . ."

Between High Holders? If true, that was something Lorien had conveniently forgotten to mention to Alastar.

". . . more than a few factors are beginning to withdraw deposits. Rumors are circulating about the stability of the Banque. That's despite the knowledge that I have sound backers . . ."

"Such as your father?"

"Not just him. Others also. Over the past week, word is passing in various quarters that Weezyr's banque will fail as well. The failures wouldn't hurt the High Holders. They'd benefit because they could escape paying their debts."

"Especially if no one but another High Holder could bring them before a justicer." Alastar's voice was sardonically dry. "Just who are these High Holders?"

"I'd rather not name those involved. Not yet."

"Is that because the loans were confidential, and the conditions included the stipulation that you not disclose their names publicly?"

Estafen nodded, if reluctantly. "It goes beyond the Banque, Maitre, well beyond . . ." Estafen looked meaningfully at Alastar.

Alastar wasn't quite sure exactly where the factor's hint was leading. "And if you don't have those golds . . ."

"What can I do? I cannot lend golds I do not have, unless I issue notes I may not be able to redeem. . . . Karl is talking about building another furnace to provide the coke to smelt the iron that Vaschet needs to make the tires and rifles that he has received orders for . . ."

Rifles? Why would the army need more rifles when it had five thousand fewer soldiers than ten years earlier? Rifles hadn't changed that much.

". . . Maartyn cannot purchase the horses and barges he needs to carry the clay for his bricks. Wylum cannot purchase the contracts on wool and cotton for his mills. Yet if I issue notes, without the golds I am owed by High Holders . . ." Estafen offered a dramatic shrug.

Alastar understood. He should have understood sooner. "Before long, the Banque D'Excelsis will fail. You, and possibly your backers, will be ruined, and many other factors will suffer."

Estafen nodded again.

"You mentioned that Factorius Vaschet has received orders for what must be significant numbers of rifles . . . so many that Karl needs to expand his ironworks."

"It's not just rifles. He makes wagon springs and the iron tires for the wheels, all sorts of parts."

"He used to forge sabers for the army, too."

"Not anymore. They put blades on the rifles, bayonets, they call them."

Then again, maybe rifles have changed that much. Still . . . "I wonder who else needs that many rifles." Alastar had an idea, but wanted to see what Estafen might say.

"I don't know. I didn't ask Vaschet. He probably wouldn't have told me anyway. He keeps his plaques held close."

"What exactly do you expect me to do?" Alastar asked quietly.

"Something about it, Maitre. At least, let Rex Lorien know what those high-handed bastards are up to. It can't be good for him if they think they're above his laws. They might not even be able to pay their tariffs."

"He's been looking into that, but he hasn't mentioned the part about petitions that claim only debts between High Holders are subject to the jurisdiction of a justicer." Alastar paused. *Except that* locus dominatus *amounts to the same thing.* "What about gaming debts? Do you think any who've borrowed from you have used the golds for that?"

"I don't lend to factors or their families without recourse." Estafen shrugged. "You hear about factors' problems. Not all of them, but most. With High Holders . . . it could be poor harvests . . ." His smile turned crooked. "It's hard to say no to a High Holder or his son."

"I assume High Holder Delcoeur has borrowed from you or Weezyr."

For a moment, Estafen frowned, then replied, "A few times. Never more than a hundred golds. He always repays. Complains about the interest. I just listen."

"I take it that some of them owe you thousands . . . if not more."

"One or two."

"If they were relying on their harvests, they won't be able to repay you."

"That's why I'm here. Several are talking about wanting to borrow more on the strength of next year's harvests in order to pay their tariffs to the rex. I don't have that much to lend, especially if their friends don't even pay the interest."

"Have they threatened you?"

"Not directly. I just get the feeling that things could get uncomfortable."

"Will your banque fail in the next few days?"

"No, Maitre. We have reserves, and matters could always improve, but if all the High Holders decide they can renege on their debts . . ."

"You see things going in a dangerous direction."

"Very dangerous, sir."

"Is there anything else I should know, Estafen?"

"I cannot think of anything else."

Alastar nodded, thinking. Finally, he stood. "I do appreciate your making me aware of the situation."

"I thought you should know. By your leave, sir?"

Alastar chuckled. "I'm scarcely a rex, Estafen. Just keep me informed."

"That I will, sir."

After the banker-factor had departed, Alastar moved toward the window, through which blew a warm harvest breeze. Estafen wasn't yet in great danger, but he'd claimed the matter was urgent. *And it is, or will be, if Lorien grants those petitions.* Alastar shook his head. "Maercyl . . ."

After several moments, the imager second hurried into the study, closing the door behind him. "I'm sorry, sir. Elmya . . . she's here, sir."

"Dareyn . . . has he taken a turn for the worse?"

"I don't know. She didn't say, just that she needed to talk to you."

"Of course I'll talk to her. While I'm doing that, would you arrange for my mount and two escorts? I need to go see Rex Lorien immediately."

"Yes, sir. Thank you, sir." With a relieved smile, Maercyl turned and opened the door.

Alastar stood as the spritely silver-haired woman strode purposefully into the study.

Elmya had dark circles under her eyes, but those eyes were focused directly on Alastar when she stopped before the table desk and inclined her head politely.

He gestured for her to sit, then said, "Matriana . . . we all have been worried about Dareyn . . ."

"He's not dying, Maitre. But he's not what he was. The flux . . ." She shook her head. "Like as he will be if he does come back to work, and the same if he doesn't."

"What if he came in for a glass or so each morning to work with Maercyl? Until he gets better."

"He'll not be getting that much stronger, Maitre."

"We should let him make that decision." *If he will . . .*

"That *might* work . . ."

"If we promise to send him home before he gets overtired?"

"Thought you might understand. I'll tell him that once he's better he's to come for the mornings until he gets his strength back." Elmya shook her head. "He'll complain that he should have been the one talking to you. As if he'd want to tell you he's not got the strength he once had."

"We'll try not to overtire him."

"My thanks to you, Maitre." She nodded and departed in quick sure steps.

Elmya had barely left when Akoryt peered into the study. "Sir . . . might I have a moment?"

Alastar gestured for him to enter. "A few moments, but I'll have to leave before long. Something has come up, and I need to let Lorien know."

Akoryt frowned.

"It's not about the Collegium, but there's more trouble between the factors and the High Holders. I'll explain in detail at the next senior imagers' meeting. What did you need?"

"Ah . . . it's not about needing. Secondus Frydrek is missing. He didn't come to instructionals this morning. Howal and Jaims said he went to get a pastry from the woman on the east riverwalk."

"They're not supposed—" Alastar shook his head. It wouldn't be the first time a student imager had been tempted by a pastry, and he doubted it would be the last . . . even after his warning to the students. But then, there were always a few who either didn't listen or didn't think rules applied to them. "He didn't get on the wrong side of Ashkyr, did he?"

"I thought of that. Ashkyr was with Maitre Tiranya the whole time. Frydrek just didn't come back. I've checked with the patrollers. No one has seen him."

"What about the bridge monitor?"

"She didn't see him, either. Orlana's not the kind to slack off, either."

"Can he handle concealments?"

"He's never been able to do it with me. That doesn't mean he couldn't. I've had the feeling that he could do more, but he's not the kind who likes to push himself."

"From his reports, he's not a troublemaker."

"Good student. Pleasant. Moderately talented, but a touch lazy."

"Make sure all the bridge monitors keep an eye out for him. Let me know when you find out something."

"I will. I'd be less worried if Oestyl and Glaesyn hadn't been followed just the other day."

"But in full morning light?"

"There was some heavy mist early on."

"Do what you can."

After Akoryt left, Alastar frowned. Why would anyone be targeting junior imagers? Even juniors could be dangerous, and the Collegium hadn't done anything to take sides in anything lately. Not publicly, anyway.

Alastar headed for the main entrance to wait for his mount and escorts.

The bells in the Anomen D'Rex were ringing the ten bells of the noon glass as he rode up the drive to the white stone steps of the entry to the Chateau D'Rex. While Alastar had been taking a slight risk in riding to the chateau without knowing whether Lorien was available, he usually was. Even if he hadn't been, Alastar could likely have conveyed his concerns to Lady Chelia, to whom Lorien listened carefully. Most of the time, anyway.

But Lorien was in his study.

"Why are you here now? I didn't request your presence."

Alastar dropped into the center chair opposite the rex. Given the sharpness of Lorien's words, he wasn't about to waste time on pleasantries. "There's another nasty aspect to that petition to attempt to remove High Holders from the jurisdiction of the regional justicers. Factor Estafen brought it to my attention just before I came here. He's the one who established the Banque D'Excelsis years ago. High Holders are borrowing from the banques all across Solidar and refusing to pay, or at least pay on time, and they also aren't paying the default interest . . ." He went on to explain, ending with, ". . . so it's much more than what Lenglan and the High Council claim."

"I was afraid it was trouble. Half the time you come unannounced, it's trouble. They'll ruin all Solidar," said Lorien sourly. "You and Sanafryt don't always agree, but on this you both do. That means more trials and tribulations after I deny those petitions. I'll also have to make it clear to all the justicers that High Holders are subject to the courts for all matters involving golds or commerce." He sighed. "I might even have to execute one or two to make the point."

"They've been taking bribes from High Holders to deny claims?"

"Some do. Some don't. For those that want to live better than they should, I can't pay them what the bribes bring in. They're all honest enough for most claims and petitions."

"Except for those involving wealthy factors and High Holders?"

"What else would you expect?"

"Maybe the Collegium should review their decisions," said Alastar with a harsh laugh.

"Be careful there, Maitre. I just might consider it . . . except that half of them would resign immediately, and those who would replace them would be worse." Lorien began to cough, a wracking, almost retching, sound. After several moments, he took a small swallow from the beaker on the goldenwood desk. "Tonic's worse than cheap ale."

"Is that cough getting any better?"

"Some. The tonic helps. Chelia makes sure I don't eat too much in the way of sweets or gravies." Lorien shook his head. "Sanafryt is already drafting my absolute denial. I'll have him add wording that declares that the High Holders are specifically under the jurisdiction of the rex, the justicers, and the High Justicer for all matters of commerce, trade, and anything else involving golds and claims. He'll use all the advocate's language. Thank the Nameless it's not a public proclamation with all those therefores and legal terms." He looked at Alastar. "You know that half the High Holders will threaten rebellion."

"Threats won't be the problem."

"Don't let it get out of hand . . . like the last time."

"We'll do our best, but . . ."

"Is that all?"

"For now."

"Good. I'm going to the private gardens."

Alastar rose. "Thank you."

Lorien's nod of dismissal was almost perfunctory.

By the time Alastar returned to the administration building it was two quints before second glass, and, as he approached his study, Maercyl stood from behind the small table desk and cleared his throat.

"Yes? Did Akoryt return with any news about Secondus Frydrek?"

"No, sir. Maitre Alyna left a message for you. High Holder Zaerlyn and his daughter have arrived. When you are free, they will be at the Maitre's dwelling." Maercyl just stood there, as if he had a question he dared not ask.

"Didn't you send word to those at the bridges that we were expecting him? And let Maitre Alyna know?"

"Yes, sir, but . . ."

"You didn't expect him to be our guest?" Alastar smiled. "Didn't you know? He's Maitre Alyna's older brother. He's the one who helped her learn surveying, mathematics, and geometry. They've corresponded for years."

"But . . . sir . . . he's here."

"Not all High Holders are wary of the Collegium, Maercyl. Too many are, we both know, but not all of them." He paused. "Has Maitre Cyran been around?"

"No, sir."

"If they need me, especially Maitre Akoryt, I'll be at the Maitre's house."

"Yes, sir."

Alastar was still thinking about what he'd learned from Estafen and Lorien—and worrying about Frydrek—when he walked up the steps to the covered front porch of the dwelling that was his . . . at least so long as he happened to be Maitre.

He glanced up to his left to see Alyna with her brother, where both had been seated on the shaded east side of the porch before rising to greet him. Although Alastar had never met Zaerlyn—or Zaeryl, as she called him—there was enough of a family resemblance that Alastar had no doubts that the two were related. The High Holder was taller than his sister, if several digits shorter than Alastar. His eyes were brown, rather than black, and his brown hair was silvered, not surprisingly, since he and Alastar were roughly the same age.

"Welcome to Imagisle, High Holder Zaerlyn," said Alastar.

"Zaeryl, please. We are family." Zaerlyn's smile was warm and open. "I've wanted to meet you for years, and I'm so glad I decided to come with Malyna."

"She and Lystara are in the parlor, getting acquainted," added Alyna. "We've settled Zaeryl's men in the stable guest house. It's a little tight, but that way Jienna can feed them as well." She gestured to the empty third chair. "Jienna will be bringing lager and refreshments in a moment. I told her to serve the girls first."

"A very good idea." Alastar seated himself, as did the other two.

"How was your day, dear?"

"Until now, breakfast was the best part," replied Alastar dryly. "The three of us should talk about it later, after dinner, in the study." He turned to Zaerlyn. "How was your journey?"

"Much easier than your day, I fear. Malyna is an excellent horsewoman, and her company made most of the travel enjoyable. We all will miss her, I most of all."

"How are her surveying skills?" asked Alastar.

Both Alyna and Zaerlyn laughed.

"She is . . . adequate in those. She does like mathematics, and she is excellent with the clavecin."

"Unlike her aunt," said Alyna.

"You were better than you let on, Alyna. You just disliked being forced to display talents like, as you put it, a filly being studied for breeding purposes."

Alastar could well imagine a young Alyna saying just those words.

"Did Mother really say that?" asked Lystara, appearing just behind Zaerlyn, with Malyna standing behind her.

Alastar managed not to smile at his daughter's skill with a concealment as he studied the two girls.

With her brown hair and black eyes, a trim but not excessively slender form, Malyna could have been Alyna's younger sister . . . a much younger sister. As Malyna stood beside Lystara, who was nearly as tall as her cousin, despite being almost three years younger, Alastar could see what Alyna had said earlier, that their daughter did in fact show many of his characteristics. He just hadn't seen them before.

Alyna frowned. "I thought you were going to stay in the parlor."

"You said we could join you for refreshments, if we asked. We came to ask."

"It's not polite to sneak up on people with a concealment, especially family," Alyna said quietly but firmly. "It's also showing off, and that is not polite, either."

"Yes, Mother. I won't sneak up on family again. Not without permission. Might we have refreshments with you?"

"You may, but you'll need to bring two more chairs from the west porch."

"Thank you, Mother." Before she turned away, Lystara had trouble concealing the mischievous smile that she had obviously inherited from her mother.

Alyna looked at her brother, but did not speak until the two girls were out of earshot. "Are you certain you want Malyna under the same roof as Lystara?"

Zaerlyn laughed. "I wouldn't have it any other way."

"I thought you might say that. You know that they won't be in the same instructionals most of the time?"

"I hadn't thought they would be . . ." After a pause, Zaerlyn lowered his voice. "I hadn't realized . . . how precocious . . . I mean as an imager . . . Lystara is."

"She takes after her father in that," said Alyna, smiling sweetly.

Alastar shook his head. The days ahead—*the years ahead*—were going to be more interesting than he'd ever anticipated when he'd fallen head over heels in love with a High-Hold-born imager with a quiet demeanor and a mischievous smile.

9

Two quints past seventh glass found Alyna, Zaerlyn, and Alastar gathered in Alastar and Alyna's study, with Alastar concluding his description of both the problems Solidar and the Collegium faced, particularly the problems with the banques, as well as the events of his day. When he finished, he turned to Alyna. "Is there anything you'd like to add?"

"Not to add. Do you think Lorien will actually deny those petitions as strongly as he said he would?"

"He's been known to dither, but his resignation over the words and his anger about the High Holders trying to subvert the Codex Legis are a good indication that he just might do what he said and do so quickly." *Unless he has second thoughts, which unfortunately he does too often.* Alastar glanced to Zaerlyn. "Does any of this have to do with what you wanted to discuss?"

"Unhappily . . . it does. Not directly, perhaps, but . . . I'm concerned about Ryel. I've heard . . . a few things."

Alastar nodded and waited, much as he wanted to press.

"Calkoran has some contacts in Montagne . . . he's heard that Cransyr made several visits to Regial's holding over the past year . . . and Cransyr and Ryel have met several times as well."

"Regial? Lorien's brother Ryentar?" Actually, Ryentar was only Lorien's half-brother, but with Asarya's death, few, if any, actually knew that, although Alastar had no doubts that there had to be some who suspected it. Still, with Ryentar's marriage to the youngest daughter of High Holder Caervyn and the subsequent birth of a daughter and a son, he seemed to be behaving himself, although Alastar had some doubts that Ryentar could ever be totally trusted.

"The same."

"Possibly some plot of Cransyr's . . . or Ryel's?" asked Alastar.

Zaerlyn shook his head. "It might be coincidence. Ryel never was that close to Ryentar when they were young. I'm not sure they ever even met."

"I worry about whether it's coincidence, when all three of them dislike both the rex and imagers."

Zaerlyn looked to his sister.

Alyna nodded. "I was rather harsh on Ryentar. So was Alastar."

"I never understood why Ryentar and Lady Asarya were exiled. You only wrote that they were plotting against Lorien."

"Lady Asarya wanted Ryentar to be rex." Alyna looked to Alastar, who nodded. "She conspired with a renegade senior imager and an army commander. They were the ones who set off Antiagon Fire in the Anomen D'Rex at the memorial service for Rex Ryen. "They were trying to remove Lorien, the marshal of the armies, and the senior commanders. They also set it up so that if Alastar survived, the imagers would be blamed for Lorien's death. It almost worked."

"I never knew all that." Zaerlyn's glance at his sister was mildly accusing.

"That was my decision," replied Alastar. "At the time, I didn't think executing the recently bereaved widow of the rex and the younger brother of the rex—especially given the unpopularity of the late Rex Ryen—would have been well taken. It seemed better to let people believe that it had all been an army plot against Lorien and the Collegium, and that Lorien was providing well for his younger brother, if removing him from temptation. Most High Holders knew that Lady Asarya had not gotten along that well in the Chateau D'Rex, and stayed well away from it as much as she could. So the fact that she accompanied Ryentar to Montagne wasn't exactly seen as unusual."

"No. That was what I'd thought."

"Now . . ." mused Alastar, "I have to wonder . . ."

Zaerlyn frowned. "I can't say that I like having been deceived, but even if there is a plot between those three, you did what was needed at the time."

"Even if it does turn out to make matters more complicated now," added Alyna.

"Is there anything else about Ryel or other High Holders?" asked Alastar. "Anything to do with claims before regional justicers?"

"Not about Ryel. Cransyr and his father and grandsire have always felt that the justicers shouldn't have any power over High Holders. That was something Calkoran told me."

"Did he say why?"

"No. He just said it went a long ways back. He didn't know why."

"Obviously, High Holders don't forget much," said Alastar dryly. *Whether they learn anything from what they remember is another question.*

"When everyone else keeps track of old scores, it's dangerous to forget," observed Zaerlyn.

"And it's more dangerous for those of us who don't even know what those scores are." Alastar paused, then asked, "What proportion of High Holders do you think are having difficulty with their finances right now?"

"I'm not the best one to ask. We've never really relied on the harvests from the lands. We take a smaller amount from the tenants than most do, except for Ryel and Calkoran. I'd judge the three of us are well suited to weather hard times, regardless of what happens. Some of the others . . . I'd judge—it's really a guess—between two and three out of ten will have trouble this year. Even more if crops and weather are bad again next year. That's here in old Bovaria and in Montagne. I couldn't speak to the east or west, and the northeast holders rely more on timber and mining. I hear that the harvests are solid in areas around Piedryn and Cheva."

"What proportion of High Holders are like you—getting more from trade and factorages than from lands?"

"One in five, from what I've seen."

"Four out of five might be inclined to follow Cransyr, then," suggested Alyna.

"Half that, at most," replied Zaerlyn.

"That's still something like three hundred very unhappy High Holders, and a good number of them are within a hundred milles of L'Excelsis."

"You didn't mention the problems with the gaming," interjected Alyna.

"What's new about that?" Zaerlyn snorted. "There have always been too many sons, especially younger sons of High Holders, who've wagered too much too unwisely."

"The problem seems to be that they're now losing, often badly, to the sons of wealthy factors because they can't raise the stakes at plaques and bones high enough to scare off the factors' sons."

Zaerlyn frowned. "I don't see . . ."

"The proprietors of the gaming houses here in L'Excelsis have forbidden weapons and are maintaining guards outside the houses. Several offspring of merchants and factors have been attacked or are missing. Oh . . . and someone is buying enough rifles that Factorius Vaschet is expanding his workrooms and forges to meet the demand."

Zaerlyn shook his head, if with a rueful smile. "You do know how to give a man pause, Alastar."

"It's your turn, Zaeryl. Alyna said there was something about the porcelain factorage . . ."

"Oh, that . . . it's not about the factorage. It's about the coal we use to fire the kilns. We used to buy it from Rhennalt, but his lands, those that were left, and the coal mine, went to his daughter, or her husband, and Staendyn sold them to Factorius Karl for something less than their fair value. Maraak attempted to offer more, paid over two years, but Staendyn wasn't interested. He wanted the golds as soon as possible. Maraak asked his son, who was handling the matter, why they'd turned down the higher offer. Young Staendyn told him that his father couldn't be bothered with operating the mine, that there was an immediate need for the golds, and that sooner or later, they'd reclaim the lands. He didn't say buy back or repurchase, but reclaim."

"I don't like the sound of that."

"Neither did Maraak. He looked into it, and, in the time before Rex Regis—"

"High Holders had the right to reclaim their historic properties at the cost for which they were sold?" guessed Alastar.

"That's right. Anytime within five years." Zaeryl frowned. "How did you know that?"

"I didn't. It was a guess based on everything else going on. Tell me . . . is Staendyn close to Cransyr?"

"They're both on the High Council. You know that. How close they are on a personal basis . . . I have no idea. Why?"

"Because Cransyr seems to be behind, or at least supporting, all sorts of efforts and petitions to restore the 'original' rights of High Holders."

"Cransyr must know that Lorien's not stupid enough to allow that."

"I would hope so," replied Alastar. "Are you paying Karl more for the coal?"

"Of course. Not a huge increase, but enough that Staendyn could have recouped the cost of buying the mine within five to ten years . . . and less than that if Karl keeps raising prices. Maraak's looking around for other lands we might be able to buy that have coal on them. Developing a mine would be expensive initially, but . . ."

Alastar nodded. "I can see that."

"Maraak and Zaeryl have always been very practical," said Alyna sweetly. "I'm sure they'll manage. If you wouldn't mind . . . tell us more about Malyna."

Zaeryl laughed. "You've heard enough about coal and lands and your least favorite High Councilor, I take it?"

"For now," replied Alyna.

"As you've seen, she's quiet, too quiet. All the same, like you, Alyna, there's a fierce desire to do anything she does perfectly. She's not a natural musician, or wasn't. She kept working with the clavecin and Master Heldryk until even he admitted she was outstanding. She's not as fond of the outdoors as you are. That might be because almost any flower makes her sneeze and her eyes run."

"That's good to know . . ."

"Do you think she'd object to being fostered with us, rather than being with the other girls?" Alastar knew he had to be the one to ask that question. "We'd thought . . . assumed . . . but . . ."

Zaerlyn smiled broadly. "She's talked about nothing else. When I put her to bed tonight, she said she already felt close to Lystara. Lystara's been so welcoming. Even I saw that."

"Sisters or cousins don't always get along," said Alyna, "after the first enthusiasm."

"In that, Malyna is very much like you. You almost never change your first impressions of people. In your case, it works out, because you've never been wrong. I'd even wager that you took one look at Alastar and—"

"Zaeryl!"

Alastar could see that his wife was actually blushing. He immediately asked, "How did you discover she was an imager?"

"I didn't. She has always been so much like Alyna that I've been watching for years." Zaerlyn laughed softly. "And she knew I was watching. I never saw her image anything. She just walked up to me a month ago and imaged a perfect copy of my seal, right in front of me. Then she told me she was ready to go to join her aunt Alyna at the Collegium."

Even Alyna looked stunned, if only momentarily, before she asked, "You never saw any signs?"

"Alyna . . . Father never saw any signs with you, either, not until you imaged five yards of brass surveying chain all at once and passed out."

Alastar raised his eyebrows. "You mentioned the chain, but not that you'd imaged five yards of it at age ten."

"I didn't want you to think I was that stupid."

"At age ten, we were all stupid."

"You weren't."

Alastar laughed. "I was stupid when I was far older than ten. You know that. You weren't."

"I'd have to agree with your husband. About you, that is."

"Tell us more about Malyna."

"The day after I discovered she could image and informed her that I would be the one bringing her here, she imaged a silver necklace for Mairina. She was careful and thoughtful, because she used silvers she'd saved. It was simple, but really quite beautiful. Mairina sobbed and sobbed—but not until we'd retired to our chambers."

"How did she know to use the silvers?" asked Alyna.

"I told her. Years before. She is so much like you that I worried. So I told her—I admit I was guessing—but I told about all the dangers you faced and how so many imagers died in the old days because they didn't even know the basics. You wrote me about those. Wasn't that just in case . . . ?"

"It was." Alyna smiled almost shyly. "Just in case."

Close to another quint passed before the three left the study, and Alastar and Alyna retired to their chambers.

"You had a special upbringing, even for a High Holder," Alastar said gently. "You've said that you felt that there wasn't as much closeness with Zaeryl . . . but it's clear . . ."

"We've become closer as we've gotten older, even if it was only through letters. I did worry that there might be another imager in the family."

"You were right to worry."

"It's a little frightening to see Zaeryl comparing the two of us."

"There are similarities. There always are in families. There are also differences."

"We'll have to watch about the flowers."

Alastar nodded. After a moment, he said, "I didn't want to bring this up downstairs, but do you think that Ryel knows that Ryentar is his half-brother?

"I think he knows now. I don't think he knew earlier, certainly not at the time Lady Asarya was trying to make Ryentar rex. I wouldn't be surprised if she let Ryel know when it became clear that Lorien and you weren't ever going to let her return to L'Excelsis."

"That makes sense, but she had to know that would be taking a risk."

"She would have, but her life was in L'Excelsis . . . and in her hopes for Ryentar," Alyna pointed out.

"Then you think that Ryel arranged her death?"

"Dearest, it could have been Ryentar, Lorien, or Ryel. They all would have had reasons. Ryentar possibly most of all."

"Why would Ryel . . . ?" Alastar broke off. "Of course. If Ryel and Cransyr want the High Holders to rise against Lorien, the last thing Ryel would want is to have it known that he's related to Ryentar and the re-gial family. It also means that Ryel has been plotting with Ryentar, the most noble High Holder Regial, for at least several years."

"Because Asarya died three years ago? We don't know that for certain."

"There's a great deal we don't know. But when it croaks like a frog, jumps like a frog, and swims like a frog . . ."

"Enough about frogs, my very dear Maitre . . ." She glanced toward the bed.

Alastar was more than happy not to talk about frogs.

10

On Meredi morning, Alyna walked Malyna and Lystara to the administration building to introduce her niece to Akoryt, in his capacity as Maitre of Studies, so that Akoryt—and Alyna—could determine what instructionals Malyna needed and didn't, and in what areas, if any, that personal tutorials might be more appropriate.

Zaerlyn was on his way to pay his respects to High Holder Cransyr.

And, as he waited for Cyran to appear, Alastar was reading through the copy of *Veritum* that Maercyl had left on his desk. The first news item he read was about how the popularity of gaming had greatly increased in the past year and how the higher table stakes had resulted in more than hard feelings . . . and possibly some "unexplained disappearances." Since the newssheet didn't blame anyone, Alastar couldn't see immediate repercussions. The second story was one that probably should have appeared much earlier, and it was about how High Holders were attempting to assert privileges revoked by the first Rex Regis to avoid paying their just debts. The brief article also noted that neither banking factor would comment on the matter, and that suggested High Holders just might be threatening those banking factors.

At that moment, Cyran walked into the study and gestured to the newssheet that Alastar was setting on the side of the desk. "I read the newssheet's views on the disappearances. It won't be the last. Heisyt said there was trouble last night, but he couldn't say anything yet."

"Just what everyone needs." Alastar waited for Cyran to sit down before asking, "What about our own disappearance?"

"I talked with Akoryt just briefly this morning. There's still no trace of Frydrek. After Akoryt told me yesterday, I asked Captain Heisyt to keep an eye out. They likely won't find anything. If he'd been killed for a few coins, they'd have found his body by now."

"I can't see that anyone would gain anything personally from killing him and hiding or disposing of his body."

"You think it's someone who hates imagers?"

"Or someone with a point to prove," replied Alastar. *Such as Cransyr or another angry High Holder.* "Can you think of another reason?"

"Could Frydrek have imaged bad coins to someone? I know they're not supposed to image coins, but some don't listen."

"Frydrek was never any problem that way, according to Akoryt. He did have a weakness for the fried pastries. Even if he had imaged a copper . . . he was good enough to image a decent one of solid copper. So that wouldn't have been a problem. Coppers are coppers."

"Could he have fallen into the river? With the water so high and wild?"

"If he went into the river, it's far more likely he was pushed . . . but the unlikely is certainly possible. Right now, all we can do is warn the students and lower-level imagers to be especially careful." After a moment, Alastar added, "There's one other thing. You might have seen or overheard—we've just gotten another imager, another High Holder's daughter. Alyna's niece, in fact."

"I'd heard that from Belsior. He was on duty last night. If she takes after Maitre Alyna, she'll be strong."

"Alyna and Akoryt are talking to her and testing her now. She's almost thirteen. She kept her ability hidden from her father until she told him she was ready to come to the Collegium, then imaged a perfect duplicate of his seal right in front of him."

"Ha!" A broad grin crossed Cyran's face, then faded. "Will that pose a problem . . . with Lystara?"

That wasn't really what Cyran meant, Alastar knew, but Cyran was far too kind to more than allude to the fact that Alyna had almost died having Lystara and could have no more children. "Lystara and Malyna seem to get along well, and it appears that Alyna is more than happy to deal with both of them."

"That would be good. Alyna kept to herself when she first came here, until Tiranya arrived. A friend does help, especially with the girls. They can be far crueler, in a quiet way, than the boys."

"More often than the boys, but we've known some boys just as cruel." Alastar couldn't forget how Bettaur had plotted against Taurek.

"Alyna has mentioned that," said Cyran. "Is there anything else you need from me?"

"Not at the moment. I'm still worried about the problems between the High Holders and the factors and merchanters, but there's not much else we can do, not unless something happens."

"Do you think that's going to be an immediate problem?"

"It could flare up in days or simmer for years. That likely depends on how Cransyr handles matters, and how the factors react." Alastar rose from behind the desk, waited for Cyran to stand, and then followed him out of the study, where he turned to Maercyl. "Any messages?"

"No, sir," replied Maercyl.

"Have you any word from Dareyn?"

"I stopped by their cottage this morning, as you requested. He says he'll be here tomorrow to help me out. Elmya says not before Vendrei."

"I'd wager on Elmya."

"So would I, sir."

As Alastar returned to the study, he continued to worry, not only about poor Frydrek, but about the growing conflict between the High Holders and the factors, especially since it had been almost two days since he'd heard from Lorien. When Lorien delayed in doing anything, that was almost always a sign of either dithering or trouble, if not both.

A quint later, Alyna and Akoryt arrived in the study and seated themselves before Alastar's table desk.

"Malyna's waiting out in the anteroom," Alyna said. "We need to talk freely."

"That bad?"

Akoryt shook his head. "That would be far easier."

"How good an imager is she?" Alastar asked.

"Right now," replied Akoryt, "she's effectively a third. There are some kinds of imaging she doesn't know, but she'll have those down in weeks, if not sooner, once she's shown and instructed. With any amount of training at all, she'll be a top third in a month. In another two years, if not sooner, she'll have the ability to be a Maitre D'Aspect."

Not that she should be at that age, reflected Alastar.

Akoryt waited several moments before continuing. "That won't be the biggest problem."

"Oh?"

"I've been working with Lystara, on and off, for the past few weeks. She's not only better than Malyna in technique, but she's stronger."

"You're sure?" Alastar didn't want Akoryt exaggerating Lystara's abilities, although he'd never felt the Maitre D'Structure was the type to do that.

"I went over concealments with her yesterday. She can do more with them than some Maitres D'Aspect."

"She figured that out just last week. On Meredi."

Akoryt frowned. "She figured it out . . . herself?"

"She heard Shaelyt talking about light to the thirds," said Alyna. "That got her to thinking."

"I don't envy you two." Akoryt ran his hand through his short-cut but unruly red and silver thatch, then cleared his throat. "As master of students, I really do believe Malyna should be fostered with you and Alyna . . . and Lystara. I realize there may be some charges of favoritism . . . but . . . I think I can defuse much of that."

"By having them prove what they can do in instructionals?" asked Alyna.

"Would you suggest something else?" Akoryt's voice was amused.

"No."

"There is one other problem I can foresee," Akoryt continued. "With that much ability, they'll both need as much physical strength as we can give them . . . without straining them."

"If you pick them out and do that . . ." began Alyna.

Akoryt shook his head. "It's something I've been thinking about. I was going to suggest some additional training for a number of the student imagers, roughly ten and older." He looked at Alyna. "You and Lystara run every morning. I'd like to have the girls over ten join you." His eyes went to Alastar. "You and I could do the same for the boys over ten, since the older male students are already running with us. We could add an exercise session for each group after the run. We'd have to push back breakfast and instructionals a bit. Some of the boys, especially, are . . . heftier than they should be."

"So am I, probably," admitted Alastar.

"It wouldn't hurt some of the other woman imagers, either," added Alyna.

After another awkward pause, Akoryt spoke again. "Have you decided . . . about Malyna?"

"We've decided, but the final decision is up to her," said Alyna. "You know that."

"There's another problem. If Malyna's a third . . . and Lystara is only a second . . ."

"We'll tutor Lystara as necessary," declared Alastar. "She needs to spend some time as a second. There are some instructionals she could take with the thirds. That happens with a few others. We'll explain that to her." *Somehow.* He couldn't help but think that parents of non-imagers didn't have to make as many explanations, but then raising imagers necessitated a different approach in some areas. The trick was to know where, and Alastar still wasn't certain he knew all he should, although he had been far more confident about that before Lystara began to image things.

"You two seem to have thought this out."

"'Seem' is precisely the right word," said Alastar ruefully. "Is there anything else?"

Akoryt shook his head.

"Then we'll offer Malyna her choice and let you know."

"If that's all . . . ?"

"Not quite. What about Charlina? Can she actually detect someone under concealment?"

"Yes. I even had Shaelyt and Cyran approach her. She could sense exactly where they were."

"Now . . . if she'd work harder at other things . . ."

"She is. The fact that you told her that she had a valuable talent seems to have made an impression."

"All the attention doesn't hurt," added Alyna. "I hope she's working that hard in a month . . . and in a year."

"Don't we all? Thank you," said Alastar, adding with a tone of cheery sardonicism, "You can escape now. Have Malyna come in."

Akoryt smiled and stood.

Moments later, Malyna entered the study, wearing the grays of a student imager that she had donned for the first time that morning, her eyes on Alastar.

"If you'd sit down, Malyna," Alastar said, "we need to talk over a few things before you head off to begin your studies."

Malyna sat on the edge of the chair, if only for an instant, before easing herself into a position that was nearly identical to that of Alyna.

Alyna looked to Alastar, then to Malyna, before speaking. "Malyna, you know that your uncle is the Maitre of the Collegium, and that he has to approve who lives where?"

"Yes, Aunt . . . Maitre Alyna."

Alyna smiled gently. "In private, I'll always be your aunt. Promise me that."

A glimmer of a smile appeared then vanished. "Yes, Aunt Alyna."

Alastar felt awkward, but Alyna had insisted that he treat their niece as any other student imager of the same age. "You know . . . I hope you know . . . that Alyna and I want you to live with us and with Lystara. I cannot tell you how much that is our wish. But . . . you are now an imager. Our wishes are not sufficient . . . unless you also want to live with us. Many of the student imagers do not have the choice of where to live, but any who are over the age of twelve and living on Imagisle with parents or guardians have that choice of living at home or with other students. So you also have that choice."

"I can choose?"

"You can," affirmed Alastar.

"If I don't choose to live with you, where would I live?"

"With other girls your age in one of the girls' cottages."

Alastar could see the tension in Alyna . . . and even apprehension.

Malyna smiled. "I like being an imager, even a very new one. How could I not choose Aunt Alyna . . . and you? I'd choose you even if I had to sleep on the floor in Lystara's room. I know you wouldn't do that . . . but your house feels . . . warm. I can't imagine it any other way. I really can't."

"It won't be easy, sometimes," Alyna said. "Just like your father, we have rules. Some of them are not so strict as those you grew up with, and some are much stricter. There are reasons for those, and those rules apply to every student imager. That is because imaging can be so dangerous when it is misused that it can kill you . . . or others."

"Father told me that. I think I understand." Malyna turned to Alastar. "Thank you for giving me a real choice."

"We've been looking forward to having you." *More than you may ever know.*

"Now, Tertia Malyna," said Alyna, "it's time for you—"

"I'm really a third?"

"That's what Maitre Akoryt determined from all those tests and exercises. You still have a lot to learn to be a high-level third."

"But I am a third?"

"You are a third, and you need to join the other junior thirds at their morning instructionals." Alyna stood.

After a moment, so did Malyna.

"I'm sure I'll be back later," said Alyna.

Alastar was afraid she would be . . . and that he knew why.

He was still thinking about what he could say to his daughter when Maercyl appeared once more at the study door. "Factor Hulet is here. He appears unhappy."

"Have him come in."

Alastar had barely stood and finished the invitation when the tall factor burst into the study like a winter wind. Despite his flushed face, his gray eyes were hard. "Another factor's ward has been taken. That's twice this week."

"Taken?" asked Alastar, although he suspected he knew exactly what Hulet meant.

"Snatched, kidnapped, grabbed off the street."

"When and how did this happen, and what does it have to do with the Collegium?"

"You know very well . . . or your senior imager does. Commander Murranyt told him about the first grabbing. No one's yet found a trace of Youvyn."

"I knew one young man had reportedly been forced into a coach, and that he was a factor's son. The Collegium is not the Civic Patrol, Factorius. I am definitely concerned and worried about the growing tensions between the High Holders—"

"Tensions? Those spoiled bastards are killing our boys because . . ." Hulet's entire body was shaking.

"Because your boys are better at gaming"—*and perhaps cheating*—"than their boys are?"

"They won't pay their debts, and neither will their spoiled brats! And now those brats are resorting to killing."

"We both suspect that might be true," said Alastar calmly, "but what proof do we have?"

"Whose side are you on, Maitre?"

"Solidar's side. That means looking to the laws." *First, anyway.*

"Namer take the laws! Laws are useless unless they're equal for everyone. They're not."

"That's the issue before the rex." Alastar paused momentarily. "Just what are you asking me to do?"

"Find a way to put the arrogant bastards and their arrogant sons under the same laws as the rest of us."

"According to the Codex Legis, when it comes to high crimes, they already are."

"Then get our high and mighty Rex Lorien to enforce the laws that way!"

Hulet's hard and penetrating voice, his commanding height, and his intensity made it more than clear to Alastar that the factor was accustomed to using his presence to intimidate others and get his way—no matter what.

"I can only recommend . . . and I've been doing just that."

"Recommend harder, or louder. Or image some sense into him."

As if you haven't been trying for years?

"If one of your relations . . ." Hulet shook his head. "Enrique was my sister's boy, and the son of a good man who died too young, cheated out of his patrimony by those bastards. When he won . . . from that same family, that was fair, but . . . I've said enough. You know what to do." With that, Hulet turned and strode out of the study, leaving the door wide open.

Alastar just stood there for several moments.

Should you request a meeting with Cransyr? Alastar shook his head. The disappearance of two factors' sons was deeply disturbing, but there was still no evidence that the two were dead. *And there likely never will be.*

By the time the study door opened at just after fourth glass, and Alyna, followed by Lystara, entered, Alastar still had received no word about Frydrek and no messages from Lorien.

"I thought we three should talk before we return to the house."

With one glance at Lystara's face, Alastar had no doubts about the matter to be discussed. "I think we should." He took one of the three chairs in front of the desk and sat down, waiting for Alyna and Lystara to do the same before he said to Lystara, "You look a bit upset." *And that's an understatement.*

"Father, it's not fair!" Lystara stopped as she saw Alastar's frown.

"What is it that you think is so unfair? You don't have to shout so loudly that the whole Collegium can hear."

Lystara clamped her mouth shut.

Alyna looked to Alastar and mouthed, "Give her time."

Alastar waited . . . and waited.

Finally, Lystara said, her voice trembling—with anger, Alastar suspected—"I'm a much better imager than Malyna . . . and you made her a third."

"How do you know that?" asked Alastar.

"I just do. She can't do concealments. I asked her."

"You're absolutely right. Maitre Akoryt told us that you were a much better imager than Malyna. But I'd didn't make her a third, although I could have. Maitre Akoryt made that judgment. He also said that you were more than good enough in terms of imaging to be a third. The three of us decided that, while we will all tutor you in imaging and other things, and you can take some instructionals with the thirds, it would be best for you to remain a second for a while. Would you like to tell me why you think that is so?"

"No."

Alastar again waited.

"Lystara . . ." said Alyna gently.

"All right. I'm smaller than some of the seconds, and I'm smaller than almost all the thirds. But Malyna's barely taller than I am."

"Is she physically stronger than you? Not in imaging, but in carrying and lifting things?"

"I suppose so."

"That's another matter that Maitre Akoryt is concerned about. We're going to add some things to your training, and that of the other student imagers over ten. That includes you. The others will join the morning run . . . and after that there will be an exercise class to build up physical strength."

"You're saying I need to be stronger. That doesn't have anything to do with imaging."

"It has a great deal to do with surviving imaging," said Alastar.

"Dear . . ." said Alyna. "Do you remember what happened to your father when he used imaging to stop the rebellious troopers?"

"He almost died. You said." Lystara's voice was flat.

"If he hadn't been as strong as he is, he would have died. You need to be physically stronger. Also . . . you need to see how the seconds and thirds act. You've already said that you don't want the seconds to think you're a baby. . . . How do you think the thirds will be? Do you want them saying that you're only a third because you can image and your father is Maitre?"

Lystara pressed her lips together, but did not reply.

"We won't stop you from learning imaging," added Alastar, "but you'll have to do it more carefully until you're bigger and stronger."

Abruptly, Lystara stiffened. "You think I'll do something stupid, don't you?"

"Not stupid," replied Alastar. "Your mother and I worry about your doing something that you know how to do that is more than your body can take. Could you lift the big chest in our room . . . or hold it over your head? You know how to lift."

"It's not the same . . ." Lystara's voice trailed off.

"Isn't it?" asked Alyna.

After several moments, Lystara said, "It's like that, but it's not the same."

Alastar managed not to smile. "You're right, but it is a matter of strength."

"How long do I have to stay with the seconds?"

"How long do you think it should be?" asked Alyna.

"Until spring . . . unless you think I could be a third sooner."

"Won't that depend on you?" Alyna's voice was gentle.

"I suppose so. You think I'm not ready to act like a third. I could do that."

"If you can, then perhaps you can join Malyna and the other thirds sooner."

"I still don't think it's fair."

"Sometimes what's right doesn't seem fair," said Alastar, thinking again, as he had for years, about how many troopers had died in the senseless attacks on Imagisle . . . all because two men believed they'd been treated unfairly, and their acts had unfairly condemned thousands of troopers to an even more unfair death. "Sometimes, even, what's right isn't fair."

"That doesn't seem right."

"Your mother and I struggle with that all the time. So does Rex Lorien." *Sometimes, anyway.* "At times, doing what's right creates unfairness, and at times, trying to be fair creates evil or wrongs someone else. Or even hurts the person you're trying to be fair to."

"That's me, isn't it."

"Yes," Alastar admitted.

"As long as you admit it's not fair . . . but I don't have to like it."

Alastar wanted to take a deep breath and a sigh of relief. He didn't. "That's correct. You don't have to like it." *We all just have to deal with it.* He cleared his throat. "We should start for home."

"We should," agreed Alyna, standing.

"Where's Malyna?" asked Lystara.

"Maitre Tiranya walked home with her," replied Alyna. "We didn't know if your uncle Zaeryl would be back, and Jienna has her hands full fixing dinner."

"Malyna wouldn't be any trouble."

"That's true," said Alyna, "but it gave Maitre Tiranya some time to get acquainted with Malyna and tell her some of the things she needs to know."

"Third things."

"And some other things that you already know so well that you wouldn't even think she wouldn't know them . . . like all the rules for student imagers."

Lystara nodded. "What are we having for dinner?"

"Pork cutlets, with fried apples, and lace potatoes."

"With the stinky cheese."

"With the stinky cheese," affirmed Alyna, giving Alastar a fond smile as Lystara stood and headed for the study door.

Outside the administration building, a brisk but warm wind was blowing from the southwest, and Alastar could make out clouds to the south.

"We might see some more rain tonight or tomorrow," he observed.

"We don't need any more."

"No," declared Lystara. "I'm tired of imaging mold off the stone steps."

"It's good practice," said Alastar cheerfully.

Lystara grimaced, but did not look at either of her parents.

When they reached the front porch of the Maitre's house, Malyna hurried out to meet them. "I've been here less than a quint." She paused, then swallowed. "Aunt Alyna . . . where might I be sleeping?"

"In the same room where you have been, we'd thought."

A pleased smile appeared. "Could Lystara help me unpack the rest of my things and help me put away my grays?"

"Could I?"

"You could," replied Alyna. "Dinner won't be for a while. We'll be in the parlor."

Alastar raised his eyebrows.

"I think you need a lager. I certainly do."

"Can we have some with dinner?" asked Lystara.

"A little or watered wine. You can choose."

"Thank you."

The two girls were upstairs well before Alastar and Alyna settled into the comfortable armchairs in the parlor, each with a beaker of dark lager.

"That wasn't as painful as it could have been," offered Alastar in a low voice.

"It was painful enough."

"I'm sorry. I know . . ."

"I know you know, and I thought I was ready, but when she asked if she could choose . . ."

"I could see how you felt." Alastar paused. "She seems well behaved."

"She sees too much, about people. More than Lystara. Lystara sees more about the physical side of the world."

"Lystara's younger."

Alyna just looked at her husband.

"She's more like you than Lystara is in that regard. Is that what you're saying? Why do you think that?"

"Mairina's also part Pharsi."

"You never mentioned that."

"It never came up, and there wasn't any reason to say anything until I realized Malyna was coming. Mairina's the sister of Zaeryl's friend Calkoran. Actually, they became friends after Mairina and Zaeryl married."

"That makes Arion and Malyna cousins."

"I know. I told her that the other day."

Alastar managed to look hurt. "And you didn't tell me?"

Alyna laughed. "You don't do the hurt look well. You do much better with the impassive expression."

"Calkoran . . ." mused Alastar, "that does explain some of the imaging ability."

"Some thought Zaeryl was marrying below his stature."

"And you?"

"I've never met her, but from what Zaeryl wrote, and writes, they both seem happy. So many aren't."

"Like the late High Holder Ryel?"

"And a few others." Alyna took another swallow of the lager. "Do you want to tell me what happened today?"

"If you don't mind, I'll save it until after dinner. Zaeryl should hear some of it, and I'd just like to hear about your day."

"I can do that, if you're ready for a few expressions of exasperation concerning a certain mathematics instructional . . ."

Almost a glass later, the girls came down the stairs.

"It's sixth glass," announced Lystara.

Meaning that it's late for dinner during the middle of the week. "We were waiting for Malyna's father."

"We'll wait a bit longer," said Alyna.

"Uncle Alastar . . . ?"

"Yes?"

"Could I talk to you . . . alone?"

Lystara tried to conceal a puzzled expression.

"Of course." Alastar glanced to Alyna. "We won't be long."

Alyna offered a knowing smile. "We'll be here."

Alastar stood and walked out to the hall, where he gestured toward the study door, then followed his niece inside and closed the door. He did not sit. "What is it, Malyna?"

"Lystara's as good an imager as I am, isn't she? Perhaps better, even?"

"Maitre Akoryt has tested you both. He thinks so. Some of that is because Lystara didn't have to hide her imaging ability."

"Lystara is only a second . . ."

"Did Lystara talk to you about it?"

"No, sir. When I told her that Maitre Akoryt had made me a third, she just said, 'I'm only a second.' I could tell she was upset."

Alastar wanted to shake his head. *With two of them . . .* "Being a second or a third or a maitre isn't just about imaging abilities. That's the most important part, but it's not the only part. There are other parts. Lystara needs to learn those other parts. As soon as she does, she'll be a third."

"She'll always be better."

Alastar managed not to stiffen. "You don't know that. You're both young."

"I know." Malyna paused. "Just like Aunt Alyna knows things. I knew Father would bring me here. I saw it years ago. It wasn't a dream, either; I saw it, but I didn't realize that was what it was until we rode up to your house, the Maitre's house. I didn't tell Father that. He worries too much."

She has the family farsight? "You've seen other things like that, haven't you?"

Malyna nodded.

"It might be a good idea if you talked about them with Alyna, you know."

"I thought I would, but I wanted you to know. I also wanted you to know about Lystara."

What have you gotten yourself into, Alastar? "Thank you. That was most thoughtful, although Alyna and I don't keep secrets from each other. We decided against that . . ." Alastar laughed softly, "*She* decided against that when we first met and liked each other. It was a very good decision. For both of us."

"That's good. Father and Mother don't keep secrets, either."

"We should join the others. I thought I heard someone come in. Your father might have gotten back in time for dinner."

In fact, Zaerlyn was standing in the parlor talking to Alyna and Lystara when Alastar and Malyna returned.

"Might we please eat now?" asked Lystara.

"I think that might be managed," agreed Alastar, "provided you two student imagers agree to tell us about your day, especially the good parts."

Malyna smiled. Lystara shot a plaintive glance at her mother.

"We could add a few bits about the good part of our days," added Alyna.

"That we could," agreed Zaerlyn.

The dinner conversation was light and cheerful, and Lystara even ate the cheese that coated the lace potatoes without comment or commentary.

Immediately after dinner, the three parents saw their daughters to bed, but Alastar and Alyna were the first to come back downstairs.

He glanced up the stairs, then said in a low voice, "You know what Malyna wanted to talk about?"

"That she's a third, and Lystara's not?"

"How did you know?"

"Malyna wants things to be fair, too."

"That's definitely a family trait."

"And you don't worry about it, dearest?"

Alastar winced.

"I thought as much."

At that moment, Zaeryl came down the stairs. "Malyna had to tell me about her day. She's very excited that she's an imager third. She also said she got to choose to stay with you. I think that made her feel more like a grown-up." He looked at his sister. "I imagine that was hard for you."

"A little."

"More than that, I think."

"We should go into the study," said Alastar. "There are some things you need to know and others we'd like to know."

"The way you say that, Alastar, worries me."

"We all should be worried."

Once the three were seated in the study, with the door firmly closed, Alastar looked to Zaerlyn. "What did Cransyr have to say? If anything?"

"He wanted to know why I was in L'Excelsis, since it was well known that seldom, if ever, did the holders of the house of Zaerlyn leave Rivages. I told him the truth, that I'd brought my youngest daughter to the Collegium. He offered condolences and sympathy for my loss, then asked me if I really believed that the Collegium was the best place for the children of High Holders who were imagers. I was curious to hear what he might have to say. So I asked him what might be a better alternative, since, especially in the case of daughters, it was unlikely that any heir to a High Holding would be terribly pleased to marry an imager, and that in the case of sons, a son who would be the heir might find it difficult to engage with other High Holders."

"And?"

"He agreed. He did say that it was a pity that no consideration was given to those of higher birth in their ranking at the Collegium. Then we talked of trade and the difficulties of establishing factorages of any size or significance at High Holdings located far from cities, high roads, or rivers. I pointed out that there was no barrier to a High Holder purchasing land in other areas and establishing a manufacturing or trade factorage there. Again, he agreed, but pointed out that such tended to lower the High Holder in the eyes of factors and merchants, and that, in turn, might lead to greater erosion of the historic rights of High Holders, which had already been eroded more than enough."

"Did he mention the issue of debts to factors, merchanters, and banques?" Alastar asked.

"Only indirectly. He made a comment that the Codex Legis needed to be amended to deal with the financial obligations and tariffs of High Holders differently from others, since High Holders did not have the same latitude in buying or selling lands as did others. I don't, as I'm certain Alyna has told you, see matters that way. That may be because we are too close, a mere handful of generations, to our less than distinguished elevation from factoring . . . and we have retained and expanded all those facilities so that we would not fall into the trap that led to our obtaining the holding in the first place."

Alastar managed not to smile at the gentle irony in Zaerlyn's voice. "Did he say anything about factors?"

Zaerlyn shrugged. "What you would expect . . . that they think only of making golds, that they have little respect for tradition, heritage, and, of course, good breeding, which, all too often translates into in-breeding."

"Did he mention anything about the Collegium?" asked Alyna.

"He did ask if I'd met you. I said I had, and that you seemed competent enough and very to the point. He declared that competence without vision would fail Solidar, but did not offer specifics. He also added, rather offhandedly, that it would be unwise for the Collegium to ally itself with the various Factors' Councils across Solidar, but that he was certain that the Collegium Maitre would eventually come to that conclusion. We did talk at great length about the difficulties of managing lands properly. He was most firm on the subject of the tendency of tenants to milk everything they could from any High Holder who was less than vigilant."

"It sounds most delightful." Alyna's voice was false-honey-sweet.

"He saw me off, offering again his condolences for my having to surrender a daughter to the Collegium. I could be mistaken, but I don't think he knows that my sister is a senior imager and married to the Collegium Maitre."

"How could he not know?" asked Alastar.

"Easily," replied Alyna. "I've never mentioned exactly from what High Holding I came, and Maitre Fhaen never wanted it known. Everyone thought it was proper that the widowed Maitre should marry a talented spinster imager . . . and that was it. Given how you feel about Cransyr, you likely haven't mentioned your wife to him, or to any of the High Holders. It's been almost thirty years since I came here. People forget."

"That might be to our advantage," pointed out Zaerlyn. "What did you want to tell me?"

"First, your daughter is, as we all suspected, a very talented imager. . . ." From there, Alastar and Alyna filled Zaerlyn in on the day's events.

Alastar finished briefing Zaerlyn with the information about both the missing student imager and the second kidnapped factor's son. ". . . and Hulet was clearly enraged, as he had a right to be, given that the second young man, if I heard him correctly, was his nephew, but he stormed off before I could draw him out."

"However right he may be," said Zaerlyn, "the Factors' Council of L'Excelsis shouldn't have a chief who is a hothead."

"Some of the younger factors thought that Elthyrd was too accommodating."

"Did you think so?"

"No, especially not at first. Even so. I doubt that Elthyrd would find the current situation any more to his liking than Hulet has. I can't see either accepting what Cransyr has in mind, but I do need to talk to Elthyrd." Alastar stifled a yawn. It had been a long day.

Less than half a glass later, when it became clear that they were merely restating what they had initially discussed, all three left the study.

When Alastar closed the door from the hall to their sitting room, he turned to Alyna. "What do you think?"

"Zaeryl's worried. His sympathies are with the factors, and he won't side with the council, but he'll try not to get openly involved."

"What would you suggest?"

"Wait. Let everyone else act. If the Collegium starts anything . . ."

"We'll be where we would have been the last time if we had acted first."

"Perhaps not that bad, but not good, and doing anything now will just make matters worse."

Their eyes met, and both smiled . . . expressions between sardonic and cynical. Then they laughed, and Alastar wrapped his arms around Alyna.

11

After breakfast on Jeudi morning, Lystara and Malyna set out through a light mist that might either turn to rain or vanish by later in the day. Alastar and Alyna followed shortly.

"Has Zaeryl said anything to you about when he intends to depart?" asked Alastar.

"No. I don't think he'll stay much longer. He already mentioned that he dislikes leaving Mairina for long. He might not even have come with Malyna if Mairina hadn't insisted."

"He would have come. He's more worried about the coal supplies than he's saying."

"I thought . . ."

"You thought what, dear?"

"That he has plenty of golds in reserve."

"For this year, and for ten years to come. Then what?"

"And that's why your family has done so well. What do you think he's worried about? That a factor has the coal lands or that Staendyn and Cransyr want to change the rules of land sales?"

"Neither one is good. Factors like to sell short-term. Father always negotiated contracts on a guaranteed delivery basis. With some flexibility in price, of course. There aren't any other working coal mines upstream of the porcelain factorage on the River Glace. The cartage for bringing in coal by wagon . . ." Alyna shook her head.

"What about Staendyn and Cransyr? Why does that worry him?"

"Staendyn's ancestors wanted our holding because it's close to the River Aluse, and the lands are better."

"And one way or another, in the long run, he'll still try to get it?"

"Zaeryl worries about that. He wondered why Staendyn married Rhennalt's daughter, with all the debts Rhennalt had run up, at least until he discovered that Rhennalt's only son was sickly, and that Juyna's sister was not quite right in the head."

"When you mention all that, I can see why he worries."

"We're a worrying family."

"I have noticed that." What Alastar hadn't considered was the extent to which at least some High Holders used every possible tool. "I assume Staendyn has a mistress or two . . . or the equivalent?"

"Zaeryl says several of the housemaids are quite attractive."

"I'm gaining an even greater appreciation of why you and Malyna are not displeased that you're imagers."

"I'm glad you said 'greater.'"

"So am I."

Alyna smiled.

When the two approached the table desk where Maercyl presided, the older second stood. "Good morning, Maitre . . . Maitre Alyna. I stopped by Dareyn's cottage." Maercyl smiled. "He and Elmya both agree that he can come in for a while tomorrow morning."

"That's good to hear. I'd like you to send a messenger to Factor Elthyrd to see if I could meet with him this afternoon, preferably at first glass."

"Yes, sir."

Alastar and Alyna entered his study, since it would be another half quint before the senior imagers' meeting began.

When Alastar and Alyna entered the conference room at just before seventh glass, the other nine senior imagers were all seated and waiting.

Alastar looked at Akoryt. "Any word on Frydrek?"

Akoryt shook his head.

Alastar then seated himself at the head of the table between Cyran and Alyna, cleared his throat and began. "As I think most of you know, Secondus Frydrek disappeared on Mardi morning after crossing the east bridge in the mist to get a fried pastry. No one, including the Civic Patrol, has seen a trace of him since. Last week, Oestyl and Harl found themselves being followed by a horseman. They gave him the slip. Those two incidents are why we've asked all student imagers not to leave Imagisle alone for the present."

"Have there been any threats against the Collegium, or has anyone made any statements that would have greatly offended anyone?" asked Obsolym. The use of the word "anyone" was a courtesy, since everyone knew that only Alastar could have made any statements, offensive or otherwise.

"Not that I'm aware. I've made no statements to the factors, High Holders, or Rex Lorien about any of the problems facing them, except that the Collegium is interested in a solution fair to all."

"Some High Holders might interpret that as being against their interests," offered Arion.

"That's possible," replied Alastar. "The High Council met yesterday, but I've not heard any word about what they discussed or proposed. In all likelihood, there will be more petitions or appeals of rulings made by justicers against High Holders. There appears to be a concentrated effort by a number of High Holders to reclaim privileges and rights they believe they had prior to the imposition of the Codex Legis by the first Rex Regis, and especially to remove themselves from the jurisdiction of the justicers except to settle disputes between High Holders. So far, Rex Lorien has not acted on any of the petitions."

"That sounds like they want each High Holder to be rex over his holding," observed Shaelyt.

"It appears that way," agreed Alastar.

After a moment of silence, Tiranya asked, "Are those High Holders acting on their own, or is the High Council behind this?"

"It's possible, even likely, but we don't have any proof. What is clear is that a number of High Holders want to keep the factors subservient. The factors are getting tired of being discriminated against, and a number of them likely have a greater stockpile of golds than do many High Holders."

"Are you suggesting that the High Holders are trying to escape their debts by getting the rex to invalidate the Codex?" asked Arion.

"Not all High Holders, but enough to cause more than a little trouble. We'll need to watch this closely." Alastar wasn't about to get into the squabbles between the sins of High Holders and factors at the gaming table, not unless that situation worsened. He turned to Gaellen. "Have any more students come down with the green flux?"

"Only one more. So far."

"Good."

The remainder of the meeting dealt with more mundane matters, such as the cleanliness of the rooms used for instructionals, and ended in less than a quint.

As soon as Alastar left the conference room and returned to his study. Maercyl appeared in the doorway to the anteroom. "Oestyl just returned, Maitre. Factor Elthyrd would be more than pleased to see you at his factorage at first glass."

"Thank you, Maercyl. If you'd arrange for my mount and escorts at half before the glass."

"Yes, sir."

Almost another glass passed, and there had still been no messages from Lorien, and that worried Alastar a great deal, even as he concentrated on checking the progress of the various primes and seconds, and the reports from the maitres who instructed them. Just before ninth glass Maercyl brought in a sealed envelope.

"It's from Factor Estafen, the messenger said."

"Thank you."

Alastar opened the missive and began to read.

Maitre Alastar—

I apologize for the haste of this message. I have not the time to make it precise and neat. I've just received word that Factor Hulet was killed his morning when he went to see High Holder Laevoryn at Laevoryn's town dwelling here in L'Excelsis.

I do not know the circumstances. I do know that one of the missing young men was Enrique D'Hulet. He was Hulet's nephew and ward. Hulet was his guardian. Word is that Laevoryn's son lost over 200 golds to Enrique on Mardi evening at Alamara's. Later that night Enrique vanished.

Patrol Commander Murranyt is on his way to ascertain what happened. I thought you should know immediately.

Estafen D'Factorius

Alastar reread the short note, then looked to Maercyl. "Send for Maitre Cyran immediately."

Cyran must have been nearby, because he stepped into the study within moments. "Was another factor's son snatched?"

It's worse than that." Alastar handed the note to the Maitre D'Esprit. "You can read for yourself."

"You're right," said Cyran when he handed the single sheet back to Alastar. "What do you need from me?"

"In about a glass, I'd like you to try to find out from Murranyt just what happened between Hulet and Laevoryn—or what Laevoryn claims occurred. See if you can discover what the commander thinks happened as well."

"You don't think that will be the same?"

"Do you?"

With a sardonic smile on his lips, Cyran shook his head.

"I'm guessing from what Estafen wrote and from what Hulet said yesterday that Laevoryn's son snatched and likely killed Hulet's nephew and that Hulet confronted Laevoryn and that Laevoryn killed the factor. There's also the possibility that Laevoryn somehow ruined the missing nephew's father. Hulet was fond of the young man. I could tell that from the way he acted when he reported his disappearance."

"Do you know anything about High Holder Laevoryn?"

"Outside of what I've told you? No. If you can find out more, that would be good."

"I'll see what I can do."

"Thank you."

Once Cyran had left, Alastar made quick visits to talk to Thelia and Obsolym, but neither could add any information about either Enrique D'Hulet or High Holder Laevoryn.

Noergyn and Coermyd were waiting with the gray gelding when Alastar left the administration building. After crossing the east bridge, the three headed south on the East River Road and covered the distance of somewhat less than a mille to Elthyrd's factorage in little more than a quint and a half. When he reined up before the small central building flanked by large two-story warehouses, Alastar was reminded just how close the factorage was to the water, although the barges tied to wharves were empty, as if they'd been recently unloaded or were about to be loaded.

After dismounting, he handed the gelding's reins to Coermyd, then walked into the small building. Once inside, he stood for several moments before Elthyrd appeared.

"You're early."

"There weren't as many wagons on the East River Road."

Elthyrd gestured toward a doorway to the right and behind the long counter.

The two entered the spare study that held little more than a table desk, a small bookcase, and chairs, two before the desk and one behind it. Elthyrd settled behind the desk. "You asked for this meeting."

"I did. Have you heard from Estafen this morning?"

"Yes." Elthyrd's voice was wary.

"About Hulet?"

"You asked for the meeting before I found out. How did you know?"

"I didn't. I asked for the meeting before I knew. I was worried that Hulet was going to have problems. He stormed out of my study yesterday because I wouldn't immediately do something about his nephew's disappearance."

"He didn't always think before he acted. I warned him about that when he became chief factor . . . told him there were times to act and times to wait. Have to know the difference between those times."

"What do you think the Factors' Council will do next?"

"We'll meet tomorrow. I can't say what will happen. There are a lot of hard feelings building." Elthyrd paused. "What will the Collegium do? What will you tell Lorien?"

"That there are hard feelings building." *And that the High Holders are asking for trouble.*

"That's all?"

Alastar laughed softly. "Of course not, but I'm not about to advise him on what to do beyond denying the various petitions High Holders have made to attempt to exempt themselves from all laws except those laid down by themselves on their own holdings."

"They've actually petitioned Lorien on that?"

"They haven't been quite that direct. There are several petitions dealing with exempting them from justice decisions requiring them to pay factors and . . ." Alastar paused as he saw Elthyrd stiffen. "Hulet didn't mention that to you?"

"He only said that they were trying to weasel out of their debts."

"They're also trying to extend their privileges of low justice to include capital and major offenses so that the only disputes involving High Holders that would come before any justice would be those between High Holders and those could only be determined by the High Justicer."

"I would suggest, Maitre, that you *demand* Lorien deny those petitions."

"As we both know, it will just delay matters and make it harder if I demand anything. I would prefer to advise him on what would happen if he approved those petitions. One almost immediate result would be that scores of factors would be unable to pay significant amounts of their tariffs to him because they cannot collect just debts from High Holders. I might even be able to suggest that he should revise the Codex Legis to require forfeiture of lands and property held by High Holders for failure to pay debts."

"I'll leave the details to you, Maitre, but the factors of Solidar won't stand for the kind of high-handed arrogance that the High Holders are engaging in. We do have our ways of making that known."

"What? Close all the exchanges to High Holders?"

"That would only be the beginning. They're not nearly as self-sufficient as they think they are."

"Can I hint at that to Lorien?"

"Whatever will get him to listen."

Alastar nodded. "One other question. I've heard that Vaschet has received orders for a rather large quantity of rifles. Do you know anything about that?"

"Not directly. We did sell him some fine grade walnut several months ago, in Mayas, I recall."

"For rifle stocks?"

"Walnut's used for cabinetry mostly, but since Vaschet isn't in the cabinetry trade . . ."

"Do you have any idea who's buying the rifles?"

"I asked him why he wanted walnut. His answer was 'Because I do.' I didn't press."

Alastar chuckled. "With an answer like that, I wouldn't push, either. Is there anything else I should know?"

"Can't think of anything at the moment. I know where to find you if I do."

Alastar stood. "Thank you."

"More than welcome. Try and get Lorien to be reasonable."

"I'll do my best."

Elthyrd walked out of the factorage with Alastar and watched as the imagers rode away and back toward Imagisle. By a quint before second glass, Alastar was back in his study.

No messages had come from either the High Council or Lorien, and that was anything but good. Cyran did not return until two quints past third glass, by which time Alastar was getting more worried, not so much about Cyran, who could certainly take care of himself, but about what the delay portended.

"What did you find out?" asked Alastar, standing as soon as Cyran entered the study.

"It's as bad as you thought. Maybe worse." Cyran settled into the middle chair. "Murranyt asked . . . well, he demanded that I tell no one but you and requested that you keep the information to yourself for now."

Alastar nodded as he reseated himself. That meant what Murranyt thought had occurred was not what Laevoryn had told him.

"High Holder Laevoryn claimed that Hulet forced his way into Laevoryn's mansion and attacked him. Laevoryn shot Hulet in self-defense. That's what he told Murranyt."

"Did Hulet have any weapons?"

"Murranyt didn't know. Hulet was shot from above, because Laevo-ryn claimed he had to retreat partway up the staircase because of Hulet's vehemence."

"Because Hulet forced his way in, no one is going to challenge that claim."

"Murranyt didn't say that."

"He doesn't have to. The High Holders will stand behind Laevoryn. Lorien isn't about to pick a fight with the High Holders over something like this. It's going to enrage the factors. Elthyrd as much as said that. He knew about the killing, but not the circumstances. When he finds out from Estafen the rest of what happened, he'll likely be even more furious."

Cyran raised his eyebrows.

"According to Hulet, who is the missing young man's guardian as well as his uncle, Enrique was swindled out of his patrimony by Laevo-ryn or his father. Hulet also hinted that Enrique had won a sum from Laevoryn's son just before his nephew disappeared. Estafen's note said the sum was two hundred golds."

"That's an enormous sum to be wagered."

"But it's a pittance to a High Holder. Sums like that change hands every night at Alamara's." At the same time, Alastar recalled that Factoria Kathila had told him that Laevoryn was one of the less well-off High Holders, and he wondered if Laevoryn was also one who owed Estafen golds.

"But a son losing that much to a factor's ward, not even a son . . . ?"

"It's more likely the scorn the son would face, both from his peers and his father, that he'd been so badly bested by a mere merchant brat. I doubt we'll ever know whether that played a part." *You might discover if Laevoryn is one of those hovering on the brink of ruin.* "Did you find out anything more about Laevoryn?"

"Murranyt was surprised by the house. It's expansive enough, he said, but it's in an older area north of the Boulevard D'Este. Laevoryn doesn't believe High Holders should engage in commerce. He made some com-ment that his family wasn't about to soil their hands by stooping to factoring or manufacturing, and that no mere grain factor was going to get away with attacking him."

"Anything else?"

"I talked to Heisyt later, but he didn't know anything, except there had been word that young Laevoryn spent a lot of time at Alamara's and wasn't that good at either plaques or bones. He did even worse at Tydaael's. He also said it wasn't a death worth looking into, not over a pair of spoiled brats' gaming."

"It sounds like Murranyt doesn't want a fight with a High Holder. I can't totally blame him. Even if Laevoryn's son was a natural gaming dupe, and likely Enrique couldn't resist the temptation of fleecing him. Not when his uncle had probably made him well aware of how his father had lost everything."

"Have you heard anything from our beloved Rex Lorien?"

"Not a word. If I don't hear anything by tomorrow morning, I'll have to ride to the chateau and chase him down, if I can. Sending messages that I want to see him is worse than useless when he doesn't want to see me, and I'm not about to put what I need to tell him in ink."

"I can see that," replied Cyran.

Immediately after the senior imager left, Akoryt appeared, just to let Alastar know that a small holder from the east of L'Excelsis had appeared with his eleven-year-old son, who was clearly an imager, and that he'd apprise Alastar of the boy's talents in a day or so.

Alyna arrived in the study at two quints past fourth glass. "How was your day, dear?"

"Outside of the fact that the chief factor was shot and killed after bursting into High Holder Laevoryn's mansion, or that the reason he did was that Laevoryn's son likely murdered Hulet's beloved nephew because the nephew fleeced young Laevoryn at bones? Or that the factors are ready to do something drastic against the High Holders? Or that Lorien's likely dithering over the High Holder petitions? Or that there's no trace of poor Frydrek? Not too bad, otherwise. And I've probably skipped over a few things. How was yours?"

"Only moderately exasperating. Some seconds who still don't want to learn basic geometry, and two thirds who burst into tears whenever I suggest that they should have known the answers to the questions I asked. One boy and one girl, by the way." Alyna sat down in the chair closest to the window. "Now . . . tell me all the details you left out."

Alastar did, and what he said took more than two quints before Lystara and Malyna appeared in the doorway.

". . . and it's just a matter of time . . ." He broke off when he saw the two girls.

"What's just a matter of time, Father?"

"What happens after what has been a very long day. Speaking of time, we should be heading home for a good dinner."

"You always leave us out of the interesting parts."

"You'll find out why when you get older." *Because the interesting parts are the ones that are often dangerous.*

Lystara looked from Alastar to her mother and then back to Alastar. "Will you tell us then?"

"Yes."

"How much older do we have to be?"

"When you're a maitre on your own."

"Father . . . that won't be for years."

"That's right."

"Your father's right," Alyna said firmly but quietly. "It's time to go. You two can lead the way."

Neither Alastar nor Alyna said anything as they left the administration building and walked through the damp heat of the late afternoon up the west side of the double avenue on which the cottages for married maitres were located. The tall trees shading the stone-paved road kept the sun off them, but Alastar was still sweating within moments of leaving the building. He concentrated on trying to hear the conversation between the two girls.

". . . *always* does that."

"So do my parents," replied Malyna. "I wish I could do concealments like you can."

"Father and Mother would know. They always know."

Alastar smiled to himself. That feeling wouldn't last.

Zaerlyn rose from where he had been sitting on the east side of the front porch as the four walked toward the steps. "This evening I won't keep you waiting."

"We're home a little early," replied Alyna. "We'll all be waiting for dinner. It's cooler out here."

Once chairs were gathered together, Zaerlyn looked at his daughter. "Tell me about your day."

"It was a day. We ran and got washed up and dressed and ate breakfast . . ."

Much later, after dinner and getting the girls to bed, the three adults met in the study, where Alastar briefed Zaerlyn on what had occurred as a result of Enrique's disappearance.

When Alastar had finished, Zaerlyn frowned. "I can't say I understand why young Laevoryn was so rash."

"You mean that there are other better ways to deal with uppity merchanter types?" asked Alyna gently.

Zaerlyn flushed. "I wouldn't have put it that way, but . . . yes."

"Factoria Kathila told me that Laevoryn is not all that well resourced for a High Holder, and young Laevoryn has been losing large sums, and losing them consistently," said Alastar. "You wouldn't happen to know whether he's facing difficulties, would you?"

"Not really. Except that he doesn't have any factoring activities, and his lands are all here in old Bovaria . . ." Zaerlyn shrugged. "It could be that his son is one who can't stop gaming, and feared his father's wrath."

"So he and some friends snatched Enrique, killed him, took his winnings, and disposed of the body?"

"It could happen, but it seems so stupid."

"I've noticed, begging your pardon, that with some High Holders, arrogance makes them stupid. I think I mentioned the case before Lorien, where Lenglan beat his wife to death and crippled Farlan's son . . . and feels that it was self-defense?"

Zaerlyn laughed sardonically. "You did. And if some High Holders hadn't been that stupid I wouldn't be a High Holder today."

"None of this is going to help the High Holders with Lorien, do you think?" asked Alyna, looking to Alastar.

"If he doesn't get too arrogant himself, it won't, but he's not saying anything, and it looks as if I'll have to force myself on him tomorrow. He needs to know just how bad matters could get."

"Are things really that bad? Just because two or three young men vanished . . . you're acting as though Solidar is about to erupt in a war between factors and High Holders."

"I could be wrong. I could be very wrong," admitted Alastar. "But Cransyr seems determined to restore power to the High Holders, and make the factors totally subservient to them. Lorien doesn't understand how dangerous the situation could become. Almost all the grain and root crop stocks in the midsection of Solidar are in factors' warehouses, and someone is ordering large numbers of new rifles. I doubt it's the army."

"Then . . . ?"

"If I had to guess, and it's just a guess, those grain and produce factors are hiring and arming guards because they believe that they'll need them."

"How bad could that be?" asked Zaerlyn.

"If Elthyrd is right, any High Holder who doesn't have a stock of golds laid up, or some very good neighbors, if not both, may face a very long winter and a spring without enough seed for planting. That's in the middle of Solidar and in the northeast. I can't speak to the south or the southeast. The factors may refuse to sell grain, and other produce, as well as iron, copper, or tin except for golds and at very high prices."

"Why iron or copper?"

"To make those High Holders who have factorages pay more. They're tired of paying more in tariffs and getting less, and they can't trust High Holders to pay their debts. So, if it's not bought with golds . . ."

"Won't Lorien do anything about that?"

"What? If he uses the army and kills unwilling factors, how will that help? There are too many factors spread across Solidar. The only people he can use the army against, effectively anyway, are the High Holders, and he doesn't want to do that, because he can't collect tariffs from the others, and he can't use the army against enough of them to seize enough golds to keep things going. That's because the holds are so spread out."

"You don't paint the most cheerful picture, Alastar, but I see what you mean." Zaerlyn paused, then cleared his throat. "I'll be leaving in the morning. I've already told Malyna. I'd planned to stay longer, but . . . she's settling in . . ."

Alastar thought he understood. Alyna nodded.

". . . and I have to say, with what you've told me, I need to get back to Rivages as soon as I can. Maraak and I need to work out something to obtain coal-bearing lands—even if the cost is significantly higher than we had planned to pay."

Alyna frowned.

"There is a holding . . . we'd thought the price too high. Now . . . it's better to pay and have an assured supply." After a pause, Zaerlyn went on. "Some High Holders may be . . . may live in the past. I don't want to be one of them. No matter what happens, we're likely to lose access to the coal we're now getting, and the land isn't going to get cheaper. We'll also have to make provisions so that we can put guards on our barges if we need to." He looked at Alastar. "That is, if you're right."

"I hope I'm wrong, and I'm trying to keep things from getting worse, but using imaging or imagers directly right now would be like throwing gunpowder and lamp oil onto a bonfire. Both the factors and far too many High Holders absolutely believe that they have been wronged and want things to change, and they want the Collegium on their side."

"Which side do you favor?"

"Neither. Too much of Solidar is effectively still governed by High Holders. The factors would like nothing more than to destroy all of the High Holds and the High Holder system, and that would be a disaster."

"You don't sound happy with either, Alastar."

"Too many High Holders revere and want to maintain absolute unbridled power, and too many factors believe in obtaining as many golds as possible regardless of the costs to everyone else."

"Are imagers any better?" Zaerlyn's voice was level.

"At heart, no. In practice, at the moment at least, yes. To survive we've had to hold the powers we have in check and work for everyone's betterment, as we could. We've had to compromise and even bend and scrape and bow. We've had to kill innocents and let some of our own innocents be killed so that High Holders and factors would realize that we only used our abilities in self-defense . . . to maintain our independence without seeking power over others."

"You're rather eloquent for a man—"

"Zaeryl." Alyna's voice was like ice. "Don't."

The High Holder paled.

"Everything Alastar has said is true. You don't have to like it. You don't have to agree, but your survival and Mairina's depend on what Alastar can do to keep the anger and rage on both sides from turning into complete carnage. Cransyr's arrogance makes him stupid. Lorien is barely competent, and has only survived because Alastar and Chelia are there to guide him. The factors are fed up with being trampled on by High Holders, and they control too many of the supplies High Holders need and have too many golds to be forced back into a subservient position."

Zaerlyn bowed his head. "My apologies." He looked at Alyna. "Some have said you're almost as powerful as Alastar. You two are—"

"No. We're not. We might be strong enough to keep the damage within some bounds, but there will be damage. It's already too late to avoid."

"But . . . only a few young men have died. Surely . . ."

"Those deaths," replied Alastar wearily, "are not a cause. They're a symptom." Even as he spoke, he wondered if he was seeing more than was really there. "Do you honestly think that the factor who bought those coal lands would ever return them willingly to Staendyn? In his boots, would you? Do you think any factor is going to loan golds to a High Holder the way things are going, knowing he may never be repaid. Or would you extend golds to most other High Holders, if the only way to get repaid was by bringing the matter before the High Justicer? Within weeks, the price of flour and bread will climb again. Will the High Holders pay the prices the factors want? Will the factors reduce prices after what the High Holders are demanding?"

"Nothing will happen that quickly," said Zaerlyn.

"Possibly not," conceded Alastar. "But will that make matters better when winter comes? When wagons have trouble traveling even the high roads? When what has been laid aside gets even more scarce and the prices get higher? If Lorien demands lower prices, the factors won't comply. They'll lower prices on a bushel and find another way to charge more, and the army can't be everywhere. Neither can imagers."

"I hope you're wrong."

"So do I, but I have my doubts."

"I think we've whipped this horse enough," said Alyna quietly. "We're going to have problems, but none of us know whether they'll be difficult or even more so. Zaeryl has a long ride tomorrow." She looked to Alastar. "And you have to explain all this to Lorien."

A faint smile crossed Zaerlyn's lips before he said, "I agree. We've said all we can, knowing what we do." With that, he nodded to Alastar, then turned and left the study.

Once a tired Alastar and a weary Alyna had retired to their sitting room, she looked at him. "Now you see, I think."

"About Zaeryl, you mean? That while he can understand in his mind what might happen, he's still a High Holder at heart, albeit more enlightened than most?"

"More enlightened than the vast majority of them."

"I don't think he still understands how bad this could get. It's not like a war, or the rebellion of the army, or a few High Holders trying to force the rex not to raise tariffs."

"Those weren't exactly good." Alyna sank into one of the armchairs.

"They all occurred in or around L'Excelsis. What happens if there are fights and riots in a score of cities and towns? The Civic Patrols don't have enough men to deal with that sort of thing, and the army commanders are predominantly from High Holder backgrounds, while most of the field grade officers are from merchanter or factor backgrounds."

"Zaeryl did point out that nothing has happened yet."

"You think I'm overreacting?"

"You're usually right about this sort of problem."

"But because no one else sees it all, including your brother, they think I'm overreacting?"

Alyna nodded.

And Lorien thinks he has trials now. Alastar shook his head. "You're saying that I need to keep my mouth shut about how bad this could be until things get bad enough that others can see it as well."

"It might not hurt."

Alastar laughed softly but ruefully. "You're doubtless right about that. I'll just tell the senior imagers that things could get worse, but we'll have to wait and see."

Alyna rose. "We both need some sleep." She paused. "Sleep, dearest."

Alastar wasn't about to argue.

On Vendrei morning, Alastar, Alyna, and Lystara said their farewells to Zaerlyn and then retreated from the front porch of the Maitre's house to the study to allow Malyna space and time to say whatever she wished—or not—to her father.

"Did Malyna say anything to you about her father leaving?" Alastar asked Lystara.

"She said she would miss him, but there was no place for her besides here. She's glad we're here."

Alastar wondered if that would last, but merely nodded.

"No matter what she says," Alyna added, "she'll be sad for a time. Please be kind to her."

"I know that, Mother. She cried some last night. She won't talk about it."

Like someone else you know. Alastar did not voice the thought, but did offer his wife a sad smile.

In return, he got a barely noticeable headshake.

Before long, Zaerlyn moved toward his mount, and the holding guards who waited, and Alastar, Alyna, and Lystara joined Malyna on the porch, each offering a final good-bye before watching the High Holder ride down the avenue toward the East Bridge.

Then Lystara and Malyna began the walk toward the administration building, followed shortly by Alastar and Alyna. Once they reached it and Alastar saw Alyna on her way, he checked with Dareyn and Maercyl, but there were no messages and, for the moment, no new problems needing his immediate attention, and he had time to check the new entries on his copy of the master ledger before he left the Collegium on his unannounced visit to Lorien.

He'd barely opened the ledger when Maercyl appeared.

"Maitre Bettaur . . ."

". . . wishes to see me," finished Alastar. "I only have half a quint or so, but he's welcome to it." He stood because he wanted to keep the meeting short.

In moments, Bettaur appeared, nodded respectfully. "Sir . . ."

"You're inquiring about your request, I take it?"

"Yes, sir."

"Normally, I would have decided, but as you doubtless know, Maitre Zhelan died, and I have to consider the matter of his successor. Until I make that decision, I don't think it would be prudent to decide on your request."

"Yes, sir. I understand that. If . . . if you decide to send someone from here to be maitre there, we would accompany that person . . . that is, if you agree that we could go to Westisle."

Alastar smiled. "I appreciate your willingness to be accommodating, and I promise, once I decide on the new Westisle Maitre, I'll also have an answer for you."

"Thank you, sir. I do appreciate it."

Alastar moved slightly toward the door.

Bettaur caught the gesture and inclined his head again. "I won't bother you again about this, sir. I do appreciate your considering it."

Once Bettaur had departed and closed the door, Alastar took a slow deep breath.

At two quints after seventh glass, accompanied by Harl and Noergyn, Alastar rode away from the administration building. His departure was later than he would have preferred, but timed to arrive at the Chateau D'Rex near eighth glass, since Lorien tended to be in a foul mood earlier in the day. At the same time, arriving in the afternoon on Vendrei risked not finding Lorien because he was out riding—and trying to arrange a meeting when Lorien didn't want to see Alastar meant that days might pass, and in the end, Alastar would end up riding to the chateau without an appointment in any event in order to corner the rex.

Upon reaching the chateau, Alastar dismounted, handed the gelding's reins to Harl, absently brushing away a mosquito, and started up the immaculate white stone steps to the main entry.

As he reached the top, an older chateau guard—Guard Captain Churwyl—hurried toward Alastar. "Maitre . . . how might we assist you?"

Not a good sign, not at all. "I'm here to see Rex Lorien."

"He's not at the chateau, Maitre," replied the guard captain.

"Do you know where he is?"

"He rode out into the hunting park a short time ago. Where, none of us could say."

"How short a time ago?" asked Alastar mildly.

Churwyl did not reply, and his eyes did not quite meet Alastar's.

"Were, perhaps, your men ordered to report to the rex immediately if I were to appear?" Alastar waited.

After a long silence, the captain replied. "There have been orders to that effect for several days."

Not a good sign, not at all. After a long moment, Alastar said, "Then I will see the Lady Chelia. Please do not tell me that she is not in the chateau."

Churwyl swallowed, then moistened his lips. "The rex said . . ."

"I do not care what the rex said. I will see her. Now. You can escort me, or I can find my own way. Those are your choices, Captain, and you will have fewer than that if you attempt to divert or detain me. Is that clear?"

"Yes, Maitre." The captain's resigned tone expressed the sense his only choice was which death faced him. "This way. I believe she is in her private salon."

The salon was the same room in which Alastar had once verbally fenced with Lady Asarya, and one he had not visited since, although the upholstery for the loveseats and armchairs had been changed from silver and green to soft blue accented with cream, giving the chamber a far warmer feel.

"Maitre Alastar . . . I thought I might be seeing you." Chelia rose from the delicate secretary set against one wall, closing the slanted desktop with a graceful gesture. She was an attractive woman, tall and well proportioned, if fully figured even after three children and years of living with Lorien, which had to have been a strain. Her face was slightly square-chinned with a barely noticeable dimple, a straight nose, a fair but not pale complexion, blond hair, and brilliant blue eyes. Her smile was warm and welcoming, as her father's reputedly had been, and her eyes went to the guard captain. "Thank you, Captain Churwyl."

As Churwyl departed, leaving the salon door ajar, Chelia gestured to the armchairs, then made her way to one and seated herself, waiting for Alastar to sit before saying, "You must have something important to say, and something Lorien would prefer not to hear. You hope, I presume, that I might be able to convey it to him."

"I have no doubt that you are able to convey whatever you wish, Lady. The only question is whether he will hear the words you speak and wish to understand what they mean."

Chelia offered a nod of acknowledgment, not necessarily one of agreement. "Go on."

"Yesterday, a High Holder shot and killed the head of the Factors'

Council of L'Excelsis. Two nights before, the High Holder's son lost two hundred golds to the factor's nephew. The nephew was forced into a closed coach later that night and is likely dead. The nephew was greatly loved by the factor, and the young man's father had been ruined years earlier by the High Holder. The High Holder claims he was justified in shooting the factor because the factor entered his dwelling uninvited and likely with force, although he carried no weapons. This is the third time in the last few weeks that a young merchanter or factor has vanished. At the same time, a number of High Holders have not only refused to pay debts owed to factors and to both the Banque D'Excelsis and the Banque D'Aluse, but also have lodged petitions with your husband claiming that they are exempt from the jurisdiction of regional justicers and, in fact, even the High Justicer, unless the dispute or offense involves another High Holder."

"In practice, that has largely been the case," Chelia observed.

"But not in law, as set forth in the Codex Legis. Moreover, if the factors cannot collect debts from High Holders, many either cannot or will not pay their tariffs this fall. Also, it is likely that the most powerful factors will refuse grain and other provisions to High Holders . . . and take other steps."

"So you believe that Lorien should deny all the High Holder petitions." Chelia's words were not a question.

"I would suggest that he return them, without specifically denying them, by stating that, under the Codex Legis, High Holders are subject to regional and high justice, and that such will remain the law unless the Codex is changed."

"Will that satisfy the factors?"

"They would obviously prefer a stronger statement, but a stronger statement is not necessary."

"You know he seldom discusses such matters with me."

"I know that he listens to you if that is what you wish."

"He has . . . occasionally."

"Has your brother expressed any views on such matters?"

Chelia's first response was a soft laugh. "My brother, the present High Holder Ryel, has not spoken to me since the day after our wedding."

"I am sorry to hear that."

"Do not be. It was my desire, not his. Lorien has never invited him to the chateau, again, at my request. I was more than glad to leave Rivages."

For a moment, Alastar was at a loss for words.

"That is the first time I have seen you speechless, Maitre. You wonder why I tell you this? It is simple. I would not wish you, particularly you, to associate me with any of the rest of my blood relations, and especially in times such as these."

"I appreciate that clarity, Lady, but I must say that I never made any such assumption, which is why I sought you out when your husband vanished at my approach."

"He vanished at my suggestion."

Alastar frowned, if but for a moment, then nodded. "I see. In this, you are wiser than I have been."

"No. As the saying goes, we must play the plaques we are dealt. You must seek out the rex. He must not—"

Alastar held up his hand. "Say no more. That way . . ."

"Thank you." Chelia smiled. "Are there any other small bits of information that I should know?"

"A student imager vanished in the mist the other day when the river was running high, and two others were earlier followed on their return to Imagisle. I also understand that the gaming houses in L'Excelsis have decided to hire guards to keep order outside in the environs of their premises . . . having something to do with young men of High Holder background no longer being able to force out other young men by making exorbitant bets . . ."

Chelia nodded.

". . . and someone, I can't recall who, mentioned that he had overheard words about reclaiming sold lands under the rights High Holders had before the Codex . . . and apparently, a number of people must have decided to begin hunting with rifles, since one factor has increased his production of heavy rifles . . ."

"Ah . . . Maitre . . . I so envy you that you get to hear such interesting things, while I am so less worldly than you."

That was something Alastar strongly doubted, not when she had grown up in the Ryel High Holding.

"How is your wife . . . and your daughter?"

"They are both well. Lystara takes after both of us, and that is enough to keep us both occupied. What of your children?"

"Charyn is no longer a child. He is riding with his father. Bhayrn will be before that long. Aloryana . . ." She laughed ruefully. "I may be better equipped to deal with sons . . . having had mostly brothers."

"What about Khanara?"

Chelia raised her eyebrows. "She might as well have been a brother. She was better in the saddle than any of them."

"Did she ever marry? I don't recall . . ."

"No. She remained with my brother."

Alastar got that message. "All that Lorien says about Aloryana suggests that she is special."

"For him, she is. What about Lystara? Isn't she special to you?"

"I suppose all daughters are to their fathers, but I'm not her best friend. I'm her father. Often, I suspect, she wishes I were not."

Chelia smiled again. "It's good to talk to you. It doesn't happen often. Is there anything else . . . ?"

"Other than the fact that the High Holders hate the factors and the other way around? With all the assorted details? And that all our children are presently healthy? I think not."

"Then I should not keep you, Maitre. When Lorien makes up his mind on those matters, I will remind him to send you a message so that you won't have to ride all the way from the Collegium."

A polite way for her to suggest to him that you'll keep showing up until and unless he does something. "Thank you. I do appreciate that." Taking the hint, Alastar rose and inclined his head.

Chelia also stood, again smiling. "If I do not see her until the Year-Turn Ball, please extend my warmest regards to your lovely and incredibly capable wife."

"That I can do."

Alastar inclined his head a last time and made his exit from the salon. Once he was a good ten yards from the door, heading toward the main entrance, Churwyl reappeared and escorted him back to where Harl and Noergyn waited at the foot of the entry steps.

The three immediately turned eastward and rode down the gentle grade of the paved lane to the ring road and onto the Avenue D'Rex Ryen. They passed the Anomen D'Rex just as the bells of ninth glass rang out.

"That didn't take long, sir," offered Noergyn.

"Sometimes, it does. Sometimes, it doesn't." Alastar wasn't about to mention either that Lorien had not been there or that he had met with Chelia . . . for all too many reasons.

"Ah . . . sir," offered Harl, riding on Alastar's left, "has there been any word about young Frydrek?"

"No. I have my doubts that we'll ever know."

"Why would anyone do that to a student imager?"

"I don't know. Weren't you and Oestyl followed coming back to Imagisle one evening last week?"

"Yes, sir. But he was only following, and we gave him the slip. You think someone's out after imagers?"

"It could be. That's why I've had Maitre Akoryt suggest to every imager who can hold shields to do so when they're away from the Collegium and that students always go in pairs or groups."

"We haven't done anything, have we, sir?"

"Not that I know of, but there have always been people who don't like imagers."

Harl didn't say more, but his questions rekindled Alastar's own concerns. He'd been careful not to take any sort of publicly stated position favoring either the High Holders or the factors, and outside of Alyna, the only others to whom he'd even hinted at what he felt were to Lorien and, most recently, to Chelia. *Is someone just assuming you're going to favor the factors?*

Alastar was still pondering the matter when they crossed the West River Road and rode onto the causeway between the river road and the Bridge of Desires. Just as the gelding's hooves touched the stone roadbed of the bridge, from nowhere, something slammed into Alastar's shields, rocking him forward in the saddle, almost jamming his nose and visor cap into the gelding's mane. That impact was followed by a second.

"Keep your shields!" he ordered, expanding his own shield to cover the gelding as he turned back toward the West River Road. He scanned the nearest sections of the road itself, but outside of several wagons that seemed not to even have noticed anything, there was no sign of a shooter—for the impacts had to have come from a heavy rifle.

"Sir!" called Noergyn. "Harl's hurt."

Alastar immediately turned toward Harl, extending his own shields to cover Harl even before he rode up beside the third.

"It's not bad, sir. My shields . . . stopped the first one . . . slowed the second." Harl pressed his right hand against the back of his left shoulder, just above the shoulder blade.

"Is it bleeding a lot?"

"I don't think so . . ."

"Then you and Noergyn ride to the infirmary—as fast as you can!" Belatedly, he asked Noergyn, "Did you get hit?"

"There was one shot that hit my shields."

"Get moving and hold your shields!" Alastar wanted the thirds across the bridge before the shooter, if he had remained hidden nearby, could reload, since most heavy rifles held five cartridges in the magazine. Harl hadn't been turning white, but that could change in a moment.

Once the two thirds were on their way, Alastar concentrated on methodically studying the entire area west of the causeway, including the riverbanks north and south of the bridge. A half quint of scrutiny revealed nothing, and he finally turned the mare back toward Imagisle, reaching the stables another half quint later. He turned the mare over to one of the student imagers working under Petros and hurried toward the infirmary.

He had no more stepped inside than Noergyn rushed toward him, stopping abruptly.

"Sir." The third swallowed. "Harl's dead."

"Dead?" The wound hadn't been bleeding that much. How could Harl have died in little more than a quint?

Behind Noergyn, Gaellen walked toward the two. The healer maitre for Imagisle was shaking his head, more to himself, Alastar thought.

"Maitre . . ."

At Gaellen's single word, Noergyn stepped back, and made to move away, but Alastar motioned for him to remain, then said, "What happened? He didn't look that badly wounded."

"He wasn't. The bullet was poisoned. There were signs of bleufleur, but it couldn't have been that alone, because he had a seizure as well."

Not only bullets, but poisoned bullets as well?

"How long ago was he shot?"

"About a quint. We were coming back from the Chateau D'Rex. We were fired on as we started across the Bridge of Desires. I couldn't see anyone, not in the open or on the riverbank. Harl's shields stopped the first shot and slowed the second . . ."

"I thought as much. His shields and grays slowed it enough that it didn't penetrate more than a digit. But he was struggling to breathe when Noergyn practically carried him in. Then he convulsed." Gaellen shook his head again. "There wasn't anything I could do."

Alastar winced, before another thought struck him. "If I'd only known, if I'd just imaged the bullet out . . ."

"It might not have helped. The impact likely spread the poison beyond the bullet itself."

But it might have . . .

Gaellen looked to Noergyn. "It's a good thing your shields held."

"Very good," agreed Alastar, still wondering if he had just immediately imaged out the bullet . . . *That won't do any good, but if it happens again . . .* "If you can, without endangering yourself, save the bullet." Alastar not only wanted to confirm that it came from a heavy rifle, although that wouldn't tell him whose heavy rifle it might have been, but also something about the bullet might tell who had made it.

"I can do that."

Alastar and Noergyn walked out of the infirmary together.

"I didn't know, Maitre. We rode as fast as we could, but then . . . when we got to the infirmary, Harl was white, and his arms and legs weren't working. Not like they should . . ."

"You couldn't have done any more," Alastar said gently.

"Sir . . . why would anyone do anything like that?"

Alastar didn't answer the question the way he could have—that until Quaeryt had created the Collegium most imagers died unpleasant deaths. "There are always people who think that killing people they don't like will make their lives better. Over the long run, it never does. Even killing people who killed others out of hatred isn't much better, necessary as that is."

By the time Alastar strode into the administration building it was a quint before noon. Both Dareyn and Maercyl looked up from where they sat, side by side, at the table desk in the anteroom.

"Maercyl, find Maitres Cyran, Akoryt, and Alyna, and have them meet me here as quickly as possible."

"Yes, sir?" Maercyl's face showed puzzlement.

"Someone fired a heavy rifle at us when we were returning from the chateau. Harl looked to be slightly wounded, but the bullet was poisoned, and he died at the infirmary."

"He died, sir? Harl?"

Alastar nodded. "About summoning . . . ?"

"Oh . . . yes, sir!" repeated Maercyl before turning and hurrying off almost at a run.

Alastar turned to Dareyn, who still looked pale. "How are you doing?"

"Just fine, sir."

"That's good, but you're only supposed to work half a day for a while. Once Maercyl returns, I think you should head home and rest. After this, especially, I may need you more tomorrow morning than this afternoon."

"Sir . . ."

"Dareyn . . . even if you think you're doing well, Elmya wants you home. Think of me. Do you really want me to have to explain why I let you talk me out of what she and you agreed to?" Alastar managed a mournful expression.

After a moment, Dareyn smiled. "Two quints past the glass, sir?"

Alastar managed a grin he didn't feel. "That wouldn't be stretching it too much."

Alyna was the first to arrive, but before she could say a word, Akoryt followed her. Alastar motioned them both into the study.

"Are you all right?" demanded Alyna.

"I'm fine. Someone shot at the three of us just as we started across the Bridge of Desires. Harl's shields held up against the first shot at him, but collapsed partly at the second. He took a minor wound, less than a digit into the back of his shoulder. But the bullet was poisoned. He died just after he got to the infirmary. Gaellen thinks there might have been two separate poisons in the bullet. I'll tell you all the details as soon as Cyran arrives . . . and some of what happened at the chateau."

Alyna looked intently at Alastar, an expression not quite a glare.

Fortunately, Cyran appeared in the study doorway at that moment.

"Please close the door and join us."

Cyran did. "I heard someone shot at you. Do you know who?"

"No. Whoever it was shot from a concealed position from behind us . . ." Alastar went on to describe what had happened from the time of the first shot until he had left the infirmary. ". . . and I immediately had Maercyl get the three of you."

"Do you think the shots were aimed just at you?" asked Cyran.

Alastar shook his head. "There were two that hit my shields, two that hit Harl's shields, and one that hit Noergyn's. That many shells, spaced across the three of us, when our backs were turned. That doesn't seem like an attack on me."

"Not after Frydrek's disappearance, and the fellow who was following Oestyl and Harl. . . . Could Harl have been the target?" asked Cyran.

Alastar shook his head. "Then all five shots should have been at him, because the shooter wouldn't have known right away that he'd hit Harl. Harl just had the misfortune to be in the wrong place twice." *Except it turned out to be far more than mere misfortune.* "The immediate question is what steps we should take to protect Imagisle and the Collegium. Especially with someone shooting poisoned bullets at imagers." He waited.

"For now, we'll have to restrict the students to Imagisle," Akoryt said. "Most of them don't have shields strong enough to block a bullet."

"Most of the longtime seconds don't, either," Alastar pointed out, "and likely a good number of older thirds would fare about as well as Harl."

"When you leave Imagisle, your escorts will have to be those with strong shields," added Alyna.

Or go without escorts.

"Shouldn't we have two monitors at each bridge?" asked Cyran. "For a time, anyway? Until we know more?"

"That makes sense." Alastar frowned. "We'll need to design and image stone guard boxes for each bridge. If the monitors are in the open . . ." He looked to Alyna. "Can you do that? Can we image a glass strong enough to stop a bullet?"

"I can try."

"What else?"

"It's hard to say what might be effective," mused Cyran, "when we don't know who's behind it or where they'll strike next."

"We'll have to assume that they'll continue to strike at imagers who are alone or who can be targeted from cover. . . ."

Although the three discussed the matter for another quint, by then it was obvious to Alastar that there was little point in continuing, and he called an end to the meeting, sending Cyran and Akoryt off to pass the word.

When they were alone in the study, he turned to Alyna. "What do you think that you weren't saying?"

"That you never said what happened at the chateau."

"Lorien wasn't there. In fact, Chelia sent him off as soon as he received word I was approaching the chateau. . . ." Alastar recounted what happened when he met with Chelia, as close to word-for-word as he could recall, then waited for her reaction.

"She's probably right. The longer Lorien can appear to be treating the situation dispassionately, the better. From their perspective."

"Do you think we should press Lystara and Malyna on learning shields?"

"Lystara can handle concealments," replied Alyna. "A shield of some sort shouldn't be a problem."

"But how strong is another question."

"She'll take it as a challenge. We'll just have to watch carefully so she doesn't overdo it."

"Like her mother?"

"You're not going to let me forget that, are you?" Alyna offered the mischievous smile that Alastar loved.

"Not entirely. You're so perfect otherwise."

Her laugh expressed total disbelief.

"Can you image those sentry or guard boxes?"

"I'll have them done this afternoon. I'll have to see how strong I can make the glass, though. What are you going to do?"

"Think for a bit. Have Cyran talk to the Civic Patrol. Then ride out and talk to shopkeepers along the West River Road. It could be that someone saw the shooter." Alastar didn't know what else he could do, but he felt he had to do something.

"Please be careful."

"As careful as I can be."

After Alyna left, Alastar made his way to the armory, where Cyran had always had his study, and where the senior imager of the Collegium preferred it to remain.

"I thought I might see you." Cyran stood beside his table desk, polishing a saber, although Alastar wasn't certain that Cyran had ever used it.

"Do you think it would be useful for you to talk to Heisyt or Murranyt about the shooting?"

"Heisyt would be better. He knows some of the thirds. He should be around the main patrol station this afternoon."

"I'd appreciate that."

"What are you going to do?"

"Talk to shopkeepers and crafters along the West River Road."

"They might have seen something. They'd talk to you, I think."

"Meaning that they won't say much, but I might get a bit more."

Cyran chuckled. "Something like that."

"You talk to the patrol, and I'll talk to some people, we'll meet at a quint before seventh glass tomorrow—unless we discover something we need to act on immediately."

"That makes sense to me."

Alastar nodded and headed to the nearby stables, where he saddled a chestnut mare. Then, regardless of appearances or custom, he rode out over the Bridge of Desires alone. His shields were strong enough to withstand the impact of a heavy rifle, and he didn't want to risk anyone else.

The closest shop to the bridge was that of a cooper on the northwest corner of the Avenue D'Rex Ryen. As Alastar reined up outside, the gray-haired man who was sweeping the paving stones in front of the entry looked up then stepped back. Alastar decided not to dismount, at least not for the moment. "Have you been here since midmorning?"

"Begging your pardon, Maitre . . . I don't hear so well."

Alastar repeated the question, raising his voice.

"Been here the whole time, Maitre. Is something the matter?"

"Not with you. Earlier today, an imager was shot as he started to ride across the bridge." Alastar had decided against mentioning the poisoned bullets or Harl's death. That might provide too much encouragement to the shooter or those behind him. "I was wondering if anyone heard anything or saw anyone with a rifle."

The cooper frowned, then shook his head. "About that time I was working inside. Wouldn't hear much anyway. My ears aren't the best."

"Was there anyone else who might have seen or heard anything?"

"You might try Doryan." The cooper gestured to the shop to the north. "Dry goods don't make as much noise as tools."

"Thank you." Alastar turned his mount northward. Since there was no one outside the small dry goods shop, he dismounted and tied the mare to the railing in front of the porch and walked inside. He noticed that the bins beside the door, which likely had held dried beans or possibly even rice, were empty, and that he saw a single large barrel of flour near the back of the shop. On the right wall were rows of largely empty baskets.

A small dark-haired man looked up, then looked again. "Maitre . . . I don't know as we'd have anything . . ."

"I take it that business has been better," Alastar said gently.

"If it weren't for the lace collars Sephia makes"—the shopkeeper shook his head—"right now we'd be better closing the shop and tending the garden.

"It's not that bad, Dael." A muscular woman looked up from the table in the corner and what appeared to be a repeating scallop lace collar laid set within a type of frame Alastar did not recognize.

"Almost." The man looked to Alastar. "Maitre?"

"I'm looking for information. Earlier today, around two quints before noon, someone shot at and wounded one of my imagers as he started across the bridge. I wondered if either of you saw or heard anything."

The shopkeeper shook his head.

Alastar looked to the woman.

"I wondered about that." She remained seated at the table, but lowered the crochet hook slightly—at least that was what Alastar thought it was—before going on. "It sounded like someone had dropped some planks outside. Not quite, but sharplike. I looked out. There was a blond-headed fellow with a staff hurrying past the window there, and then he was gone. I asked Dael to look out back, but he didn't see anything."

Alastar looked to the shopkeeper.

"I didn't hear anything. Sephia's got better ears."

"You didn't see him when you looked?"

"Took me a moment to unbolt the back door. Wasn't anyone in the back alley. I looked both ways."

Alastar turned back to Sephia. "Can you tell me anything more about the man you saw?"

"He wasn't big, and he wasn't small. He wore a brown shirt. I didn't see his face because he was past the window when I looked out. He was walking fast. He wasn't running, though."

Although Alastar asked more questions, within a fraction of a quint, it was clear that Sephia had seen what she had said—and no more.

"Thank you," he finally said, stepping forward to the counter and laying a half silver on it. "I appreciate your taking the time and telling me what you saw."

"You don't have to pay us," protested Dael, if weakly.

"I don't have to," replied Alastar with a smile, "but I choose to. If you see the man again and send word to me . . . then there will be more."

"Ah, Maitre . . . I know you must be one of the imager maitres, but where . . ."

"Oh, I'm terribly sorry. That's my fault. Just have the message delivered to Maitre Alastar. I'll pay the messenger as well."

"Alastar . . ." mused the shopkeeper uncertainly.

"Alastar? You're the Maitre of the Collegium?" asked Sephia.

Alastar nodded.

She swallowed. Dael paled.

"Thank you both for your help." With a smile, Alastar turned and left. *Another reminder that you're still not doing enough to make people aware of the Collegium.* But there were only so many glasses in a day, a week, even a month.

Three glasses later, as he stepped back into the anteroom outside his study in the administration building after having talked to more than a score of shopkeepers, or their assistants, or apprentices, or children, Alastar knew little more than what he'd discovered from Sephia the lacemaker—that a blond man carrying a "staff" that was probably a rifle might have been the shooter. And only one other person—a skinny boy who could not have been more than eight or nine—even recalled seeing the blond man with the "staff."

He could have been sent by anyone, reflected Alastar, *the army, the High Holders, or a disgruntled factor out to stir things up.* He offered Maercyl a pleasant smile and asked, "Have there been any messages or letters?"

"No, sir."

Still nothing from Cransyr or Lorien. Not that Alastar had expected anything from Lorien immediately after his visit to Chelia, given how easily Lorien could be miffed if he felt he were being slighted. "Thank you."

Alastar was still thinking matters over when Alyna appeared in the study at two quints past fourth glass. He took one look at her and said, "You need some dark lager. Now. And some bread and cheese."

"All three are done."

Alastar took her by the arm. "We'll talk about it after you get some color in your face."

Alyna nodded. "I'd forgotten . . ."

That was obvious, but Alastar refrained from saying so. That was also for the best since they encountered Lystara and Malyna in the main corridor outside the anteroom to his study.

"We're going to the dining hall," Alastar announced. "Just to feed your mother."

"Can we have something?" asked Lystara.

"We'll see," replied Alastar.

"Perhaps a little," murmured Alyna.

When they entered the dining hall kitchen, one of the assistant cooks hurried forward.

"Yes, Maitres?"

"Dark lager and some bread and cheese for Maitre Alyna, Narlana," Alastar said. "Quickly, please."

"Yes, sir. We'll bring it right out."

Alastar led the way to a table at the side, the one for the thirds, had it been a regular mealtime. They had barely seated themselves when Narlana returned with a pitcher of dark lager and a beaker, as well as a platter with half a loaf of bread and a wedge of cheese, along with a kitchen knife. She set everything in front of Alyna.

"Thank you," offered Alastar with a smile as he immediately half-filled the beaker and handed it to Alyna.

Another kitchen worker appeared with a tray holding three additional beakers and set those on the table, then scurried off. The pallid Alyna immediately took a slow but deep swallow of the lager, followed by a mouthful of bread and cheese.

Alastar filled two beakers slightly, perhaps a fifth full, and set one in front of Malyna and the other before Lystara, then said, "Just take sips. That's all the lager you get."

"Dear," said Alyna quietly, "have some lager. Your eyes are getting reddish."

Alastar obeyed, half-filling his beaker and taking a swallow. It did taste good.

As some of the paleness left Alyna's face, she cut a small slice of bread for each girl, along with a chunk of cheese. She cut a healthy slice and a much larger piece of cheese for Alastar.

After a time, Alastar turned to Malyna. "This is what happens when you image too much, but not enough to knock you out or kill you. When you feel faint or weak, it's time to stop . . . and get some nourishment, and rest if you can." He ate another mouthful of bread and cheese.

"Father . . . who was the imager who was killed?"

"Where did you hear that?"

"Everyone knows. Someone shot through his shields with a poisoned bullet, and no one can leave Imagisle. Who was it?"

"Harl."

"I only met him a few times. He was nice."

"He was a good man." *Too good to die from a poisoned bullet in the back.* Not that there was any good way to die, so far as Alastar was concerned.

"Who did it?" asked Malyna.

"We don't know. He was shot twice. His shields stopped the first bullet. They partly collapsed with the second shot. He was scarcely wounded, and there was no sign that the bullet had been poisoned. He died less than a quint after reaching the infirmary. Maitre Gaellen couldn't do anything." *But you might have been able to . . . if you'd known.*

"Did they shoot at you?" asked Lystara.

"They hit my shields," Alastar admitted.

"Mother and Father carry their shields all the time," Lystara said to Malyna.

Alastar looked to Alyna, questioningly.

She nodded, then cleared her throat. "Your father and I thought that it's time to see if you and Malyna can learn the beginning steps of creating and holding shields."

"You're worried," declared Lystara.

"We are," affirmed Alastar.

"When will we start?"

"That depends on how we feel," said Alyna firmly.

"How do you feel about the sentry boxes you imaged?" asked Alastar, not wanting to dwell on the concerns behind the decision to see if the girls could learn shields earlier than either he or Alyna would have preferred.

"The sentry boxes were easy. The glass . . . I'm not sure what it is, but you can look through it just like glass." Alyna took another swallow of the dark lager. "I'm feeling much better. I think it's time to head home." She stood.

So did Alastar and the girls.

13

After dinner, Alastar and Alyna took Lystara and Malyna out onto the east side of the front porch, where, in the twilight, a nearly full Artiema was rising over the trees.

"You two may or may not be ready to create or handle shields," began Alastar. "It's different for every imager. Some imagers learn early and some learn late. Given your abilities already, you will both be able to create shields. It's only a question of when. A shield is a way of using your imaging ability to keep anything from touching you, and there have been some very unusual shields and ways of using them developed by imagers over the years. Some imagers have even developed different types of shields." He paused and glanced at Alyna.

"Whatever kind of shield you develop won't be very strong at first," added Alyna. "Strong shields take at least a year to develop, and perfecting them will usually take much longer."

Alastar let an object drop from his hand—except the polished oblong of goldenwood stopped short of the stone tiles of the porch because it was attached to a length of twine he still held. "We'll start with this. Lystara . . . I'll hold this high and then swing it toward you. Try to stop it. Do not image it away or damage it. Just stop it."

"How do I do that?"

"Some imagers say they harden the air. Others create a net only they can see. One or two . . . do other things." Alastar wasn't about to offer what those other things were, since most of them had turned out to be counterproductive. He stepped toward his daughter. "Ready?"

Lystara nodded, her expression almost grim.

Alastar swung the polished billet of wood toward her.

The billet slowed, but did not stop. Lystara jumped back.

Alastar reclaimed the wooden oblong. "You did something. Let's try again." He launched the billet once more.

This time the billet stopped in midair, bouncing back and then to the side, before again swinging down toward Lystara's side. She jumped sideways.

"That's better, but you have to keep the shield in place. Try again."

The third time, the wooden billet stopped, then edged forward slightly.

"I stopped it, but it didn't stay stopped."

"Still, that's better," said Alastar. "You can rest for a moment." He turned to Malyna. "You try now."

The older girl squared her shoulders as if Alastar held a weapon.

He swung the small goldenwood billet toward her, and the wood slowed, then stopped.

"Good." Alastar nodded. "It will be faster this time." Rather than just let the billet swing down toward Malyna, Alastar pushed it faster.

Again, the billet slowed, and then stopped, as if caught in a net, but it stopped much closer to Malyna.

"You see that it got closer to you when it was going faster?"

"Yes, sir."

"Try to stop it farther away from you this time."

Malyna nodded.

Alastar again launched the wooden billet.

Once more, Malyna stopped it, but not noticeably farther away than the second time. "That's hard."

"It is," agreed Alyna. "A few more tries by each of you, and then we'll stop for the day. You'll need to practice every day, but we don't want you trying to stop objects of any sort unless one of us is with you."

"Is that clear?" asked Alastar.

Both girls nodded.

After another half quint of practice, both girls were clearly tiring.

"It's time to stop, now, I think," said Alastar, winding the cord around the goldenwood billet.

Lystara looked at her father. "Could I see the cord for a moment, Father?"

Curious as to what his daughter had in mind, Alastar handed the cord and the billet to her and watched as she unwound the cord and let the billet dangle. Then the billet moved to one side . . . and swung back. The arcs became larger and larger, then stopped abruptly. Lystara carefully rewound the cord and handed the billet and cord back to her father.

"What were you trying to find out?" he asked.

"I just wondered how much I could make it go if I used imaging to push it, just a little, like swinging on a rope." Lystara paused. "That ought to be good for something. I'll have to think about it." Abruptly, she walked to the east end of the porch and pointed to the north. "Look! The glow-bugs are out. Can we go look at them?"

"Not tonight," replied Alyna. "It's already late. Some other night."

"Promise?"

"We promise."

Alastar was still thinking about both promising to let them see the glowbugs and whatever it was Lystara had in mind from swinging the wooden billet when Alyna escorted the girls inside and upstairs to wash up and get ready for bed.

He remained on the porch as twilight faded into night, standing and moving to the railing, watching as Artiema continued to rise. He continued to worry over the shooting. Who had anything to gain from trying to kill imagers, especially given what an angry imager could do? *Unless they honestly believed that they could destroy or severely cripple the Collegium.* Did Cransyr and the High Holders believe that? Or whoever had ordered rifles from Vaschet . . . who was someone that Alastar definitely needed to talk to even more after what had just happened with Harl. Or were the disappearance of Frydrek and the shots at the three of them, especially just as Alastar was returning from the Chateau D'Rex, a warning of sorts, to show what could happen if the Collegium became involved in the conflict between the High Holders and the factors? All that suggested that High Holders were behind the attacks, because they were the ones trying to regain old privileges.

Alastar heard steps and turned, admiring Alyna as she walked from the front door to join him. "How are they?"

"Tired. Lystara's excited about trying to learn shields. It took a bit to settle her down. I think Malyna's worried. I talked to her for a bit."

"Worried about shields . . . or everything?" Alastar suspected the latter, given their niece's seeming similarity to Alyna.

"Everything, of course. She worries she won't be a good imager. She's afraid her father doesn't understand the dangers ahead."

"Does he?"

"I'm afraid he doesn't want to, but he does understand the danger Ryel represents, thank the Nameless."

"And he's one of the more enlightened High Holders . . ." Alastar kept his voice low, knowing that the upstairs windows were open. He shook his head, then said. "You had me worried this afternoon."

"I wasn't that—"

"You were," Alastar said firmly.

Alyna smiled. "Perhaps . . . but it was good to see how much you care."

"I've always cared."

"I know. It's one of the things I love about you." Her smile faded. "You had a very serious expression."

"After what happened thirteen years ago and what's happened since, I would have thought that the High Holders would have come to understand—"

"They have," interjected Alyna quietly, but firmly. "They now understand that Solidar is changing and that they will come to have even less power, and they don't like it. Even Zaeryl didn't care for the coal lands going to a factor. Didn't you catch that?"

"I thought he just didn't like paying higher prices."

"That, too."

"Neither Lorien nor Cransyr has bothered to let me know what they are doing, and it's been a week since the High Council met. Everyone is waiting for someone else to make a move."

"As are you," Alyna pointed out. "If you haven't heard anything by Lundi, perhaps you should pay Cransyr a visit."

"Unannounced, you think?"

"With some, that might reveal more. With Cransyr, I doubt he will reveal much that he does not wish to share."

With that, Alastar agreed. "What about Lorien?"

"Once you visit Cransyr . . ."

"I can use that as a reason to visit Lorien—this time at seventh glass. He couldn't even find his saddle that early."

"The guards may have orders not to let you in."

"I hope he's not that foolish." Alastar sighed.

"So do I, dear, but that side of the family hasn't retained the intelligence of the first rex regis."

At times, Alastar still found it amazing that he was married not only to a descendant of the sister of Bhayar, the first rex regis, but to a descendant of the first maitre of the Collegium. "That's become apparent. I can only hope that Charyn is more perceptive than his sire."

Alyna nodded, leaving unsaid the possibility that Charyn becoming the next rex might well not occur until Alastar was no longer alive, given that he was almost fifteen years older than Lorien.

"I'd also thought of visiting Factoria Kathila tomorrow to see what she might know about poisons, and who might produce them in quantity."

"Quantity?"

"I have my doubts that just five bullets were poisoned." He paused. "But I did promise some boot or shoe buckles . . ."

"You need a geometric design?"

"If you would . . . and I thought you should come with me . . . so I don't overcommit."

"Wise of you." Alyna's voice was humorously dry.

"I try."

"I'll make you a design after breakfast tomorrow."

"The other matter is that the Factors' Council was supposed to have met today. I've had no word about that, but then, Elthyrd wouldn't necessarily feel bound to let me know anything."

"He didn't send you any messages, did he?"

"No."

"Then they didn't decide anything, or he decided he wasn't about to let you know what they decided."

"I think I'd prefer the first," Alastar said dryly. "I can send him a message, letting him know about what happened to Harl, and asking if he or the council might have any information about why someone would shoot at imagers returning to the Collegium."

"That might be better than going to see him again so soon, and you wouldn't have to leave Imagisle by yourself immediately, since he wouldn't take to my accompanying you there."

"You're right." He offered a grin. "And you're worried, too." He put his arms around her, and hers went around him.

14

Once he was in his Collegium study on Samedi morning, after checking
with Akoryt to make sure that all student imagers understood that they
were restricted to Imagisle until further notice, Alastar immediately wrote
a short letter to Elthyrd explaining about the shooting on the previous
day and the use of poisoned bullets, and noting that he thought the factors
should be aware that such weapons were now in use. He closed by
expressing the concerns he shared with the factors about the unhappy
circumstances that had led to Hulet's death.

After having Maercyl dispatch the letter, with instructions to assign
a third with strong shields, Alastar made his way to Thelia's small study.

"What is it, Maitre?"

"As you have doubtless heard, Tertius Harl was killed by a poisoned
bullet yesterday when someone fired a rifle at three of us. According to
Maitre Gaellen, the poison was possibly a combination of bleufleur and
something else that causes convulsions. While poisons have always been
a part of Solidaran life, this is the first time I know of that a bullet has
been poisoned."

"And you're asking me?"

"Your mother deals with oils, scents, and other substances. What I'd
like to know from you is whether she would have any knowledge of the
various poisons and their sources in more than minute quantities . . . or
whether asking her about that would be tantamount to a deadly insult."

"As far as I know, she has never dealt in poisons as such. Some substances which her factorages use can be quite dangerous, but I've never
heard of any of them being employed as poisons. They smell too odoriferous to be useful that way. She often does know what is being traded
or offered. I doubt that she would be offended by a request for information. She is most practical."

"Thank you. That will be useful."

With that, Alastar returned to his study and picked up the square of
paper with the precise geometric design that Alyna had so carefully
inscribed just after breakfast that morning, and made his way to the

Collegium factorage, largely deserted in the morning, except for Tertius Akkard, the smith who was principal assistant to Maitre Arthos.

"Good morning, Akkard. I need a bit of silver for some imaging. Scraps or even ore will do."

"We got some ore on Mardi, sir. I don't know how good it is."

"I'll find out for you."

"Maitre Arthos would be obliged, sir."

"Lead the way." Alastar followed Akkard from the workroom and to the far south end of the building where the forge and the anvils were located.

Akkard pointed. "In that barrel, sir. Well . . . and the others behind it as well."

Alastar surveyed the rocks in the first barrel, some of which had dark squarish metallic-looking lumps surrounded by white crystals, and some of which just looked like ordinary rock. He decided to concentrate on imaging out a lump of silver, roughly a fifth the size of his palm.

Moments later, an oval silver shape sat on the anvil. Alastar had only felt a momentary flash of light-headedness, but he shouldn't have felt that. He turned to Akkard. "I'd be careful with that ore. It doesn't seem to have that much silver in it."

"It never does, sir. That lump is a lot more than Maitre Arthos would ever try."

"I'm afraid that shows how little I know about ore."

"What are you going to do with it, Maitre . . . if I might ask?"

"Image something out of it to repay a favor." Alastar smiled. "Come along." He walked from the forge area back to the empty workroom, picking the end of the table where the light shone through the window onto the polished wood.

There he set down the lump of silver and then laid the paper with Alyna's geometric image on it beside the lump. Once more, he concentrated, focusing on replicating the design exactly. In an instant, beside the slightly diminished lump was a single shimmering boot buckle. In another moment, a second lay beside the first.

Sensing the heat from the pair, Alastar left them on the table and looked to Akkard.

"They're . . . beautiful." It was almost as if the third didn't want to use the word . . . or that he wasn't sure what to make of the design.

"Thank you. They should serve the purpose. Now . . . how are you doing with Maitre Arthos?"

"Very well, sir."

"I take it you prefer the forge to escort duty?" Alastar concealed a smile, but only for a moment, then added, "I'm glad you do." He took a small box from his jacket pocket, opened it, and eased the buckles into the box, and then returned the box to his pocket. He put the silver lump and the design in his other pocket. "Thank you."

"My pleasure, sir."

By the time Alastar returned to his study, Alyna was waiting.

"I had Maercyl ready the horses. I told him we wouldn't need escorts."

"Thank you. I appreciate your coming with me." He took out the box and handed it to her. While she opened the box, he set the lump of silver and the design on the table desk.

"Very stylish," Alyna affirmed, replacing the top on the plain wooden box and returning it to Alastar. "They're worth more than what you received."

"Probably, but I expect more today."

Her eyes went to the silver lump, questioningly.

"I imaged raw silver from some of the ore Arthos had. I overestimated what I needed, but since I'd done it, I thought we might find a use for it."

"No more silver adornments for the factoria."

"No, dearest." Alastar smiled innocently. He had other ideas.

At the rap on the study door, both looked up.

"Your mounts are ready." Dareyn paused, then asked, "No escorts, Maitre?"

"Not for short rides right now. There would be more danger to them than to us." *And the last thing we need is more imagers being killed.* Alastar adjusted his visor cap.

The two walked out to where Kaylet, the lead ostler under Petros, held their mounts.

"Good morning, Maitre Alastar . . . Maitre Alyna."

"Good morning, Kaylet. Thank you."

Again, as he watched Alyna mount, Alastar enjoyed seeing the grace with which she did, then hurried into the saddle himself, before they turned westward.

As they neared the west side of Imagisle and the South Bridge, Alastar studied the sentry box that Alyna had imaged, a solid stone structure with a window facing the bridge, and a heavy wooden, but iron-bound door at the back. Alastar blotted his forehead with the back of his hand

and looked again at the stone monitoring station. There were even angled ventilation ducts.

The third manning the box watched them from behind the transparent window.

"That's an imposing sentry box, especially with all the vents."

"I believe that was the idea."

"It might even stand up to a cannon shell."

"It might, but I wouldn't want to be inside when it did."

A quint later, the two reined up outside the low brick-walled structure just off the West River Road west and well south of Imagisle. Alastar couldn't help but note that the factorage windows were clean and actually shone in the morning light.

The same young girl in gray waited on the front step of the factorage. As before, she opened the door for Alyna and Alastar.

The white-haired woman who sat behind the table desk in the small anteroom looked startled, but only for a moment. "Maitres . . . let me tell the factoria you're here."

Alastar merely nodded and slipped his visor cap under his arm.

The older woman reappeared immediately, walked down the hall, returned with a chair which she placed in the factoria's study, and then gestured to the door.

After looking to Alyna to indicate she should go first, Alastar followed her into the study, closing the door behind them.

Factoria Kathila was already standing behind the jet-black table desk.

"I apologize for our calling uninvited," said Alastar, "but I don't believe you've met my wife, Alyna."

"I have not, but I've heard much of her prowess. I had not realized you were also so attractive." Kathila smiled, an expression seemingly without guile or undercurrents, at least to Alastar, as she motioned for them to seat themselves.

"Nor I you," replied Alyna as she sat down, "although I should have realized it, given your daughter's beauty and abilities."

Alastar seated himself without speaking.

"You're most kind, Maitre Alyna."

"Not kind. Accurate."

"What information do you seek? I presume that is why you're here."

"It is," began Alastar. "I don't know if you've heard, but a junior imager was shot with a poisoned bullet yesterday. He died almost immediately from the poison, most likely a mixture of bleufleur and another substance that causes convulsions. The wound was little more than superficial. A number of shots were fired, and all the bullets were poisoned." That was strictly speculation on Alastar's part.

"And?"

"While I understand that you do not deal in such substances, you would have the greatest breadth of knowledge as to who might or whose facilities might have the capability of casting or forging the hollow bullets and making larger quantities of such poisons." What Alastar wasn't saying, but what would certainly be obvious to the factoria, was that if no one in the factoring community happened to be making the bullets, whoever it might be was likely a High Holder.

"I could scarcely speak to the matter of weapons. In fact, the only factor I know who has any familiarity with those is Vaschet. Poisons? Every factor in L'Excelsis likely has substances that could poison someone in some fashion."

"That is doubtless true," replied Alyna, after a glance from Alastar. "Most of those substances would not kill someone in moments without any odor and in such small amounts that they could be carried by a bullet."

"That is, as you say, true enough, but the most effective poisons are those gathered from herbs and plants, although I have heard that the skins of certain frogs from Otelyrn contain a deadly venom. Very few factors have lands vast enough to gather the herbs and plants sufficient for the quantities of poison necessary for scores of bullets, let alone hundreds. While the root of a single bleufleur contains enough poison to kill a man, I do not know of anyone foolish enough to grow scores of them. It takes the pits of about thirty wild apricots to make a fatal dose of pitricin, but that is for a liquid that can be placed in food. I understand that it is not nearly so effective if applied in other ways, and the amount required would be much greater . . ." After another half quint, Kathila paused, then concluded, "I trust you can see why I believe it unlikely that any factor in L'Excelsis would be involved in creating poison bullets."

"What about smallholders outside L'Excelsis?" asked Alastar. "They would have access to the plants."

"They could certainly make pitricin or bleufleur, but bleufleur in particular is dangerous to handle in large quantities. Spilling the liquid on an arm could kill a smallholder. Only someone with access to land and a special factorage . . ."

"That's not quite an accusation of High Holders," suggested Alastar, his voice lightly humorous.

"You asked, Maitre. I have answered as honestly as I know how. Do you disagree?"

"You do make a case for a greater probability that the poisoned bullets came from a High Holder, but at the moment, it only appears that it is more likely."

"In time, Maitre, a succession of likelihoods becomes a certainty."

"You have been most helpful," Alyna said warmly, glancing to Alastar.

"Most helpful," he agreed, easing the wooden box from his jacket pocket and extending it across the desk.

Kathila took the box. "Might I open it now?"

"I hope you would."

The factoria eased off the wooden top. Alastar could see the slight widening of her eyes before she said, "They're magnificent . . . and the design . . ."

"Alyna created the design. They're pure silver."

Kathila inclined her head slightly. "Thank you. I may just keep these, at least for a time." After a pause, she added, "There is not a factor in L'Excelsis who has not said that you are a man of your word. This is a splendid example of that." Her voice darkened as she went on. "I fear that too many High Holders do not understand that, and we all will suffer."

"I hope not," replied Alastar.

"One can always hope, while continuing to prepare for the failure of those hopes." Another silence followed. "Is there anything else?"

"I think not." Alastar rose, as did Alyna. "We thank you for your time and knowledge."

"And I, for your word, and the silver that supports it."

Neither Alastar nor Alyna spoke until they were mounted and headed north on the West River Road.

"She knows more than enough to poison most of L'Excelsis," Alastar declared wryly. "She's not someone we need as an enemy."

"You just discovered that, dearest?"

"Let's just call this morning confirmation, both of her abilities and the fact that she has nothing to do with it."

"She has the abilities, regardless of what she said, but I would agree with you. No matter what she conveys to Thelia, she would do nothing that might harm her."

"Assuming she is correct, and I'm assuming that," said Alastar, "that only narrows those with the ability and proximity to half the High Holders in and around L'Excelsis."

"Half? Because the other half aren't competent enough or don't have lands near enough or any real factorages?"

"It might be a bit more or less."

"Likely less."

"Make certain your shields are strong," Alastar said as they continued north toward the south bridge. "If anyone is likely to shoot, it will be when we're near the bridge."

"Do you think they will?"

"Whether they do or not will reveal something."

"Whether the clouds cover the sun or not reveals something."

"If the shooter is present and after senior imagers, he will shoot. If he does not shoot, why then, he is either not present or looking for more vulnerable imagers as targets."

While Alastar could not help but feeling tense and very much like a target, the remainder of their return to the Collegium was uneventful, and he was back in his study at a quint past ninth glass.

Just after midday, as Alastar was wondering if it might be safe to leave the heat of the administration building, since it was end-day once the bells struck noon on Samedi, Belsior, the duty maitre for Samedi, rushed into the study. "Maitre! Someone's shot at juniors by the Bridge of Desires!" Then he turned and ran from the study.

Alastar followed at a run, if not at the headlong sprint exhibited by the younger maitre. Despite his regular morning runs and the exercise sessions added by Akoryt, he was breathing hard and sweat was running off his forehead and into his eyes when he reached the grassy swale between the causeway leading to the bridge and the raised stone walk that ran just behind the west riverwall.

A student imager lay sprawled on his back on the grass just below the stone walk. He did not move, and his eyes were open. An imager third—Glaesyn, Alastar recognized belatedly—was sitting on a stone bench, with a female student imager holding something against his shoulder.

Belsior was talking to the two at the bench. ". . . was he hit . . ."

As soon as Alastar reached Glaesyn and the two others, he immediately demanded. "Show me the wound."

Orlana, the student third, answered, "I'm trying to stop the bleeding."

"That can wait for a moment." Alastar gently but quickly moved Orlana's hand and the cloth—likely her scarf—and studied the wound. The shell wasn't visible, but there wasn't that much blood . . . *Last time you waited.* "This could hurt." He concentrated.

Glaesyn shuddered and uttered a low, "Oooo."

A bloody lump appeared on the stone pavement.

"Don't touch it!" snapped Alastar. "Orlana and I will get Glaesyn to the infirmary. Belsior . . . get all the juniors and anyone else away from the riverwalls. Get anyone you can to help. Find a maitre to man the sentry box until I can get back. Oh . . . use oilcloth or a lot of fabric to pick up that bullet and have someone bring it to Maitre Gaellen. And send someone to find Maitres Akoryt and Cyran. Have them meet me at the infirmary."

"Yes, sir."

As Alastar helped Glaesyn to his feet, he caught sight of the student sprawled on the grass on his back, an expression of shock or surprise frozen on his dead face. He recognized Lyam, a second, a good solid student. Then he turned to Orlana. "You can press that scarf against the wound again."

With Orlana on one side and Alastar on the other, they managed to walk Glaesyn to the infirmary, although his steps were uncoordinated, almost shambling.

Gaellen was waiting.

"I imaged the bullet out. Belsior or someone will be bringing that. I might have done some damage, but I tried to keep the imaging to the area around the bullet."

"They kept shooting . . ." mumbled Glaesyn. "Two of them . . . couldn't hold full shields . . . then they were gone . . ."

"How many shots?" asked Alastar.

"Nine or ten," said Orlana. "Maybe more."

"Enough," said Gaellen. "Get him into surgery."

Alastar and Orlana guided Glaesyn the few yards to the surgery.

Once Gaellen had Glaesyn on the table, Alastar guided Orlana back outside the infirmary and under the shade of the nearest tree. "Tell me everything you can remember."

"We were walking along the riverwall path near the bridge," said Orlana. "It's been so hot, and there's always a breeze on the west side of

Imagisle, and the summer flowers haven't faded. I heard something—it was like a shot—and Maitre Akoryt had said that we needed to drop to the ground if we heard shots. I went down on my hands and knees. Lyam—he just laughed at first. Maybe he didn't hear the shots. Maybe he didn't know what they were . . . then one of them hit him. He said something like 'I'm shot.' He was hit again . . . and he fell. He just lay there. Glaesyn was on bridge duty, and he came running out of the box. Whoever it was fired at him, and they kept shooting. Glaesyn jerked, like something hit his shields. Then he staggered down the slope and sat on the bench. . . . I called for help, and Thoms came running. I sent him for the duty maitre . . . and then I tried to stop the bleeding until you and Maitre Belsior came."

"Is there anything else?"

"I . . . I don't think so."

"If you remember anything, please let me know."

"I will, sir."

"Stay away from areas where you can be seen from the far banks of the river."

"Yes, sir."

As Orlana left, Alastar turned toward Thoms, whom he now recognized as the second who had been carrying the basket.

"I gave the basket that had the bullet to Osfuerk. He's Maitre Gaellen's assistant. I told him that the bullet might have poison in it."

"Thank you, Thoms. I appreciate it."

"Thank you, sir."

Since he didn't see Akoryt or Cyran yet, Alastar walked back into the infirmary to see if Gaellen had done what he could for Glaesyn. He was afraid that he hadn't arrived soon enough and that his removal of the bullet had either been too late or too violent.

Pacing back and forth along the corridor several yards from the surgery, Alastar waited almost a quint before Gaellen emerged.

The healer looked at Alastar. "He might make it. He's not getting any weaker, and his breathing isn't getting worse. You did the right thing in imaging out the bullet. His shoulder is going to take a long time to heal, and he may have some trouble moving it as well as he could. Then again, he might not. He wouldn't be moving anything if you hadn't gotten it out. There was still poison in the shell."

"Can you tell what it is?"

"It smells like bleufleur, but there's something else in it."

"Did he say any more about the shooting?"

"He wanted you to know that one of the men was blond and he wore a brown shirt and trousers. The other man also wore brown. Both had rifles. They were on the knoll to the north of the bridge on the far side."

And no one saw them until they started shooting? "Thank you. Can he talk?"

"He was rambling for a bit, but that settled down. I'd let him rest for a time."

"Then I'll be back later."

Gaellen just nodded.

Since neither Cyran nor Akoryt had arrived, Alastar left the infirmary and started toward the administration building when he saw Alyna, accompanied by Lystara and Malyna, headed toward him. They met some twenty yards from the main door of the administration building.

"Someone was shot. Who?" asked Alyna.

"Secondus Lyam was killed. Glaesyn was wounded. I imaged the bullet out. Gaellen thinks his chances are good. The bullet was poisoned. It appeared that Lyam was struck twice and both bullets were poisoned. One of the shooters was probably the man who killed Harl."

"Did you see him?" asked Malyna.

Alastar shook his head. "He was long gone by the time I got there. They shot from that knoll on the west side of the river north of the Bridge of Desires. I sent for Akoryt and Cyran, but I haven't seen either yet."

"It is Samedi afternoon," Alyna said, the tone of her voice between dry and sardonic. Then she smiled. "I'm glad you're fine. Is there anything I can do?"

"Just have Tiranya keep the young women away from the riverwalks and exposed places for now."

"Every shot has been taken from the west bank of the Aluse," Alyna pointed out. "That's likely because the shooters can get to hidden places more easily without being seen."

"We can't count on them not sneaking into buildings on the east bank."

"That could come next." She nodded. "You have things to do. We can talk later."

Alastar had just turned to make his way to the administration building when Akoryt hurried toward him. "Maitre! I just heard. . . . What about Glaesyn?"

"Gaellen thinks he might make it."

"What do you need from me?"

"For now, I think it's best that anyone on Imagisle avoid open spaces where they can be seen from across the river—unless they have very strong shields or they're posted in one of the sentry boxes."

"That's making everyone a prisoner of sorts," replied Akoryt.

"It's better than losing more imagers. We also need to have concealed maitres watching the west bank during daylight hours to see if they can spot and capture—or wound—the shooters." At Akoryt's expression, Alastar asked, "Do you have a better idea? We still have no idea who the shooters are or who is behind the shootings." He had some strong general suspicions, centered on the thought that most likely to be involved were High Holders, possibly a group of them.

"Except that they are very good shots," Akoryt pointed out. "That means that they've been well trained, and they're likely not from the army, because that would be too easy to discover."

"Unless they're former army sharpshooters. There are likely scores of them around. The question is not only who they are, but just how many shooters there are and what is their ultimate goal, if there is one, besides destroying the Collegium."

"Isn't that enough, so far as we're concerned?" asked Akoryt.

"More than enough for us, but not enough to get Lorien to act willingly, or to get others to back that action . . . and if we act against anyone but the shooters . . ."

"Too many will turn against us. That means we have to catch some of the shooters."

"Which is why we need maitres posted in places where they can catch or kill a shooter in the act—and recover a rifle with poisoned bullets in it . . . or a dead shooter carrying such ammunition." Alastar offered a wintry smile. "See what you can do. If any maitre questions your assignments, send them to me."

Akoryt chuckled. "If I say that they can come to you . . . not a one will."

"One or two might."

Akoryt shook his head. "I don't think so."

"I won't keep you, but I want maitres watching from where they can't be seen beginning within a glass. Oh . . . I almost forgot. There have to be poisoned bullets up where Glaesyn was hit, because most of them bounced off his shields. They need to be collected. If someone picks one up and isn't careful . . ."

"Yes, sir."

Once Akoryt was on his way, Alastar headed back to the infirmary where he found Gaellen.

"How is Glaesyn?"

"His shoulder hurts like the Namer hammered it with a sledge he says. I gave him some willow powder with water. That's about all I dare give him with bleufleur in him."

"Can I talk to him?"

"For a little while. He's in the first room beyond the surgery. Don't upset him, if you can help it."

"I'll try not to."

When Alastar entered the small room, Glaesyn was in the bed, but propped up in a sitting position.

"How are you feeling—besides having a very painful shoulder?"

Glaesyn looked over. "Maitre . . . thank you. Maitre Gaellen says I wouldn't be here if you hadn't imaged out that bullet."

"I don't know about that. I do know . . ." He almost said that when he hadn't with Harl, it had been a mistake. "I did know that your chances were better if I got it out. I wanted to ask you a few questions about anything you noticed about the shooters. You said they were on the knoll?"

"Yes, sir."

"How many were there?"

"I didn't see any at first. That was why I left the box. I thought they might have been more to the north. They were in brown. They kind of blended into the brush on the knoll. I didn't see anyone at first, until one of them shot. It hit my shields, but I saw a puff of smoke. The next shot hit my shields, and then there was another one. I only saw two of them."

"You think there were more?"

"Yes, sir. They fired more than ten shots without stopping. I only saw the two. They had on brown hoods. Except the hood fell back when one of them was running back toward the road. I didn't really see him until it did."

All in brown and hooded—along with three shooters, all with poisoned bullets, that definitely suggested some thorough advance thought and planning. "Could you tell if they had mounts or a coach waiting?"

"No, sir."

"Was there anyone on the river?"

"I didn't see any barges or boats, sir."

Although Alastar took his time with additional inquiries, Glaesyn could add nothing to what he had already revealed.

Alastar left the infirmary with more questions than answers and headed back to the administration building to write out a few more instructions for Akoryt, such as removing the brush from the knoll and a few other places along the west bank of the river. He also wondered where Cyran was and when he might show up.

15

The remainder of Samedi passed without incident, and Cyran did appear, if a glass later, because he'd been working in the forge with Arthos, trying to replicate the construction of the poisoned bullets, and hadn't even heard all the commotion. He'd only found out when he'd gone home and Meiryl had told him. He did inform Alastar that making the bullets required a good deal of skill.

Most of Solayi passed without incident, although Akoryt did come to the Maitre's house briefly in midafternoon to go over the schedule of maitres who would be watching and monitoring the east and west banks of the River Aluse for the next week.

Almost before Alastar realized it, it was after dinner—since dinner was always in the late afternoon on Solayi—and time to set out for the anomen. Alastar wasn't looking forward to going, since the service on Solayi evening would also serve as the memorial for Harl, who had no relatives near L'Excelsis, and for Lyam, who had been a foundling raised from the age of seven at the Collegium.

"Don't forget your mourning scarves, girls," Alyna called up the steps, adjusting her own black and green scarf.

"Aunt Alyna . . . I don't have one," Malyna called down from the top of the stairs.

"I thought you might not. There's one on your dresser."

"Oh . . . I didn't see it."

"I doubt that," murmured Alyna to Alastar. "She never misses anything. She said something about dark colors . . ."

"What about them?"

"I didn't hear the rest. She thinks her skin is too dark."

"She has the same wonderful skin you have. She's already very pretty. Before long, we'll have to worry about the young men."

"Your judgment is suspect, dear. Her skin is darker than that of most young women from a High Holder background. She's aware of that."

"It doesn't matter here."

"She wasn't raised here . . ." Alyna turned as Lystara came hurtling down the steps and raised her voice. "It's about time. Malyna?"

"I can't get the scarf right."

"Bring it down. I'll fix it."

"Yes, Aunt Alyna."

Alyna just looked at Alastar, not quite rolling her eyes.

When Malyna reached the bottom of the stairs, she extended the black-trimmed dark green scarf. She did not look up as Alyna adjusted it.

"Remember. It covers your hair until the memorial part of the service is over. If you're not sure, just do as I do."

"Yes, Aunt Alyna. I understand." Malyna's tone was submissive, resigned, and close to quiet defiance.

"Rules are rules," Alyna said firmly. "Your personal sense of taste in dress is secondary to the customs of the Collegium . . . and to the respect due to two young men who died too young and too cruelly. Now . . . we need to go."

As they walked down the steps and then along the west side of the split avenue that led to the administration building and to the anomen south and west of it, Alastar and Alyna let the girls lead the way. Noticing that Malyna squared her shoulders, as if she faced some trial, he gestured to his wife.

She leaned toward him and murmured, "Ignore it."

Alastar nodded, but wondered if he'd see the same sort of maneuvers with Lystara, then decided it was all too likely, and the only question was how soon.

Once inside the anomen, Alastar, Alyna, and the girls moved to the front and to the left side. Although the nave was already crowded, the students and imagers moved aside to allow Alastar to take the place where they always stood.

When the last chime of the glass died away, Chorister Iskhar took his place in the middle of the sacristy dais. "We are gathered here together this evening not only for worship, but also in the spirit of the Nameless, in affirmation of the quest for goodness and mercy in all that we do, and in celebration of two lives ended too soon by senseless violence. We are here to remember Lyam and Harl, and to give thanks for their lives."

The opening hymn was "The Glory of the Nameless."

Then came the confession, followed by the charge from Iskhar. "Life is a gift from the Nameless, for from the glory of the Nameless do we come; through the glory of the Nameless do we live, and to that glory do we return. Our lives can only reflect and enhance that glory, as did that of Lyam and of Harl, whom we honor, whom we remember, and who will live forever in our hearts and in the glory of the Nameless."

Another hymn followed—"In the Footsteps of the Nameless."

> *When we walk the narrow way of what is always right,*
> *when we follow all the precepts that foil the Namer's blight . . .*

Then Iskhar said, "Two imagers died this week, one on Vendrei, another on Samedi. Tertius Harl was a solid and dedicated young imager who was shot in the back as he escorted the Maitre back to the Collegium. . . ." The chorister went on to talk of Harl's honesty and dedication, before turning his words to Lyam. "Secondus Lyam was a promising student. He worked hard, and he was noted for his cheer and warmth. There were few indeed who did not respond to that warmth and openness. . . ."

When he finished telling about Lyam, Chorister Iskhar paused, then said, "At this time, we wear black and green, black for the dark uncertainties of life, and green for its triumph, manifested every year in the coming of spring. So is it that, like nature, we come from the dark of winter and uncertainty into life which unfolds in uncertainty, alternating between black and green, and in the end return to the life and glory of the Nameless. In that spirit, let us offer thanks for the spirits and the lives of those two fine young men who died for us," intoned Iskhar, "and let us remember them as each was, not merely as a name, but as a living breathing individual whose spirit touched many and in ways only the Nameless can fully fathom. Let us set aside the gloom of mourning, and from this day forth, recall the glory of their lives and the warmth and joy they have left with us . . ."

When he heard the words "warmth and joy," words he had heard too often since he had become Maitre, Alastar asked himself how he was supposed to set aside the gloom he felt with each imager who died, merely because each was an imager. At the same time, he could sense that most of the women had let the mourning scarves slip from their hair, and Malyna was among the first.

From there, Iskhar began his homily with a question that had certainly occurred to many at the service.

"Why does the Nameless permit the wicked to kill innocents like Harl . . . or like Lyam? Harl was a good man, with no personal enemies.

Lyam was a good person and a good student, who worked and studied diligently. Why? Why these two? Bad things do happen to good people. We all know that. Why don't bad things happen to bad people? They do, but we do not notice those, or if we do, we tend to say that such evil people deserved what they got. But Lyam did not get what he deserved. Neither did Harl. How do we answer that question?"

Iskhar paused. "To those who love and grieve, there is no good answer. Rholan the Unnamer claimed that there could only be greatness and virtue if evil existed, for greatness and virtue can only exist in the choices to do good and struggle against evil . . ."

Alastar managed not to frown. That wasn't exactly what Rholan had said, not as he recalled . . . or not all of what the Unnamer had reputedly said. Rholan had suggested, if not said directly, that "evil" was a value judgment placed on an event by those who witnessed it or suffered through it, and that even the events judged most vile and evil by some might have value when viewed in a larger context . . . or over time, when even a "good" event might turn out to have enabled a far greater evil— and that most judgments were premature.

Alastar had more than a few doubts about that, if indeed, he recalled what he had read accurately. He doubted there was any great good coming from the killing of young imagers.

After the homily came the closing hymn, traditional for a service containing a memorial—"For the Glory."

> For the glory, for the life,
> for the beauty and the strife,
> for all that is and ever shall be,
> all together, through forever,
> in eternal Nameless glory . . .

Once the last words had died away, and Alastar and Alyna left the anomen and walked back toward the Maitre's house, some ten yards behind Malyna and Lystara, Alyna said quietly, "You looked preoccupied during the homily."

"I was, but not as preoccupied as you were when you looked at Linzya. She doesn't look that far along. She doesn't even look like she's with child."

"She's one of those who doesn't show . . . but that wasn't what I'm worrying about. She came alone, but Tiranya and Shaelyt joined her."

"That's right. I didn't see Bettaur." Alastar frowned. "He wasn't duty maitre today. That was Celiena . . . no . . . sorry, today was Dylert."

Alyna smiled, widely enough that Alastar could see her expression even in the darkness. "You don't have to remember who is duty maitre for every day of the year."

"It's better if I do. I noticed that you stopped Akoryt before he left the house this afternoon."

"I did. I'm going to be one of the watchers."

"You don't . . ."

"I don't, but I should, and I might see more than some of the junior, or even some of the senior maitres."

Left unsaid was the fact that Alyna could likely do more if she happened to see something happen. Alastar wasn't totally happy about that, but he couldn't argue with either her reasoning or her abilities.

"I asked for times when the younger juniors might be free and wandering Imagisle, since they can't wander anywhere else right now."

"You think they're targeting the juniors?"

"That's not the question. Whether they're shooting at any imager or more at juniors, the juniors are the ones who need more protection."

"You can't protect them from the first shots," he pointed out.

"No. But protecting them from the later shots would have saved Harl and kept Glaesyn from being wounded."

"You have a good point." He laughed softly. "But then you usually do."

"There's one other thing," she said.

"Oh?"

"You were right."

"About what?"

"A number of the younger male imagers kept looking at Malyna. It wasn't just curiosity, either."

"Of course they would," Alastar replied with a smile. "She looks much like you, except you're more beautiful."

"You're too kind."

"Hardly . . . just accurate." He reached out and took her hand as they continued the walk home.

By seventh glass on Lundi morning, Alastar and Coermyd were already riding south on the East River Road. Alastar had kept his eyes open, but had seen no signs of shooters or other people who looked suspicious, but that didn't mean that some shooters weren't in position somewhere, only that he hadn't seen anyone. He would have preferred to undertake his unscheduled visit to Factorius Vaschet by himself, but since he felt he needed at least one other imager, he'd picked Coermyd, whose shields were as strong as those of many maitres.

"Might I ask, Maitre, why we're going to the ironworks?"

"Because the ironworks also apparently produces rifles, and I'd like to know who might be purchasing them." Alastar didn't mention that it was more than a little unusual for an ironworks to be producing finished goods, especially something like rifles that required precision crafting. Because of this, he'd placed several additional items in his saddlebags, including several coils of rope, which would come in useful if he needed to tie the gray somewhere and proceed under a concealment shield.

Coermyd nodded thoughtfully, but did not ask any more questions.

Vaschet's ironworks was located on land bordered to the west by the River Aluse and on the south by a stream that fed into the river. According to the map Alastar had consulted before leaving the Collegium, just short of the ironworks the East River Road turned farther east and angled toward a stone bridge over the stream, while a smaller road circled westward around a hill to the ironworks.

What Alastar did not expect when he and Coermyd followed the road leading from the East River Road was that even from half a mille away, he could see the smoke from the blast furnace set into a low hill and almost feel the rhythmic impacts of the forge's drop hammer. Nor did he expect the stone wall around the works, and the heavy iron-bound wooden gates with two gatehouses, one on each side of the gates, as well as a guard standing post before the gates.

"Check your shields." Alastar did just what he'd ordered Coermyd to do as he rode toward the guard, halting a good five yards away.

"The ironworks is closed to outsiders . . . Maitre."

"That may be, but I'm here to see Factor Vaschet."

"The factor won't be seeing no one, Maitre. He never does. That's just the way it is."

Alastar smiled easily. "I'm not no one, and I will be seeing him."

Two more guards stepped out of the shade beside the left gatehouse. They leveled heavy rifles at the two imagers.

Alastar imaged both weapons out of the guards' hands. "He will see me . . . and you can wager your life on that not happening . . . and some substantial chunks of the factorage as well." Alastar rocked in the saddle as something impacted his shields, a jolt that had enough power behind it that he wondered if he might get a bruise from it. He immediately turned to see another guard aiming at him from the second guardhouse. He imaged an iron dart through the shoulder of the guard, pinning him to the wooden structure. The rifle dropped, its polished barrel striking the ground first, followed by the solid wooden stock.

Alastar scanned the area for more armed guards, then turned his attention to removing the gate supports from two stone posts.

As the double, iron-bound, wooden gates toppled forward, a fourth guard appeared, this time from the other gatehouse. He brought his rifle up quickly, but not quickly enough, because Alastar also imaged that away.

The first gate guard looked from one side of the gap left by the fallen gates to the other side, taking in the three remaining once-armed guards . . . and the guard hanging from the guardhouse, who had gone limp . . . and was likely dead, Alastar realized from the dark stain across his pale tan uniform.

"Hasn't anyone told you that it's not a good idea to shoot at imagers?" Alastar asked.

The four remaining guards looked blank.

"Which building is the one where I'll find Vaschet?"

For several moments, none of the four answered.

Alastar waited.

The first guard finally spoke. "His study is in the building north of the river loading dock, beside the new factorage."

"The one that makes the heavy rifles you just tried to use?"

"It's the new factorage. That's all we know."

Alastar had his doubts, but nodded, and then walked the gray gelding across the iron-bound solid wood gate that lay atop the paving stones.

Once he was clear and on the road leading into the steelworks, he said, "Keep an eye behind us."

"Yes, sir. Right now, they're just watching. One of them is looking at the gates you brought down."

Alastar studied the compound. Ahead and partway up the hill was the blast furnace, with a waterwheel on one side. Below and to the east of the furnace was an expanse of sand, with trenches into which the molten iron was tapped off, and where it cooled into a sow and pigs. The forge, he realized belatedly, was actually east of the blast furnace along a millrace that powered another waterwheel, the one that doubtless operated the forge's drop hammer. Immediately to his right were several long two-story buildings that looked like barracks, except that the infrequent windows were all barred.

He glanced back at the wall bordering the gates, a wall close to three yards high. He thought he saw glints from the top. *Broken glass set in mortar?* Was Vaschet using prison laborers? How, when that was forbidden, except for High Holders on their own holdings?

Alastar wondered if he would have to drag Vaschet out of his study, but the tall black-haired and broad-shouldered figure who stood on the porch of the structure just north of the river loading dock had to be Vaschet.

Alastar reined up several yards from the porch. "Good morning, Factorius Vaschet."

"How did you get in here, Maitre? The ironworks is closed to outsiders." Vaschet's voice was loud, pitched to carry over the considerable background noise.

"After your guards started shooting at me," replied Alastar in an equally forceful tone. "I took down the gates."

"You'll pay for those . . . and for any prisoners who escape."

"Use of prisoners at hard labor for hire is forbidden."

"So? The ironworks is outside L'Excelsis."

"What does that have to do with anything? You still can't use prisoners."

"I know the laws, Maitre. More to the point, how do you propose to pay for or repair my walls and gates?"

Alastar sighed, loudly, then realized that the noise from the drop hammer in the forge behind him and from the factorage to his right meant Vaschet couldn't even hear something that soft, even if the factor had been listening, about which Alastar had some considerable doubt. "We'll talk about that after you answer a few questions. That's why I came out here to talk to you."

"You've talked. You can leave. After you reimburse me for the damage you've caused."

"Stop being an idiot, Vaschet. You don't want to make me any angrier than I am."

"You force your way in here, and expect me to be reasonable?"

"I didn't use force until your men started shooting. That makes you the unreasonable one. Not me. Now . . . back to why I'm here. I'm looking to know who bought how many of those new heavy rifles you're manufacturing and to whom you've been selling them."

"What heavy rifles?"

"The ones coming out of the new building over there." Alastar gestured. "The factorage you built with the golds you borrowed."

"Estafen tell you that? Be the last time I deal with that useless stripling."

"Who's buying all those rifles?"

"I don't tell the names of my buyers, and no imager or even the rex is going to make me tell."

"I've had two young imagers killed and another wounded by your heavy rifles, and I'd like to know who bought those rifles so that I can deal with them."

"I can't do that, Maitre. I won't. I've given my word. It's worth more than yours. In golds."

"Your word is void if someone has used your rifles to murder someone. And if you don't tell me, you become an accomplice under the law."

"Now . . . I wouldn't be knowing that. It's just your word . . ." A wide and false smile followed the words that Alastar could only have described as even greasier than Vaschet's slicked-back hair. "And the law . . . well, sometimes the law just doesn't apply."

"I've never been afforded the luxury of lying, Vaschet. Let's try again. Who has been buying large quantities of those rifles?"

"That's something you won't find out from me."

"Why not? Has someone threatened you if you tell?"

"No one threatens me. No one."

"Or do you lose special terms and privileges if you reveal your customers? I'm not interested in telling anyone."

"Doesn't matter. Wouldn't matter if the rex put his army at the gates.

And you certainly don't want every factor in Solidar angry at your little Collegium."

"You're assuming that they'll all agree with you. They won't."

"Maybe. Maybe not. But you're not getting names. Not from me."

Alastar could see that no amount of words would convince the factor. Without uttering another syllable, he clamped shields around the factor and held them tightly until the factor turned red, then toppled forward. After dismounting and tying the gray to one of the porch posts, he took out one of the coils of rope from his saddlebags and tied up the factor, who was beginning to rouse by the time he was thoroughly trussed.

"You will pay for—"

Alastar pulled a greasy kerchief from the factor's heavy leather vest and stuffed it in the man's mouth, then looked to Coermyd. "If he manages to ungag himself, gag him again."

"Yes, sir."

"And if anyone attacks you, kill them with an iron dart. Don't hesitate. Not with all the rifles around."

Still holding shields, Alastar opened the door to the building. Inside was an anteroom. Something struck his shields, and he staggered slightly before in the dimness he saw a massive figure swinging a short-handled wide axe at him.

Alastar imaged an iron dart through the guard's eye, then stepped aside as the man toppled. The wooden floor vibrated when the body struck. Seeing no one else in the anteroom, Alastar moved to the door to the left and behind the empty table desk where the overlarge guard had presumably been sitting.

The comparatively small chamber appeared to be Vaschet's study. Alastar began to search for the equivalent of ledgers. There weren't any on the shelves of the single bookcase, nor in the two drawers of the modest desk. There was, however, a wooden cabinet fastened to the wall with iron straps, and a heavy lock through iron hasps fastened the doors shut. Alastar imaged away the hasps and opened the doors.

Rows of ledgers were racked there.

It seemed as though a quint had passed before Alastar found four with entries dated in the last year. Two appeared to be supply ledgers, another an account of payments received, and the fourth the current master ledger, or a copy of it. Alastar took all four. He didn't want to linger at the ironworks. Too much had already not gone as planned.

Because you couldn't believe Vaschet would be so intransigent?

He hurried, if cautiously, out of the study and back outside.

Vaschet glared at Alastar from where he lay on the porch.

"I'll return these after I've had a chance to study them." Alastar smiled pleasantly. "It would have been much easier if you'd simply told me what I needed to know."

"Sir . . . there are more guards headed this way. Maybe a whole squad of them. They've got those rifles."

"Then we should go." Alastar put the ledgers in the saddlebags, making sure they were secure, and then untied the gelding and mounted. "Keep right alongside me."

"Yes, sir."

Alastar extended his shields just enough to cover Coermyd as well. He wasn't certain that the third's shields would be able to withstand repeated heavy fire. *Will yours?*

The oncoming guards were over twenty yards away, but reined up in a staggered formation, and raised their rifles.

More than twenty guards? That wasn't something Alastar had planned for at all. He immediately imaged a cloud of pepper and salt mist across the faces of the guards, followed by even more pepper. "Coermyd! Charge!"

The two galloped toward the guards. All the guards fired simultaneously. Alastar felt as though his entire body had been squeezed through Vaschet's drop hammer or rolling mill, and a reddish mist seemed to hover in front of his eyes.

With another set of shots hammering him, he struggled to hold his shields, as he and Coermyd bore down on the middle of the ranked guards, three of whom immediately tried to scatter. When Alastar's shields momentarily struck some of the riders and mounts, a wave of blackness threatened to rise over him. He somehow pushed it back as he and Coermyd burst through the second rank, knocking at least one rider off his mount.

He slowed the gelding to a fast walk when he neared the fallen gates, but there was no sign of the gate guards, except for the one dead body still hanging from the one gatehouse. After they were a good half mille from the ironworks, and Alastar could feel the blackness rising toward him, he finally released his shields, realizing that he hurt and ached all over.

He was also breathing heavily, as if he'd run all the way around Imagisle, and he felt more than a little faint.

"Sir . . . might I ask . . . are those ledgers you brought with you?"

"They are."

"They wanted to kill us because you took some books?"

"I'm hoping those ledgers will tell us who else has all those heavy rifles. Vaschet must have had a good reason for us not to know. That suggests great wealth and power are behind the shootings." *Not that you didn't already know that.*

After all the difficulty Alastar had gone through to get the ledgers, he definitely hoped that the entries in them provided at least some information about who had bought Vaschet's rifles. But given the abbreviated notations he observed, translating the almost cryptic symbols into something usable was likely to take some effort . . . and likely expertise and knowledge he lacked.

When they neared the East Bridge, Alastar eased his mount alongside Coermyd. "You're going to have to shield me. Taking all those bullets . . ."

"Yes, sir."

At just after two quints past noon, Alastar and Coermyd rode back across the East Bridge, only to find a grim-faced Akoryt hurrying toward the sentry box

"Keep riding until you're well clear of the bridge and out of sight from the east bank." The Maitre D'Structure turned and walked beside the gray gelding.

"What happened?" asked Alastar, trying to raise his shields once more, and failing. "Cover me with your shields. Mine are gone. Coermyd covered me coming back."

"Gone? What happened?"

"We got fired on by a squad of Vaschet's guard. All twenty or so fired simultaneously. What happened here?"

"We lost Paolyn, one of the younger gardeners. He was trimming bushes north of the East Bridge. He was shot twice."

"Poisoned bullets?"

"Who knows? The second shot hit him just above the ear. The worst part is that he was working where he couldn't be seen from the east bank of the river."

"Was the shooter in one of the taller buildings?"

"He had to be, but Paolyn was working alone, and none of the maitres working this side of Imagisle discovered his body immediately. Actually, Bettaur and Ashkyr found him."

"Bettaur and Ashkyr?"

"Bettaur's taken an interest in him. It seems to be helpful. His studies have improved, and so has his attitude."

Will wonders never cease?

Akoryt stopped and gestured. "There. He was found over between those bushes. The only buildings you can see from there are the River Inn and the old port tower that's part of the building where they print that newssheet—"

"*Veritum?*" asked Alastar as he reined up.

"—and Cyran and I already searched both buildings. No one in either building saw anyone on the upper levels." Akoryt shrugged. "That doesn't mean they weren't there."

"Could the shooter have used a boat and climbed the riverwall?"

"It's possible. He would have to have been very careful, because no one saw him, and there are no tracks."

"No one saw anything? Not even the maitres on duty?"

"No, sir."

Another half quint of questions by Alastar and answers by Akoryt revealed little more, and after Akoryt finished the informal briefing, Alastar rode directly to the administration building, where he dismounted and retrieved the ledgers before leaving the gelding with Coermyd with instructions to water the mounts and return to the administration building in two quints. Then he hurried inside, although he still felt faint . . . and slightly dizzy.

Maercyl jumped to his feet as Alastar entered the anteroom, carrying the stack of ledgers. "Maitre!"

"Is there anything else urgent besides the shooting? Any messages from Rex Lorien?"

"No, sir."

Somehow that didn't surprise Alastar, knowing as he did that Lorien would avoid meeting with him for as long as possible. "Please find Maitre Thelia and have her join me as soon as possible. If Maitre Cyran appears, have him come in. Oh . . . and could you have someone bring me a large beaker of dark ale? Soon, if possible."

"Are you all right, sir?"

"I will be." *You hope.*

Once in his study, Alastar set the ledgers on the desk in a row, then sat down. For several moments, he just sat there. Finally, he opened the first. He leafed through several pages before he came to a pair of entries that might reveal something about Vaschet's sale of rifles.

| 25 Juyn 402 | 100 R-2 | Ag/R | 250G |
| 4 Agostos 402 | 120 R-2 | Ag/C/CHH | 300G |

If "R-2" means rifle and "G" is a gold . . . Alastar shook his head, thinking.

"Maitre, you wanted to see me?" The slender maitre of accounts stood in the study doorway.

"I did. Come in, and please close the door." Alastar stood and motioned for Thelia to join him. He pointed to the ledgers.

Her eyes went to the ledgers, widening as she took in the four volumes.

"These are the ledgers I took from Factorius Vaschet. I believe he's somehow involved in dealings with at least one High Holder and manufacturing something of value for them that he doesn't want anyone to know about. He refused to tell me anything. Rather than follow my feelings, I limited my treatment of him to removing them. After glancing through the pages of this one, I have my suspicions, but I'd like you to take a good thorough look and tell me what all the numbers and comments tell you about Vaschet's ironworks and factorage."

"Maitre . . . you realize that the Factors' Council will be incensed at your taking the ledgers?"

"They may be. I don't know that I had any real choice. We lost another person today, a young gardener named Paolyn, and we still have no idea who is behind the shooters. I told Vaschet about the shootings, and he could have cared less. All he cared about was keeping secret the names of those who bought the rifles."

At that moment, there was rap on the door, and Maercyl stepped into the study carrying a large beaker of dark ale. "Sir . . ."

"Thank you." Alastar immediately took the beaker, raised it to his lips, and took a long slow swallow before setting it down.

The study door closed behind the retreating Maercyl.

"You were saying," prompted Alastar. "About secrecy . . ."

"For some goods, that is indeed the custom." Thelia paused, then added, "Maitre . . . these are more precious to Vaschet than all but his firstborn son."

"He'll get them back. As I told you, I promised him that . . . although I'm not so certain that he deserves that much consideration."

"The Factors' Council will not see it that way."

"You mentioned that. Why not? I'm not giving the information to another factor or a High Holder . . . or even to Rex Lorien or his Minister of Finance." Alastar took another swallow of lager. He thought some of the dizziness and faintness was subsiding.

"That is good, but most factors won't see it that way. They believe that anyone who would steal private ledgers cannot ever be trusted."

"While I believe that anyone who would refuse to provide information that would halt the killing of innocent students cannot ever be trusted, especially when it comes to golds and power." Alastar half-shook his head, stopping as he realized that the motion renewed the dizziness, and gestured to the ledgers. "Take them and see what you can discover. I have another visit to make. I'll see what you've been able to find out when I return. That will likely be around fourth glass."

"I'll do what I can, Maitre."

Alastar closed the open ledger, watching as Thelia picked up all four ledgers and carried them out of his study and through the anteroom into the hallway that led to her small study.

Less than a quint later, Alyna appeared, closing the study door behind her, eyes intent and fixed on Alastar. A water bottle was in her left hand. She glanced to the empty beaker.

"At least, you had enough sense to have some lager. I brought some more."

"That's my second beaker," he admitted. "They did help."

"Alastar D'Imagisle! You are fifty-two years old. You are not a young man. Why on Terahnar did you think you could prevail over twenty men aiming heavy rifles at you?"

"I did manage." Alastar almost grinned at the concern in her voice.

"Barely. Akoryt said you looked three steps from death's front door, and your eyes are still pinkish . . ."

"Who would have expected a private army, even a small one, at a factorage?"

"Alastar . . ."

"They surprised us as we were leaving. The guards at the gate I expected, but . . ." He started to shrug, but stopped as twinges ran through his back and shoulders. He managed to keep a rueful smile in place.

"You are to be careful. You are." She uncorked the water bottle and poured more lager into the beaker.

"I'll do my best."

"You need to do better than that. Promise me."

Alastar knew better than to argue.

"You need to stay here and recuperate."

"I can't. I need to see Cransyr immediately."

"Without shields?"

"I can take a junior maitre. Once I'm inside the Chateau D'Council, nothing will happen, and I will have enough strength to ward off anything Cransyr might do."

Alyna sighed. "You are the most stubborn . . ."

"It does take one to . . ." Alastar grinned.

Alyna just shook her head.

A good quint later, Alastar, Coermyd, and, at Alyna's insistence, Belsior, who was also shielding Alastar, were riding north on the West River Road and were nearing the Nord Bridge on Alastar's second unscheduled visit of the day, this time to see High Holder Cransyr. The early-afternoon sun beat down as if it were midsummer, rather than closer to late harvest, and Alastar kept having to blot his forehead and to adjust his visor cap. Less than half a quint later, after the three imagers crossed the Boulevard D'Ouest, Alastar concentrated on the Chateau D'Council, now visible slightly less than a half mille ahead on the left. The iron gates were closed.

The gates remained closed, and when the two reined up outside the ironwork, the pair of guards in their maroon livery looked out warily, then opened the gates.

One said, "High Holder Cransyr did not mention he would be receiving, Maitre."

"That's correct. He is not formally expecting me. He will not be surprised to see me, however."

The pair exchanged quick glances, but said nothing as Alastar, Belsior, and Coermyd rode past and up the stone entry lane to the receiving portico.

The footman who awaited Alastar at the portico was also in maroon and nodded respectfully as Alastar dismounted and handed his mount's reins to Coermyd. "High Holder Cransyr requested that you be shown to the study, Maitre. He will see you there."

"Thank you." Alastar wondered if Cransyr had actually expected him or had merely observed his entrance from the windows of the main-floor study.

When Alastar entered the study, Cransyr stood beside his desk. As seemed to be the case every time Alastar had seen the High Holder, his comparatively short silvered-blond hair was swept back without a strand out of place. His narrow-set blue eyes, seemingly harder-looking than usual, which Alastar would once have thought close to impossible, fixed on the Maitre and then looked away almost dismissively.

"You might have requested a meeting, Maitre Alastar. However, since you are here . . ." He gestured toward the armchairs with a motion both precise and contemptuous, then walked to one and seated himself.

Alastar smiled easily as he took the other chair, nodding pleasantly but not speaking.

After several long moments, Cransyr looked sharply at Alastar. "I assume you have something to say."

"I do. How many High Holders are arming their private armies with rifles purchased from Factorius Vaschet?"

Alastar noted just the slightest stiffening and hesitation before Cransyr replied.

"Private armies? Armed with weapons purchased from a factor? Even on the surface, that's preposterous. No High Holder would ever subject himself to being dependent upon a factor, particularly now."

Alastar nodded again. "I thought that might be the case, but, assuming what you say is true, that does raise another interesting question. Just who might be using the latest heavy rifles to shoot at imagers, especially young imagers? Oh . . . and attempt to shoot them in the back? That would seem to be against the reputed honor of High Holders, but the factors insist that it is also against their standards of honor."

"I cannot believe that you have the temerity even to suggest a comparison between High Holders and mere factors, Maitre Alastar. I would have thought better of you. . . ."

"You must admit, Cransyr, that it poses an interesting puzzle, but it becomes more than interesting when one considers that several innocent young imagers have already been killed by these rifles that no one seems to want to admit even exist, let alone admit that they or their peers might actually possess and use."

"It is outrageous that you—"

"Please dispense with the protestations and the outrage. The rifles exist. Those who are shooting and killing young imagers exist. Were young High Holders being killed, I am more than certain your outrage would far exceed what I have expressed."

"Very well." Cransyr smiled. "There's a myth that imagers cannot be easily killed. Yet from what you tell me, three have been killed in the past few days. Why . . . at that rate, there wouldn't be any left in a year. Fancy that."

And if you don't stop this and they decide on mass fire, things will really worsen. "Please don't tell me that you have no knowledge of who might be creating a private army."

"I wouldn't do that, Maitre. Any High Holder might be doing that, especially if Rex Lorien continues his attempt to restrict or eliminate the traditional powers of High Holders."

"Lorien hasn't restricted any powers. He hasn't changed the Codex Legis with regard to the High Holders. He's merely enforced the limits set forth in the Codex Legis."

"Those limits restricted the traditional powers."

"They may have, but that wasn't Lorien's doing, and you're being disingenuous in making that claim."

"If Lorien insists that High Holders are subject to every common justicer in Solidar, that will be an unacceptable restriction."

"At present, that is a matter between the High Council and the Rex," Alastar pointed out, "and if any High Holder is found to be attacking imagers on those grounds—"

"Spare me the threats, veiled or otherwise, Alastar. If you had any solid proof, you wouldn't be sparing with me."

Alastar shrugged, managing not to wince. "That's your problem, not mine."

"That's as much as admitting you have no proof."

"I don't believe I said or intimated that."

"Acting without proof will anger many. You really don't want to anger all the High Holders."

"I wouldn't think of angering any of them." *Possibly removing a few of them.*

"I find that hard to believe, given your past actions."

"You shouldn't." Alastar stood. "I appreciate the time you've spent with me."

A hint of a frown flickered across Cransyr's forehead as he rose. "You came to make unfounded assertions and ridiculous claims?"

"No. I came to discover what I needed to know."

"Just what might that be?"

"As I said . . . what I needed to know."

"Maitre Alastar . . . if you act precipitously without proof . . . you will regret it."

"High Councilor . . . I fully understand that. You of all High Holders should know that the Collegium does not act without solid reasons." Or proof, *even if action is required to find that proof.* Alastar smiled politely before nodding, and then turned and headed for the study door. He could feel Cransyr's eyes on his back as he departed.

In another three quints, more or less, Alastar was back at the Collegium, walking into Thelia's small study.

She looked up from the ledger before her and started to stand. "Maitre . . ."

Alastar motioned for her to sit back down, then took the chair across the desk from her. It did feel good to sit down. "What have you found out, if anything?"

"The factor doesn't want anyone to know much about his activities. The entries are almost a cipher in themselves." She paused for a moment before adding, "It does appear that he was struggling until about three months ago, assuming the ledgers are accurate."

"What happened then?"

"There was an entry for a thousand golds, which appears to have been a deposit on future goods. That's if I've interpreted it correctly."

"Would you show me that entry?"

Thelia paged back in the ledger, frowning as she did so, before finally stopping, and then running her finger down the columns. "Here . . ."

Alastar read the line:

15 Mayas 402   Dep/ret   Ag/XXX   1000G

The "Xs" were so heavy that they, clearly by intent, blotted out the letters that had originally been placed there.

" 'Ag' with the slash following it usually means the funds were received by or the goods delivered to an agent or intermediary for a third party," added Thelia.

"Why would the second entry be blotted out if Vaschet never intended anyone else to see the ledgers?"

Thelia smiled and leafed to the next page, pointing out another entry:

5 Juyn 402   Loan/BE   ----   400G

"He had to show the ledgers to Estafen at the Banque D'Excelsis?"

"That's what I'd suppose, Maitre, but it's only a guess."

Alastar paged forward to the entries he'd noted earlier. "What do you make of these?"

| 25 Juyn 402 | 100 R-2 | Ag/R | 250G |
| 4 Agostos 402 | 120 R-2 | Ag/C/HHC | 300G |

"The numbers have to be how many units were sold, but there's no way of telling exactly what 'R-2' happens to be, except that it must be made of precious silver or even gold, because at two and a half golds apiece . . ." Thelia looked to Alastar. "Or it could be spices, but you said these were ledgers from Vaschet, and he's an iron factor."

"Can you think of anything made of iron that is that costly for each item and sold in that great a quantity?"

"No, sir."

"What about heavy rifles?" suggested Alastar. "He does have a new factorage that produces them."

"That is possible." Thelia paused. "But he must have been doing this longer than just this summer. He couldn't have built the factorage in a month and then made that many rifles."

"Not in that short a time," Alastar agreed.

"There might be more indications farther back." Thelia looked sheepish. "I had to deal with some problems with kitchen provisions so I've only been able to study this for less than a glass."

"See what you can find and let me know in the morning."

"Yes, sir."

Alastar stood and stretched. His entire body was sore and aching. While he'd had more and more times in the last year or so when his back was sore, and he wasn't happy about that in the slightest, all the aching and the muscle pain had to have come from the impact of all those bullets on his shields at the same time. *And that's more than a little worrisome.*

He nodded to Thelia, and headed back toward his study, wondering if he'd ever find out the whole story about the rifles . . . or anything else.

17

Alastar awoke early on Mardi, or at least early enough that he was one of the first to arrive for the run around Imagisle. He was also rested enough that he did manage to be among the first of the men to finish, if further behind the leader than usual, unsurprisingly, given the bruises that had shown up on his body. Alyna finished a good hundred yards in front of everyone else, as she usually did, and even farther in front of him than normal.

But then you weren't at your best this morning . . . and she is fifteen years younger and built like a natural runner. That thought wasn't terribly comforting, because it reminded him that he was no longer a young man, as had Alyna . . . and yesterday's events. *Or not so young as you think you are.* He was also well aware that he hadn't been that far in front of either Lystara or Malyna, and that it likely wouldn't be all that long before Malyna would be running as fast as Alyna.

He was still half-pondering that after breakfast and as he and Alyna walked toward the administration building, when she asked, "How sore are you?"

"More aching than sore."

"I still can't believe—"

"I'll try to be more careful. As I said before, seeing a factor with what amounted to a fortified factorage and a small private army wasn't exactly expected."

"There's likely to be more of that," she pointed out. "Just what will you do if you find the High Holder behind the shootings?"

While the question might have appeared simple, it wasn't, Alastar knew. "Capture him, if possible, and force him to stand trial before a justicer." *And make sure that he's convicted of murder and treason.*

"Do you think any justice would convict him . . . and if one did, would any High Holder think that the conviction and execution was anything but forced by the Collegium?"

"Some might, but most would think exactly the way you've voiced it." He paused. "In a way, it wouldn't matter, so long as the precedent is set and enforced. People, even High Holders, tend to forget the circumstances of the past and remember the results."

"We may be very busy seeing that such precedents are continued," she replied dryly.

"Do you have a better approach?"

"No," Alyna replied with a short sardonic laugh, "although wiping out any High Holder who is part of this rebellion would be my second thought."

"Perhaps a combination . . . but we have to find out who's behind it."

"You know Cransyr is. Finding out the others and proving any of it will be harder."

"We both know that." Alastar looked ahead to where Malyna and Lystara were entering the administration building. "They look happy this morning."

"They weren't so happy last night when we drilled them on shields."

"No . . . but they were so tired that they slept soundly." More soundly than Alastar had, that was certain, since no part of his body had felt without sore spots or bruises.

With shared smiles, the two parted once inside the administration building.

Both Maercyl and Dareyn were waiting in the anteroom when Alastar entered.

"I'll need a few words with Akoryt and Cyran in about half a quint, after I talk to Maitre Thelia. If you two could arrange for that . . . and for a mount and one escort. I'll be going to the Chateau D'Rex after I finish with Akoryt and Cyran. Oh . . . any messages?"

"No, sir."

Reflecting that it would have been too much to expect any response from Lorien, Alastar made his way to Thelia's small study. When he entered it, he could immediately see that she must have come in early, because the ledgers were spread across her desk, and she had a sheet of paper on which she had written what looked like a list.

"Have you been able to wrest any more information out of those ledgers, anything that might be useful to the Collegium, anyway?"

"A few, Maitre. Possibly more. There's no sign that he contracted to deliver rifles—if that's what the 'R-2' refers to—before the first sale of fifty rifles in mid-Juyn. There was a payment there of a hundred golds as well. The buyer was just listed as 'R/ag/A/W.' After that, there was the sale and delivery you pointed out. That was in late Juyn. He also received a shipment of walnut wood in late Mayas."

"How do you know it was walnut?" asked Alastar.

"There are some things where everyone uses the same abbreviations."

About when Elthyrd said he'd sold some to Vaschet. "That makes it even more likely that 'R-2' means heavy rifles."

"I thought it might, sir."

"Is there anything else?"

"Vaschet started buying soap from my mother."

"Soap? Why would an iron factor buy soap?"

"It's often mixed with water to cool and lubricate turning benches drilling into metal."

"Rifle barrels?"

"It could be . . . or any kind of drilling into iron or steel."

"That doesn't give us another factor who might know more," Alastar pointed out.

"Have you considered who manufactures cartridges, and who is buying them?"

Alastar wanted to shake his head. "No. That's an excellent idea . . . except I don't even know who has a brassworks."

"There are two in L'Excelsis that I know of. Cuipryn is the most likely. He has the best rolling mills . . . or so I've heard."

"Do you know where his brassworks is located?"

"It's on the west bank of the Aluse about three milles south of the Sud Bridge. There's a stream that enters the river there, and his works are on the north side."

"Might I ask . . . or does your mother sell tallow and oils . . . ?"

"She does. I had to know where many factorages and works are located."

"Thank you."

"You're most welcome, Maitre."

As Alastar left her study, he was thinking that Cuipryn's brassworks was yet another place to visit . . . or perhaps he could send Cyran. Whoever went needed to be a maitre with strong shields. *And you definitely haven't fully recovered your shields.*

Cyran and Akoryt were waiting in his study. Alastar didn't bother to sit down, although he closed the study door before he began to speak.

"The ledgers confirm, for all practical purposes, that Vaschet is manufacturing and selling large quantities of rifles. His entries are partly in cipher, and that means that those entries don't provide any proof of who is buying the rifles." He turned to Cyran. "I'd like you to ride south to Factor Cuipryn's brassworks—Thelia can tell you where it is if you don't know—and see if you can find out if he is manufacturing brass cartridges for those rifles and who is buying them."

"I'll do what I can, sir."

Alastar turned to Akoryt. "I don't think the sniping is going to stop. They may not be shooting every day, but we need to keep maitres on duty for now. Who are the ones on duty today?"

"Ah . . . Maitre Arion will be in the west this morning, followed by Maitre Alyna in the afternoon. Arion has very strong shields. On the East Bridge will be Maitre Shaelyt . . ."

Alastar hadn't realized Alyna would be on duty immediately, although she had mentioned on Solayi that she would be one of the monitors on Mardi. He listened until Akoryt was through. "Good. There's one other thing. Do you have some thirds with good shields and who can hold at least blurring concealments for a good time?"

"Three or four . . . maybe one or two others."

"I'd like them to watch the Chateau D'Council and take notes on every High Holder who visits for the next few days. They'll have to note livery colors, and a number of other details to determine who the High Holders are."

Akoryt frowned. "Even so . . ."

"I can help some. Ryel's colors are black and silver. I'll write down that and the others I know in a moment. If High Holders are behind this, it's likely some might actually visit Cransyr. Then, they might not, but at the moment, we don't have much else to go on."

"I can see that."

"After we finish here, I'm headed out to see the rex. He might actually be there this morning."

"I think I'd rather see Factor Cuipryn," said Cyran dryly.

Alastar and Konan crossed the Bridge of Desires at two quints before eighth glass, later than Alastar would have liked, given the time it had taken him to write the listing on High Holders. As he turned his mount onto the Avenue D'Rex Ryen, he noticed the wall of gray clouds to the northwest. *Three glasses before the rain arrives?* He doubted that he'd be at the Chateau D'Rex anywhere near that long, not given Lorien's apparent desires to avoid meeting with him.

Just before they reached the ring road around the chateau, Alastar turned to Konan. "We'll use blurring concealments from here until we rein up at the chateau."

"Yes, sir," replied the third, if raising his eyebrows in question.

"The rex often seems to find other pursuits when his guards inform him that I am on the ring road riding toward the chateau."

"Yes, sir."

Alastar kept his smile to himself.

No sooner had Alastar dropped the blurring shield at the chateau entrance than Guard Captain Churwyl immediately appeared hurrying down the stone steps.

"Good morning, Captain," offered Alastar cheerfully.

"The rex is not expecting you, is he?" asked Churwyl.

"He should be expecting me, although he hasn't requested my presence."

"Should I announce you?"

"Not until I'm at the door to his study," replied Alastar as he dismounted and handed the gray's reins to Konan. As if to punctuate Alastar's words, the gelding whuffed. From the corner of his eyes, Alastar caught Konan's inadvertent smile.

Churwyl trudged up the steps beside Alastar and then through the entry hall and to the grand staircase.

Surprisingly, at the top stood Chelia, wearing a blue riding jacket and trousers. "You apparently avoided his lookouts, Maitre."

"I thought there might be a few. I shouldn't be that long. Not long enough to delay your ride by much."

"He may change his mind about riding . . . now."

"He might, indeed," agreed Alastar. "If you were looking forward to it, I do apologize, but it might be for the best, since it may rain in a few glasses."

"Don't let me keep you, Maitre."

Alastar nodded and headed for the north corridor, absently wondering why Chelia had made a point of being there. *To let you know that Lorien was indeed trying to avoid you? Without saying a word about it?* That was certainly possible.

At the door to the study, Alastar turned to the guard captain.

"Maitre Alastar, Your Grace," announced Churwyl.

Alastar did not wait for Lorien's response but opened the door himself, stepped into the study, and closed the door.

"You might have had the courtesy to request a meeting?"

"So that it could be postponed, delayed, or avoided? No, thank you." Alastar dropped into the chair across the goldenwood desk from Lorien. "I haven't heard anything about those petitions."

"I'm still considering them."

"Don't. Rule against the High Holders in all cases."

"That's easy enough for you to say."

"So far I've had three young imagers shot and killed and others wounded. It's almost a certainty that High Holders are behind it. High Holder Laevoryn killed Chief Factor Hulet and claims it was self-defense. Whether you want to admit it or not, the High Holders are beginning a rebellion to void all the limits placed on them by the Codex Legis. They're also obviously trying to weaken or destroy the Collegium. Neither set of actions will benefit you . . . or Solidar."

"That may be . . . but there's no proof of who's doing all this."

"The High Holder petitions are proof enough. Your own Minister of Justice knows that."

"Sanafryt doesn't wish to sign an opinion at present."

"So they've threatened him as well?"

"He just says I should sign the opinion. I'm not an advocate."

No . . . just Rex Regis. "You are the final authority."

"That may be, but . . . there are so many ramifications, Maitre. So many . . . and all lead to differing trials. I'm so tired of no one being happy with anything."

"The High Holders won't be happy with anything. You give in, and they'll just want more, and before long you'll have a civil war, and then no one will be happy."

"No one's happy now."

"Many of the people are happy . . . or at least content that Solidar is not in turmoil. They're the ones you don't hear from. The ones who complain are those with wealth and power, and they always want more, except tariffs, and there, they always want lower levies."

"That doesn't lessen the trials."

Alastar nodded, even though he wanted to squeeze shields around Lorien or dowse him with ice water. He also wondered, not for the first time, how Chelia put up with Lorien. "It doesn't, but you still need to deny those petitions . . . and fairly soon."

"I'll do it in my own good time. You want them denied sooner, you take over as rex."

"You know that won't work."

"Then stop badgering me."

Alastar decided not to press directly. "There's another matter about the shootings of my imagers. I'd be curious to know if Marshal Wilkorn ordered new heavy rifles for the army."

"That's absurd!" Lorien's voice rose. "You're suggesting that the army . . ."

Alastar shook his head. "I'm just trying to figure out why Vaschet built a new factorage to manufacture rifles. If Wilkorn ordered newer rifles—"

"He didn't." Lorien frowned. "I suppose you need to know. One of his subcommanders did. He ordered a thousand. He didn't have the authority, and the army didn't need any more, except for a few for sharpshooters. Wilkorn canceled the order, except for fifty of them. We had to pay Vaschet an extra hundred golds for the cancellation. He complained bitterly that he'd built a new factorage based on the order and that we ought to pay for that. Wilkorn said an indemnity payment of a hundred golds was more than enough. Alucar said it was far too much."

"If the army didn't need the rifles . . ."

"There was some confusion about that. Wilkorn insisted that he'd never approved it. The subcommander insisted he had an order with Wilkorn's signature. I wouldn't even have found out about it except that Alucar asked why the army was paying Vaschet damages. Wilkorn wanted to relieve the subcommander, but decided against it after we reviewed the matter."

"Do you remember who the subcommander was?"

"Do you expect me to remember that? I don't even know who's in charge of the Collegium after you and Cyran . . . and I suppose your wife, since she's also a Maitre D'Esprit. I know Wilkorn, Vice Marshal Vaelln, and Sea Marshal Tynan. I'd recognize other names if I saw them, of course."

Alastar had his doubts that Lorien was that ignorant. "I'm sure you know a few more than that, after all these years."

Lorien dismissed Alastar's words with a gesture, then smiled. "There's one other disturbing matter, Maitre. The factor Vaschet has lodged a complaint against you with the High Justicer."

"Oh? About what?"

"He claims you destroyed the gates to his ironworks, and killed several guards, as well as stole his ledgers. Not to mention assaulting him."

"When I went to visit him, his guards threatened me. I removed their weapons. Then several other guards shot at us. In defending ourselves, the other imager and I may have killed one or two guards, but we tried not to hurt any more than necessary, but when we tried to leave we were attacked by a full squad of men armed with heavy rifles. I did borrow Vaschet's ledgers because he refused to discuss to whom he was selling the rifles being used to kill young imagers."

"Hmmmph" was Lorien's only comment.

"I also discovered that Vaschet is using prisoners as laborers in his ironworks, which is why the walls of the works are fortified."

"So long as the prisoners don't come from L'Excelsis—"

"Nonsense!" snapped Alastar. "It's a violation of the Codex Legis for anyone other than you and High Holders to imprison people, and High Holders can only do so for less than two months under low justice." *Even if we both know that provision is observed more in the breach than by compliance.* "And only to their own people on their own lands."

"Are you saying that you expect the High Holders to submit to the High Justicer when you do not?"

Alastar looked directly at Lorien and image-projected authority and fury.

Lorien shuddered. "Don't—"

"Stop playing plaques with me! You don't want to make the right decision because it's not comfortable, and you hate being uncomfortable. Right now anything you do will make you uncomfortable. You need to deny those petitions, and you need to do it today. You need to do it because it's what's right; it's what's best for Solidar; and because if you think you're uncomfortable now, you don't want to know just how un-comfortable you'll be if you don't." Alastar paused, for just an instant. "Is that clear, Lorien? Very clear?"

Lorien swallowed. "You didn't have to make a scene."

"You didn't have to be so obtuse. That makes us even. I was rude; you were obtuse." Alastar smiled coldly. "I expect all those petitions that ask you to exempt High Holders from justicing or which would increase their powers and privileges to be denied. Today."

"You wouldn't . . ."

"I would. Ask your father."

Lorien paled. "It's that important?"

"Yes." *More than you know . . . and all this dilly-dallying around has only made matters worse.* But that was the danger in trying not to overmanage Lorien.

"I'll sign. But this will only cause more trouble."

"You're right, but it will cause less trouble than not signing. I'll wait while you sign every last one."

In the end, Alastar spent almost another glass at the chateau, making certain the petitions were all denied and that Minister Sanafryt made copies and sent out the denials.

Then he rode north from the ring road with Konan, heading for army headquarters and Marshal Wilkorn.

Wilkorn was in, not that Alastar expected otherwise, and when Alastar entered his study, he rose slowly from behind the wide desk from which he had directed the army and navy of Solidar for the past thirteen years. "Greetings, Maitre. What troubles bring you here? Don't tell me it's just a friendly visit."

"How about a friendly visit to discuss troubles with which the army, so far as I know, is not directly involved?"

The white-haired marshal gestured to a chair and reseated himself carefully. After all the years, he still favored the leg injured in the troubles that had led to Lorien's becoming rex. "Tell me about it."

"Someone has been using heavy rifles to shoot young imagers. They've also targeted me . . ." Alastar went on to give a brief summary of what had occurred, including the armed guards at Vaschet's factorage, then finished by saying, "When I talked to Lorien earlier today, he mentioned something about an order of heavy rifles that had never been authorized, but he didn't seem to know much about it . . . or at least not want to talk about it."

"That doesn't surprise me. I still don't know exactly everything. It all began when Minister Alucar sent a message asking why we needed to draw three thousand golds for a thousand new rifles. Procurements of that magnitude have to go through him, you know."

Alastar nodded. "And?"

"We still had a thousand rifles that have barely been used, and that's after the thousand we shipped to Ferravyl."

"Who in Ferravyl needed a thousand heavy rifles?" asked Alastar. "I thought most of the army in the south was in Solis?"

"Solis turned out to be a mistake. Well, not a mistake, but a miscalculation. A number of the pirates in the Southern Gulf had developed bases within the Sud Swamp, and it's easier to access the north end of the swamp from Ferravyl. For one thing there are the old stone roads that date from the time of the Naedarans, not to mention all the old barracks and quarters and stables that we've been maintaining. So we moved a regiment there from Solis two years ago. The swamp is harder on equipment, and last spring Commander Aestyn asked for the rifles so that he could rotate them, continuous maintenance, you know. We had the extras. So why not?"

"I can see that."

"You can see why I wouldn't have approved anything like purchasing another thousand rifles, right now, anyway. So I summoned Hehnsyn. He's the subcommander in charge of procurement. For almost fifteen years, he's had an excellent record. He's been effective. He's improved procurement . . . likely saved us thousands of golds . . . could be more. He even had an order with my name on it. The signature was mine. But I never signed it. I know I didn't. There would have been no way I'd have signed something like that. Or sealed it. Hehnsyn couldn't explain it. He even had a cover memo from Commander Marryt."

"Your chief of staff?"

Wilkorn nodded. "Marryt swore he never signed that, either."

"Who could have taken your seal and forged your signature? Or Marryt's?"

Wilkorn shrugged. "A good forger, I suppose. Possibly Hehnsyn, even, but he couldn't have done the seal . . . and he had no reason at all to do something like that. It's under lock and hidden, as is the special wax I mix myself. Anyway, the whole episode bothered me a lot, especially since we ended up ordering fifty rifles and paying damages. The new R-2 rifles are better, but not worth half a gold each more, and not when we have an additional thousand perfectly good R-1s for an army that won't likely do much fighting except against a few pirates or the occasional peasant riot."

"What did you do with Hehnsyn?"

"Cautioned him. He has a perfect record . . . and since he is the younger son of High Councilor Cransyr . . ."

"Did you mention that to Lorien?"

"How could I not, Maitre? I wanted to transfer Hehnsyn to other duties. The rex said that he had enough problems with the High Holders without creating more."

Alastar nodded slowly. "He does have problems with the High Holders, especially with Cransyr." He paused. "Vaelln and Tynan . . . I understand that Vaelln comes from a factoring background, and you once said that Tynan came from a merchanting family."

"That's right. Tynan's the fourth son. If his sire owned as much in land as he does in ships, he'd easily be a High Holder. According to Tynan, his father says that land just costs too much, both to buy and to manage, and that the return is poor at best."

"I assume you're watching Hehnsyn?"

"For now. When things die down, I think a tour in the south, along the Southern Gulf, or out of Ferravyl, ferreting out the landings of what pirates are left, would be good for him." Wilkorn smiled wryly. "I thought about putting in for my stipend, but then, with this and what Lorien said about the High Holders, I decided to put that off for a year or so."

"Have you told anyone?"

The marshal shook his head. "You're the only one."

"It might be best . . ."

Wilkorn nodded.

"How much better are the new rifles?"

"They're better, but not enough to make a difference except to a sharp-shooter aiming at targets more than four hundred yards away. You can load them faster, as well. We'll end up buying more, but not for a while."

"Several others have bought over two hundred of them. I'm thinking they were bought by High Holders."

"I can't say I like the sound of that, not if they're the ones who shot your young imagers." Wilkorn frowned. "And why would a factor be using that many of them?"

"I don't know, and that bothers me. I can't see him targeting young imagers. That seems more like High Holders. In that light, you might keep an even closer eye on Hehnsyn."

"I can do that." Wilkorn sighed. "Hate it when Lorien gets involved."

"That makes two of us."

After more general conversation, and a few parting pleasantries, Alastar left the headquarters building, and he and Konan began the ride back to Imagisle.

As he neared the Bridge of Desires, just before second glass, Alastar was struck immediately by the two imagers positioned beside the sentry box on the Imagisle side of the bridge, neither of whom was Alyna. When he reached the middle of the bridge he could see that one was Akoryt and the other was Taryn, who immediately called out, "Maitre Alyna is fine."

Which means that someone else has been shot.

Alastar said nothing until he reined up beside the sentry box and looked down at Akoryt. "Who got shot?"

"Primus Wrestyl. The shooter hit him in the back of the skull. If Maitre Alyna hadn't been there, we might well have lost another student imager."

"How did it happen?"

"They were over there on the slope. It's shielded from the north and west, but the shooter was under that tree to the south on the west side of the river. It's the only place anywhere that could have hit the two. It's a tiny space. The shooter must have waited for glasses."

"You said 'two.' "

"Alyna saw Wrestyl fall, and she did something to protect Boltyn. Then, because she couldn't see the shooter from the sentry box, she ran onto the causeway to the bridge and imaged a hail of iron darts, then froze him in place. There was another shooter, but no one ever saw him. He loosed at least ten shots at Alyna. Taryn and I crossed the bridge under full shields and brought back the body and the first shooter's gear. The body's in the surgery. It wasn't the blond man."

Ten shots at Alyna? Alastar managed not to swallow.

"No one saw the other shooter," added Taryn. "Even Alyna didn't see him, but she pointed us to where he had to have been. She'd imaged more darts, but didn't know if she'd hit the second man. We checked the area around where we thought he was, and found nine spent cartridges, but nothing else. Well . . . some blood, but it wasn't enough to stop him from getting away."

"Or from someone helping him get away. Were there any signs of mounts?"

"There was no way to tell if they had them tied up behind the shops. No one remembers seeing anyone in particular. It's a busy place. People tie up mounts, visit the shops, and then leave."

"Where's Alyna?"

"At the surgery . . . or maybe in your study. She said she'd be there after she learned what she could from Gaellen."

Alastar decided to ride directly to the administration building, not only to see whether Alyna was there, but to discover if there were any other messages. Once he left his mount with Konan and made his way toward his study, he found that Maercyl was alone in the anteroom.

"Dareyn gets tired in the afternoon," the second explained. "Maitre Alyna is in your study, and you have a message from the Factors' Council."

"Thank you." Alastar took the sealed missive and entered the study, looking to Alyna as he closed the door behind himself. "Are you all right?"

"Tired, but I'm fine. I've already had a lager." Alyna remained seated in the middle chair before the desk. "How about you?"

"I had to lose my temper with Lorien and stand over him while he wrote the denials of all the High Holder petitions," Alastar began as he sat down in the chair beside Alyna. "Then I went to see Marshal Wilkorn . . . and discovered that one Subcommander Hehnsyn, a junior son of Cransyr, had ordered a thousand heavy rifles for the army—without authorization—and that when Wilkorn tried to relieve him of his duties, Lorien insisted that he not do so, because he said he didn't want any more trouble with the High Holders. When I mentioned the rifles to Lorien, he did say that the army had had a procurement problem with them, but denied knowing the subcommander who made the order in Wilkorn's name, yet Wilkorn insisted that Lorien not only knew, but directed him not to relieve Hehnsyn. Most disturbing was the fact that someone duplicated Wilkorn's seal and signature without his knowledge."

"Why would Hehnsyn do such a thing? What would it gain him?"

"It wouldn't gain him anything, but Vaschet claimed he never would have built the new rifle facility without the large order from the army . . . and he demanded damages for what he regarded as cancellation of the order. Wilkorn ended up buying fifty rifles and paying a hundred golds in damages. He admitted that the new rifles are more accurate at a greater distance."

"With the result that High Holders now have over two hundred new heavy rifles they wouldn't otherwise have. What is Wilkorn going to do about Hehnsyn?"

"Watch him closely for now."

"That's probably better for the moment."

Alastar had no doubts that Alyna had ideas about what should happen to Hehnsyn. "I talked to Akoryt. He summarized what happened. What else was there that you didn't tell him? Besides taking something like ten shots to your shields?"

"Not much."

"How badly are you bruised?'

"I'm sore all over, but there aren't any bruises. Not yet anyway."

"And it was more like fifteen shots," suggested Alastar.

"It might have been, but one at a time is different from twenty at once . . . twice. I wasn't counting. I just wanted to kill some of the shooters so that they wouldn't think they could keep firing away with impunity. After I made sure that Boltyn was all right." She smiled faintly. "I also didn't want anyone left to shoot at you. Your shields still aren't fully recovered."

"Probably not. Besides the one you killed, Akoryt said you wounded another one."

"Good. He should die."

Alastar raised his eyebrows. "Poisoned iron darts?"

"Of course. I studied the bullets they used. It wasn't hard to duplicate them. It's also easy to refine bleufleur with imaging. I even think I might be able to image it directly. Anyone who goes around shooting young people and children deserves what they get." She paused. "Tiranya knows how to do those darts also. She said she'd teach Shaelyt."

"Just Maitres D'Structure for now, I hope."

"Of course."

Alastar had his doubts about that, but decided not to comment. "You know Cyran has been working with Arthos to copy those bullets . . ."

"You want me to see if it can be done with imaging?"

"They have to fit snugly, but not too snugly, into a rifle barrel."

"We don't use rifles."

Alastar nodded. "I know. I'm thinking ahead."

"Oh . . ."

"I hope it doesn't come to that. Oh . . . one other thing." He lifted the missive. "I also just got this from the Factors' Council. I haven't read it. I forgot to tell you that Vaschet has lodged a complaint against me for forcing my way into his ironworks, a complaint that doubtless overlooks his own myriad offenses. I imagine this is a protest against my high-handed acts."

"I wouldn't wager against you." Alyna smiled sadly. "You were high-handed, you know?"

"I'm aware of that, but if I had been polite it would have taken weeks to get the information, and with four young imagers dead already, I felt that haste and high-handedness were necessary. Do you disagree?"

"No. You might as well find out what the council thinks."

"They won't be happy," predicted Alastar as he slit open the envelope with his belt knife. He began to read.

Maitre Alastar—

*Factorius Vaschet has made a disturbing claim—that you forced your way
into his ironworks, destroying costly gates in the process, that you killed three
guards in doing so, and that you removed private financial records over his
objections.*

*While the council understands your concerns about discovering who might be
using the rifles produced by Vaschet, it feels that your actions could be a prosecutable
offense under the Codex Legis. If a satisfactory explanation is not forthcoming, the
council will be obligated, under its charter to protect its members, to seek a
hearing before the High Justicer . . .*

Alastar shook his head, then continued reading.

. . . to seek recompense and possible punishment.
We look forward to your early response.

The signature was that of Elthyrd, as acting chief of the Factors'
Council of L'Excelsis.

Alastar handed the missive to Alyna and waited as she read it.

"He's being pressed by Vaschet . . . and others."

"Vaschet's an idiot. I'm the one trying to protect their interests, and
they want to make it harder for me?"

"Golds can make any man an idiot. But Vaschet's not an idiot. He's
been forced to make the complaint and petition by whichever High
Holder or Holders bought the rifles. In all likelihood . . . didn't you tell
me that Thelia thought he would have failed if he hadn't been backed in
building the new factorage?"

"She thought it was possible."

"The complaint splits the factors, or could, at a time when they should
be united. Thelia did tell me she was afraid you didn't fully understand
just how angry your taking Vaschet's ledgers would make some factors."

"So I was set up by Vaschet and whatever High Holders are backing
him?"

"That likely wasn't the initial purpose, but Cransyr's a complete
opportunist, and you gave him the opening."

"If I hadn't . . ."

"Dearest . . . I agree that it had to be done. You could have spent days
or weeks otherwise, but it does create certain problems."

"Like having some factors think I'm just like the High Holders."

"Not all High Holders."

"No. Your brother wouldn't do that, and neither would Calkoran . . . or a few others.

"More than a few, but a lot of them don't pay much attention to what happens in L'Excelsis."

"Not until it's too late."

"There is that."

"I never asked you what you found out about the shooter."

"I had Thelia look at his garb. The cloth was fairly new. It comes from Montagne, in the same region as Cransyr's lands. So does that particular dark brown dye. I didn't recognize the rifle, but it is very new. The exterior of the barrel is octagonal. That suggests that they used a flat grinding wheel, rather than a turning bench."

"Vaschet?"

"That would speed up production. It would also leave the turning benches free for more precise work."

Once again, Alastar was struck by how much Alyna knew about so many things. "You had those in Rivages?"

"And at the porcelain works."

"What about the shooter?"

"There were some silvers in his wallet, and he had a good knife. Old and well-used, but a good blade. Solid leather boots. Gaellen said they were like the ones used by the army."

"It's sounding more and more like someone, maybe several High Holders, have built a small fighting force."

"I'd have to agree—"

At that moment, there was a rap on the door.

"Maitre Cyran is here," announced Maercyl.

"Have him come in."

Cyran entered, a satisfied look on his face, and closed the door.

"From your expression, you must have discovered something. What might that be?"

Cyran grinned wryly. "That Thelia's directions needed a little help, and that Cuipryn doesn't think much of Vaschet. He was happy to tell me who bought up all the cartridge cases he machined. It won't help us much, though."

"Vaschet?"

The Maitre D'Esprit nodded. "Exactly. Cuipryn only supplied the empty cases. Vaschet actually makes the complete cartridges and the bullets."

Which means he's also likely the one who made the poisoned bullets, using bleufleur from Cransyr or another High Holder.

"Did anyone else buy any?" asked Alyna.

"The army buys some every season. It varies."

"Did you find out when he sold them to Vaschet?" Alastar could only hope he did, because he hadn't asked Cyran to find that specific.

"Actually, I did. He even checked his ledgers and then wrote out the sale dates and amounts."

"That was helpful."

"It might be because his cousin's son is a junior imager."

"Who?"

"Eshtyl. He's a second who works for Petros. Cuipryn was worried because he didn't visit this past Samedi. He was happy to know that Eshtyl was safe . . . and not very happy about the shootings." Cyran extended a sheet of paper.

Alastar took it, studied it briefly, then stood. "Excellent. Let's go see Thelia." He looked to Alyna, questioningly.

"I'll wait here. Three of us in her study would be cramped."

"You're sure?"

Alyna nodded.

In moments, the two senior imagers were entering Thelia's study.

She looked up. "Yes, Maitres?"

"We need you to find transactions in Vaschet's ledger that occurred on these dates for roughly these amounts."

Thelia frowned.

"Vaschet bought the cartridges from Cuipryn, and he likely resold them at a profit to someone else."

"Now?"

"Now," said Alastar firmly, handing her the sheet. "Here's the information."

Neither Alastar nor Cyran said a word as the maitre of accounts opened Vaschet's master ledger. After a time, she glanced up. "It looks like he coded the cartridges as 'CC.' The golds match, but the numbers are way off."

Alastar remembered something. "High or low?"

"The ones in Vaschet's accounts are too high."

"Cuipryn likely charged him by the pallet, while Vaschet broke the pallets down and charged by the case. See if dividing by twenty works."

After several moments, Thelia replied. "Twenty doesn't work. Twenty-five does."

"Can you tell to whom he sold them?"

"He's using the same codes for the cartridges as for the rifles, and the dates are the same or within a few days."

Which doesn't tell us all that much. At the same time, Alastar was fairly certain that the HHC code was for the High Council, but there were more than a few High Holders whose name began with 'R,' including Ryel.

After another half quint, Thelia said, "I can't find any other codes like that."

"Thank you." Alastar paused. "If you'd make a copy of that sheet for your use and return the original?"

"Yes, sir."

Alastar and Cyran walked back to the anteroom.

"Is there anything else you need from me, sir?"

"Not right now." Alastar laughed. "I'll likely think of something after you go, but I can't think of anything."

After Cyran turned, Alastar reentered his study, closing the door. Alyna waited.

"The cartridges went where the rifles went, but . . ."

"There's no proof besides initials."

He nodded. "I need to write a response to Elthyrd and the Factors' Council. If you wouldn't mind waiting and reading over what I write."

"I can do that. The girls are at the factorage with Tiranya."

More than two quints and several drafts later, Alastar read through what he hoped would be his final draft.

Elthyrd D'Factorius
Chief (Acting)
Council of Factors, L'Excelsis

I understand that Factor Vaschet has lodged a complaint against me, as Maitre of the Collegium Imago, for acts undertaken on Lundi, 9 Erntyn, 402, A.L., to wit:

    1. Forcibly entering his ironworks, destroying two gates in the process.

    2. Attacking and killing three guards.

    3. Assaulting Factor Vaschet.

    4. Removing certain ledgers.

In response:

1. Two imagers removed the gates and entered the ironworks after they were attacked by eight armed guards who opened fire with heavy rifles. One guard was killed when the imagers defended themselves. The gates were removed, not destroyed.

2. When one imager attempted to locate Factor Vaschet a second guard attacked that imager with a blade. The imager killed the guard in self-defense.

3. Factor Vaschet was asked to reveal who had purchased large quantities of the heavy rifles used to kill four imagers to date. The imager was not inquiring about costs, profits, or any private financial information. Vaschet refused to divulge that information and threatened the imager.

4. The imager restrained Vaschet and removed certain ledgers, with the promise that they would be returned, and without divulging financial information to any other factors or High Holders.

5. When leaving the ironworks, the two imagers were again attacked, this time by roughly twenty guards also armed with heavy rifles. It is possible that another guard might have died as a result of the imagers' departure. The imagers did not attack the guards, but merely rode through the formation.

Further, it is noted that bringing an action against the Collegium might be unwise since: (1) Factor Vaschet was observed to have been operating a prison and using prisoners to operate facilities at the ironworks, a practice forbidden under the Codex Legis. Should that be the case, the entire ironworks could be confiscated by the rex; (2) by failing to disclose the purchaser of heavy rifles used to murder four imagers, Factor Vaschet could be brought before even a regional justice as an accessory to murder.

Under these circumstances, it is suggested that any complaint be withdrawn, and that Factor Vaschet be investigated for his own violations of the Codex Legis.

After rereading the reply, Alastar handed it to Alyna. "Will this suffice?"

She read it slowly, then looked up. "You could still be prosecuted."

"I could, but do you think the council will press under the circumstances?"

"It's unlikely, but right now, who knows? When will you send it?"

"Tomorrow morning, unless you think I should send it now."

"Tomorrow. Wait to sign it until then . . . when you're certain. That's soon enough. We should go home. We both need a good meal with the girls, and they need us to be there."

Alastar could see that. He smiled and extended a hand to Alyna. She took it and rose, although she did not need the assistance, for which Alastar was most grateful, for more than one reason.

18

After dinner on Mardi evening, Alastar went to the private study in the Maitre's house and jotted down a note to remind himself to ask Cyran if there had been any more trouble between young factors and High Holder's offspring, something he'd meant to do on Lundi. The two girls were already practicing shields with Alyna on the front porch, which was cooler than it had been, with a dry wind blowing out of the northeast, which kept the mosquitoes away, by the time Alastar joined them.

"How are they doing?" he asked his wife in a low voice.

Alyna smiled. "Throw something at Lystara."

Alastar glanced around, but saw nothing small enough. He wasn't about to throw a chair . . . or his belt knife. After considering a moment, he fished a copper out of his wallet and lobbed it at his daughter. The coin angled away from her a good third of a yard from her body. "That's good, Lystara."

"Take this," suggested Alyna, extending one of the wooden wands used to train imagers with sabers, "and swing at her."

Alastar looked at his wife quizzically.

"Go ahead."

Alastar took the wand and walked toward Lystara. He swung at her, gently. At a third of a yard from her body, the wand slid to one side. Alastar tried once more, using slightly more force. The same thing happened again.

"You can swat harder," said Alyna.

Alastar did. All that happened was that the wand slipped off Lystara's shields so quickly that, for a moment, Alastar was off-balance. He caught himself and lowered the wand. "Do you feel any pressure on you when I strike your shields?"

"Just a little."

"All right. I'm going to hit them harder." This time Alastar struck with much greater force, if downward at a slight angle, so that if Lystara's shields failed, the blow would pass by her shoulder.

Her shields didn't fail, but shunted the wand to the side, so that

Alastar pitched forward and struck her shields with his right forearm . . . and found himself twisted away from his daughter. He had to take three steps to keep from falling, and probably would have anyway if he hadn't been able to grab the porch railing. His back spasmed for a moment, but he managed to hide the wince from Alyna. He definitely hadn't fully recovered from the attack at the ironworks.

"Are you all right, Father?"

"I'm fine." Alastar felt even more chagrined when he caught sight of Alyna's amused smile. "Those are some shields." He looked to Alyna. "I don't know any way to test them farther without the possibility of injuring her."

"I had that problem, too."

"Can I stop, now?" asked Lystara. "I'm getting tired."

"Yes, dear," replied Alyna.

Lystara exhaled noisily, and then took a deep breath.

"What exactly are you doing?" Alastar asked. "Your shields aren't solid, and they're not angled. It's almost like you're sliding what hits them aside."

"That's sort of it," replied Lystara. "I can't hold a shield like you, Father, or Mother or Malyna. Not for very long, anyway. I'm still not strong enough. So I was thinking about the concealment shield."

"Your concealment shield, you mean?"

"Yes, sir."

"But bullets and hard objects aren't the same as light," Alastar said mildly. Although he now had an idea what Lystara had done, he wanted to hear her explanation.

"I've got a whole series of little shields. They can be tilted and slipped. Each little shield tilts, and that tilt moves the object sideways, and if I have lots of little shields . . ."

Alastar nodded. "That's a good start. Do you have to think about each one sliding?"

"No. They're all linked from the beginning."

"That's even better. You need to keep practicing so that you can hold them all the time."

"So someone can't surprise me?"

"That's right."

"It's time for you to wash up, Lystara, and get ready for bed," said Alyna.

"Ohhh . . . already?"

"We worked with you first. Now we need to work with Malyna."

"Tomorrow night"—*if we remember*—"we'll work with Malyna first," said Alastar. "We'll try to alternate."

After Lystara headed inside and up the stairs, Alyna turned to Malyna. "Raise your shields. Your uncle will tap at them with the wand."

"Are you ready?" asked Alastar.

Malyna nodded.

Alastar kept pressing at Malyna's shields for a bit less than half a quint. At that point, Malyna stepped back. "I can't hold them any longer."

Alastar lowered the wand. "Just take a deep breath and rest for a bit. Then we'll go through it again."

"Uncle Alastar, I get tired so quickly when I'm holding shields."

"Most young imagers do," replied Alastar, "and you haven't been really working at imaging all that long. That's why you need to practice them when you're tired. That's what strengthens your abilities."

"Why does Lystara have different shields than I do? I tried what she said she does, and nothing happens." Malyna blotted the perspiration from her forehead with a kerchief that she quickly slipped back into her trousers' pocket.

"Each imager—those who can even do shields—approaches shielding a little differently because each of us thinks a bit differently. Most imagers create barriers. Some can create softer barriers that change into full shields if they're touched—"

"Can you do that, Uncle Alastar?"

Alastar shook his head. "No. I just have to hold full shields whenever I might be attacked."

"Which is all the time outside the Maitre's house," added Alyna dryly. "Now . . . you've rested enough. It's time for another session."

After another half quint, Malyna was exhausted and perspiration was running down her face.

"That's enough for tonight," said Alyna. "Go get washed up and ready for bed."

Once the older girl was in the house, Alyna turned to Alastar. "What do you think?"

"She looks to have the talent of a maitre, possibly even a Maitre D'Structure. We'll just have to see, though. What do *you* think?"

"She'll keep Lystara on her toes."

"Oh?" Alastar knew exactly what Alyna meant, but wanted her to say it.

"You know exactly what I mean. Lystara's worked harder and made more progress in the last week than in the past few months. We should talk about that later." She glanced toward the upper level of the Maitre's house.

Alastar nodded, then said, "What you did this afternoon was remarkable."

"You would have done the same."

"Not nearly so effectively, I think." *Especially right now.* "There are times when, no matter how strong you are, and you've proved how strong an imager you are, technique is more important. I wouldn't even have thought about poisoned darts. I didn't, as a matter of fact. Or spraying the area with them."

"It only seemed fair, and I felt that if I even wounded one of them . . . well, they'd get exactly what they planned for young imagers."

Alastar turned slightly and found he was looking eastward, where red-tinted Erion was nearly full and rising over the trees. *The moon of the hunter.*

"What are you thinking?" asked Alyna. "You have that faraway look in your eyes."

"Erion . . . the hunter, and I have to wonder who is the hunter and who is the hunted."

"We're the hunted, until we become the hunters."

"After we discover whom to hunt," Alastar said dryly.

"You will; you always do." Alyna paused. "I hear signs of . . . I need to check on the girls." With that, she turned and headed inside.

Alastar shook his head. *Never in your wildest dreams did you think you'd end up in a household with three imager women.* But he smiled.

Once the girls were in bed, hopefully sleeping, Alastar and Alyna retired to their own sitting room, except that Alastar found himself walking to the window, and then toward the closed door to the upper hall.

"Sit down and stop pacing," said Alyna gently. "When you do that, you always have something on your mind. Talk to me."

Alastar sat down, turning toward her. "I've got a lot of things on my mind. First, where did she ever come up with that idea for shields?"

"She told you. She thought it up."

"Ten-year-olds don't usually think up things like that."

"Your daughter does. In that, she's like you."

Alastar laughed, if softly. "Oh . . . poisoned darts?"

"So . . . she might take after me . . . a little."

He shook his head.

"She's curious about everything," Alyna went on. "Remember when she imaged those wooden flutes . . ."

". . . to see if the diameter of the center affected the sound," finished Alastar, "all because of the players she saw in the square, and she didn't believe our explanations."

"The other night . . . the business with the cord, what was that all about?"

"I don't know, exactly. She was using imaging at the top of the arc to give the billet a push. Why, I don't know, except I think she was thinking about ways to multiply the effect of her imaging, because she's not as strong as she wants to be." He grinned at Alyna. "She does sound like—"

"Enough of that, Maitre of the Collegium." The words were said warmly and affectionately. "What else is on your mind?"

"The fact that we still don't know who is behind the shootings. I forgot to tell you that Akoryt is posting scouts who can do concealments to watch the Chateau D'Council. It might be a waste of time, but, right now, I can't think of anything else that might help."

"It's only been five days . . ."

"It seems longer . . . a lot longer. And the fact that Lorien hasn't been exactly forthcoming lately isn't exactly helpful."

"He doesn't want trouble with the High Holders. The last time a rex defied them he ended up dead."

"That was because his father wouldn't compromise."

"Exactly. And now you're telling him not to compromise."

"The situation is very different."

"To us, but not to Lorien. He's not . . ."

"The brightest plaque in the deck? No, he's not, and I'm worried that he's becoming less bright these days."

"Like his father?"

"Let's just say that the heritage of the first Rex Regis has fared better through daughters."

"You can be so sweet, at times. If all those junior imagers knew . . ."

"Better they don't." *And it's definitely better the High Holders and factors don't know.* "How do you think Malyna's coming?"

"You're changing the subject."

"Yes, I am." Alastar offered a grin.

"She's adjusting well. It doesn't hurt that she and Lystara are so different . . . but I worry. She's already a bit more outgoing around the other thirds, and some of the boys . . ." Alyna shook her head. "I've asked Tiranya and Linzya to let me know if any of them make untoward advances . . ."

"You think that would be a problem . . . so soon? She's not that old."

"She's old enough, dearest. That's not the problem I foresee. She still doesn't have enough experience with imaging. If some advances are indeed untoward, she might overreact . . . and she's strong enough to hurt some of those thirds."

"I can see that might be a problem . . ." He shook his head. "And we'll have to go through that with Lystara.

"Not that problem," Alyna returned. "Lystara's shields are already strong enough, and her control precise enough that she won't hurt anyone inadvertently . . . as long as she's not tired."

"Or angry," added Alastar.

"There is that . . ." Alyna looked inquiringly at Alastar.

"The anger comes from me, I'm certain."

"I know. You've been kind with me, and gentle, but when those you love are threatened . . . or young imagers . . . I'd not wish to be anyone who made such threats. The High Holders don't understand that . . . not even Zaeryl. I think Mairina does, but that might be her heritage . . . or, then again . . ."

Alastar kept listening.

19

On Meredi morning, Alastar had no sooner dispatched Coermyd to take his reply to the Factors' Council—except he directed the third to deliver it personally to Elthyrd at his factorage—than Cyran appeared at his study door.

Alastar waved him in. "You have that look. What else has gone wrong this morning?"

"Not this morning. Last night."

"Go on."

"A High Holder's son decided to take over driving his carriage from the coachman. He ran down a factor's son. The youth was killed. He might have died shortly after. That's not clear. The young man's older brother slit the throat of the High Holder's son. Then he disappeared."

"Which High Holder and which factor?" asked Alastar. "How did you find out?"

"I asked Captain Heisyt to let me know of any trouble between High Holder and factor offspring. He's been more than happy. He doesn't much care for most of the High Holder youngbloods. Oh . . . the father of the dead youngblood is High Holder Paellyt. The supposed killer's father is Naathyn. He builds most of the wagons and coaches—and the costly carriages—here in L'Excelsis."

"I take it that the one who got his throat slit wasn't beloved?"

"Heisyt didn't know about that. He'd heard that young Paellyt owed a lot to Alamara's, maybe even to Tydaael's. The younger Naathyn had cleaned out young Paellyt at bones, then left. Young Paellyt followed."

"If he'd lived, young Paellyt would have claimed it was an accident," said Alastar sourly. There was something about Paellyt, something he'd heard. He tried to remember. . . .

"There's not much doubt about that," replied Cyran.

Kathila! Alastar finally recalled that she had said something about Pa-ellyt being one of the less endowed High Holders, one of those who might face ruin as a result of the crop failures. "It might have something to do with the fact that his father's finances are less than solid at present. I take it that the Civic Patrol hasn't found the surviving Naathyn offspring?"

"I doubt that the patrollers are trying all that hard."

Alastar could understand that, given that the Civic Patrol was funded by the Factors' Council, and that most patrollers weren't all that fond of High Holders. "The patrollers? What about Commander Murranyt?"

"Heisyt said the commander ordered them to bring in the killer."

An order most patrollers wouldn't exert any extra effort to follow, Alastar suspected. "Did Heisyt have anything else to say?"

"Besides wishing that the High Holder brats didn't think they were entitled to everything under two moons? No, not really."

Alastar shook his head. "This is going to make matters worse, even if I can't predict exactly how." He rose. "I suppose most of the other senior maitres are already in the conference room."

"Most of them. Gaellen's still at the infirmary." Cyran followed Alastar through the side door into the conference room.

At that moment, Gaellen hurried through the other door, closing it behind himself and seating himself at the last seat near the foot of the table.

After settling himself at the head of the table and glancing at Alyna, who offered the tiniest of headshakes, Alastar waited for several moments before beginning. "As all of you know, we've had four imagers shot and killed, and one wounded since the last meeting of the senior maitres. The shooters appear to have been using new heavy rifles produced by Factor Vaschet . . . who has proved to be less than cooperative in disclosing who bought those rifles . . ." Alastar quickly explained the basics of what had happened with Vaschet and the subsequent complaints made by the factor to both Lorien and the Factors' Council. He did mention the impact that massed firing had on shields, but not the extent of his own injuries. When he finished, he asked, "Any questions?"

"Why is the Factors' Council pressing you on this?" asked Shaelyt. "Don't they know that, without the support of the Collegium, Lorien would give in to the High Holders?"

"I've talked this over with Maitre Thelia, and one of the freedoms the factors value the most is the ability to keep what they have and do confidential. If the Factors' Council doesn't at least protest . . ."

"Seems like that was planned by the High Council," grumbled Obsolym.

"I doubt that the High Council would do anything so overt," replied

Alastar, "but they're not beneath looking the other way and letting an individual High Holder do something like that."

"That's very much the way the High Council works," added Arion.

"What about Rex Lorien?" asked Khaelis.

"He doesn't want trouble with the High Holders. It appears that he's concerned. He may be thinking that his father's stubbornness with the High Holders led to his death."

"Does he think that much?" murmured someone, but Alastar couldn't tell who.

"What about the shootings?" asked Obsolym. "Surely you must have some idea who might be behind it?"

"Ideas, yes. It's almost certainly a High Holder, if not several. But which one? Cransyr, or one of the other four councilors? Or any one of eight or ten others who have expressed unhappiness or filed petitions? Or someone with a grudge that we haven't even considered?"

"Ah . . . is there anything that might be done to gain that information?" ventured Tiranya.

"In fact, Maitre Cyran is working with the Civic Patrol, and I've asked Maitre Akoryt to post scouts to observe the Chateau D'Council." Alastar looked to Akoryt. "Do you have anything to report?"

"Not yet, sir."

"Does anyone else know anything or have any thoughts about who, specifically, might be behind the shootings?"

There were several headshakes, but no comments.

"Until further notice, all imagers without strong shields are to remain on Imagisle and in places where they cannot be observed from the outer banks of the river."

"Does that include instructional activities on the river?" asked Khaelis.

"It does, unless your shields can cover all those you're instructing."

"That might be a bit much, sir. Thank you."

"Maitre Akoryt will continue to maintain and post the watch schedules for the senior imagers . . ."

The remaining routine matters took almost another glass before Alastar called the meeting to a close.

Akoryt lingered after the others, except Alyna, had left the conference room. "There is one other matter I didn't wish to bring up in the meeting."

Alastar nodded.

"As you requested, I've occasionally talked with Tertia Charlina. She's noticed that there have been even more instances of someone moving around in the imager factorage under a concealment. The person did not reveal himself or herself."

"Can she tell whether it's the same person all the time?"

Akoryt shook his head. "She says she's working on that, but right now, she cannot."

Alastar had a thought, but kept it to himself. "All I can say is to keep checking. It does sound like the situation is encouraging Charlina to develop her abilities more, and that's not bad at all. Or am I being too optimistic?"

"Not at all. I think she's encouraged by the idea she has a unique talent. She's begun to work more on shields, and she can hold them and concealments much longer. She can also sense another concealment even when she's holding shields. I'm working to get her able to do all three at once."

"Excellent!" Alastar didn't have to feign enthusiasm.

"That is very good," added Alyna. "Very good."

"I wouldn't have known if you hadn't told me she could detect concealments," Akoryt added.

"That was just good fortune," replied Alastar.

"A little more than that, Maitre, I think. If there's nothing else . . . ?"

"Go," said Alastar cheerfully. "I won't keep you."

With a nod, Akoryt turned and left the conference room.

Alyna and Alastar had just entered his study when Dareyn appeared in the study door, a pair of missives in hand.

"One is from Rex Lorien, the other from Westisle."

"Thank you." Alastar took the sealed envelopes, then studied the white-haired third. "How are you feeling, Dareyn?"

"Much better, sir. Not back to where I was, but better."

"I'm glad to hear that. Very glad."

"Thank you, sir."

Once Dareyn returned to the anteroom, Alastar slit the envelope from Lorien, extracted the sheet of heavy paper, and began to read.

Maitre Alastar—

It has been brought to my attention that the eldest son of High Holder Paellyt was murdered by the son of a factor last night, and that the Civic Patrol appears *unable to find the miscreant. It is not to anyone's advantage to have this situation unresolved.*

With your long-standing ties to the factoring community, you should be able to deal with the difficulty and dispose of it before it creates even greater difficulties than those that you and the Collegium now face. We look forward to hearing that you have done such.

The signature and seal were that of Lorien.

But why didn't he summon you to see him if he's so concerned? Alastar suspected that Lorien didn't want to give Alastar any excuse to see him personally any sooner than absolutely necessary. That also suggested that Lorien was attempting to play both sides. *Which will only get him—and the Collegium—in deeper trouble.* Alastar sighed softly and handed the sheet to Alyna. He waited while she read it, abruptly realizing something else. For Lorien to have written and dispatched the message as early as he had meant that someone had informed him either late the night before or very early in the morning. *And Lorien isn't a morning person.*

She looked up from the sheet, shook her head, and handed it back. "He doesn't understand. Or he knows something we don't."

"How about both?" asked Alastar dryly. "And the fact that someone beholden to the High Holders is keeping him informed."

"We've been thinking that the shootings are targeted just at the Collegium. What if the shootings are to make a point to him as well?" asked Alyna. "What if he's received an indirect message to that effect?"

"That if the imagers can't stop the shootings of imagers, how could we protect him and his family?"

"Isn't that possible?"

"It's all too possible. And it makes a great deal of sense, unfortunately. But why wouldn't he . . ." Alastar shook his head. "Knowing Lorien . . . he isn't sure who he can trust."

"He can trust you."

Alastar shook his head. "He can only trust me to do what is right for Solidar, and he knows that. All this means is that it's even more important to discover who's behind it, but trying to find out which High Holder or High Holders are is like trying to find a copper dropped in hog slop." Should he send out more scouts? With more than twenty High Holders having holds within fifty milles of L'Excelsis, and reportedly another eighty or so with town homes or chateaux nearby, trying to investigate all of them quickly would be impossible, since Alastar only had ten senior maitres and perhaps another twenty maitres and imagers with the skills and shields to search undetected. *Still . . . if you don't learn something in the next day or so . . .*

"That metaphor tells a great deal about how you feel about High Holders, dearest."

"Only about some," he replied sheepishly.

She grinned, all too briefly. "I need to get to my mathematics instructional."

"What about geometry?" Alastar realized that was a stupid question, because geometry was in the afternoon.

"That's this afternoon, remember?"

"I'm sorry. All of this . . ." He gestured vaguely.

"I understand."

After Alyna left, Alastar realized he had not opened the second envelope. *What other problems does Voltyrn have?* With a sigh, he opened the second envelope, extracted the missive, and began to read.

> *Maitre Alastar—*
>
> *While we realize that making a decision on Maitre Zhelan's successor does require thought, those of us here in Westisle would fervently hope that you can see your way to make that decision in the near future, since we did our best to forewarn you about the possible need . . .*

Alastar shook his head. *Has it been that long?* He tried to remember. It had been late in Agostos, the last Thursday—not quite two weeks ago—and the letter in his hand had been sent almost a week ago. *Why is he pushing for a decision?*

Admittedly, Voltyrn had no idea of all that was occurring involving the Collegium, but how could he not know that pushing Alastar wasn't likely to help his cause. And Alastar hadn't cared that much for Voltyrn years ago, thinking him a smarmy weasel even then.

Is he trying to upset you? Or is he that stupid?

Alastar walked to the half-open window, but the air was so still that there was no breeze whatsoever.

Finally, he decided to walk to the East Bridge, holding full shields, now that he had them back, even if holding them for long was a slight strain, just to see if he could draw fire . . . and perhaps learn more, or even kill another shooter. When nothing happened, he walked to the

Bridge of Desires and did the same thing, making certain he was most obvious, but there wasn't a single shot. Nor did he see anyone who looked like a possible shooter, not that he would have expected that.

He returned to his study, deciding to wait, at least another day before starting expeditions to the chateaux of various High Holders. As always for him, waiting was the hardest part. *Even if it is the best strategy at times.*

Just before fourth glass, Akoryt reappeared and entered Alastar's study. He closed the door before speaking. "I sent Belsior to keep watch on the Chateau D'Council. He just returned. He actually used shields and concealments to get inside the gates. He didn't enter the chateau, but he was able to overhear a conversation between a chateau footman and a messenger. The messenger wore green and gray livery, by the way . . ."

Green and gray? High Holder Meinyt?

". . . and they were talking about how the High Holder's illness meant he wouldn't be able to attend the meeting tomorrow afternoon. They didn't mention the time." Akoryt paused. "Belsior had to be cautious and careful. There were several guards in maroon carrying heavy rifles."

"They were actually carrying them? Ready to shoot?"

"Yes, sir. Belsior was getting tired. He was afraid his shields or his concealment might fail, and he didn't want to reveal himself. So he left when the messenger did. He just returned. He was as pale as a frog's underbelly. I sent him to the mess."

"Good and thank you. Did he see any other livery colors or other possible High Holders?"

"No, sir. There was one other messenger, who wore scarlet and black, but Belsior didn't hear him say anything."

"Scarlet and black? I've never seen those colors. Have you?"

"No, sir."

"Is there anything else I should know?"

"I don't think so."

"I'll need Belsior tomorrow, from about noon on, so don't have him do anything in the morning."

"Yes, sir." Akoryt raised his eyebrows.

"Don't say a word."

The younger maitre grinned. "I wouldn't think of it."

When Akoryt left, Alastar went to find Obsolym to see if he knew what High Holder might have livery of scarlet and black, but the older maitre had already left for the day. He was just entering the study when Lystara and Alyna appeared.

"How was your day, Lystara?"

"It was good, except we didn't get to practice imaging on the water. How long will we have to stay away from the river?"

"Until we can find and stop the men that are trying to shoot at young imagers." Alastar paused. "I have a question for you. I'm not angry, but I need to know something. Have you been practicing and using a concealment any of the times you've been at the imager factorage?"

"Is this important?"

"It could be."

Lystara sighed. "Most times. Just a little bit, though. If I disappeared for long, Tertia Linzya would get upset and start looking. I've been really quiet."

"I'm glad you're practicing, and you've obviously gotten very good . . . but I'm going to ask you not to do any more concealments in or around the factorage for the next month. There's a reason for that, but I can't tell you yet."

"Can I still practice concealments?"

"In other places, but not during instructionals, and not to eavesdrop on maitres . . . or other imagers."

"And if you do hear something you shouldn't, if you think it's important," added Alyna, "you're to tell one of us. If it's not, you're to keep it to yourself. You know what I think about gossip."

"Yes, Mother . . . Father."

At the slightest sound, Alastar turned and said, "That goes for you, too, Malyna."

The concealment vanished and Malyna stood just inside the study door. "I thought you couldn't see me."

"We couldn't," said Alastar. "That didn't mean I couldn't hear you."

"Oh . . ."

"That's why you have to be quiet, especially inside, if you don't want to be discovered."

Alyna looked to Alastar.

He nodded.

"I think it's time we left for home. It's been a long day."

And tomorrow will be even longer.

As Alyna and Alastar walked from the administration building, she asked, "Why did you make Lystara promise not to do concealments in the factorage? Because someone else might be?"

"Charlina told Akoryt that there's been even more of it. I didn't think about Malyna, but if you'd ask the same of her . . . ?"

"I can do that. She likes to be helpful."

Alastar smiled.

"I hate it when you smile like that." Then Alyna laughed.

So did Alastar.

20

Much, much later on Meredi evening, Alastar and Alyna sat on the porch, one of the few cool places, and one where finally there was enough of a breeze to keep the mosquitoes and moths from bothering them excessively.

"There's something on your mind . . ." she ventured quietly.

"Several things. I didn't have a chance to tell you. The other letter was from Voltyrn. He's urging me to choose a successor to Zhelan. Immediately. He didn't make it quite that obvious. Almost, but not quite. He must have written it even before he could have received any response to his letter about Zhelan's death."

"He wants to be Maitre."

"He wants it that badly, and that suggests I shouldn't choose him, but send someone from here." Alastar shook his head. "I haven't really even had time to think about it in the past few days."

"You haven't wanted to."

"You're right. It will be a thankless job for anyone from here."

"Bettaur would love it."

"He's too junior and not even a Maitre D'Structure . . . but you know that. It's still disturbing."

"What else?"

"Akoryt had Belsior scouting the Chateau D'Council today."

"You'd mentioned that you were thinking of that."

"He discovered there is a meeting tomorrow afternoon . . . and Meinyt is ill, and will not be attending, and there are guards with the new heavy rifles on duty at the chateau."

"Then they're about to act . . . fairly soon . . . and Meinyt's not ill, not from what you said about your meeting with him."

"Unless Cransyr found a way to poison him. I thought he was too honorable to get involved, and, apparently, I'm guessing, Cransyr felt the same way and took steps to keep him from being involved."

"Do you know that?" Alyna's words were low, with a tone between sadness and amusement.

"Of course not." Alastar's soft laugh was ironic. "Meinyt likely didn't realize how serious Cransyr was, and also didn't want to say anything until he was certain. That's often the problem with waiting until you're certain."

"That's why you're going to do something tomorrow."

"I didn't say anything about that."

"You didn't have to. Can I do anything?"

"Only if something goes wrong, and I don't return. Then you and Cyran are to destroy the chateau with the High Council—excepting Meinyt—in it. He likely won't be there anyway. Remove permanently any High Holder who objects. Explain to Factoria Kathila and Factorius Elthyrd that the High Holders were about to depose Rex Lorien, destroy the Collegium, and take total control of Solidar."

"I'd appreciate it if you'd take enough care so that such a bloody eventuality isn't necessary. Are your shields even up to what you plan?"

"I'm mostly planning on eavesdropping. They're certainly up to that. After that . . . even if nothing happens, things will get bloody."

"If so . . . I'd prefer the blood were on both our hands, and that our hands remain warm. So would Lystara and Malyna."

Alastar glanced up at Erion, the reddish moon that was nearly full. "That makes all of us, I think."

21

The first thing Alastar did upon reaching the administration building on Jeudi was to seek out Obsolym, who was dusting his table desk when Alastar appeared.

"Beloved Maitre, what obscure bit of information do you seek?"

"I don't know that it's obscure. I just don't know. Would you happen to know what High Holder might claim scarlet and black for his colors?"

"Scarlet and black . . . hmmm. Scarlet or red—that's common enough. Courage, breeding, blood . . . but black, the sinister side of family and nature, as a significant part of livery or a banner?" The old Maitre D'Structure shook his head. "Oh . . . there have been those who did. Green and black, at one time, those were the colors of the house of Ryntar, as I recall. And silver and black are Ryel's colors, but I can't think of another High Holder who uses black, or even scarlet and black." Obsolym laughed. "Then with fifteen hundred High Holders spread across Solidar, who could know all their colors? Some don't even claim colors. I know Calkoran doesn't. Neither did Guerdyn nor does Lhullyt . . ."

"If you happen to recall or come across that, I'd appreciate your letting me know."

"I probably won't, not anytime soon, but if I do . . ."

"Thank you." Alastar headed back to his study.

Akoryt and Cyran were waiting in the anteroom, talking with Dareyn and Maercyl. All four stopped as Alastar entered.

Dareyn picked up an envelope from the table desk and offered it to Alastar. "This just came from the High Council."

"Did the messenger say anything about a response?" Alastar took the envelope.

"No, sir."

"Thank you." After motioning for Akoryt and Cyran to follow him, Alastar walked into the study and to his desk, where he remained standing as he slit open the envelope and extracted the single sheet.

Absently, he noticed Akoryt glancing at the two water bottles set on the desk, bottles filled with dark lager. "Refreshments for later, if necessary."

He began to read.

Maitre Alastar—

In view of our shared concerns, the High Council would like to invite you to a meeting at the Chateau D'Council on Lundi, the sixteenth of Erntyn, at the first glass of the afternoon, in order that we might discuss the possibility of an amicable resolution of at least some of the differences of opinion about the meaning of certain sections of the Codex Legis.

We look forward to seeing you then, or if that time is not agreeable, to another time you might suggest.

Alastar nodded and passed the letter to Akoryt. "Read it, and then let Cyran see it."

"Yes, sir."

After reading the short missive, Akoryt passed it to Cyran, frowning as he did.

Cyran looked mildly puzzled when he returned the letter to Alastar. "That seems to suggest that it's all merely a mild disagreement."

"I'm certain that's exactly what Cransyr wants us to think. He's trying to keep us from acting, and that means we need to, possibly sooner than I ever intended." Alastar knew that was shading matters quite a bit, but he went on, "As you two may already have guessed, Belsior will be helping me infiltrate the High Council meeting this afternoon. While I expect to return, in the instance I do not, as I've told Maitre Alyna, you're to destroy the Chateau D'Council and remove all the High Councilors except Meinyt. You may also have to remove Commander Marryt and Subcommander Hehnsyn, who turns out to be a younger son of High Holder Cransyr. I trust those actions will not be necessary, but if something fatal occurs to me, those removals will be the minimum necessary to keep the High Holders in check."

Cyran swallowed. Akoryt merely nodded.

"You will take care, sir?" Cyran finally said.

"As much as I can. If I can discover more about which High Holders are those with control over what have to be private armies, we may be able to limit the damage." *And then again, defeating this so far subterranean revolt may require ever greater force than any of us would wish.*

"You could be there a very long time. . . ." Cyran pointed out.

"That's unlikely. I would doubt the meeting will take more than a glass, two at most." Alastar shrugged. "I could be wrong."

"You couldn't just invite yourself?"

"Then I'd learn nothing. We've already had too many young imagers shot, and we still have nothing on who did it." Cyran's question reminded Alastar exactly why Cyran being Maitre would not have been good for either the Collegium or Cyran himself. If necessary, Alyna could keep Cyran on task. *But you definitely don't want matters to end up that way.* Which meant he would need to be very, very careful. "Just have Belsior here at two quints before noon, with our mounts."

"Yes, sir."

Once the two left, Alastar walked to the window, where he glanced at the high hazy clouds, a possible indication that the day might be cooler that most of those of the previous week. He was debating whether he should also pay a visit to Elthyrd and Kathila when Dareyn appeared with a missive in hand.

"From Rex Lorien?"

"No, sir. From Factor Elthyrd."

Alastar took the envelope, and Dareyn immediately withdrew as Alastar walked back toward his desk before opening it and beginning to read.

Maitre Alastar—

After receiving your explanation about events which precipitated your actions at the ironworks of Factorius Vaschet and those which occurred during your visit, I thought it best to send a copy of your explanation to the other members of the council for their information before the council makes any decision on whether to pursue the matter further.

 You must realize that the personal sanctity of factor accounts is something of great concern, and that some factors regard those accounts as highly as those they employ, if not more so. At the same time, the council does not wish to see L'Excelsis become a battleground between thus-far-unknown forces and the Collegium. We trust that, before the Factors' Council deliberates the matter, the Collegium will be able to provide additional clarification of the situation without divulging whatever information may be in the ledgers you borrowed.

Alastar snorted. *In short, don't tell anyone what you've discovered about Vaschet's less than savory dealings with High Holders, but please bring all this to an end immediately.*

And don't let the High Holders take back all the privileges revoked by the first Rex Regis. And, oh, yes, do it all in the next few days so that we can get back to making silvers and golds.

For a moment, just a moment, Alastar wondered if it would be less trouble just to seek an agreement with the High Holders. *Except that would only prolong the inevitable and make it more bloody in the long run . . . and something that Lystara and Malyna would have to live with, if the Collegium could even survive under those circumstances.*

By the time Belsior arrived, Alastar was more than ready to leave the Collegium, and he was walking out toward his mount, carrying the water bottles, even before Belsior reined up outside the main entrance to the administration building. Alastar put the water bottles in the saddlebags, then mounted immediately and turned the gray gelding westward toward the Bridge of Desires.

"Maitre Cyran never said what you needed from me, sir."

"That's because I never told him," replied Alastar, adjusting his visor cap. "I'll explain as we ride. We're headed to the Chateau D'Council. You're going to watch and hold my mount, under a concealment, of course, while I make my way inside and observe what I can of the meeting that is supposed to take place. If all goes well, then I will return, and we will return to the Collegium knowing more about the conflict to come."

Belsior nodded, although a quizzical look flashed across his face.

"You wonder why I'm talking of conflict when all you've seen is a few imagers being shot? What you haven't seen is the head of the Factors' Council being shot down by a High Holder, hundreds of new heavy rifles passing into High Holder hands, anger and resentment resulting in quiet killings of young men, both factors and High Holders, an effort by the High Holders to remove all restraints on their actions and make them effectively equal to the Rex . . . and quite a few more matters which I'm not about to reveal at the moment."

"Might I ask why all this is happening now?"

"Because we've had two years of terrible harvests here in the middle of Solidar, and a number of High Holders are facing ruin, while the factors are largely prospering to the point that some are wealthier than High Holders. As a group, the factors are becoming more prosperous and the High Holders less so, and the High Council wants to put a stop to it . . . and they'll try to destroy the Collegium to do so, especially if we weigh in on the side of the factors . . . which, in the end, is the only way to preserve the Collegium. Rule by the High Holders would destroy Solidar in the end, just as happened with Antiago."

"Sir?"

"History, Belsior. Antiago was effectively ruled by the Autarch and the High Holders. They were called something else, but effectively they were High Holders. The Autarch made a few imagers his tool for controlling the High Holders, but the imagers were essentially slaves. By keeping any High Holder from getting too powerful, Antiago as a whole was weak and became easy prey for the first Rex Regis. Most of the Antiagon imagers died as a result."

"Oh . . ."

"History doesn't repeat itself exactly, but the patterns do, if they're allowed to." As he rode up the causeway and onto the bridge, Alastar studied the west bank of the river and the West River Road. "Make sure you're carrying full shields from here on."

"Yes, sir."

"We'll raise blurring shields once we pass your favorite bistro, and then ease into a full concealment when we near the chateau. . . ." Alastar went on to explain what he planned and what he required of Belsior.

After crossing the bridge, the two rode north on the West River Road. Several blocks north of the Bridge of Desires, they passed the bakery and the bistro.

"Blurring shields, now."

"Yes, sir."

The day was milder, and there was even a breeze out of the north, for which Alastar was grateful, even though he was still wearing his lightest grays. Little more than a quint later, the two crossed the Boulevard D'Ouest, avoiding several heavy wagons headed eastward toward the Nord Bridge. Alastar's gray gelding tossed his head once, as if he had smelled or heard something that displeased him, then settled down.

Alastar glanced toward the Chateau D'Council, a half mille ahead on the left. "Time for a full concealment." He drew his mount closer to that of Belsior and lowered his voice even more. "We'll rein up at the corner of the wall. From there I'll walk to the gates, under a concealment. Then I'll just follow whoever comes first inside. Later, when I leave, I might have to create a diversion. Wait a quint after that if I don't show up immediately. Getting out undetected might be a little trickier."

"Yes, sir," murmured the junior maitre.

Alastar could see the guards inside the gates, but neither even looked in the direction of the concealed imagers as he dismounted and handed the gray's reins to Belsior. Then he walked slowly and as quietly as possible beside the stone wall toward the gates, finally stopping some five yards from the gatepost.

Alastar had to wait more than a quint before a coach appeared, slowing in front of the tall, wrought-iron gates. As the driver, in pale blue livery, halted the coach, Alastar eased from beside the wall and walked to just behind the back wheels, thankful there was no footman at the rear, not that there usually was, but Alastar had worried that the footman's stand might be occupied by a guard.

"High Holder Staendyn . . ." announced the driver.

The two guards in maroon opened the gates, and Alastar kept close to the middle of the rear of the coach as it moved through and onto the stone-paved lane between the formal gardens. The pace was slow enough that Alastar could keep pace at a fast walk that slowed gradually to bring the coach to a halt under the covered portico. He moved around the wheels and to the side of the stone steps.

Four guards in maroon and carrying heavy rifles flanked the main entryway, but the same footman Alastar had seen earlier greeted the High Holder with a deep bow, then retreated to one side of the door as Staendyn descended from the coach.

Alastar stepped behind the hatchet-faced and angular High Holder in his pale blue doublet and matching breeches, with cream hose and boots, and followed Staendyn up the stone steps, across the portico, and past the footman into the circular high-ceilinged entry hall beyond the bronzed double doors.

Alastar could see the footman twitch, but the man said nothing as Alastar followed the High Holder, still trying to step lightly. Staendyn moved decisively down the corridor and took several steps into the receiving study before halting.

Alastar stopped as well, surveying the room. Only two sets of armchairs were set around a conference table that had replaced the usual low table, a clear indication that Meinyt was not expected.

Cransyr turned from where he stood by the window. "Greetings."

"Was this really necessary, Cransyr?"

"How could it not be, Staendyn? We are engaged in an enterprise, if you will, that will remake all Solidar."

"You think Alastar and the Collegium will stand by idly?"

"Not idly, but by the time they understand what is at stake, it will be too late. We're already ringing their little isle with hundreds of marksmen. That will totally isolate them. You've seen their reaction. Maitre Alastar is not the maitre he once was, and Cyran . . . well . . . he wishes to be liked all too well."

"I understand Alastar's wife is also powerful."

"She's only a woman."

Only a woman. Alastar reminded himself to relay that comment to Alyna, as he eased away from Staendyn, who had moved toward the conference table. Both men turned as a third figure, dressed in dark blue, entered the receiving study, and Alastar took the opportunity to position himself in the inside corner of the room between two bookcases, listening intently.

"Olefsyrt . . ." offered Cransyr.

"Cransyr. I take it that Meinyt won't be here."

"It's best for his health that he's not."

"Hah . . . after I heard he met with Maitre Alastar, it's probably for the best."

"Are your forces ready?"

"They're positioned within an easy glass of Lorien. Our . . . friend has been most cooperative."

"As if he had much—" began Staendyn, but broke off as Souven entered the study.

"We might as well be seated," announced Cransyr smoothly.

The footman quietly closed the study door as the four High Holders settled around the table.

"To begin with," said Cransyr, "do any of you know about any signs that anyone not involved knows anything about our . . . efforts?"

"Paellyt has been asking when the High Council is going to do something to put the factors in their place," said Olefsyrt. "He's been most insistent."

"What did you tell him?"

"That we needed to wait until Lorien denied all the legal petitions before deciding on a course of action. He already knew that Lenglan's petition had been dismissed."

"Just tell him that he'll be among the first to know when the High Council decides to consider the matter," replied Cransyr. "Just keep him quiet for a while. The last thing we need is a hothead like Paellyt getting the Collegium stirred up. It's much better that they remain turtlelike on Imagisle."

"Are the letters to all the High Holders of influence ready to go?" asked Staendyn.

Cransyr gestured to the table in the corner opposite the one where Alastar stood within his concealment. "Ready to dispatch. There's a stack for each of you."

Alastar judged that here were close to a hundred envelopes there.

"They outline—" began Souven.

"All our grievances against that idiot Lorien, and against the meddling of the Collegium, and the reasons for our actions, just as you insisted." Cransyr's words were both mellifluous and smoothly delivered.

"What about the Army High Command?"

"Just as I explained. High Holder Caervyn's assistance, direct and in-direct, and that of his sister, will prove helpful in the last stages of our efforts to restore High Holders to their rightful position, as will that of our other ally, who while unable to join us physically at the moment, for reasons we all understand, is more than eager to accept a less active role in governing than his soon-to-be predecessor."

As the last section of the puzzle clicked into place, Alastar just stood there, stunned, yet not exactly surprised.

The question in his mind was not what to do, but how exactly to accomplish it . . . and how to do so in a way that left the cause and who-ever was behind it . . . *ambiguous.*

"What about the Collegium?"

"That, too, will take care of itself, as we planned," declared Cransyr.

"But . . ." began Souven.

"Enough. We all have work to do."

Staendyn nodded, and began to stand.

Alastar realized he was almost out of time. With that, he imaged a block of wood into Souven's heart, followed by blocks into the hearts of Cransyr, Olefsyrt, and Staendyn. He might have learned more by waiting, but he likely never again would have had the opportunity to take out all the top conspirators at once. *And who knows how much damage will be done even now?*

Still holding a concealment, he eased to the door, then gently opened it and peered out. The footman stood in the archway between the en-try hall and the corridor, but because the door opened inward, he had apparently not noticed. Alastar eased out into the corridor, trying to close the door silently, but there was still a slight click.

The noise was loud enough that the footman turned and began to walk toward the study, slowing as he saw the door was closed. Alastar moved quietly toward the main entry, staying on the far side of the corridor from the footman. The main door was closed.

Alastar paused. Any effort to open the door would definitely alert the footman, if not others in the chateau. Still . . .

He readied himself, then moved to the door, opening it swiftly, but as quietly as he could. There was only a low grinding, barely audible, but the footman turned and started toward the door.

Alastar stepped out onto the portico, and immediately imaged his best imitation of an oversized cannon shell into the receiving study—with a white-hot iron splinter going into the charge. As he did, he moved out far enough that he was beyond the four armed guards before flattening himself on the stone tiles.

Crummmptttt!

After a moment, Alastar looked around. The armed guards stood frozen, then rushed toward the entry. Avoiding them, Alastar climbed to his feet, moving toward the steps down to the stone lane, avoiding the three coaches lined up under the covered roof. His eyes went to the study windows, all of which had blown out, along with a substantial amount of masonry. Surprisingly, at least to Alastar, the stories above the study did not seem to be that damaged.

Which means secondary measures are necessary.

Alastar imaged a flaming ball of oil into the center of the study, then hurried down the lane as flames burst from the shattered windows. His head throbbed, painfully, and all the soreness that he thought had left his muscles returned, uncomfortably, but not agonizingly, most likely from the effort of imaging from behind shields and a concealment.

The gate guards gaped, then rushed toward the chateau.

Alastar slowed to a fast walk, but kept moving. He had to lift the gate bolt himself and shove the gate open enough to squeeze out, but no one was even looking in his direction. Black and gray smoke continued to billow out of the study windows, and flames were also shooting up the front of the chateau.

He dropped the concealment as he neared the corner of the wall.

"Sir . . . ?"

"It's me." Alastar replaced the concealment and continued onward until he almost bumped into Belsior's mount. "Expand your concealment a bit."

Belsior did, and Alastar took the gelding's reins and mounted, then turned in the saddle and extracted one of the water bottles. "We need to get back to the Collegium. Things are even worse than we thought. There may already be a hundred or more sharpshooters around Imagisle. If not, there likely soon will be. That's just the beginning." He turned the gelding to head back south along the West River Road.

"What happened here, sir?"

"It looks to me like someone planted a cannon shell in the Chateau D'Council. Doesn't it look that way to you?"

"Ah . . . yes, sir." After a moment, Belsior spoke again. "If four of the five councilors were there, won't that . . . stop matters?"

"You'd think that it would, but, in this case, there are at least three other High Holders involved, and we have no idea where they are." *Not to mention whatever Marryt and Hehnsyn are already doing.* "We'd best maintain at least blurring shields from here until we near the bistro north of the Bridge of Desires. Then we'll have to resume full concealments."

"Yes, sir."

"How are you holding up?"

"A blur concealment for a while will help, sir."

"Good." Alastar glanced back. There was no pursuit, not that he expected any, but relying on expectations wasn't the way to survive anything chancy. He uncorked the water bottle and took a swallow. Warm or not, the dark lager was welcome, and he kept drinking, intermittently, until they neared the Nord Bridge and the Boulevard D'Ouest, when he replaced the water bottle in the saddlebag.

"From here on," Alastar told Belsior, "keep your eyes open for sharpshooters, in any position that might bear on Imagisle. Or anything that looks in the slightest fashion out of the ordinary." That was easy enough to say, but Alastar wasn't certain he'd noted the terrain and buildings on the west bank of the Aluse intently enough to recognize minor discrepancies.

He needn't have worried. Even from north of Belsior's "favorite bistro" on the West River Road, Alastar had no trouble making out the revetments flanking the causeways to the Bridge of Desires and the south bridge—or the angled iron shields that topped them, with slots through which heavy rifles could be fired. He judged that there were

two companies in sight, one at each west bridge, and most likely another at the east bridge.

Just as obviously, there were no horses and riders, no carriages, and
no wagons on the West River Road south of the bistro and neighboring
bakery.

"Why are they doing that?" asked Belsior.

"I'd guess the idea is simply to keep imagers on Imagisle." Alastar
wasn't totally guessing, not with what he had heard at the Chateau
D'Council. "The question is what to do with them."

"They've been shooting at imagers," said Belsior.

"That's true. But they've been ordered to shoot at imagers. The High
Holders who suffered the unfortunate consequence of having a cannon
shell explode before them gave that order. Besides, what happens if we
kill all of these men when most of Solidar will consider them to only be
doing their duty? Does that help the Collegium?"

"Ah . . . probably not." Belsior paused, then asked, "But do most
people care?"

Alastar laughed. "Good point. Probably not, but it's better not to get
in the habit of unnecessary killing. Why don't we at least start by imaging lots and lots of fine red pepper into the revetments around the Bridge
of Desires? Once we get closer, I'll take the revetments on the north side,
and you do the ones on the south side."

"Yes, sir."

The two continued riding south until they were less than fifty yards
from the end of the north revetment, when Alastar said, "This is close
enough." He reined up. "Ready to image pepper?"

"Right now?"

"Now." As he spoke, Alastar image-flooded the fifty- to seventy-yard
length of the revetment with a mist of red pepper so thick it looked like
a red fog. As he studied the results, another thought struck him, something that he should have realized earlier—to make all those iron shields
had required a great deal of advance planning.

A very great deal.

As he watched the revetment, he also realized that considering the
implications of that would have to wait. There had to be close to fifty
men in the revetment on the north side of the short road leading from
the West River Road to the causeway, and perhaps twenty crawled out,
keeping low and trying to make it to and beyond the West River Road

without drawing iron darts from the imager sentries. Most carried their weapons.

Alastar had to say that he was both impressed and concerned— impressed by the ability of so many men to remain confined with that much red pepper and concerned that there had been no response from Imagisle. He glanced to the revetment on the south side. Only about ten men were fleeing, again with weapons. He imaged again, this time a myriad of tiny white-hot iron needles—into both revetments.

More men began leaving the revetments when a tall blond man stood up, and shouted, "Hold your ground! Pepper and needles won't kill you, but I will!"

Alastar imaged, regretfully, flaming oil around and onto the man, who was likely the equivalent of an undercaptain, who immediately sprinted toward the river. Alastar put an iron dart through his skull.

At that, the remainder of the armed shooters withdrew, in various degrees of order or disorder.

"Now, we'll see about the south bridge revetments."

"Ah . . . yes, sir."

Alastar could almost hear the queasiness behind Belsior's words. "In these circumstances, one graphic and grisly death is much to be preferred to a hundred neat killings. We can hope the shooters in the southern revetments are more amenable to dispersal."

Alastar turned the gray gelding southward. Belsior followed, then drew up beside Alastar without speaking.

Not quite a half mille farther south, Alastar reined up at the eastern edge of the road. "This should do. Ready?"

"Yes, sir."

While the red pepper fog was not sufficient to clear the revetments, the white-hot iron needles were. As the shooters retreated, however, Alastar image-projected his voice across the retreating shooters. "We were merciful. This time. If you return and attempt to shoot at Imagisle, each of you will die!"

Once the last of the brown-clad riflemen had departed, Alastar dropped the concealment, but not his shields, and urged the gelding onto the causeway. By the time he and Belsior crossed the south bridge and reached the end of the causeway on Imagisle, Alyna, Shaelyt, and Tiranya were waiting for them.

"We need an immediate meeting of the senior maitres," Alastar declared before turning to Belsior. "For the moment, until we can send some junior maitres, you have the defense of the south bridge. It's not likely you'll see anything soon, but who knows, the way things have developed. Let Shaelyt and Tiranya have your mount, and Alyna will ride double with me. It's not that far."

Belsior immediately dismounted, while Alastar helped Alyna up to ride behind him, not that she needed much assistance. In moments, the gelding was at a fast walk toward the administration building.

"What was the reason for allowing those shooters to set up to block the bridges, not that it hurt that much in the end—although we'll have to do something about those on the East Bridge. I assume they've got people there, too."

"They do. Cyran thought we should wait before doing anything, since they weren't shooting at anyone," said Alyna. "I agreed that we should wait, but no longer than fourth glass."

"Maybe I should deal with the East Bridge before—"

"*We* should deal with the East Bridge." Alyna turned in the saddle. "Tiranya, Shaelyt, get the others together for a senior maitres' meeting. Akoryt's at the Bridge of Desires. We'll go to the East Bridge."

When Alyna and Alastar were somewhat farther from Tiranya and Shaelyt, she demanded, "Now . . . what happened at the Chateau D'Council?"

"A cannon shell apparently exploded in Cransyr's receiving study . . ." Alastar gave Alyna a brief summary of what he'd heard and done.

When he finished, she said quietly, "Then there's more, much more, about to occur."

"Lorien and his family are in danger. That's for certain. But we need to disperse the shooters on the East Bridge quickly and then meet—a short meeting. I'd thought about just taking some maitres to the Chateau D'Rex immediately, but . . . well . . . I needed to think about it, and to make sure all the senior maitres understand what's involved. But it has to be quick."

"Lorien doesn't deserve saving."

"No, but Solidar deserves not having a war of succession, especially given who wants to succeed him."

"I'll grant that." Alyna's laugh was short and acerbic. "Ryel has to be behind this."

"I'd judge so, but we haven't seen any sign of that."

"Would we?"

Alastar didn't bother answering the question as he reined up well back from the East Bridge.

Cyran hurried toward Alyna and Alastar as they dismounted from the gelding. Standing closer to the bridge were three other imagers, including Taurek and Khaelis, and another man that it took Alastar a moment to recognize—Julyan. "They moved in iron shields all across the end of the bridge."

"Have they shot at anyone?"

"They've hit my shields twice. I tried to suggest that they should leave or face the consequences. I didn't want to do more until I knew how you had fared with the High Council." The Maitre D'Esprit raised his eyebrows.

"The meeting had an explosive conclusion. Something like cannon shell hit the study where they were meeting, just after they'd concluded an agreement to marginalize the Collegium and replace Lorien. Now . . . let's remove these annoyances."

"You're not going to—"

"I hope not." Alastar walked to the end of the causeway. Immediately, he felt the impact of a bullet on his shields . . . and it was painful. *Get this over.* He looked to Alyna, beside him. "Fine red pepper as thick as fog."

She nodded, and the reddish mist seethed along the line of iron at the east end of the bridge. As had been the case on the western bridges, a minority of the shooters behind the shields staggered back. "White-hot iron needles, hundreds of them."

More shooters retreated.

"Not enough," said Alyna, concentrating.

Abruptly, a narrow pillar of oil-fueled fire flared directly behind the middle of the iron wall across the east end of the bridge, and a curdling scream followed.

Alastar image-projected his voice. "The rest of you have a count of ten to leave."

More shooters departed, but not nearly enough.

"You're not imagining more right now. I'll do it." Alyna's voice was hard.

Given how he felt at the moment, Alastar let her image two more pillars of flame. Screams followed.

The remaining shooters sprinted away from the iron wall.

Alastar turned to Cyran. "Do you have any other maitres besides the three?"

"Julyan and Taurek . . . and Khaelis. He was the only other senior I could find quickly."

"Julyan and Taurek will have to keep watch. They can use iron darts if anyone's stupid to try to attack. I'm gathering all the senior maitres for a short meeting."

"Yes, sir." Cyran's eyes drifted from Alastar to Alyna, and then back to the greasy black smoke still rising from where the pillars of fire had been.

Alastar walked over to Julyan, who was slender, if muscular, with copper-red hair and green eyes, unlike the broad-shouldered and burly Taurek.

"Sir?"

"Did any shots hit your shields?"

"Just two, sir."

"Did the impacts hurt? Are you having any trouble with your shields?"

"No, sir. Well . . . they were like a shove, but they didn't hurt. I was more concerned about keeping the students back. Some of the riflemen were shooting everywhere." Julyan didn't quite meet Alastar's eyes.

"Did you get him with a dart?"

"Oh, no, sir. Maitre Cyran said we weren't to hurt them. I imaged away parts of the rifles of two of them. They mostly stayed behind those big shield after that."

Alastar refrained from grinning, although it was hard, given the twinkle in Julyan's eyes. "Good thought. Very good thought." He motioned Taurek over to join them. "You two will need to guard the East Bridge for a time. Don't let anyone you don't know personally cross. Try not to kill anyone—unless they do something foolish and try to shoot you or anyone else."

"Yes, sir."

"Good."

With a smile, Alastar turned and walked back to rejoin Alyna.

Less than a quint later, and after having had some hard bread and lager, Alastar stood at the head of the table in the conference room.

"It has been an interesting day. . . ." After a sardonic grin, he swiftly outlined what the High Council had planned and revealed, then concluded, "When it was clear the meeting was ending, I slipped out. I had just reached the main entry when what appeared to be a cannon shell shattered the study windows. The ensuing fire spread quickly. Under the circumstances, Belsior and I did not choose to remain, especially given what I had learned. You all know what happened here."

"How could they not have known what an imager could do?" asked Khaelis.

"What happened was thirteen years ago," said Alyna dryly. "What did anyone who survived actually see? There was an explosion in the Anomen D'Rex, a short battle along the west bank of the Aluse, in which thousands of rankers no factor or High Holder knew or cared about, and some senior officers and a few High Holders died. We cleaned up most of it in days. There were no lasting scars, and while the names changed, and tariffs went up, everything stayed mostly the same. It didn't help that we cleaned it up too soon."

"None of the present High Council saw any of that," added Alastar. "People tend to forget or minimize what they haven't seen in person. That's likely why peace only lasts so long. Now, I need a small group to accompany me to the Chateau D'Rex. Cyran, I'll need your imaging strength, and Arion, Khaelis, Shaelyt, and Taryn. That should be sufficient for now. Maitre Alyna will be in charge here until we return. It's possible some of the army might attack; it's equally possible that nothing more will happen here. Any questions?"

"Might I ask—" began Obsolym.

"Whatever it takes to keep our rightful and not-terribly-perceptive rex upon his throne," replied Alastar. *Though the Nameless knows it's a throne he scarcely deserves.* He stood. "Anything else?"

There wasn't.

At roughly two quints after fourth glass, Alastar and his group of senior maitres rode from the Boulevard D'Rex Ryen onto the ring road . . . and found the stretch between them and the Chateau D'Rex deserted. Alastar glanced back, his eyes lingering briefly on the saddlebags that contained the remaining water bottle of dark lager, then to the northern stretch of the ring road before centering on the chateau.

"Full concealment and shields!" Alastar ordered, even though all of the five other maitres should have been holding shields already. "Keep the concealment far enough out, and stay close enough that you can see me." He turned the gelding toward the lane that led up to the Chateau D'Rex.

Before he had ridden even twenty yards south on the ring road, he could see more of the iron wall-shields, similar, if not identical, to those used in the attempt to blockade Imagisle. There weren't that many more than at Imagisle, perhaps half a score at most, and they were set at intervals around the Chateau D'Rex.

That makes no sense at all. Why were perhaps two companies, three at most, besieging the chateau? *Because they're there to keep Lorien from escaping until reinforcements arrive?*

"We need to rout those shooters immediately," Alastar declared, "before any reinforcements arrive. We'll circle behind them and attack."

"Red pepper, sir?" asked Cyran.

"Just to get them more out in the open. Then use iron darts or anything else that will kill them."

Cyran's mouth opened. "We'll already be behind them."

"They're attacking the ruler of Solidar. Their lives are forfeit anyway. Since it's likely they'd run off and join the other rebels, I really don't want to fight them twice. Do you? Or do you want them to sneak back to Imagisle and shoot more unsuspecting junior imagers?"

"No, sir."

"We'll use red pepper fog to get them out from behind the shields, then iron darts," ordered Alastar, raising his voice, "but not until we're closer. Remember, we don't want to fight them twice."

He kept riding, studying the position of the iron shields as they neared the two lanes that led up to the chateau. "Cyran, you, Arion, and Taryn, take out the attackers around the rear of the chateau. Head up the lane to the stables. Khaelis, Shaelyt, you two join up with me. We'll take the ring road behind those in front and strike from the rear."

As they rode nearer to the chateau, and then past the stone way that led up the gentle slope to the main entry, Alastar continued to survey the position of the attackers, spread across the lawn between the entry drive and the formal gardens that extended across the southern section of grounds encircled by the ring road. He also realized that he had not heard a single shot being fired. Just as he had observed that, several shots punctuated the comparative silence. He glanced toward the chateau, but couldn't see whoever had been the target. Then a chateau guard looked out the main entry, and more shots peppered the stonework, but the guard retreated, apparently untouched, and closed the door.

When Alastar reached the foot of the ring road, he turned the gelding through the stone posts and onto the path that split the gardens, motioning for Khaelis to move to his left and Shaelyt to his right. "When we reach the end of the gardens, we'll rein up and attack. First with a thick red pepper fog, and then with iron darts. Shaelyt . . . you take the two shields and the attackers on the right. Khaelis, you take the two on the left. I'll get the others."

"Yes, sir."

Despite the crunching of hooves on the gravel of the path, when Alastar reined up just outside the gateposts at the north end of the gardens, flanked by Shaelyt and Khaelis, none of the shooters stretched out behind the iron shields, rifles half ready, even turned, although they would have seen nothing.

"Image pepper fog," ordered Alastar.

In moments, swathes of reddish fog filled the space behind the shields, and shooters began to stagger upright, most of them retreating away from the chateau and toward the imagers.

"Iron darts!"

As Alastar concentrated on taking out shooter after shooter, for an instant, he felt almost guilty, then shook his head. None of the shooters had felt guilty in killing innocent students, and they were now attacking the Chateau D'Rex.

"Imagers!"

"Where are they?"

"Behind us somewhere . . ."

Several of the attackers sprinted away from the gardens and toward the drive. Alastar's imaged iron darts brought them down, one after another. He could see several shooters behind the shields on his left lifting rifles and beginning to shoot in the direction of the imagers.

"Khaelis! Take out those shooters!"

One of the shooters firing toward the imagers collapsed, then another.

Alastar kept imaging.

In less than a quint, there were only bodies sprawled on the lawn around the iron wall-shields. Alastar doubted that even a handful of the company of snipers had survived, although he had seen one man in the dark brown uniforms dart into an alley to the west before he could react.

"Drop the concealment. Hold your shields," Alastar commanded. His head throbbed so much he could barely keep his voice level. "Forward at a walk." He was concerned that some of the shooters might have crept behind the iron shields on the chateau side, but there was no movement as the three advanced.

"Sir . . . maybe I'm missing something," began Khaelis in a low voice, "but you went to some lengths not to kill the shooters who were attacking Imagisle . . ."

"And I had you kill every one that we could here?" replied Alastar. "Who were they attacking here?"

"The rex."

"Exactly." At the confused look on Khaelis's face, Alastar went on. "The Collegium is not part of the government of Solidar. It's barely mentioned in the Codex Legis, and largely only to allow the maitre to adopt laws for the Collegium that cannot be less strict than the laws promulgated by the rex, but may be more so. We can defend ourselves, but wholesale slaughter would not set well. Had we known that the rex was under attack, that might have been a different question. With the rex, however, there's no question. The rex is the ruler and head of state. An attack against Imagisle constitutes assault, murder, and various other offenses. An attack against the rex is treason and rebellion, and any response to those is largely justified." Alastar was overstating the situation somewhat, but he doubted that anyone, least of all Lorien, was going to call him on the finer points. "Since they have committed rebellion, we no longer have to be so circumspect."

When the three imagers reached the paved area at the bottom of the steps up to the main entry, a voice called from above.

"Is that you, Maitre Alastar?"

"Is that you, Churwyl?"

"Yes, sir."

"Good. You can come down here once Maitre Cyran and the others arrive."

"Ah . . . sir?"

"We've flushed out the shooters in the front, and Maitre Cyran is working on those on the north side of the chateau." Alastar turned when he saw Cyran, Arion, and Taryn appear as if from nowhere, clearly the result of their having dropped their concealments.

He waited until Cyran reined up a yard or so away.

"We got rid of them." Cyran offered an expression of distaste.

"They would have shot anyone they could have," replied Alastar, "just the way they did with our young imagers. How many were there?"

"Eighty or so."

Alastar nodded. "Not quite a company back there, perhaps two in all. How many escaped?"

"Maybe a handful. They made it to the stables, and then went out the west door and used the wall on that side for cover. Arion got one or two when they looked up, but I'm fairly certain a few escaped." Cyran frowned. "How did they think that they were going to take the chateau with a few companies?"

"I don't think they did. I have a very uneasy feeling that they expected reinforcements . . . and that those reinforcements still might be on the way."

"That makes more sense," agreed Cyran.

"I need to talk to Lorien and let him know what has happened. Keep everyone here and ready. If those reinforcements arrive, do as much damage as you can, until I get back. If you need to, withdraw into the chateau."

"Yes, sir."

Alastar didn't miss the hint of resignation in Cyran's voice, but he turned toward the chateau. "Guard Captain Churwyl . . . you can join us now."

After several moments, one of the heavy brass-clad doors at the main entry opened, and the guard captain appeared, then hurried down the steps. He stopped two steps above the pavement, so that he was close to eye-level with Alastar. "You got them all?"

"About a handful escaped. Most didn't. When did they surround the chateau?"

"Right around noon. These wagons appeared. Men in brown started carrying those iron shields into position. Other men in brown started shooting at the guards on the steps here. In less than a quint, they had the shields set up and they were settled in behind them. We did get a messenger off to Army High Command, but . . . you can see . . . no one came."

"If troopers had come, they might not have been the ones you expected." Alastar's smile was cool. "I need to see the rex. I assume he's unharmed?"

"Yes, sir. He's . . . unharmed."

And doubtless furious. "Then we should tell him what happened." Alastar dismounted and handed the gelding's reins to Shaelyt, then looked to Cyran. "I'll be as quick as I can be." Turning back to Churwyl, he said, "Lead the way, Guard Captain."

"Yes, sir."

Alastar followed Churwyl up the steps and into the chateau, keeping his shields fully up, if close to his body. That took somewhat less effort. When he crossed from the top of the grand staircase to the north corridor that held Lorien's study, he thought he caught a glimpse of Chelia in the half-open door at the end of the corridor.

Churwyl reached the door and immediately announced, "The imagers destroyed the attackers, sir."

"I saw that! Tell me something I don't know!" Lorien's voice was so loud Alastar had no trouble at all hearing it even through the heavy wood of the closed door.

"Maitre Alastar is here to see you."

Alastar opened the door and strode into the study, leaving Churwyl to close it behind him.

Lorien stood by the north window, glaring at Alastar. "It took you long enough! Where's the sow-begotten army?"

"I don't recall your sending for us," Alastar replied dryly. "We came because we thought there might be trouble. That was after the High Council—except Meinyt—declared their support for your successor. It was also after some three hundred armed riflemen besieged Imagisle behind iron shields like those surrounding the chateau. It did take us a while to deal with those matters."

"Deal with? You'd better not have come up with some mealy-mouthed agreement—"

"Something like a cannon shell hit the receiving study of the Chateau D'Council just as the meeting formalizing their conspiracy to overthrow you, destroy the Collegium, and suppress the factors was coming to an end. None of the four conspirators survived. Meinyt, I suspect, is still under High Holder guard. At least several other conspirators—including Caervyn—were not at the meeting, and it's likely that some of the army was part of the revolt, but we haven't had time to find that out."

"Why not?"

"Because we were dealing with the High Council, an attack on Imagisle, and making certain you and your family were safe. That is a fair amount for one afternoon."

"Who else besides Caervyn?"

"Most likely his son. Commander Marryt is Wilkorn's chief of staff. And since Cransyr's son was instrumental in that business with the rifles . . ." Alastar wasn't certain how much more he really wanted to say at the moment, especially since anything else would have been speculation. "As for others, that may take a day or two to discover."

"It's treason. That's what it is, and every last one of them should be drawn and quartered . . . or burned alive, if not both."

Alastar did not comment on the physical impossibility of doing both. Nor was he about to mention the fact that Caervyn's daughter was married to Ryentar. Even mentioning that was likely to send Lorien into a rage.

"Did you let any of the bastards outside escape?"

"We killed almost all of them. Three or four might have escaped."

"You should have gotten them all." Lorien paused. "Still . . . I have to admit, with over a hundred of them out there, only letting four escape likely wasn't bad."

"No . . . not with only six imagers on the spur of the moment."

Behind Alastar the study door opened, and Taryn hurried through, an envelope in hand. "Maitre, sir," said Taryn, ignoring the red-face Lorien, "this is an urgent message from Marshal Wilkorn. Maitre Dylert brought it. He and a company from the Army High Command just arrived. The army had a rebellion, too."

As Lorien gaped, and Taryn slipped out of the study, Alastar quickly opened the message and began to read.

Maitre Alastar—

I regret to inform you that two battalions have rebelled against my command and that of Rex Lorien. One battalion is now apparently under the command of Subcommander Hehnsyn and the other under Commander Marryt. Both departed High Command early this afternoon after a series of explosions in numerous buildings across the base. I regret my tardiness in reporting these developments, but the collapse of part of the main headquarters building and other damages effectively imprisoned me and severely injured Vice Marshal Vaelln. Sea Marshal Tynan is, of course, in Solis.

In the course of his departure, Subcommander Hehnsyn also removed close to 1,000 of the spare heavy rifles and a considerable amount of ammunition. Both battalions marched south. Scouts report that they appear to be continuing along the river road in the direction of Caluse.

Caluse? As soon as he thought the question, Alastar was afraid he knew the answer, but he wasn't about to say anything until he had confirmation from Wilkorn.

Following our discussion this past Mardi, Vice Marshal Vaelln and I began a thorough review of procurements and transfers of field officers over the past year and a half. It appears that the majority of field grade officers and company commanders in the two battalions are either junior sons of or otherwise related to various High Holders. I would not have considered the matter earlier, but it appears the fact that Commander Aestyn is the second son of High Holder Breussyrd may also bear on the gravity of the situation.

Aestyn—the commander who requisitioned a thousand more rifles—and who is in command of the post at Ferravyl? The more Alastar was discovering, the less he liked the picture that information was painting.

The remaining two battalions here at headquarters remain completely loyal, and we stand ready to support the rex in any fashion that we can. I trust you will convey this to him, since I felt using your services might be more reliable.

When he finished reading, Alastar handed the sheet to Lorien.

The rex read through it, his face seemingly flushing more with each word. "This . . . it's outrageous! How could they . . . ?"

"You're the one who ordered Wilkorn not to replace Hehnsyn . . . as I recall," said Alastar icily.

Lorien glared again, but did not speak.

"You're fortunate," Alastar said calmly. "If that cannon shell had not exploded at the Chateau D'Council, I expect that both those battalions would have arrived here to reinforce those shooters. That was likely the original plan."

"Why are they heading to Caluse?"

"To join up with the regiment commanded by Aestyn at Ferravyl and the other rebels, likely already on the way from Ferravyl . . . and to make use of all those stolen rifles . . . and the thousand others Aestyn requisitioned earlier this year, supposedly for maintenance purposes. If I'm counting correctly, the rebels are backed by a considerable number of High Holders and have no less than three thousand trained troopers armed with heavy rifles and heavy rifles enough to equip another two thousand men."

"I told you that the High Holders were nothing but trouble," declared Lorien.

"And I agreed with you, and suggested that you not give into them."

"What good did that do?"

"It may have hurried their plans and resulted in the death of four of the chief conspirators, among other things."

"That's not enough."

"It's better than their being able to cause more trouble," Alastar pointed out.

"If you don't have anything else to add, I've had enough trials for today."

Alastar didn't argue, but inclined his head, then turned and left the study.

When Alastar stepped out through the main entry of the chateau, a Solidaran officer stepped forward and inclined his head. "Maitre Alastar . . . Major Luerryn. We've deployed two companies to protect the rex and the chateau. Marshal Wilkorn sends his apologies for not being here personally, but he suffered a broken arm and some formidable bruises in the explosions."

"I'm very glad you're here, Major. The marshal's letter indicated that the rebel battalions were headed south. Is that still the case?"

"We believe so. We've posted scouts well south of L'Excelsis on the West River Road that leads to Caluse to alert us in the event that changes."

"I appreciate that. I'm certain that Rex Lorien will as well."

"Is there anything else you'd suggest, sir?"

"Not at the moment. Now that you and your men are here, we'll be returning to Imagisle. If you need assistance of the kind we can provide, don't hesitate to send a messenger."

"Thank you, sir."

When Alastar reached the bottom of the steps and then mounted, Cyran looked at him inquisitively.

"We're heading back to see what else has happened." *And what else you've overlooked.* There had to be aspects of what happened that Alastar didn't know or had overlooked because even two regiments of rebels weren't enough to overthrow Lorien, and whoever was behind the rebellion had to have known that. Alastar also had the sinking feeling that he might just have played into their hands by killing the four councilors.

How could you have known? Because it was too obvious? Too easy?

He turned the gelding eastward and started down the stone drive toward the ring road, half-dreading what might be waiting for him at the Collegium.

When Alastar finally reined up outside the administration building on Jeudi afternoon, it was already two quints past fifth glass, and he found Alyna striding out to meet him even before he began to dismount.

"Are you all right?" she asked immediately.

"I'm fine. A bit sore." *And that's an understatement.* Alastar wouldn't have been as sharp as he was, he suspected, if he hadn't drunk the entire second water bottle of dark lager on the way back from the chateau.

She studied him intently. "You're stiff. I can see that, but your eyes aren't pink. That's good."

"I was good. I managed to drink my lager. What about you?"

"No more attacks since we routed the riflemen in midafternoon."

"Good." Alastar turned to Cyran. "Since there haven't been any more attacks here, have everyone ride to the stables, and then return here for a brief meeting. Oh, and gather as many senior maitres as you can find."

"Yes, sir."

"Ah . . . would you mind taking the gelding and have the ostlers unsaddle and groom him."

Cyran laughed. "I think we can manage that."

"Thank you." Alastar handed over the reins, then turned back to Alyna. "We might as well walk to the conference room."

"We can. Now . . . what happened at the chateau?"

"Not as much as could have . . ." From there Alastar gave her a brief account of all that had happened, as well as what he had learned from Wilkorn's message and from Major Luerryn, ending up with, "All that suggests an effort well planned by a High Holder not on the High Council."

"By someone who at least half-expected the possibility of you removing the High Council," replied Alyna. "That means they've thought this through. They may even have wanted the council removed because that would leave the High Holders leaderless . . . and willing to follow whoever was ready to lead."

"Which means I've been set up." *Again.*

"Removing Cransyr and that lot wasn't the worst thing that could have happened to Solidar," commented Alyna dryly as they walked toward the administration building.

"No . . . but it suggests that our real problems may be just beginning."

"There's another aspect to that," Alyna said slowly. "Bettaur is missing. So is Ashkyr."

Alastar just raised his eyebrows. He wasn't totally surprised, not the way matters had revealed themselves over the past few days. *But Bettaur? Right now?* "Are you certain he left? That something didn't happen to him?"

"Two horses and riding gear are missing."

"Why would he go now?"

"It has to have something to do with this revolt. It's the only thing that makes sense."

"When do you think he left?" Alastar opened the door for Alyna.

"Sometime soon after you did. Petros noticed the extra mounts were missing, and he came and asked how many imagers were with you. It took about a glass to discover who wasn't accounted for."

"You think his asking to be transferred to Westisle was just a blind of some sort?"

"It could be . . ."

"Have you talked to Linzya?"

"Only briefly. I thought it might be better if we both did. She didn't know that he was gone until I told her."

"After the meeting, then." Alastar turned and walked to the table desk in the alcove off the entry foyer where the duty maitre or the secondus assisting him was always posted after fifth glass. He recognized Davour. "Where's Maitre Chervyt?"

"He's eating, sir. He said he'd be back in less than a quint."

"When he gets back, I'll need you to find Tertia Linzya. Maitre Alyna and I would like a few words with her in my study around sixth glass."

"Yes, sir."

"Thank you."

Alastar and Alyna continued on, walking down the corridor and then into the anteroom and on into Alastar's study, where he took off his visor cap and set it on the corner of his desk. "How are the girls?"

"They're fine. They're at the house." Alyna tilted her head. "Do you think that Breussyrd or Caervyn were the ones who masterminded the revolt?"

"I haven't met either, so all I can say is they're certainly a part of it.

I'd wager there are others, including Ryel, most likely." Alastar had no ideas about who anyone else might be, but he had the feeling that there were indeed others. "We can wait in the conference room." Leaving his cap on the desk, he walked to the door from his study, opening it for Alyna, and then following her into the chamber and standing beside the chair at the head of the table.

Before long, somewhat more than a quint after Alastar had returned to the administration building, Cyran and Akoryt appeared, followed by Tiranya. Within moments, all the senior imagers, with the exception of Gaellen, were seated around the conference table.

"Does anyone know where Gaellen is?" asked Alastar.

"He's in the infirmary," said Tiranya. "One of the juniors fell out of the hayloft in the stables and broke some bones."

"Then we might as well begin. I know today has been a long day. Tomorrow will be as well. The first thing in the morning I'll be taking a small group of maitres back to the Chateau D'Council to see what else we can discover there. Arion, Khaelis, I'd like you two to accompany me, along with two Maitres D'Aspect with strong shields." He turned to Akoryt. "Perhaps Belsior and Taurek?"

"Seliora actually has the strongest shields of the Maitres D'Aspect besides Taurek."

"Then Seliora and Taurek. Cyran, I'd like you and a strong third of your choice to find Factor Elthyrd and escort him to the Chateau D'Council to meet us there. Tell him it's a matter of extreme interest to the Factors' Council. Don't accept his attempts to decline, and tell him that I told you that. If need be, put shields around him and bring him unwillingly." Alastar cleared his throat. "For those of you who haven't heard, a company of riflemen besieged the Chateau D'Rex, and two battalions of army troopers revolted and have left L'Excelsis, presumably to meet up with other rebel army units coming from Ferravyl in support of a revolt led by High Holders. In addition, Bettaur and Ashkyr and two mounts are missing. They apparently left almost immediately after the last of the attackers here fled. Does anyone know why they might have departed." Alastar looked around the table.

There were only headshakes.

"If anyone discovers anything about that let me, Cyran, or Alyna know. For the time being, no one is to leave Imagisle without informing me or Maitre Cyran." He paused again. "Is there anything I should know? Any questions?"

"What should we do with those iron shields the riflemen left behind?" asked Taryn. "Petros carted them into the storage yard behind the factorage."

"They belong to us. So do the rifles they left behind. The rifles go to the armory, if they aren't there already. The iron shields can be used any way that makes sense, but, again, see me or Maitre Thelia about it before you do." Alastar rose. "That's all for this evening. The group with me will leave no later than seventh glass tomorrow morning."

Linzya was waiting in the anteroom when Alastar and Alyna left the conference room.

Alastar could see traces of red in her eyes. "If you'd come into the study. We need to talk to you. It shouldn't take too long."

"It's about Bettaur . . . isn't it?"

Alastar nodded, stepping aside and motioning for her to enter the study, where Alyna was rearranging the three chairs that were normally lined up before the desk into an arc. Linzya hesitated, then took the chair on the end closest to the window. Alyna took the chair beside her, leaving Alastar the chair most directly facing Linzya.

"You know Bettaur has left the Collegium," Alastar began. "It's likely he took a mount and that Tertius Ashkyr went with him."

"I heard that."

"Did he say anything to you recently that might have suggested why he left?"

"About a week ago, he asked me if I'd mind if we went to the Collegium in Westisle. I told him that if that was what he wanted, it was fine with me. He asked me not to tell anyone because he was going to ask you, and he didn't want anyone else to know."

"Did he say why he wanted to go?" asked Alyna gently.

"He said he was tired of the senior maitres looking at him as if he'd done something wrong. He also said he would have been a Maitre D'Structure already, like Maitre Arion, if things were fair."

"Did he ever say why he thought things weren't fair?" asked Alastar.

"No, sir. It had to be the problems he had with Taurek years ago. He didn't mention it, and it wasn't my place . . . I mean, if I brought it up, he'd think that I was . . ." Linzya swallowed, then snuffled. "He's always been so good and kind to me. He taught me how to speak better, and how to write a real letter. He's always been gentle . . . I didn't want ever to say anything that would hurt him. . . ."

"What about the last few days?" asked Alyna. "Did he say anything that might have indicated he was disturbed or upset?"

"I don't remember anything like that. I really don't."

"Did he say anything about Tertius Ashkyr?"

"He did say he understood how Ashkyr felt. He said he intended to do what he could to help him through his troubles."

"Did Bettaur go out much in the evenings?"

"Almost every night. He'd go out at night and practice. Sometimes so late that I was asleep when he got back. Sometimes not."

"Practice?" asked Alastar. "Imaging?"

Linzya nodded. "I followed him the first few times. It was stupid of me. He went to the south end of Imagisle. He stood there. He did things like imaging fire on the water. He imaged water from the river into a block . . . and let it fall, except there was ice on the water, and it all splintered away."

"You didn't keep following him then?" asked Alyna.

"I did for the first few days, but not after that. He was so dedicated. He said he needed to be as strong an imager as anyone, and practicing was the only way."

"Did he go anywhere else at night?" asked Alastar. "Do you know?"

Linzya hesitated, then finally said. "Sometimes . . . I think. One night he came back and his grays smelled like smoke . . . like at the inn when I was little. But most of the times he was practicing."

"How do you know that?" asked Alyna.

"When he practiced, he'd smell . . . well, sweaty, and he'd drop into bed and be asleep almost before I could say a word to him. That's how tired he was."

"Did you ever ask him where he'd been when he wasn't practicing?" asked Alastar.

"Not like that, sir. I did say that his grays smelled like he'd been to an inn that one time. He said he'd found out that the steward where he grew up was visiting his son, and he went to see him. He said he wished he hadn't. I didn't smell that smoke again."

"Has he been practicing ever since you were married?" Alyna smiled sympathetically.

"Before that, I think. When he was courting, he'd come to talk to me some nights, but other nights he'd say he had to practice imaging."

"Did you two ever leave Imagisle together, besides going to a bistro or places nearby?" asked Alastar.

"Oh, yes. He was teaching me to ride. He made arrangements with Maitre Petros. He got me a real gentle mare. We'd ride mostly along the West River Road. One time we rode almost to this big mansion. He said it was the chateau where the High Holders met. He said it was too bad that imagers couldn't live like that. I said we did all right, and that I felt safer on Imagisle. He said that if we lived in a chateau I'd feel just as safe."

"Did he say anything else about the chateau?"

Linzya shook her head. "He told stories about the river and how he had a boat when he was a boy. He had a horse, too. He rode so well. I felt like I was bouncing. Well, at first. I got better. He said so, too."

"Was he any different this morning?" asked Alastar.

"No, sir. He kissed me like always when I left for the imager factorage, and he said he'd see me later. But . . ." She shook her head, and her eyes brightened.

Alyna glanced to Alastar.

"I think that's all we need to know, Linzya," he said. "Thank you." Alastar rose and looked to Alyna, who stood as well.

"I'll walk out with you," Alyna said warmly.

Alastar watched as the two left, wanting to shake his head. From all that Linzya had said, and from the way she had said it, Alastar had the feeling that Bettaur had indeed been an almost perfect loving husband. *So why had he left? Had everything with Linzya been an act? Or . . .*

When Alyna returned, Alastar asked, "How is she?"

"You know as well as I do, dearest."

"She's incredibly upset and trying not to show it."

Alyna nodded.

"So what do you think about Bettaur?"

"After all this . . . I don't know what to think. My instinct is that Bettaur's capable of almost anything, and yet from what she's said, and from what Tiranya's heard, he's treated her like a High Holder's lady, maybe even better. He even asked her permission, in a backhanded way, about going to Westisle."

"So why did he and Ashkyr leave this afternoon?"

"What's your guess?" countered Alyna.

"Something was likely to be revealed as a result of what happened at the Chateau D'Council that involved Bettaur, and he felt he couldn't risk it being known."

"But why would he even want to be involved in something as chancy as a High Holder revolt?"

"Why indeed? Except who might be the only possible pretender to succeed Lorien?"

"Ryentar, of course, but Bettaur doesn't know they're related."

"But someone else does, and that someone may well know Bettaur's parentage . . . and may have used it against him."

"Ryel. He's certainly capable of masterminding this." Alyna paused. "I can certainly see Ryentar wanting to take advantage of the situation, enough that he could be used as a tool, although it would be exceedingly dangerous for him to travel close to L'Excelsis."

"He wouldn't have to if his half brother set it up," Alastar pointed out.

"Ryel? He's certainly capable of any sort of treachery."

"That makes an unfortunate kind of sense, but there won't be a single piece of paper to tie him to any of this."

"Of course not. Everyone else will serve as tools and take the risk."

"Without evidence, another death of any sort . . ." Alastar shook his head. "We can prove even less of this."

"Does anything else make sense?"

"Not that I know of at the moment. I still feel that there's a part of this that we're not seeing."

"That may be, but we need to get home. Jienna is holding dinner, and we have two impatient young ladies. Your eyes are also turning pink, and you're limping a little."

"Then we should go."

They had barely left the study when Chervyt appeared.

"Maitre . . . Davour said that you were looking for me. I went to get a quick bite to eat . . ."

"Even duty maitres have to eat," said Alastar with a smile. He still recalled the night that Chervyt had lost his lover, during the time of troubles, but from that tragedy, the young man had certainly recovered. He'd applied himself with even greater effort. "I'm hoping that the evening will be quiet, but, if it's not, don't hesitate in the slightest to send for me."

"I won't, sir."

"Good."

After they were away from the administration building, Alyna said quietly, "He's strong, but he's very sweet."

"He's very diligent, too."

Half a quint later, Alastar and Alyna walked up the steps onto the porch of the Maitre's house, only to see Malyna and Lystara waiting beside the door.

"You said you wouldn't be long," declared Lystara.

"What happened at the chateau?" asked Malyna.

"We'll talk about both later," said Alyna. "Wash your hands."

"We already have."

"Then let us wash ours," said Alastar with a smile.

Malyna and Lystara were waiting by the door into the dining room when Alastar and Alyna returned. In moments, everyone was seated, and Jienna appeared with a pitcher of dark lager and a basket of warm bread. She quickly returned with a large casserole dish, which she set before Alyna.

"You may each have half a beaker of lager," Alastar announced. "It has to last through dinner."

"Thank you, Father." Lystara smiled.

While Alastar poured the lager, Alyna quickly served the girls what amounted to a shepherd's pie, then Alastar and herself.

No one spoke for a time until Alastar said, "We usually don't talk about imager matters at dinner, but these are not normal times. So Alyna and I are going to ask you two some questions." He noticed that Lystara immediately looked up from her platter, clearly interested. Malyna looked wary.

"Lystara . . . what have you noticed about Ashkyr?"

"He's a third. I don't see much of him, except he takes mathematics tutorials with the seconds. He doesn't like being with any of us, except for Ilora. That's because she's pretty. He looks more at her than at Maitre Arion. Howal doesn't like him. He says Ashkyr's sneaky."

"Do you think that?"

"I wouldn't know. He avoids me. I mean Ashkyr does. So does Howal, mostly."

"Have you seen much of Ashkyr outside of tutorials?"

"He runs in the morning. He's faster."

"What about you, Malyna?" asked Alyna.

"I don't care for him. I don't know why. He's strange. He thinks Maitre Bettaur is wonderful, though."

"Oh?"

"He said Maitre Bettaur was teaching him ways to be a better imager. Paemyna asked him what, but he wouldn't say."

"That's the way it's supposed to be," replied Alyna. "Personal lessons stay between the teaching maitre and the student, until the student is examined by Maitre Akoryt."

"It was just the way he said it, like it was something special."

"What about today? Did either of you see Ashkyr?"

"He left the factorage a little after third glass," announced Lystara immediately. "Tertia Linzya and Tertia Charmina were having us practice making fibulas. That was to keep us busy. They didn't even notice when I imaged one out of wood. I kept it, and then I made one out of woven steel wire, except it's so shiny that it looks like silver."

Alastar managed not to roll his eyes, asking almost in spite of himself, "How did you manage that?"

"It's like . . . weaving. You just have to keep the pieces right in your thoughts. Like concealments or shields, except much smaller."

Alastar nodded. "Did you see Ashkyr after that?"

Lystara shook her head.

"Did you, Malyna?" asked Alyna.

"He wasn't imaging what he should have been. He imaged a tiny knife, and then he imaged a sheath for it and slipped it inside his shirt. That was just before he left. I thought, I couldn't be certain, but I thought Maitre Bettaur asked for him. I couldn't see them. Whoever it was, Tertia Charmina wasn't pleased. She frowned, anyway."

"Have you ever noticed anything about either Maitre Bettaur or Ashkyr?" pressed Alyna gently.

"Maitre Bettaur's too handsome . . ."

Alastar managed not to break out laughing, smothering even a smile, especially since words like those had come from Alyna's mouth years earlier.

"Is there anything else?"

"I can't think of anything else."

Although Alastar and Alyna asked questions for perhaps half a quint longer, neither girl added much to what had already been said. Then Alastar gave a quick summary of the day's events.

In time, Alyna announced, "Dinner was late. So you two need to wash up and get ready for bed."

"So soon?" asked Lystara.

"No . . . so late," replied Alastar.

"Oh, Father . . ." Lystara did not quite pout when she left the table.

Malyna hid a smile as she followed her cousin.

After several moments, Alastar turned to Alyna. "What do you think?"

"Besides the fact that you almost burst out laughing?"

"She sounded so much like someone else."

"She did . . . and you did manage not to give that away . . . too much, anyway."

"What do you think about Bettaur and Ashkyr?"

"That we don't know enough. What about you?"

"You're right, but I'm afraid that whatever happens, there are some things we'll never know."

24

Alastar was at the administration building early on Vendrei morning, and the first thing Dareyn said to him was, "Best you read what's in *Veritum*, sir."

"That bad?"

"I don't think so, but you never know what folks will think."

Standing behind the white-haired second, Maercyl nodded.

As soon as Alastar reached the corner of his desk, he set down the water bottle filled with dark lager that he had brought with him and immediately picked up the newssheet and began to read, concentrating on the parts that concerned him.

> . . . apparent cannon shell explosion that killed four of five councilors . . . but no trace of a cannon found . . .
>
> . . . attacks on both Imagisle and the Chateau D'Rex by armed men wearing brown uniforms with heavy rifles of the type used by the army . . . dispersed by red fog . . . most attackers killed by iron darts of the kind used by imagers . . .
>
> . . . rebellion or desertion of two battalions of troopers from Army High Command headquarters . . .
>
> . . . full company of troopers now guarding the Chateau D'Rex . . .
>
> . . . no justicing action taken against High Holder Laevoryn for his cold-blooded killing of Chief Factor Hulet . . .

Alastar frowned as he read the short story, which suggested that Laevoryn and his son had committed double murders, both of Hulet and of the missing Enrique D'Hulet. Given Laevoryn's arrogance and apparent viciousness, the newssheet was taking a bit of a chance. *Except they only implied the first murder.* Still . . . He continued reading.

> . . . rifles reportedly manufactured by Factor Vaschet . . . denies he has any part . . . factorage fortified and possibly using prisoners as labor . . . against Codex Legis . . .

. . . High Holder petitions designed to reassert ancient privileges denied by Rex Lorien just before all this occurred . . .

. . . does this sound like a power grab by High Holders . . . or just an undeclared war against the factors and people of Solidar?

. . . not one word from anyone on the Factors' Council of L'Excelsis . . .

Alastar set down the newssheet. Whoever the publisher was, he wasn't going to have many friends among the High Holders . . . or many others.

Cyran appeared in the study door. "Everyone's ready, Maitre."

"I'm ready as well." Alastar picked up the water bottle and joined Cyran on the walk to the stables. "Has anyone heard anything about Bettaur or Ashkyr?"

"Not a single word. You might ask Taurek . . ."

"He still keeps an eye out for Bettaur?"

"Wouldn't you?"

Alastar offered a short laugh, then said, "You may have to be forceful with Elthyrd, but he needs to come to the Chateau D'Council." Alastar actually had no logical reason for that, or not one that he could put to words, but he felt strongly that it was absolutely necessary, and usually when he disregarded such feelings he ended up regretting it.

"We can do that."

As Cyran promised, the horses and junior maitres were ready and waiting when Alastar and Cyran reached the stables. In less than half a quint, Alastar, Taurek, and Seliora were riding over the Bridge of Desires toward the West River Road. Alastar appreciated the comparative coolness of the day created by the thickening clouds, but suspected that he and the others might end up riding back to Imagisle in the rain.

"What do you think about Bettaur's disappearance, Taurek?"

"What should I think, sir?" asked the muscular and black-haired Maitre D'Aspect.

"Whatever you've observed, and please don't tell me you haven't watched him for years."

Alastar could sense Seliora's amusement, but her face revealed nothing.

"Ah . . . sir . . . ever since that . . . incident, I have never seen Maitre Bettaur do a single thing that was the slightest contrary to good and proper conduct. Nor have I ever seen or heard of him doing or suggesting others do anything contrary to the rules of the Collegium."

"Neither has anyone else, so far as I know, but you didn't answer my question."

"I've never seen Bettaur do anything that was not calculated. If he acted to leave the Collegium of his own free will, then it was part of something well considered and thought out. If he bowed to the suggestions of another, that other person must have had great power and influence in ways I cannot comprehend."

"What you're saying is that he either left as part of a large and well-thought-out plan, or was influenced or forced to leave by someone with even greater influence than the Maitre of the Collegium."

Taurek smiled ruefully. "I guess I am, sir."

"What do you think, Seliora?"

Seliora, a young woman partly of Pharsi heritage with her brown eyes, and smooth honeyed skin, offered a wry smile before saying, "I'd have to agree with Taurek. I've never seen anyone so self-possessed and so in control of himself, and yet so able to project warmth and caring."

"Did either of you see him yesterday?"

"Except at the noon meal, no, sir," replied Taurek.

Seliora shook her head.

After they crossed the Boulevard D'Ouest, Alastar said, "Remember. Full shields until we're back at the Collegium."

"Yes, sir."

Before long, the three were riding up to the iron gates of the Chateau D'Council. The two guards who stood behind the iron gates of the Chateau D'Council looked at each other, then at the three imagers . . . and opened the gates.

"Ah . . . Councilor Meinyt is acting as head of the High Council, Maitre."

"Is he here?" Alastar would have been shocked if Meinyt hadn't been.

"Yes, sir. The steward sent for him yesterday afternoon."

"Are there any other High Holders here?"

"No, sir."

"There will be several other imagers arriving before long. I thought you'd like to know." Alastar offered a friendly smile before easing the gelding forward onto the stone drive between the formal gardens. Apparently, the chateau was better built than Alastar had realized, or had more stone and less timber in its interior walls, or the staff had been effective in stopping the flames, if not all three, because, while the front walls were blackened around the shattered and blown-out front study windows, the remainder of the structure seemed intact.

When he reined up below the covered portico, for the first time ever, there was no footman there. He dismounted and handed the gelding's reins to Taurek.

"If anyone fires at either of you or attacks you, remove them."

"Yes, sir."

Alastar walked up the steps to the main entry, only to discover two men posted in the recesses beside the front door. They were uniformed in green and gray, rather than in maroon, but they carried heavy rifles in addition to sabers.

"Where did you come by the rifles?" asked Alastar.

"The previous guards left them, sir. Council Meinyt thought Culosh and me ought to use them, seeing as we each did a term in the army."

"What happened to the previous guards?"

"Councilor Meinyt sent them all to High Holder Cransyr's lands. Said he didn't care how they got there."

Alastar could see that, but before he could ask another question, Meinyt stepped out onto the portico.

"I thought I might see you, Maitre. I wondered if you might have been at the meeting here yesterday."

"I wasn't invited. Even more interestingly, I was invited to a High Council meeting scheduled for next Lundi. As you may have heard or read, the Collegium was rather involved yesterday with an attack on Imagisle, and then we ended up dispersing more attackers who were trying to keep Rex Lorien from leaving his chateau. Then we received a message from Marshal Wilkorn that two battalions deserted and are headed southeast. They are commanded by sons of High Holder Cransyr and High Holder Caervyn." Alastar smiled politely. "What might you be able to add to that? I understand you were not here yesterday."

"I was rather high-handedly detained by a squad from Cransyr's private army, many of the remainder of which were dispersed or killed by you and your imagers. Given what happened here"—Meinyt gestured in the direction of the study—"it appears my detention was not without some benefit."

"Do you have any idea what the departed four were planning?"

"We should retire to the parlor. The study is totally unusable."

As the two entered the chateau, Alastar said conversationally, "From all the signs of fire, I'm surprised that that there wasn't more damage."

"The interior walls are masonry, and the door was closed and had a bronze core. The staff kept it from spreading until it burned out. Everything inside burned to ashes."

"I never would have known that," Alastar admitted.

"Nor I," said Meinyt, gesturing to the first door off the north corridor.

Once inside the parlor, whose windows opened onto a garden courtyard, Meinyt took one of the pair of armchairs. He did not sit back, but leaned forward slightly, looking at Alastar, who had taken the chair opposite him. "I have my own ideas as to why you're here, but I'd like to hear your reasons."

"Simply to make sense of a confused situation," replied Alastar. "Four of the five High Councilors are killed; the Collegium is attacked after that; the Chateau D'Rex attacked even later; and then two army battalions desert, both commanded by the sons of High Holders, and one of those sons is Cransyr's. The battalions leave L'Excelsis. It's almost as though some other High Holder . . ." Alastar shrugged.

"It does. I can assure you that I'm not that High Holder, assuming that is the case. I was very much held captive in my own house, and my entire staff will vouch for that. Anyone who came was told that I was not receiving and quite ill." Meinyt snorted. "The way things have turned out, most who don't know me will believe the worst. You realize that I will be offering my resignation from the High Council immediately, remaining only until successors for all five seats are chosen. If I don't, then the deaths of the other four will be laid at my feet—even if no one says a word."

"You're still effectively the head of the High Council for now," Alastar pointed out.

"Unfortunately." Meinyt cocked his head and looked directly at Alastar. "What do you have in mind that I should do? Isn't that why you're really here?"

"I'm here to see what can be done to put down an unwise rebellion with the least fuss and loss of life."

"A rebellion about which I know nothing."

"You do know the grievances voiced by Cransyr and others."

"I do. I understand how they feel—or felt. I told them they could not turn back history, not without destroying the Collegium . . . and that seemed unlikely." Meinyt barked a short laugh.

"Did Cransyr say anything to that?"

"He said that there might be ways around that . . ." Meinyt smiled sardonically. "When I asked him how he planned that, he said it was unlikely that even the Collegium would be able to go against the will of the rex, the Army High Command, and the High Council."

"Even assuming that," Alastar mused, "it would only postpone the difficulties with the factors."

"Although he did not say so, I think Cransyr would have begged to differ, Maitre."

"You're likely right about that. What did you say to him?"

"That I had my doubts, just as I have doubts you will be able to resolve the matter without more bloodshed."

Alastar smiled coolly. "I'm only aiming at the least bloodshed possible, since there are already close to two hundred High Holder riflemen dead." *And there might even be more than that.* "There is one other small detail you might be able to help with. One of my scouts noted a rider—a messenger, it would seem—rising into the grounds of the Chateau D'Council several days ago. It might mean nothing, but the rider was in livery of scarlet and black. The historian of the Collegium could find no record of such livery, but he noted that many High Holders do not have hereditary colors. He also confessed that, with something like fifteen hundred High Holders, he was far from conversant with any sizable number. I wondered if you might know."

"You have been watching the chateau?"

"It would not have been prudent to do otherwise," Alastar pointed out.

"Then what did your scout see . . . yesterday? About the explosion?"

Alastar shrugged. "Less than what I imagine all the retainers here saw. He heard an explosion. He rode closer. He saw flames. He heard guards yelling that the Council had been attacked . . . or words to that effect. He reported that it appeared likely that the High Councilors had been either wounded or worse. I read the accounts in *Veritum* this morning and decided a visit was in order. We are here."

"I see."

"And about the scarlet and black livery?"

"The only livery that I know of that embodies scarlet and black is that of High Holder Regial—scarlet for the regial blood, and black for the disgrace. He wrote that he wanted those colors to flaunt his lineage, or something like that, I understand. He didn't have to inform the Council, but he did."

Alastar felt like nodding. *Another piece of the puzzle.* "When was that?"

"Years ago. Before I was on the council. Olefsyrt told me about it." Meinyt frowned. "You're certain about the colors?"

"My imager was close enough to the messenger to be very sure."

"I can't say I'm happy about that." Meinyt shook his head.

"Regial's lands aren't that far from Cransyr's, I imagine. They're both in Montagne."

"You *are* sure about the colors and the messenger."

"The scout was one of my best."

"I don't imagine you have many that aren't," said Meinyt wryly. "I'm certain you've thought about the possibilities, then."

"Only in the last few moments, when you informed me of Regial's colors. The attack on the Chateau D'Rex . . ."

"What else?" asked Meinyt.

"Two imagers also left the Collegium in haste after they heard about what happened here. They've never met High Holder Regial, or even been anywhere near him." Alastar didn't want to lie outright. "But the timing disturbs me."

"It would disturb me, too, in your position. As I recall, a renegade imager caused the Collegium considerable difficulty when you first became Maitre. To have that happen again . . ."

"Exactly," agreed Alastar.

A knock on the parlor door was followed immediately by a retainer in green and gray easing the door open and saying, "High Holder Meinyt, Maitre Alastar . . . Maitre Cyran and Factorius Elthyrd have arrived."

Meinyt looked to Alastar. "Your doing?"

"I admit to it. You both have your positions because your predecessors were killed. In the case of Elthyrd, definitely by a High Holder. In the case of the High Council, the killer or killers remain to be found and identified."

"I doubt that any proof will ever be found identifying whoever it was." Meinyt looked openly at Alastar. "It's been like that before, I understand." He rose and turned toward the retainer. "Have them join us."

Alastar stood.

The door opened wide, and Cyran stepped inside, gesturing for Elthyrd to enter, and then closing the door and joining the other three.

Elthyrd looked from Meinyt to Alastar. "Why did you insist on my being here?"

"Because I wanted both of you together," Alastar replied. "As soon as possible. You're both very practical, and you both see that times are changing in Solidar, even if you, Elthyrd, think the changes are too slow, and you, Meinyt, worry that they are coming too swiftly for most High Holders."

"You do have a way with phrases." Elthyrd's words were tart.

"I also would like us to share knowledge and information in order to keep the coming bloodshed to a minimum."

"Coming bloodshed?" Elthyrd glanced in the direction of the burned-out receiving study. "Hasn't there been enough?"

"There may have been," replied Alastar, "but it's less than what's about to happen. . . ." He went on to explain about Commander Aestyn, the extra two thousand heavy rifles, and more than two thousand armed troopers, with the rebel units most likely consolidating forces and then heading back to L'Excelsis. "And to add to that, there's a possibility that two imagers *might* have thrown in with the rebels, if for reasons that are anything but clear. I say they might have, but they might not have. Right now, we don't know, and it's better to assume the worst."

"Two imagers . . . that doesn't sound that bad," offered Elthyrd dryly.

"The presence of one renegade imager thirteen years ago resulted in the death of almost a regiment of largely innocent troopers, the fracturing of the regial family, and the death of most of the Army High Command," replied Alastar in an even drier tone. "That's an example of why imager justice is far more stringent than that of the rex or High Holders." He couldn't help but wonder if he'd erred on the side of being too lenient with Bettaur years before. *But you can't undo what's done . . . and besides, you don't know why he left or what he's doing.*

"How strong are the two imagers?" asked Elthyrd.

"A junior maitre and a third," replied Alastar. "Now that over three hundred men with heavy rifles manufactured by Vaschet have attacked both Imagisle and the Chateau D'Rex, I trust the Factors' Council will drop the idea of bringing me in front of a justice for borrowing Vaschet's account ledgers."

"We haven't discussed the matter. Not formally."

"It might be best not to discuss it. I'd rather not be forced to bring Vaschet before a justicer for aiding and abetting revolt and treason, and I'm certain he'd prefer that."

"He might. He won't be happy."

"He'll be a lot less happy if all the details come to light in a justicing hearing."

"I thought you might say something like that, Maitre."

"It might also be best if he disclosed which High Holder or Holders provided him with prisoners for his ironworks."

Meinyt half-opened his mouth and then closed it before speaking. "Is that true?"

"He had fortified walls and prisoners, and the prisoners did not come from the Civic Patrol, which means . . ."

Meinyt and Elthyrd exchanged glances.

"I have another unpleasant task," announced Alastar. "I suggest that you two discuss how you intend to work out a means whereby High Holders will pay their debts, both to factors and to banques, and how factors will refrain from destroying High Holdings by excessive charges for grain and other crops."

"You're not offering a choice, are you?" asked Meinyt.

"No. I don't expect you to come up with an immediate solution. I do expect an agreement to work out that solution. Cyran will escort Elthyrd back to his factorage when that agreement is reached."

"Might we ask your task?" inquired Meinyt.

"I need to confront Rex Lorien about certain matters, before the details slip his mind." Alastar smiled at Meinyt and then Elthyrd. "Good day." He turned and walked out of the parlor, then out of the chateau toward his mount and his escorts.

Less than two quints later, the three were riding up the entry lane to the Chateau D'Rex, toward the main entry, now guarded by a squad of troopers.

The squad leader looked at Alastar, almost helplessly. "Sir . . ."

"I know. You're not supposed to allow anyone inside without permission or something like that. I'm Maitre Alastar. Chateau Guard Captain Churwyl knows who I am. So do Rex Lorien and Lady Chelia."

At that moment, Churwyl hurried down the white stone steps. "That's Maitre Alastar. He's always welcome here." The guard captain looked to Alastar. "I had a feeling you might be here today, Maitre."

Alastar looked to the army squad leader. "Maitre Taurek will remain here with your men and our mounts. Maitre Seliora will accompany me."

"Yes, sir."

Alastar turned to Churwyl. "We're here to see Rex Lorien."

"I'll escort you." The guard captain offered a sympathetic smile.

Alastar dismounted, as did Seliora, slightly awkwardly, reminding Alastar that she had not ridden that much. He just hoped she wasn't too sore on Samedi, but he also had the feeling that a number of the maitres might be riding more than they usually did over the coming weeks.

"Might I ask why you need me?" asked Seliora softly as the two walked up the steps behind Churwyl.

"I may need you to fetch someone, and you may need shields to require their presence. Also, you're said to be perceptive, and I definitely need another pair of perceptive eyes. It should go without saying that you're to maintain shields at all times in the chateau."

Seliora nodded.

As they made their way through the main entrance and foyer, then up the grand staircase, Alastar was reminded again of just how tall the blond maitre was. He also wondered about her parentage, although the Collegium records only showed that she had been a foundling raised by a Pharsi couple in Mantes.

The chateau guard posted outside Lorien's private study stiffened as he saw the group approaching.

"Both of you?" asked Churwyl.

"Just me for the moment. Maitre Seliora will wait here in the north corridor until she's needed."

"Maitre Alastar," announced the guard captain, opening the door.

Alastar stepped inside the study, amused at how quickly the door was closed behind him.

Lorien looked up from the goldenwood desk. He did not stand.

Alastar took the middle chair across from the rex, but did not speak as he seated himself.

"So you finally decided to explain matters. I am rex, you know?" Lorien's jaw trembled, most likely a sigh of suppressed rage, Alastar thought.

"Explanations go two ways, Lorien," replied Alastar. "Let's start with your telling me which High Holders were informing you of matters like the death of Paellyt's son, well before I found out . . . or the fact that the Collegium was having trouble stopping the shooting of innocent student imagers . . . or my difficulties with Factor Vaschet . . ."

Lorien did not answer, but looked toward the window.

Alastar waited.

After what seemed a quint, but was perhaps a tenth of that, Lorien looked back at Alastar. "No one informed me directly. Chelia got messages. Not too often, except in the last few weeks. She doesn't know from whom."

"But she suspects who the sender might be."

"You'd have to talk to her." Lorien tightened his lips and jaw.

Alastar stood up again and walked to the study door and opened it. "Seliora, please find Lady Chelia and bring her here."

"Yes, sir."

Alastar left the door ajar and walked back to the goldenwood desk. He did not sit, but stood with his back to the window so that he could watch Lorien and the study door. "What else haven't you been telling me, besides the fact that you knew very well that Hehnsyn was Cransyr's son and that he had deliberately ordered those extra thousand rifles?"

"Am I supposed to tell you everything?"

"I generally don't care to hear what you had for breakfast. I do think I should hear when you decide to do a favor for the head of the High Council, especially since he's been plotting with other High Holders to replace you with someone else as rex."

"That wasn't obvious at the time." Lorien's voice was sulky.

"No, it wasn't," agreed Alastar, "but it was obvious even then that Cransyr had anything but your best interests in mind, and when his son does something suspicious . . . You should at least have allowed Wilkorn to shift his duties."

"Given him a battalion, perhaps? To lead against me?"

"He took a battalion anyway," Alastar pointed out, "but it would have reduced the number of heavy rifles in the hands of High Holder private armies." He looked up as the door opened, and Chelia entered the study, followed by Seliora. *Two very different blondes.*

"You requested my presence, Maitre Alastar?"

"I did." Alastar saw Seliora turning to leave the study and said gently, "Maitre Seliora . . . it would be best if you remained."

"Not exactly an impartial witness," sneered Lorien.

"Rather a perceptive observer," countered Alastar.

The sneer vanished from Lorien's face, as if Alastar's words had unsettled him, but, after a moment, he said, "You're acting like you're the rex. Again."

"That happens when you don't." Alastar could see Chelia stiffen ever so slightly and turned more toward her. "Chelia, Lorien has indicated you received messages about the death of Paellyt's son and about the shootings of student imagers."

"I did."

"Why didn't you let me know?"

"Whoever wrote the notes said that it would be best if I didn't . . . that Charyn, Bhayrn, or Aloryana could just as easily be shot as a student imager . . . more easily, in fact. The writer said that what he was disclosing was information already known to the Collegium, but not known to the rex."

"Suggesting without saying so that I was not to be trusted in informing Lorien and not-so-subtly encouraging him not to share information with me."

"I never suggested that."

"You didn't have to. All you had to do was show the notes to your husband."

"What was I supposed to do?" snapped Chelia. "If you couldn't protect your own imagers, how could I count on you to protect my children?"

"You couldn't. That was exactly what the writer wanted you to think. Who is the writer?"

"The notes were never signed."

"How did you receive them?"

"They were left in the stable in my saddlebags. I had one of the guards watch them, but they never saw anything. Never. But the messages were there."

Alastar nodded slowly. "That also reinforced your concerns."

"You would have felt the same."

"Now . . . back to my question. Who was the writer?"

"I told you. They weren't signed."

"I think you have a very good idea who the writer is, even without his signature, even if his hand happened to be disguised."

"If you know . . . then why ask me?"

"I suspect . . . and what I know points to only one person . . . but I don't know."

Chelia did not speak.

"Does he want to be chief councilor?" pressed Alastar.

"For the sake of the Nameless, no. That would be too obvious. He's never liked being obvious, unlike . . ."

"His sire?"

Chelia gave the faintest nod. "I've said nothing."

"No . . . you haven't," Alastar agreed. *Not that it will make much difference now.* "Your children will likely be as safe as you are for the present."

Chelia frowned.

"There's a rebel army that will soon be headed toward L'Excelsis.

I wouldn't be surprised if High Holder Regial happened to be the titular commander."

Lorien gaped, if but for an instant. "He wouldn't dare."

"You think not? The day before the receiving study at the Chateau D'Council holding some of the High Holder conspirators exploded, a messenger in scarlet and black livery either delivered to or received a message from the High Council, if not both. I doubt it was coincidence."

Chelia paled. "He wouldn't . . . couldn't."

Alastar knew to whom she was referring. "I'm afraid he likely has, Lady Chelia."

"I knew he was an untrustworthy bastard, but treachery like this . . ."

"He is willing to use anyone," Alastar pointed out, "including his sister." *And both half brothers.* "So is Ryentar. The two of them are a match made in the Namer's parlor."

"What are you going to do?" Chelia demanded.

"Work with Marshal Wilkorn to defend you and your husband—and L'Excelsis—from that army." *And its allies.* "When that is done will be the time to reduce further the power of the High Holders."

"None too soon," declared Lorien.

"No, it's not," agreed Alastar. *Let's hope that it's not too late.*

What also worried him was how much he had not seen, and the fact that the High Holder behind the rebel plot had foreseen too well what had happened thus far. Someone that bright had to know just how powerful imagers were—and planned for that as well. And Alastar had no idea what that part of his opponent's plan was. That was another reason why he needed to meet with the marshal once he left the Chateau D'Rex. He could only hope that Wilkorn could shed some light on events, but that might prove to be a vain hope.

He rose. "I'll do my best to keep you informed." Then he turned and motioned to Seliora.

25

By a quint before second glass, Alastar, Seliora, and Taurek were less than half a mile from the gates of the Army High Command.

Alastar turned to Taurek. "Your father was a commander, wasn't he?" Alastar knew that, but didn't want to presume too much.

"Yes, sir."

"Was he posted here?"

"No, sir. Well . . . not as a commander. He was posted to Estisle when I was little. He was the base commander there."

"Wasn't that unusual?"

Taurek laughed. "He asked for it. Figured he'd never make commander any other way, and he didn't much care for all the second sons of High Holders who were always jockeying for position here."

"He'd just taken his stipend, as I recall, when I became Maitre. Is he . . . ?"

"He's fine. He was when he sent his last letter a couple of weeks ago. He keeps his hand in by training merchanter ship guards. Says he doesn't miss L'Excelsis at all, especially the High Holders' sons who become officers."

"We just might recommend to the marshal that there be a limit on the number of them in senior officer positions here in L'Excelsis. It wouldn't hurt if they spent more time in places like Tilbora or Solis, or Estisle."

"You know, sir, it wouldn't hurt to have a branch of the Collegium in Estisle."

"I've thought about it." Alastar smiled. "Are you jockeying to head it up?"

"No, sir." Taurek grinned. "Not until I'm at least a Maitre D'Structure. But I do know a bit about Estisle. My da walked me over every street and out every pier, both in Nacliano and Estisle."

"We'll talk about it after this mess is over . . . and after you become a Maitre D'Structure."

"Of course, sir."

Alastar looked toward the gates. Beyond them, where stood two guards with rifles, Alastar could see a faint haze, or perhaps a thin wreath of smoke. As he started to rein up, a squad leader emerged from the gatehouse.

"You're Maitre Alastar, sir?"

"I am."

"Go on in. The marshal left orders that if you showed up, he'd like to see you. You know where the headquarters building is?"

"If it survived and hasn't moved in the past year," replied Alastar dryly.

The squad leader smiled. "Same place, sir. It's got some holes in it now, though."

"Thank you." Alastar inclined his head, then urged his mount forward, noticing that the gelding tossed his head just slightly as a vagrant puff of air carried an acrid odor to him.

As they neared the headquarters building, Alastar saw a gaping hole at one side, where he thought Wilkorn's study had been. A handful of rankers were already busy with picks and hammers, breaking apart the rubble and stacking the good bricks in neat piles.

When he reined up in front of the building, he couldn't help smiling at the polished brass of the main entry. Then he turned to the junior maitres. "If you'd wait here, but hold your shields. I hope I won't be too long."

He dismounted and tied the gelding to the hitching rail, then walked toward the steps.

The trooper on duty started forward, then caught sight of the imager grays and stepped back. "The marshal is in the procurement study, sir."

"Thank you. Where is that . . . from where his study is . . . or was?"

"It's two doors to the left, sir."

"Thank you."

Two more troopers studied Alastar as he crossed the center hall and turned to the left, but did not move toward him. A third trooper rose from behind a narrow table in the corridor, obviously moved there temporarily. "I'll announce you, Maitre." He turned and opened the door slightly, "Maitre Alastar is here, sir."

Alastar was vaguely amused. Clearly his description had been passed around headquarters. "Thank you." He stepped past the table and opened the door, entering the study.

Although Wilkorn's left arm was splinted, he rose from behind the small desk, if somewhat slowly, but before Alastar could gesture for him to remain seated. "You look to be in better shape than I am, Maitre."

"For which I have to admit that I'm grateful," returned Alastar humorously.

Wilkorn settled back into his chair. "I don't know whether to be angry at the Namer-damned High Holders or just relieved to survive."

"Maybe you should just promote more sons of factors," said Alastar, "and post the offspring of High Holders in out-of-the-way installations."

"I'm giving that great thought. Vaelln would, too, I suspect."

"How is he? Your message said he was severely injured."

"Not quite so bad as we thought, but he was cut up all over, and there was a lot of blood. The surgeon thinks he'll recover fully before I will."

"How many troopers do you have ready to fight?"

"Two battalions, but five companies to a battalion. We've had to restructure, but they'll fight, and they'll fight well. I put Commander Maurek in charge." Wilkorn coughed and cleared his throat. "Frigging dust. Still everywhere. I heard that a cannon shell wiped out four of the five High Councilors." He smiled. "Had to be a pretty good gunner to hit a window with one round and no ranging shots."

"Perhaps someone placed the shell there and set it off with a fuse of some sort."

"Anything is possible, I suspect. Not that I'm going to worry about a single misplaced shell when I've got two missing battalions, and two thousand stolen rifles to worry about."

"I have the feeling that Commander Aestyn . . ."

"So do I. No proof, but with two High Holder brats running in the direction of a third, who used maintenance to get an additional thousand rifles, I'd be a fool to think anything else." Wilkorn frowned. "You and your imagers took out a whole regiment years back. They have to know that."

"I've thought of that. Right now, we have two missing imagers. One of them . . . let's say . . . might have ties to a High Holder . . . and even to one High Holder Regial . . ." Alastar went on to give his version of the messenger in scarlet and black. ". . . and then there's the problem that someone was sending notes to Lady Chelia providing her and Lorien with information about the killing of young student imagers . . . and the fact that initially we were unable to do anything."

"Implying that Lorien shouldn't back the Collegium . . . or something might happen to their children."

"That was the conclusion I drew, and the one they did."

"Who is that someone?"

"The notes were unsigned and the hand disguised. It has to be a High Holder, but she couldn't name him."

"Probably her brother or someone acting for him. That's just the sort of indirect scheming that family is good at . . . and they'll sacrifice their own as quick as anyone else."

"That's the most likely possibility, but there's no way to tell, and probably less chance of proving it."

The marshal snorted. "Could be he's worse than his sire, and that's saying something."

"How soon do you think we'll see their forces?"

"That depends on how much they've got in the way of reinforcements and where they're coming from."

"I'd wager that all the reinforcements are already with Aestyn and on the way toward L'Excelsis from Ferravyl."

"A good week, most likely." Wilkorn frowned again. "Might be longer. They've got to be bringing cannon."

"Because cannon are the only weapon a good imager can't stop?"

"That's the way I see it."

It was also the way Alastar saw it, although he hadn't initially thought of cannon. "Did Aestyn also requisition cannon to use against the pirates in and around the Sud Swamp?"

"He did, and I granted the request, the more fool I."

"Might I ask when?"

"Last Mayas."

In *Mayas? How long have they been setting this up?* Much longer than Alastar wanted to think, that was clear. "Do you have cannon to deal with theirs?"

"Not what they have. We moved most of them to Solis and the port cities." Wilkorn looked to Alastar.

"At my recommendation, I know."

"Nothing like being sunk by your own guns, is it, Maitre?" Wilkorn's words were warmly ironic.

"You do have some, I take it?"

"An even half score."

"That might be enough. Do you remember what Chesyrk attempted. . . ." Alastar went on to explain, outlining how it might be possible to use one past rebel tactic against the latest rebels.

Less than a quint later, he left headquarters and mounted the gray for the return to Imagisle.

"That didn't take too long, sir," offered Taurek as the three imagers rode toward the gates.

"Longer than I would have liked, but Marshal Wilkorn does have some capabilities that we can adapt." *At least, I hope we can.*

"Do the High Holders really believe they can win?" asked Taurek.

"Those who are rebelling believe they will lose if they don't fight," replied Alastar. "The rex has turned down their petitions. Those petitions asked for the reinstatement of their ancient and excessive rights, not that they believe they were excessive."

"But all of them have so much."

"Many would have to sell lands to pay those debts, and if they sell enough to pay, they well might not hold enough to be High Holders. They feel threatened, and those with power who feel threatened are always dangerous."

Seliora nodded, while Taurek just shook his head.

Just before fourth glass, Alastar walked into the anteroom in the administration building to find Cyran waiting for him.

"Come on in." Alastar motioned for the senior imager to join him in the study. "When did you get back?"

"About a glass ago."

Alastar shut the study door and asked, "How did matters go with Elthyrd and Meinyt?"

"They're not happy men, either of them," replied Cyran.

"I don't want them to be happy. I want them to get on with developing a working relationship between factors and High Holders."

"You made that clear enough. Meinyt is willing to work with Elthyrd, but he wanted me to convey to you that there's little if anything he can do about the rebels, and unless or until they come to terms or are defeated, nothing that he and Elthyrd agree on can be implemented. He did have one good suggestion, and Elthyrd agreed with it."

"What was that?"

"There should be a council of factors for all of Solidar just as there is a High Council."

Alastar nodded. "That makes sense. It will probably have to start as a coordinating and advisory group."

"That's just what Elthyrd said."

"At least we've got those two talking." Alastar shook his head. "Now all we have to do is defeat a rebel army that has enough cannon to pound down almost any imagers' shields."

"They have cannon?"

"That's what Wilkorn believes. Far more than he has, ever since a certain maitre suggested that the cannon at headquarters might best be employed elsewhere." Alastar's last words carried a certain amount of rue.

"How could you have known?"

"I should have seen that times were changing and that the old ways of the High Holders couldn't last, not unless they changed and became more like factors. Some have, but most haven't, and they're afraid and angry at what's happened, and they blame the Collegium and the rex. They think we've helped the factors at their expense, when all we've done is to keep the High Holders from squashing the factors. The High Holders don't see it that way, of course. Most of them don't, anyway."

"How soon will they attack, then?"

"Wilkorn thinks it will be at least a week. It might be longer. Cannon slow things down."

"What do you think we should do?"

"I'd like to have you, Akoryt, Alyna, and me meet tomorrow morning at seventh glass to talk over some of the things we might be able to do. I need to think before we meet, and it might be better if we all do."

Cyran nodded.

"Has anything else happened?"

"Nothing out of the ordinary, that I know of."

"That's somewhat reassuring." Alastar's tone was dry. "Then I'll see you in the morning. Leave the door open."

Once Cyran left, Alastar looked at the master ledger, then shook his head. With the accuracy Thelia applied to the Collegium's accounts, he really didn't need to study the ledger as much as he did, and he certainly wasn't in the mood, anyway.

He couldn't help worrying that, as far as the rebels were concerned, they knew something he didn't, and that bothered him. *Perhaps in the meeting tomorrow . . .*

"You're looking very thoughtful."

Alastar looked up as Alyna stepped into the study.

"I'm worried, I have to say."

She smiled warmly. "You've always worried a lot. Did you find out anything more from Lorien? I assume that's where you went. You'd mentioned that at breakfast."

"I saw Lorien and Chelia, and then went to see Marshal Wilkorn."
He summarized what he had learned. ". . . and all that means matters
are worse than we expected."

She raised her eyebrows.

"I've confirmed that they're worse. I can't prove it. I may never be
able to prove it, but guess who's likely behind all of this?"

"High Holder Ryel."

Alastar nodded. "And he's likely enlisted Ryentar to the cause, most
likely promising that he can be rex."

"The messenger in scarlet and black? Those are his colors as High
Holder Regial? That makes sense, given his attitude. Do you think Ryel
has also co-opted Bettaur?"

"It's possible, but I have no way of knowing."

"That may be, but is there any other explanation?"

"I can't think of one," Alastar admitted.

"How do they think they can defeat the Collegium?"

"With a great number of cannon."

"That didn't work last time," Alyna pointed out.

"We had the advantage then."

"We did?"

"They were attacking us, and we knew where their positions were,
and they didn't know where ours were. They also didn't know what we
could do, and their cannon were lightly guarded. This time, their cannon will be heavily guarded, and they may even have two imagers."

"That shouldn't be enough, and Ryel has to know that."

"I know that, and so do you, and so does he, and that makes me wonder what we've overlooked."

"Maybe that's what he wants us to think."

Alastar shrugged.

"You're not thinking well. Your eyes are pinkish again. Let's go collect the girls and go home. You need some lager and some quiet."

Alastar didn't argue.

After returning to the Maitre's house, he did indeed have a lager, and
then a solid dinner, and it was solid, with potato dumplings, no doubt
because the root crops, such as potatoes, hadn't suffered nearly so much
as the grains and maize. When the main part of the meal was over, he
gave Lystara and Malyna a brief summary of the day's events, beginning
with his meeting with Meinyt and Elthyrd, followed by the meeting with
Lorien, and then the meeting with Marshal Wilkorn. He did avoid men-

tioning anything about Ryel and the twisted family relationships, involving Chelia, Ryel, Ryentar, and Bettaur.

Lystara immediately asked, "Why do the High Holders want things to be the way they were? Most people were poorer and unhappier, weren't they?"

Alyna and Alastar exchanged glances before she nodded to him, if with the hint of a smile.

"Most people were, but the High Holders were more powerful, and they could do almost anything they wanted, especially in the parts of Solidar that used to be Tilbor, Telaryn, and Antiago. They also had more of the golds. Now the factors and even some crafters have more golds, and some of the High Holders have less. They don't like that. This isn't true of all High Holders. Your uncle Zaerlyn, for example, has done quite well, but that's because his family has always stayed in factoring and manufacturing as well."

"Isn't his family ours?"

"We are all part of a large family," Alastar agreed.

"How many High Holders will join this rebellion, Uncle Alastar?"

"Right now, we know of at least ten, and there are probably another ten, although that's just a guess."

"That's not very many. There are more than a thousand High Holders."

"If we don't defeat them, it's enough to unseat Rex Lorien and change the laws, and weaken the Collegium, if not destroy it."

A puzzled expression crossed Malyna's face.

"Most people really don't care who's rex, just so long as their lives aren't upset and they aren't put in danger or impoverished. They worry more about putting food on the table, clothes on their back, and a roof overhead . . . and about being able to walk the streets safely. That's a simplification, but it's true for most people. The factors want to be able to build bigger factorages and make more and better things." Alastar paused for a moment, trying to summarize his answer. "If the High Holders defeat the army and the Collegium, and remove Rex Lorien and make someone else rex, and nothing else changes, most people won't want to fight anymore because it won't gain them anything . . . and those who wanted to make things better will have been defeated or scattered." *Or dead.*

"That's . . ." Malyna shook her head, apparently unable to find a suitable adjective.

"That's human nature," added Alyna. "Only a small fraction of people in any land determine what happens. When the first rex regis decided to unify Solidar, he had only a small army and a handful of imagers. We were fortunate that he had good ideas. Others have had bad ideas. The ancient Naedarans turned against their imagers, and everything collapsed. That's often why it's important to stop people who have bad ideas before they get too far. That's what your uncle is trying to do."

"But Rex Lorien really isn't that good a rex, is he?" asked Malyna.

"No," replied Alastar, "but he's better than the kind of ruler that the High Holders want. They want someone who will allow them to do anything they want. They wouldn't even have to follow the Codex Legis."

"So . . . all this fighting and killing is just to keep things from getting worse?"

"And to maintain things in a way so that they can get better in time," added Alyna. "That's important."

"You're not learning imaging all at once, are you?" asked Alastar.

"I understand that, Uncle Alastar."

"You're fortunate you do," said Alyna. "Most people have trouble with that. They either think nothing will change, or they want everything better immediately."

"Anyway," concluded Alastar, "that's what happened today, and why we think it happened. So far, at least."

"You have a few quints before bed," said Alyna, "and you can play plaques, or read, or talk with us on the front porch."

"Can we go and see the glowbugs?" asked Lystara. "There are hundreds of them tonight, all around the north garden. They're everywhere."

"Everywhere?" asked Alastar skeptically.

"Except really near the house. Can I show Malyna? They don't have glowbugs in Rivages."

Alastar looked to Malyna, then to Alyna. "You don't?"

"No, Uncle Alastar."

"Almost never," corrected Alyna. "Not unless the winter was mild, and only a few."

"There are hundreds out there tonight. You promised. That was a week ago. They won't be that bright many times. You did promise . . ."

"She is right," Alyna said with a smile. "They won't last that long. . . ."

Alastar laughed softly and rose from the table. "Then you should go before they do."

"Really? We can?"

"As you pointed out, Lystara, we promised."

Alastar and Alyna followed the girls out onto the front porch and then around to the east side. From there, in the deep twilight, they all could see a haze of points of light spread like a carpet across the grassy slope a good three hundred yards to the north behind the house.

"Remember, you need to move quietly and slowly," said Alastar. "The glowbugs can sense movement, and if you disturb them, they'll stop glowing."

"I know that, Father." With that Lystara hopped down the side steps, followed by Malyna, who wore a bemused expression.

"Should we go with them?" murmured Alastar.

"We can watch from here," replied Alyna, in an equally low voice. "If they go beyond the hedges in the middle of the slope, then we'll follow, under a concealment."

"We'd better start now, then," replied Alastar wryly. "I don't see that Lystara's going to be stopping until she reaches the river."

The two went down the steps and began to walk after the girls.

"It's a lovely night," Alyna said. "Just warm enough and the slightest touch of a breeze."

Alastar felt that it was a touch too warm, and he would have personally liked a stronger breeze. "If there happened to be more of a wind, we wouldn't be seeing all those glowbugs."

"But the glowbugs are beautiful," Alyna pointed out. "We really don't see them that often, and we almost never take time to enjoy them."

Alastar had to admit she had the right of that.

Twilight was fading into early night as they followed the girls, under the faint light of Artiema, three days past full and on the wane. Alastar began to pick up the pace as the girls started up the stone steps in the middle of the grassy slope.

Although Malyna and Lystara were walking evenly and carefully, the point lights from the glowbugs closest to the steps began to fade as the pair climbed step by step.

"You're right," murmured Alyna. "She won't stop until she reaches the riverwall."

"Or until she runs into some juniors looking for privacy."

"Or the monitors patrolling to assure that privacy doesn't go too far."

The girls reached the top of the steps and kept going. Alastar and Alyna followed and then continued along the stone walk that led to north-point, the northern tip of Imagisle. Lystara and Malyna stopped suddenly some ten yards from the riverwall. Just as abruptly, the glowbugs in the waist-high hedge bordering the walk below the raised riverwall flickered, starting on each side of the stone walk that led directly to the slight protrusion in the riverwall that was the only indication that it was the northernmost point of the wall. The light-points rapidly darkened on both sides, until there were only scattered glimmers.

To the right, a good five yards to the right of Lystara, Alastar saw shadows outlined against the faint shimmer of the river to the north, shadows climbing over the top of the riverwall.

Then there was a gasp.

"What have we here?" The rough voice, low as it was, carried enough for Alastar to know it didn't belong on Imagisle.

Without even looking at each other, Alastar and Alyna both began to run.

Within moments, Alastar could see a figure holding a girl—but the girl was neither Lystara nor Malyna, while another held a young man who struggled. In fact, he could not see either girl. A third dark-clad man held a rifle aimed at the struggling youngster.

At that moment, the rifle seemed to fall apart, and the girl spun away from the man who had held her. Two more men vaulted onto the riverwall, both holding rifles.

Alastar imaged iron darts into both, as did Alyna, and both men plunged forward onto the stone walk, their rifles crashing and spinning away.

The man whose rifle had broken lunged toward the youngster still held captive, a knife in his hand, but slowed as a mist surrounded his head. Then he screamed, as needles appeared across his face. Blood spurted from one eye as a spike, rather than a dart, appeared there. He staggered, then sagged to the ground and was still.

The man who had held the girl crumpled, an iron dart protruding from his skull, a startled expression frozen on his face.

Yet another dark-clad figure jumped onto the riverwall, swinging his rifle around, but before he could bring it to bear, or Alastar could image, the rifleman stiffened, tottered, and fell back.

Alastar wasn't sure he heard a splash, and that worried him. He sprinted to the wall and looked out. Despite the faint light from Artiema, he could not clearly make out how many men remained on the barge-like craft that the two sailors on the prow were pushing away from the riverwall even though they were only two yards below him—a yard more than would have been the case farther south along the riverwall. Rather than guess, he imaged away a chunk of the hull below the prow, then imaged a spray of iron darts across the deck of the craft. A second and more targeted spray followed when he saw two figures still standing.

Then he imaged away part of the upstream side hull, watching as the craft dropped lower in the water. There was no motion on the deck of the flatboat as the current slowly carried it away from Alastar, first scraping against the stone riverwall and then sinking lower while it drifted away from the stone, slowly gaining speed.

Alastar turned, scanning the area, but could see no one except Alyna and the boy and girl . . . and the five bodies.

"Girls," said Alyna calmly, "you can drop the concealments."

Both Lystara and Malyna appeared—Lystara less than a yard from the female student imager, Malyna by the hedge.

As he walked toward the others, Alastar belatedly recognized the young man and the girl. "Davour, Ilora . . . just what were you two doing this close to the riverwall?" He shook his head. "Don't bother answering. There should be some disciplinary punishment, but I think you've both been through enough tonight. You'll walk back with us in a few moments." He looked to Lystara. "You used your shields to push Ilora to safety, didn't you?"

"That was all right, wasn't it?"

"It was well done. Very well done. It might have gotten very unpleasant after that if your mother and I hadn't decided to follow you when you kept heading up the steps toward the riverwall—which you should not have done, either." He looked around. "Who imaged the pepper mist?"

"I did," admitted Davour.

"And the spike to the eye?" Alastar looked to Malyna.

"How did you know?"

"It wasn't likely to be anyone else." He looked to Ilora. "The needles?"

"Yes, sir. I'm still not good with darts."

"If you are in a situation like that again, and I hope you're not, make sure some needles go into the eyes."

"Yes, sir."

"Who broke the rifle?" asked Alyna.

"I did," said Lystara. "That was a mistake. I was trying to get it to explode in his hands. It didn't work."

Alastar frowned, then walked over to where the two pieces of the broken rifle lay, leaning down to inspect them. "Not so much a mistake as a miscalculation. There was a small explosion or fire here." He straightened up. "Davour. I don't feel much like running. Hurry to the duty maitre and inform . . . her"—it took Alastar a moment to remember that Celiena had the duty—"what happened here. She'll need to have the duty disciplinary squad come up here and take care of the bodies. You wait there for me."

"Yes, sir." Davour hurried off, south along the stone walk and then down the long and gradual staircase.

Alyna moved to the wall and looked out across the river. "There's no sign of anyone else."

"Good." Given the currents around the north end of Imagisle, Alastar hadn't thought that someone would have tried to land a flatboat there.

He went from one body to the next, looking closely. All wore the same dark brown uniforms, and all the rifles were seemingly identical. Then he quickly searched each, looking for something that might easily identify from where they came. He found nothing of the sort. He also only found seven coppers among all five bodies.

Finally, he straightened. "We might as well head back now that you girls have seen the glowbugs. After we collect all the rifles. We don't want anyone fiddling with them. There's already been enough excitement this evening."

26

While Alyna herded the girls back to the Maitre's house, Alastar escorted Ilora back to the girls' cottage occupied by the student seconds, and then made his way to the administration building. Once there, he instructed Celiena on what needed to be done, and by whom, before he headed back home. Because almost a glass had passed, the girls were in bed, although he doubted they were sleeping. Alyna immediately poured them each a dark lager before they moved to the main-floor salon.

Trying to be faintly humorous as he settled into one armchair, Alastar said, "That's one glowbug viewing that Lystara and Malyna won't ever forget." He took a slow swallow of the lager.

"We'll likely remember it more vividly, dearest."

"You're probably right. We were fortunate . . . in more ways than one. Do you know which girl suggested concealments so quickly?"

"Each said the other did."

"Lystara put her shields to good use, but all of them, even Ilora and Davour, did well. Although those two had no business being there."

"What did you tell them?"

"Just about that. I also told each of them separately that, if anything like that happened again, they'd get double the disciplinary punishment. I'll need to have Akoryt note that."

"Have him note it, but have him remove the note in a season if they're good."

"That's probably better," Alastar admitted. "Tonight worries me. More than a little. We don't have enough imagers, especially those with good shields, to patrol every yard of the riverwall, and with the river so high the wall itself doesn't provide as much protection as when the river is at its usual level, or lower."

"After this, they may not try again . . . or not soon."

"I hope you're right, but we'll still need regular patrols along the northern riverwall."

"You know that the word will be all over the seconds and thirds by tomorrow afternoon about Malyna and Lystara?"

"I worry about that as well. It was bad enough that Malyna killed the one brown-shirt. I don't like the idea of the younger imagers seeing just how easy it is."

"I wouldn't worry about Malyna. She's sensitive, but practical. She only did it when she saw Ilora was about to be attacked."

"The good thing, if it can be called good, is that the brown-shirts don't have any idea how close they came to being successful."

"They might have killed Davour. I'm not certain about Ilora," replied Alyna. "If they'd come farther south, they would have reached us, and then the same thing would have happened. The walls here have stopped cannon shells."

"Except it would have been messier, and Jienna and others would have been in danger."

"That's true, but the result would have been the same from the point of view of the brown-shirts."

Alastar wasn't so sure about that, but then Alyna had been as quick as he'd been, if not quicker, and she had certainly been deadly. "How was Lystara?"

"She was fine. She didn't even think about killing any of them. She just wanted to protect Ilora. Ilora has been friendly to Malyna."

"Not too friendly, I hope."

"Dearest, you can't worry about everything."

"Isn't that the task of the Maitre?" he asked, not quite sardonically.

"Within reason, even if we do live in most unreasonable times."

"I have to wonder just how many brown-shirt companies there are left around L'Excelsis."

"You think they're that close?"

"They have to be. None of the dead brown-shirts had that much in the way of personal items. That tells me that they're quartered not all that far away."

"You can't search every High Holder's estate around L'Excelsis."

"No . . . but maybe something will happen that will suggest who might be quartering them."

"Would the boat show anything?"

"I'd doubt it, but it's probably milles downstream by now. And if none of the brown-shirts we found had anything on them . . ."

"None of the bodies on the boat—if there are any left—would, either," said Alyna.

"At the time, I didn't think about saving the boat."

"You also can't think about everything when your daughter and niece are in the middle of a fight. I wouldn't have thought about saving the boat, either."

Alastar took a long swallow from the beaker. The dark lager was good, he had to admit. "I just wonder how many High Holders are involved."

"More than you know, and fewer than you fear."

Fewer than you fear? That wasn't much comfort, given that he feared hundreds of High Holders might join in the revolt if he and Wilkorn couldn't put down the rebels fairly quickly. He took another swallow of the lager. Then he frowned. "How did you come out in imaging poisoned bullets? I never did ask."

"It's very time-consuming, and even I had to image against a template. Why?"

"Wilkorn's troops will be outnumbered when we meet the rebel regiments. If we had enough special bullets . . ."

"But poisoned bullets? In a full battle?"

"They started using them. Against students . . . children. I'm not feeling terribly charitable. I'd like to use the special bullets against High Holders and rebel officers."

She nodded. "I'll see what we can do." After a moment, she added, "You need to finish your lager . . . slowly . . . and then get some sleep. You have too many bruises . . . and don't tell me you don't."

Alastar couldn't argue with that.

By Samedi morning, when Alastar and Alyna walked into the administration building slightly before seventh glass, Alastar was feeling much better than he had the evening before. A solid night's sleep, despite some disturbing dreams, followed by a good run that helped with the residual stiffness, a thorough washing-up—even if the shower was cold—and a solid breakfast, had left him in a much better frame of mind.

Much of that feeling departed when he saw a concerned-looking Cyran waiting for them outside his study. "I have the feeling I'm not going to like what you're going to tell me."

"I won't like telling it," replied Cyran dourly, "especially after what happened to you and your family last night."

Maercyl and Dareyn exchanged worried glances, but neither spoke as Alastar gestured toward the study door. None of the three said a word until they were inside the study with the door closed, and Alastar looked to Cyran.

"The smaller problem is *Veritum*."

"The newssheet?"

Cyran nodded. "The entire building burned down last night—all of the old port tower on the east side of the river where they print the newssheet. They have that . . . it's like a grape press, but they can make a hundred copies in a glass or so. I don't know how it works. The old fellow who was the watchman died in the fire. Heisyt says that two of the street urchins saw men in brown leave the building right before the flames came up. The fire brigade barely managed to save the River Inn. They wouldn't have been able to, except the river's still high and they could use the hand pumps and hoses."

"No one else saw anything?"

"Celiena was the duty maitre, and she watched it to make sure it didn't spread, but there wasn't much that she could do from here, especially since the duty squad was dealing with bodies."

Alastar understood that. Imaging water was difficult, especially in quantities and over any distance. "Has the newssheet gotten any threats?"

"Heisyt didn't know of any."

"I'd wager that our High Holder rebels don't like the news that *Veritum* has been reporting." If that were the case, it wouldn't have surprised Alastar. "And it's likely the attempted raid on Imagisle was also to keep us busy."

"I'd thought that myself," said Cyran.

"What else?"

"At some time around ninth glass last night, more of the shooters in brown uniforms attacked Factor Naathyn's factorage and coach works. They killed Naathyn and his wife and three of their children. Then they burned everything."

"How does Heisyt know it was the brown-shirts?" asked Alyna.

"Some of the servants and an apprentice escaped. Heisyt's certain that it's because the Civic Patrol hasn't been able to find Naathyn's oldest. He's the one who slit Paellyt's son's throat."

"Did they find him last night?"

Cyran shook his head. "None of the servants has seen him since the night Paellyt's son used a coach to run down Naathyn's next-to-eldest son."

Alastar frowned. *If we'd only removed all of the shooters who attacked Imagisle.* But he hadn't expected them to act so boldly against others, such as Factor Naathyn, or even against Imagisle. *But that you should have expected.* "How many men were there?"

"The servants didn't know, except it was a lot. They burst into the house and shot everyone in the bedrooms, Naathyn, his wife, and the rest of the children. Two boys. One of them was only seven. Three daughters, too."

"Were there any threats?" Alastar felt like he was repeating himself.

"Heisyt didn't know of any." Cyran paused. "He told me that there are broadsheets being posted by High Holder Paellyt. They say that he will pay two hundred golds, no questions asked, for anyone who turns young Naathyn over to him . . . or to the Civic Patrol. The broadsheets also promise that Paellyt will insist on a fair hearing before the High Justicer."

"That's very interesting," said Alastar.

"Interesting?" Cyran's eyebrows lifted. "The young man wouldn't live to see the hearing."

"You think the Civic Patrol is that corrupt?" asked Alyna.

Before Cyran could answer, there was a knock on the door, and Dareyn announced, "Maitre Akoryt."

"Have him come in."

As soon as Akoryt closed the door, he asked, "You all know about the fires?"

Alastar nodded. "They were both set by the brown-shirts, according to the Civic Patrol, and they killed a watchman at *Veritum* and all of Naathyn's family except for the son they wanted. That's all we've discussed. Cyran was telling us about Paellyt's handbills. Did you hear about those?"

"Yes, sir. They're everywhere."

Alastar gestured to the chairs. "We might as well sit down. Do either of you think Paellyt really wants young Naathyn alive?"

"I think Paellyt would rather have him in the Civic Patrol gaol," replied the Senior Imager. "Otherwise he'd have to make sure he stayed alive."

"Where, if something befell him in gaol, Paellyt could blame it all on the Civic Patrol," said Alastar.

"Two hundred golds? That's a great temptation," Akoryt pointed out.

Except for someone very wealthy, with other objectives, reflected Alastar, but all he said was, "It is indeed. We'll have to see if anyone is tempted."

"You don't think someone will turn him in?" asked Akoryt.

"I think many people would like to in order to get those golds, but that's not the question. The question is whether the person sheltering him is going to be tempted."

"Or would trust Paellyt to pay," added Alyna dryly. "Paellyt may not have two hundred golds to spare."

That brought another thought to Alastar's mind. "What if someone else put up the golds? Knowing that the factors might not want to give him up?"

"Another way to stir up more High Holders against the factors and the rex?" suggested Alyna.

"The thought had crossed my mind. Printing up all those handbills wasn't without a cost, either."

"When were they printed?" Alyna asked.

"Heisyt said they started seeing them yesterday," replied Cyran.

"Before the attack at Naathyn's," said Alastar. "That's also interesting. It could be that the handbills were posted to divert attention from

Paellyt . . . or to provide an alibi of sorts so that he could claim that he had nothing to do with the attack and that he just wanted justice for the death of his son."

"Or," suggested Alyna, "the attack was carried out to make the point that mere justice was insufficient to remedy the loss to the High Holders . . . that a single dead High Holder youngblood was worth the lives of the entire family of the factor whose son revenged the death of his brother."

"By the time we sort that out," said Alastar dryly, "the whole rebellion may be over, one way or another." He looked to Cyran, then Akoryt. "Have Alamara and Tyndaal had any more problems?"

"They've both added more guards outside," replied Cyran.

"All that will do is keep problems from happening near their gaming," observed Alastar, "not that you could expect more from them. They're interested in business, and they cater to money, not either High Holder or factor youngbloods exclusively. Is there anything else you've discovered . . . about the fires or that bears on the rebellion?"

"Vaschet has closed the gates at his ironworks," said Akoryt. "He'll only receive ore or send out iron by water."

"Do you know why?"

"The word is that he's furious the Factors' Council won't support him against you, Maitre. He's also working the rifle factorage twenty glasses a day."

"Those rifles aren't going to the army or other factors, I'd wager," said Cyran. "You think we should sink some of his barges headed downriver? That's where the rebels are."

"I don't much care for Vaschet, but we're likely to be facing the rebels before Vaschet can make that many more rifles, and another action against him really won't set well with the factors."

"Do the factors matter that much, sir?" asked Akoryt.

"They don't. Elthyrd does. He's backed the Collegium. If we undercut him, we may be back to dealing with another hothead like Hulet. If the rebellion drags out . . . then we'll have to reconsider. The question is what we need to do next . . . and the supplies we'll need to do it."

At the mention of supplies, Akoryt looked puzzled.

"If we have a rebel army marching toward L'Excelsis," replied Alastar, "it might be a good idea to stop them before they get in cannon range of the Chateau D'Rex or Imagisle. That means we'll need to have enough horses and supplies to accompany Wilkorn's battalions when they leave in a few days. We also need to discuss how many imagers should comprise our force and who exactly those imagers should be."

"Are you thinking about sending all the senior maitres?" asked Cyran.

"A goodly number, but not all. I was thinking you and I would definitely go, and Maitre Alyna and Maitre Gaellen would definitely stay. We need to talk about the others."

"If I'm staying on Imagisle," declared Alyna, "then out of Tiranya, Seliora, and Celiena, two of the three should go."

"Which two would you suggest?" asked Alastar.

"Tiranya and Seliora—they have the strongest shields and the most experience."

"I should go," declared Akoryt.

"Also," Alastar said, turning to Cyran, "Alyna will need to show you how to image some special bullets. She's already been imaging some."

A frown creased Cyran's forehead.

"She'll explain later. It's a possible way of making the rebel leaders pay in the same way we have. It may also offset some of the numerical advantage that the rebels have."

In the end, the four decided that the twelve imagers who would accompany Alastar in support of Wilkorn's forces would be Cyran, Akoryt, and all the other senior maitres except Gaellen, Obsolym, and Shaelyt, Shaelyt being excepted because Tiranya was going and they had a five-year-old son. From the junior maitres, they decided on Belsior, Chervyt, Dylert, Julyan, Seliora, and Taurek. After that, Alastar divided the imagers into two groups, one under Cyran, and the other under Akoryt, although Alastar knew he'd likely be in command of that group most of the time.

Then came two quints of discussion about supplies, and additions to the early list that Alastar had given Thelia.

When Cyran and Akoryt had left, Alyna turned to Alastar. "I could do as much as Cyran could."

"You can do more," replied Alastar. "But the Collegium will need a strong maitre if we fail or even if we succeed and don't survive. Cyran isn't that strong in standing up for the Collegium, and we both know it. If I send others out and don't accompany them, then I'll be faulted for not having used the full strength of the Collegium . . . and . . . there are Lystara and Malyna."

"At least you put them as the last reason."

"Do you disagree?"

Alyna sighed. "I don't. It's necessary. I understand that. But I don't have to like it. I'd feel better going and leaving you here." She shook her head. "We both know that wouldn't work."

"Would you suggest I do something differently?"

"Just make sure Cyran shares every risk that you do. You've protected him from his shortcomings for years. If necessary, let him make the sacrifices."

"One way or another that won't be—"

"Alastar!" Alyna glared. "Would you please listen to me? Don't dismiss my concerns. The Collegium can do without Cyran. If you won't save yourself for the good of the Collegium, just think of what my life would be like both missing you and having to deal with Cyran as Maitre . . . and just how much sadness your daughter would feel."

Alastar was silent for several moments. While he had no doubts that Alyna was strong-willed, even he was surprised, not so much by the words themselves, but by the vehemence behind them.

"Now . . . do you understand, dear one?" Alyna said gently as the silence dragged out.

Alastar did.

28

Solayi morning was quiet, and there were no messages from the duty
maitre, for which Alastar was most grateful. He and Alyna did enjoy
breakfast later than usual, and took a leisurely walk around Imagisle with
the girls—still with full shields—and he finally was feeling that he could
again carry them without strain.

Later, he spent time in their personal study, considering and refining
the details of the plan for the imager force to accompany the army . . .
including trying to consider as many possible contingencies as he could,
while Alyna went to visit Linzya.

That time was to be not entirely quiet, as he discovered when he
heard raised voices from the parlor. Rather than just burst in, he raised
a concealment and tiptoed out of the study and across the hall where he
peered into the parlor. There, Malyna and Lystara sat across the folding
plaques table they had set up.

"You can't play an imager when you still have blues in your hand,"
insisted Malyna. "You have to play a blue or another chorister."

"You can play imagers anytime," replied Lystara testily.

"You cannot."

"You can, too."

Malyna folded her plaques and set them facedown on the worn but
time-polished goldenwood. "I'll play with you when you want to play
by the rules."

"You imaged that chorister," declared Lystara.

"I did not."

At that point, Alastar dropped the concealment. "Lystara, you're
accusing Malyna of cheating by imaging."

"She did."

"Turn all the plaques face up. Now."

At the chill in Alastar's voice, both girls turned their plaques up.

"Spread the discard pile." When they had done so, Alastar asked, "Are
there two blue choristers?"

"No, sir."

"Malyna, count the plaques aloud and slowly."

"Yes, sir. One, two, three . . ." The last plaque she counted was number fifty . . . as it should have been.

"Now . . . there are no extra cards, and every suit has ten plaques. Is that correct?"

Both girls nodded.

"Watch." Alastar concentrated.

Three more chorister plaques all appeared—all blues. A moment later, one was red, another black.

"Pick up the new choristers, and handle each of them, both of you." Alastar waited, then asked, "Do they feel any different?"

Malyna shook her head, and then Lystara did.

"Why did I stop your game, and why did I do what I did?"

Lystara frowned.

After a moment, Malyna spoke. "You showed us how easy it would be for an imager to cheat at plaques."

"It's not quite that easy, but a good imager could keep track of what plaques have been played and what have not, and in some cases, change the plaques in his hand in order to win. But that is cheating, and there is always the risk of duplicating a plaque in someone else's hand. Besides being unfair, why is playing plaques for any stakes—gambling—absolutely forbidden to imagers?"

"Because people would think an imager was cheating even if he wasn't?" asked Malyna.

"Wasn't that what you did, Lystara?" asked Alastar.

"Yes, sir." Lystara's voice was resigned, just short of being sullen.

"How many young men have been killed in the last month because someone thought they were cheating."

"Five?" questioned Lystara.

"Between three and five, depending on whether you count the retaliation as caused by the charge of cheating." Alastar was guessing on the exact number, but felt he was close enough. "Now what would be the reaction if imagers were doing it?"

"It wouldn't be very good," admitted Lystara.

"Now . . . you can play plaques, if you play by the rules, or you can go to your rooms and read. It's up to you. If you don't want to play plaques, you need to put away the table and chairs."

"I'll be good," said Lystara.

"Promise?" asked Malyna.

"I promise."

Alastar managed not to sigh and eased back to the study. He hadn't wanted to mention that there was an imager party game that involved seeing who could image and re-image plaques while match-wager was played. Any player could strike a bell—and if the plaques didn't match up, the bell-ringer won points, but if they did, every other player received a point. It had been popular at Westisle. Alastar hadn't seen it played at Imagisle, but he suspected something like it had probably developed.

Less than a glass later, Alyna returned.

"I see the girls are still playing plaques."

"They are now. Lystara accused Malyna of cheating by imaging. We had a lesson. I hope it took. They had a choice of reading in their rooms or playing nicely."

"I'm sure the lesson took. You have a way of doing that."

Alastar had his doubts about that. If his lessons took so well, he wouldn't have had to give them so often. *Except most young people need repetition . . . and more repetition.* "How is Linzya doing?"

"As well as you might expect. She doesn't understand why he left without a word to her, but she can't believe that he's part of the High Holder rebellion."

"What else could it be? We've gone over the possibilities. Nothing else makes sense."

"It doesn't seem to, but sometimes what makes sense is how things turn out, and sometimes, if far fewer times, what seems to make sense is totally wrong."

"You're withholding judgment?"

"I suspect you're right, but I'm leaving open the possibility that Bettaur might not be as bad as we think."

"I'd like to think so, but in even the best case, he's going off on his own, and that's not exactly encouraging."

"You've often gone off on your own, dearest."

"But not without telling you," Alastar replied before quickly adding, "Not since we've been married."

"You were older when we married, and so was I."

Older, but not necessarily wiser. "That's true, and there's little we can do. Bettaur could be anywhere."

Before Alyna could reply, there was a knock on the door. "Mother . . . you promised you'd play plaques with us when you returned."

Alyna looked to Alastar and murmured. "Four-hand?"

He nodded.

"Your father and I will both play."

"Good!"

Alastar couldn't help smiling.

After a glass or so of playing plaques, followed by dinner, it was time for the evening services at the anomen.

As the four left the house, Lystara said, "I wish we didn't have to go to services on Solayi. They're so long."

"They're very short here," said Alastar. As he saw Malyna nod, he asked, "How long are they in Rivages?"

"Much, much longer. Chorister Aumyn never stops talking."

Lystara looked at Malyna, almost unbelievingly, before saying, "Doesn't everyone fall asleep?"

"We couldn't," replied Malyna. "Father would ask us about the homily when we got home."

"Maybe we should do that here," said Alastar, managing to keep the smile out of his words.

"Father . . ."

"That actually sounds like a very good idea," added Alyna.

Lystara shot a glare at Malyna, then began to walk faster, as if to leave the older girl behind. Malyna continued at the same pace. After a hundred yards, Lystara stopped and waited for her parents and Malyna to catch up.

When they did, Alyna looked hard at Lystara and said one word. "Enough."

Lystara seemed to shrink. "I'm sorry, Mother."

"Your apology is accepted. I expect no more displays like that."

"Yes, Mother . . . Father."

Alastar kept the nod and amusement he felt to himself. He never wanted to receive one of those looks from Alyna.

The anomen service followed the usual pattern, and Alastar followed his usual practice of listening, joining the chorus of refrains and responses and barely singing . . . until Iskhar got into the evening's homily.

"Does the Nameless value a man or woman by how much land over which they hold sway? Or how many golds are laid up in their strong-room? By the other side of the coin, why should the Nameless value more the poor if that poor man is a beggar who could work and will not because what tasks he could receive pay for are beneath his sense of self-worth? As Rholan once said, 'Worth is not measured by what one has or does not have, but by what one does with what one has.' That is why imagers have a greater obligation than many others. Imagers have an ability that others do not, and to waste that ability or to misuse it in the quest for power or wealth is one of the worst forms of Naming. . . ."

As Iskhar went on, Alastar wondered about what the chorister had propounded. Should a poor man or poor woman be forced into labor that destroyed body and spirit simply because they were poor? More than a few imagers had come to the Collegium relatively young and unable to read or write, or with few skills. Even those who were limited in their imaging skills and ended up doing other tasks ended up with a far better life than they would have had. How much worth, even if measured just by accomplishments and not wealth or power, was often the result of chance, of the parents to whom one was born and what they did . . . or could not do?

He was still mulling over those thoughts as he and Alyna walked back toward the Maitre's house after the service, letting Malyna and Lystara lead the way.

"You were deep in thought in the latter part of Iskhar's homily," observed Alyna.

"I was thinking about worth, about how sometimes, what one can accomplish is as much a matter of chance as choice."

"You had little, and you've accomplished much."

"I was loved and treated as well as my parents could manage, and because I could image and was willing to work hard, I have been able to do what I have done. It was mere chance that I am an imager. My father was a good man, and he was an intelligent man, but he came from little, and fortune deserted him. He worked his entire life until he could no longer work, and he died penniless. I have accomplished more than he did. Am I a better man than he was? I doubt it."

"You are a good man who has risked his life for others. You have returned the Collegium to a position where young imagers can have a better future. I cannot compare you to others I never knew. Such comparisons are hateful. As far as I'm concerned, they're just another form of Naming."

Alastar laughed softly. "That is a far better homily than what Iskhar offered . . . and much shorter."

Alyna smiled and took his hand.

When Alastar woke on Lundi morning, the sky was so dark that he thought it was too early to be rising, but the thunder and the pounding of rain on the slate roof of the Maitre's house explained the darkness. A roll of thunder reverberated through the bedchamber, but did not rattle the sturdy window frames.

"How heavy is the rain?" asked Alyna, slowly sitting up in bed.

"Bad enough that we won't be running this morning, and if it continues for more than a glass or two, bad enough that there won't be any grain crops left to harvest anywhere around L'Excelsis."

"Just as the local High Holders thought they might be able to salvage some of their crops," she added. "I hope it's not this bad in Rivages."

"Your brother doesn't rely as much on harvests, I thought."

"He doesn't, but that doesn't mean he won't suffer from too much rain. He'll have to buy grain to feed the tenants and the livestock if it gets bad enough."

"At least, Lystara will be happy she doesn't have to run this morning."

"And unhappy that she'll have to wear oilskins to get to her instructionals," said Alyna, swinging her feet onto the rug beside the bed.

Alastar peered out the window. "It does look like this is coming from the north. I'm going to go out and see if it's having any effect on the river . . . or rather if it rained north of here and that has already affected the river."

"You wear your oilskins."

"I know." Alastar grinned. "Otherwise, a certain young lady will ask why she has to wear them if her father doesn't. I'll wash up and shave after I get back." He pulled on his exercise clothes and boots, then headed downstairs, where he donned his oilskin and headed for the front door.

Once he stepped out onto the porch, he noticed one thing immediately—there wasn't that much wind. The rain was coming down heavily, but not in sheets, and it was falling close to straight down. Already, the walks and the stone-paved ways were miniature streams flowing toward the river, with enough depth that Alastar was walking through ankle-deep water. The fact that all of Imagisle had been graded in a way to assure that the water drained—and that the walls and drains still functioned well after four centuries—was just another indication of the skill and foresight of Quaeryt and the original imagers.

Alastar turned toward the eastern side of the isle, since it was marginally closer, and since he also wanted to see how the buildings on the east bank were faring. From the riverwall, he could just barely make out the east bank. The water level was a little less than half a yard higher than it had been the day before, if he remembered accurately, getting all too close to overtopping the riverwalls, and the water was definitely moving faster. That wasn't good. On the other hand, there wasn't likely to be another attempt at a raid using flatboats, not soon, anyway.

Alyna was dressed in her grays and at her desk in the study when he returned. "How is it?"

"The river's rising, but not too fast, and the water level is still half a yard below the lowest point on the riverwalls. If it rises much more, there will be flooding in parts of L'Excelsis."

"On top of everything else."

"The rain might slow the rebels down some."

"Optimist." The word was said affectionately. "Go get washed and dressed. I'm hungry. So is Lystara."

Alastar smiled as he hung up the oilskin and then started up the stairs.

Somewhat more than a glass later, after breakfast and wading through the water and continuing rain, Alastar and Alyna—and the girls—finally reached the administration building.

Maercyl was alone at the table desk in the anteroom. "I stopped by Dareyn's cottage. I suggested that it might be best if he didn't come in until the rain stopped. He was going to come, but Elmya and I persuaded him that the last thing he needed was to wade through water."

"Thank you. I think that was for the best, and I do appreciate your looking out for him. I suspect Elmya did as well."

"I got that feeling, sir."

"Are there any messages?"

"Not yet, sir."

Alastar nodded and then walked into his study. It was just as well there were no messages. If there had been, given the weather, they wouldn't have held good news. He hadn't been in his study more than two quints, most of which he had spent studying the maps of the roads and towns along the River Aluse south of L'Excelsis, when Maercyl rapped on the door.

"Factorius Estafen is here and would like to see you, sir."

That can't be good. "Have him come in." Alastar rose as the comparatively young banking factor entered the study.

Estafen appeared slightly haggard, and there were circles under his eyes that Alastar did not recall from his previous visit less than two weeks earlier, although his black beard remained well trimmed. The lower parts of his trousers were wet, and the leather of his boots was dark with water.

"Good morning, Maitre."

"You're looking a bit concerned."

"You're being most polite. Let me say that I'm not at my best, and I'm likely to be even less so. That is why I am here. You did request that I keep you informed." Estafen's tone was sardonic.

Alastar gestured to the chairs and reseated himself, waiting until Estafen was settled before speaking. "Tell me about it."

"It's simple, Maitre. No High Holder will pay me what he owes me. Every High Holder who owes me has declared that he will not abide by the rex's denial of the petitions. Nor will any of them submit to the decrees of any justicer requiring repayment."

"You can point out to other High Holders that you cannot lend to them if those who owe you will not pay . . . or are all the High Holders refusing to pay anyone anything at the moment?"

"It appears to be that way here in L'Excelsis. Elsewhere, I cannot say."

Estafen's reply did not surprise Alastar, but did remind him about the need to follow up on Meinyt's idea for a Factors' Council that covered all of Solidar—when the time came. "How long can you hold out? It's likely that anything the rex and the Collegium can do may take several weeks to accomplish what is necessary."

"If we don't make any more loans, and if too many factors don't want too many of their golds back . . . a month, maybe two." Estafen shook his head. "Oh . . . and then there's Vaschet. He also has declared he will not pay when his note comes due because the Collegium and the rex have almost ruined him. He sent a message telling me to collect from you."

"One way or another, he will pay," Alastar said quietly.

"Ah . . . there is the question of when."

"There is," agreed Alastar. "You might have to run an ironworks or sell it to someone who can."

Estafen swallowed.

"That is," Alastar continued, "if Vaschet chooses not to pay his just debts." He smiled pleasantly. "I do appreciate your letting me know about this decision of the High Holders. It's a matter I need to discuss with Rex Lorien. It's likely he'll be even less happy with them than you are. Is there anything else I should know?"

"No, sir." Estafen paused. "I do hope you are successful in resolving this without it taking all harvest and fall."

"I doubt it will take that long . . . but, unhappily, anything is possible." Until it is not. Alastar stood. "Again, I want to thank you for the information."

"I won't say it was my pleasure, sir, but I'm glad to have been helpful."

After Estafen had left, Alastar told Maercyl to find him a third with strong shields or a junior maitre, whoever was immediately free, to act as an escort, and then pulled back on his oilskins and headed for the stables. Even after he had saddled the gray gelding, and had one of Petros's assistants saddle another mount, he had to wait almost half a quint before Dylert hurried up at almost a run, his boots splashing through the water, although the rain was not coming down so heavily as it had earlier.

"I'm sorry, sir. I just got word. Most of the other maitres have applied imaging or instructionals right now."

Alastar should have thought of that, given that it was late morning. "That's all right. Mount up. We're headed for the Chateau D'Rex. This will be your second visit in less than a week, but this time, you'll probably only be waiting with the mounts. Since there might still be shooters around, I need an escort with strong shields."

"Yes, sir. Maercyl said so."

Alastar didn't say more until they were riding up the approach causeway to the Bridge of Desires. "Do you still have a scar from that lamp-oil burn?"

"Ah . . . sir, I'd hoped . . ."

"That I'd forget it? How could I? It was one of the first instances of misguided student imaging after I became Maitre. I'm sure you'll remember the first time something like that happens when you're duty maitre—if it hasn't happened already." Alastar frowned. "You were duty maitre on Solayi—the day after the old river port tower caught fire, weren't you?"

"No, sir. Celiena was. But I was out that night, and I saw the flames. One moment, there was just some black smoke and the next flames were everywhere. I told Maitre Cyran that it wasn't natural. It couldn't have been. Thelia agreed. She said some sort of oils had to have been used, probably oily rags."

"Thelia? Years ago . . ." Alastar grinned.

Dylert flushed. "I knew she was special then."

"If you still think so, let her know you do."

"Ah . . ."

"You have? Good." Alastar wasn't about to ask whether the two either were very good friends, sweethearts, or even more intimate. That was their affair. And sometimes friendship turned into love, as it had with Tiranya and Shaelyt, and sometimes it didn't. What he did know was that people didn't share appreciation nearly enough . . . and that he often was guilty of exactly that.

Before long, the two turned their mounts onto the Boulevard D'Rex Regis, much changed from what it had been when Alastar and the Collegium imagers had built it thirteen years earlier. Now it was lined with shops of the better crafters and merchants, and there were even cafés here and there, not that anyone was outside under the awnings with the rain continuing to fall.

After a time, Dylert cleared his throat. "Sir . . . the word is that Bettaur fled Imagisle."

"Bettaur and Ashkyr are missing. So are two mounts. At present we have no idea beyond that. Do you know anything more that might shed light on the matter?"

"No, sir. Well . . . not directly."

Alastar nodded, then said, "But you have an idea?"

"It's not that, sir. Last week, I couldn't help but overhear a few words between Bettaur and Ashkyr. Bettaur said something like it was important not to do things that gave people the wrong impression because most people never got over that impression, and that it was almost impossible to change their minds unless you did something truly outstanding. I didn't hear more than that. It just made me think."

"Do you think he knew you could hear him?"

"I don't see how. I was on the other side of the wall on the south side of the stable. I didn't even see who it was until several moments later when I saw the two of them walking toward the East Bridge."

"Did you tell Thelia or anyone else?"

"Only Thelia, and she promised she wouldn't tell anyone else, except you, if you asked."

"What did she say?"

Dylert grinned. "That Bettaur would have to do something really outstanding to change her mind."

"What do you think?"

"Bettaur might do something really good, but he'd do it so people would think better of him, and not because it was good."

"That's not always the best motivation, but if wanting to improve people's opinion of you makes you do good things, it's certainly better than the alternatives." *Especially where Bettaur is concerned.*

"Unless you do things that people want you to that they think are good and aren't," suggested Dylert.

"That can be a problem," agreed Alastar. "Do you and Thelia talk about things like that?"

"Sometimes. She thinks about that more than I do."

"She's a very bright woman. You're fortunate. But then, you were fortunate she was around just before I met you for the first time."

Dylert grinned sheepishly.

A little more than a quint later, Alastar and Dylert rode up the rear lane to the stables of the Chateau D'Rex, since Alastar wasn't about to have Dylert and the horses waiting out in the rain. After persuading the ostler to let them use the stables, not that doing so was difficult, Alastar dismounted and made his way to the rear entry and then inside, where he removed the oilskin and his soaked visor cap and handed them to one of the footmen before making his way up the grand staircase to Lorien's study.

"What's the problem now? Besides all this rain that no one needs?" asked Lorien sourly even before Alastar sat down in the chair across the desk from him. "I'm not certain I want to know."

"Estafen visited me this morning. He's the one who created the Banque D'Excelsis."

"You mentioned him earlier. Some of the High Holders wouldn't repay him."

"He just told me that all the High Holders now refuse to repay any debts to him or to other factors. They say they won't pay any debts until all their ancient privileges are restored." What they said was they wouldn't pay because Lorien had denied their petitions, but it amounted to the same thing, and Alastar didn't want Lorien focused on the petitions.

"Those self-centered ingrates! I'd have the whole High Council exe-cuted for that, except all the ones who first demanded that are already dead. They think their tariffs are high now. Wait until after you and the army take care of them."

"It might be better to issue a decree stating that the failure of any High Holder to pay all debts owed to any party, whether that party is a High Holder, factor, holder, merchant, or crafter will subject that High Holder to whatever measure the rex deems appropriate to repay that debt, but no measure can exceed twice the value of the debt owed."

"Make that thrice." Lorien frowned. "Are you sure you can deal with all of them?"

"No. Not all of them. They're scattered all over Solidar, but most of them either don't have or cannot afford much in the way of arms and armsmen at present. Once we put down the rebels, then the army and the Collegium can take on those who owe one by one . . . if it even comes to that. If necessary, an execution and confiscation of lands in a few cases might make the point." Alastar was feeling less and less chari-table toward the High Holders the more he learned about what many of them seemed to want.

Then again, if Vaschet were any example, many of the factors likely weren't much better.

"Where are the rebels?"

"Somewhere south of Caluse at this point." That was really a guess on Alastar's part, but he was fairly certain he'd know as soon as Wilkorn did. Since he hadn't heard anything, it was likely that they hadn't joined up with Aestyn's regiment yet.

"I can't believe they'd do this."

"Has Chelia received any more messages?"

"Not a one."

That tended to confirm one of Alastar's suspicions about who could deliver messages to the chateau stables and remain undetected.

"Who should I give Cransyr's lands to . . . and those of the other three?"

"Wait and see. Given that Cransyr was head of the council and that his son was part of the army rebellion, you can get away with confiscat-ing his lands. The other three might prove a problem because there's no proof—"

"No proof? With a rebellion going on?"

"There's nothing I know of remaining that would tie them to the rebellion. Anything that might have done so didn't survive the fire at the Chateau D'Council."

"Convenient for their heirs. . . . Now what should I consider for next year's tariff levels?"

Alastar could tell he wasn't leaving the chateau for a time.

30

By Mardi morning, the rain had subsided to a drizzle and then to a mist, allowing Alastar and the group of imagers assembled by Akoryt to manage a morning run, if avoiding all the low spots on Imagisle that resembled miniature lakes, while brushing away more than a few mosquitoes. The River Aluse was little more than a yard below the top of the riverwall—and that was the highest Alastar had ever seen it. Because the air was warm and damp, Alastar, Lystara, Malyna, and Alyna were all thoroughly soaked all the way through by the time they walked up the steps to the Maitre's dwelling after their run, a run that once more had left Alastar lagging his wife.

"At least it looks like it's going to clear up," Alyna observed, stopping on the porch and looking eastward.

"If it does, the river might not overtop the walls. I can hope, anyway," returned Alastar. "Downstream will be worse, especially around Reyks. The ground there is barely higher than the riverbanks."

"Why did the rebels go that way, then?"

"Because the road is good. It was built before the time of Rex Regis, but Quaeryt and his imagers improved it even more. Their bridges still look like they have been built in the past few years."

"You still wonder about him, don't you?"

"I do." Alastar blotted his forehead with a sleeve that was not quite dripping wet. "Even Gauswn's journals only give the slightest hint of what he was like and what else he did that we'll never know about."

"Isn't that true of everyone once those who knew them are gone?"

Alastar laughed softly. "Thank you."

"You're welcome." After a pause, she said, "We need to get ready for breakfast. We can't eat like this."

Alastar couldn't have agreed more.

By the time the four had washed up, dressed in grays, eaten breakfast, and left the house, the rain had stopped completely, and Alastar could see patches of blue between the clouds to the northeast. He just hoped that they wouldn't have more rain at least for a few days.

Once at the administration building he immediately went to find Thelia to go over the supply list he had planned for the small imager force to accompany Wilkorn's troopers. That took little more than a quint, and he then headed back toward his study. When he walked back into the anteroom, Maercyl stood waiting, holding an envelope. "This just came by army courier."

"Thank you." Alastar took the envelope and entered his study, where he immediately opened it, and began to read, concentrating on the body of the text.

> Scouts report that the rebel battalions continued through Caluse. They halted on Samedi for the night at Reyks. They continued on Solayi toward Nordeau. It would appear that they will occupy the old army quarters there. My judgment is that they will wait at Nordeau for reinforcements, possibly either from local High Holders or from Commander Aestyn's regiment.

> If they do march back north along the West River Road, my plan would be to meet them north of Caluse at a point where the terrain favors us. South of Caluse, the land is boggy and soft, and now that will be even less suitable.

> We will inform the Collegium and Rex Lorien daily on the position of the rebel forces.

How long will they wait in Nordeau? Alastar wondered if it might not be better to attack them immediately, but he was no strategist or military tactician. Then, too, it might be better to let the rebels do all the marching—or most of it—especially given the recent weather. The mosquitoes were already bad enough in L'Excelsis. He couldn't imagine what they'd be like in Reyks or Nordeau, especially with the red flies that infested the reeds along the river south of L'Excelsis.

In the meantime, there was the problem of the brown-shirts that apparently still remained in or around L'Excelsis. Alastar nodded, then walked to the study door. Both Maercyl and Dareyn looked at him.

"If you could, send someone to tell Maitre Cyran I need to see him. If he's giving an instructional or otherwise occupied, it can wait until he's finished."

"Yes, sir," said Maercyl, rising.

Alastar returned to the study, still thinking over the possibilities.

Cyran appeared a bit less than three quints later, hurrying into Alastar's study. "I hope I didn't delay anything. I was working with Arthos on something."

"Image-forging?"

Cyran nodded. "What do you need?"

"I've been thinking about the brown-shirts. Even after the army battalions left, even after we killed most of the lot attacking the Chateau D'Rex, there were those that attacked Imagisle, those that fired the port tower, and the ones who laid waste to Naathyn's factorage and family. That means they're still around. Does the Civic Patrol have any idea where they might be lodged or hiding?"

"I've asked Heisyt. He doesn't know. They appear, and then they're gone."

"It has to be fairly close to L'Excelsis, if not inside the city. I'd wager it's also fairly close to the Collegium."

"You think so, sir?"

"The fact that so few people see them suggests they aren't riding very far, and that they know the city. They vanished almost immediately after firing *Veritum* . . ." Alastar paused. Just why had they set fire to the old port tower that had held the newssheet printing works? Who would have cared most about a newssheet?

"Sir?"

"You'd mentioned that High Holder Laevoryn had a place north of the Boulevard D'Este. Do you know anything about it?"

"No, sir. Not any more than Commander Murranyt told me."

"I'd appreciate it if you'd find out. I'd like to see how large the stables are there."

"You think . . . ?"

"I have no idea, but the brown-shirts belong to High Holders. It won't hurt to look at a few of their places to see which High Holders might be quartering them."

"Wouldn't that be . . . rather obvious?"

"If anyone is looking, but I imagine lots of riders enter most High Holders' establishments. What if the grounds are extensive enough that there are other gates or entrances?" Alastar shrugged. "It can't hurt to look." *Especially since there's not much else we can do until we know what the rebel army is doing.* "Do it quietly."

"It might take a while."

"For the moment, it appears that we do have time. Until the High Holders do something else, or some factor or his son decides they've had enough of some High Holder or his offspring."

"You don't sound enthused about either."

"I'm not. The High Holders don't care much who gets hurt in their efforts to hold on to their power. The factors want more golds, and they don't care much who gets hurt so long as they obtain more golds."

Cyran stood. "I think I'll better find out just where Laevoryn's estate is. Do you want me to have scouts explore it?"

"I'd rather take a look first."

"I'll find out as soon as I can."

"Thank you." Alastar did not rise as the senior imager left the study. *Why was Cyran so eager to leave? Because he doesn't like it when you're so cynically accurate? Or because he thinks you're on the edge of fury?* Then again, in a way, Alastar was on the edge of fury, aimed at both High Holders and factors, not to mention Lorien on the side. *Can't any of them see that life is changing and the old ways aren't working?*

He was afraid that he knew the answer.

After Alastar was certain that Cyran was well away from the administration building, he made his way outside and then walked swiftly to the west riverwall to check the water level. The swirling dark gray-blue water remained just a little over a yard below the top of the stone walls. Mixed among the water, frequent whitecaps, and dirty foam were branches, leaves, occasional planks or boards, and other debris. He didn't see any bodies, either of animals or otherwise, but he had no doubts that he might have if he'd stayed and looked long enough.

When he returned to the administration building, he couldn't help thinking about Westisle. Why had Voltyrn inquired twice, the second time before Alastar could have sent a response, even had he been minded to reply instantly? From what he'd seen earlier, from the correspondence from Zhelan, and from the tone of Voltyrn's missives, Alastar was getting a very strong impression that Westisle needed a maitre from L'Excelsis. The question was who? And even if he had decided he wasn't about to send that maitre off to Westisle until the High Holder rebels were dealt with, one maitre probably wouldn't make a difference, but there was little point in risking it, especially given that the rebellion had been planned months in advance, if not longer, and there might be yet other surprises. *Might be?*

Cyran did not return until two quints past noon. He wore a wry expression on his face as he settled into the chair across from Alastar.

"I had to wait to see Murranyt, and he really didn't want to tell me much."

"I take it that he finally did."

"He wasn't happy."

"Why not? Merely telling you where Laevoryn dwells isn't Terahnar's greatest secret. Or do you think he's been pressed to keep away from anything dealing with Laevoryn and High Holders?"

"He did say that he wished Hulet had never set foot in Laevoryn's mansion. He's also not terribly pleased with the Collegium. Several people were wounded, and one died, from stray bullets fired when those shooters attacked Imagisle."

"He's less than pleased with us . . . when we were attacked then, and again on Vendrei evening?"

"That was just my impression. I didn't press."

"It's likely better that you didn't. It almost sounds like he's related, if on the off side of the blanket, to some High Holder . . . or taking a few golds from one."

"That was my thought as well. I did find out where Laevoryn's mansion and grounds are, though . . . after I hinted that it would be much easier than if I had to stop every patroller on the north side of L'Excelsis."

"Let's go take a look." At Cyran's dubious expression, Alastar added, "Using concealments, of course." He stood. "We might as well head out now."

Since Laevoryn's L'Excelsis dwelling was north of the main part of the city, Alastar and Cyran rode out over the East Bridge and turned north on the East River Road. Once they crossed the Boulevard D'Este, they raised blurring shields. A half mille north of the Nord Bridge, the main road curved to the east, leaving little more than a narrow, if well-paved, lane paralleling the river.

"Laevoryn's main gate is off of the main road," said Cyran. "The servitors' gate is at the end of the lane."

"Let me guess. His predecessors didn't want their access to the river blocked by the East River Road."

"I wouldn't know," replied Cyran, "but it makes sense."

"For a High Holder. We'll look into the servitors' gate . . . under full concealment." As they rode forward at a slow walk, Alastar noted that there were no trees near the wall, itself a good three yards high, either inside or outside and along the lane. Given the apparent age of the wall stones, that suggested that Laevoryn and his predecessors had definitely valued their privacy.

When they were within ten yards of the gates, Alastar murmured to Cyran, "Wait here." Then he continued on toward the guardhouse.

The guard posted there wore livery of a pale lavender. He was also gray-haired and looked to be almost half asleep. Alastar eased his mount forward until he reined up only about a yard from where the gates joined, each formed of plain iron bars running vertically in an oiled timber frame. There was no visible chain or lock, suggesting a simple drop bar on the inside. He stiffened as he caught sight of two more guards, wearing the brown uniforms with which Alastar had become too famil-iar, seated on a bench beside the paved drive leading from the gate into the grounds. Each had a heavy rifle in hand.

The two looked bored, but one suddenly frowned and looked up. "Did you hear something?"

"Just a rider going by."

"I don't see anyone." The guard who had spoken stood, rifle in hand, and moved toward the gates, peering one way and then another. Finally, he turned and walked back toward the bench.

Alastar eased the gray away from the gate, his eyes still on the brown-shirt guards.

The one stopped and turned, looking at the gate again, before shrug-ging and returning to the bench.

Alastar continued to walk the mount back until he was inside the scope of Cyran's concealment. Keeping his voice low, he said, "We'll ride past the main gate now."

"What did you find out?"

"Two additional guards in the brown-shirt uniforms with rifles posted just inside the gate."

"You thought you'd find them, didn't you?"

"After I thought about *Veritum* being burned out, I felt it was likely."

As they rode back south and then rejoined the main road, where they resumed blurring shields, which had the advantage of letting others see a pair of riders, Alastar kept studying the wall that surrounded the es-tate. By the time they could see the front entry gate, Alastar judged that they had covered almost a mille, and he had not seen any other gates or breaks in the wall that remained a constant three yards in height.

The two rode another two hundred yards before approaching the main entry, a much more elaborate structure with two gates with fluted iron grillwork topped on each side with a wrought-iron crest, whose center depicted a flower that Alastar did not recognize, crossed by a saber. The gatehouse was inside the gates, with two guards posted, both wearing the lavender livery. Alastar could not discern any other guards, but that didn't surprise him, since, if there were any, he doubted they would be visible to passersby on the well-traveled East River Road.

Once past the entry, Alastar continued to study the wall until they had covered another fifty yards, when he asked, "What did you notice about the main gate?"

"Besides the fact that it was locked and there were two guards there on the inside? There wasn't much I could see beyond that."

"Think over what Murranyt told you about how Hulet died."

Cyran frowned, then, after several moments, replied, "Murranyt said that Hulet forced his way into the house."

"Exactly how would an unarmed factor have been able to force his way through those gates and guards? Especially when the guards are inside the gates?"

"It would seem rather difficult."

"More than a little. Now we need to find out how much farther Laevoryn's grounds extend."

After riding another half mille, Alastar could see just ahead a cornice rising from the top of the wall. As he drew nearer, it became clear that the cornice marked a corner and that the wall turned there and headed due west, seemingly all the way to the river, or at least the riverbank. Alastar reined up opposite the corner and studied the wall for several moments, then turned the gelding to head back south.

"What now?" asked Cyran as he eased his mount around to keep position with Alastar.

"I think it's time we paid a visit to Commander Murranyt. We'll need to stop by the Collegium to pick up an escort who can handle the mounts."

"You want me to accompany you?"

"Absolutely. Otherwise, he'll claim to me that you misunderstood what he said."

"Have you ever met Murranyt?"

"A few times, but only in passing."

Three quints later, after a stop on Imagisle to collect Tertius Beltran, the most available junior imager, the three imagers rode south from the East Bridge some eight blocks before reaching Fedre Street and turning east toward Civic Patrol headquarters, little more than a block east of the river, in a yellow brick building of two stories barely twenty yards wide.

Alastar and Cyran reined up and dismounted in front of the single door, positioned five yards from the west corner of the building, and handed the reins of their mounts to Beltran before entering the building.

Inside the well-oiled but battered oak door was an anteroom that stretched five yards on each side of the door. Benches set against the front wall flanked the entry. Directly opposite the door and in front of an archway was a large desk, behind which sat a beefy patroller. Beside him, on a stool, sat a much younger patroller.

Cyran stepped up to the seated patroller, who looked up impassively. "Maitre Alastar is here to see the commander."

"Actually, both the senior imager and I are here to see him," Alastar added. "It's not a social call."

"Sandryt," growled the duty patroller to the younger one, "go up and tell the commander that Maitre Alastar and Maitre Cyran are here to see him."

Sandryt immediately stood, ducked through the archway, and started up the stairs to the second level.

"Don't suppose it's anything good that brings imagers here," said the duty patroller.

"I suppose," returned Alastar cheerfully, "it's like most matters that concern the patrol—good for some and much less than that for others . . . and always presenting challenges for the patrollers on the street."

Within moments, the young patroller was back. "This way, Maitres."

Alastar and Cyran followed him up the stairs to a narrow corridor and then to the second door on the right. Alastar let Cyran enter first, then closed the door.

Murranyt did not rise, but gestured to the two chairs across the desk from him. "To what do I owe the dubious honor of hosting the two senior imagers of the Collegium?"

Alastar settled himself before replying. "We're here to learn of any progress the patrol might have made in finding the brown-shirts who murdered Factor Naathyn and a number of student imagers . . . oh . . . and not to mention killing the watchman and burning the old river port tower . . . or landing on Imagisle and attempting to kill two student imagers."

"L'Excelsis is a big place, Maitre Alastar," replied the commander. "There are more than a few places for lawbreakers to hide."

"That's true." Alastar offered a nod that he hoped was understanding and sage. "L'Excelsis is a large city, and I can understand how difficult it must be for your patrollers to search out single criminals who look like everyone else and who can hide almost anywhere. What must make it even harder is that often no one knows a crime was committed until later, and even when someone does see the crime and the killer, they find it difficult if not impossible to describe the man."

"We do our best."

"I'm more than certain your patrollers do in fact attempt to do their very best, as they can in their circumstances." Alastar paused just slightly, before going on. "What puzzles me in the case of the brown-shirts is that they all wear the same uniforms, and there are scores of them, if not more. Many of them have mounts, and they commit their offenses in groups. Their victims, and those they have attacked, with the single exception of the watchman at *Veritum*, have either been from a factoring background, from a regial background, or imagers. Does not that pattern suggest something?"

"It could suggest anything," replied Murranyt cheerfully.

"To a stable-mucker, perhaps, but certainly more to an experienced Civic Patrol officer, unless, of course, the officer had reasons for not wishing to perceive the pattern."

Murranyt's eyes narrowed. "That would seem ungenerous, especially—"

"From an imager. No, I'm actually being very, very generous, Murranyt, incredibly generous. If you don't think so, you might consult with High Holder Guerdyn or Marshal Demykalon or Commander Chesyrk."

"I didn't allow you to see me to be insulted."

"No, you didn't. You allowed me to see you because, if I wanted to see you, I would, and you know that . . . unless you're incredibly stupid, and I don't believe that for a moment." Alastar smiled. "I might even be more generous and congratulate you on your long service to the Civic Patrol, were you to announce your decision to request your stipend."

"And if I don't." Murranyt wasn't quite sneering.

"One way or another, the Factors' Council will be most interested in hearing how Chief Factor Hulet could possibly have forced his way through either of the gates at Laevoryn's estate, considering he was unarmed, and there were not only estate guards there, but that those same gates are also guarded by the brown-shirts that the Civic Patrol seems totally unable to find, when a mere imager with no experience in patrolling could locate them in less than a glass."

"Threats don't move me, Alastar."

"I wouldn't think of threatening you, Murranyt. I've never made a threat in my life, and I'm not about to now." Alastar stood. "I would suggest that you review my words very carefully."

"You don't want to deal with anything directly. I know your kind."

Alastar laughed. "You flatter me."

Cyran stood, shaking his head.

"You, great senior imager," said Murranyt, "just how did I flatter the honorable maitre?"

"You suggested that . . . that he was skilled in scheming. Perhaps he has that ability, but from what I've seen, he's never asked anyone to do what he hasn't already done."

"I'll give you one additional thought, Murranyt," added Alastar. "I could care less about you, after what it's clear you've done. I just would prefer that the Civic Patrol only have a shadow over its past after you leave than outright proof of treachery and betrayal."

"I'll leave when I decide."

"One way or another," replied Alastar with a pleasant smile, "you are absolutely correct." He looked to Cyran. "It's time to leave." He turned and walked from the small chamber.

Cyran stood there for a moment, gave the faintest headshake to the commander, and then followed Alastar. Just outside the building, he said, "I don't think Murranyt understood what you meant."

"That's because he didn't want to." Alastar didn't say another word until he was mounted and the three imagers were riding toward the East River Road. "We'll ride out to see Marshal Wilkorn."

"We could deal with Laevoryn ourselves."

"We could, but that would cause other problems. What I have in mind, if Wilkorn agrees, will make Laevoryn the traitor instead of an imager victim."

"That would be better."

Slightly more than two quints later, the three imagers reined up outside the main army headquarters building more than two milles north of the Chateau D'Rex. Again, Beltran remained with the horses when Alastar and Cyran dismounted and made their way inside past a trooper, who stiffened as they passed.

"They don't question you," murmured Cyran.

"Unlike Murranyt," replied Alastar in a low voice as he turned to the left after leaving the entry foyer.

"Is the marshal expecting you, Maitre?" asked the ranker, who immediately stood from behind the table set in the hallway outside the small study in which Wilkorn had most recently seen Alastar.

"No, but the matter is urgent."

"Yes, sir." The ranker turned and rapped on the door. "Maitre Alastar, sir."

While Alastar couldn't hear the response, the ranker opened the door and stepped back. "He'll see you, Maitres."

Alastar let Cyran enter first, then closed the door.

Wilkorn remained seated, but gestured toward the chairs in front of the desk with his unsplinted hand and arm. "What new problems or information are you delivering? With the two top imagers, it must be serious." His words were delivered in a half-humorous tone.

"I'd like to borrow two squads of troopers and their captain or undercaptain."

A twisted smile crossed the marshal's face. "I can't imagine you'd need their protection."

"Not their physical protection, but their authority to deal with rebel forces."

"Oh?"

"There's a High Holder named Laevoryn who has a number of armed brown-shirts quartered on his estate grounds. Since the brown-shirts attacked the rex . . ."

". . . and since you don't have the legal authority to invade a High Holder's lands, but the army can pursue traitors and rebels . . . I take it that's what you have in mind."

"Something along those lines. Also, there's an interesting link to Commander Murranyt, the head of the Civic Patrol. . . ." Alastar explained what had happened involving Laevoryn and Murranyt's response.

"I've seen enough not to be surprised at anything, but . . ." Wilkorn shook his head. "You could remove him, and no one would be able to do anything."

"Which means that Laevoryn has the same ability . . . or an even greater hold over Murranyt," suggested Alastar.

"When do you want those squads?"

"How about in a glass?"

Wilkorn laughed. "We can do that. It will be a good exercise for them."

"I'll accompany them. Cyran will go back to the Collegium and gather some maitres to meet us."

"Maitres? You need more than you two?"

"We're going to try to shield your troopers. I'd rather not have any casualties among your men, or as few as possible. We may need every man later." Alastar quickly added, "We can't do that in a large pitched battle with hundreds of men and cannon. Only a few imagers have that ability, and how many men they can protect is very limited."

"I've wondered about that for a long time . . . ever since I heard that you'd managed to survive the Antiagon fire that killed Petayne and all the others."

"We think that's why the brown-shirts were targeting students and younger imagers."

"From their point of view that makes sense. Kill the young ones before they get strong enough."

"That's why Quaeryt set up the first Collegium."

"Quaeryt? That was his name?"

"It was. He was actually married to the sister of the first rex regis."

"That explains a few things."

It really didn't, but Alastar wasn't about to offer the detailed explanation, especially since he really didn't know it, and doubted that anyone in centuries had. Instead, he turned to Cyran. "You need to ride back with Beltran and assemble our force. Two senior maitres besides you, but not Alyna, and two or three strong junior maitres. "We'll meet where the lane to the rear gate and the East River Road diverge."

Cyran nodded. "We'll be there."

Once Cyran had left the study, Alastar turned back to Wilkorn. "Is there any recent news about the rebels?"

"I'm waiting for a report from the scouts. I'll let you know."

"I do need one other favor."

"Oh."

"A water bottle filled with dark lager."

The marshal chuckled.

31

Wilkorn was better than his word. At two quints after third glass, Alastar and two squads of mounted troopers rode out through the main gates of the High Command. Beside Alastar rode Weidyn, whose graying hair proclaimed that he'd worked his way up from a ranker to captain. At the head of the second squad, halfway back in the column, was squad leader Remaylt, a more grizzled trooper even than Weidyn.

When Alastar had described the mission and what he expected, Weidyn had merely nodded, then asked, "Are we to act as patrollers or troopers?"

Alastar's response had been blunt. "Troopers as far as the brown-shirts are concerned. Shoot any brown-shirt who doesn't surrender. That includes those who try to flee. We've fought them twice. Three times would be too many. Anyone else . . . don't shoot unless they have a weapon and threaten."

"Any other orders, Maitre?"

"No one on the grounds, buildings, or dwelling is to leave except by my command. Use whatever force is necessary."

"Whatever force?"

"No more than necessary, but if they get shot, they get shot."

After the short briefing, Alastar had no doubts about why Wilkorn had selected Weidyn's company and ordered the captain to command the two squads.

Once Alastar's force was riding eastward toward the Nord Bridge, he asked the captain, "How did you come to be an army officer, Weidyn?"

"My grandsire was a stone mason, and my da named me after him, thinking I'd follow that path." The captain laughed. "I was good at breaking stones, but not shaping them. My da said that the only place a fellow got paid for destroying things was the army. He was half right, but my being a stone mason would have been all wrong."

"You've been in . . . what? Fifteen years?"

"Eighteen. I made squad leader just before you destroyed fourth regiment. I was transferred to twelfth company, third regiment. Never did care much for Commander Chesyrk, even when he was a major. I was glad more for the transfer than the promotion. Learned a lot chasing pirates through the Sud Swamp, but didn't care for the hot and damp. Got breveted to undercaptain there, though."

"And you were good enough to keep the rank, clearly."

"Marshal Wilkorn was looking for company officers with field experience to head up training. That's how I made captain five years back."

"I thought it might be something like that." Alastar took out his water bottle and drank. He didn't want to have to image while not feeling his best.

"I've heard that you train imagers like troopers. That so?"

"In a similar fashion, but it takes longer because they start usually between age eight and thirteen, although some come to the Collegium younger, and some very few later. We run them, exercise them, and make them learn how imaging works, then start them on improving their imaging slowly. It takes about six to ten years for a student to develop solid basic abilities. Those who can do more become maitres, usually in their twenties, although a few manage that earlier. Too much imaging can kill an imager. We still lose a few who think they know better."

"Lose? Like dying?"

"Three things happen to young imagers. They do what they're supposed to and succeed. They die. Or they're blinded because they become a danger to others."

Weidyn stiffened just slightly, then laughed softly. "You mind if I pass that on to our recruits? Some of them might find it . . . useful to know that there's an outfit where those who fail die or go blind."

"And it's headed by another gray-hair."

Weidyn didn't reply, but his smile was wry.

Slightly after fourth glass, Alastar and Weidyn led the two squads across the Nord Bridge and then north on the East River Road. As they neared the meeting point where the lane branched off from the main road, abruptly a group of six mounted imagers appeared, the result of their dropping their concealments.

"That's a handy trick," observed Weidyn.

"It's useful for small groups, but like all imaging, the larger the area involved, the more difficult it is." Alastar quickly made out Cyran, Tiranya, and Khaelis, then Belsior, Dylert, and Taurek.

"One of your maitres is a woman?"

"They fight as well as the men, and some are better than the men of equivalent position. Tiranya's very good. For those who are married, we try not to have husband and wife in the same battle at the same time." Alastar smiled wryly. "Sometimes it doesn't work out that way, but so far we haven't lost both."

"You're married?"

"My wife is the third-ranking imager. She's quite able. She's in charge of defending Imagisle. Have the squads halt. You and I and Remaylt will meet with Senior Imager Cyran. That should only take a few moments." Alastar reined up at Weidyn's commands, then rode forward several yards and stopped again, motioning for Cyran to join him.

In turn, Weidyn gestured, and Remaylt rode forward to join the captain and the two imagers.

"The plan here is simple," Alastar began once the four were gathered in a rough circle. "There aren't any gates except at the front and rear of the estate, and the walls run all the way around it. The group headed by Maitre Cyran and Captain Weidyn will attack through the front gate. The group headed by squad leader Remaylt and me will take the rear gate. Cyran, you, Khaelis, Belsior, and Dylert will accompany and shield Captain Weidyn and his squad. You're to remove the front gates and enough of the walls on each side so that you can lead the squad in quickly, but don't make the gap more than ten yards wide. Otherwise, you may have trouble holding shields across the front. I'll take Tiranya and Taurek, and we'll break through the rear gate. Image a fireball above the main house when you're in position. When I image one in return, we'll both attack. Oh . . . use blurring shields getting into position, but not concealments."

"Yes, sir."

"If High Holder Laevoryn gets into this, try not to kill him, because it would help to get answers from him, but don't take chances. He's already killed the chief factor in cold blood. As I've said before, anyone in a brown uniform or with a weapon is fair game unless they surrender and throw down their weapon. Any last questions?"

The other three all offered headshakes.

"Then let's head out. Cyran, send Tiranya and Taurek over."

"Yes, sir."

Weidyn nodded to Alastar, then turned and signaled for his first squad to join up on him. Alastar eased the gelding to the side and then rode toward second squad, turning his head and calling, "Tiranya, you and Taurek ride directly behind the squad leader and me."

"Yes, sir."

Several yards before second squad, Alastar reined up, and in moments, the two other imagers took position behind him. Then Remaylt drew his mount alongside Alastar.

Alastar nodded to Remaylt, then eased the gelding forward, raising a screen concealment in front of the small force.

After they had ridden a few yards and turned onto the lane, Remaylt asked quietly, "Begging your pardon, Maitre, but how much fighting experience do your imagers have? I notice they carry sabers."

"They've all had training with the blades. Those are mainly for self-defense, for when they're too exhausted to image. All of the imagers here have used imaging to kill. I doubt that any of them have accounted for less than at least half a score of brown-shirts . . . or, years ago, troopers who rebelled against Rex Lorien."

Remaylt looked inquiringly at Alastar. "And you, sir?"

"He destroyed an entire regiment," said Tiranya from where she rode.

The squad leader looked puzzled.

"Then why do we need troopers?" said Alastar. "Because that kind of imaging destroys pretty much everything, and when you're trying to find out who's an enemy and who is not, that gets difficult if there are no survivors and no records or evidence. Also, the High Holders who aren't rebels might consider flattening an estate somewhat excessive." Alastar wasn't about to mention that, while Quaeryt might have been able to wield that much power, he himself never had and probably couldn't. "Do you see that discolored stone in the wall ahead?" He pointed to the wall on his right. "We'll halt there. It's about twenty yards from the gates, and I'll keep holding the screening concealment until we get the signal from Cyran."

Remaylt offered another quizzical look.

"A full concealment hides one from anyone who's looking from any direction. A screening concealment only conceals what's behind the screen from anyone looking toward it, in this case, the gate guards. It doesn't take nearly as much effort."

"The gate guards can't see us?"

"No, but they can hear us," replied Alastar in a lower voice, slowing the gelding as they neared where he wanted to stop. "We need to stop talking."

Remaylt turned in the saddle, saying in a low voice, "Silence in the ranks. Pass it back."

After he reined up and the imagers and troopers waited, Alastar kept watching the sky above the roof of the main structure . . . and watching. Finally, when what seemed to have been a glass passed, but was likely only a quint, if not less, a fireball appeared.

Alastar imaged a second fireball into the sky, near but not too close to the first one, already fading.

"I'll take out the gates. Tiranya, Taurek, extend your shields two yards on a side. Once we're inside the gate, move to the outside of the column to give the troopers a clear field of fire." With those words, Alastar imaged away the gates and the gateposts, dumping them in the lane, since moving was easier than destroying. "Forward!" He moved the gelding at a fast walk.

"Rifles ready!" added Remaylt.

As Alastar neared the gap in the wall where the gate had been, he looked for the gate guard, but did not see him immediately—until he passed the small guardhouse, where the man was crouched as low as he could be. Two brown-shirts, presumably those on duty by the bench, had stood and began to fire at the oncoming troopers, but, so far as Alastar could tell, the imagers' shields—including the one he had extended to cover the middle of the advance—had stopped any bullets from hitting the troopers. The shots were scattered enough in timing and so few that Alastar barely felt the impact.

The two brown-shirt sentries were not so fortunate, going down almost immediately.

"Keep moving!" Alastar ordered. "Along the lane to the main buildings!"

The paved lane from the gate ran due east, and ahead about fifty yards, brown-shirts were forming up. Several began to fire at Alastar and the army troopers. This time, Alastar could feel the impact of the bullets on his shields, and he decided to move faster, easing the gelding into a trot.

"Hold station on the Maitre!" ordered Remaylt.

Even more brown-shirts appeared, several taking cover behind garden bushes and low walls. Another squad or so of the brown-shirts appeared in good order, with one rank kneeling and firing and the rear rank standing and firing. The impacts on Alastar's shields came more rapidly and were starting to become painful. In turn, he imaged iron dart after iron dart. He was glad that the brown-shirts weren't concentrating their fire on him or the other two imagers.

The fire from the squad behind Alastar took its toll as well, fairly

quickly and by the time his force was within twenty yards of what remained of the brown-shirt formation more than a score of bodies lay
sprawled beside the lane, possibly as many as two-score, and the surviving brown-shirts were withdrawing. Some continued to stop and fire.
Some just ran for cover.

As he continued to lead the advance, Alastar kept targeting those
brown-shirts who attempted to fire at the army troopers. He also kept
trying to discover the building or buildings where they had been quartered, finally seeing what looked like a stable to the south of the lane, almost against the wall separating the High Holder's estate from that part
of the East River Road that ran east to west. He wasn't quite certain until
he saw two brown-shirts running along the path to the building. *Should
you send some troopers there?*

He shook his head. He had only twenty-five troopers, and splitting
up his force—and imagers—even more wasn't the best of ideas.

"Sir? The brown-shirts are dead or wounded, or they've fled."

"We'll ride to the main buildings and meet up with Captain Weidyn
and the other imagers."

Alastar found Cyran and his force drawn up behind a stone wall, one
that Cyran had clearly imaged somewhat higher.

"Half the squad—with Khaelis and Belsior—is on the northwest
side covering the rear," explained the senior imager. "The few brown-
shirts that survived withdrew into the hold house. They've barred
the doors. They did stop shooting after we used darts on anyone who
tried."

"That doesn't surprise me. I'd like you and your imagers to accompany and shield squad leader Remaylt and his squad while they search
the grounds and either capture or disable any remaining brown-shirts."
Alastar turned to Weidyn. "Assuming that's not a problem for you,
Captain."

"It would be our pleasure. It's not often that we get the chance to put
a rebellious High Holder in his place." Weidyn paused then asked, "What
might you have in mind for me and the other squad?"

"We're going to invite ourselves inside, of course, once Cyran
and Remaylt assure us that the grounds are clear of brown-shirts. In
the meantime, we'll make certain no one inside has any ideas about
leaving."

Once Cyran and the three other maitres had left with Remaylt's squad,
and Tiranya had gone to replace Khaelis and Belsior, Weidyn moved his

mount closer to Alastar and said, "I have a feeling you don't have the greatest respect for High Holder Laevoryn."

"Let's just say that I currently know only one other that I believe deserves even less respect."

"Do you know any, if I might ask, who do deserve respect?"

"Yes. I have met a few who are deserving of respect." *Far fewer than you'd like.* "The problem with all forms of power is that they tend to make those who have whatever power they have arrogant, and arrogance in its extremes differs little from stupidity."

"What about imagers?"

"Imagers are no different from others in their feelings. We try to point out to them when they're young that imaging does not bestow power, only ability, and that because young imagers are vulnerable, without the Collegium they would all be servants to arbitrary power. In turn, the Collegium does its best to keep the use of power from being capricious or arbitrary."

"Is not the Maitre usually the most powerful imager? What keeps you from being arbitrary?"

"Some would claim that I am. I try not to be, and I listen to my senior maitres, to Rex Lorien, to the Factors' Council, and to as many others as possible, whether or not I agree with them. I also keep in mind that no one today, except a few imagers, even knows the name of the most powerful imager who ever lived, and who will likely be the most powerful ever. He had the wisdom not to abuse great power, to remain as much in the shadows as he could, in order that the imagers who followed would have a relatively safe place to live and work."

"The first Maitre? How do you know that? Don't people always imagine the greatness of the past?"

"You've thought about that, I can tell. But there is some evidence remaining. The maitre's dwelling was imaged in that time. It was shelled during the last days of Rex Ryen. The shells didn't even scratch the walls. The same is true of the Chateau D'Rex. For all the bullets fired at it, ever since the first Rex Regis and just a few days ago, there is not a scratch on those walls. The riverwall around Imagisle is the same. It's true that I am likely the most powerful imager alive today, and possibly in the past generation or two. I can do none of that. Nor has any other imager since that time been able to."

For several moments, Weidyn was silent. "Yet I saw bullets bounce away from your imagers."

"We'll all likely have bruises tomorrow, if we don't already. A cannon shell would destroy even the strongest imager. That is why imagers need the Collegium."

Weidyn nodded. "I've some thinking to do."

Alastar decided he'd said enough. *If not too much.*

While he waited, he studied the hold house, an imposing structure with red stone walls that rose three stories, if the narrow windows and heavy shutters on the lowest level of the center section of the dwelling suggested that the basic structure dated back centuries. The wings had far larger windows, but the entry portico was narrow, only wide enough for one coach, and was unroofed.

Almost a glass passed, with no shots at the troopers—before imagers and the second squad returned, and the white sun was not that far above the trees to the west. Alastar had long since dismounted and tied the gelding to a tree. He stepped forward, as did Weidyn, to hear Cyran's report.

"There are nine wounded in their quarters," Cyran reported. "Half will likely make it. We counted fifty-two bodies. One of the wounded said that there had been a company here. They lost almost an entire squad Vendrei night in the attack on Imagisle. The company captain is in the hold house with the High Holder."

"Now that you're back, Weidyn and I and Tiranya will go in. Four troopers with rifles should be sufficient accompaniment. Your job, and that of the remaining troopers, is to make sure no one escapes."

"We can do that."

Once everyone was in position, Alastar walked across the narrow drive to the portico and up to the polished bronze doors of the entry. Behind him came Weidyn and Tiranya, then the four troopers, rifles in hand and ready. He tried one door, then the other. Out of politeness, he tugged on the bellpull. There was no response. Rather than destroy the doors—the bronze surface had been cast into what he imagined was the familial crest—he imaged away the brass where he thought the lock-plates or bars might be. Then he tugged at the doors. They opened a hand's-width, enough for him to see the three bars. He imaged out the midsection of each and opened the doors. Behind them was a polished oak door. It was also locked or barred.

Alastar sighed, them imaged away an entire section of the door—the side away from the hinges, then pushed. The door swung inward. He stepped into the octagonal foyer, which had square archways on each side. He heard the shots as he felt the impact on his shields and saw three brown-shirts standing at the base of the lavender marble staircase at the far side of the foyer. He imaged three iron darts, each through an eye of a shooter.

He did not see any other shooters as he took several steps toward the staircase with its polished bronze balustrades before stopping well short of the bodies. He could sense Weidyn, Tiranya, and the troopers behind him as they entered and then stopped.

A single figure descended from higher on the wide staircase and stopped on the third step. The man had sandy blond hair, shot with silvery-gray, and a face that was totally nondescript, if clean-shaven, except for pale watery gray eyes holding an intensity Alastar had seldom seen. He wore a lavender coat over a darker lavender-purple shirt. Both his trousers and his cravat matched the coat. One hand was behind his back, the other extended in a mocking gesture of greeting.

Alastar waited.

"Welcome to Voryn, unwelcome as you are. You must be the redoubtable Maitre Alastar, able to walk through hails of bullets unscathed."

"Then you must be High Holder Laevoryn, famed for shooting down unarmed men and siring sons who kill anyone who happens to best them at their own gaming."

"One is demeaned, not famed, for disposing of the unworthy."

Alastar was struck by the combination of Laevoryn's visual intensity and the deep smoothness of the man's voice, but not struck enough not to reply. "That right was removed from High Holders four hundred years ago, Laevoryn."

"Who are you to declare that? No rex can take away inalienable rights. No piece of paper, no proclamation by a weakling rex can do that. Not to me, not to any High Holder. Those were and are our rights by birth."

"The first Rex Regis was anything but a weakling, but this isn't a debate." Out of the corner of his left eye, Alastar saw Weidyn and Tiranya move to that side of the octagonal entry hall as if they were trying to study both the chamber that lay beyond the archway and watch Laevoryn as well. "Where is the brown-shirt captain?" asked Alastar conversationally.

"I shot him for incompetence. He failed," replied Laevoryn. "His job was to help bring down that insufferable weakling Lorien and to protect Voryn."

"Then we will be taking you into custody. You will appear before a justicer on charges of treason and murder."

"I may not stop you, Alastar the long-winded, but no mere captain will ever take me into custody." The hand came from behind Laevoryn's back, revealing a large pistol, which he immediately fired at Weidyn.

Tiranya staggered with the impact on her shields, but then straightened.

Three of the four troopers fired, all but the one directly behind Alastar, and Laevoryn staggered, then pitched forward onto the green-and-white marble floor. His head hit the stone with a sickening crunch.

"Tiranya?"

"I'm fine. That pistol . . . it hit my shields harder than a rifle bullet."

Weidyn moved forward and scooped up the pistol that had skidded across the marble floor from the High Holder's hand. "It's a special design. Single shot, with a bullet half again as big as a heavy rifle slug."

"That's why he aimed at you, then," said Alastar. "He knew Tiranya was shielding you, but he thought her shields wouldn't be strong enough to stop that bullet." He glanced into the chamber on his left, apparently a receiving parlor. There was no one in it. Nor was there anyone in the chamber to the left, which looked to be a reading room of some sort. "Now we need to go through the house, a room at a time."

All they found in the central section of the dwelling on the main level were the bodies of three more brown-shirts, each with an iron dart through an eye, and the body of the brown-shirt captain.

Weidyn looked up from the captain's body and shook his head, but he didn't speak.

The north wing of the dwelling was empty of furniture on the main-floor level, as it was on the upper levels. In fact, by the time Alastar and the others had finished going through the house and bringing the three surviving family members down to the receiving parlor, it was clear that the older main section and the sitting rooms and bedchambers on the second level of the south wing were the only chambers in regular use.

While the four troopers watched Laevoryn's son, daughter, and wife, Alastar went back to the study that seemed to hold the ledgers for the estate. After half a quint, he shook his head and hurried outside to find Cyran.

"What do you need?" asked the senior imager.

"I need you to return to Imagisle with Tiranya and Belsior. Send Maitre Thelia here as soon as possible with two imagers who have strong shields. I'm hoping she can go through the ledgers and find out more than I could see."

"You think she'll find something?"

"She either will, or she won't. Either will be useful, because Laevo-ryn was supposedly having a hard time paying all his expenses. All the vacant and empty rooms here would seem to confirm that it was enough of a hard time that his son murdered Factor Hulet's nephew over a gam-bling debt of perhaps two hundred golds, and Laevoryn shot Hulet dead . . . under rather dubious circumstances. Yet Laevoryn was main-taining almost a full company of brown-shirts here? How could he af-ford their food, ammunition, uniforms, and rifles, not to mention how the matter of paying them? We'll need three maitres here to help the army maintain control until Maitre Thelia finishes her examination of Laevoryn's expense ledgers. I'd thought Khaelis, Dylert, and Taurek. While you do that, I'll be talking to the family."

"We'll take care of it."

"Thank you."

After Alastar had seen Cyran, Tiranya, and Belsior off, Weidyn approached.

"Sir?"

"Yes?" Alastar grinned sheepishly. "What have I forgotten that you're about to remind me about?"

"There's close to sixty bodies scattered on the grounds."

"And it's hot. What would be the best way to handle that?"

"Since they're rebels, we'd just hold a service for all of them and do a joint pyre. We'd collect all the personal effects and take them to head-quarters for any family to claim."

"That sounds fine to me. Is there anything I should do as a part of this?"

"Well, sir, the senior officer is usually the one who says a few words. I'm not much for speaking . . . and it wouldn't hurt to get a good start to the flames."

"I can do that. About when would that be?"

"First full glass after sunset. Seventh glass."

"All the bodies but the High Holder's. I'll leave those arrangements to his family."

"Yes, sir."

"I know he's a rebel, too, but I don't see much sense in offending High Holders any more than necessary. Lumping his body in with the others would be throwing oil on the flames . . . even if he more than deserves it."

The captain nodded. "I can see that, sir. How long will we be here?"

"No longer than tomorrow morning. Earlier, if you want to ride back at night."

"The men would rather stay. There are provisions and quarters. I'll set up a watch and patrol rotation and get them to work on the pyre."

"I appreciate it, Captain."

"Our duty, sir."

When Weidyn left to set up his patrols of the grounds, Alastar returned to the main house. Three troopers were stationed in the octagonal entry foyer. They inclined their heads politely as Alastar passed and walked into the receiving parlor.

Lady Laevoryn, a slender dark-haired woman dressed in an off-white dress with lavender trim, sat in one of the armchairs. Her daughter, also slender and black-haired, sat in the side chair she had obviously moved to be next to her mother. She wore a tan riding jacket, matching trousers, and even tan boots. The daughter immediately looked away from Alastar as he walked toward them. The son stood by the front window and turned his back on Alastar.

"Lady Laevoryn . . . one of the servants indicated that you have another younger son who is visiting relatives?"

"Yes." The single word was clipped and cold. "What have you done with my husband?"

"His body is laid out on oilcloth in the first lower-level bedroom in the south wing, one of the ones that was closed. We'll be gone by the morning at the latest."

"I would have thought you'd make some great display."

Alastar chose not to respond to her words, instead asking, "What can you tell me about the men who were quartered here?"

"Why should I talk to you? You're the reason why my husband is dead, and my life is in shreds."

"Your husband is the reason for that. If he hadn't supported the rebels, murdered Factor Hulet, and attempted to kill Captain Weidyn, he'd still be alive."

"What choice did he have? What choice did any of us have?"

"Would you care to explain why a High Holder and his family had no choice?"

Lady Laevoryn was silent.

"Was it because, with the drought and the ruinous rains, the lands no longer provided the golds necessary to live as in the past? Others faced drought and less income without resorting to rebellion and murder."

"You'll never understand."

"Understand what? That there haven't been enough golds for years? That more golds come from factoring and manufacturing than from lands? That because the wealthy factors bought cheaper grain in the east and carted it here, prices stayed lower than they would have, and what crops there were didn't fetch the prices they once would have?"

"They're greedy gold-grubbers, all of them."

"Most people need golds to live."

"They think of nothing else. They understand nothing of art or poetry or music."

"What composer's work do you find most enjoyable to play? I assume you do play because the clavecin in the salon looks to be a beautiful instrument."

"I prefer not to discuss music, or any other pleasantry at the moment."

"Then tell me why your husband agreed to take part in this ill-considered rebellion."

"He didn't believe it ill-considered, but necessary."

"Could you tell me why he thought it so necessary?"

"Isn't it obvious?"

"Perhaps to you and to him, but not to most of the rest of Solidar."

"All that matters to Lorien and to the factors is golds. Golds and more golds. Tradition is nothing. Culture is nothing. Being responsible for the lives and futures of tenants and crafters who have served a family for generations is nothing. All the factors want is more golds, faster and faster. They use golds to destroy others so that they can amass more."

"Many of them do seem to live for little more than the pleasure of amassing golds." Alastar couldn't disagree, in general, with her observation.

"If you think that, Maitre, why do you side with them?"

"I don't side with either the High Holders or the factors. I side with the Codex Legis and the structure it represents. There are a number of factors who are as displeased with me and the Collegium as you are."

"What a pity."

"You're angry because your husband was killed. I'm angry because the brown-shirts here killed four innocent students at Imagisle, as well as a young gardener and several others. None of them had done anything against you, your husband, or any High Holder. Then those brown-shirts attacked the Collegium—twice. We attacked no one. And you sit here, steeped in self-pity, but you have lived in a gorgeous estate, amid fine furniture, with fine fare upon your table . . . and you complain because your husband had to pay for the killings he supported and made possible. You know nothing and wish to know nothing beyond a narrow world of privilege."

"You're no better, Maitre. You live in a fine house yourself."

"I didn't always, Lady, and I remember those years well." Alastar looked to the daughter, most likely two to three years older than Lystara. "I imagine you ride well."

"I'm not talking to you."

Alastar refrained from pointing out that she just had and walked toward the young man, who had his father's sandy hair, if somewhat lighter in color, but the dark blue eyes of his mother.

Before Alastar could say anything, young Laevoryn turned and asked, "How long will you be defiling my hold?"

"With that attitude, young Laevoryn, it might not be your hold for long."

"You wouldn't dare."

"Don't try my patience. You're in enough trouble in your own right, and as the heir to a rebelling High Holder, young man, you have no rights at all. Unless Rex Lorien is merciful, he could give the entire High Holding to anyone he pleases and leave you and your family with nothing."

"That is unacceptable."

"So was your killing of Enrique D'Hulet."

"I didn't lay a blade or bullet on him."

"I'm certain you didn't, but whatever you did, it certainly shouldn't have been over a mere two hundred golds. Did you ever tell your father?"

"That is a shameful accusation." Those icy words came from Lady Laevoryn.

"Nothing accurate is shameful, except to the one who has committed the act, but then, what your sire did to Factor Hulet was shameful as well. Killing the unarmed seems to run in the family." Alastar turned back toward Lady Laevoryn.

She did not meet his eyes, nor did her daughter.

Alastar doubted that either felt shame, only that they preferred to dismiss him as someone who could not possibly understand the trials of a High Holder. *In that regard, there's little difference between them and Lorien.*

Distasteful as it was, he addressed Lady Laevoryn. "You can have your servants fix you dinner. Eat it in the breakfast room. Then retire to your chambers."

Again, none of them spoke in return. Alastar was just as glad that they didn't. He returned to the study and resumed his search of Laevoryn's papers, initially without much success. Then, in a side drawer inside a small leather folder, he found several cards and sheets of paper. He read through them one after the other, his eyed picking out the key phrases.

> . . . *appreciate your support in the matter discussed last night, and we will consider what might be done* . . .

That one was signed by Cransyr, but not dated. There were no specifics on "the matter."

> . . . *in addition to the sum agreed upon* . . . *must convey an appreciation for a quiet and permanent resolution* . . .

Whatever the resolution was remained unmentioned, and the note was unsigned.

> . . . *with thanks for the swiftness of disposal* . . .

That card was signed with a symbol Alastar did not recognize. Several other notes and cards and even a long letter followed a similar pattern. In some cases, he noted, the signature had been inked out. Clearly, Laevoryn had "repaired" matters for either golds or to call in favors. One of the last cards was more intriguing.

> *In return for the tonic, it will be taken care of as you wish.*

The undated card was signed only by an "M." Alastar frowned. *Murranyt?* What had been taken care of, and in return for what?

The thought of Murranyt called up when Strosyl had died. It had seemed so ironic that a man who had come up from a street patroller, dealing with the worst types, had died from a case of the red flux, especially in the prime of life. He looked at the card again, then replaced it in the small folder, which he tucked inside his summer gray jacket.

At three quints past sixth glass, Khaelis informed Alastar that Thelia had arrived, accompanied by Tiranya and Belsior.

Alastar hurried to meet Thelia outside, where he dismissed Tiranya and Belsior to return to the Collegium and then escorted the accounts maitre into the dwelling through the octagonal foyer to the study that held the ledgers. Gesturing to the ledgers on the desk and those remaining on the shelves, he said, "They're all yours, metaphorically speaking."

"What am I looking for?"

"Evidence that Laevoryn was participating in the High Holders' revolt. He had a company of brown-shirts quartered here, most likely those who destroyed Naathyn's family and factorage and fired the old port tower . . . and attacked Imagisle last Vendrei. My guess is that someone else paid him to do it. One whole wing of this place is closed off, as is half the south wing. The rooms in the north wing are without furnishings, and I'm fairly certain that young Laevoryn either arranged for the death of Hulet's nephew or killed him himself over a two-hundred-gold gambling loss."

Thelia nodded. "He might have handled all that in coin. There'd be no trace of it in the ledgers."

"That's all right as well, because it shows, in a different way, that he was at least cooperating with the rebels, and it would also show that the rebellion went beyond the four High Holders who died in the explosion at the Chateau D'Council. While you're doing that, I'll be going through his desk and files to see if there are any messages or letters that reveal anything. I'll try to stay out of your way."

"I can use the side table."

"Thank you." Alastar paused. "This might have nothing to do with it, but you grew up around oils and essences. Are you aware of any poison that has an effect similar to the red flux?"

Thelia shook her head. "I don't know of one." She frowned. "There is a tonic that they caution against using when you have the flux. It makes things worse. It's really good for consumption and the wheezes, though."

Alastar nodded. *Suggestive, but far from proof.* He returned to his own search.

Slightly before seventh glass, still not having found anything amid Laevoryn's papers that might have confirmed his treachery in ink, Alastar left the study and walked around the ancient dwelling and down the lane to a wider stone-paved space where the troopers had erected a truly massive pyre. The bodies were evenly spaced out.

Weidyn was waiting.

"Where did you find all the timber?"

The captain smiled. "Here and there. We didn't destroy anything, except for two old run-down sheds that were empty. We did take as much oil as we could find and soaked some of the greener timber."

"Did you find anything that would indicate who paid them or where they came from?"

The captain shook his head. "I recognized one. Served one term and left service a year ago. Good with a rifle and sharp. Didn't much care for the army. I never knew where he came from. The others? Personal things. A handful had letters, but there was nothing to indicate where they came from. A lot were older, probably former rankers. They didn't have much coin."

"That suggests they were either from around L'Excelsis or that they were paid in advance where they were enlisted and left the coins with their families . . . or perhaps both."

"That'd be my thought, too, Maitre." Weidyn cleared his throat.

"I'm ready." Alastar stepped forward. As Collegium maitre, he'd presided over a few pyres, if for individuals.

Four troopers stood around the pyre, to the north, south, east, and west. Each held a burning torch.

Alastar began. "Life is a gift from the Nameless, for from the glory of the Nameless do we come; through the glory of the Nameless do we live, and to that glory do we return. Each of these men lived his life as best he could, and all judgments now belong to the Nameless. May they be remembered for who they were and what they did, and may each remain in memory for his deeds and kindnesses, not merely as an empty name."

He gestured to the troopers, and as they lowered the torches, he offered the final words. "As each of these men was born in warmth, so is it fitting that they leave their mortal form in fire and return to the life and glory of the Nameless." With his last words, he imaged a fireball into the center of pyre.

He stood there for a time as the flames mounted. He knew he couldn't have afforded to handle the situation otherwise, especially since the brown-shirts he'd allowed to flee and survive the first large attack on Imagisle—the one using the angled iron shields doubtless manufactured by Vaschet—had merely gone on killing others and doubtless would have continued to do so. Yet he had a hard time understanding why such men would serve the ends of those who wanted to keep everyone subservient to their every whim. *Are times that bad for the able-bodied poor?*

Alastar feared that they were, that the majority of either factors or High Holders could have cared less about the lives lost to support abusive personal power on the one hand and the often abusive pursuit of golds on the other.

When he was certain that the flames were sufficient for the task at hand, he turned and walked back to the hold house, the pyre providing enough light that his shadow stretched out before him.

As he entered the study once more, he noticed that the pale lavender hangings somehow not only failed to lighten the study, but almost seemed to absorb the light from the pair of wall lamps and the one on the side of the desk, giving the chamber a feel of insubstantiality that conveyed, in Alastar's opinion, a sense of evil. *But your feelings about the Laevoryn clan just might be affecting your feelings.*

After perhaps another half quint of searching, Alastar found—wedged in the back of the bottom drawer of a side table—a single half-sheet of paper with but two lines upon it . . . and no signature or initial. There was also no date.

> *Here is the latest payroll. The captain will render an accounting as well.*
> *Keep them busy. The Collegium needs to be kept occupied.*

Alastar read the words again, then smiled, if ironically. The writer definitely had doubts about Laevoryn's probity with funds. Unfortunately, the precise scrip could have come from any wealthy individual's hand . . . or from a clerk.

At almost three quints past eighth glass, Thelia looked up from the side table. "I've done what I could, Maitre Alastar."

"Did you discover anything?" Alastar noted a smudge of ink on her forehead and could see the tiredness in her eyes.

"I went through the ledgers as quickly as I could with some care. That's what you requested. There's no indication of any payments other than land rents and various banalities, and all those payments are meticulously noted. What is interesting is that the expenditures listed in the provisions and supplies ledger are far greater than those entered in the master ledger, as if some were not part of estate expenses."

"That discrepancy is a good indication that he was being paid to quarter the brown-shirts." Alastar frowned. "Is there something like a pay ledger?"

"There is, but it only deals with estate servants. Payments to factors and tradesmen are listed in the general expense ledger."

"What about personal disbursements for Laevoryn or his family?"

"There are payments to tailors and seamstresses, carters, a coppersmith, a silversmith, and others. There's nothing stating that Laevoryn gave golds or silvers to himself or others, and there's nothing that shows a statement of assets or golds."

"That may be another reason why he's been in financial difficulty . . . or that account ledger is somewhere else." Alastar took a slow deep breath. "Calculate the difference between the actual outlays on provisions in that ledger and the amounts entered in the master ledger."

"I've already done that, for the last three months. It's been running about a hundred golds a month."

"That's about right for food for eighty to a hundred men. Gather up your papers with the calculations. We're going to head back to Imagisle. I need to brief Weidyn first, but that won't take long."

"We're just going to leave?"

"What else should we do? There aren't any rebel fighters left. Laevoryn is dead. We've discovered what little we can. And some of us need to get ready for a trip south along the river." *Among other things.* Alastar stood, all too conscious that he was sore in more than a few places . . . and would likely be even sorer by morning.

On Meredi morning, Alastar had to force himself through his morning run, and, as he'd known would eventually happen, both Alyna and Malyna finished ahead of him, despite the fact that a brisk cool wind out of the northwest kept him from feeling too overheated.

As they walked back toward the Maitre's house, Alyna said, "You didn't want to talk about yesterday much last night."

"I was tired." After a moment, he added, "I still can't get over the sense of entitlement that Laevoryn had, and that his family still has. They're worse than Ryen was, and people called him Rex Dafou."

"I couldn't believe all the notes in that folder. But why did he keep it?"

"So he could remember who owed him what. All the notes or cards that were signed or initialed were suggestive but hold no real details. Like the card I suspect was from Murranyt. For anyone to use them as proof they'd have to have discovered things far more incriminating. There's just enough there so that Laevoryn could remember. The ones with details had the signature or name thoroughly blotted out. I'll need to brief Lorien on all that after the senior imagers' meeting."

"He won't be happy."

"He'll be less happy if I don't."

Alyna nodded.

"Later, I'll meet with Elthyrd . . . when I can. I think I'll take that card with me."

"You might image a copy."

"That's not a bad idea. Do you have any other suggestions?"

"You might let Factoria Kathila know. If you merely tell her, and don't ask or suggest anything, she'll be in your debt . . . and not the other way around."

"That's a very good idea."

"I do have some."

"More than that. How are the special bullets coming?"

"Slowly. Remember, imaging and checking against a template is anything but swift."

That didn't surprise Alastar. He looked ahead to where Malyna and Lystara were hurrying up the steps to the Maitre's house. "They look happy."

"I'm glad they enjoy one another so much."

Alastar nodded, his thoughts on the day ahead, which he knew would be even longer than he planned—something was bound to come up.

Even so, by the time he'd washed up and shaved, eaten a hearty breakfast, and he and Alyna had left the house for the administration building, he was feeling more cheerful, at least until he looked to the southeast, where it seemed to him that more clouds were gathering.

"I hope we don't get more rain. Those clouds . . ." He shook his head.

"They do look like they might bring showers."

"You're being optimistic."

"It doesn't hurt."

Alastar agreed—mostly.

Before long they were entering the administration building.

Dareyn looked up from the table desk as Alastar and Alyna approached. "There's a dispatch from Marshal Wilkorn." He held up the envelope.

"Thank you." Alastar took it. "Is there anything else I should know?"

"Not that I know of, sir."

Alastar and Alyna entered the study, Alyna closing the door behind them, while Alastar slit the envelope with his belt knife, extracted the dispatch and began to read.

Maitre Alastar—

On Lundi evening, the rebel forces mustered in Nordeau appeared to be readying to depart. Earlier on Lundi, they sent scouts north on the road to Caluse. At this point, the total force approximates close to two and a half regiments, and a number of cannon. They have ample supply wagons . . .

After he finished reading the dispatch, Alastar handed it to Alyna, then waited until she handed the dispatch back.

"I worry about the cannon," she said.

"We'll have to see if we can do what we did before."

"What if they space them out? They'll have far more than we faced when Chesyrk attacked."

"We have more strong imagers."

"They may have some of their own—Bettaur and Ashkyr possibly."

"Do you have any better ideas?" Alastar asked. "I'm open to any suggestions."

"Outside of finding a way to make them concentrate their forces near a river . . . no, not at the moment."

There was a knock on the door.

"Ah . . . sir, I believe all the other senior maitres are in the conference room."

"Thank you." Alastar moved to the door that led to the conference room directly, opened it, and followed Alyna in before taking his place at the head of the long table.

"I want to keep this meeting short. Most of you know what happened at Laevoryn's estate, but for those of you who don't, we took down the gates and discovered that he'd been quartering and feeding an entire company of brown-shirts. They fired on us, and the imagers shielded the two army squads. When it was all over, there were more than sixty dead brown-shirts, and Laevoryn still tried to kill Captain Weidyn. The troopers killed Laevoryn. We found evidence that someone else was funding Laevoryn so that he could pay, quarter, and feed the brown-shirts. We couldn't determine who that was, other than it was likely another High Holder. I'll be reporting all this to Rex Lorien immediately after we finish. Also, Commander Murranyt of the Civic Patrol has proved to be rather reluctant to deal with Laevoryn despite the likelihood that he had suspicions.

"Marshal Wilkorn's latest dispatch indicates that the rebels were preparing to leave Nordeau, but had not left by Lundi evening. They have more than two regiments of troopers, possibly three, more than half mounted, and a substantial number of cannon. It is likely that our force will have to depart on Vendrei or Samedi, unless we hear otherwise from the marshal. Other than that, not much has happened," Alastar finished sardonically.

"Do we know where any other High Holders stand?" asked Cyran.

Alastar smiled wryly. "Right now, the only other High Holders I have knowledge of are High Holders Zaerlyn and Meinyt, neither of whom is supportive of an armed rebellion." He turned to Arion. "Have you heard anything?"

"I have received some correspondence from my family," replied Arion, "and my sire is strongly opposed to any armed opposition to the rex or the Collegium. Indications are that the majority of High Holders along the River Aluse are opposed to taking up arms against the rex, and so far none have sent armsmen."

"Thank you. That's good to know." Alastar glanced down the table, his eyes stopping on Gaellen. "How is Glaesyn faring?"

"It will be several weeks before the wound fully heals. It may be months before he can use the arm and shoulder as well as he could before. It might be longer . . ."

"And it might be never?" suggested Alastar.

Gaellen nodded, almost grudgingly, before adding, "He would have died otherwise."

That still didn't make Alastar feel much better.

"Should we still keep the students on Imagisle?" asked Akoryt.

"For now," replied Alastar. "I'd like a better sense of whether we've removed all of the brown-shirts from L'Excelsis before we let them venture off Imagisle. For the older imagers, I'd suggest that if they feel they must leave Imagisle, they have a good reason, that they do so during the day, and that they don't do so alone. We can reduce the number of patrols and go to one additional maitre on duty for now."

There were reluctant nods around the table.

After a few more questions about schedules, Alastar called an end to the meeting, and he and Alyna returned to his study.

"I was initially surprised at some of what Arion said," offered Alyna, "until I thought it over."

"You mean," replied Alastar, "that Ryel is personally opposed to taking up arms, but not opposed to others doing so . . . or to sending golds to those who do?"

"Cynical of me, I know," returned Alyna. "It goes against all the teaching of Rholan and the precepts of the Nameless." Her smile was patently and falsely sweet.

Alastar almost laughed but managed just to shake his head. "Iskhar would be so disappointed with the low esteem in which we hold our most noble High Holders."

"No, he wouldn't. He'd only be disappointed if we voiced it in public."

"You're probably right about that." Alastar stopped as he heard the knock on the door. "Yes?"

Maercyl opened the door and handed him an envelope. "Sir, this came from High Holder Meinyt of the High Council."

"Thank you." Alastar took the envelope. He did not sit down as he slit the envelope, took out the missive, and began to read.

Maitre Alastar—

I have just received word that High Holder Paellyt was foully murdered on his own lands yesterday. He was apparently checking on the condition of a prize mare when his throat was slit. The killer has not been found, but his family has reason to believe the death was the work of a disgruntled factor . . .

Alastar nodded. He would have been very surprised if he didn't know exactly who the killer was.

. . . Incidents such as this can only make the majority of High Holders more restive and less amenable to a resolution of the conflicts between the High Holders and the rex, I believe it would be very much in the interests of the Collegium, the rex, and the High Council if we could meet at your earliest convenience to discuss this and other related matters in hopes of coming to a resolution, rather than having misunderstandings fuel the spread of the current High Holder displeasure with Rex Lorien and the Collegium. While repairs are ongoing at the Chateau D'Council, I will be at my residence.

Current displeasure? That's a bit of an understatement. Alastar took a deep breath. While he just wanted to shake his head, it sounded like he needed to talk to Meinyt immediately, whether or not he wanted to.

He handed the letter to Alyna. "This isn't totally unexpected, but . . ."

She read it quickly, then looked up. "You're right. He likely deserved it, but it's going to enrage the High Holders even more."

There was a second knock on the door.

"Trouble comes double," said Alyna sardonically.

Dareyn eased the door ajar. "A messenger just arrived from the chateau, sir." He extended an envelope.

"Thank you." Alastar took the envelope and slit it open. The message was short. Very short.

We would appreciate seeing you at your earliest convenience this morning.

Beneath the words were the letter "L" and the regial seal.

Alastar handed the sheet to Alyna.

"That's about as close to a command as he's made recently."

"I suspect he's just discovered what we did yesterday. I'd best head out. He usually isn't up all that early."

"No . . . only on the days when it's inconvenient for you." Alastar offered a wry smile.

Three quints later, he was striding along the upper north corridor in the Chateau D'Rex, accompanied by Captain Churwyl.

From somewhere came the scent of roses, most likely from Lady Chelia's private sitting room, thought Alastar. *She might need every distraction from Lorien these days.* "He's not been pleased with much, I take it?" Alastar kept his voice low.

"I couldn't speak to that, sir."

Alastar took that for an affirmative. "Until we get the High Holders firmly in hand, he may not be too pleased about much."

Churwyl did not reply, not that Alastar expected that he would.

When they reached the study door, Churwyl nodded to the guard on duty, rapped on the door, and announced, "Maitre Alastar to see you, your Grace."

"Send him in."

The guard opened the door, and Alastar entered. As was almost always the case, the door was quickly closed behind him. He walked to the desk and seated himself across from Lorien.

"You're prompt enough this morning. Why didn't I know about what you did yesterday? Marshal Wilkorn sent me a dispatch about your requisitioning his troops to attack and invade a High Holder's estate." Lorien's voice began to rise as he continued, "Wasn't that beyond the scope of the Collegium? Don't you think I have enough trials with High Holders as it is without your making matters worse? Why do you persist in this?"

"I didn't let you know yesterday because we didn't finish dealing with the rebel brown-shirts until past eighth glass last night. I was setting out to see you this morning when I received your message. As for why I am persisting, as you put it, it's because that estate held a company of the same kind of brown-shirts who attacked the Chateau D'Rex. They were the same brown-shirts that destroyed the factorage and family of Factorius Naathyn and destroyed the river port tower . . . and killed nearly half a score of innocent young imagers. The last thing you need is a rebel force here in L'Excelsis while another one is marching toward you from the south."

"You still should have informed me. There is the small matter of my being the rex, and your acting as if you were by ordering my troopers to attack a High Holder."

"We didn't attack a High Holder. I requested troopers from the marshal after we discovered the brown-shirts on Laevoryn's estate. The troopers have the authority to investigate and deal with rebels. We did not know that they would attack. We never attacked High Holder Laevoryn personally, but he attempted to kill Captain Weidyn. As a result, Weidyn's troopers shot Laevoryn. Imagers did not attack Laevoryn. He died because he committed an overt act of rebellion against you."

Lorien's glare faded . . . somewhat. "At least you've thought this one out. More than what should have been done in dealing with my brother. Pardon me, my half brother. Do you realize what a trial it is, how totally unsuitable it is, to be married to my brother's half sister?"

"At the time, it would have caused more trouble."

"At the time. What about now?"

"What do you suggest we do? The only proof we have is a messenger in your brother's livery. If you execute him on those grounds without more proof, you'll have an even bigger rebellion on your hands, and not because he's your brother, but because he's a High Holder. That's why I wanted Wilkorn's troops—because the brown-shirts fired on them, and that's an armed rebellion by men in the same uniform that attacked the chateau here. Not even your worst enemies can say you exceeded your authority or rights in attacking Laevoryn's estate. He was harboring armed troopers who attacked your chateau. He died in the act of rebellion." Alastar knew he was going over the same ground again, but it seemed necessary. *More than necessary.*

"They can't have been the same ones. You and your imagers killed most of those."

Alastar did not sigh, much as he wanted to. "There is a rebel army raised and funded by High Holders. All of the rebel troops that have so far appeared and attacked in L'Excelsis have been uniformed in brown. Your troopers attacked troopers wearing the same uniforms after hearing reports that those brown-shirts attacked more student imagers, killed an entire family and burned a factorage, and then fired the old port tower. Those brown-shirts did not surrender, but immediately fired upon your troopers. Those are more than grounds enough for your actions."

"My actions?"

"The actions of troopers under the command of Marshal Wilkorn, who is your marshal of the army."

"The High Holders won't like it."

"The ones who aren't already rebelling will accept it. It doesn't matter what the ones who are rebelling think because they've gone so far that nothing except defeat in battle will stop them."

"Why are they so willful?"

"Because many of them are losing power to the wealthier factors. They want you to change things back to the older ways so that they won't. For the most part, the factors are the ones who are making things better. They're paying more and more in tariffs, while the High Holders are demanding lower tariffs. As the number of High Holders declines, so will the total amount of golds collected from them. In fact, from what you've said previously, that's already happening." Alastar paused, then said, "There's one other matter."

"Another trial you've foisted on me?"

"No. Another trial foisted on you by High Holder arrogance. You may recall I'd mentioned the burning of Naathyn's factorage by the brown-shirts. Well, it seems that was because . . ." Alastar went on to explain the events and the report he had just received about Paellyt's death.

Lorien snorted. "I'd like to see a few of them cut up like that. If the boy survives, maybe I should grant him Laevoryn's lands and assets." His brief smile faded. "There's something else. Minister Sanafryt tells me that in several pending hearings, High Holders have refused to appear, or even to have advocates representing them appear. I cannot have that. I won't!"

"It might be best to concentrate on putting down the armed rebellion first. After that, the army will be free to deal with individual High Holders, and there shouldn't be many complaints if Marshal Wilkorn requests the assistance of imagers in order to reduce the bloodshed."

"I don't like it."

Alastar decided to wait.

Finally, Lorien said, "I can see why it has to be that way, but I'm still not happy. It's just another unnecessary trial."

"It's a trial," Alastar admitted. But one that is necessary and one that had to happen sooner or later, given how arrogant many of the High Holders are.

"We've talked enough. I'm going to walk in the garden to get the stench out of my nostrils." Lorien stood.

So did Alastar. "By your leave?"

"Go. Try not to surprise me again."

"I'll do my best, but I won't be speaking for the High Holders." Alastar inclined his head, then turned and left.

Once he left the chateau, he headed down the white stone steps that still showed no wear and no marks from four hundred years of service, the thought of which again called up a certain wonder about Quaeryt. *How on Terahnar did he do all that he did?*

Coermyd was waiting with the gray gelding at the foot of the steps at the edge of the paved area for coaches and mounts. "Back to the Collegium, sir?"

"No. We're headed to High Holder Meinyt's. Did you see anything interesting while you were waiting?"

"Everyone watches you, sir." Coermyd shrugged. "Other than that . . . there were wagons and coaches on the ring road, and there weren't any other visitors to the chateau."

"There usually aren't too many," Alastar replied as he mounted and turned the gelding eastward down the paved entry lane to the ring road, heading toward the Boulevard D'Ouest. The clouds he had barely glimpsed earlier were now forming an even line across the sky to the southeast, but didn't seem to be moving that swiftly. *And if they hold rain, that means it will rain for a long time . . . too long.*

At the northernmost point on the ring road, Alastar turned onto the Boulevard D'Ouest, heading east. What Alastar saw as he rode—that everything in L'Excelsis seemed to be just another day—reinforced his belief that most people could have cared less who ruled Solidar, just so long as the ruler didn't upset their lives too much. *Or at all.* Only those with golds, factorages, or lands really worried about who ruled . . . and imagers, because those with power could destroy the Collegium, and in time, essentially enslave imagers.

When the two reached the West River Road, they turned north, and shortly thereafter, turned northwest on a narrower if stone-paved road that bordered the unnamed stream. In less than a quint, they rode through the stone gateposts, whose iron gates were drawn open, and up the stone-paved lane to the small covered portico on the east side of the two-story gray stone structure overlooking the stream.

As before, a footman in green livery trimmed in gray appeared at the top of the portico steps as Alastar reined up. "Welcome, Maitre. High Holder Meinyt thought you would be here early this afternoon. Let me escort you to the study." The footman turned to Coermyd. "There is water for the mounts and some refreshment for you in the rear courtyard."

"Thank you." Coermyd nodded, then urged his mount forward, tugging gently on the gray gelding's reins as well.

Meinyt was standing by the window, looking downhill to the south at the stream beyond a low stone wall, when Alastar entered the study. The High Holder turned and gestured to the chairs set on each side of a circular table. "I appreciate your response."

"You did express a certain sense of urgency," replied Alastar as he seated himself. "It seemed proper to respond in like fashion."

"You sound as though it was not necessarily that urgent."

"Were you aware of the situation that led to High Holder Paellyt's slaughter? And to several other deaths?"

"There was a confrontation over gaming by Paellyt's son and a young factor. That doesn't justify murder."

"You're right." Alastar nodded. "It doesn't. Especially in these circumstances, which aren't what most High Holders would want to hear. I'm most gratified that you do." Alastar doubted that was the case, but decided to offer the compliment as an entry to the larger story. "The second son of Factorius Naathyn bested Paellyt's eldest in bones. Paellyt's son then took steps to run the young man down with his coach. The younger Naathyn died on the street. The older Naathyn slit the throat of Paellyt's eldest in return and then went into hiding. Last Jeudi evening, those brown-shirted thugs armed by Cransyr, Laevoryn, and other High Holders attacked Naathyn's coachworks and home and killed Naathyn and all members of his family—except the eldest son, who wasn't there. I imagine he's the one who slit Paellyt's throat, and I can't say I blame him."

"You seem to be justifying violence on the part of the factors, Maitre."

"I could say that you seem to believe that High Holders have the right to kill anyone who bests them at gaming. I trust that's not what you meant."

"I never said—"

"No . . . it's your instant reaction. Enrique D'Hulet was also likely killed by young Laevoryn, and Laevoryn shot Factorius Hulet, who was unarmed, in cold blood. Rather than ask why all these High Holders felt that they had to kill factors, you immediately focused on the violent reaction to the killings. The High Holders involved acted as if the laws didn't apply to them. Isn't it rather coincidental that a significant number of High Holders have petitioned or supported the petitions to exempt High Holders from justicing—except before the High Justicer when the matter is between High Holders?"

Meinyt started to say something, then stopped.

Alastar waited. When Meinyt did not speak, Alastar went on. "On Mardi we tracked the brown-shirts back to High Holder Laevoryn's estate. Because the brown-shirts had already attacked Imagisle and the Chateau D'Rex, Marshal Wilkorn dispatched troopers to deal with the brown-shirts. Rather than surrender, they attacked the troopers. When the troopers defeated the brown-shirts, High Holder Laevoryn appeared and immediately walked up to the army captain commanding the troopers. He insisted that he had every right to use the brown-shirts as he saw fit and to kill any lesser factor or individual who infringed on what he saw as his rights, those being the ancient rights before they were limited by the Codex Legis. Then he aimed a pistol at the captain and fired. The troopers with the captain returned fire and killed Laevoryn. The captain was fortunate enough to survive."

"Laevoryn was being extreme, it does appear."

"So was Paellyt's son, and so was Paellyt."

"Many High Holders feel that Rex Lorien has applied the provisions of the Codex Legis in a fashion that will destroy them and their heritage over time."

"For all his faults, and those of his sire, both of which are many, neither has exceeded the limits of the Codex. Nor have there been any recent increases in tariffs. What has occurred is that as factoring and manufacturing methods have improved, many High Holders have not adopted those improvements. As a result, those High Holders have debts they cannot repay, often to factors. Their response is to blame the rex and the factors . . . and at times the Collegium."

"Has the Collegium changed so much, Maitre?"

"Not so much as I would prefer, and not so much as will continue to happen, but we now have a factorage, and we are selling goods to the point that we require far fewer golds from the rex. We're also not blaming others for the changes that have occurred."

Alastar waited once more.

Finally, Meinyt spoke. "I was not fully aware of all the circumstances that led to High Holder Paellyt's death, but the manner of his death disturbs me nonetheless. Yet I can see that the death of the younger Naathyn and the deaths of nearly all his family are even more disturbing. What would you suggest to the High Council that will succeed me in the months ahead to prevent more such misunderstandings? Even as I understand that revenge fueling further revenge can only make matters far worse, I also see that many High Holders only see their futures as less prosperous than their past."

"I don't have a simple answer to that," Alastar admitted. "I do believe that some of these issues need to be resolved between the High Council and the factors without recourse to violence, and I believe they could be if the factors of Solidar created their own equivalent of the High Council. That is something that you suggested. I think it is a good suggestion, and I will press that upon the Factors' Council of L'Excelsis. Perhaps also, the High Council and the factors could agree on the rates of interest that would not be considered excessively usurious . . . as well as other matters."

"That might be a start . . . assuming that Rex Lorien can put down the armed insurrection of the most disgruntled High Holders."

"Another part of the solution, of necessity," added Alastar, "may have to be the dispossession of High Holders who refuse to accept the limits of the Codex Legis . . . and perhaps a change in the requirements to be a High Holder so that the amount of land required might be offset by other physical assets. If factors felt that some possibility for acceptance . . ."

"That would set ill, initially, but I can see the possibilities . . ."

Almost another glass passed before Alastar left Meinyt's comparatively modest mansion.

After Alastar mounted the gelding and he and Coermyd rode out through the open gates, he said, "We're headed to Factor Elthyrd's factorage."

"Yes, sir."

Alastar had planned to meet with Elthyrd in any case, but now he not only had to brief the acting head of the Factors' Council but also try to lay the groundwork for what would follow the revolution. *Assuming that the High Holders don't prevail.*

Because Elthyrd's factorage was less than a mille south of Imagisle on the East River Road, it was simpler to take the West River Road, then cross the river at the Sud Bridge, and turn south on the East River Road. Again, Alastar studied the clouds, which covered almost a third of the sky and seemed darker than they had earlier.

Before long, they were entering the compound that held Elthyrd's factorage. Over the thirteen years that Alastar had known Elthyrd, the factorage had changed little. At the center was the small building flanked by large two-story warehouses, although a third warehouse had been added several years before, south of the southernmost warehouse, and one pier had been widened, where men were using a crane Alastar had not seen before to unload one of the low barges tied there, and lowering lengths of timber onto a flatbed cart with two mules in traces, ready to carry the timber to one of the warehouses.

Alastar reined up in front of the small building, where he dismounted and handed the gelding's reins to Coermyd. "I hope this won't take too long." Then he walked into the small building and found the anteroom empty. Recalling where Elthyrd's study was, he moved toward the doorway behind the long counter. While the door was open, Alastar could see that no one was in the small study that held little more than a table desk, a small bookcase filled with what looked to be ledgers of some sort, and three chairs—two in front of the desk and one behind it. He turned just as Elthyrd hurried through the front door.

"You might give a poor factor some notice, Maitre."

Alastar could sense a slight irritation behind the humorously spoken words. "I thought you'd rather meet sooner without notice than later with notice."

"You're right about that." Elthyrd walked past Alastar and into the study.

Alastar followed and closed the door behind himself, then sat in one of the chairs in front of the desk. "I've spent most of the day with Lorien and High Holder Meinyt."

"What do you have to tell me?"

"Where the rebels are and how many of them there are, and other developments here in L'Excelsis."

Elthyrd nodded. "Go on, if you would."

"The rebels have nearly three full regiments and supporting cannon. They'll be leaving Nordeau to march on L'Excelsis shortly, if they haven't already. They outnumber Lorien's forces three to one, if not more."

"Can you imagers make up the difference?"

"We hope to, but cannon make that more difficult. The other problems lie in what has happened with the High Holders here in L'Excelsis. Have you heard about Paellyt?"

Elthyrd nodded.

"Then I won't repeat that. I will tell you about the remaining brown-shirts here in L'Excelsis and what happened . . ." Alastar went through all the events, including what he had learned about Murranyt. When he finished, he asked, "Has anyone ever looked into the events surround-ing the death of Murranyt's predecessor?"

"Not in the way you have." Elthyrd frowned. "I don't doubt you. But the proof's not exactly iron-plated, if you know what I mean."

"You might want to look at this." Alastar took out the card that he had removed with the others from Laevoryn's study and laid it on the desk in front of Elthyrd.

"It is suggestive," Elthyrd said as he looked up.

Alastar reclaimed the card. "For the moment, I'd just like you to think about it. There's no point in pursuing it until after we deal with the rebel High Holders."

"You talked to Councilor Meinyt?"

"Earlier today. He's not a happy man. He mentioned again his sugges-tion that all the factors across Solidar need to form their own council."

"Be hard on those selected."

"It might be, but it would give you all a voice directly with the rex, and you'd have more power because he'd know that all the factors were behind you." Alastar smiled. "That can wait a bit . . . but not too long, not if you want to reduce the influence of the High Council."

"Sounds like you don't think it's a choice."

"That's up to you and the other factors."

Elthyrd sighed. "You make a suggestion, and going against it never works out." He took another deep breath. "I'll talk to the others on the council." After a pause, he asked, "You have any more news or sugges-tions?"

"I'm afraid that's all."

Elthyrd stood. "By the way, appreciate your advice to Estafen."

As he rose, Alastar replied, "I appreciate what both of you have done."

"The same to you, Maitre."

Alastar nodded, turned, and walked out of the building to where Coermyd waited.

"Are we headed back to Imagisle, sir?" The imager third glanced up at the dark clouds that covered almost half the sky.

"I'm afraid not. We need to visit one more factor this afternoon. If we're fortunate, we might be able to finish before it starts raining again."

Alastar felt in some ways that he was just riding back and forth, since this time they rode back north to the Sud Bridge, across it, and then south to Kathila's factorage, a ride that took just over a quint before Coermyd and Alastar reined up before the low brick-walled building just off the West River Road. This time Alastar did not see the young girl in gray, and he made his way inside by himself, slipping his visor cap under his arm as he did so.

The older woman smiled and nodded as Alastar appeared. "Maitre, I'll tell her that you're here."

As she stood and walked down the corridor, Alastar had the feeling that his arrival was not entirely unexpected, especially when she returned and gestured in the direction of Kathila's study.

This time the factoria did not rise from behind her jet black desk when Alastar entered the study and closed the door, but merely gestured toward the chairs.

"You were expecting me, I see." Alastar eased into a chair.

"I thought it was likely."

"Have you talked to your daughter recently? In the last few days?"

"Not since this morning," replied Kathila almost acerbically. "She did mention that she spent much of the evening with you at High Holder Laevoryn's."

"Then I presume you know what we found there?"

"Outside of arrogant High Holders and rebel troopers? No. Thelia never discusses anything that is not known outside the Collegium unless she's been instructed to."

"I had thought as much, but I've never told her that."

"I doubt that is often necessary," replied Kathila dryly.

"Since you are a member of the Factors' Council, I thought you might like to know more about what has occurred over the past few days, beginning with a series of brown-shirt attacks in L'Excelsis and Imagisle and our discovery that a number of brown-shirts were being quartered on High Holder Laevoryn's estate in L'Excelsis . . ." Alastar went on to describe the boat attack on Imagisle, the destruction of Naathyn's factorage and family, his meeting with Murranyt, and then the events at Laevoryn's estate.

"None of that surprises me greatly," said Kathila.

Alastar nodded. "Were you aware that Laevoryn likely had a . . . private arrangement with Murranyt?"

"That would not precisely astound me, either."

"Considering that Sostryl, who was Murranyt's predecessor, died of the red flux, I thought you might find this card, which I discovered in Laevoryn's study, of some interest." Alastar laid the card on the polished jet wood surface in front of Kathila. He watched closely as she studied it.

The factoria's eyes might have widened slightly, and she did look up with an amused smile. "Again, I cannot say I am greatly surprised. But then, I was opposed to Murranyt's appointment as head of the Civic Patrol."

"Why, might I ask?"

"He had almost no experience as a street patroller. He started as a clerk, and spent five years there. When I looked into his references, it turned out that most of them were older and had died, some even before he became a patrol clerk."

"And no one listened to you?"

"They listened and nodded, and then pointed out that he had greatly improved the operation of patrol procurement and reduced the overall costs of operating the Civic Patrol without requiring fewer patrollers."

"Very factor-like requirements," observed Alastar reclaiming the card.

"I prefer factor-like requirements in a factorage. I would rather have safety and fewer malefactors on the streets and prowling the alleys."

"That would seem most reasonable, and I would agree. But I am not a factor."

"You run an efficient factorage, Maitre. I've seen that."

"I know enough to let those who can run it do so." Alastar smiled. "In any case, you now know why I wished to see you."

"You've told me what you want me to know. That is likely not why you wished to see me."

"But it is. I wanted you to know what I discovered. I've also informed Elthyrd of what you know. Now . . . it has been a long day already, and I would like to return to Imagisle before another deluge pummels L'Excelsis."

"I certainly will not keep you," said Kathila, standing and glancing momentarily toward the window, "but I have my doubts as to whether you will reach the Collegium before being drenched."

Alastar stood and inclined his head to her. "That may be."

In fact, it was.

He and Coermyd had ridden less than half a mille north on the West River Road before a soft heavy rain began to fall.

33

The rain lasted until well after midnight, and, again, there were shallow ponds and puddles everywhere on Jeudi morning, as well as scattered fog and mist. Even so, Alastar and the others did manage the morning run, and he was soaked through and through from the warm damp and the standing water by the time he finished. Alyna and Malyna seemed to fly over the water while he and Lystara had slogged through it. At least, it had seemed that way to him.

He'd only been in his study less than a quint when Dareyn brought in the first message of the day, delivered by army courier. Knowing it had to be from Wilkorn, Alastar read it immediately.

> Maitre Alastar—
>
> I have just received reports that on Mardi afternoon, the rebel forces set out from Nordeau. If they maintain standard pace, they will reach Caluse by Lundi around midday.
>
> We intend to depart headquarters at sixth glass tomorrow. That will allow us a day and a half to reach a point north of Caluse ideal for an attack on the rebels and another two days and a half to prepare. Should they decide not to take the west road north, we will be able to withdraw more quickly than they to L'Excelsis, since the East River Road north of Caluse is narrow and parts remain unpaved and rutted. Also, the ancient three-span bridge at Caluse is very narrow. We could easily shell it and destroy it, or render it unusable by other means, if we think it would be to our advantage.
>
> It would seem preferable for the majority of the imagers to be near the van, but the army will defer to the Collegium in the positioning of imagers . . .

When Alastar finished reading the long dispatch, he had Maercyl summon Cyran, Akoryt, and Alyna. While he waited, he took out his maps and considered what Wilkorn had written. Should the imagers be that concentrated? Or would several groups be preferable?

Two groups, not several.

Alyna was the first to arrive. As she settled into the chair closest to the window, she looked at Alastar and said, "The High Holders are advancing on L'Excelsis, aren't they?"

"Moving toward L'Excelsis, at least. How did you know?"

"Maercyl said you'd gotten a dispatch from the marshal, and you summoned me, Cyran, and Akoryt. That was the obvious conclusion. There are others, but, knowing you, none of the others were probable."

As she finished speaking, Cyran and Akoryt entered the study. Akoryt closed the door.

Alastar gestured toward the chairs and then waited for the other two to sit down before beginning, "The High Holder force is moving toward Caluse. We're leaving in the morning."

"I had a feeling it wouldn't be that long," said Akoryt.

"Are you sticking with the same twelve imagers you picked earlier?" asked Cyran.

"Unless something has changed that I don't know about. Has it?"

"Not that I know of." Cyran smiled sheepishly. "I mean, much has changed, but nothing that you don't know."

"We'll need to have everyone ready at the stables. We're to meet up with the main force where the Poignard Road meets the West River Road at seventh glass."

Akoryt frowned momentarily. "That's where the river bends and heads due south, isn't it?"

"It is," replied Cyran. "South and west of the barge piers."

"That's only a ride of three quints at best," offered Akoryt.

"I think you're suggesting that being ready at fifth glass is perhaps early?" Alastar smiled warmly.

"I might be at that," replied Akoryt.

"Two quints before sixth glass, then?"

"That should provide more than enough time," said Alyna.

"Can any of you think of anything I need to do before leaving tomorrow?"

Akoryt and Cyran exchanged glances. Both shook their heads.

"If you do, let me know. Otherwise, get on with your preparations. First off, Akoryt, you make sure that all of those going are told and know when to muster. Then go over the equipment and gear listings with each one."

"Yes, sir. I went over the gear with each yesterday."

"Good."

"Cyran, you have the bullets in special cartridge cases?"

"Yes, sir."

"Make sure someone is watching them all the time, once we set out."

"Alyna, how many of those bullets did you two manage to image?"

"A thousand."

"And they're all to tolerances for the heavy rifles?"

"That's why there are only a thousand. We also fired some using the captured rifles. There didn't seem to be a problem."

Beside her, Cyran nodded.

Akoryt gave the faintest of headshakes.

"I don't like it, either, but I'd rather try to take out the leadership than slaughter the rebel troopers." Alastar just hoped he didn't have to use the bullets on troopers, but he wasn't about to rule that out, not if it meant the difference between putting down the revolt and not doing so.

"When you put it that way . . ."

"Exactly," said Alyna.

Another quint passed before Cyran and Akoryt left. When Alastar and Alyna were alone in the study, he turned to her. "You know I'm not pleased about possibly having to use those bullets."

"I know."

"I won't if I don't think it's necessary."

"You may not have a choice. We both know that."

After Alyna left, Alastar turned to Dareyn, the only one in the anteroom. "I'll be going over some matters with Maitre Thelia. After that, in about two glasses, I'll need an escort and a mount—but not the gray. He needs to rest today."

"Yes, sir."

"Thank you." Alastar then walked back to Thelia's study, where he spent slightly more than two quints going over the last details of arranging the supplies and the two wagons necessary to carry them.

When Alastar returned to the anteroom, Maercyl said, "Beltran and your mount are waiting by the main entrance."

"Thank you." Alastar paused. "Is Dareyn all right?"

"Yes, sir. He's helping Maitre Obsolym." Maercyl smiled. "He's almost back to where he was."

"We don't want him overdoing things."

"No, sir. I've threatened to tell Elmya when he pushes himself too hard. That seems to work."

Alastar laughed, then turned and headed for the main entrance.

As he approached the horses, Beltran, who stood between the two, holding the reins, said, "Good morning, sir."

"Good morning. We won't be riding far. Just over the East Bridge and south to the Banque D'Excelsis. After that, we might ride another few blocks." Alastar took the reins of the chestnut mare from Beltran and mounted.

As he rode across the East Bridge, Alastar checked the water level in the river—still roughly a yard below the top of the riverwall, and far higher than he would have liked. He would have been surprised if more than a few fields and lands south of L'Excelsis weren't flooded, and that could change everything in terms of what Wilkorn had planned.

When they reached the Banque D'Excelsis, Alastar took a good look as he dismounted. The narrow stone building appeared far better than it had the first time Alastar had seen it some thirteen years earlier. Then the gray stone had been covered with years of smoke and grit that had given it almost the color of charcoal. Now the light gray stone was clean, and the bars that covered the windows were painted a shiny black. A stone plaque with the letters stating BANQUE D'EXCELSIS had been set into the stone above the door several years back, recalled Alastar, replacing the older signboard. The brass on the heavy oak door shimmered. Two guards, with sabers at their sides, stood just inside the entrance. Both looked at Alastar, then inclined their heads.

Inside the door was a small foyer, its floor of gray marble. Beyond the square arch at the rear of the foyer was a single large chamber, at the back of which was a counter. The top of the counter was graced by a bronze railing fastened to a bronze plate, with bronze bars connecting the plate and railing. At three places, there were openings in the bronze bars, and behind each sat a man in a green jacket, presumably on a high stool.

"Maitre Alastar . . ." Estafen appeared from somewhere to the side and walked forward, stopping a yard away. "You honor us."

"I have to say that you've definitely improved the building . . . and especially the interior, I suspect."

"You're kind. Might I ask . . . ?"

"I'd like a few words with you, preferably not in public."

"Of course. This way." Estafen led the way to a very small study, one with just a circular table and two chairs, a single bookcase, and two file chests on narrow tables. He closed the door behind Alastar, then gestured to the table and chairs.

As he took one of the chairs, Alastar observed that both chairs were positioned so that whoever sat in either could see the door.

Estafen took in Alastar's glance and said, "Some of those with whom we do business very much wish to keep their plaques close to their jackets."

"I've found that a great many factors share that feeling."

"Might I ask what you have in mind, Maitre?"

"Commander Murranyt."

"Oh? In what regard?"

Although Estafen's expression remained pleasant, Alastar could definitely sense a tension that had not been present a moment before.

"I recall that his predecessor died of the red flux. Most people don't."

"That's true. Most have it as children."

"I also discovered that there is a tonic that, helpful as it may be in dealing with other illnesses, actually makes the red flux much worse. Why this may be of interest is that in searching the study of the late High Holder Laevoryn—who supported armed brown-shirts against Rex Lorien—I came across this." Alastar laid the card on the table before Estafen.

The financier read it slowly, then looked up. "It is suggestive."

"In more ways than one . . ." Alastar gave a brief summary of his meeting with Murranyt, concluding, "so you can see why I have certain concerns."

"I would suggest that you are not the only one, but . . ."

"Unpleasantnesses tend to occur to those who cross the commander?"

"Something like that."

"I've been getting that impression." Alastar smiled pleasantly. "That's really all I wanted to say. It's not a matter with which I'm likely to concern myself or the Collegium until we finish dealing with the High Holder rebels."

"And that is likely to happen . . . when?"

"As matters now stand, within the next few weeks . . . possibly sooner." Alastar stood.

"Is what you showed me something you wish kept between us?" asked Estafen as he rose.

"I have no problem in others knowing the contents of the card, or the fate of the previous commander. I would appreciate that any others not be informed of how you came to see it."

Estafen nodded. "There are a few . . ."

"I believe I understand." Alastar inclined his head slightly. "Until later."

Estafen inclined his head in return.

Alastar had thought about conveying similar information to Alamara the younger, but after seeing Estafen's reaction decided against it. He also had his own preparations to make for the battle ahead. He just hoped it wouldn't turn into a campaign.

34

While Alastar had hoped to get back to the Maitre's house by third glass, word about his departure had apparently spread, and more than a few imagers appeared at his study door with various matters they felt needed decisions or resolution before he left. Some things did indeed need resolution—such as Petros's concerns about the continually rising prices for hay and feed grain, although in the end, there wasn't much of a choice besides trying to negotiate the best prices, but Alastar did have to make sure that Thelia knew he had approved the purchases to come.

When he finally reached the Maitre's house, it was well after fourth glass, and he was wondering what he'd overlooked. With so many aspects of the Collegium, there had to be something. Not that he worried overmuch. Alyna was more than capable of dealing with matters in his absence.

Deciding what to take from all the gear he had assembled was the next step. He squared his shoulders and headed up the stairs to the sitting room. After glancing around, he set out his saddlebags, then laid out the two sets of grays he'd already decided upon—one to wear and one spare. The two were his oldest, since he suspected that neither would be worth wearing after what was likely to happen.

At that moment, Alyna appeared. "You'd hoped to be home earlier."

"I did."

She handed him an oilskin jacket. "This might take up less space than your full-length one."

"I hate the idea of taking an oilskin, even the shorter jacket," declared Alastar. "It's still heavy and takes up space, and everything in that saddlebag will smell of fish oil."

"Dear . . . after two days everything will smell, and we've not had a week in the last two seasons when it didn't rain at least once, and sometimes almost every day."

"If I take it, it won't rain."

"That alone is reason enough . . ."

Alastar folded the jacket and put it in one of the saddlebags. "I do have two water bottles for lager."

"Good. What about spare boots?"

Alastar gestured toward the boots and smallclothes on the side table.

Even with Alyna's help and suggestions, or perhaps because of them, Alastar didn't finish packing his gear until two quints past sixth glass, and it was a quint before seventh glass before Jienna announced that dinner was ready.

Once everyone was settled around the table and Alastar had filled his beaker and Alyna's, and given each of the girls half a beaker of the dark lager, he took a sip and cleared his throat. "Tomorrow morning, as you know, I'll be leaving with most of the senior imagers, except for your mother and aunt, and Maitres Shaelyt, Gaellen, and Obsolym. We'll be traveling with the army battalions in order to stop and defeat the High Holder rebels. They left Nordeau on Mardi afternoon." He served Alyna two of the gravied pork cutlets, then took two himself before passing the platter to Malyna.

"Why is Maitre Shaelyt staying here?" asked Lystara. "Is he hurt?"

"No, he's not," replied Alyna, "but Tiranya has stronger shields, and they have a child. That's another reason why I'm staying here. We need to keep some senior maitres here in case some of the rebels decide to attack Imagisle." She broke off a chunk of bread and handed the basket to Alastar.

"You're a stronger imager than Maitre Cyran, aren't you?" asked Lystara.

"I don't know that's ever been determined," replied Alyna.

"Your mother will be better at dealing with the factors, the High Holders, and Rex Lorien," declared Malyna.

Alastar managed not to choke on his lager. "That might be true, but it's not something that either of you should *ever* mention to anyone except the four of us. Is that clear?" His voice was chill as he spoke.

"Yes, sir," chorused both girls.

"But it is true, Uncle Alastar, and she is a stronger imager," Malyna added.

Alastar wasn't quite certain how to respond to that, but he couldn't not deal with it. "She is. Almost everyone knows it, but declaring how good an imager anyone is doesn't happen to be the wisest thing to say in public, at least most of the time." *Particularly if the imager is a woman.*

"That's only true if the imager is a woman," Malyna replied.

"It's true for all imagers. It's even more true for a strong woman imager."

"How can something be more true, Father?" asked Lystara. "Aren't things either true or not true?"

Alastar could see Alyna trying not to smile. "You're absolutely right, Lystara. What I should have said is that most men don't like to admit that a woman is better or especially that she is stronger in something in which men think men should be the strongest."

"Men are vain about being strong," murmured Malyna.

"Most men are," agreed Alastar, "just as most women are vain about the way they look." *And just as most women worry about losing their looks, most men worry about losing their strength . . . or their power, if they don't have great physical strength.* He wasn't about to say that aloud, outnumbered as he was at his own table . . . and not with the ramifications of his words that Alyna might think about.

He cut another bite of the cutlet and followed it with a mouthful of fried apples, and then dipped his bread in the apple drippings. He was going to miss Jienna's cooking.

"I'm glad you mentioned the vanity of men, dear," said Alyna dryly.

"I admit it. Men are vain. Most of their vanities differ from those of women, although I've known some men so vain about their clothes and appearance . . ." He shrugged, thinking that completing that thought was definitely unwise.

"So vain that no woman could compare?" asked Alyna, a glint in her eye.

"I said nothing of the sort." Alastar took refuge in another swallow of lager.

"I would hope not," she replied. "I do find it interesting that the birds where the males have the most gorgeous plumage are those who do the least in rearing their young and also that the most effective birds of prey are those where the males and females differ the least."

"By that reasoning Quaeryt was very wise in insisting that imager grays be essentially the same for men and women. I have no doubt that Vaelora made her thoughts known there."

"I doubt she had to."

Alastar laughed. "In turn, I have no doubt of that, coming as you do from her lineage."

"You're a wise man, dear." Alyna grinned.

So did Malyna.

"Is there dessert?" asked Alastar.

"Tonight? Of course. Jienna's apple cobbler."

Alastar was definitely going to miss Jienna's cooking.

Much later, after the girls had retired to their rooms, where they were hopefully sleeping, Alastar and Alyna sat in their sitting room, sipping the last of the lager in the beakers they had brought upstairs.

". . . still wonder what part, if any, Bettaur plays in all this," mused Alastar. "I'd have no doubts whatsoever if it weren't for Linzya. You've never been fond of him. Nor have I been, but . . . something . . ." He shook his head. "Am I getting that old, that I'm not seeing what's before me?"

"No. You see what's before you, and it doesn't fit. I have the same problem. I don't trust Bettaur. I never have. I likely never will. But Linzya has always been perceptive, and every detail suggests that, for whatever reason, he loves her, and that, because of her, he wants to prove we were wrong about him."

"It still doesn't make sense."

"Some things don't, dearest. Ever." She took the last sip from her beaker. "It's getting late."

"I know."

"I've said it before, but I have to say it again. Please be careful. You're . . ." She shook her head.

"I'm what? Getting older? Not as strong as I used to be?"

"Not yet . . . but you've even said that you don't recover as quickly anymore."

Alastar wasn't sure he'd ever said that, although he'd felt that way over the past few weeks. And Alyna's "not yet" was an indirect way of suggesting that he probably wasn't as strong as he had been ten years earlier. "Then it's a good thing that I've got a bunch of younger maitres who are stronger than they were ten years ago . . . and recover more quickly."

"It's a very good thing, and it's time they learned just what it costs to protect the Collegium. Actually, it's past time. I think your choice of who is accompanying you and the troopers was very wise."

"Even if I didn't include you?" he asked lightly.

"Your choices are wise. I can't argue with them, much as I'd like to. But . . ." Alyna paused letting the silence draw out to punctuate the words that followed. "If you do something foolhardy, that will mean I'll have to prop up whatever male succeeds you as Maitre. That will weaken the

Collegium so much it may not recover. That's even truer because of the decline of the imagers at Westisle."

"Which is no one's fault but mine."

"That can be remedied . . . if you survive the battle or battles to come." She stood, walked to his chair, and took his hand. "It is late, and you do have to get up early . . ."

Alastar understood what she wasn't saying. He stood, then took her other hand, and imaged out the oil lamps.

35

Alastar had to struggle out of bed on Vendrei morning, even though it was less than a glass earlier than he usually rose. But then, he and Alyna usually didn't stay up so late as they had the night before. *Or is it because you're getting older?*

After he and Alyna had a quick breakfast, and Jienna had filled the water bottles with the best lager he'd likely have for who knew how long, Alastar swung the saddlebags over his shoulder and looked to Alyna. "Time to go."

"I'll walk with you. You didn't think I'd let you out of my sight any sooner than necessary, did you?"

He smiled. "I'd hoped you wouldn't."

As the two walked through the gray light of early morning toward the stables, Alastar couldn't help thinking how differently the rebellion had developed from the time of madness that had marked the end of Rex Ryen's rule . . . and how many more High Holders were now involved.

Back then it was only about tariffs. He almost shook his head. The "simple" issue of tariffs had resulted in the death of the marshal of the army, the rex, and the head of the High Council, not to mention an attempted officer mutiny within the army, and the deaths of more than a regiment of troopers. Now . . . the struggle over golds, privilege, and power had combined into an armed High Holder rebellion.

"You're awfully quiet," observed Alyna.

"Just thinking about how small the troubles of when I became maitre were compared to what we face now. I certainly didn't see them that way then."

"The stakes are higher now. High Holders were secure in their position then. Now many are not, and all of them worry. They worry more because they see the Collegium as powerful and as a potential enemy."

"Then there are factors like Vaschet," mused Alastar.

"The factors and the High Holders share a similar belief. They both believe that power should be determined by who has the most golds, property, and other physical resources. Most of them resent any other source of power and would destroy it if they could."

"Or they believe that golds should be able to purchase it. But since the rex controls the army"—*or some of it*—"and the Collegium controls imaging, and the Collegium places the freedom and safety of imagers above golds, even though we both know it's not that simple . . ."

". . . only the Collegium has the power to keep them both from ruining Solidar in their single-minded pursuit of lands and golds," concluded Alyna. "Is that what you're suggesting?"

"Something along those lines. But that's not all. The Collegium has taken impoverished children who have very limited imaging abilities and given them the skills to do other things. So far I don't see most High Holders or factors doing that unless they see it bringing them more golds than such training costs." He snorted. "They always plead an inability to do that when times are hard, and then claim they can't do it when times are good because they have to save for when times are hard. That means that doing things for everyone's good can only be done by the rex and the Collegium."

"That means higher tariffs and dissatisfaction," pointed out Alyna. "That's not exactly the most cheerful thought to set out on."

"No . . . but it might be more useful in not letting me get too sympathetic toward anyone." Alastar's words were sardonically spoken.

"Stay sympathetic to me and the girls . . . and all the imagers who need your leadership . . . and remember what I said about Cyran." She paused. "I definitely mean that."

Still recalling the vehemence with which she had spoken, Alastar said, "I'll remember. There's no way I could forget."

"Good."

As they neared the stables, Alyna reached out and squeezed Alastar's hand. "Just take care of yourself."

"I'll do my best."

"No. Just do what I said."

"I will." He wasn't about to argue with the iron in her voice.

Just at the edge of the stable yard, Alastar halted, turned, and put his free arm around Alyna. Her arms went around him for a long moment before they separated, and he crossed the yard to where Kaylet had the gray saddled and ready for Alastar.

"Thank you."

"My pleasure, Maitre."

Alastar surveyed the yard, finally locating the two supply wagons, nodding as he noted the two spare mounts on short lines from the second wagon. After that, he fastened the saddlebags in place behind his saddle and glanced around the yard, looking for Cyran, before realizing that next to Alyna stood Shaelyt, holding the hand of his and Tiranya's son. The boy looked toward his mother, who had just fastened a kit bag behind her saddle and was leading her mount toward Alastar.

From the other side of the yard came Cyran, followed by Akoryt, and suddenly, or so it seemed, the stable yard was filled with imagers and their mounts. Alastar had already assigned the imagers to two groups, one headed by Akoryt, with the other two senior maitres being Arion and Khaelis, and the junior maitres being Dylert, Seliora, and Taurek. The second group was Cyran's, and the senior maitres were Taryn and Tiranya, with Belsior, Chervyt, and Julyan as the juniors.

"Imagers!" ordered Alastar, using imaging to boost his voice. "Form up on your group leader." Then he walked his mount over to meet Cyran. "Good morning."

"It's not bad for being early," replied Cyran.

"Not too bad. Now . . . when we join up with the army, I'll ride near the van with the first group of imagers, and you'll ride with the second group between the first and second battalion. Later, depending on what Wilkorn's scouts report, you and the second group may be needed with the rearguard. Once we take up whatever position Wilkorn determines is to our advantage, we'll evaluate that and decide where we can be most effective."

Cyran nodded. "It would be useful to know just where their cannon are."

"Very useful and most necessary, preferably well in advance. I've already stressed that to Wilkorn. Of course, everything could and probably will change." *More times than any of us would prefer.* "Any questions right now?"

"No, sir."

"Then I'll join Akoryt and the first group, and we'll lead the way." Alastar mounted the gray and rode across the yard to Akoryt. "Is everyone here with all their gear?"

"Yes, sir."

"Then we need to ride out, with shields in place."

"On the Maitre, shields in place," ordered Akoryt, turning in the saddle.

"Forward!" Alastar ordered, then glanced to the north side of the stable yard where Alyna still stood. Their eyes met for a long moment before Alastar glanced at Shaelyt, who had put his son on his shoulder so that the boy could see Tiranya as she rode out of the stable yard. Then Alastar returned his attention to the lane that led to the south bridge.

Three quints later Alastar was easing his mount alongside that of Marshal Wilkorn, who had halted the army column. Less than two fifths of a mille to Alastar's left were the west river barge piers, which would have cast shadows in the low morning light except that the waters of the River Aluse were so high that they left no space for shadows. He could also smell the mixed odors of spilled and ruined cargoes, a miasma redolent of rotting leaves, putrefying fish, garlic, spoiled cheese, and other less identifiable scents.

"Morning, Maitre." Wilkorn wore a light green army riding jacket . . . or half wore it, since his left arm remained in a splint.

"The same to you, Marshal."

"You wonder why I'm here, Maitre? So do I. I'm not a land marshal, and I don't claim to know tactics. That's why Commander Maurek is here. I retain the right to override him . . . or to order him to listen to you. I doubt that will be necessary." Wilkorn chuckled. "Truth is that I'm here because there's nothing I can do at headquarters. Besides, this way Maurek doesn't have to send messengers to me."

"And you don't have to wait and worry, wondering if you should have been there."

"There's one other reason." Wilkorn offered a crooked smile.

"You don't have to worry about informing Lorien until it's over."

"We can talk about that on the way. We'll have time. We have two overlarge battalions, one of mounted infantry commanded by Major Luerryn, and one of foot commanded by Major Rykards. Where do you think your imagers should be positioned?"

"For purposes of both attack and defense, we have two groups. On the march to Caluse, I'd suggest one group in the van, the other halfway back, between your battalions. I'll be with the first group. Once we near Caluse, obviously, we'll need to adapt to the terrain and situation." *And where the cannon are.*

The marshal nodded. "That's fine for now. Get your imagers in place. We'll move up to give the first group space in front of first company. That way we can talk and your imagers will be close to the front—except for the scouts and one squad. Supply wagons go before the company handling rearguard."

"I'll get them in position." Alastar turned the gray and rode back to Cyran, relaying the marshal's orders, then watched as the second group and supply wagons made their way north along the side of the road to take their positions. When he was satisfied, he turned to Akoryt. "You and first group will be taking station directly behind the command officers, and ahead of first company. In other words right behind me. That's why they're opening that gap."

"That's good."

Alastar nodded. "On me." He urged the gray forward toward where Wilkorn and the commander who had to be Maurek waited.

Once the imagers were in position, with Alastar on Wilkorn's left, the marshal nodded to Maurek, who rode on his right.

"Column! Forward!"

Wilkorn did not speak until they had ridden almost half a mille, then cleared his throat. "I noticed you've got two women imagers in your force." The marshal's bushy eyebrows rose.

"They're good. Better than some of the men."

"Still . . ."

"We have to use as many of our best as we can," replied Alastar. "If the rebel High Holders win, in a generation it's more than likely that the Collegium will be almost powerless, and in three, it may not even exist. The women know that."

"Have they been fired upon?"

"The two here have been, as have all those who are maitres. The two we brought have been under fire or were among the maitres who shielded Captain Weidyn and his men when they entered Laevoryn's estate."

"Every imager fights?"

"No. We train them all to fight, in case Imagisle is attacked, but off the isle, we only send those who can. Some of those are women."

"How effective is the training for those who aren't the best?"

"The night when the brown-shirts sent a squad to attack Imagisle, they ran into two student seconds. One temporarily blinded one attacker, and a young female imager killed him. After that, senior imagers killed the rest of the attackers."

"All of them?" asked Maurek.

"So far as we know," replied Alastar.

"You don't give much quarter, I see," said the commander.

"Not when they're attacking children and students. Remember, almost all the imagers in Solidar are in one of two places. We can't afford much generosity when we're attacked."

"That's something that more than a few High Holders and a rex have learned, rather fatally," added Wilkorn.

"That's also why we're here," said Alastar. While Wilkorn knew that, Alastar had some doubts as to whether Maurek did. "The rebel High Holders wish to destroy the Collegium and all the imagers."

"Might I ask why?"

"Because we've supported the rex and opposed their efforts to regain their ancient powers, which would allow them, among other things, to execute capital punishment without recourse to a justice and make it impossible for a factor or tradesman to use the justicing system to seek redress against them."

"They really are seeking that?" Maurek's tone was close to incredulous.

"A number filed petitions with Rex Lorien seeking restoration of the powers removed by the first Rex Regis with the Codex Legis. Lorien denied all of them."

"You see," said Wilkorn jovially, "Lorien can do the right thing when it's important."

"Will wonders never cease?" replied the commander, almost under his breath.

Alastar looked past Wilkorn and Maurek and ahead, where he saw a whole section of flooded fields to the right of the road. Although the fields were higher than the river, they weren't that much higher, and they were lower than stone-paved road, which acted like a dam, catching all the runoff. The tops of the stunted maize were yellow and extended barely half a yard above the murky water.

"We've been asking all the questions," said Wilkorn. "Is there anything you'd like to know?"

"I do have one question," replied Alastar. "How will the rebel commanders and subcommanders benefit from their mutiny against you and the rex? What about their men? That may seem simplistic, but I can see how the High Holders would feel they would benefit. I can even see how Aestyn, Hehnsyn, and Marryt might benefit. But what about the other officers and rankers? What were they told . . . or promised?"

"The usual, I'm sure," replied Wilkorn, "promotions, bonuses, and plunder, all larded with the idea that they'd be part of returning Solidar to its former glory. Remember, Marryt and Hehnsyn have been transferring officers, senior squad leaders, and squad leaders for almost a year. That was to obtain forces inclined to follow them."

"Does that mean your forces are more inclined to follow you and Commander Maurek?"

"More likely Maurek," replied Wilkorn with a smile.

"You give me too much credit," said the commander with a laugh.

"Too little, I fear."

Just from seeing the interplay between Maurek and Wilkorn, Alastar felt strangely relieved, perhaps because he sensed they worked well together. He just hoped that proved true in battle as well.

36

Just after noon, still riding beside Wilkorn, Alastar spotted three riders moving toward them from the south. All wore the pale green uniforms of Solidar. *But then, so would the rebel forces.* But it was highly unlikely that three rebel troopers would ride up to a column of Solidaran regulars, and far more likely the troopers were scouts or couriers.

Less than half a quint later, Wilkorn halted the column as the couriers rode up. One of the troopers handed a dispatch to Wilkorn, then moved to the west side of the river road, waiting.

The marshal read the dispatch, then looked to Alastar. "The rebels are still well south of Reyks. They were slowed because one of the old bridges washed out. The whole bridge just tipped on its side, like it was one solid piece." Wilkorn shook his head. "Never heard of anything like that. They had to march five milles west to ford the river—the Sommeil."

"What about the number of troopers?" asked Maurek.

"Three regiments, or close to that." The marshal handed the dispatch to the commander, waiting for Maurek to read it.

"Thirty cannon," added Maurek. "Aestyn's regiment had twenty. They must have gotten some from Solis, likely earlier this year."

"I agreed to it last Fevier," said Wilkorn dryly. "So Aestyn could position them more effectively."

Maurek handed the dispatch back to Wilkorn.

"Since we're making good time," said the marshal, "and since they're not, we'll push on to where we'll meet them. We'll probably not make it until sixth glass, but we won't have to make and break camp. Overall, that will give us more time to prepare."

Alastar shifted his weight in the saddle. He had the feeling that a number of imagers would need that time to get over being saddle-sore. He'd been riding enough that he'd only be slightly sore. *You hope.*

Wilkorn nodded to Maurek.

"Column! Forward!"

By the third glass of the afternoon, Alastar was still riding in the same position beside Wilkorn as he had on and off for most of the day. Despite making liberal use of the lager in his water bottles, he was still hot. He blotted his forehead with his sleeve and then adjusted his visor cap.

Something glinting in the distance to the southwest caught his eye. After a time, the shimmer faded, and he realized that the shimmer or glint must have come from the large lake that was still somewhat indistinct because of the haze that seemed to be everywhere. He'd heard the name and seen it on the maps, but it took him a moment to recall it. "Is that Lake Shaelyt?"

"That it is," replied Maurek. "Not good for much. Shallow and swampy. Yellow catfish are about the only decent fish you can catch there. Before long we ought to be able to see the hamlet on the north. It's hard to pick out the cots, with all the trees. I've heard that the hamlet was once bigger. That was when the lake was once larger and deeper. Maybe all this rain will help."

"Only the rushes and reeds," said Wilkorn dryly.

Alastar kept looking but almost two quints passed before he could make out the cots to the northwest of the lake, farther from the water than he would have thought. "What's the hamlet called?"

Wilkorn and Maurek exchanged glances.

Finally, Maurek replied. "I haven't the faintest idea."

Just ahead, Alastar saw a narrow dirt lane angling off the main road to the south and then more southwest toward the hamlet. Although he could not make out where it led much beyond the hamlet, he thought it might curve into the heavy forest that rose beyond the swamp on the west side of the lake and seemed to border the west shore of the lake as far as he could see.

Over the next glass and a half, the river road ran along the top of a low ridge that followed the course of the River Aluse and roughly parallel the eastern edge of Lake Shaelyt, although the lake was almost two milles from the road. When the road reached a point even with the southern shore of the lake, it began to slope gradually downhill, even as the ridge narrowed and dropped off more steeply to the west.

After they had ridden another mille, the road began a gentle rise, and Alastar saw ahead another lake, this one far narrower than Lake Shaelyt, perhaps half a mille across at the widest point, and not nearly so long, possibly only two milles or so. He glanced to the west, shielding his eyes with his hand, because the sun was so low in the sky. The fields north and east of the lake were waterlogged and muddy, and Alastar had the feeling that any crops planted there had either been washed out or drowned well before they could have been harvested. Before long the grade of the road lessened even more so that the rise was barely percep-tible.

At the top of the gentle rise, Wilkorn halted the column.

"On the northern slope—the one we just rode up—that's where we'll wait for them," Wilkorn announced. "It's not perfect, but it's the best location for us anywhere along the river between L'Excelsis and Nordeau."

Alastar surveyed the position. With the river less than a hundred yards to the east of the road, there was no danger of being surprised from that quarter. The southern end narrow lake lay just about a mille away and was slightly downhill from the flat area just to the west of the river road. The eastern side of the lake was almost all a reedy marsh with no clean shoreline. That, too, would restrict the rebels' maneuverability, although not as much as Alastar would have preferred. As with Lake Shaelyt, the far side of the lake was heavily forested.

By making camp on the northern slope, also, the marshal's force wouldn't be nearly so visible to scouts, especially if Maurek ran patrols a few milles farther south.

The ground to the southwest of the road held fields and small hold-ings, with cots and outbuildings scattered here and there. Ahead, per-haps two quints of a mille, Alastar could make out a side road that ended at the river road. From the river road it headed due west, gradually slop-ing down toward the fields and scattered cots. A thousand yards or so west, it split, or joined another narrower road running north parallel to the river road, leading northwest to the long narrow lake that they had ridden past several quints earlier.

"The rebels are at least two days away?" Alastar's words were barely a question.

"At least. More likely three."

"I assume we don't want to move into Caluse." While Alastar had good reasons why they shouldn't do so, he had not discussed the matter with Wilkorn, simply because he'd had more than a few other thoughts on his mind until they had left the Collegium.

"No," replied Maurek. "It's a river town, and there are too many temptations. It's also got narrow streets, and that would work against us. All the old tacticians thought that was ideal, and it is—if you're fighting with blades and axes. With rifles, it's another story, unless you take over every house. Then they bring in cannon, and you're buried in debris, and you've let them kill the people and destroy everything that brings in tariffs."

"It also gives them another reason to hate the rex," added Wilkorn. "We also don't want a battle there because all the troopers may be wearing green."

"The local people won't pay any attention to the scarlet and black armbands the rebel troopers are wearing," added Maurek.

"You didn't mention those before," Alastar said calmly, although he didn't feel as calm as his words. "Does Lorien know?"

"Not yet. Our daily dispatch will inform him. That was in the scouting report we got earlier today."

"So they're fighting for the rex who will restore tradition and strength to Solidar?" asked Alastar sardonically.

"I'm sure it's something like that," agreed Wilkorn. "The one who will make everything wonderful."

"For the High Holders, anyway," replied Alastar.

"When things aren't going well, many will follow anyone who promises he can make things better, especially without more hardship, and who seems to have the arms, the golds, and the troopers."

"That's why it just might be a good idea to get to work setting up," declared Maurek.

Alastar and Wilkorn exchanged amused smiles.

On Samedi morning, Alastar woke up slightly sore and stiff, not unexpectedly, considering that he'd been sleeping on the ground. The leaves and pine needles under his ground cloth hadn't helped all that much, although the night had been warm enough that the only use for his blanket had been to keep the flies and mosquitoes from attacking too much of his anatomy. He woke thirsty, and while the replacement dark lager he'd imaged into his water bottles slaked his thirst, it was extremely bitter, unsurprisingly, since that wasn't a kind of imaging he'd done much of in years, and he'd never been terribly good at it back then. But it was definitely safer than river water.

Once he had washed up and shaved, he walked around trying to remove some of the stiffness from his back and legs, and then made his way to the imagers' supply wagon where the teamsters had prepared a breakfast of sorts—a hot porridge, not-quite stale bread baked the previous morning, a handful of dried fruit, and overstrong hot tea. As Alastar tendered his mess kit to the teamster doing the serving, he saw that Seliora and Tiranya had already been served and stood at the side of the wagon, eating and talking. He could catch only a few words.

". . . years since I ate anything this bad . . ."

". . . better than the early slop I got . . ."

Alastar thought they both were smiling, but the smiles vanished as he walked toward them, mess kit in one hand, his tin mug in the other. "Good morning."

"Good morning, Maitre," they both replied.

"Is there any news about the rebels?" asked Tiranya.

"I haven't heard anything since yesterday. How are you two feeling?"

"Sore," admitted Seliora.

Tiranya nodded in agreement.

The three of them had finished eating and had rinsed their mess kits with water from a bucket provided by the teamsters, and Alastar was still sipping his way through the tea when Cyran and Akoryt appeared. Both had apparently already eaten.

"Do we just wait here?" asked Akoryt.

"In general, yes. We'll hold this position."

"Just stand and wait, or walk and wait?"

"Among other things, we could think about new and deadly ways to kill or wound the rebel forces—and try them out well away from the rest of the army . . . and wait," replied Alastar. "War is much like imaging. A great deal of preparation, a flurry of action, and more waiting, with time, hopefully, to recover and prepare for the next part of the fight."

"Will they even attack? Couldn't they just withdraw and march up the east side of the river?" asked Cyran.

"Oh, they could, but there's no ford and no bridge between Caluse and L'Excelsis, and the road is better on this side. With all the rain over the past season, no army is going anywhere fast except on a paved road. If they took the east side of the river we could withdraw back to the Sud Bridge, cross and be in position at least two days before they arrived, and they'd still have to attack."

"What about waiting us out?"

Alastar smiled wryly. "Strangely enough, time is on our side. Armies have to be fed and paid. Even the wealthiest High Holder could not support three regiments for months, and some of the rebels, if not most, are short on golds. Oh . . . they have vast lands, but with two years of poor harvests, even the wealthiest are limited. Just to pay and feed three regiments costs several thousand golds a week, and they're likely already short on supplies since Ferravyl was provisioned for one regiment, not three. The two battalions that left L'Excelsis likely used most of their provisions in joining up with Commander Aestyn's regiment. Sea Marshal Tynan is loyal, and he holds Solis. We're blocking them from reaching L'Excelsis, of course. With all the rain and flooding along the river, what they can get from the locals is also limited.

"They have to triumph and remove the Army High Command and Rex Lorien quickly, within a month, two at the outside. The longer they wait, the fewer resources they have, and the more Wilkorn can bring to bear. It's a desperate gamble, a high-stakes wager, and if they can pull it off, it will change Solidar forever, and for the worse for everyone—except the High Holders."

"All because they want powers they never had, and no High Holder has had in hundreds of years?" Akoryt sounded exasperated.

"That's not totally true. At least on their own lands and in more than a few instances, a great number of High Holders haven't changed all that much, but they see that they'll have to, and they don't want to. They see their entire way of life as being destroyed . . . and they're right." Alastar snorted. "It's past time that they changed. Well past time."

"Right now . . . in the meantime," began Tiranya, "isn't there something more we can do?"

"As a matter of fact, there is. I'll need to talk to the marshal and Commander Maurek first, but I do have some ideas." Alastar bolted down the last of his tea, trying not to wince, then turned to Akoryt. "If you get group one ready to ride . . ." He smiled. "As I recall, you were the one who didn't want to stand and wait."

"Yes, sir." Akoryt grinned sheepishly.

Alastar turned and walked to the bucket, used it to rinse the tin cup, then carried his mess kit and cup back to where his gear was and put them in the saddlebags. He set out to find Wilkorn.

That wasn't terribly difficult, since the marshal turned out to be less than a hundred yards away, seated on a camp stool under an awning, looking at maps set out on a collapsible table. Maurek stood by his shoulder. Both looked up and stopped talking as Alastar approached.

"Good morning, Maitre," offered Wilkorn. "You look like a maitre on a mission."

Alastar stopped about a yard from the table. "I've been thinking about ways the imagers might be able to make a difference even before the rebels arrive. . . ." He smiled politely.

"What do you have in mind?" asked Wilkorn.

"What I have in mind will depend on the terrain. I'm certain that your scouts are excellent, but they're not imagers. There are likely places we might be able to use imaging to reduce the number of rebel troopers well before they reach our position here. There might be other possibilities as well."

"I could assign a squad . . ." ventured Maurek.

Alastar shook his head. "We can deal with any small forces they may send, if they're even close enough to do that right now. What we can't deal with is massed force and concentrated cannon fire. The more we can reduce their numbers . . ."

"Would you mind if a couple of my scouts went with you?" asked Maurek.

"That would be good." Alastar should have thought of that himself. "That way they could let me know if something isn't feasible and offer their experience."

"You're not taking all the imagers?" asked Wilkorn.

"Just one group. The second group, under the command of Maitre Cyran, will remain with the command company."

"When will you leave?" asked Wilkorn

"As soon as we can."

"I'll let the sentries and patrols know, and I'll send the scouts to where your mounts are tied," said Maurek.

"Thank you." Alastar inclined his head, then turned and strode back to where Akoryt and the first group were saddling up. He hoped Cyran was nearby. The Maitre D'Esprit was. Alastar, after saddling his gray, gathered the first group of imagers and Cyran together.

"We need to do some scouting ourselves," Alastar said.

Cyran raised his eyebrows, but both Akoryt and Taurek nodded.

"We're outnumbered. I'd like to find ways to reduce the number of attackers before they get here. We can't do that effectively unless we can find a number of places from which we can attack or where we can conceal some of our troopers and allow them to open fire on the rebel troopers. We'll also have two of Commander Maurek's scouts with us. They should prove useful in keeping me from selecting less than optimal locations for troopers." Alastar looked to Akoryt. "Have your group mount up. I'll be with you in a moment." Then he turned to Cyran. "While we're gone, have your group practice. See how far they can image pepper in a thick mist. You might also try smaller but still lethal darts at a distance."

Cyran nodded. "We can do that."

Alastar had barely mounted the gray and started the group forward, up toward the top of the rise when he saw two troopers riding toward them. He motioned for the two to join him.

The first trooper, narrow-faced and dark-haired, reined in a yard away from Alastar, matching pace with the gray. "Maitre, senior scout Landesh." He gestured to the round-faced younger trooper. "This is scout Quellyn. Commander Maurek said we were to accompany you."

"We both thought your experience would be useful. We're going to do a different kind of scouting. We'll be looking for places where our imaging can attack the rebel column where they can't respond effectively. We'll also be searching for places where we could conceal a company of troopers in almost plain sight and from where the troopers would have a field of fire that could remove a great number of rebel troopers in a very short time. We know what we can do. We don't necessarily know if what we think would be ideal for troopers would work."

"Yes, sir."

"Now . . . there's a road, a lane really, on the south side of this rise? It heads west. Can you tell me more about it?"

"Well, sir, it goes west a fair distance, could be three to four milles."

"Are there any lanes or the like heading south off it?"

"Just one. Could be a mille and a quint or so. There's a dirt track that heads south. It peters out at a small creek. There are the ruins of a bridge there. On the other side you can see where the track goes on."

"Good. We'll start there." Alastar saw the puzzled expression cross Landesh's face. "Don't worry. You'll see. Now . . . if you'd ride with me, Landesh, and tell me everything you've seen about the terrain between our position and Caluse, I'd be most appreciative."

"Yes, sir. Hard to know where to start."

"How far does the road descend from our position before it levels out . . . or start to rise?"

"Steepest part of the road is the half mille just south of us. After that, it sort of flattens out . . ."

Alastar listened intently, asking questions as necessary, for the quint or so that it took them to reach where the narrow dirt lane ended. A handful of rotted posts protruding from the reedy grasses on each side of the creek were all that remained of what had once been a bridge. The distance from bank to bank was roughly fifteen yards, but most of that was composed of the marshy grasses surrounding the creek and the creek banks themselves. The actual watercourse was no more than three or four yards wide.

"You can see, sir. We tried to go through it, but the bottom's a soft sandy mud. Quellyn's mount near-on got stuck."

"I can see how that could happen." Alastar turned in the saddle. "Seliora, would you image a stone pier on this side of the creek. Put its base a yard from the water and make it deep. The top should be wide enough for a wagon or two horses."

"Yes, sir." Seliora eased the dapple forward and reined up. Lines appeared in her forehead, then vanished.

A slab of stone appeared a good three yards wide. Immediately, the top was covered in white. Almost as suddenly mist swirled up from the stone, and Alastar felt a cool breeze sweep across him. He rode forward and to the side of the narrow lane. The pier looked solid. "Good."

"Would you like me to do the other side?" asked Seliora.

"No. It's better if you rest. There may be more to do later. Taurek, please match her pier with one on the other side."

As Seliora moved her mount back, the broad-shouldered and stocky junior maitre moved his forward. In moments, an identical stone pier stood on the far side.

"Also good," declared Alastar. "Now, Khaelis, a stone arch and road-bed to connect them."

As the arch and span appeared, it vanished in white mist, and thin sheets of ice appeared on the slow-moving water before breaking up. More mist rose from the water.

"Arion, roadbed and fill to connect to the pier on this side."

"Yes, sir."

Akoryt eased forward. "I can do that on the other side."

"If you would."

Alastar studied the nearly completed structure, then spoke again. "Dylert, railings and posts on each side, a yard and a half high."

"Yes, sir."

Alastar had been intermittently watching the two scouts as the imagers created the small bridge. Both appeared to be stunned. "We should wait until the ice melts."

"It's too warm for ice," replied Landesh, "but it's there."

Quellyn nodded in agreement.

When the last of the mist and ice cleared away, only a fraction of a quint later, Alastar turned the gelding toward the bridge. "Now . . . let's see where this lane leads." He couldn't help but notice that the two scouts held their mounts back slightly, as if to see if the causeway to the bridge and the center span both held. They did.

Possibly a quint of a mille later, Landesh cleared his throat. "Maitre, sir . . . ah . . . are there not many bridges that could use repair?"

"There are, and we've repaired and built some. Imagers built the entire Boulevard D'Rex Regis some thirteen years ago. We've repaired sewers in L'Excelsis and built buildings. But there are only so many imagers who can do what these six did." He laughed gently. "And how many roads and bridges are there in Solidar?"

The scout frowned for a moment, then nodded. "Never thought of it that way."

Quellyn, on the other hand, still looked puzzled.

Alastar turned his full attention to the lands on each side of the dirt lane, whose sides were overgrown in places by creeping clingweed, a certain sign that few horses had passed and few cattle or sheep had been grazed nearby. The field to his right looked to be a pasture of some sort, but there was no sign that anything had been grazing there, at least not recently, while the field to his left held maize that was higher than the gelding's withers, but the plants that grew on the lower ground nearer the river had yellowed leaves at their base, while those nearer the lane were much taller and entirely green. *Too much water nearer the river?* He shook his head. He'd been raised to learn about the sea, not about crops.

The maize and pasture gave way to bushes, clearly planted to be harvested, although Alastar saw no signs of berries. They might have been blueberries, since they ripened early, but he wouldn't have known a blueberry plant from a redberry or a greenberry. Beyond the bushes, there was another field, filled with yellowing or tan plants that looked to have been flooded out, but the amount cultivated was only halfway to the embankment that held the river road, and the rain had turned the last hundred yards between the dead plants, most standing in several digits of water, into what looked to be a shallow pond.

Alastar signaled a halt and reined up. He turned to Landesh. "The river road seems fairly exposed from here."

"A company formed up here would be just as exposed to their fire, and they'd see us long before they marched into range."

"What if they couldn't see you?"

"But they—" The senior scout broke off his words. "You could hide a company?"

"If they stayed in a tight formation."

"The rebels couldn't see muzzle flashes?"

"No."

Landesh pursed his lips. "They'd still know we were here somewhere."

"Would they charge through that water? If they did, wouldn't it slow them down?"

A slow smile crossed the scout's lips. "A hundred yards of knee-deep water and mud. That'd slow anyone down. They might send lancers, but they'd want to ride around the water."

"If they went north, they'd have trouble with all those berry bushes. And if the marshal sent mounted infantry to man the ambush, they could mount up and withdraw before the rebels ever got too close," suggested Alastar. "Think about it." He eased the gelding forward.

For the next half mille, a large and overgrown woodlot covered the ground on each side of the narrow lane, which now rose somewhat and showed greater signs of use, unsurprisingly to Alastar, given the scattered cots to the west. But beyond the woodlot, he saw another flooded area beside the river road. Not only that, but because the lane was higher, any troopers posted on the lane would actually be firing down on the road, and any attack on the troopers would have to be through deeper water followed by an uphill slog.

Alastar looked to Landesh.

"Be even better here, sir."

"What if we did both?"

"They'd likely act quicker the second time. Might be better to have our men fire from the saddle."

Alastar could see that, but he still wanted to see where the lane led.

The imagers kept riding for another mille. While the river and the river road angled slightly more to the southeast, the lane kept heading south. Then, from the top of the next rise in the lane, Alastar could see a hamlet or small town. He judged it to be another two milles away. At the bottom of the rise, the lane widened into more of a road, with cots on plots of land spaced much more closely together. He looked eastward. Even from the rise, he could barely make out the river road. *But you can . . . barely.* "It looks like the lane or road goes to that hamlet before turning back east and meeting with the river road."

"Yes, sir. We came down the river road and took it to the hamlet. The locals told us this lane just ended, and only a few small holders lived on it."

"The rebels would get the same answer, but they might not believe it."

"Be easy enough to put a scout right here. Quellyn could let us know when the rebels reached that bend, and if some were headed to the hamlet."

"That's a very good idea." Alastar smiled. "I think we can head back now."

38

Alastar had hoped to meet with Wilkorn and Maurek when he and the imagers returned so that the three of them could talk over what he had discovered on his scouting mission and work out what he had in mind, but both Wilkorn and Maurek were out doing their own scouting. Then the two senior officers held a meeting with the battalion commanders. In the end, Alastar wasn't able to gain a moment with Wilkorn until after the imagers and troopers had been fed. Even then Alastar had to hurry to catch up with the marshal, who was walking up the road and had almost reached its crest. Maurek was nowhere to be seen.

"Thought I'd see how the road looked in low light," offered Wilkorn.

"You don't think they'll attack at dawn or dusk?"

"You can't ever tell." Wilkorn stopped at the edge of the road's crest, looking southward across the fifty yards stretch immediately before him, a section with an incline almost imperceptible, one so gradual that the paving stones looked almost level.

Alastar waited.

"Understand you've been looking for me," Wilkorn finally said. "How did your scouting mission go?"

"Fairly well. I've located several places where we could conceal a company, and they could open fire on the rebels, but where the rebels wouldn't be able to get to our company before we could withdraw."

"I'd like to hear more." Wilkorn's tone was even, neither encouraging nor discouraging.

"You know that road partway down from the crest of the road, the one that heads almost due west . . ." Alastar went on to describe the terrain and what he and the scouts had worked out as a rough plan of attack.

When Alastar finished, Wilkorn frowned slightly, then said, "I like the idea, and we could spare a company, but getting a full company moving and then set up again in a space of less than three milles might be asking too much, especially on that narrow a lane. There's also the problem of mounts. They take up space. If you have the men mounted, so that they can move—"

"I see your point," Alastar replied. "We couldn't conceal mounts and men unless the horses were farther away, and then all the men couldn't get to their mounts, and if they're mounted there wouldn't be enough space for a full company."

"My thought would be to place two squads in the first position and have the other two squads wait near the second position . . . I'll talk it over with Maurek, see what he thinks. We can work something out." Wilkorn glanced away.

"There's also something else," Alastar added. "It's not as pleasant."

"What's the problem?"

"It's not a problem. It's an opportunity. You remember the poisoned bullets that the brown-shirts used to kill our imagers?"

"I do."

"We've managed to duplicate a thousand cartridges just like them. We thought they might be useful for whatever company you wanted to employ them. I'd think they'd likely be more useful at closer range after initial contact, but how they're used is up to you. There is one restriction. I've heard that sometimes troopers chew bullets to make them more deadly. These shouldn't be chewed. They can be handled, but not chewed."

The marshal winced, and a slightly appalled expression crossed his face. "That doesn't feel right . . ."

"No, it's not. It's nasty; the Nameless would call it evil; and those poor misguided rankers don't deserve it—but our rankers, the factors, and the people of Solidar certainly don't deserve what those Namer-cursed idiots commanding those poor rankers will get if we lose."

"I can't argue that. I don't like it, but I can't argue it."

"Think of it this way: If Aestyn had better bullets, would he hesitate to use them? Or Hehnsyn? Or Marryt?"

"I can't argue that, either." Wilkorn shook his head. "Maurek and I will have to talk it over, but I'm inclined to have the company assigned to you and your imagers be the one with those bullets. Do you have any objections to that?"

"No. That makes sense." *For a great number of reasons.* First of which was that while the bleufleur killed quickly, its effect wasn't instantaneous.

Wilkorn smiled sadly. "I would have to end up commanding in a war where both sides are fighting for what they believe is their very survival."

"The High Holders believe that, and they're wrong. Most of them will survive as High Holders for generations, if not longer. They just won't have the power they once did. If the Collegium fails, in three generations, imagers will be being killed or be in hiding again, and Solidar will suffer the loss of all we provide, which costs almost nothing."

"You really think that?"

"No. I know it. Name me another land on Terahnar where imagers are not slaves or in hiding."

Wilkorn frowned, then shook his head once more. "After all these years, I should know better than to argue with you."

Alastar managed a laugh. "You weren't arguing, only questioning, and it was a fair question."

"It was a question I shouldn't have asked. I already knew the answer. Must be getting old."

"You're not that old," protested Alastar.

"My muscles ache when I ride all day. My bones ache, even when they're not broken." The marshal glanced down at his splinted arm. "I worry when I know there's nothing to worry about, and I let a rebellion happen under my own eyes and didn't see it. That's another reason why I have to be here."

"Who could have imagined—"

"You did." Wilkorn shrugged. "I didn't. If anything happens to me, make sure that Maurek is the next vice marshal. He'll be a good successor to Vaelln."

"You'll likely be in a better position than I will to assure that."

"That could be, and then it might not be." The marshal smiled. "I need to find Maurek and talk some matters over with him."

After leaving Wilkorn, Alastar walked slowly back toward where the rest of the imagers were settled in. Wilkorn wasn't that much older than Alastar, perhaps five years . . . maybe slightly more than that. *And he thinks he's getting old?*

39

Alastar slept even less well on Samedi night, even though he was more tired, most likely because he kept worrying about what lay before him . . . and the imagers. While he could still image as strongly as ever—at any one time—he had the feeling that he didn't quite have the resilience and stamina he'd once had. That had been reinforced by the awareness that it took him longer to recover from heavy imaging. He also worried about what other stratagems Ryel and Ryentar had in mind, or possibly had already put in play. Then there was the matter of Bettaur, who had clearly been doing his best to increase his strength as an imager—and who had likely thrown in with the rebels. And behind it all was the feeling that the High Holders wouldn't have rebelled if they hadn't believed that they had a decent chance of prevailing.

After Alastar woke and ate, he went over the strategy that he and Wilkorn had developed with both Akoryt and Cyran, although he made it clear that only one imager group at a time would be away from the main body. Even as he did so, he half wondered if Commander Maurek might make additional suggestions . . . or find some reason that it wasn't feasible—which was certainly possible.

Once he was sure that both Akoryt and Cyran understood what he had in mind, he spent much of the morning working with both groups on imaging iron darts—refining the size and shape so that each imager was more effective . . . and so that each would use less strength when they needed to image those darts against the rebels. That was as much because he couldn't think of anything else that would improve the imagers' chances of affecting the battle or battles to come. He also worked on getting them to alternate imaging so that three of them could maintain a steady stream of darts. Then he had them work on thick fogs of red pepper mist.

In early afternoon, when the imagers, including himself, were tired, but not totally exhausted, he went looking for Maurek since he hadn't heard from either the commander or the marshal. This time, he found Maurek leaving the mess area.

Maurek spoke first. "Good afternoon, Maitre. I saw you were working your imagers this morning." He paused. "Some of what you were
working on seemed . . . ah . . . fundamental."

"It was. Imagers are highly trained to work as individuals. We seldom work as groups. That's required . . . infrequently, while other skills
are required continually."

"Hadn't thought about that."

"Marshal Wilkorn and I talked last night . . ."

"He told me about your suggestions, and his modifications. The idea
sounds like it should work. I haven't decided which company to use."
Maurek smiled. "I'm thinking of Captain Weidyn's company. He's worked
with you before, and he reported on those events favorably."

"We'd be more than happy to work again with the captain and his
company," replied Alastar.

"I'll inform the captain that he'll be reporting to you until further
notice. We would appreciate your informing either me or the marshal
of any evolutions you plan before beginning them. That's so that we
have an idea of where you'll be and what you have in mind . . . since I
understand that where imagers are involved, one may not see all that is
happening."

"I'll report any independent action we take."

"I appreciate that, Maitre."

"Do we have any idea where the rebel forces might be? The marshal
said he didn't expect them until around midday tomorrow."

"We still don't have any reports." Maurek frowned. "We sent scouts
south of Caluse yesterday. They should have returned by midday. They
haven't."

"You think they were ambushed?"

"There were four of them—they work in two-man teams. There
aren't any clouds in that direction. The water level in the river is down
a little, not up. It's possible that they'll be back shortly, and it may be
that the rebels are moving more deliberately than we thought. They do
have almost a regiment of High Holders' forces, and they're not used to
army evolutions."

"You're still concerned," offered Alastar.

"I am. If they're not back by fifth glass, I'll be worrying that they ran
into a larger advance force." The commander shook his head. "They were
experienced men. If they ran into trouble, at least one of them should
have been able to escape. If one didn't, that could be a real worry."

"Do you have other scouts headed that way?" asked Alastar.

"I sent out a full squad early this morning. They're scouting both the river road and the side roads and looking into ways that Aestyn might send troopers to try to flank us."

"Like the lane we looked into?"

"And anything else. After dealing with the pirates along the Southern Gulf, he's had more experience than any of us with ambushes and unusual maneuvers or tactics. I did insist that some of the scouts lay well back and report if anything happened to their comrades." His mouth curled into a wry smile. "Complete information is best, but I made the point that incomplete information was far better than no information at all."

"Especially since we have no information at all at the moment."

"That's another worry."

"You do have more than a few," agreed Alastar.

"You can expect Captain Weidyn before too long." Maurek glanced to the south.

Alastar took the hint. "Thank you. We appreciate your assigning a veteran captain. I'll let my imagers know."

After Maurek headed south along the road, past the various companies, Alastar headed back to find Cyran and Akoryt. Unsurprisingly, they were standing in the shade of an ancient oak that dominated a wooded patch some twenty yards from where the imagers mounts were tethered. Given the bright and hot harvest afternoon sunlight, he couldn't say that he blamed them.

"I met with Commander Maurek a little while ago. We'll be working with Captain Weidyn again. I imagine it won't be too long before he arrives. He's a very solid officer. We couldn't do better."

Cyran and Akoryt both nodded.

Alastar wasn't in the least surprised when Captain Weidyn appeared striding along the edge of the stone-paved river road less than half a quint later.

Weidyn stopped a yard or so from Alastar, inclined his head. "Maitres, Fifth Company reporting."

"It's good to see you again, Captain," replied Alastar. "We have a plan, but it will take both imagers and your men to implement it."

"Commander Maurek said you had an idea for reducing the number of rebels before we met in a full battle."

"We do. We replaced a ruined bridge in order to gain access to a lane that parallels the river road . . ." Alastar went on to explain.

When he finished outlining both the terrain and the proposed plan of attack, Weidyn nodded, then said, "Begging your pardon, sir, but while I trust your judgment on this, I'd feel that we could do this better if one of my senior squad leaders and I rode out and looked over that lane."

Alastar refrained from smiling at the way Weidyn had phrased his concerns without ever seeming to impugn his own assessment. "That's an excellent idea. I might suggest that one of the imagers accompany you and that you do that immediately. If you feel that another tactic might be superior, we'll need to make changes, the sooner the better. If not, then I'd prefer any tracks on the road not be too recent when the rebel scouts appear. I'd assume there's a chance they'll scout the lane as well . . . although they might not if the locals in that hamlet tell them that the bridge is out."

"I appreciate the offer of an imager, sir. That way we could move faster with fewer men. We'll meet him . . . or her . . . here in a quint, if that's satisfactory?"

"That will be fine. It will likely be Arion. He's a senior maitre. He has very strong shields."

"Thank you, sir. By your leave?"

Alastar nodded. "I'll look forward to hearing what you have to say . . . and any recommendations you may have."

After Weidyn strode away, Akoryt looked to Alastar. "He doesn't totally trust your judgment, does he?"

"He shouldn't," replied Alastar. "I'm an aging imager who's never been in a war or trained for one. More important, he might just see something I overlooked. He spent some time as a squad leader digging out pirates from the Sud Swamp. You'd better have Arion get ready. Weidyn will be here when he says."

While Akoryt went to tell Arion of his task, Alastar imaged a simple wooden chair with very short legs, then eased it against the trunk of the oak and settled into it. He was so tired that he dropped into a doze deep enough that he didn't even hear Arion and Weidyn leave.

He woke more than a glass later, feeling less tired, but somewhat stiffer. Walking up and down the road helped with the stiffness, and some more of the bitter lager cleared his head, enough so that he felt considerably better when Weidyn, the squad leader, and Arion returned at roughly two quints past fourth glass.

Weidyn dismounted, handed his mount's reins to the squad leader, and walked to join Alastar. Arion turned his mount toward the tielines for the imagers.

Weidyn's face held a slight smile.

Better than a frown or an impassive expression. "What do you think, Captain?"

"It's a good plan . . . if you can keep the squads concealed. There are some changes that might make it more effective."

"I'll have five imagers with me. That will be more than enough for concealment. We won't be able to offer as much shielding as we did at High Holder Laevoryn's. We could do that there because we covered the narrow front of the column. With your men spread and mounted . . . that will be harder, but their muzzle flashes and any smoke won't be seen."

Weidyn nodded thoughtfully. "Any shielding is better than we'd get in the regular order of battle."

"What are your suggestions?"

"If the situation allows in the first ambush—the southern one—we should wait until the vanguard is partly past us . . ."

Alastar listened as Weidyn laid out his suggestions, then replied, "I'd agree with all of them, except for the last one. Not that it's not an excellent idea tactically, but a concealment only affects the eyes, and attempting to wait that long and then move everyone would create enough noise to give the rebels a better idea of where we are. Also, once the company moves, so does the concealment, and that leaves dust and tracks visible, which point to where our forces are. Both of those will put too much strain on the imagers, and they won't be able to hold that large a concealment and any shielding at all."

Weidyn nodded. "I had not considered that."

"You wouldn't have known. For obvious reasons, especially given how few imagers there are, we tend not to let others know of our limitations." Alastar kept his tone wry.

Weidyn smiled, if briefly.

"We need to discuss one other matter, Captain," Alastar said quietly, moving away from the others.

Weidyn followed. "Yes, sir."

"You know we're greatly outnumbered."

"Three to one, I've heard."

"I don't know if you heard, but the brown-shirts that your men fought at High Holder Laevoryn's estate had been using special bullets to kill students and young imagers."

"Sir?"

"If the bullet isn't immediately removed, within a fraction of a quint, whoever is shot with one will almost certainly die in less than two quints, possibly sooner."

"The rebels are using those kinds of bullets?"

"No, not any longer." Alastar paused. "It may be worse than that. We have a thousand cartridges like those. I mentioned this to Marshal Wilkorn. He thought those cartridges would be most useful to whatever company supported us in this attack. The effect would be less in an all-out battle."

For a long moment, Weidyn did not speak. "The commander mentioned special bullets. He didn't say they were poisoned."

"The poison's inside the bullet. It won't hurt your men—except they shouldn't chew the bullets. I've heard that sometimes troopers have done that."

"I've kept my men from doing that. The Gulf pirates sometimes did." Weidyn paused. "More than sometimes."

Alastar waited.

Finally, Weidyn spoke. "Might I ask what you think of the bullets, sir?"

"I don't like the idea of using them. I wouldn't even have considered it as a possibility until the High Holders' brown-shirts started using them to kill students and imagers. Yet the fact that they would use them tells me that they'll do anything to overthrow the rex, suppress the factors, and destroy the Collegium. If that happens, almost everyone in Solidar will end up living at the pleasure of one High Holder or another. Given that . . . and the fact that we're outnumbered three to one, I don't see much of a choice." He paused, just slightly, then went on. "If the rebels were farther from L'Excelsis, we could keep fighting delaying actions. But as I see it, they have to win, and win quickly, and they'll keep pressing if we withdraw, and a withdrawal could so easily turn into a rout."

Weidyn nodded slowly. "Some of that I'd thought about. The rest of it makes sense. I don't like it, either. It's a choice between the Namer of the night, and the Namer of the day." His laugh was sardonically bitter. "Best we go with the bullets and the Namer of the day." After a moment, he said, "I'd prefer to tell the men that the bullets are special and extra-powerful, and to make every shot count because we only have ten cartridges of those for each man."

"That's true enough." *So far as it goes.*

"If it's all right with you, sir, I'll have the squad leader who's the company armorer get the cartridges tomorrow morning after I've had a chance to brief all the squad leaders."

"That makes sense to me, and you've got much more experience in dealing with troopers than I do. Thank you, Captain."

"Appreciate your plain words, sir. Thank you."

Alastar watched as the captain turned and left. *How many more distasteful decisions will there be?* The way matters were going, he already knew.

Too many.

40

A chilly breeze came up on Solayi night, and by Lundi morning, mist and fog filled the air. While the higher area where the imagers were camped was clear, the lands to the west were mist-shrouded, and patches of fog and mist wreathed parts of the road to the south. The sky overhead was clear, and Alastar thought that the sun would burn off the fog by midmorning if not sooner. While the teamsters, who were doubling as cooks, prepared breakfast, Alastar went to find Wilkorn or Maurek, and instead found a trooper looking for him.

"Maitre, sir, the marshal would appreciate a few moments of your time. . . ."

"Lead on," replied Alastar, deciding against mentioning he'd been looking for Wilkorn.

Both the marshal and commander were in the command tent when Alastar slipped inside, standing and looking at a large map laid out on a camp table. Both turned immediately.

"You were looking for me, Marshal?"

"We were. Maurek told you yesterday that we hadn't heard from the first scouts we sent out. We still haven't. The second set of scouts hasn't reported back yet, either. I've posted full squads three milles to the south on all roads and lanes that might lead to us. I'd be interested in hearing what you make of that."

Maurek nodded.

"By what I make of that, are you asking if my missing imagers might have something to do with it?"

"You have mentioned concealments, and I can't see any other way that so many scouts would fail to report."

"Certainly, one of the two missing imagers is capable of handling a large enough concealment to hide several squads—if they were fairly close together—but he doesn't have the capability of being in more than one place at a time. If the rebels could figure out where your scouts were headed and there was enough time . . . I suppose it's possible he could have thrown up a concealment that allowed the scouts to pass a force that would then have them surrounded and their escape blocked."

"How would you deal with that possibility?"

"Space the scouts a quint of a mille apart, but each in sight of the one before him. If the lead scout disappears while he's on the road, it's likely he's passed through a screen concealment."

"How long could this imager hold such a concealment?"

"That depends on how large it is. One across the river road and on the shoulder covering a squad of troopers . . . easily a glass, probably longer. Large shields, on the other hand, wear out even the strongest imagers quickly." Alastar only paused for a moment before asking, "But couldn't the rebels do the same thing by using a wooded area close to the river road and waiting for the scouts to pass?"

"They could," admitted Maurek, "but it seems unlikely that none would escape."

"The rebels have a much larger force."

"Either way," said Wilkorn, "it's disturbing."

"So we still don't know where the rebels are?"

"We know that they're not yet within five milles of Caluse," replied Maurek. "Otherwise . . ."

"That's almost a day away, then," observed Alastar.

"It might be two," said Wilkorn, "or they might be wanting to create that impression while they send part of their forces westward."

"And bring them through that gap between Lake Shaelyt and the smaller lake just to the northwest of us?"

"We have scouts posted there, just in case," replied Maurek.

"Can your imagers sense when there is another imager hiding behind a concealment?" asked Wilkorn.

"That is a very rare talent. At present, we have one very young imager who appears to have that ability, but she is young and can only detect concealments that are within a few yards. That wouldn't be helpful here."

"I was hoping . . ." admitted the marshal.

"Is there anything else I should know?" asked Alastar.

"You know what we know." Wilkorn offered a crooked smile. "Little as it is. We'll let you know more as soon as we do."

When Alastar returned to the imagers' area, he immediately gathered them all together. "There are two things you all need to know. The first is that we will be supplying Fifth Company with some special cartridges. Fifth Company is the same company that we assisted in dealing with the late High Holder Laevoryn, and we will be supporting the company in dealing with the rebels. For those of you who haven't heard, Captain Weidyn is very experienced. His troopers only know that the cartridges are more powerful. That is true, and that is all anyone needs to know. Is that clear?" Alastar paused and surveyed the imagers one by one before continuing.

"For your information, they were imaged by Maitres Cyran and Alyna. The second matter is that the rebels are at least fifteen milles away. We don't know more than that because a number of the scouts the marshal dispatched yesterday have not yet returned, and it's possible that they were ambushed. That means you all should remain fairly close to our muster area because it is possible that some of the rebel forces might be nearby." Alastar paused. "Are there any questions?"

"How many of their troopers are mounted, and how many are infantry?" asked Tiranya.

"We don't know precisely yet. Of those who deserted from army headquarters, less than a third are mounted infantry. The first reports from scouts last week indicated that only about a quarter of the forces supplied by the High Holders appear to be mounted. That may have increased since then."

"Do we know if Bettaur or Ashkyr are with the rebels?" asked Taurek.

"We don't have any information either way. It might be best to assume that they are, or at least keep the possibility in the back of your minds."

"Besides the early operations with Fifth Company, sir," asked Dylert, "what exactly will we be doing?"

Alastar suspected that question had come as much from Thelia as from Dylert, although he honestly didn't know just how much the junior maitre had discussed matters with Thelia. "What we're expected to provide is opportunistic support and attack. As we've already discovered, there's a limit to how many heavy rifle bullets most imager shields can take. Leading a charge might sound glamorous, but you can't lead without being somewhat visible to those you're leading, and a force large enough to be effective is going to leave traces and be heard, even under concealment. After the first few uses of concealments, bullets will be flying everywhere. So we'll be doing things like moving close enough under shields and concealments to fire their cannon shells and ammunition.

Or perhaps torch their provisions, or any number of other operations that will create losses to them while incurring as few as possible, hopefully none, to the imagers involved. Remember . . . there are only twelve of you, and likely close to five thousand troopers on both sides. If any of you have other ideas along those lines, I'm open to suggestions."

"Thank you, sir."

"Now . . . get something to eat."

As Weidyn had promised, immediately after breakfast a squad leader from Fifth Company appeared with a handcart—and the captain was with him. Both carried heavy rifles.

Alastar walked them to the first supply wagon where Cyran was waiting with ten wooden boxes set out on the tailboard.

"There they are," said Alastar.

"Do you mind if . . ." The squad leader looked to Alastar.

"You'd like to look at the bullets, to make sure that they won't foul your barrels?" asked Alastar gently.

"Yes, sir."

Alastar nodded to Cyran, who took one of the wooden boxes and handed it to the armorer.

"Awfully nice for a cartridge box," observed Weidyn, glancing at the other nine boxes. "Men will be wanting them when they're empty."

The armorer slid the top open just enough to remove several of the cartridges. Then he lifted his rifle, swiveled the breech, and inserted the cartridge. He inspected the fit carefully, then swiveled the breech down, checking the closure, before he looked to Alastar.

"We've fired at least a score of rounds from heavy rifles. You can fire how many you want, but each one you fire is one less with which to kill rebels. Each one was specially made, and there aren't any replacements." Alastar smiled pleasantly. "When you fire, just make sure the bullet won't ricochet and hit someone."

"I'd like to walk over to the river and see if I can find some wet sand or mud to fire into."

"Go ahead," replied Alastar, "but if you want to look at the bullet afterward, put on some gloves. Then wash them when you're done. The residual from the charge could burn your fingers even when the bullet's cold." That was as much as Alastar was going to say, and it was true in a way.

"That charge won't foul a barrel, will it?"

"No," replied Cyran. "We actually fired close to two score cartridges from one rifle."

"Maitre Cyran works with forging and metals, turning benches and tolerances," added Alastar.

"Go ahead," said Weidyn. "We'll wait here." Once the armorer was out of earshot, he added, "He's very conscientious. He'd feel better firing an entire box. I told him that wasn't possible."

"Oh . . . it's possible," replied Alastar dryly, "but the cost of his certainty would likely be the greater possibility of deaths among his men and comrades."

"Rushing weapons can be dangerous," pointed out Weidyn. "It can cost lives."

"You're right. It usually does. But if we wait until we're absolutely certain the cartridges won't create problems, the revolt will be long over . . . one way or the other. The question is whether the new weapon saves more lives of our troopers than it costs. We think the special cartridges will . . . and since we're hazarding our imagers to help in the matter, it's not as though we're not sharing that risk."

"I did point that out to the armorer."

"But you're letting him come to the right decision his way," said Alastar with a smile.

"Most times, it works better when you let them know the entire problem, or as much as you can."

Alastar thought he heard three shots, but he wasn't certain.

More than half a quint passed before the armorer rejoined the three. He looked to Weidyn. "Sir, they don't seem to foul the barrel. The bullets crack when they hit, but they don't fragment. They don't scar the barrel, and they seem more accurate than the ones we're using."

Alastar noted the smallest of nods from Cyran.

"Then they'll do?" asked Weidyn.

"As far as I can tell, sir."

"Then load them up. We'll wait to issue them until just before the evolution. We might be ordered to some other duty first."

"Yes, sir."

"I'll be with you in a few moments."

Once the armorer was on his way with the ammunition boxes loaded on the hand cart, Weidyn turned back to the imagers. "That's as good a statement as you'll ever get from Aloisyn. The better accuracy may help as much as your other touches." He paused. "Usually, something that's individually made . . ."

"Each cartridge and each bullet was imaged to a precise template," said Cyran. "If you take care, the results can be very precise."

"So it seems." Weidyn inclined his head. "You will inform me when we know more about the coming evolution?"

"As soon as we know," promised Alastar.

The two imagers watched as Weidyn strode northward toward his company.

Alastar cleared his throat. "You and Alyna really worked on finish and balance, didn't you?"

"That was her doing. I experimented a bit with the composition. Arthos had a few ideas, also."

At that moment, a junior squad leader hurried up, inclining his head to Alastar. "Sir, the marshal and the commander thought you should hear the latest scouting report."

"We'll talk more later," Alastar said to Cyran before turning back to the trooper. "Lead the way."

As Alastar neared the command tent, he saw two rankers waiting outside with a squad leader and decided that the three, or at least the rankers, were scouts. When he entered, Wilkorn and Maurek were seated on canvas camp stools, side by side looking at the same map they had been studying before. Both rose.

"Have the scouts come in," ordered the marshal.

The two rankers Alastar had seen outside the command tent entered, stiffening to attention in front of the camp table. "Sir."

"You two were the only ones to return from a scouting mission. Is that correct?" asked Maurek.

"Yes, sir."

"How did that happen?"

The taller man looked at the shorter.

The shorter scout cleared his throat nervously. "We were with second squad, third scout company. We rode though Caluse before dawn this morning. We didn't see anyone. Saw smoke from chimneys, like folks were fixing breakfast. Some teamsters at the brewery were rolling barrels up a ramp onto an old dray. South of town, the captain sent each squad a different way. He and first squad went south on the river road. We went with first squad for more than a mille, might have been another half mille past the milestone. That was where the captain told the squad leader—that's Plessat—for us to scout the side road that headed off. That's what Plessat said, anyway. Once we were away from the main road, Plessat detailed me and Borkel here, to fall back two quints. Told us that if anything strange happened, anything happened to the rest of the squad, we were to hightail it back to camp and report. Maybe a mille out, we came to another road, a good wide road. Not paved, but graveled some. Plessat took the squad south on the side road. Looked like anyplace else we've been seeing. Fields, cots, woodlots. Musta been another two milles on . . ." The scout looked to Borkel.

"A quint more'n two milles, seemed to me."

"That was when it happened, right after they road past this orchard, apples, I think. I was looking right at the others. Like I blinked, most of the squad was gone, excepting Fedor and Daffyr. They were maybe twenty yards back of the others. Then, suddenlike they were gone, too. Like they weren't there at all."

Wilkorn and Maurek looked to Alastar.

"What happened then? Did you hear anything?"

"Next thing we know, Fedor appears, except he's riding toward us, low on his mount. Then there were lots of shots, and he and his mount go down. Leastwise, I swear on the Nameless that's what we saw. Except we're looking, and he disappears, like he'd never been there."

Borkel nodded.

"Anything else? Horses? Voices?"

"We were more than half a mille away, sir."

"Where did the shots come from?" asked Alastar.

"They must have come from the orchard. Leastwise, I couldn't see anyone anywhere else. Don't see how the squad disappeared, though." The scout shook his head. "Just gone, and then Fedor shows up, and then he's gone. Enough to make a man question his eyes. Maybe all his senses, too."

"What did you do then?"

"Like we were ordered. We turned our mounts and rode like the Namer was after us. When you see a whole squad disappear . . ." The shorter scout shook his head, then looked to Borkel. "Best you finish."

"Well, sirs," said the taller scout, "we went back to the main road, but we didn't see the rest of the company. I mean, we saw the traces showing them heading south on the river road. Weren't no traces coming back, and we had orders. So we rode back here. We didn't see no sign of any other troopers, theirs or ours, till we got back to our picket lines."

"You didn't see traces or tracks of other horses on that side road?" asked Alastar.

"No, sir."

"Could you tell how many shots were fired at Fedor?"

"Sounded like two squads, maybe, but all at once. Then there weren't any more."

"Did anyone fire at you?"

"Not so as we could tell, sir."

Alastar and the two senior army officers continued the questions for almost another quint, but neither scout could add much to their initial report.

Finally, Wilkorn said, "I think we've covered this in enough detail. All I'd like to add is my appreciation for your carrying out your orders. If you two hadn't done so, you would have been shot or captured, and we still wouldn't know what had happened."

Once the scouts had left the tent, the marshal asked Alastar, "What do you make of all that?"

"I think we can assume that at least one of our missing imagers has thrown in with the rebels."

"How did they manage that?" asked Maurek.

"The imager used a screen concealment across the road. The rebel troopers were in the orchard, most likely at the very edge. Once the squad passed, the concealment was shifted so that both your troopers and theirs were concealed. One scout tried to escape, and was shot. Since the two who escaped didn't hear shots until then, I'd assume that the scout squad was greatly outnumbered, with at least a full company aiming rifles at them, and decided that discretion was the better part of valor. That's just a guess, of course."

"I can see that," replied the commander. "I don't like it. They just surrendered?"

"You think they should have chosen to get killed for nothing when the fight is between the rex and a bunch of High Holders?" asked Wilkorn sardonically. "When they're in an impossible position?"

Alastar found his thoughts were similar to those of the marshal.

"I still don't like it," declared Maurek.

"We'll just use it," said the marshal. "Spread the word to all the troopers that the rebels are shooting scouts, and that so far out of all the scouts only two have returned. Get the point across that while those men once may have been comrades, they'll now kill their former comrades without even blinking."

Has it come to that? How could it not, given the anger of the High Holders?

"We still need to decide how to deal with them," pointed out Maurek.

"Does the road where the scouts were ambushed lead to that hamlet south of where we planned the first ambush?" asked Alastar.

"That's what we were looking at when you came in," replied Wilkorn.

"I was just wondering . . ."

"That was our thought as well," said Maurek.

"What if we tried the same thing on them . . . but south of the hamlet?" asked Alastar.

"Were you thinking of some of your imagers with Fifth Company?" Maurek frowned. "Even with imagers, and the lane as narrow as it is, that could be a real problem with just one company if they sent a battalion that way. Aestyn's cautious that way, and so is Marryt."

"Two companies at least," said Wilkorn

"Major Luerryn, too," added Maurek. "That's for the troopers. Luerryn will listen to you. You impressed him, Maitre."

"Let's look over the map and the earlier scouting reports," said Wilkorn. "We need to give this some thought.

Alastar had the feeling he was in for at least a glass of deliberation and planning.

41

Early Mardi morning found Alastar saddling the gelding. He'd already imaged both water bottles full of the barely passible dark lager that was the best he could manage when Cyran appeared.

"I don't want to seem insubordinate, Maitre, but might it be more prudent if I took second group with Major Luerryn's forces?"

Alastar suppressed the wry smile he felt. He knew from where that question had come, but he didn't ask Cyran. "It's a good thought, but I think I'll need your support a great deal more a little later." At Cyran's expression, he added, "I appreciate your concern, but, as I'm sure Alyna may have indicated, I don't always recover from heavy imaging as quickly as I did a few years ago. That means the more time I have between imaging, the more effective I'll be . . . and the more all of us can do together. So it's likely that I'll be asking you and second group to handle whatever the next task is. If you go first, on the other hand . . ."

Cyran nodded, and a brief smile followed. "I just wanted you to know."

"I understand, and I'm very grateful." *And Alyna will be also . . . if matters work out anywhere close to what we've planned . . . which they likely won't.* "Make certain second group rests, but keep them close together so that if you have to mount up it won't take long."

"Yes, sir." Cyran still wore a concerned expression when Alastar mounted and formed up his group.

Alastar, Akoryt, and the imager of first group left the encampment at sixth glass, directly behind Weidyn and his first squad, with Major Luerryn and Alastar riding side by side at the head of first group, followed by the remainder of Fifth Company and then Eighth Company. Slight wisps of mist swirled around the edges of the River Aluse, and the air was cooler than it had been in days, but then, less than two weeks remained before the end of harvest and the beginning of fall.

"How far in front of the main force do you think the rebels' advance companies are?" asked Alastar once the formation was headed west on the narrow road leading to the lane with the rebuilt bridge.

"Anywhere south of Caluse," replied Luerryn. "They could be even farther north if they're taking the side roads. I wouldn't anticipate the main forces on the side roads. They're too soft for all the cannon and the supply wagons."

"What's the largest force you'd put on the side roads?"

"In one formation? Two companies."

"That's why we've got two?"

"The commander and I do tend to think alike."

"What about Commander Aestyn? Or Hehnsyn or Marryt?"

"From all I've heard and seen, Hehnsyn's very traditional. I don't know anything about Marryt. Aestyn . . . he got the command dealing with the pirates in the Sud Swamp because he's more adventurous. He'd put cannon on flatboats and bombard pirate camps from the middle of a bog where the pirates couldn't even get to the boats."

Although Alastar nodded, what Luerryn said about the rebel commander bothered him more than a little. "I assume the marshal knows that?"

"That's why he picked the spot he did. No swamps, no bogs, no backwaters, no terrain any higher anywhere close."

But Aestyn likely knows that, mused Alastar.

Once they had turned off the west-heading road and onto the dirt lane, Alastar studied the sides of the lane, checking the clingweed to see if it showed more traces of horses, but he couldn't see much of any change since the last time he had ridden there. Nor was there any sign of riders as they passed through the berry-bush fields, while the first flooded field showed a slightly lower water level than before and more exposed mud.

Weidyn ordered scouts out to go through the ill-tended woodlot, but they discovered nothing. Nor were there any signs of large numbers of riders on the part of the lane leading to the second flooded field between the lane and the river road. The only recent tracks were those of four or five mounts, most likely those of Weidyn, a few troopers, and Arion.

So far . . . so good.

As Weidyn's squad rode up the low rise to the crest from which Alastar had observed the hamlet situated several milles north of Caluse, Alastar could feel his guts tightening and he checked his shields once more, wondering if they'd be met be a hail of rifle fire, but nothing of the sort occurred, and Luerryn called a halt, which Alastar would have suggested if Luerryn had not already ordered it.

"A bit more than two milles to that hamlet," observed Luerryn. "The road widens at the bottom of here. Unless my eyes fail me, there's a narrow hedgerow just this side of the hamlet and that rubs west and then turns more to the south. The hedgerow keeps going south, but there's another road going west off of it."

"My eyes must have failed me," Alastar replied wryly. "I didn't see the hedgerow at all. I can see it now."

"It's easier in morning light. The long shadows help."

Alastar wasn't so sure that he would have picked out the hedgerow without Luerryn's assistance, especially given that trees and bushes lining the lane were uneven, and even had gaps in places, but couldn't help but wonder what else he might have missed. He didn't think his eyes were that much worse than they had once been. *But how would you know?*

He glanced toward the bottom of the rise to the south, where the lane widened, and then beyond. It was definitely possible that the second lane Luerryn had pointed out might afford another route for the rebels, possibly even connecting to the side road described by the two returning scouts. "Could they make better time by sending the mounted units on the side lanes?"

"Probably not, but they could pick up a lot more forage, and it would make it easier for them to try an encircling maneuver. I don't see any dust, but there won't be much, except on the river road, not with the ground as damp as it's been."

Alastar looked downhill and watched as the two scouts rode along the road south from the rise and toward the point where the hedgerow joined the south road. They reined up, and one took out a blue banner on a short pole and waved it.

"Looks like it's clear so far. Thought it should be, but you never know," said Luerryn. "Column! Forward!"

As Alastar rode beside the major, he looked ahead to the hedgerow that bordered the lane heading west from the narrow road on which they rode. It wasn't that tall as hedgerows went, a little less than three yards and appeared to be somewhat shorter farther west, but he wondered why that was the only hedgerow in the area. "I don't like riding past a side road that we haven't scouted."

"There wasn't any sign of riders or wagons on the road around the hamlet," Luerryn pointed out. "Just one full mounted company would stretch several hundred yards along these lanes and roads. Could an imager hide that many riders?"

"Most competent imagers could conceal a squad. A very good imager could conceal a company. More than that would be hard for any length of time."

More than a quint went by while they rode past small cots, an apple orchard, and what Alastar thought might have been a stand of pear trees, before they neared the hedgerow.

Alastar looked to his left, in the direction of the river. A low berm with a level top almost the width of the road bordered by the hedgerow ran the two milles or so toward the river, joining a raised flat field or space just short of the trees immediately to the west of the river road.

Once Luerryn and Alastar reached the half crossroads, the major signaled a halt and turned to the Maitre. "What do you think?"

"I think I'd like to take a look down the side road."

"Then we should send a scout in front of you."

Alastar frowned. "That might be dangerous for the scout."

"It undoubtedly will be. The marshal has far more scouts than imagers."

Alastar managed not to wince at the major's pragmatism. "And scouts are more expendable than entire companies."

"That, too. I'll send a squad with you. The squad leader will be Helm-nyn. How many imagers will you take?"

A polite way of saying that you're not going alone. Alastar kept his smile to himself. "Two. Arion! Seliora!"

Luerryn gestured and a trooper rode forward.

In less than half a quint, the small formation turned onto the hedge-row road. The scout was already a good hundred yards ahead. Then came the three imagers—all abreast—with the mounted squad close behind, led by squad leader Helmnyn.

The sound of the gelding's hoofs on the road changed, and Alastar looked down. The lane was stone-paved, although a thin layer of dirt covered the stone, and some of the pavers were missing and others were cracked, suggesting that the road was indeed old. He looked up and glanced back toward the river, but the imagers riding behind him blocked his view.

"Sir?" asked Arion.

"Nothing. I was just thinking." Alastar suspected that the old road had once run along the berm right to the river, and that the flat area had held buildings, perhaps a place where cargoes could have been loaded or un-loaded off riverboats. But *who had built it? When? And where had it led?* There were certainly no cities, and no sizable towns to the south and south-west.

Alastar smiled, shook his head, and returned his concentration to the road ahead.

As the imagers and as Helmnyn's squad continued westward, Alastar kept his eyes moving, noticing that the section of hedgerow through which the scout was passing was more even, seemingly all the same, and didn't have the breaks he had observed from the rise in the road. The scout rode deliberately, almost stiffly, still a hundred yards ahead. Alastar couldn't blame the man for feeling like he was a target. He well might be.

For a moment, the scout appeared to disappear, then reappear.

"Company! Halt!" Alastar ordered, projecting his voice. "Recall the scout!" In a much lower voice, he added, "Helmnyn, pass the word quietly. Ready arms."

Alastar continued to watch as the scout turned his mount, but there was no flicker or change in the trooper's appearance. *Did you imagine it?* He didn't think so. Then, abruptly, he realized something else. *The hedgerow where the scout had been is far too regular.* "Arion . . . just west of where the scout turned, image a cloud of red pepper across the lane and on both sides of the hedgerow. Into the hedgerow a bit."

"Into it, sir?"

"I have my doubts that it's as solid as it looks."

"Yes, sir."

An almost impenetrable red fog filled the road a hundred yards ahead. For several moments, nothing happened. Then the fog seemed to move, and congeal over figures. Part of the hedgerow vanished, leaving gaps on both sides of the narrow road. In those gaps Alastar could see ranks of mounted troopers carrying rifles and wearing crimson and black arm-bands. Despite the momentary chaos caused by the cloud of red pepper, all too many of those rifles were pointed in the direction of the imagers and the single squad that accompanied them.

In moments, several rebel troopers began to fire at the imagers.

"Seliora! A screen concealment in front of us."

Abruptly, the rebel force vanished as well, but the scout remained in sight less than thirty yards away, now spurring his mount toward the imagers.

"More red pepper, and hot iron needles to the gaps on each side of the road!" Alastar turned in the saddle. "Squad leader! Have your men fire mounted-rider-high into those gaps in the hedgerow. Rapid fire!"

"Yes, sir." Squad Leader Helmnyn raised his voice. "On my command! Rider high. Into the gaps! Fire!"

Alastar rocked in the saddle as several bullets ripped into his shields, then imaged hundreds of wooden darts into the gaps in the hedgerow, followed by hundreds more, knowing that using wood would take far less effort than iron, even as he heard the thunder of hoofs pounding toward his small force, and as the fleeing scout rode past Seliora.

"Squad leader! Fire down the road!"

Alastar had to guess, but imaged a shield across the road a yard high, anchoring it to the stone beneath the surface, roughly fifteen yards in front of himself, holding it as he waited.

The wait seemed interminable, but was likely only a tiny fraction of a quint before the first rebel riders appeared, brandishing sabers and out-riding the screen that had concealed them—before their mounts plowed into the low shield, going down and spewing the first and second ranks of riders onto the road. Then the concealment vanished totally, and all Alastar could see was the lane before him filled with riders jamming up behind those thrown by the road shield or killed by bullets or darts.

"Arion! Seliora! Use wooden darts! Wooden darts! Take down as many as you can!"

More rebel troopers, many unable to move, slumped in their saddles. The carnage grew, until a trumpet sounded from the west, and the rid-ers in the rear of the rebel force began to turn and ride back west, a ride that began to resemble a rout.

As soon as Alastar could see that the rebels had passed the gaps in the hedgerow, without flowing out into the surrounding fields, he dropped the road shield and ordered, "Turn and withdraw! Back to the crossroads."

He'd already visually studied the retreating rebels and scanned the fallen, but he hadn't seen any figure in gray, although there definitely had been an imager with the rebels.

As for what else he and the imagers could do, there wasn't any-thing else but to withdraw. They were outnumbered by the two or more companies that looked to comprise the rebel force, which made pursuit a less than optimal option, especially given the heap of dead and wounded men and mounts resulting from the combination of the road shield, iron needles, wooden darts, and rifle fire, a heap that effectively blocked the narrow road from hedgerow to hedgerow. Alastar could also see other fallen troopers and riderless mounts in the gaps between the hedgerows, most likely casualties from the first attack by Alastar's small force.

As Helmnyn's troopers, the imagers, and Alastar rode back toward Luerryn and the bulk of the two companies, Alastar stood in the saddle to survey the squad. From what he could make out, there were two bodies draped over saddles, and another trooper binding his arm.

His squad-sized force had taken out half a company, possibly more, but he had the feeling that doing the same thing again would be even harder. *Which means you'll have to come up with something else.*

The only problem was that by the time he and his force had rejoined Luerryn's main force and Alastar had quickly explained to the major what had happened, including the fact that there had definitely been an imager with the rebel forces, he still had no idea of what else he might try, and it was hard to think about that with Luerryn's continuing questions.

"They had rifles. Why didn't they use them?"

"They did, at first. They killed at least two of Helmnyn's men and wounded another, possibly more, but when they started to fire, Seliora raised a concealment, and Helmnyn's men fired into the gaps where the rebel troopers were waiting even though they were under a concealment. They were crowded together, and we did some imaging to make it hard for them to use their rifles—"

"How did you manage that?"

"It's hard to hit people when you're breathing red pepper, your eyes are watering, and you can't even see anyone to fire at," said Alastar dryly. "I'm certain that the plan was to let us pass, trap us in the hedgerow, and then wipe us out."

"There has to be a larger force on this road. What do you have in mind? Or should we withdraw?"

Alastar didn't feel that withdrawal was a good idea, not when the rebels—or some of them—had been upset and disorganized. "We should press on for the moment. If there is a larger force, it will be somewhere that an imager doesn't have to maintain a concealment for a long time. The road ahead doesn't have any orchards or woodlots immediately ahead of us, not until close to the hamlet. We can always withdraw if it's clear there's a massive force. Besides, our job is to whittle down their forces before we get into a full battle with both armies." Alastar didn't say anything about the dangers of being the whittler. He turned in the saddle.

"Akoryt, pass the word. If we need lots of darts—you and the imagers can do them out of wood. Just push them harder."

"Yes, sir."

Luerryn cleared his throat. "Column! Forward!"

The three scouts, already two hundred yards ahead of Weidyn and the lead squad, resumed their even pace, as did Weidyn and the vanguard, riding past a narrow dirt path leading to a weathered cot some thirty yards back on the west side of the road. On the north side of the cot was a shed, and beside it a woodpile, on top of which sat a large white and black cat, looking intently at the riders. A scattering of fruit trees rose behind the cot. The door to the cot was closed, and likely barred, Alastar suspected.

As the troopers and imagers rode south along the packed clay road, still damp enough that the riders raised no dust, they passed more cots, mostly located on the west side of the road. Alastar still could not make out where the hamlet was, except it had to be beyond the scattered trees at least another two milles south. He studied the ground ahead. To the left stretched rows of what looked to be bean plants. The large field was almost level, although the southeastern corner looked to be slightly higher. To the right was pastureland, stretching back slightly over a hundred yards. Beyond the pasture was a large orchard, but Alastar had trouble making out what was between the trees, although the split-rail fence on the north side of the orchard was clear and distinct.

A blurring shield!

He immediately glanced back to the left, but farther south, a good three hundred yards, to an unmortared wall of stacked stone, beyond which the land rose slightly. His eyes went immediately to the three scouts on the road ahead, who were nearing the point opposite where the wall ended.

"Order a quiet 'ready arms,' and then a loud halt," Alastar said. "There are troopers in that orchard over there."

"How many?"

"I have no idea, except it's probably a lot. I also wouldn't be surprised if there's another company or two behind that low hill several hundred yards ahead on the left. Can you give orders for the troopers to fire once we're opposite the orchard? That will allow most of them to fire, won't it?"

"We can stagger files so that they all can . . . but what about the rebel troopers ahead of us?"

"What would you suggest?"

"Not riding any closer to them yet," replied Luerryn, before raising his voice slightly. "Ready arms. Pass it back." After several moments, he called out, "Column halt! Stagger files! Rifles right!"

Alastar studied the orchard ahead once again. "I think we ought to attack before the troopers on the far side of that rise decide to make us defend or get routed."

"Do you think it's wise?"

Alastar laughed softly. "No, but everything else I can think of seems even more foolish." *All because you didn't believe that they'd split the two imagers that they have . . . or risk them so early.*

"I have to agree." Luerryn gave a wintry smile, then ordered, "Column! Forward!"

"Imagers. Prepare to image pepper into the first five yards of the orchard ahead on the left."

Alastar checked his shields, convinced that shots would ring out any moment as the vanguard drew even with the edge of the orchard some hundred yards back from the road. There were no shots, but Alastar could definitely make out that a blurring shield was in place.

"We're getting close to the best firing position," murmured Luerryn.

Alastar cleared his throat, then swallowed. "Khaelis, Dylert, Taurek. Fill the first five yards of that orchard with red pepper. Make it thick and hot. Now!"

A swathe of red fog filled the front of the orchard.

"Column halt! Open fire!" ordered the major. "Fire at will!"

Alastar immediately noticed that a five-yard swathe of the orchard showed no red mist at all. "Major! The area where there's no red mist. Have as many men as you can target that area now."

At first, only a few scattered shots came from the orchard, but the numbers increased. Alastar felt several impacts on his shields. More shots from Luerryn's troopers ripped into the unpeppered area.

"Dylert! Pepper that area in the orchard that isn't red. Taurek! Spray it with white-hot needles!"

As more of the red pepper fog appeared, the unpeppered area shrank to a space little more than a yard wide.

"Akoryt! Iron darts to the unpeppered spot! Imagers! Hold your shields firm."

Alastar added several iron darts of his own to those of Akoryt.

Abruptly, the blurring shield vanished, revealing spread across the less-than-hundred-yard front of the orchard at least a company of rebel troopers with their crimson and black armbands, although there were definitely gaps in their ranks, significant holes, if not so many as Alastar would have wished.

Three quick blasts on a horn followed, and the rebel troops spurred their way from the cover of the orchard toward the troopers on the road, who continued to fire into the oncoming rebels, most of whom had holstered their rifles and brandished sabers.

"Imagers! Wooden darts into the front ranks of the attackers!"

Between the heavy rifles of the troopers and the efforts of the imagers, the ranks of the rebel attackers thinned, but more kept coming from the orchard.

"More pepper into the attackers!" Alastar imaged out his own pepper spray. He was gratified to see that several riders veered into other riders, and more went down, whether to imager darts or trooper bullets, he couldn't tell.

Another horn signal echoed from the south.

"Left file!" ordered Luerryn. "Wheel out into the beans! Double up! Staggered formation! Right file! Double up! Staggered formation! Keep firing!"

Alastar kept imaging wooden dart after wooden dart, opting for projecting them with power, rather than trying to reach for iron. Occasionally, he could feel the impact of bullets or something on his shields, but not so much as he'd feared.

Then a wedge of riders charged toward him. Alastar linked his shields to the ground. For a moment, everything around him shook, before he discovered that horses and men were piled against the shields. Methodically, he imaged wooden darts into every moving figure, then expanded his aim to those farther away.

"Keep imaging the darts! Make every one count!" Alastar had no idea if any of the imagers were listening, or could even hear him.

In the end, he had no real idea how long the skirmish or battle lasted, only that at some point there was another horn signal, and the attackers withdrew. Alastar could barely see. His head felt like it was being hammered with a wooden mallet, and he felt very unsteady as he fumbled a water bottle out of his saddlebags. He had to use his teeth to extract the cork because his hands were shaking so much.

Some of the shaking subsided after several swallows, and he looked around. He was surrounded by the imagers. None of them seemed to be injured, but Akoryt was drenched in sweat, as were Khaelis and Dylert. Alastar was also, he realized. Arion merely looked disheveled and exhausted. Seliora and Taurek were both pale and shaking.

"You two were partly shielding me, weren't you?"

The burly Taurek managed a shaky grin. "Couldn't lose a Maitre, could we?" He was swaying in the saddle.

"Drink some of that lager in your water bottle before you fall out of the saddle. You, too, Seliora."

"Yes, sir . . . if I can find it. . . ."

Taurek looked so unsteady that Alastar reached out and handed his own water bottle to the junior maitre. The movement made him realize that he wasn't all that steady himself, but he managed to straighten in the saddle. "Share it with Seliora."

"Yes, sir."

Alastar managed to get out the second water bottle and uncork it without using his teeth. After another swallow, he turned southward, and scanned the area from west to east. Bodies were everywhere. So were a number of riderless horses. The air was absolutely still.

"Maitre . . ." Luerryn's voice roused Alastar from his bemused and stunned survey of the carnage.

"Yes?"

"You think we've done enough?" asked Luerryn, with a gesture that encompassed the carnage.

"More than enough. I don't think most of the imagers could image even a feather dart or stop a moth." That was an overstatement, Alastar knew, but not that much of one. "We need to move out back to camp and report to the marshal."

"I'd agree. The rebels might just be regrouping." Luerryn raised his voice. "Get the wounded on mounts! Those that aren't already. Collect all the rifles and sabers! Now! We're moving out in half a quint!"

"How many did we lose?" asked Alastar.

"More than a score are dead. Another score wounded."

Alastar winced.

"That's not bad, Maitre. Between those two companies you faced in the hedgerow and what they threw at us here, they had at least a mounted battalion."

"We must have killed . . . what . . . ? Two companies?"

"More than three. Maybe four."

Alastar had strong doubts that would happen again.

Luerryn turned his mount and eased away.

"Maitre? Thank you." Seliora returned Alastar's first water bottle to him.

"You're welcome. Are you feeling better?"

"Yes, sir. A little sore."

Alastar turned his mount toward the orchard. Taurek and Khaelis immediately moved up beside him.

"Sir?" asked Khaelis.

"We need to see if we got the imager . . . if we can even determine that."

The three imagers had to take a winding path through the bodies, and through the troopers scavenging for weapons and valuables. Alastar strengthened his shields as he neared the edge of the orchard, hoping no one armed was there, since he doubted what he had left of shields would resist more than a single shot or blow.

He could also smell smoke, most likely from the impact of bullets on wood or perhaps the white-hot needles that Taurek had imaged, but he didn't see any flames or black or gray smoke itself.

Although there was a good score of bodies in the area where the imager had been, all wore the green trooper uniforms with the crimson and black armbands, and Alastar didn't see a single face that remotely resembled either Bettaur or Ashkyr. He and the other two quickly checked the other bodies in the orchard and immediately in front of it, but saw no trace of one that could be identified as an imager before they finally rode back to the road.

Once there, he addressed all of his group. "We need to move to the front—what will be the front." Then he turned the gray and started northward along the side of the road, noticing that some of the troopers were still hurriedly scavenging.

Akoryt held back and brought up the rear.

You can't do this very often . . . and not that soon again. That thought went through Alastar's head more than once after the imagers re-formed behind the rearguard that had become the vanguard.

Before all that long, Luerryn was calling out the order, "Column! To the rear! Ride!" Then he eased his mount in beside Alastar, who said nothing, deciding to let the major do the talking.

Alastar took another swallow of lager from his remaining water bottle.

"Why wooden darts?" the major finally asked.

"Imaging wood takes much less effort than imaging iron. There were so many of the rebels. We needed more darts, and I wasn't certain we could keep imaging long enough if we did iron darts."

"Did you get those imagers?"

"I have no idea. I never saw anyone wearing gray, but they could have been wearing regular trooper uniforms so that we couldn't pick them out." *In that, they were likely smarter than you were.*

"Do you really think you can ambush them? Their ambush didn't work all that well on us?"

"I'll have to think about that." *That . . . and a lot of other things.*

Alastar took another long swallow of lager. He hoped he'd feel better before too long.

At the top of the rise in the road, he looked back toward the hamlet. Thick smoke was rising from the orchard, and he could just barely make out flames.

Frig!

But there wasn't a thing he could do now. . . .

He took another swallow of lager.

Alastar's head had largely stopped throbbing by the time he and the imagers arrived back at camp just before third glass. After he unsaddled and
groomed the gray, he made his way to Wilkorn's command tent, where
he found Major Luerryn and Commander Maurek, but not the marshal.
Maurek looked less than satisfied.

"Is there a problem?" asked Alastar.

"If I understand what Major Luerryn has reported, you routed a battalion of rebels, inflicted severe casualties, and then failed to pursue and
eliminate them. Is that correct?"

"It is," replied Alastar, deciding not to say more . . . not yet.

"They were routed, and you didn't pursue?" Maurek looked to
Luerryn.

"It didn't seem advisable, sir."

"When they were on the run? It didn't seem advisable?"

Alastar cleared his throat, loudly.

Maurek looked both surprised and annoyed. "Yes, Maitre?"

"The imagers accounted for a significant number of the rebel casualties and also provided a certain amount of protection to Major Luerryn's
forces. By the time the rebels withdrew, not a single imager was capable
of additional effort, and most could no longer provide even minimal protection for themselves." That might have been stretching the truth
slightly, Alastar felt, but only slightly.

Maurek's expression was puzzled.

Alastar refrained from sighing, and went on. "You wouldn't send a
company to chase the rebels when they had no ammunition in their rifles
and their sabers were broken. That was the situation the imagers were
in, and Major Luerryn was wise enough to recognize that."

"You wouldn't have gone?"

Alastar looked at Maurek. "Commander . . . you know what your men
and weapons can do. I know what mine can do. We killed close to two
companies worth of rebels. Possibly more. We did it with six imagers.
That was all we could do today. Let us rest, and we can fight again. Insist

that we fight when we're spent, and you'll lose most of the imagers . . .
and you can't replace them for another twenty-five years, if then. It's that
simple."

Maurek swallowed. "I'm sorry, Maitre. I hadn't thought in those terms.
It's just that . . ."

"You saw what seemed to be a lost opportunity. It was, but pursuing
it would have cost you even more dearly." *Not to mention what it would have
cost the Collegium . . . for almost no gain.*

Maurek started to say something, then stopped as Wilkorn entered
the command tent.

"How did it go?" asked the marshal.

Alastar decided to state the case for the marshal quickly before Maurek could. "We encountered a rebel force of at least battalion size . . ."
He quickly repeated what he had just told Maurek, adding, "The rebels
have at least one imager, possibly two. We have no way of knowing
whether either imager was killed or wounded. We searched the bodies
but could find no traces."

"Why not?"

"Because imagers look like everyone else. There was no one wearing
gray, and none of the dead men was either of the two who deserted."

"That could be a problem," mused Wilkorn.

"The concealment aspect is more of a problem in fights with small
forces," Alastar pointed out. "It's hard to maintain a consistent concealment over a large area and for any length of time. That was one reason
I could spot the one in the orchard."

"How did you?" asked Maurek.

"The area under the trees wasn't clear, but the trees were, and so was
the ground in front of the orchard."

"You knew what to look for," said Wilkorn. "Even after what you've
said, I don't know as I'd recognize something like that."

"After you've seen it a few times, you would," Alastar said. "Where
are the rest of the rebel forces?"

"We're getting more reports, now that the scouts are aware of the
kinds of traps the rebels were setting for them. The main force was just
south of Caluse early this morning," said Wilkorn. "Around noon it appeared that they were investing the town. They're taking their time. It
may be that the battalion you encountered was attempting to get into
position to mount a flank attack or even one from the rear. We've sent
more scouts west and positioned them well in advance so that the rebels

will advance toward them, rather than having them advance into the rebel forces."

"That would minimize the effect of possible concealments," Alastar agreed. "What's your feeling about how long they'll stay in Caluse?"

Wilkorn shrugged. "I don't see weeks. A few days. Who knows?"

"If they stay a while, then we could do something to whittle them down," suggested Alastar.

"That might be necessary, but it seems that you won't be doing much for the next day or so."

"I won't, but Maitre Cyran and group two are ready. That's another reason why it wasn't a good idea to use all the imagers at once, at least in the beginning."

"I can see that," said Maurek dryly.

"We'll decide on that once we have a better idea on what the rebels are likely to do," added Wilkorn. "Or what the next reports from the scouts show." He offered a sympathetic smile to Alastar. "You look like you could use something to eat and some rest."

"They might help," admitted Alastar.

"We'll keep you informed."

"Thank you."

Alastar left the tent and walked several paces away, until the troopers who were posted weren't looking. Then he wrapped a concealment around himself, knowing he couldn't hold it too long and slipped back to the tent, stopping just outside the canvas and listening.

". . . how much did they do, Major?" Maurek's voice was skeptical.

"Everything he said, Commander. Likely more. Most of the bodies had wooden darts in them. Usually through the eyes or heart."

"What about the Maitre? He's not a young man."

"Two of the younger ones helped shield him. I think that was so he could use all his abilities with the darts. Bodies were piled in front of him withers high."

"Would you go out again with imagers?" asked Wilkorn.

"With him . . . anytime. Facing a battalion and a half and only losing a squad . . . that just doesn't happen."

"That still leaves the rebels with two and a half regiments," said Maurek.

"The imagers did that with half their force. We'll just have to keep using them."

Alastar would have liked to hear more, but his head was beginning to pound, and he could sense he was getting unsteady. Before he released the concealment, he did manage to walk far enough from the command tent so that it wasn't likely anyone would see where he'd been.

Rubbing his forehead in an effort to ease the throbbing, Alastar walked slowly back toward the imagers' area, thinking over what he'd observed about the rebel imagers during the two skirmishes or battles. Had there been two . . . or just one? Given the timing between the two, one imager could have done both—except that placing an imager with the smaller attacking force seemed strange . . . unless the rebel commander was using the imager to strengthen the lesser force and the imager had retreated to the main force under a concealment.

Had Bettaur been there? The more Alastar considered the matter, the less he thought that Bettaur had been present. Bettaur was a stronger imager than the one he and the first group had faced, but Ashkyr certainly could have handled what they had faced, and Bettaur could certainly have persuaded the younger imager to do his best and then withdraw. With only two imagers, the rebels would likely be more willing to let them avoid danger. Or at least save them until a more critical conflict.

43

Wilkorn summoned Alastar well before fifth glass on Meredi. Alastar woke Cyran, then finished getting ready.

"Why do you want me there?" asked Cyran as the two walked toward the command tent in the gray light before dawn.

"Because there's likely a problem that requires imagers, and group one isn't up to it, and, frankly, I'm still sore and tired. So it's your turn. I did tell you this would happen."

"You did," replied Cyran with a short laugh.

"And you thought I was just placating you." Alastar grinned. "Anyway, I want to make certain that Maurek doesn't put you and group two in an impossible position. As I told you last night, he still doesn't understand, at least with his feelings, the limits to what imagers can do."

"Do any of us, really?"

Alastar smiled. "Probably not, but we're likely to be closer."

"I still don't understand why Bettaur threw in with the rebels."

"If he did, he may have felt he didn't have a choice."

"If he did? You said you faced an imager . . ."

"That's what bothered me. It was more like we faced Ashkyr, but with all the trouble Bettaur took to help the young man, why would he leave him out there alone?"

"Maybe the rebels didn't give Bettaur much choice."

Alastar frowned, considering Ryentar's personality, and the attitudes manifested in the acts of Hehnsyn, Marryt, and Aestyn, then nodded. "With only two of them, that's possible."

"More than likely, if you ask me."

What Cyran said made sense, but Alastar still had his doubts.

Both Maurek and Wilkorn were waiting in the command tent.

"Good morning, Maitres," offered Wilkorn cheerfully. "Commander Maurek has some ideas . . . and some questions." He moved toward the camp table that held a large map.

The commander already stood behind the table. "The rebels are definitely settling into Caluse, here." Maurek pointed. "They're patrolling

the river road north of the town and the side road that leads to Luasne—
that's a small town seven milles west . . . right here."

"Does the road to Luasne lead on to the hamlet where we fought yesterday?" asked Alastar.

"It does."

"Are they garrisoning Luasne?"

"Not yet, according to the scouts."

"Have any more scouts vanished?"

"No. Why do you ask?" Maurek's brow furrowed.

"That suggests they've pulled the imagers back. At least for now. Or
that they have another use for them at the moment."

"Could they have been as exhausted as yours were?" asked Wilkorn.

"That's possible." Alastar realized, if belatedly, he hadn't even considered that, possibly because it hadn't seem to him that the rebel imagers
had done all that much compared to the Collegium imagers.

"You have another group ready, I recall," said Maurek.

"We do. That's why Maitre Cyran is here."

"We have a plan to deal with the company that is patrolling the river
road to the north of Caluse," said Wilkorn. "If we attack there, it might
force them to consider keeping their forces closer together."

Alastar frowned. "I thought the idea was to fragment them so that
we could pick them off and reduce their numbers."

"We don't want them too fragmented," Maurek replied. "If they
spread into separate battalions and attack at different times and places,
that would be hard to defend."

"In any case," said Wilkorn smoothly, "we think there's a chance to
totally destroy a patrol company and then set up an ambush for the force
that comes after us. We'd like to take advantage of your imagers as much
as possible before the rebels realize that their best chance is an all-out
attack on our main force. Commander Maurek will be in command."

Alastar nodded and waited to hear what more either the marshal or
the commander had to say.

"About two milles north of Caluse," began Maurek, "the river road
swings away from the river around a huge rocky outcropping. The space
in front of the rock is bare. There's some grass there, but not a lot, and
no trees, and no cover. If your imagers could conceal a company there,
and in the open space north of the outcropping, we could put several
squads in plain sight on the road in the open . . ."

Alastar and Cyran listened as the commander laid out the plan.

"What do you think?" asked Wilkorn when Maurek had finished.

"It sounds like a good plan," replied Alastar, "but you'd be splitting the imagers into two groups."

"We're only asking for concealments," pointed out Maurek. "We could wipe out at least a company."

Alastar looked to Cyran. "You're going to be the one implementing it. What do you think?"

"How long is the outcrop . . . how far does it go beside the road?" asked Cyran.

"About half a mille."

"How much space is there between the rock outcropping and the river?"

"None. The rock is a sheer cliff straight down into the water."

"What about between the road and the rock at the west end?"

"No more than a few yards for most of the way."

"What about the west side of the road?"

"Low rocky hills. No trees . . . some bushes."

Cyran nodded slowly. "I have some ideas, but we'll have to see. When do you plan to leave?"

"Sixth glass."

"Second group will be ready."

Less than half a quint later, after the details had been finalized, Alastar and Cyran walked back toward the imager area.

"I don't have to tell you this," Alastar said, "but I will. Think of it this way. Every imager is worth a battalion."

Cyran's laugh was low and humorless. "A good thought to keep in mind with Maurek in command."

"He is right about reducing the numbers of rebels while we can . . . unfortunately."

While Cyran readied the second group, Alastar worried. He was still worrying when the six imagers rode south to form up with the three-company group commanded by Maurek. Part of that was his worry that Cyran was too defensive in his outlook.

But it could be said that you take the offensive too readily. And how much of Cyran's apparent reluctance was deference? Alastar didn't know, but suspected he might just find out over the next week or so, if not sooner.

By the fourth glass of the afternoon, Alastar found himself glancing to the south all too often, even though he knew it was hardly likely that

Cyran and the second group of imagers could return before fifth or sixth glass.

At fifth glass, Alastar noticed companies of troopers mounting up and riding south.

He immediately made his way to the command tent where Wilkorn offered a knowing glance. "I thought I'd be seeing you. We just got a messenger from Maurek. The ambush went well, and they're on the way back. He's being chased by almost a mounted battalion. We're sending reinforcements."

"The imagers?"

"That's all I know."

"Maurek had almost a battalion when he left here," Alastar said. "If the ambush went well . . ."

"He wouldn't withdraw if it weren't absolutely necessary."

From the commander's words the day before, Alastar had no doubts about that, but a withdrawal raised other questions. Had the imagers run into trouble? Or was more than a battalion in pursuit? Yet there was little he could do . . . except gather the first group of imagers if it became necessary.

At two quints past sixth glass, a messenger galloped up to the command tent. Before he could even dismount, Alastar and Wilkorn were standing there.

"The rebels saw the reinforcements and turned back, sirs. A little less than three milles south of here."

"Thank you. You can go."

That was all that Wilkorn said, but Alastar could read the relief in the marshal's face and posture.

Once the messenger had ridden off, the marshal shook his head. "That's closer than either of us planned."

"Everything's been that way."

"From the beginning." Wilkorn shook his head. "Told you, Maitre, that I was getting too old for this sort of thing. Even with two good arms." He glanced down at the still-splinted arm.

Almost another glass passed before the vanguard of the returning troopers rode up the road and into the encampment. Alastar made his way toward the imager encampment, then waited and watched, counting the riders as Cyran reined up. He hurried toward the Maitre D'Esprit. Cyran wasn't pale. He was ashen, his face a sickly gray.

Alastar didn't ask. He just grabbed Cyran's empty water bottle from his saddlebag, uncorked it, and imaged it full of passible if bitter dark lager, then thrust it at the Maitre D'Esprit. "Drink! Now!"

Cyran didn't argue.

Alastar glanced across to the other five. Tiranya was merely pale, as were Taryn and Belsior. Chervyt's face and neck were grayish green, and Julyan's skin looked white.

Alastar made his way to Chervyt first. "Have you had any lager?"

The Maitre D'Aspect just looked at Alastar blankly. Alastar immediately took the junior maitre's water bottle and imaged dark lager into it, then returned it with the same command he'd given Cyran. He did the same with Julyan. When he turned toward Tiranya, she shook her head. "Just a little. We shared what I had."

Alastar still filled all the water bottles. None of the three remaining imagers protested.

More than a quint passed while Alastar and the imagers of the first group helped unsaddle and groom the mounts of the returning imagers. Both Chervyt and Julyan had to be helped from the saddle.

In time, Alastar and Cyran sat at the base of an oak that had seen better days, scattered yellow leaves clearly showing that it had suffered from the earlier drought despite its closeness to the river.

"What happened?"

"We won . . . but we almost didn't survive the victory." Cyran took another swallow from the water bottle he still held. "You image lousy lager, Alastar . . . except it's better than what I can do."

Alastar forced himself to wait.

"The ambush . . . went fine. The company patrolling the road was infantry. They marched right into the crossfire Maurek set up. They lost almost the whole company right off. But there were two companies on the hills, under a concealment, and they opened fire, ripped right into the lead ranks of Maurek's men—even if they couldn't see them."

"But . . . if they were there . . . why wait?" Alastar didn't understand.

"The company that walked into the ambush . . . they weren't troopers—serfs, tenants, prisoners . . ."

"They sacrificed a hundred men . . . in cold blood?"

"That was the plan." Cyran offered a ragged grin. "We upset it a bit. Between Maurek's reserves and the imagers, we pretty much took care of the two companies on the rocky hills. The problem was that the rebels brought in two more companies from the northwest, and another two from Caluse."

"What did you do?"

"Imaged a bridge along the east side of the road, got our imagers together and formed a shield wedge. We used the wooden dart trick to cut through the two companies to the north, and between us and the troopers, we broke through. Likely killed more'n half of those troopers, but we had three mounted companies chasing us, and the troopers were running out of ammunition. A lot of it was passed to the rear-guard. Rear-guard kept up running fire on the rebel troopers behind us. Slowed them down, and cost them more troopers. It was a long ride back. We were too exhausted to image anything, and we only stopped for fractions of a quint at a time. The rebels didn't turn back until a couple of milles south of here. They saw the reinforcements coming from the north, decided maybe they'd lost enough."

"How many troopers did Maurek lose?"

"A good company's worth, maybe more."

"And the rebels?"

"Wouldn't be surprised if it cost them close to a battalion."

"So they might outnumber us by only two to one?"

"It's better than before." Cyran took another swallow of lager. "This isn't bad. Not after a while."

"No lager's that bad if you drink enough . . . until any lager's too much."

"Probably ought to stop. Namer-damned rebels . . . never saw so many bodies, so much blood. Don't think any of the others ever did, either." Cyran forced a grin. "Good thing it's your turn tomorrow, Alastar."

"I told you I had a feeling."

"I know. I hate it when you have those feelings."

"So do I." Alastar stood. "You need some sleep. I know I do, and I haven't had anywhere near the day you've had."

"That's not a bad idea. Not at all." Cyran stood slowly. "I feel as old as you."

"I'm not that much older than you. Just five years."

"That's what a fight like that will do."

As Cyran walked away, Alastar stood there, looking to the bloody orb of Erion, hanging just over the trees on the east side of the river. *Hunter's moon . . . or killing moon?*

He shook his head. He did need sleep.

44

By sixth glass on Jeudi morning, Alastar and Cyran were once more in
the command tent with Maurek and Wilkorn.

"We need to hit them quickly," insisted Maurek. "Keep them off-
balance. Make them feel that it's not safe for them to stay that long in
Caluse. If you could strike in the town itself, while they're regrouping . . ."

"We could certainly use concealments around the town, but we'll
need some support, and there are only a few roads and lanes that lead
into Caluse. I can't imagine that the rebels are going to leave them un-
guarded after yesterday. We could easily get close to any guard forces,
but we'd likely end up in a battle with them, especially if they decide to
stand their ground."

"Yesterday I had some of the scouts looking. They've found some
back lanes that join the main road west from Caluse less than a mille
from the town. That's less than half a mille from one of their encamp-
ments."

"How did they get so close without trouble?" asked Alastar.

"Not much difference in uniforms except for the armbands. We picked
up a score or so of them along the way. I thought they might be useful."

The offhanded way Maurek mentioned the armbands impressed
Alastar. "How many extra milles will we have to ride?"

"Not that many. You can take the same lane where you replaced the
bridge and stay on it until just past the point where you fought the first
skirmish, and if you ride across one bean field, you can get on decent
lanes that will take you there." Maurek pointed to the map. "Here is
where you fought. Now . . . if you go this way . . ."

Alastar saw the possibilities. Still . . . "Those lanes are narrow. If we
get trapped—"

"My best scouts looked into that. There's no easy way to get a large
force to those lanes, except by the ways you're going. If you send scouts
ahead, you can just withdraw if they see a large force. Once you're in the
territory they patrol . . . well . . . we've got enough armbands for the lead
squad. You've said that they only have a few imagers. Are they going to

waste one on a side lane when they need to worry about the river road and the larger ways?"

Alastar had to admit that Maurek had a point there. "Are there cannon at that encampment?"

"There are, but they can't bring cannon to bear that quickly," Wilkorn said.

"That wasn't why I asked. I still don't see the point of risking imagers just to kill even another company's worth of rebel troopers. If we can destroy even some of their powder and cannon . . . that's very much another matter."

"You'd have to get much closer . . ."

"We'd need fewer troopers and fewer imagers. A squad at most," suggested Alastar. "And the armbands would be most useful."

Maurek frowned.

"We won't get close enough to do what we need to do with a larger force."

"He's right about that," added Wilkorn.

"When do you want to leave?"

"The sooner the better."

"You'll have a squad in two to three quints, if not a little sooner," said Wilkorn, a faint smile on his lips.

Once Alastar and Cyran were away from the command tent, Cyran looked to Alastar, "Are you sure I shouldn't be doing this?"

"No, but Maurek's right. This is something that needs to be done quickly, before someone realizes it can be done . . . and I've been successful at doing this before. You could do it . . . tomorrow or the next day."

"What if the rebels have thought about the possibility?"

"It's unlikely. Even if Bettaur is on their side, he wasn't privy to it when we did this the last time."

Cyran smiled. "That's true. He was in a detention cell or under watch."

"Who in the first group has the strongest shields and can hold them the longest?"

"Arion and Seliora. She's not quite as good as some of the others with darts and the like, but her shields are at the level of Maitre D'Esprit. Arion's strong all-around."

"Then I'll take them . . . and lots of lager."

It was a quint before seventh glass when Alastar, Arion, and Seliora headed out, accompanied by the squad from Fifth Company led by Remaylt. While Alastar hadn't requested Remaylt's squad, that decision made sense, since the troopers had worked with the imagers before and knew about concealments and shields.

They covered the mille to the dirt lane in little more than a quint, then headed south. When they reached the bridge that the imagers had built, Alastar turned to Remaylt, riding beside him. "From here on, we'll be riding under a concealment, the way we did at High Holder Laevoryn's. That's why there's no point in sending scouts ahead. You might want to pass that back. We'll rein up while you do." Alastar eased the gray to a halt.

"I've told them that was likely, but I'll let them know."

While Remaylt rode back along the lane, talking to the troopers, Alastar turned in the saddle. "Seliora, Arion, I'd like you two to alternate holding a concealment over the entire group from here on."

Seliora nodded. "I'll start."

"Alternate every quint or so."

"Yes, sir."

Once Remaylt returned, Alastar eased the gelding forward and across the stone bridge. He kept checking the road and the creeping clingweed on each side of the lane, but it appeared few horses had passed since his last withdrawal along the lane. He noted that while standing water in the fields had dropped more, the two sites that he'd originally picked for ambushes still looked usable for those purposes.

Before that long they reached the point where the river and the river road angled slightly more to the southeast, while the lane kept heading south. He slowed the gelding as they came to the crest of the next rise in the lane, but when he reached the top, he could see no sign of rebel troopers on the stretch leading to the hamlet. Nor did he see any on the side lane between the hedgerows. The blackened remains of the apple orchard where the rebels had hidden were far more obvious.

As he rode down the rise, Alastar had to look carefully before he spotted the bean field they would cross to get on a lane more than a hundred yards to the east. *At least, you hope that's the right bean field.*

The slight breeze out of the southwest carried a slight odor of wood smoke and burned wood, suggesting that there still might be embers smoldering in some of the blackened trees. When they passed the orchard, Alastar had a better idea why the fire had burned so hot. The trees had been old, if not ancient.

He tensed some as they neared the hill behind which the rebel reinforcements had hidden, but there was no one there—except a gray-haired woman who looked toward the road in a puzzled fashion, and then hurried westward toward the nearest cot.

Finally, Alastar spied the corner of the stone wall that marked the end of the lane he was seeking. He turned the gray off the lane and tried to pick the widest space between the rows of bean plants. Even so he could see that the gelding's legs were causing some damage to the immature beans. *Immature?* He glanced over to Remaylt, riding down the open row beyond his.

"Isn't this late for beans?"

"Those are bush beans. They plant two, maybe three crops a year." *Another thing you didn't know.*

At the end of the field, Alastar turned south along a small irrigation ditch until he reached the overgrown beginning of a lane that was more like a dirt path. For the first hundred yards, brush and dead branches lined the way, leaving only enough room for a single horse. Then the overgrown lane joined another that angled southeast. At that point, Alastar reined up and turned to Remaylt. "Time to put on the armbands. Seliora, Arion, and I will hold concealments just for ourselves."

"Yes, sir. Armbands in place!"

Once the troopers all had their crimson and red armbands in position, Alastar led the way, passing through another set of orchards, before the lane turned southwest to curve around a large stock pond, although Alastar only saw five cattle grazing on the too-short grass. From the stoop of a cot on the east side of the pond, a dog barked, almost continuously, until a man yelled something.

More than a glass passed as Alastar and the squad navigated the twisting lane, overgrown and barely passible in more than a few places. He could see why Maurek thought it might be useful.

At some time past ninth glass, Alastar reined up less than fifty yards from the road west from Caluse in a space shaded by tall trees, elms, he thought. He adjusted his visor cap and blotted his forehead. The day had become hot, more like summer than late harvest. "Have something to drink. We'll wait a bit and then ease forward."

After taking several long swallows of lager, Alastar began to watch the road. A squad of riders in trooper green with black and crimson armbands rode past, heading west. Then a farm wagon pulled by a single donkey passed the entrance to the lane, heading east toward Caluse.

Two more troopers rode by, messengers from their sashes.

Alastar turned to the squad leader. "Remaylt, you and the squad are going to have to wait here with Seliora. There are too many riders and wagons for us to bring a full squad, even with the armbands. Someone would ask about that large a group once we got to the encampment."

Remaylt looked to protest.

"There's no help for it. If something happens to us, Seliora can get you back safely, but we fully plan to return with you. I'm not exactly eager to attempt the impossible."

"Yes, sir."

"Seliora . . . you know what to do."

"Yes, sir."

"Arion, we might as well get on with this. Keep your concealment large enough so that you can see me."

"Yes, sir." Alastar raised his own concealment and then eased the gray forward, keeping to the edge of the lane. When he reached the end of the lane and the edge of the main road, he slowed, then reined up as four troopers rode past heading east.

The troopers didn't even look in their direction.

"Now," Alastar said in a low voice, walking his mount out and across to the south side of the road where he turned eastward, riding practically on the shoulder. He'd ridden little more than three hundred yards when he saw the black and crimson ensign flying from the portico of the large two-story dwelling—almost a mansion—on the west side of the encampment, overlooking the sea of tents that stretched back from the south side of the west road. He couldn't help but smile. *Of course, Ryentar would take the best dwelling he could find. Should you see if he's there?*

Reluctantly, he shook his head. Ryentar was as much a figurehead as anything else, just another tool used by Ryel, and removing him wouldn't solve the problem of all the other High Holders or the army and its artillery. *Just as removing most of the High Council didn't help.*

"Sir . . ." murmured Arion.

"I'm considering our options. I'd wager that the cannon will be close to the road and on higher ground. There will be more wagons or limbers and horses nearby. Can you see anything like that?"

"Not from here."

The two continued to ride at a pace faster than that of wagons so that no one would run into them. While there were sentries outside the mansion, they were posted at the gates some ten yards back from the road, and neither looked in the direction the two imagers, possibly because there was enough noise from the encampment that began less than thirty yards from the low stone wall separating the dwelling's gardens from what had been fields on the east side. As Alastar passed the stone wall, he looked back again. Several men, possibly officers, stood under an awning on a rear terrace of the large dwelling.

He frowned. *Perhaps . . . just perhaps . . .* He looked at the rows of tents, then glimpsed a line of wagons. That was likely where the powder might be. Then he looked more toward the east end of the encampment. There were plenty of tents there, but he didn't see all that many troopers. In fact, he didn't see any—except a few posted along the front row of tents, those nearest the road. The west end of the encampment, however, was thronging with troopers. He wanted to shrug. He couldn't do anything about troopers who were out on maneuvers or whatever.

Turning his attention back to the western end of the encampment, he said to Arion. "The wagons . . . on the right . . . let's move closer."

At that moment a trooper ran across the path, slamming into the gray's withers. "Watch it, trooper!" snapped Alastar, hoping the voice of command would startle the man enough that he wouldn't catch the slight differences between imager grays and the trooper grayish green, or the imager's visor cap and an officer's visor cap.

"Oh . . . sorry, sir."

"Get on with where you were headed."

"Yes, sir." The trooper fled.

Alastar almost let out a sigh of relief and continued on, trying to foresee others who might run into them, but the grounds were crowded. "Blurring shields," he finally said. Another risk, but necessary. He could hope that the troopers would just see an image of two officers riding through the area.

The first line of wagons were clearly supply wagons, but to their right were cannon limbers and beyond them, neatly lined up in rows, were what looked to be twenty cannon. *Too much metal to easily destroy them.* His eyes continued to search for the power stocks, finally locating a set of wagons surrounded by sandbags, some fifty yards away, with a good ten troopers stationed there, all with rifles at the ready. He thought he saw boxes that could hold shells.

"Can you image hot iron into those boxes of shells and the general area, from where we are now? And hold your shields?"

"Yes, sir."

"I'm going to do something else first. Then when I tell you, image white-hot iron everywhere you can." While trying to draw on the powder stocks farther uphill, Alastar imaged an imitation of an oversized cannon shell into the room immediately behind the terrace of the mansion—with a white-hot iron splinter going into the charge. Then he ordered, "Hot iron into the power stocks and cannon."

Even before he finished speaking, an explosion from the mansion shredded the upper rear wall and the awning. Alastar saw one figure flung outward over the terrace railing. Belatedly, he began to image hot iron. For a moment, nothing seemed to happen. Then his shields were hammered, and hammered again . . . and again.

His ears were ringing with the sound of explosions that seemed to keep occurring.

"We . . . need . . . to get out of here."

"Yes, sir . . . don't think I have any shields left."

"I don't, either." Alastar immediately turned the gray and urged him into a fast trot, as if he were headed toward the mansion.

Arion followed.

Shells continued to explode behind them, and Alastar thought he glimpsed flames as well. All around them, a welter of shouts and orders filled the air. Not totally surprisingly, amid the chaos, they reached the lane without being noticed. He could still hear intermittent explosions, seemingly coming from the direction of the rebel encampment.

Alastar dropped the blurring concealment as they neared Remaylt.

The squad leader gaped for a moment. "Maitre . . . sir? Is that you?"

Alastar wondered if he truly looked that disheveled. "Who else would it be? We're back. We left a mess. Let's go. We need to get away from here before the rebels recover and start looking."

"Yes, sir. Squad! To the rear. If you'd move to the front, sir?"

Alastar nodded. "Seliora?"

"Yes, Maitre?"

"You're the only imager here who can raise protective shields. We got a little too close to the powder."

"A little too close? Both of you—your grays are singed. Some of your hair, too."

Alastar hadn't noticed.

But on the long ride back, he noticed the odor of burned hair more and more. He also worried about the fact that even more than a glass later, as they passed the burned orchard, he still could not hold the slightest of shields for more than a few moments, even after drinking most of the dark lager from his water bottles.

The odor of burned hair still filled his nostrils when, another glass later, he reined up with the other imagers and dismounted to see Cyran hurrying toward him.

"Are you all right?"

"Do I look that bad?"

"Tired. You smell a little like burned hair and cloth." The Maitre D'Esprit glanced at the gray. "Or it might be your horse."

"Both. I am tired. Exhausted. Arion probably is as well, and we're a little singed. I think we set off most of the powder and even some of their cannon shells. Maybe more than that. Seliora had to shield Arion and me on the way back."

"You're sure you're all right?"

"I'm in one piece, without wounds. I'm tired and sore, and I need to report to Wilkorn. You should come with me."

Cyran motioned. "Dylert! The Maitre needs to meet with the marshal. If you would take care of his horse."

"Yes, sir."

"Thank you, Dylert." Alastar nodded to the younger maitre. "I do appreciate your help." *Especially after a day like this.*

Alastar's legs ached even more by the time he and Cyran reached the command tent, although they had walked only a few hundred yards. Alastar didn't bother announcing them; he just walked into the tent where the two senior officers sat on camp stools behind the table with the maps.

While Maurek said nothing, Wilkorn frowned as he looked at Alastar. "Did you ride through a fire or something?"

"Not exactly. We managed to reach the rebel encampment just west of Caluse. We likely destroyed most of their powder and shells. The explosion of powder and shells killed a number of troopers and also killed at least some of the senior officers . . ."

"Do you have any idea of the casualties?" pressed Maurek.

"We weren't in any condition to stay around and count. Neither Arion nor I had shields enough to matter left after the blast. There were several hundred officers and troopers in the area, but the wagons were sandbagged, and that likely limited the effect of the blast near the ground. There were still some shells exploding when we escaped the encampment and began the ride back here."

"You couldn't tell—"

"You wouldn't have been able to tell, either," said Alastar. "The explosions from the powder cases or magazines kept going off. Men were yelling. Horses were screaming. Officers were shouting orders, and there was smoke everywhere. Some flames, too."

"Before all this began, what did you see at the encampment?" asked Wilkorn.

"There were rebel troopers riding everywhere. The cannon were neatly drawn up with the wagons and limbers on the west side of the encampment . . ." Alastar went on to describe what he had seen of the encampment, including the mansion that had appeared to serve as a headquarters. "Since it didn't seem as though we'd have much time before we were discovered, or before one of the rebel troopers who bumped into us and got inside the blurring concealments reported something to senior officers, as soon as we located the cannon and powder, we immediately torched everything we could and then made our escape."

"Did anyone chase you?"

"No one besides those few troopers even noticed us."

Almost two quints passed before Wilkorn and Maurek finished with their questions and Alastar and Cyran walked back toward the imagers' area.

From somewhere drifted a fragment of song, sung loudly and slightly off-key, not that Alastar was one to judge, given that he seldom could remain on tune, even with the hymns to the Nameless that he'd sung since he'd been a boy in Westisle.

> . . . a holder boyo came to town
> a-riding in his carriage,
> slapped a silver on a cheated plaque
> and called it noble marriage . . .

Absently, Alastar wondered from which gaming house that song had originally come.

"They didn't mention any plans for tomorrow," observed Cyran. "Or what they want from us."

"That's because they didn't expect us to be that successful. I'm certain that they'll want something by tomorrow morning . . . or even later this evening." *And whatever it might be will likely be even more dangerous.* But Alastar didn't voice that thought. All he really wanted was something to eat and some time to rest . . . and sleep.

45

Although Alastar slept soundly, more like the sleep of the dead, when he woke on Vendrei morning, it felt as though every muscle and bone in his body ached. More worrying was the fact that he could only raise the weakest of shields.

He thought the breakfast of dried ham and milk gravy over biscuits, with hot too-strong tea, helped, but not enough to make that much difference with his shields. After he finished eating, standing by the teamsters' wagon, he turned to Arion, who had eaten earlier but who was still sipping tea from his tin cup. "How are you feeling this morning?"

"A touch sore, sir. Otherwise, I'm all right."

"What about your shields?"

"I'm not quite at full strength, but almost."

"That's good. With some moderate fortune, you won't need them today." Alastar managed a cheerful smile, thankful that Arion seemed not much worse for the wear.

As he walked away, he caught sight of Chervyt and Julyan, standing together, seemingly bantering with Dylert and Taurek. *Were you ever that unconcerned?* Then again, Chervyt probably wasn't as unconcerned as he appeared, not after his loss in attacks on Imagisle thirteen years earlier.

Alastar shook his head, worried about how long it might take him to recover . . . and what Wilkorn and Maurek had in mind for the imagers.

Much as he didn't really feel up to it, he walked south to the command tent and made his way inside. Wilkorn turned from where he had been talking to Maurek. "Yes, Maitre?"

"What are the rebels doing right now?"

"They're still cleaning up the mess you made," said Wilkorn.

"That's not all," added Maurek. "There's only about a regiment left in Caluse, and the scouts can't find a trace of troopers anywhere else. There are tents in the west encampment, but almost no one is there."

"Half of the encampment wasn't there. . . ." Alastar stopped. There had been no trace of imagers either. "Are all three—or two and a half—regiments still in Caluse? Have your scouts actually seen the troopers?"

Wilkorn frowned.

"The scouts only confirmed a regiment or so," said Maurek.

"I wondered about the lack of troopers in the eastern rows of tents, yesterday, and there was no sign of any imagers. Now, if your scouts are seeing troopers—"

"You think the imagers are covering the movement of a large group of troopers?"

"I wouldn't be surprised if the troopers left in Caluse are the High Holder volunteers, and that Aestyn's best troopers are moving north somewhere to the west of us at this moment. Can they get all the way to L'Excelsis without using the river road?"

"Not quickly." Maurek pointed to the map on the table. "They'd have to circle Lake Shaelyt to the west, but the ground to the north and west of the lake is mostly marshes, unless they wanted to go almost twenty milles west."

"So they have to go through that hamlet on the northwest side of Lake Shaelyt and back to the river road to get to L'Excelsis faster than you would?" asked Alastar.

"Or they could take the road between the smaller lake just north of us and Lake Shaelyt, replied Maurek, "but that would be awfully close to us."

"That was likely their original plan," suggested Alastar, "before they lost all that power and much of their ammunition."

"Original plan?" questioned Maurek.

"Either way, I think we need to withdraw at least to the highest point on the road north of Lake Shaelyt," declared Wilkorn.

"I don't like giving up this position. We're still outnumbered," said Maurek.

"That's not your biggest problem," said Alastar quietly, angry at himself that he hadn't seen what all the empty tents had really meant. "If they get around us, they'll take the Chateau D'Rex, and remove Lorien. They'll make Ryentar rex, and then we'll have to take them on while they hold the chateau—which is almost impregnable," declared Alastar. "Most people don't like Lorien that well, and the Codex Legis gives the rex the power to change the laws. If Ryentar immediately restores the ancient powers of the High Holders . . ."

Maurek looked stunned.

"Frig . . ." muttered Wilkorn. "We're moving out now! I'll have two companies moving in a quint. Can your imagers be ready in the van?"

"We'll be ready."

"Maurek, get scouts out to the west."

"Yes, sir."

In less than a quint Alastar found himself riding north along the river road with Wilkorn, immediately in front of the imagers and directly behind a squad from Weidyn's Fifth Company, acting as vanguard. The remainder of Fifth Company rode behind the imagers, followed by Major Luerryn and Eighth Company.

"Aestyn likely planned this from the start—tricky bastard," Wilkorn was as much muttering as talking. "Set us up here. Then bring up the cannon and pound at us, while the bulk of his force swings behind us. If we had to withdraw after the cannon were in place, we would have been under attack on two fronts. If we'd held, then he would have gotten between us and L'Excelsis, and we've have had to attack a superior force, and he would have been free to withdraw to L'Excelsis and do exactly what you suggested. If we don't cut off that battalion, he still could." After a moment, the marshal added, "Good work with the cannon. Without that, we'd have been in even more trouble."

"I wish I'd realized about the empty tents earlier," Alastar admitted.

"My scouts didn't pick up on it, and you were in the middle of explosions."

Alastar couldn't help but wonder what else he'd failed to notice . . . and should have.

Almost two glasses passed, and by that time, Alastar and the imagers were well north of their former encampment and roughly a mille south and two milles east of the northern end of Lake Shaelyt. They were also a great deal hotter, and the air was still, although Alastar could see a line of dark clouds to the northeast that seemed to be creeping toward them. At that moment, he also saw a single trooper, most likely a scout, riding swiftly south on the river road toward them. The scout rode immediately to Wilkorn, who did not slow his mount, but motioned the scout to ride beside him.

"What can you report?" asked the marshal.

"There's more than a battalion of mounted infantry three milles west of the hamlet, sir. They're moving at a fast walk. There's a lot of dust on the road farther behind the battalion, all the way into the forest on that road that cuts through it. The others are trying to find out more, but lead scout Vactyr sent me to tell you about the battalion."

"Good. Now head back and post yourself where you can watch the hamlet. Let me know as soon as you can whether that battalion stops at the hamlet or keeps moving. We'll be on the high ground northeast of the hamlet on the river road."

"Yes, sir." The scout inclined his head, then turned his mount and headed north along the road."

Wilkorn turned to Alastar. "We're between two and three milles from where we need to be to stop them, and they're closer to six." He shook his head. "Good thing we headed out when we did. Need to send a messenger back to Maurek to tell him to push."

While Wilkorn summoned a messenger and briefed him, Alastar tried to make out the terrain immediately ahead. According to the maps, most of the area north of the flat land surrounding the hamlet was swampy and marshlike, and the downpours over the previous month doubtless had only made the marshes even less passable. Even so there was between a quint and two quints of higher solid ground on the west side of the river road, which stretched for several milles before widening out into the higher fields south of L'Excelsis.

Meaning that you have to get into position just north of the road from the hamlet and hold that ground to keep the rebels from getting through.

"Are your imagers ready to do what they can if that battalion tries to break through?" asked Wilkorn, his voice interrupting Alastar's study.

"All but one or two." Alastar wasn't about to admit that he was one of those not at full strength.

"We may need every one of you."

Alastar nodded.

Less than a glass passed before a messenger galloped up along the shoulder of the road shouting, "Message for the marshal! Message for the marshal!"

Whatever it is, thought Alastar, *it's not good news.*

Wilkorn gestured. "Here! Over here!"

The messenger pulled in beside the commander.

"What is it?"

"Commander Maurek is under attack by at least a battalion. He's sent the remainder of Major Luerryn's battalion to join you at a faster pace. He will close with you as soon as he can."

Wilkorn looked like he wanted to swear, but he only nodded. "Thank you. Tell the commander we will be holding the road north of Lake Shaelyt in order to keep the lead elements of the rebel forces from proceeding to L'Excelsis."

"Yes, sir."

Once the messenger was headed back south, Wilkorn snorted. "It might have been better if we'd just invested that hamlet over there."

"It would have been harder to do the damage we did from here," Alastar pointed out.

"True enough, but there's a price for everything." Under his breath, with words Alastar could barely hear, the marshal added, "Especially overlooking the obvious. Too frigging old for this."

At the risk of intruding on what might have been meant as private musings, Alastar said quietly, "If two gray-haired men hadn't said a few things, Rex Lorien would likely be facing certain removal."

"And if a gray-haired marshal hadn't let himself be persuaded, we'd be in good position and not racing to be outflanked." Wilkorn shook his head, then said, "Doesn't matter. Regrets are a waste of time and breath."

Within another quint, a trooper rode forward to Wilkorn. "From Major Luerryn, sir. Eighth Company has rearguard, sir."

"Convey my thanks to the major."

"Yes, sir."

As Alastar, Wilkorn, and the imagers reached a point where the small hamlet lay due west and the point where the side road joined the river road was less than two quints of a mille ahead, Alastar looked at the narrow side road more intently. There was something about the road. The mille and two quints or so that were closest to the road appeared like any other dirt road. So did the next quint mille, but there was something about the grass and bushes on each side, as if a light breeze were blowing. His eyes traveled farther west, where he could see the first ranks of the mounted infantry—no more than two companies—riding past the hamlet at a steady pace, still almost three milles from the river road.

What happened to the rest of the mounted infantry? He studied the narrow road again. *Frig! They're under a concealment and moving at fast trot, most likely.*

"Marshal . . . the first two or three companies of the rebels' mounted infantry is halfway to the river road. They're riding under a concealment. Send the vanguard and imagers. We can at least slow them."

"Sowshit! The whole Namer-fired column can do two quints at a full trot." Wilkorn raised his voice to a shout! "Column! Forward! Full trot!"

Alastar turned in the saddle and said back to Cyran and Akoryt, "Can you see where the bushes and grasses are moving, even though here's no wind? I'd wager that's half a battalion under a concealment."

"Won't take that wager."

"I'm guessing. We'll have a little time after we form up. Make sure they all have some lager. They'll need it."

"Yes, sir."

Less than a full quint later, the column halted with the southern end of the column positioned just north of the side road. In moments, Wilkorn was re-forming the two companies into a wedge formation. Alastar positioned the imagers on the right side, close to the northern end of the formation, where they could use imaging if the rebels attempted to squeeze between the formation and the marshland some two hundred yards west of the imagers.

Then he addressed the imagers. "I don't want any of you wasting your strength. When the attacking troopers get close enough, and I order darts to the attackers, I want you, Arion, to put a dart in the eye of the trooper on the far right side of the front rank. Dylert, count one, and take the next trooper. . . . Keep doing it that way as long as you can. After that, those of you in back, aim for troopers nearer the rear. Those in front, aim for the middle. . . ." When Alastar finished his instructions, he eased his mount back and positioned himself behind and just slightly to one side of Seliora, something he felt strange about. *But she has strong shields, and you won't be doing anyone any favors by getting killed needlessly.*

As the attackers neared, as evidenced by the motion of the grasses and brush, and the sound of hoofs, the concealment of the oncoming troopers remained in place. That worried him. *Exactly what are they concealing?*

It couldn't be cannon, not at the pace at which they rode up the almost imperceptible slope toward Wilkorn's waiting troopers.

When Alastar judged that the lead elements were just over two hundred yards away, and just past the flat yellow marker he had imaged beside the road, he ordered, "Junior maitres! Red pepper fog! From the marker to fifty yards back! All the way across the road."

The vague outlines of troopers appeared, coated in red mists . . . and then the concealment vanished. The attackers were packed into a tight formation five abreast.

Apparently seeing the tight formation, Wilkorn immediately ordered, "Fire at will!"

For all the bullets flying toward the attackers, not a single attacker dropped or staggered, which explained why the attackers were formed up so closely, although Alastar did not see any obvious imagers.

"Keep firing!" Alastar projected.

The lead ranks of the attackers raised their rifles and fired, not all that swiftly, and some were definitely having trouble seeing and aiming. At the same time, a few of Luerryn's troopers had been hit.

"More pepper!" Alastar ordered.

Abruptly, the lead riders among the attackers began to fall, and those behind turned the attackers toward the gap between the imagers and the marshy lands to the west, as if aiming to squeeze into the open space and sprint for the river road.

"Imagers! Measured darts to the attackers. Now!"

Ten of the first twelve riders went down, and then more behind them.

Just as suddenly a burst of flame appeared over the front rank of the defenders. For an instant, Alastar gaped, not believing what he'd seen, then used what imaging strength he had to drop it back onto the attackers. "They're imaging Antiagon fire! Image it back onto to their troopers!" He found himself breathing hard, but not feeling weak. *Not yet.* He also realized that he'd missed a small part of the Antiagon fire that had dropped on several of Luerryn's troopers, turning them into charred figures, at least one of whom was still moving and screaming.

Another gout of flame appeared, but one of Alastar's imagers flung it in a line across the troopers aiming for the gap. Then more of the attackers went down with darts in them. The pace of fire from the defenders picked up.

After another burst of Antiagon fire flew toward the defenders, but was imaged back across the rebel troopers trying to get to the river road, charring several ranks, a horn sounded, and the attackers turned and began to withdraw.

Only when it was clear that the attackers were truly withdrawing did Wilkorn order, "Hold your fire!"

Alastar surveyed the area between the imagers and the marshes. A quick count suggested more than a hundred of the attackers' mounted infantry lay dead or likely dying just there. Farther to the south the carnage was even greater. For a moment he wondered why the rebels hadn't persisted. Some very well might have gotten through. *But not enough to proceed to L'Excelsis and do what they had in mind.* He looked out to the west. The rebels were indeed withdrawing to the hamlet at the northwest end of the lake.

Wilkorn rode up to Alastar and reined in his mount. "Were those yellow-greenish flames Antiagon fire?"

"That's what it seemed to be," replied Alastar. "The last time I saw that was when Chesyrk used it on the Army High Command at Ryen's memorial service."

"Hehnsyn and Marryt were both junior officers then," said the marshal. "But . . . I thought it took an imager to create it."

"They could have taken the formula. They've obviously had an imager for a while."

"Nasty stuff."

"We might see more of it."

"So long as you and your imagers can handle it, that may be the least of our problems. I just got a messenger from Maurek. They held off the rebels, and he's moving to join us. It appears that the rebels have re-formed and are following, and they've been joined by the regiment of High Holder troopers from Caluse. They have five cannon, from what his scouts show."

"How many do we have?"

"Eight. We had to leave two in L'Excelsis. One turned out to be flawed, might have exploded if we used it, and someone damaged the other one . . . ruined the trunnion on one side. Could have been done years ago."

"You might think about spacing the cannon out," suggested Alastar. "The rebels might try what we did this evening or early tomorrow morning."

"I've already planned for that. We'll also be using earthworks and putting the foot behind them. That way they can fire from cover with minimal exposure. I hadn't thought we'd be able to do that."

That comment puzzled Alastar, given that firing from cover seemed far preferable to firing from a position where one was fully exposed. "Why not?"

"They have greater numbers. I would have thought that they would attack in waves and from angles and in places where we couldn't afford to dig in, for one reason or another. If we had dug in, they just would have gone around us, and the effort would have been wasted. This way, they've boxed themselves in."

Alastar frowned, then almost nodded, but because he wanted to hear what Wilkorn had to say, he replied, "Aren't we the ones boxed in?"

"That's true, but we've shown that we can whittle them down with far fewer losses than they've taken. They're running out of time and men, and resources. They feel they have to break through and win."

"If they do, Lorien is finished." *And the position of the Collegium will be close to untenable.*

Wilkorn laughed harshly. "We both know that losing Lorien as rex would be no great loss. Putting his brother on the throne at the beck and call of the High Holders would be a disaster for Solidar. That's why both of us know that we have to use this situation to destroy the rebels or weaken them so greatly that they're not only defeated, but perceived by other High Holders as defeated."

"The only problem with that," Alastar pointed out, "is that the only High Holders directly linked to the revolt are all dead, except for Ryentar. Lorien might be able to make a case against Caervyn, but he's the only one besides Ryentar for whom there's any real proof. The only one living, besides Ryentar, that is."

"What a frigging mess." Wilkorn shook his head.

Alastar thought the marshal's assessment was exceedingly understated.

"They'll likely attack early tomorrow. That's Aestyn's preference. Usually, anyway. We'll talk later."

Alastar turned his mount, only to see that Cyran and Akoryt had eased their mounts closer. "How much did you two overhear?"

"Enough," said Cyran dryly.

"How is everyone?"

"All the imagers are close to full strength," replied Cyran.

Akoryt nodded.

"In case you didn't overhear it all," said Alastar, "it appears that the rebels are massing all their forces. Wilkorn believes they'll make an all-out attack early tomorrow morning. You two talk it over, and see if you can come up with anything else we should do. We'll get together later. I need to find Captain Weidyn."

"Yes, sir."

Weidyn wasn't that hard to find, since he was less than a hundred yards away, standing at the edge of the road, clearly having left his mount elsewhere . . . or had it shot from under him.

"Maitre . . . what can I do for you?"

"I was wondering. Have you issued those special bullets?"

"No, sir."

"It might be a good idea to do so before tomorrow."

"Much as I dislike the idea, sir, I'm afraid you're right. Especially after they used that yellow-green fire."

"Antiagon fire."

"Is that what it was? I heard about that, but I never saw it before. Nasty stuff. Where did they get it?"

"Subcommander Hehnsyn or Subcommander Marryt must have gotten the formula from army files and persuaded a renegade imager to make it." More likely to image it, but that was something that Alastar didn't want to get into.

"Is there anything else, sir."

"Not right now." Alastar smiled pleasantly and turned his mount back toward where Cyran had gathered the imagers.

46

Alastar woke well before the sun on Samedi morning. Knowing that he would not sleep longer, no matter how long he lay on his makeshift bed, he slowly rose and stretched, trying to get the aches and soreness out of his muscles, trying to ignore all the reminders that he wasn't as young as he liked to think he was. He checked his shields . . . and was relieved that he seemed able to hold them without strain. The last thing he needed was to be unshielded or to have to rely on one of the other imagers for protection.

There was neither a glimmer of light to the east nor were there many night sounds outside of the chirping of crickets. Unlike birds, crickets didn't stay quiet unless someone was moving and close enough to step on them. Erion was still fairly high in the western sky, but gibbous, while Artiema, nearly full, was close to setting. *The hunter's moon will see the day hunt.* A sardonic grin crossed Alastar's lips and vanished.

Once he was fully dressed, he walked toward the upper level of the low earthwork revetments set in a semi-circle, careful to stay well back from the troopers manning them as he looked first south along the river road, and then westward toward the hamlet, where he saw several points of light that had to be fires, most likely cookfires. Although he, Cyran, and Akoryt had discussed possible imager tactics the night before, none of them had come up with anything new. The only questions were those relating to when to use what tactic or ability and how to space out which imagers were dealing with the attackers so that some were always ready to step forward.

Alastar had no doubts that the day ahead would be long, one way or another, as he made his way to the imager wagon for an early breakfast, most likely of porridge and tea. Cyran was already there, not totally surprisingly.

"The rebels had their cookfires going early this morning," said the senior imager after a mouthful of porridge. "What sort of imaging do you think we'll face today?"

"I wish I knew. There's only so much two imagers can do, but Bettaur's as strong as a Maitre D'Structure."

"We haven't seen that sort of strength yet." Cyran sipped tea from his tin cup. "They're probably saving him for something special. Where do you think we'll be?"

"Most likely in two groups, but not too far apart, and under a concealment so that they can't target cannon at us . . . at least until we can get rid of their cannon, one way or another. The objective today is simple. Destroy every possible rebel ranker and officer. We don't want to have to fight another battle."

"No tactical victories, then?" Cyran offered an exaggerated smile.

"Not unless they're total."

"And you'll promise not to make any heroic sacrifices so that I don't have to tell Alyna?" While Cyran's tone was humorous, Alastar could sense a certain concern behind the words.

"No heroic sacrifices, I promise. I'd like to have the rebels make heroic and futile sacrifices."

"That makes two of us," returned Cyran.

After eating hurriedly, Alastar made his way to the command tent.

Wilkorn was there alone, sitting behind the camp table where a small lantern illuminated the map spread before him. He looked up. "Morning, Alastar. How does it feel to be one of the two gray eminences . . . fighting a revolt that never should have been, caused by pride, ignorance, arrogance, and greed?"

"About the same as you do, I imagine. Except I feel gray, and not much like an eminence of any kind. But hasn't every revolt or war been caused or fueled by pride, ignorance, arrogance, and greed?"

Wilkorn laughed harshly, then winced, and adjusted the sling that still held his broken arm. "Any that I've ever heard of. To win will require the greatest slaughter I'll ever be a part of, and . . . and if we lose, the same will be true. The pity of it all is that almost all of those who created this mess are either already dead or will never be called to account—except by the Nameless . . . if there even is a Nameless."

"Can you tell if Ryentar is here?"

"The scouts report a group flying his banners, and it appears to be the command group. Well back, of course."

Alastar wouldn't have expected any less of Ryentar, whether as the disinherited brother of the rex or as High Holder Regial. "He must be confident, then, because his life is forfeit just for being this close to L'Excelsis."

"From what I've seen and from what you've said, he's never lacked for either confidence or arrogance. It runs in a certain bloodline. Aestyn's in actual command. I'm certain."

"And Ryentar's here to inspire the rebels . . . to lead them into a new and better day for Solidar . . . and especially for the High Holders."

"Of course." Wilkorn straightened, wincing slightly. "How do you plan to deploy and use your imagers?"

"The best way I can think of is to get rid of their cannon and kill as many of them as possible. Here's what I have in mind. . . ."

All that Alastar said took far less than half a quint. When he finished, he looked to the marshal. "Does that upset anything you and Maurek had planned?"

Wilkorn shook his head. "Except for the cannon, Maurek feels that the later the imagers can be used the more effective they'll be. So what you've outlined goes with what he's planned, even to where you intend to muster your imagers."

"Then I'd better get back to them."

Wilkorn was back looking at the map even before Alastar had left the tent.

By the time the eastern sky was graying, columns of rebel foot and mounted infantry were moving from the hamlet and from an encampment to the south toward Wilkorn's forces.

Major Rykards's foot rankers manned the revetments of the defenders, their rifles in hand, while Luerryn's mounted infantry was mustered to the east of the river, partly shielded by the slope down to the water, with Fifth Company to the north, behind where the imagers would be, Eighth Company farthest to the south, with the other mounted infantry companies between them. The eight cannon were in sandbagged pits, their muzzles barely visible even from a few yards away . . . and their powder trunks and ammunition well out of sight. *That ought to make their imagers work to even find them.*

Alastar had gathered the imagers, not yet mounted. He looked over the junior maitres—copper-haired Julyan with his ready smile standing beside Chervyt; Chervyt, who had lost a lover in the last mess, but still was there to give all he had for the Collegium; then Dylert, so steady and determined; Taurek, burly, broad-shouldered, and more than accomplished enough to be a Maitre D'Structure; Seliora, who probably should have been one already; and finally, Belsior, not the most gifted, but hardworking, and enormously pleased to be an imager at all. To one side were Cyran and the senior maitres—Arion, Khaelis, Tiranya, and Taryn.

"Our task in the coming mess is to see what we can do to take out the rebel cannons . . . and hold back as much as possible until later in the fighting . . . when we're likely to be more effective . . . and less easily targeted if we can't take out all the cannon . . ."

Three quints later, Alastar rode toward the south end of the revetments, accompanied by Arion. Once on slightly higher ground, under a concealment, he and Arion reined up.

"We're looking for cannon . . . and for ammunition wagons or powder trunks. Since the ground slopes away from us rather gently, and there aren't any real hills or hillocks, we ought to be able to find them now that we're getting better light."

"Yes, sir."

Alastar was still looking when Arion spoke again. "Sir? Do you see those three bushes four hundred yards or so down the road to the hamlet?"

"I do."

"About three hundred yards, I guess, due south, there's what might be a revetment, concealed by bushes, and there are wagons. One of them looks like a long trunk on carriage wheels."

"That's a powder trunk." Alastar squinted. After several moments, as the early-morning light strengthened, he could make out what seemed to be the muzzles of two cannon, but only the one powder trunk. "I can only see two cannon."

"That's what I see. Just two of them. I don't see anything like that emplacement anywhere nearby."

"Let's look on the other side of the hamlet road, then." Alastar shifted his attention northward, toward the ground just south of the marshlands.

Once again, Arion spoke first. "Do you see that place in the marsh where the reeds are higher?"

"Yes."

"Fifty yards back and a little to the left . . ."

"I see them. Three cannon muzzles. Two powder trunks. The trunks are half hidden in the reeds." In both instances, once Arion had pointed them out, Alastar had had no trouble seeing them. But *you couldn't see them first.* "Can you image something that far?"

"If it's small."

"Let me see what I can do." Alastar focused on the emplacement near the reeds, since it was slightly closer, if still a good seven hundred yards. He concentrated on imaging a single very thin, white-hot, iron needle inside one of those magazines. Nothing happened. He took a long swallow of lager, waited a bit, and tried again . . . with no better success. The third time, the wagon exploded. How much damage resulted, Alastar had no way of knowing, given that white smoke wreathed the entire area.

"There must have been a lot of powder there."

"Enough, anyway."

"How did you do that, sir?"

"A thin, very thin, white-hot iron needle inside the powder trunk. Why don't you try that on the other emplacement?" Alastar blotted his suddenly perspiring forehead with his sleeve. Imaging a hot iron needle that far had been work. *A lot more work than something like that used to be.* That was something he really didn't want to think about. Instead, he watched Arion concentrate on the rebel emplacement.

"Needle's not that hard . . . harder to aim."

After a time, a second explosion and a cloud of white smoke marked where a powder trunk had once been.

"Excellent!" Alastar estimated that the younger maitre had likely imaged more needles than Alastar had, but Arion had merely appeared annoyed, rather than flushed.

"That was tricky."

Technique helped, Alastar decided, as Gauswn had once written about Quaeryt, but there was no doubt he didn't have quite the raw power he'd once been able to summon. "Tricky, but effective. Let's get back to the others and hope that they can't come up with more powder." In point of fact, Alastar had had no intention of trying to destroy any cannon, not given the distance and the imaging effort it would take just to destroy the powder, without which a cannon was just a big bronze tube.

Alastar couldn't help but notice the line of black and crimson banners near the rear of the rebel forces. Behind the banners was perhaps a half company mounted in black uniforms, trimmed in crimson. At least, that was the impression Alastar got.

He continued to study the advancing forces, beginning to re-form about three-quarters of a mille from the arc of the revetments holding Wilkorn's troopers. If the formations of the rebels were any indication, their battle plan was simple. One group would advance north along the river road, and two would advance across the sloping grasslands. Between the two forces, apparently readying to advance eastward on the east side of the road from the hamlet to the river, was a much smaller force, little more than a squad with a wagon, except the wagon was being pushed by a team of oxen. All of that pointed to a direct and headlong advance against riflemen in protected positions, which seemed suicidal, given how exposed the attackers would be.

Concealments. The rebels were already forming up far enough away from the defenders that accurate fire would be difficult, even for Wilkorn's few cannon. Then the rebel imagers would raise concealments, and the attackers would move quickly in a mass rush to get as close to the defenders' revetments as possible, most likely within a few yards.

"You need to get back to the other imagers," declared Alastar, "and I need to see the marshal immediately. Tell Maitre Cyran that we may need a great deal of pepper far sooner than anticipated."

"Yes, sir." Arion turned his mount toward the river.

As Alastar rode toward the command tent, he still wondered why a cart pushed by oxen was moving into position between two of the three masses of attackers. *It has to have something to do with the attack.* He just couldn't figure out what, although he had no doubt it would become blindingly obvious at the most inopportune time.

When he reached the command tent, he handed the gelding's reins to one of the troopers standing guard and hurried inside. Maurek and Wilkorn immediately turned.

"I don't know if this is going to happen," said Alastar, "but the rebels are forming up for an all-out attack. That's not as suicidal as it seems. . . ." he explained quickly.

"What can your imagers do?" demanded Maurek.

"I don't know any way of breaking a concealment. We can hamper those being hidden by it, but not until they get closer to our lines, or close enough that we can hear them or determine roughly where they are."

"Why not earlier?" asked Maurek.

"It wouldn't do much good, and it would tire the imagers. First, we can't see where they are, and we don't have enough imagers to image pepper everywhere. Even if we were fortunate enough to hit some of them, they can move out of the spray, and we wouldn't know exactly where they were . . . not until they're almost on top of the troopers. Once their troopers reach our lines, our men would be inside the concealment

as well, and able to see all of the attackers. If the rebels keep the concealment just short of our lines, then their men won't be able to see if they
were supported or left out there all alone. Maintaining such a large concealment for a long time takes great effort. So they might drop it just
before their leading troopers reached our lines."

"Their columns are tight right now," said Maurek.

"If they go with a concealment, once it's in place, they'll likely
move to a different location or formation. It might be useful to fire at
where the column was immediately after their troopers vanish. That's
if they're in range. You might get some of them that way, while they're
still close together."

"What if they don't use a concealment?" asked Wilkorn.

"Then when they get closer we'll begin by blanketing them with pepper mist . . . and we'll concentrate on dealing with groups or attackers
that seem to be giving your troopers trouble. That won't change from
what we discussed before. What I wanted you to know was that the
attackers might seem to disappear while they were actually still moving forward to attack."

"Pass that to your officers immediately," Wilkorn said to Maurek.

"I'm on my way."

"So am I," added Alastar.

Alastar hadn't even ridden all the way back to the river road, east of
which the imagers were mustered, when the two columns of attackers
directly west of the defenders vanished from sight. The column to the
south, while drawn up and appearing ready to move, remained visible,
stationary, and out of accurate rifle range, and just dispersed enough that
cannon wouldn't be that effective.

Now what are you going to do?

Cyran and Akoryt hurried toward him as he reined up.

"They've thrown a concealment over the forces moving toward us
from the west. I'm guessing they'll hold it until their troopers are almost
on top of ours. The only thing I can think of is to move the imagers
forward, also under a concealment, and wait for their troopers to show
up. If we space the imagers out, and tell each to deal only with attackers in front of them, that would keep them from targeting the same
rebel troopers. Mostly anyway." When neither responded immediately,
Alastar asked, "Any other ideas?"

The two looked at each other.

"No, sir," Akoryt finally said.

"I knew Bettaur was strong, but . . ." Cyran shook his head.

"It's actually a good way of using only a few imagers," Alastar pointed out. Concealments are easier than shields . . ." He broke off. "Of course!"

"Of course what?" Cyran didn't hide his puzzlement.

"I saw a wagon being pushed by a team of oxen. I'd wager that the front of the wagon is armored, and that Bettaur and Ashkyr are inside. The wagon will move with the troopers, and the two imagers won't have to worry about shields—just about maintaining the concealment."

"They couldn't have thought that up on the spur of the moment," Cyran pointed out, in his always practical manner. "That would take a special yoke and harness arrangement."

"None of this revolt has been planned as a spur-of-the-moment uprising, no matter how much it seems that way. That includes all the petitions. This has been going on for years. The drought and then the late rains just made it seem that way." Alastar shook his head. "We need to mount up everyone and space them up behind the revetments, fairly far back, because they won't be able to do much until they can see the attackers. We can talk about how it all happened later." *If we manage to survive this disaster.*

Despite Alastar's concerns and worries, it still took almost half a quint before he had the other twelve imagers mounted and in position some sixty yards back from the second line of trenched earthworks, with Cyran positioned a third of the way in from the south end of the line, while he had taken a position a third of the way in from the northern end of the imagers. Each imager was separated from the next by ten yards, and, in addition to personal shields, each held a screen concealment, a yard or so in front of his or her mount, which allowed Alastar and Cyran to see them all.

When Alastar looked out to the west, he shivered at the seeming unreality before him, an expanse of grass and harvested fields that appeared empty, but over which marched a good thousand men, if not more, unseen. He could still see about half the number of rebel troopers as before, but all those who remained unconcealed were mounted, while those he couldn't see, he realized from his much earlier observations, were foot troopers. Again, that made sense, allowing the men on foot to advance at a measured pace without too much fear of being shot, while saving the faster-moving mounted troopers for action when or if the concealment collapsed.

Abruptly, at the sound of a horn, rifle shots rang out from in front of the defenders' earthworks. The sound suggested to Alastar that the attackers were still perhaps twenty yards or more back from the lower revetments.

"Imagers! Twenty yards beyond the revetments! Red pepper fog!"

Alastar watched, but saw nothing. Even though he'd expected that, it was still slightly unnerving. At the very least, he hoped, the pepper should make it harder for the attackers to see and to aim accurately . . . and, as if to validate that thought, the volume of shots slackened somewhat.

Then troopers wearing the black and crimson armbands and carrying rifles with knives fastened to them—bayonets—appeared, running toward the revetments. Immediately the defenders opened fire. Attackers began to drop, initially almost as they appeared, but there were more attackers appearing than being shot.

Alastar had ordered the imagers to hold off using wooden darts except in places where it appeared the attackers would overwhelm the second line of revetments. But it was still hard to watch when an attacker bayoneted a defender who was overcome by more attackers than he could shoot at.

The muted thunder of hoofbeats behind the imagers grew as a company of mounted troopers rode forward and past the imagers and down over the low revetments and into the mass of attackers, forcing many of them back or killing them outright.

At least a squad of the riders kept going, cutting through the foot with their sabers . . . and then disappearing. Two or three riders, or maybe it might have been more, kept coming in and out of sight as they wheeled their mounts to deal with attackers on the other side of the concealment and unseen by Alastar.

One rider went down, clearly shot by an attacker inside the concealment, and then another. Even so, the combination of troopers firing from behind the low revetments and the mounted company seemed to have blunted the attack.

A set of horn doublets came from the west, and the remaining attackers turned and sprinted back into the cover of the concealment. Five, then another five mounted troopers rode uphill out of the concealment, and joined the rest of the company in withdrawing.

A last rider, moving to join them, shouted, "Wagon-turtle! There's a wagon-turtle!" Then he slumped forward in the saddle, shot from behind.

A wagon-turtle? Alastar had no idea what that was, unless it referred to the wagon he'd seen earlier and the fact that it was armored somehow, although he only recalled seeing armor on the front of the wagon.

In what seemed like moments, there was no sign of any attackers, except for the fallen, and there looked to be at least a hundred. Alastar surveyed the double line of revetments, going from the north all the way to those on the south that ran all the way up to the river road, but there were no attackers.

Without any warning, and no horn signals, a massive wave of attackers appeared, charging out of the concealment toward the revetments. Then a company of mounted rebels charged from out of nowhere, heading toward the northeast end of the defenders' lines, clearly aiming to open a passage to the river road . . . and L'Excelsis. They weren't within a hundred yards when Fifth Company appeared in force, slamming into the rebels, halting the attack, and turning the northern end of the battle-field into a confused mass of men, mounts, and blades.

Alastar couldn't afford to watch the mounted conflict, especially since the troopers manning the revetments were clearly outnumbered.

"Imagers! Use your darts! Now!"

Attackers began to fall, one after the other, but the survivors still pressed forward, if slowly. Then another company of foot charged past the imagers, sabers in hand, and began to cut into the advance, pushing the attackers back.

"Imagers! Hold your fire!" Having no doubts that the second wave of attackers was far from the last, Alastar wanted to save the imagers as much as possible. While still watching the melee less than fifty yards away, he took out his water bottle and took a long swallow . . . and then a second.

Another set of horn doublet echoed across the battlefield, and in moments, the surviving attackers had retreated back into the concealment. Alastar glanced back to the north where the remaining attacking horsemen were breaking off the fight.

He caught a glimpse of Julyan, the youngest of the maitres in the imager force, looking westward, seemingly trying to see past the conflict and into the concealment that hid all too many of the attackers. Behind Julyan and spaced midway between him and Dylert was Cyran, looking as calm and self-possessed as he always did.

Perhaps not the most far-seeing senior imager, but certainly solid. Definitely solid, if slightly prone to wanting to please too much.

At that moment, a very small spear, actually a projectile resembling an ancient crossbow quarrel, slammed into the chest of a trooper who had turned to withdraw with the rest of Fifth Company.

A quarrel? Alastar froze for a moment. *A frigging quarrel?* That meant at least some imagers from Westisle had thrown in with the rebels, most likely Voltyrn and those he could convince. Alastar could only hope it wasn't the entire Westisle Collegium. *If you'd named him Maitre there . . .* Alastar shook his head. *You can't deal with that now . . . but you can't not deal with it . . . or at least not find out.* And since there wasn't nearly the risk of cannon or massed heavy rifle fire centered on him or the other imagers. . . .

Alastar looked right to Seliora, posted now slightly less than ten yards to the north, and then to his left, where Arion was stationed. "Arion! Seliora! Close on me! Now!"

Once the two flanked him, he said, "We're headed into the concealment, carrying our own concealment. There's at least one imager from Westisle with the rebels."

"How—" Arion broke off his question.

"They don't use darts. They use something like a small crossbow quarrel. Fifth Company just lost some troopers to quarrels. We need to do something before they commence another attack." He urged the gray forward at a fast walk. There would be time enough to hurry once they were inside the rebel concealment . . . when whatever they were dealing with was done.

The way to the concealment wasn't exactly straight, not with the horses having to wind around bodies, but when they were inside the concealment was obvious, for two reasons. First, there were only a few bodies lying in the trampled grass, and second, Alastar could see the rebel troopers re-forming—all of them, a force that looked more like four regiments than the two that the rebels were supposed to have. And that force was advancing, although it was more than three hundred yards away.

Alastar did his best to fix the relative positions of the various units in his mind, then turned his attention to the "wagon-turtle," less than a hundred yards away. The wagon did indeed resemble a giant shelled creature, with the plates of the shell being iron shields that fitted together.

"Your strongest shields," he said quietly, before imaging his equivalent of a cannon shell inside the wagon.

The explosion that followed was strangely muffled, but the upper shield "plates" of the turtle flew both outward and in some instances upward, and a cloud of white smoke wreathed what remained of the wagon. Alastar felt shaken by the impact on his shields, but not as much as he had expected. *The Westisle imagers' shields blocked some of the force.*

He could only hope that the explosion had killed or at least stunned the imagers who had created and maintained the concealment, but there was no way to tell that yet, because he and Seliora and Arion remained within the area the concealment had covered.

"Back to our revetments." He turned the gray.

Arion and Seliora kept pace.

As soon as the gray carried him back across where he thought the concealment had been, he glanced back over his shoulder . . . and smiled, if only momentarily, as he saw the entire rebel force moving toward them. "Back into position. Maintain shields and concealments."

The advancing rebel troopers, carrying their bayoneted heavy rifles, just walked steadily toward the defenders. At that point, Wilkorn's cannon began to fire. Many of the shots missed, but Alastar did see an entire squad wiped out. *Grapeshot!*

Despite the occasional devastating effect of the cannon, the rebels kept coming. At some four hundred yards away, they began to spread out, but they did not slow. When they reached a point about three hundred yards from the outermost earthworks of the defenders, Major Rykards's troopers began to fire, if deliberately and slowly.

Alastar saw more rebels begin to fall.

Then the advance changed. The attackers angled slightly, trotting and then stopping, if only for a moment, but always moving forward, the mass of foot troopers moving inexorably eastward toward the defenders. Few of the attackers actually fired their rifles, even as more of them dropped to the measured fire from Rykards's troopers.

Alastar waited until the advancing foot troopers were within less than a hundred yards before ordering, "Red pepper across the front ranks." He wished he'd said "leading attackers," because there really weren't any ranks as such, but the imagers laid down a fog of pepper that covered the first three or four yards of those advancing.

That slowed the attackers, and the rifle fire from behind the earthworks picked up. More attackers fell, but the remainder surged forward. Another company of mounted troopers charged past the imagers, past the revetments, slashing into the middle of the attack and cutting a path through the center. The attackers fell back for a time, but then, by force of sheer numbers, began to hem in the mounted troopers.

Another mounted company rode forward, coming from the reserves behind and to the south of Alastar, followed by yet another mounted company. Before long, the rebels and the defenders were so tightly interwoven in the fighting along the lower earthworks that Alastar could see no effective use of the imagers.

Wilkorn's cannon were picking off attackers farther away, but were useless against those rebels engaging the defenders around the revetments.

Alastar kept looking to the north, fearful that, in the middle of the chaos, the rebels might disengage and make a mass attack there to punch through the defenders and gain control of the river road and thus open their way to L'Excelsis, but Weidyn had moved Fifth Company slightly forward, and the fighting to the north was more scattered.

At that moment, Alastar heard a horn triplet, repeated twice, but he could see no movement anywhere to the west, including from the company or so of rebel troopers surrounding the command group—still almost a mille from the fighting—whose red and black banners drooped in the still air under the midday sun.

Midday? Had the entire morning passed already?

He kept looking, then realized that the southernmost section of the rebel forces was marching up the river road toward the left flank of the defending force, a flank greatly weakened by the use of the mounted troops to repulse and hold the earthen revetments against the massive assault from the west.

"Imagers! On me!" Alastar dropped his concealment and turned the gray to the south and slightly uphill. By the time he reached the river road itself, Cyran was riding beside him and the other imagers were directly behind them. *Solid Cyran.*

Alastar then re-created a screen concealment in front of himself.

When they reined up behind the thin line of foot that constituted the south defense perimeter holding the road, the leading rank of the rebels was still almost a hundred yards away. Directly behind the first five or six ranks was what appeared to be a moving square of iron some five yards by fifteen, pressing inexorably northward along the river road.

The last thing Alastar wanted to deal with was another set of imagers, but he couldn't imagine who or what else was inside the second wagon-turtle. He immediately attempted to image another cannon shell into the wagon-turtle . . . but it was as though he hit a wall. *A shield wall.* Then he felt something jab at his own shields, a probe followed by an immediate hail of bullets from the rebels' mounted rifles that passed over the heads of both the attacking and defending foot troopers, with at least four or five bullets slamming into his shields.

You need to stop them. He tried again to image a cannon shell, this time trying to place the shell in the rear under the hooves of the oxen. Even doing that left him light-headed, and he rocked slightly in the saddle before recovering.

The explosion was muffled, but the rear of the wagon-turtle sagged, and the entire assembly lurched to a halt.

"Commence firing!" ordered the foot commander.

Measured shots followed, a continuous and methodical barrage that tore into the advancing rebels, but it seemed that for every man who fell another, if not two, took his place. At the same time, the shots from the mounted rifles behind the advancing foot were taking a toll on the defenders. The wagon-turtle remained in place, little more than a hundred yards away, and a squad of attackers moved up and used the shields of the turtle as a safer emplacement from which to fire at the defenders.

Alastar took a quick glance to the west, but could only see a continuing seething mass of troopers—both mounted and on foot—battling it out generally just before or around the earthworks. He thought he'd only looked away a moment, but when he looked back to the river road before him, the attackers were within yards of the remaining foot defenders. "Imagers! Darts to the attackers. Those directly in front of you! Now!"

The initial stream of darts stopped the attackers cold, but only for several moments before they began to regroup.

Alastar tried something else—just imaging a constant stream of darts across the front rows of the attackers. The darts hit with such force that the bodies of the attackers piled up into a low wall.

Another horn signal sounded, and the foot attackers opened a space in the middle, and mounted riders moved forward.

Alastar found that he was breathing hard and sweating profusely, but he turned toward Cyran and said loudly enough for his words to carry, "Image a line of pikes in front of our foot, but cover them with a concealment. You take the right side; I'll do the left. Make sure the pikes are anchored to the road stones."

"I can do that."

Alastar imaged his own line of pikes in position with a concealment . . . and waited, blotting his forehead.

The riders thundering toward the defending foot were actually lancers, and Alastar could only hope that he'd imaged the pikes in place far enough out that the lances didn't still strike the first ranks of the defenders. Those defenders were firing directly at the lancers, apparently to no effect, suggesting that the Westisle imagers had imaged shields for the riders.

Tired as he was getting, Alastar imaged two more cannon shells—one on each side of the stalled wagon-turtle, but right next to the outboard panels.

The resulting explosions flung a number of the riflemen from the back of the turtle and created more smoke. Alastar also noticed that one of the lancers went down from the defenders' rifle fire, followed by another and a third—just before the horses and their riders plowed into the line of pikes. Some of the riders were flung over the pikes, where they were dispatched by the waiting foot troopers. Others scrambled clear.

Alastar, trying to conserve his strength, released his concealment on the framework holding the pikes, as did Cyran. In moments, the attacking footmen charged again, some climbing over or through the framework, while others were cut down before they could do either.

Two horn triplets sounded, and the attacking foot abruptly withdrew, but only about fifty yards. A thin line of Antiagon fire dropped onto the pikes.

While the fire seared at the wooden framework, Alastar grabbed his water bottle and took several long swallows.

Then a withering blast of rifle fire slammed into the area where Julyan and Tiranya were posted. Alastar saw the younger maitre rock back in the saddle, and as he did, a gout of Antiagon fire flared from a tightly knit group of attackers less that twenty yards from Tiranya and Julyan. Julyan's shields collapsed and he and his mount became an instant flaring pyre.

"No!"

Alastar turned to see Chervyt spurring his horse toward the source of the Antiagon fire, his shields obviously extended and strengthened, because bodies sprayed away from him and his mount. Alastar could also see bullets ricocheting as well. As Chervyt plowed into the tight group, a huge flare of Antiagon fire shot skyward and then radiated out a good five yards in all directions. The entire area was filled with small explosions, and even from where he was, behind his shields, Alastar could feel not only the impacts on his shields, but the intense heat that accompanied the eye-searing flare of light.

He blinked, clearing his eyes, even blotting them with the back of his sleeve before he could see distinctly—only to find that the attackers who had launched the Antiagon fire that had killed Julyan had vanished in the heat of that blast. So had Chervyt!

Only a glassy circle of ice remained as a result of that interaction of Antiagon fire and Chervyt's shields, and possibly the interaction with the rebel imager's shields. In the warmth of the day, that ice was already turning into a foggy mist in front of the remaining attackers.

Alastar swallowed. Two young imagers gone like that. The morning before they'd been joking . . . and he'd envied their carefree appearance.

Still trying to hold his shields and be able to attack the oncoming attackers, Alastar released his personal concealment and imaged more darts into the attackers. As he did so, he could feel more impacts on his shields, and he glanced sideways to see a hail of bullets ricocheting off Cyran's shields, some few of which were also striking his own shields. The impacts came so hard and fast that it was all Alastar could do to hold his shields against the onslaught.

Then an immense ball of Antiagon fire—one that had to have been imaged into being—arched down toward the center of the imagers, right toward Alastar and Cyran.

"Taryn!" shouted Cyran, "On me! Now!"

Before Alastar could say a word, his mouth opening to protest—far too late—Cyran and Taryn were charging toward the center of the attackers. Somehow, Cyran had imaged shields around the Antiagon fire and then re-imaged the mass out before himself and Taryn like a scythe of yellow-green fire, sweeping away and destroying everything before it. Abruptly, an even more brilliant flare of light coruscated though Alastar's eyes, momentarily blinding him, followed by a soundless explosion that almost ripped him from his saddle, then shook him back and forth.

Instantly, frigid cold enveloped Alastar, and tiny needles of ice fell like miniature spears from the sky. Foggy mists swirled everywhere.

Alastar blinked, blotted his eyes with his sleeve, and, as his vision returned, tried to make out the scene before him—except there was nothing there except a thin sheet of ice stretching almost half a mille to the south and almost that far to the west.

Nothing! Not a trace of anything, not the damaged wagon-turtle, not a single rebel or mount . . . nothing. Nothing. Not a thing moving along or beside the river road for a half mille. No troopers, no horses, not a single bush or tree. Nothing except the ice that was already cracking . . . and the swirls of foggy mist that rose from it.

A half mille of ice! Alastar had never seen that before. Nor had he seen that much destruction. More than a regiment wiped out by that swathe of flame and imaging, such power that, in the end, even Cyran hadn't been able to control it.

You did that once. But Alastar had not seen that destruction, even if he had survived. He swallowed once more. He had survived that, thirteen years ago. Now, Cyran and Taryn . . . they hadn't.

He did that to save you. Not just the imagers, not just Solidar. You. Alastar's guts twisted inside him. *And Taryn went with him.*

Looking to both sides, his eyes burning, Alastar could see the other eight remaining imagers, all seemingly motionless, as if frozen in incomprehension at the suddenness and magnitude of the destruction stretching southward from them.

Then he glanced to the west, where it appeared that the remaining rebels had broken and were fleeing, except for the company or less surrounding the rebel command group, who Wilkorn's troopers almost seemed to be ignoring. Alastar blinked. He was having trouble focusing on the command group, and even the banners seemed fuzzy and muddy, rather than of the sharp black and crimson.

A blurring concealment!

"Imagers! On me! Hold shields! Release concealments!" Alastar wasn't certain which imagers, if any, were still holding screen concealments, but they weren't necessary and he wanted all of them to be able to see him.

He turned the gelding westward, moving at a fast walk, trying to move through the bodies piled here and there, while keeping his eyes on the rebel command group that seemed to be slowly edging back along the road to the hamlet north of the lake.

By the time he and the imagers were on the dirt road and within a few hundred yards of the blur-concealed rebel command group, more than a squad of mounted troopers had joined them, flanking them on each side as they closed the distance on the withdrawing rebels. Belatedly, Alastar recognized the squad leader as Remaylt, and nodded to him. From what Alastar could tell from the brief glances around and behind him, Wilkorn's troopers held the field and were busy dealing with scattered rebels—except for a company that held the river road at the narrowest point between the marshlands and the river.

Remaylt eased his mount over near Alastar's. "Are those rebels up ahead? The ones that are hard to see?"

"I think it's what's left of the command group. We need to stop them."

"Yes, sir." Remaylt eased away.

Belatedly, Alastar turned in the saddle and recovered his water bottle. He began to drink the dark lager, still trying not to think about Cyran . . . and the other three. By the time he had finished, he felt considerably better but far from as strong as he would have wished. In less than half a quint, during which time Alastar and his force had moved to within less than a hundred yards of the retreating rebels, another two mounted squads joined Alastar's force, presumably summoned in some fashion by Remaylt.

Alastar was less than thirty yards from the rear of the rebels when the riders he pursued halted, then wheeled their mounts about. The blur concealment dropped, revealing almost a full company of troopers wearing black and crimson uniforms, doubtless Ryentar's personal guard.

Three imagers in gray were in the second rank. While Alastar couldn't be certain, he thought one of them was Voltyrn. He also thought he saw another figure in gray in the third rank, but he wasn't certain.

The black-clad troopers held rifles at the ready, not quite pointed at the imagers.

For a moment, no one spoke.

"It's over," Alastar said. "You might as well surrender."

"It is over," replied Voltyrn, riding forward just slightly. "You have almost no army left, and there are thousands of High Holders who can raise yet another army . . . and another."

Alastar almost asked, *To what point? To get more people killed for nothing?* Instead, he just said, "The time for talk is over. Surrender."

"You might as well let us go, Alastar," called out Voltyrn. "We're all fresh, and it's clear you're having trouble just holding shields."

"Not all of us," returned Seliora, from where she had reined up beside Alastar on the right.

"Not at all," added Arion from Alastar's left.

"Arms ready!" ordered Remaylt.

Instantly every mounted trooper had his rifle aimed at the black-clad troopers.

"That won't help," said Voltyrn.

Alastar wasn't about to try to image against the rebel imager, not when he could barely maintain full shields.

At that moment, Voltyrn pitched forward in the saddle, and Alastar could see an iron dart in the back of his neck. Almost instantaneously, the two imagers beside him slumped.

"Guard! Fire!" called another voice.

"Fire!" snapped Remaylt, and his troopers instantly fired. The first two ranks of Ryentar's guard went down, as did some of those farther back.

As the first ranks dropped, and the fire from Remaylt's men felled more of the black-clad guards, Alastar saw clearly the imager in the third rank—Bettaur—who was white-faced and swaying in the saddle, unable to do much more than stay in the saddle as the guard troopers further behind him tried to bring their rifles to bear . . . or to escape.

At that instant, before Alastar could react, he saw another familiar face ride forward, blade in hand, and thrust it into Bettaur, whose face contorted.

"Seliora, clamp a shield around the blond man who stabbed Bettaur."

Bettaur froze in place, an expression resembling a twisted smile on his face.

"Surrender or die!" snapped Remaylt." Drop your rifles!"

The surviving black-clad troopers began to do so. Alastar did not move until Remaylt's men moved the captives away, which took surprisingly little time. Then he rode forward to the two blond men—one with blood spreading across his imager grays, leaning forward against the neck of his mount, and the other held tight by Seliora's shields.

With Seliora on his right and Arion on his left, Alastar looked at Bettaur, taking in his white face and haggard look, and the dark circles under his eyes, realizing that the reason Bettaur hadn't been able to protect himself was that he'd likely used the last of his energy punching the iron darts through the shields of the three Westisle imagers, something Alastar doubted either he or any of those with him could have done.

Bettaur's eyes focused on Alastar, and he forced a smile that was mostly a grimace. He opened his mouth, trying to speak. ". . . was . . . the only way to stop them . . . had to make them believe . . . no one believed me . . . blackmailed . . . tell Linzya . . . love her . . . no traitor . . . never . . . was." Bettaur convulsed, trying to get out a last word, before slumping forward, motionless, unbreathing.

For a moment, Alastar could say nothing. He finally looked at the second blond man who still held a bloody blade in his hand, unable to drop it, so tight was he held by Seliora's shields.

"Loosen the shields," Alastar told Seliora. "Let him speak."

She did, and the bloody saber dropped to the trampled dirt of the road below.

"We seem to meet in the situations where you have the advantage, Maitre Alastar." Ryentar's use of Alastar's title was sardonically dismissive.

"You killed Bettaur. You cut him down from behind, but then, you've always maneuvered from behind."

"He betrayed me."

"Opposing you wasn't betraying you, not when you blackmailed him into helping you."

Ryentar grinned. "It worked, didn't it?"

"He was the best of you, and you killed him."

"He was just another imager. He wasn't one of us."

"But he was, Ryentar. You didn't know it, but he was your brother." Alastar smiled sadly. "You tried to kill your older brother and your sister. You killed your mother, I'm sure, and, in the end, you killed your younger brother."

"If it weren't for you," Ryentar said, again dismissively, as if he had not even heard Alastar's words, "it would have worked."

"And you killed your own brother because it didn't. What did that gain you?"

"No one betrays me. No one."

Alastar imaged an iron dart through Ryentar's left eye into his brain and watched him stiffen and then slump lifelessly in the saddle. Then he looked past the imagers to Remaylt. "We'll need this body as proof that High Holder Regial was here and was in command." *At least, nominally.*

"Yes, sir." Remaylt's voice was flat.

"Squad leader," Alastar said gently and firmly, "this is the second time Ryentar has caused the needless deaths of imagers and thousands of troopers innocent of anything except following orders. I had no intention of allowing the possibility of a third time. And, since we are within a hundred milles of L'Excelsis, his life was already forfeit by regial edict."

"I didn't know that, sir."

"I didn't expect that you would. I'm also thankful for all the support you and your men have provided. Without it, matters could have gone otherwise." Alastar inclined his head.

"We'll take care of the body, sir."

"Thank you. I appreciate it."

Alastar turned the gray so that he could face the surviving imagers, nodding to Seliora and then to Arion. "We need to head back, just in case we missed something."

Once the imagers were re-formed, Alastar started back along the dirt road, flanked immediately by Arion and Seliora. Akoryt brought up the rear of the imagers, riding beside Remaylt at the head of the three squads the squad leader had gathered in the effort to catch Ryentar.

"It doesn't look like there's much left to have missed." Arion gestured toward the river, where the only moving figures appeared to be the regular army troopers.

"Perhaps not, but I also need to meet with Wilkorn, just in case."

Arion nodded, then said in a lower voice. "All that you said to the High Holder . . . that was true, wasn't it?"

"I wasn't entirely convinced that he killed his mother. I said that to get his reaction. The fact that he didn't protest . . ."

". . . means that he did," finished Seliora firmly.

"You were wondering why we had to pursue Ryentar immediately, weren't you?" Alastar asked Arion.

"I did wonder, I have to admit."

"If he had escaped, he would have claimed that he wasn't there, and that the High Holders took his colors without his permission . . . and he could easily have gotten off without paying for all this. Could you imagine the outcry if Lorien had executed him without proof?"

"But you killed him . . ."

"It's not the same. He died in the battle, after killing an imager."

Arion nodded, then asked, "Do you believe what Bettaur said?"

"It must be true, mustn't it?" asked Alastar, his voice gentle. "Even Ryentar admitted it. And Bettaur killed the leader of the rebel imagers when it would have been difficult, if not impossible for us to do it without losing more imagers and troopers."

Arion looked to Alastar. "Then that's the way it was. He died . . . just like Taryn . . . and the others."

"That's the way it always was," said Seliora firmly, "and every imager who was here will insist on it."

Alastar smiled inside, if faintly, knowing what Seliora hadn't added—*especially for the sake of Linzya and her unborn child.* Then he looked toward the river road, where the command tent still stood, seemingly alone in light of the afternoon sun. He wasn't looking forward to learning just how great the toll on Wilkorn's troopers had been. The toll on the imagers had been far too high—six out of fifteen, counting Bettaur and presumably Ashkyr, not to mention how many rebel imagers there had been from Westisle. *All because you wouldn't name Voltyrn Maitre there.*

He kept riding and reached for his water bottle, hoping there was at least some lager remaining in it.

47

The ride back along the dirt road to the river road took almost three quints, what with avoiding bodies and scavengers. Alastar left Akoryt in charge of the imagers and rode to the command tent, simply because he was too tired to walk. Once there, he handed the gelding's reins to one of the troopers standing guard and walked inside. Maurek was talking to Luerryn.

Alastar just stood quietly, not wanting to interrupt.

Suddenly, Maurek looked past Luerryn. "Maitre, what can you report?"

"High Holder Regial died in the last part of the battle after he killed an imager. The rest of his personal guard surrendered. So far as we know, there are no renegade imagers remaining."

Maurek nodded to Luerryn. "You can go." He didn't speak again until the major had left the command tent. "What did you do up there on the south road?"

"We did our best to reinforce the foot there when the mounted infantry had to stop the attack from the west." Alastar didn't feel like explaining in detail.

"We wouldn't have won without what you did to Hehnsyn's battalion," said Maurek. "That allowed us to concentrate all our forces on Aestyn and Marryt. Some of them lost heart when they saw half a regiment had been wiped out all at once." He paused. "How did you do that?"

"I didn't," Alastar admitted. "Cyran and Taryn did. They imaged a massive blast of Antiagon fire back at the imagers who were supporting the High Holders. I can't explain what happened, except that there was apparently a massive interaction of imaging forces, and Cyran managed to channel it against the attackers. I've never seen anything like it. We lost a third of our imagers there. We lost the other two in dealing with the Ryentar's personal guard and the last of the renegade imagers from Westisle." That wasn't precisely true, but it was better stated and left that way.

"Renegade imagers?"

"It turned out that there were more than we thought, and that they came from Westisle. The two imagers missing from the Collegium were actually helping us, but they died destroying the last three renegade imagers."

"How did that kind of treachery happen? I thought you had tighter control over your imagers."

"So did I." Making his words sound wry was an effort for Alastar. "How does any treachery occur, either in the army or the Collegium?" he went on tiredly. "Usually because someone who has an excessively high opinion of himself feels slighted and is flattered and persuaded to betray those he feels slighted him. I doubt we'll ever know all the details, just as you probably won't about Aestyn, Hehnsyn, or Marryt. How heavy were your casualties?"

"Dead and wounded, close to eight hundred of ours. Over three thousand of theirs, maybe four thousand if you count what you and the imagers did earlier."

Alastar paused, then asked, "Where's the marshal?"

"He rallied two companies and led them against Aestyn . . . from the front. They shot him five times, Luerryn said, but he still broke their formation."

"He told me he had to be here," said Alastar.

"He did. He felt it was his fault that the army was corrupted."

Alastar understood too well. *All too well.* Wilkorn had felt responsible for allowing the army revolt to happen.

"He never wanted to be put out to pasture like a warhorse who outlived his purpose."

Not as a warhorse who felt enormous guilt that would have gnawed him into a slow and agonizing death. "He wanted to act, not be acted upon." That was also true enough.

"I suspect you are much the same, Maitre."

Alastar wasn't about to comment on that. "What do you intend to do with the rebel troops?"

"With the rankers and squad leaders—let them go. The rankers, even the squad leaders, don't have that much of a choice. They've suffered enough. If any want to rejoin the army a year from now, we'll look at them one by one. The officers? They swore an oath to support the rex and Solidar." Maurek shook his head. "They had a choice, and they chose disloyalty and treason. I've had everyone who survived shot. Not that there were all that many. Aestyn was killed in the marshal's attack, and Marryt probably wouldn't have survived his wounds. Hehnsyn . . . your imagers took care of him and his officers." Maurek's smile was grim. "What about your renegades?"

"So far as we can determine, they're all dead. We'll have to change all the leadership in Westisle and move some imagers from there to the Collegium in L'Excelsis . . . and go from there. Since there appears to be no immediate need for the imagers, we will return to L'Excelsis in the morning." After a brief hesitation, Alastar asked, "Have you dispatched a messenger to Rex Lorien?"

"I have. I kept the dispatch brief. I just wrote that we had destroyed the rebel force, and that all the officers involved had died in the course of the engagement. I did not mention anything about High Holder Regial. At the time, I did not know, and I wanted Rex Lorien to know that we had prevailed."

"I'll let him know about his dear brother."

"That might be for the best," said Maurek.

"If there's nothing else?"

The commander shook his head. "If there's anything else you should know, I'll inform you."

Alastar inclined his head, then turned and left the command tent. He mounted the gray and headed back north along the river road. He took his time covering the hundred or so yards back to where the imagers had tied their mounts, thinking about what he might say to them.

Even before he dismounted, Dylert was standing there. "I'll take care of your horse, sir."

"Thank you." Alastar dismounted carefully, then turned to wait as Akoryt walked toward him. Alastar couldn't help but note that Akoryt's formerly red hair was now mostly gray. *Did that just happen . . . or is it another thing you failed to notice?*

"Sir . . . I've gathered the others . . ."

"Thank you." Alastar already knew what Akoryt wasn't saying—that Alastar needed to talk to all the imagers. "Dylert offered to groom my horse."

"I'll have one of the teamsters take care of that." Akoryt motioned, and a teamster hurried to catch up to Dylert.

Alastar realized that Akoryt had already thought that out. *He'll make a good senior imager or maitre.*

The two walked toward where the others waited.

Once there, while he waited for Dylert to join them, Alastar looked across the faces of the eight surviving imagers. All of them looked the way he felt—drained and anything but triumphant. After several more moments, Dylert hurried up and stood between Belsior and Taurek.

"It's been a long day," Alastar began, prosaically, "a long week as well. In fact, it's been a long harvest season, but the worst is over. All the rebel commanders and their officers are dead. So, it appears, are the imagers from Westisle who turned on the Collegium, simply because I hesitated to appoint one of them as Maitre at Westisle." He paused. "I didn't make a choice because I had concerns about either of the most senior imagers at Westisle, and I wanted to think over who might be most suitable from the Collegium here. Then I didn't make a choice because we got involved in a war, and I didn't want to distract any of you from the problems here." He offered a wintry smile. "Obviously I was right and wrong. Right to be concerned and wrong to put off deciding." He paused once more.

"Nothing is achieved without hard work. Often that hard work ends up requiring sacrifices—of time, of pleasure, and, as it did today, of lives. All too often, those with power use that power not only unwisely, but selfishly, as if they and those like them are the only ones in all Terahnar who matter. To stop such abuses and selfish power requires greater power, of some sort, and that power may take lives, as it did today. We would all like to think of success or victory as a triumph. That is our nature. But, as happened today, sometimes the greatest victories, the most important triumphs, feel anything but triumphant. But had we failed today, all of Solidar would slowly but inexorably have sunk back into the chaos and tyranny that preceded the founding of Solidar, where any High Holder could condemn someone to die for merely displeasing him, where young imagers could be enslaved or killed, where crafters and tradesmen would ply their trade only at the whim of the wealthiest, where there would be no women of property, where no one of Pharsi blood could be certain when he or she would be hounded or killed. We did not fail, but that success, a success which feels little like triumph, would not have been possible without each and every one of you—and without the sacrifices of Cyran, Taryn, Chervyt, and Julyan—and, strangely enough, of even Bettaur and Ashkyr." Alastar paused for a long moment. "What we must do next is to assure that all the pain and sacrifice do not go in vain. We must rebuild the Collegium to be even stronger. We must assure that those imagers in Westisle never again feel that they are not part of the whole Collegium. And we must make certain that every

High Holder is held to obey the Codex Legis as it was written, and not when or where they wish to obey. These things we can do. These things we must do . . . in the name and spirit of those who gave everything for this bitter triumph."

Alastar didn't know what else he could say. He just lowered his head.

"I don't think there's more to be said," offered Akoryt quietly, but firmly. "Except one thing. None of us would have survived or triumphed without good leadership. The greatest fortune we had was Maitre Alastar. None of us should forget that. He has always put the Collegium first, and he has never hesitated to take the greatest risks on behalf of all of us. Ever."

Alastar looked up. He hadn't expected that.

Taurek and Arion were both nodding. In fact, all of them were.

Alastar swallowed. He couldn't speak for several moments. Finally, he said, "I did the best I could, but I wasn't perfect. I made mistakes, as I just told you. You will, too, when you lead. It's what you do after you make a mistake that counts."

Since he couldn't think of anything else to say, he didn't.

48

With a cool wind blowing out of the northwest, and under an overcast sky, Alastar and his surviving imagers left the site of the battle just after dawn on Solayi. They were accompanied by what remained of Weïdyn's Fifth Company. Behind them, the remaining troopers were collecting wood and timbers and building the pyres to burn the dead from both armies. All—except the rebel officers—would have a few words said on their behalf. The memorial services for Cyran and the other imagers would be offered at the Collegium anomen, sometime in the next week.

Weïdyn rode beside Alastar, behind the squad riding vanguard, with Akoryt and Tiranya riding directly behind Alastar, and the remaining imagers in pairs behind them and ahead of the sixty-odd troopers who had survived the carnage.

Beyond commands to the troopers and pleasantries, Weïdyn did not speak until they had been riding close to three quints, when he finally said, "Always wondered how the first rex regis did it. Not anymore."

"His imagers were stronger than we are," Alastar said quietly. "At least, he and Elsior were. Much stronger."

"Makes sense. Even your lady imagers . . . Remaylt told me how one just froze the bastard pretender with his saber still in his hand."

"For her, that was the easy part." Alastar chuckled. "Will you stay with the army?" He didn't want to talk about the imagers or the battle, not when he could still recall those terrible flashes of light that had consumed first Chervyt and then Cyran and Taryn.

"After this, sir . . . what else could I do? I'd like to go back to training recruits at some time." He barked a short laugh. "Could tell 'em all, honestlike, that I'd seen an outfit that made the toughest of them look soft, and one where the women were just as tough and deadly. One where everyone fought to the death. Most wouldn't believe me. A year ago, if someone had told me, I wouldn't have believed either." The captain paused. "Not a trooper who was here is ever going to forget the sight of the nine of you riding back up the road. Remaylt told me that every ranker stopped and watched when you rode past."

"I was too tired to notice," Alastar admitted.

"I figured as much. That's why I told you. Thought you ought to know."

"Thank you." *Maybe, just maybe, that might keep all of the army loyal . . . for a few years, anyway.*

Two quints before noon, Alastar reined up outside the Chateau D'Rex, accompanied just by Taurek and Dylert, and a squad from Fifth Company, the squad commanded by Remaylt, since Alastar had had Captain Weidyn escort Akoryt and the other imagers directly to Imagisle. He had just dismounted and turned to the two imagers when Guard Captain Churwyl hurried down the alabaster-white steps at almost a run, stopping just short of Alastar.

"Maitre Alastar!"

"He wants more details on what happened, I take it?" More likely, Lorien was furious that he hadn't heard more.

"Yes, sir."

"And that's an understatement?"

"Ah . . . yes, sir."

"Lead on, Guard Captain."

Churwyl winced, but turned and headed up the white stone steps.

Alastar followed.

At the top of the grand staircase Alastar caught a glimpse of blond hair from the corner of his eye. He turned to see Chelia standing outside the door to her salon. She froze where she stood. Alastar turned and walked to the north corridor and to Lorien's study door. He didn't bother to knock.

"Maitre Alastar," announced Churwyl from behind Alastar, immediately closing the door.

Lorien stood before the open north window closest to his desk. He turned and glared. "Well . . . it's nice that someone finally decided to inform me—"

"Lorien, shut the frig up." Alastar's voice was flat and cold.

The rex's mouth opened.

"Don't say a frigging word. I'm liable to image anything you say down your throat. Sit down, and I'll tell you what happened . . . all of it. Don't say a word until I'm done." Alastar dropped into the chair in front of the goldenwood desk.

Lorien actually swallowed, then sat down behind his desk, moistening his lips.

"I'm not in the best of moods, right now," began Alastar. "That's because this stupid revolt killed six imagers from Imagisle and most likely ten or so from Westisle. There are close to five thousand dead or injured army troopers, on both sides, and Wilkorn is dead. So are all the rebel officers. Maurek executed those who survived. Ryentar killed one of my imagers, and he died for it." Alastar cleared his throat. "That's the short version. Now, you're going to listen to the long version, every frigging word of it, and if you don't pay attention, you're going to be very uncomfortable . . ."

Giving Lorien the longer summary still took more than a quint.

When he finished, Alastar looked at Lorien. "Now . . . if you have any questions, I'll answer them."

"Why didn't you bring that bastard brother of mine back here?"

"Because neither he nor you deserved it. He deserved to die Namer-near anonymously in a bloody battle and not be given even the recognition of a regial execution." *Even if he was only treachery's tool.* "And after the mess you've made of things, you certainly don't deserve whatever you might get out of such a spectacle."

Lorien's jaw tightened, but he only asked, "Is there any proof that Marryt, Aestyn, and Hehnsyn are dead?"

"Maurek's not exactly charitable. He saw Aestyn's body, and stood there and had Marryt executed, although Marryt probably would have died from his wounds. Hehnsyn was incinerated in the Antiagon fire flare that turned him and his entire battalion to ashes."

"What about the other High Holders?"

"They were all smart enough to remain well away from the rebel army. Your brother was their figurehead, and if they'd defeated us, the rebel army would have removed and executed you and put him on the throne. The only High Holder you can really tie to this mess—with any sort of real proof—who isn't already dead is Caervyn. His son led the rebel army and his daughter married Ryentar. You probably ought to order his execution."

"How generous of you to allow me that privilege. What about Ryel?"

"You're going to insist that he become High Councilor, and head of the High Council."

"That scheming bastard? Never!"

"There's not one frigging shred of proof that he did anything, and not even the notes Chelia got will prove anything. Do you want him plotting from Rivages for the rest of your life? His heading the High Council will keep him where you—or the Collegium—can easily reach him. We can control him, and we will. It will also reassure the High Holders that their voices will be heard. Just have Chelia write him a pleasant letter telling him that he will be much happier and safer as a High Councilor and as head of the Council. I'm certain he'll understand."

"That's what he wants."

Alastar shook his head. "That's the last thing in all Terahnar he wants. Two of the last three heads of the council have died in office. He'd much rather plot from the shadows. There's an old saying about holding your friends close, and your enemies even closer."

"But the High Holders have to make the choice. If I even . . ."

"You don't have to say a word. If Ryel makes it known that he would serve, he'll be chosen in a moment."

Abruptly, Lorien laughed. "You're crueler even than people think I am."

"Just practical," demurred Alastar.

"Who's going to pay for it all?"

"Maurek's disbanding the rebel battalions. It will likely be a year before they're reconstituted. That will save you golds. You can also change the tariff laws so that tariffs are assessed equally on High Holders and factors—except phase the change in." Those would cover all the costs of the short war, but Alastar wasn't ready to propose more at the moment, and definitely not off the top of his head.

"What else do you have in mind?"

"Appoint Vaelln as marshal of the armies and promote Maurek to vice marshal. Never have more than one son of a High Holder as a senior officer in L'Excelsis. Three were definitely too many." Before Lorien could say more, Alastar went on. "That's enough for now. Have Chelia draft that letter. We'll go over it in a day or so." He stood. "I need to get to the Collegium for other necessary tasks." After a moment, he added, "And, Lorien, don't do anything or sign anything. Anything at all—until we meet and talk it over."

Alastar turned, but heard Lorien murmuring under his breath.

". . . more trials . . . always more trials . . ."

Alastar walked out of the study. He didn't bother to close the door.

49

Alastar did not make it back to Imagisle, riding through the light drizzling rain that begun to fall shortly after he had left the Chateau D'Rex, until well past second glass. He left Remaylt and his squad at the Bridge of Desires, then crossed the bridge with Taurek and Dylert. Rather than go to the stables or the administration building, he rode directly to the first of the maitres' cottages along the green. He reined up, more than reluctantly, dismounted, and handed the gelding's reins to Dylert, then walked up to the door. He was about to knock when the door opened.

Meiryl stood there. Her eyes were reddened. "I've been expecting you, Maitre."

"I wish I weren't here."

"So do I." Her words were barely a murmur, and she made no attempt to invite him in.

"I came here as soon as I crossed the bridge."

"You would." More tears oozed from her eyes. "He . . . said . . ." She shook her head.

"He was the most noble imager I've ever known." That was definitely true, and Alastar wanted his words to convey that. "All of us who returned owe our lives to Cyran. The Collegium owes its future to him. So does Solidar. None of that will ever make up for your loss, but I wanted you to know that."

"He . . . said . . . either you or he wouldn't be likely to return."

That surprised Alastar. "He never even hinted at that. But he wouldn't have."

"No. He wouldn't." Meiryl shook her head slightly. "I didn't want him to go. He said he had to, that the children . . . that . . ." She swallowed, unable to speak.

"He was right. Without any of those who went . . ." Alastar stopped and just stood there.

After a moment, she stepped back and closed the door.

When he climbed back into the saddle, Alastar felt exhausted, and he still had one more visit to make—at the last maitres' cottage on the green. Dismounting was an effort, but he forced himself to walk up to the door and knock.

Linzya's eyes widened, and she paled as she saw Alastar standing there. "No! No . . . it can't . . . it mustn't . . ."

Alastar glimpsed Charlina standing in the foyer behind Linzya. That Linzya wasn't alone offered him some small measure of relief. "I'm afraid it is, Linzya. He was one of the reasons we were able to defeat the rebels. He killed the last three renegade imagers from Westisle who had backed the pretender, but the effort left him without shields. High Holder Regial stabbed him in the back before we could get close enough to help him."

Linzya just stood there, not speaking.

"You should also know . . . his last words. He said, 'Tell Linzya I love her . . . that I'm no traitor and never was.'" Behind Linzya, Alastar saw a quick expression of disbelief cross Charlina's face, and he added, "I'm not making that up. If either of you don't believe me, you can ask Seliora or Arion. They were right beside me and heard what he said. And he was right. He wasn't a traitor." *Unwise and almost mad with the belief no one would ever believe him, but not a traitor.* "And he did save me." *Which is also likely.*

"He . . . did?"

Alastar nodded. "I was almost without shields at that point. Maitre Cyran was already dead, and Seliora, Arion, and I were facing three fresh Westisle imagers. Bettaur put iron darts through their shields. It took all he had."

"Then . . . he wasn't . . . he really wasn't . . ."

"No. And it's very clear that he truly loved you. He didn't want you and your child to live under a cloud . . . or under the rebels."

Tears were streaming down Linzya's cheeks, and she sobbed uncontrollably.

Charlina moved forward and put an arm around Linzya, easing her back into the cottage, mouthing to Alastar as she did, "Thank you."

Alastar waited until the door closed before he turned and walked back through the rain to the gray. As he mounted, he said to Taurek and Dylert, "The Maitre's house."

"We'll take your mount to the stable, sir," offered Taurek.

"Thank you. I appreciate it, and so will my family."

"Our pleasure, sir," added Dylert.

Alyna, Lystara, and Malyna were all standing on the front porch, waiting as he dismounted.

"If you'd take your kit, sir." Taurek's reminder was gentle.

Alastar smiled wryly. "That's a good idea. Thank you." He handed the gelding's reins to Dylert, then quickly unstrapped his gear and threw it over his shoulder before walking swiftly, or as swiftly as he could, along the walk and up the stone steps out of the rain and into Alyna's arms. The gear hit the porch floor with a dull clunk, just before Lystara wrapped both her arms around his waist.

". . . so glad you're back," Alyna murmured as she held him.

". . . makes two of us . . ."

"Akoryt told me you were safe, but I still worried."

"I had to stop to tell Meiryl. She might have already heard, but she needed to hear from me."

Alyna eased back, but still held Alastar's hand. "I think she knew already. She came to see me last night. She wanted to know if I'd heard anything. She said she'd had the most terrible feeling."

"And when she saw the others return . . ."

Alyna nodded.

"I needed to tell Lorien as soon as possible, so that he didn't do anything stupid. The Nameless knows, he's capable of it. But I went to see her first after that. Then I saw Linzya."

"Bettaur?"

"He died saving my life. I'll tell you more later." He offered a tired and ragged smile. "I'd like to wash up and change into something that doesn't smell . . ."

"I think we can manage that."

"We?"

"You and me. Do you think I'm letting you out of my sight?" Alyna turned to Lystara. "If you and Malyna would take your father's bag to the washroom."

Alastar bent slightly, not that he really needed to, and gave his daughter a heartfelt embrace, then looked to Malyna and smiled. "I'm very glad to see you, too." Malyna's smile was so much like Alyna's that he just froze for a moment. "You definitely are family."

"I'm glad."

"So are we," said Alyna. "Now . . . that bag. I need to get your father cleaned up and made presentable. We're going to have an early dinner." She looked to Alastar. "And we are *not* going to services tonight."

Almost two glasses later, later than Alyna had planned, Alastar

suspected—although she had not protested the reasons for the delay—
the two of them joined the girls at the entrance to the dining room.

"You two took too long," declared Lystara.

"Or not long enough," murmured Malyna, so low that Alastar almost
didn't catch the words.

Lystara looked puzzled.

"That will do, Malyna." But Alyna's voice was amused, rather than
cross. "We're here and it's time for dinner. We'll also break another
rule and let your father tell us everything that happened." Her eyes met
Alastar's.

He nodded, understanding what he was to offer in detail and what
would be deferred until Lystara was older. Alyna would fill Malyna in
over the next day or so.

Once they were seated, Alyna looked to Malyna.

"For the grace and warmth from above, for the bounty of the earth
below, and for all the wonders of this world, and especially for the safe
return of the one we all love, we offer our thanks and gratitude, both
now and ever more, in the spirit of that which cannot be named or
imaged."

Alastar found he could not speak for a moment. So he reached for
the pitcher of dark lager and half filled Malyna's beaker, then Lystara's,
before he filled his own. He set down the pitcher and said to Malyna,
"That was beautiful. Thank you."

"It was beautiful, indeed," added Alyna.

Jienna appeared and set a platter before Alastar, and another before
Alyna.

Alastar found his mouth watering as he saw the platter of game hens,
a half hen for each of them, with lace potatoes and fried apples, and,
of course, two baskets of freshly baked bread. "This looks wonderful."
Especially after all that dried mutton, porridge, and too-bitter dark lager.

"You said you'd tell us everything," said Lystara.

"I will," promised Alastar, "but let me drink a little good lager and
have a mouthful of the best food I've seen in weeks first."

"It was just nine days, Father."

Alyna rolled her eyes, then looked hard at her daughter.

"I'm sorry, Father."

Given Lystara's contrite tone, Alastar smiled. "I accept the apology."
He took a slow swallow from the beaker, enjoying the full but not bitter

taste before he set the beaker down. Then he served himself a game hen and passed the platter to Alyna.

When everyone's plate was full, Alastar cut a morsel of the game hen, ate it slowly, and then began, "A week ago Vendrei morning, thirteen of us rode out across the south bridge and south on the West River Road . . ."

In between bites, he told the essential elements of what had happened, but without speculation, and without dealing with the politics that lay behind many of the actions. A good two quints later, he finished, cleared his throat and refilled his beaker.

"Why did the Westisle imagers join the rebels?" asked Lystara.

"We don't know yet," replied Alastar. "Since they're dead, we may never know. I can only guess that those who did felt that they should have had greater recognition and praise than they received or that Voltyrn even wanted to become Maitre of the Collegium here."

"Did Bettaur really save your life?" pressed Lystara.

"Yes. Whatever else he may have done or not done, he saved my life and made victory possible."

"Then that makes him a hero, like Maitre Cyran."

"All of the imagers from Imagisle who died were heroes," said Alyna gently. "Now . . . the time for breaking the rules is over . . . and we'll have dessert."

Lystara nodded. Malyna glanced at her cousin and smiled.

Alastar could smell the apple pie long before it arrived.

Later that evening, well after the girls were in bed, Alastar and Alyna sat in their sitting room.

"I still have to wonder," she said. "How did they think they could possibly succeed?"

"Because they were far better prepared than we had any idea of. Just one example was the fact that Ryel, or someone, subverted close to ten imagers from Westisle."

"But Voltyrn wrote you . . ." Alyna paused. "He knew you wouldn't make him Maitre of Westisle. The letters were just to keep you from thinking about the fact that he'd already decided to back the rebels."

"That's my guess. Ryel or Caervyn, most likely Caervyn, persuaded Ryentar to join the cause. Ryel found some way to blackmail Bettaur . . ."

Alyna frowned. "I thought you said he saved your life."

"He did." Alastar gave the complete story of the encounter with Ryentar, Voltyrn, and Bettaur. "I doubt if my shields could have stopped a wooden wand at that point. As it was, breaking three imagers' shields left Bettaur defenseless, and that allowed Ryentar to run him through."

"That makes Ryentar one of the most despicable characters in the history of Solidar. He conspired with his mother to kill his own brother and half sister . . . well, half brother and half sister. Next he killed his mother so that no one could prove the first conspiracy. Then he rebelled against his brother, and ended up stabbing his other half brother in the back."

"And that's just what we know," replied Alastar sardonically. "And the worst of it was that he and Bettaur were really only Ryel's tools." He paused. "Even Laevoryn, despicable as he was, was only a tool."

"Just tools . . ." She shook her head. "I still wonder how they thought . . . or how Ryel thought . . ."

"How did the first rex regis think he could possibly unite Solidar?" asked Alastar, almost rhetorically. "He was outnumbered, and his enemies had better weapons. He didn't even have rifles or cannon. He only had a handful of imagers. Today, no one even thinks about how improbable his success was. If Ryel's scheme had succeeded, a generation from now, it would merely be regarded as a coup, the overthrow and replacement of one rex by his younger brother." Alastar shook his head. "This was so much closer than anyone will know."

"Or should know."

"I made a mess out of all this," he said slowly. "I'm not as strong an imager as I once was. I didn't see how well the rebel High Holders had planned, even to how the legal petitions played into it. I certainly didn't see what Vaschet's ironworks represented, or the treachery brewing at Westisle. My failures led to the deaths of Cyran and Taryn and all the others, even Bettaur's death. I think he really did want to go to Westisle, where no one knew him . . ."

"Do you think Voltyrn was the one who blackmailed him?"

Alastar didn't say anything for several moments. "I didn't even think of it that way." He shook his head. "I suppose there's really no way to know." He paused again. "But it doesn't matter. I made too many mistakes. I failed the Collegium, and Cyran redeemed my failure. So did Taryn, Julyan, Chervyt, and Bettaur."

"Dearest, none of them would have been able to do that if you hadn't spent years training them."

"It doesn't matter."

"Alastar D'Imagisle! You made mistakes. We all make mistakes. The mistakes you say you made were mistakes no one else even thought about or even recognized. You still saw things that no one else saw, and you managed to save Solidar when no one else could. Is there anyone else who could have done what you did?"

"You could have. You've been part of it for years."

"A part, yes, but only a part. Even if it were true, Solidar wouldn't have accepted a woman maitre." Her voice softened. "The Collegium and Solidar need you. Not for massive imaging ability, although you're far stronger than you think you are, but for the wisdom to keep more trouble from happening."

"The way I did here?" he asked sarcastically.

"The way you did here," she said quietly but firmly. "The way no one else could."

"I see I'm not going to convince you."

"You won't until you train someone able to step into your boots. Now . . . what about the Westisle imagers?"

"Ryel or one of the other High Holders must have contacted Voltyrn years ago . . . and kept in touch"—likely far more often than you did—"and that's something else we can't let happen."

"That wasn't quite what I meant. Who will you appoint as the Maitre there?"

Alastar smiled. "Who would you suggest?"

"You're Maitre. That's your choice."

He smiled at her. "We can talk about that later. I've talked enough this evening."

"You would say that." But she smiled, rose, and took his hands.

50

Well before seventh glass on Lundi morning, Alastar and Alyna set out for the administration building, walking through the rain wearing oilskins, as were Malyna and Lystara, who had left not quite half a quint earlier. Alastar didn't say much for a time, going over in his mind just how to present matters to the senior maitres, wondering how much he should say about certain things.

"I know what you said last night," began Alastar, as they neared the administration building, "but I worry. I did make mistakes, and imagers died. Am I losing—"

"Dear. Even the best make mistakes. There's no one here at the Collegium who would make fewer."

"Except you."

"We've been through that. Like it or not, you're the Maitre. Like it or not, there's no one else quite ready to take your place."

And like it or not, you're going to have to live with those mistakes, he thought. Alyna hadn't said that, but she might as well have done so. "Akoryt's close."

"Not close enough, and he's told me that himself."

"What about his being senior imager?"

"That's your decision. You're Maitre. You're meeting with him first. Ask him."

"You agree about Arion, Seliora, and Taurek?"

"Absolutely, but it's up to Arion. If he doesn't feel—"

"I know. Then we'll have to consider another way."

Another thought struck Alastar, and he sighed.

"Now what?"

"I never did anything about Vaschet . . . or that bastard Murranyt."

"Vaschet won't be a problem. There's a story about him in *Veritum.* I left a copy on the desk in your study. I thought you'd want to see it. As for the Civic Patrol . . . you have time. After all that's happened, Murranyt may decide to take his stipend quite soon."

"You speak as though you know. And what about Vaschet—"

"You can't do anything about what's happened . . . and we're almost there." She opened the door to the administration building for him.

"You do put matters in perspective." He managed a smile. "Likely another result of your training in geometry." *But more likely the result of growing up in a High Hold.*

"No more than you, dear."

Alastar doubted that, but he wasn't about to say so at that moment.

As they approached the anteroom, Alyna reached out and took Alastar's hand, then squeezed it as she leaned forward and kissed him on the cheek. "I'll see you at the meeting. There are some things I need to do, and you should read about Vaschet and meet with the others alone."

Then she was gone.

Both Dareyn and Maercyl stood outside the door to the Maitre's study.

"Welcome back, Maitre," said Dareyn cheerfully.

Maercyl nodded in agreement and smiled.

"Thank you both. Have Akoryt come in as soon as he arrives."

"Yes, sir."

Alastar took off the oilskin and handed it to Maercyl. "If you would . . . somewhere out of the way. The aroma . . ."

Maercyl smiled broadly. "Yes, sir."

Alastar left the door open as he made his way to the desk, polished and without a speck of dust anywhere. The only item on the desk was the single copy of *Veritum*.

How did they find another printing press so soon? Then he picked up the newssheet. The date was Vendrei, 27 Erntyn, and the lead story was about the rebel army marching on L'Excelsis . . . and how it was being led by commanders loyal to dissident High Holders. The headline of the second story caught his eye—IRON FACTOR MURDERED.

That must have been what she meant.

Vaschet D'Factorius was shot leaving a Factors' Council meeting on Meredi morning. He died on the spot from a single bullet that went through his eye and into his brain. Civic Patrollers found an almost new R-2 rifle of the type manufactured by Vaschet's own ironworks less than a block away. No one saw the killer.

Vaschet had been meeting with the council about his petition that the council press for legal charges dealing with damages to his ironworks incurred as part of events connected with the ongoing High Holders' rebellion. Council members declared that the matter would not be pursued, given the circumstances surrounding Vaschet's death and the fact that it was clear Vaschet had provided aid to the rebels.

A single bullet? Through the eye? Alastar nodded slowly, and a wry smile crossed his lips.

He barely had set down the newssheet and hadn't even seated himself when Akoryt appeared. Alastar motioned for Akoryt to close the door and then sat down. Once the grayed redhead seated himself, Alastar began. "You did a remarkable job over the past month."

"Thank you."

"Have you thought about being senior imager?"

Akoryt looked directly at Alastar. "I couldn't do that, sir. The only one who could fill Cyran's boots is Maitre Alyna."

"What about the fact that we're married?"

"Sir, there's not an imager on all Imagisle who doesn't know she would be senior imager if Cyran hadn't already been."

"You've been outstanding as Maitre of Students."

"Thank you, but the senior imager should be Maitre Alyna."

Alastar smiled. "Then I should bow to your judgment, which I've always trusted. I do feel a little awkward . . ."

"Don't. You should feel awkward about considering me when she is so much more qualified."

Alastar shook his head. "I said I trusted your judgment and your honesty, and you've just demonstrated why."

"You should announce it at the meeting."

"I think I can do that. What do you think about the situation at Westisle?"

"You need to send a young and strong Maitre D'Structure there, and several Maitres D'Aspect."

"Would you be interested?"

"If you wouldn't mind . . . no. I prefer working with you and Maitre Alyna, and Corlyssa hates really warm weather."

"What have I missed? Or what recommendations do you have?"

"Arion, Khaelis, or Shaelyt would do well in Westisle, but Tiranya wouldn't. She's anything but fond of either the ocean or heat."

"That leaves Arion or Khaelis."

"Either would do well."

"Anything else?"

"From what I saw, Seliora is more than qualified to be a Maitre D'Structure."

"Thank you. I'd already planned to tell her and announce that, but I'm glad that you agree."

Akoryt smiled. "That's all I have, sir."

Alastar stood. "I can't tell you how much I appreciate your support and your hard work over all the years."

"I've enjoyed it, and I look forward to continuing."

"So do I."

After Akoryt left, Alastar walked to the window, closed against the rain that had become more of a downpour, and looked out. *Even more damage to the crops, as if there's all that much left to harvest.*

There was a knock on the door, and Dareyn announced, "Maitres Arion and Seliora are here."

"Have Arion come in." Alastar turned and waited.

"Sir, you wanted to see me?"

"I did." Alastar did not sit down. "It won't take long. I'd like you to consider becoming Maitre at Westisle."

"Sir? Me? There are others more senior . . ."

"From what I've seen, you're at least as strong an imager as any, and you have a better background in the sort of dealings the Maitre must have. You also aren't likely to be flattered into defecting by rebellious High Holders."

"I hadn't even thought . . ."

"You also have the makings of a Maitre D'Esprit. So the rank would come with the title of Maitre."

Arion smiled wryly. "There is one consideration."

"Oh?"

"Seliora. We'd thought . . . I wouldn't . . ."

"If she wants to go to Westisle if you do, that would be even better. Go ask her, and then come back. I understand she's in the anteroom."

"Right now?"

Alastar nodded.

In moments, Arion returned. "She said yes. We'll go."

"Excellent!" Alastar didn't have to counterfeit satisfaction and enthusiasm. "Keep that between you two until I announce it at the meeting."

"We can do that."

"Now . . . have her come in."

"Yes, sir."

Seliora entered the office, quietly closing the door behind her. "Sir?"

Alastar smiled happily. "First, I wanted to thank you for probably saving my life several times over. Second . . . it's more than clear to me, and to every imager who was with us, that you are more than capable of everything required of a Maitre D'Structure and then some. So you're to attend the senior maitres' meeting in a few moments, where I will make that formal announcement."

"Thank you, sir." With the words came a quiet smile.

That pleased Alastar especially, because she offered no false modesty, and no protests, just a quiet acceptance of what she knew she deserved. "I understand you're willing to go to Westisle?"

"I am, particularly now."

Alastar understood that as well. "Good. There will probably be a Maitre D'Aspect going as well. That has not been decided."

"Is there anything else, sir?"

"Not at the moment." Alastar grinned. "Go tell Arion."

Seliora offered a most uncharacteristic impish smile. "I just might." She turned and left the study.

Alastar nodded. He'd always thought Seliora would turn out well. He just hadn't realized how well.

"Maitre Taurek is here," announced Maercyl.

Alastar motioned for the burly maitre to enter.

Taurek closed the door behind himself. "Sir?"

"Do you know why you're here?"

"I'd rather not guess, sir." Taurek grinned. "But I imagine it's not about creating a branch of the Collegium in Estisle."

Alastar laughed at Taurek's open and good-humored words, then said, "You're to attend the senior maitres' meeting. You've demonstrated the abilities of a Maitre D'Structure."

"Thank you, sir."

"We'll talk about Estisle in a while . . . maybe a year or so."

"Yes, sir. I won't forget."

"I'm sure you won't. Now . . . go, so that I can get ready for the meeting."

"Yes, sir."

A quint later, Dareyn announced, "The maitres are all in the conference room."

Alastar frowned. Alyna hadn't come to see him first. *Did you upset her?*

Worried as he was, he offered a pleasant expression as he walked to the side door and then entered the conference room.

All the surviving senior imagers of the Collegium were seated around the table with Alyna in her usual position on Alastar's left. The seat to his right had been left vacant. As he sat at the head of the table, Alastar looked at each imager in turn—Alyna, Akoryt, Khaelis, Tiranya, Gaellen, Obsolym, Arion, Shaelyt . . . and Seliora and Taurek. Finally, he spoke.

"Before I brief everyone on my meeting yesterday with Rex Lorien, I have a few announcements to make." He turned to Alyna. "If you would please take the chair to my right, Senior Imager Alyna."

"About time!" snapped Obsolym, the one senior maitre that Alastar would have thought the least likely to make such a comment.

The nods that ran around the table seconded Obsolym's tart comment.

"I'd also like to welcome Maitre D'Structure Seliora and Maitre D'Structure Taurek to the ranks of the senior imagers." Alastar paused. "The last matter of this nature is the appointment of the new Maitre of the Collegium at Westisle. Maitre D'Esprit Arion has accepted the post, and he will be accompanied by Maitre Seliora. At least one other junior maitre will accompany them, but that imager has not yet been determined. See me or Maitre Alyna later if any of you have suggestions." Alastar gestured. "Maitre Arion?"

Arion smiled ruefully. "My father said to make the most of opportunities. I believe that Seliora and I will certainly have the chance to make the most of what appear to be almost, but not quite, insurmountable opportunities in Westisle, just as Maitre Alastar did here in Imagisle some thirteen years ago." He smiled at Seliora. "That's likely more than I should have said."

Alastar waited for the soft laughs and chuckles to fade, then said, "I met with Lorien yesterday afternoon . . ." In less than half a quint, he summarized what had been said.

"Will he do all that?" asked Gaellen.

"If he wants to remain as rex," replied Alastar. "Charyn is almost old enough to succeed him, and Lady Chelia would be a more-than-adequate regent."

After Alastar's response there were no other questions.

"Then the meeting is over." Alastar stood, then waited as the other imagers left before turning to Alyna. "I'd like to meet with you, Senior Imager."

"I'd like that."

After they entered the study and he closed the door, he said, "You knew, didn't you?"

"I thought, but I didn't know. It had to be your decision. All yours. That was why I went directly to the conference room."

"You're likely to be as much Maitre as I am." He gestured toward the newssheet on the desk where he'd left it. "How did you find out when the Factors' Council was meeting?"

"I just asked Thelia if she'd keep me posted on whatever the council was doing. From what you said, Vaschet's the type who never thought he was wrong about anything and would keep pushing until he was dead. So he'd keep pressing with the council. We did have more than a few of the new rifles left from the attacks here." Alyna paused. "Either Lysara or Malyna could have just as easily been the ones killed by the brown-shirts. They came close enough when they wanted to see the glowbugs. You and the Collegium didn't need to worry about Vaschet. And Solidar didn't need a factor who'd stoop to manufacturing poisoned bullets. Not for all the golds in L'Excelsis."

"Very neatly done."

"I didn't like doing it, but I can still see Lyam's face." She shook her head. "And the way you looked after you came back from the ironworks."

"You're more qualified than me—"

"No. I'll be your senior imager."

"I'll need your judgment . . . and more than that."

"You've always had my thoughts."

"But the Collegium hasn't always, and it needs them, and your actions, too."

"That's one of the things I admire most about you, dearest. You respect the past. You understand the traditions, but you're not afraid to change." She offered the mischievous smile he liked so much. "Even if you are conservative in how you change . . . and sometimes need a little encouragement."

"I've thought about that, especially in the last few days." Alastar offered a faint smile. "I've done a lot of thinking. If you remember everything, and you're tied to the past, you can be weighted down and chained not only by unfilled expectations, but also by the angers, grievances, and sorrows, unable to change and improve. If you remember nothing, and all you can do is make the same mistakes, time after time, and that, too, leaves you unable to change and improve." He shook his head.

"I sound all too pretentious. It might be better said that Quaeryt was right in not wanting too much remembered."

"You're right, and so was he." Alyna nodded. "You could also say that the High Holders like Cransyr, Laevoryn, and Ryel were wrong in hanging on to a time that was long past. As was Ryentar."

Alastar frowned. "I'm not sure about Ryel. He certainly used the unattainable past to motivate the others . . . and he's emerged, largely untouched, as the de facto leader of the High Holders. Which makes him perfect to be the next head of the High Council."

"He'll accept. He has no choice."

"Do any of us?"

"You did. You didn't have to choose me."

"No." He smiled broadly. "I had absolutely no choice."

"Neither did I."

They both laughed, if softly.

EPILOGUE

"Maitre Alastar and Senior Imager Alyna," the footman announced.

Alastar and Alyna stepped into the rebuilt and refurbished receiving study of the Chateau D'Council.

The man who stood beside the ebony conference table could have been no other than High Holder Ryel, not with the fine blond hair, blue eyes, and the warm welcoming smile that seemed to embrace whoever received it. His attire was what Alastar would have expected, a formal but austere black jacket with a silver-gray shirt, and a black and silver silk cravat. His trousers matched his shirt, and his boots were black.

Alastar and Alyna walked across the black marble floor and halted a yard or so from Ryel.

"Welcome to the Chateau D'Council, although you're more familiar with it than am I, since I arrived but yesterday."

"Only the entry, hallways, and receiving study," replied Alastar with a smile. "Oh, and one parlor. You must have had the study here refurbished before you arrived."

"That seemed opportune."

"I'm pleased that you saw your way to becoming High Councilor," Alastar said.

"I fear events—and you, Maitre Alastar—left me little choice." Ryel again offered the same warm, winning, and oh-so-sincere smile that Alastar had seen too often from Ryentar . . . and Bettaur.

"That's true. Events have left all of us with few choices, and some events predictably lead to others, often with fatal outcomes. Failing to see that was a mistake Ryentar and your predecessor Cransyr both made. Your serving as High Councilor will, I am most certain, assure that the High Holders will not ever again attempt to press change upon Solidar through force of arms or spurious legal claims."

"I think we all have seen the dangers of that, and I will be more than pleased to work with a strong Collegium to assure any change that may occur will be through the laws and in accord with the Codex Legis in a manner acceptable to all."

"We are agreed in that," said Alastar almost amiably.

"Indeed," added Alyna, her eyes fixed on the High Holder, "we are." She smiled. "And we will always agree on that, I am most certain."

Ryel paused, then said, "How could it be otherwise?"

"How indeed?" replied Alyna, and her words were silvered, even as her black eyes fixed the High Holder where he stood.

Ryel's smile was thin as he nodded. "Indeed."